THE TAWNY MAN

II: THE GOLDEN FOOL

Voyager

THE TAWNY MAN

II
THE GOLDEN FOOL

Robin Hobb

HarperCollins*Publishers*

Voyager
An Imprint of HarperCollins*Publishers*
77–85 Fulham Palace Road,
Hammersmith, London W6 8JB

www.voyager-books.com

First published by *Voyager* 2002

Published by *Voyager* 2003
1 3 5 7 9 8 6 4 2

A catalogue record for this book
is available from the British Library

ISBN 0 00 716039 9

Set in Goudy by Palimpsest Book Production Limited,
Polmont, Stirlingshire

Printed and bound in Great Britain by
Clays Ltd, St Ives plc

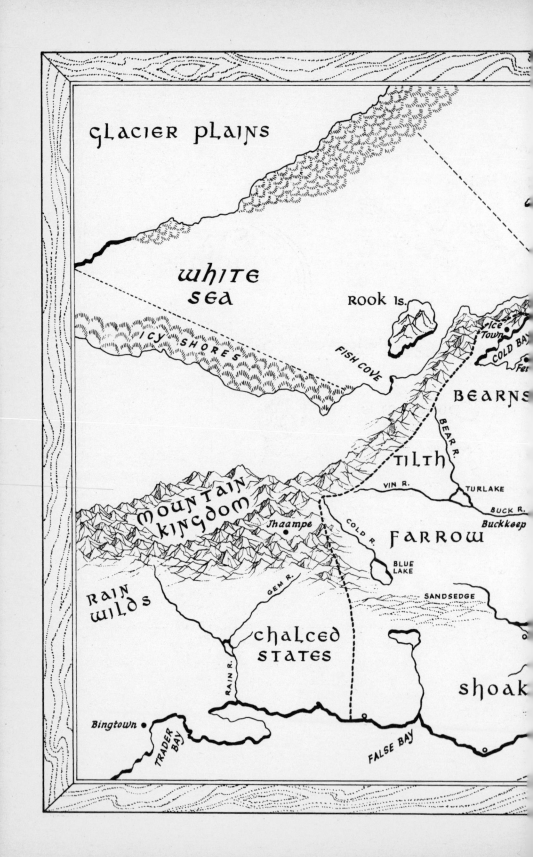

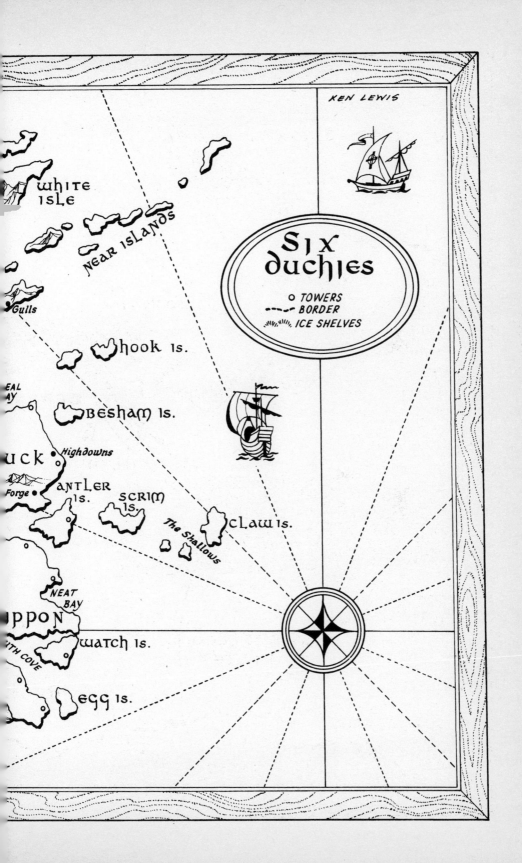

KEN LEWIS

WHITE ISLE

NEAR ISLANDS

SIX
duchies

○ TOWERS
--- BORDER
ICE SHELVES

Gulls

hook Is.

EAL
AY

BESHAM Is.

uck • Highdowns

Forge •

ANTLER
Is.

SCRIM
Is.

The Shallows

CLAW Is.

NEAT
BAY

JPPON

TH COVE

watch Is.

EGG Is.

Losses Sustained

The loss of a bond beast is a difficult event to explain to the non-Witted. Those who can speak of the death of an animal as 'It was only a dog' will never grasp it. Others, more sympathetic, perceive it as the death of a beloved pet. Even those who say, 'It must be like losing a child, or a wife' are still seeing only one facet of the toll. To lose the living creature that one has been linked with is more than the loss of a companion or loved one. It was the sudden amputation of half my physical body. My vision was dimmed, my appetite diminished by the insipid flavour of food. My hearing was dulled and

The manuscript, begun so many years ago, ends in a flurry of blots and angry stabbings from my pen. I can recall the moment at which I realized I had slipped from writing in generalities into my own intimate rendering of pain. There are creases on the scroll where I flung it to the floor and stamped on it. The wonder is that I only kicked it aside rather than committing it to the flames. I do not know who took pity on the wretched thing and shelved it on my scroll rack. Perhaps it was Thick, doing his tasks in his methodical, unthinking way. Certainly I find nothing there that I would have saved.

So it has often been with my writing efforts. My various attempts at a history of the Six Duchies too often meandered into a history of myself. From a treatise on herbs my pen would wander to the various treatments for Skill-ailments. My studies of the White Prophets delve too deeply into their relationships with their Catalysts. I do not know if it is conceit that always turns my thoughts to my own life, or if my writing is my pathetic effort to explain my life to myself. The years have come and gone in their scores of turnings,

I

and night after night I still take pen in hand and write. Still I strive to understand who I am. Still I promise myself, 'Next time I will do better' in the all-too-human conceit that I will always be offered a 'next time'.

Yet I did not do that when I lost Nighteyes. I never promised myself that I would bond again, and do better by my next partner. Such a thought would have been traitorous. The death of Nighteyes gutted me. I walked wounded through my life in the days that followed, unaware of just how mutilated I was. I was like the man who complains of the itching of his severed leg. The itching distracts from the immense knowledge that one will ever after hobble through life. So the immediate grief at his death concealed the full damage done to me. I was confused, thinking that my pain and my loss were one and the same thing, whereas one was but a symptom of the other.

In a curious way, it was a second coming-of-age. This one was not an arrival at manhood, but rather a slow realization of myself as an individual. Circumstances had plunged me back into the intrigues of the court at Buckkeep Castle. I had the friendship of the Fool and Chade. I stood at the edge of a true relationship with Jinna, the hedge-witch. My boy Hap had flung himself headlong into both apprenticeship and romance, and seemed to be floundering desperately through both. Young Prince Dutiful, poised on the lip of his betrothal to the Outislander Narcheska, had turned to me as a mentor; not just as a teacher for both Skill and Wit, but as someone to guide him through the rapids of adolescence to manhood. I did not lack for people who cared about me, nor for folk I deeply cherished. But for all that, I stood more alone than ever I had before.

The strangest part was my slow realization that I chose that isolation.

Nighteyes was irreplaceable; he had worked a change on me in the years that we had shared. He was not half of me; together, we made a whole. Even when Hap came into our life, we regarded him as a juvenile and a responsibility. The wolf and I were the unit that made the decisions. Ours was the partnership. With Nighteyes gone, I felt I would never again share that arrangement with any other, animal or human.

When I was a lad, spending time in the company of Lady Patience and her companion, Lacey, I often overheard their blunt appraisals of the men at court. One assumption Patience and Lacey had shared was that a man or woman who had passed their thirtieth year unwed was likely to remain so. 'Set in his ways,' Patience would declare at the gossip that some greying lord had suddenly begun to court a young girl. 'Spring has turned his head, but she'll find soon enough there is no room in his life for a partner. He's had it all his own way too long.'

And so I began, very slowly, to see myself. I was often lonely. I knew that my Wit quested out for companionship. Yet that feeling and that questing were like a reflex, the twitching of a severed limb. No one, human or animal, could ever fill the gap that Nighteyes had left in my life.

I had said as much to the Fool during a rare moment of conversation on our way back to Buckkeep. It had been one of the nights when we had camped beside our homeward road. I had left him with Prince Dutiful and Laurel, the Queen's huntswoman. They had huddled around the fire, making the best of the cold night and sparse food. The Prince had been withdrawn and morose, still raw with the pain of losing his bond-cat. For me to be near him was like holding a previously burned hand near a flame; it woke all my own pain more sharply. So I had made the excuse of getting more wood for the fire and gone apart from them all.

Winter was announcing its approach with a dark and chill evening. There were no colours left in the dim world, and away from the firelight I groped like a mole as I searched for wood. At last I gave it up and sat down on a stone by the creekside to wait for my eyes to adjust. But sitting there alone, feeling the cold press in around me, I had lost all ambition to find wood, or indeed to do anything at all. I sat and stared, listening to the sound of the running water and letting the night fill me with its gloom.

The Fool came to me, moving quietly through the darkness. He sat down on the earth beside me and for a time we said nothing. Then he reached over, set a hand on my shoulder and said, 'I wish there were some way I could ease your grieving.'

It was a useless thing to say, and he seemed to feel that, for after those words he was silent. Perhaps it was the ghost of Nighteyes who reproached me for my surly silence to our friend, for after a time I groped for some words to bridge the dark between us. 'It is like the cut on your head, Fool. Time will heal it, but until it does all the best wishes in the world cannot make it heal faster. Even if there were some way to disperse this pain, some herb or drunkenness that would numb it, I could not choose it. Nothing will ever make his death better. All I can look forward to is becoming accustomed to being alone.'

Despite my effort, my words still sounded like a rebuke, and worse, a self-pitying one. It is a tribute to my friend that he did not take offence at them, but rose gracefully. 'I'll let you be, then. I think you are choosing to mourn alone, and if that is your choice, I'll respect it. I do not think it is your wisest choice, but I'll respect it.' He paused and gave a small sigh. 'I perceive something about myself now; I came because I wanted you to know that I knew you were in pain. Not because I could heal you of it, but because I wanted you to be aware that I shared that pain through our connection. I suspect there is an aspect of selfishness to that; that I wished you also to be aware of it, I mean. A burden shared not only can lighten it; it can form a bond between those who share it. So that no one is left to bear it alone.'

I sensed there was some germ of wisdom in his words, something I should consider, but I was too weary and wracked to reach for it. 'I'll come back to the fire in a little while,' was what I said, and the Fool knew it was a dismissal. He took his hand from my shoulder and walked away.

It was only when I later considered his words that I understood them. I was choosing to be alone then; it was not the inescapable consequence of the wolf's death, nor even a carefully considered decision. I was embracing my solitude, courting my pain. It was not the first time I had chosen such a course.

I handled that thought carefully, for it was sharp enough to kill me. I had chosen my isolated years with Hap in my cabin. No one had forced me into that exile. The irony was that it had been the granting of my often-voiced wish. Throughout my youth, I had always asserted that what I truly wanted was to live a life in which I could make my own choices, independent of the 'duties' of my birth and position. It was only when fate granted that to me that I realized the cost of it. I could set aside my responsibilities to others and live my life as I pleased only when I also severed my ties to them. I could not have it both ways. To be part of a family, or any community, is to have duties and responsibilities, to be bound by the rules of that group. I had lived apart from all that for a time, but now I knew it had been my choice. I had chosen to renounce my responsibilities to my family, and accepted the ensuing isolation as the cost. At the time, I had insisted to myself that fortune had forced me into that role. Just as I was making a choice now, even though I tried to persuade myself I was but following the inescapable path fate had set out for me.

To recognize you are the source of your own loneliness is not a cure for it. But it is a step towards seeing that it is not inevitable, and that such a choice is not irrevocable.

ONE

Piebalds

The Piebalds always claimed only to want freedom from the persecution that has been the lot of the Witted folk of the Six Duchies for generations. This claim can be dismissed as both a lie and a clever deceit. The Piebalds wanted power. Their intent was to mould all of the Witted folk of the Six Duchies into a united force that would rise up to seize control of the monarchy and put their own people into power. One facet of their ploy was to claim that all Kings since the Abdication of Chivalry were pretenders, that the bastardy of FitzChivalry Farseer was wrongly construed as an obstacle to his inheriting the throne. Legends of the 'True-Hearted Bastard' rising from the grave to serve King Verity in his quest proliferated beyond all common sense, ascribing powers to FitzChivalry that raise the Bastard to the status of a near-deity. For this reason, the Piebalds have also been known as the Cult of the Bastard.

These ridiculous claims were intended to gives some sort of legitimacy to the Piebald quest to overthrow the Farseer monarchy and put one of their own on the throne. To this end, the Piebalds began a clever campaign of forcing the Witted either to unite with them or risk exposure. Perhaps this tactic was inspired by Kebal Rawbread, leader of the Outislanders during the Red Ship war, for it is said that he drew men to follow him, not by his charisma, but by fear of what he would do to their homes and families if they refused to fall in with his plans.

The Piebalds' technique was simple. Either families tainted with the Wit-magic joined their alliance or they were exposed by public accusations that led to their execution. It is said that the Piebalds often began an insidious attack on the fringes of a powerful family, exposing first a servant or a less affluent cousin, all the while making it clear that if the head of the stalwart house did not comply with their wishes he, too, *would eventually meet such an end.*

This is not the action of folk who wish to bring an end to persecution of their kin. This is the act of a ruthless faction determined to gain power for themselves, first by subjugating their own kind.

Rowell's The Piebald Conspiracy

The watch had changed. The town watchman's bell and cry came thin through the storm, but I heard it. Night had officially ended and we were venturing towards morning and still I sat in Jinna's cottage waiting for Hap to return. Jinna and I shared the comfort of her cosy hearth. Jinna's niece had come in some time ago and chatted with us briefly before she sought her bed. Jinna and I passed the time, feeding log after log to the fire and chatting about inconsequential things. The hedge-witch's little house was warm and pleasant, her company congenial, and waiting for my boy became an excuse that allowed me to do what I wished, which was simply to sit quietly where I was.

Conversation had been sporadic. Jinna had asked how my errand had gone. I had replied that it had been my master's business and that I had but accompanied him. To keep that from sounding too brusque, I added that Lord Golden had acquired some feathers for his collection and then chatted to her about Myblack. I knew Jinna had no real interest in hearing about my horse, but she listened amiably. The words filled the small space between us comfortably.

In truth, our real errand had had nothing to do with feathers, and had been more mine than Lord Golden's. Together, we had recovered Prince Dutiful from the Piebalds who had first befriended and then captured him. We had returned him to Buckkeep with none of his nobles the wiser. Tonight the aristocracy of the Six Duchies feasted and danced, and tomorrow they would formalize Prince Dutiful's betrothal to the Outisland narcheska Elliania. Outwardly, all was as it had been.

Few would ever know how much the seamless continuation of their normality had cost the Prince and me. The Prince's Wit-cat had sacrificed her life for him. I had lost my wolf. For close to a score of years, Nighteyes had been my other self, the repository of half my soul. Now he was gone. It was as profound a change in my life as the snuffing of a lamp makes in an evening room. His absence seemed a solid thing, a burden I must carry in addition to my grief. Nights were darker. No one guarded my back for me. Yet I knew I would continue to live. Sometimes that knowledge seemed the worst part of my loss.

I reined back before I plunged completely into self-pity. I was not the only one who was bereaved. Despite the Prince's briefer bond with his cat, I knew he suffered deeply. The magic link that the Wit forms between a human and an animal is a complex one. Severing it is never trivial. Yet the boy had mastered his grief and was stalwartly going through the motions of fulfilling his duties. At least I did not have to face my betrothal tomorrow night. The Prince had been plunged immediately back into his routine since we returned to Buckkeep yesterday afternoon. Last night he had attended the ceremonies that welcomed his bride to be. Tonight, he must smile and eat, make conversation, accept good wishes, dance and appear well pleased with what fate and his mother had decreed for him. I thought of bright lights and skirling music and laughter and loud conversations. I shook my head in sympathy for him.

'And what makes you shake your head like that, Tom Badgerlock?'

Jinna's voice broke in on my introspection, and I realized that the silence had grown long. I drew a long breath and found an easy lie. 'The storm shows no sign of dying, does it? I was pitying those who must be out in it this night. I am grateful that I am not one of them.'

'Well. To that, I'll add that I am thankful for the company,' she said, and smiled.

'And I the same,' I added awkwardly.

To pass the night in the placid companionship of a pleasant woman was a novel experience for me. Jinna's cat sat purring on my lap, while Jinna's hands were occupied with knitting. The cosy warmth of the firelight reflected in the auburn shades of Jinna's curly hair and the scattering of freckles on her face and forearms. She had a good face, not beautiful, but calm and kind. Our conversation had wandered wide this evening, from the herbs she had used to make the tea to how driftwood fires sometimes burned with coloured flames and beyond, to discussing ourselves. I had discovered she was about six years younger than I truly was, and she had expressed surprise when I claimed to be forty-two. That was seven years past my true age; the extra years were part of my role as Tom Badgerlock. It pleased me when she said that she had thought I was closer to her age. Yet neither of us really gave mind to our words. There was an interesting little tension between us as we sat before the fire and conversed quietly. The curiosity suspended between us was like a string, plucked and humming.

Before I had left on my errand with Lord Golden, I had spent an afternoon with Jinna. She had kissed me. No words had accompanied that gesture, no avowals of love or romantic compliments. There had been just the one kiss, interrupted when her niece had returned from the market. Right now, neither of us quite knew how to return to the place where that moment of intimacy had been possible. For my part, I was not sure that I wished to venture there. I was not ready even for a second kiss, let alone what it might bring. My heart was too raw. Yet I wanted to be here, sitting before her fireside. It sounds a contradiction, and perhaps it was. I did not want the inevitable complications that caresses would lead to, yet in my Wit-bereavement, I took comfort in this woman's company.

Yet Jinna was not why I had come here tonight. I needed to see Hap, my foster son. He had just arrived at Buckkeep Town and had been staying here with Jinna. I wished to be sure his apprenticeship with Gindast the wood-worker was going well. I must also, much as I dreaded it, give him the news of Nighteyes' death. The wolf had raised the lad as much as I had. Yet even as I winced at the thought of telling him I hoped it would, as the Fool had said, somehow ease the burden of my sorrow. With Hap, I could share my grief, however selfish a thing that might be. Hap had been mine for the last seven years. We had shared a life, and the wolf's companionship. If I still belonged to anyone or anything, I belonged to my boy. I needed to feel the reality of that.

'More tea?' Jinna offered me.

I did not want more tea. We had already drunk three pots of it, and I had visited her back-house twice. Yet she offered the tea to let me know I was welcome to stay, no matter how late, or early, the hour had become. So, 'Please,' I said, and she set her knitting aside, to repeat the ritual of filling the kettle with fresh water from the cask and hanging it from the hook and swinging it over the fire again. Outside, the storm rattled the shutters in a fresh surge of fury. Then it became not the storm, but Hap's rapping at the door. 'Jinna?' he called unevenly. 'Are you awake still?'

'I'm awake,' she replied. She turned from putting the kettle on. 'And lucky for you that I am, or you'd be sleeping in the shed with your pony. I'm coming.'

As she lifted the latch, I stood up, gently dumping the cat off my lap.

Imbecile. The cat was comfortable. Fennel complained as he slid to the floor, but the big orange tom was too stupefied with warmth to make much of a protest. Instead he leapt onto Jinna's chair and curled up in it without deigning to give me a backward glance.

The storm pushed in with Hap as he shoved the door open. A gust of wind carried rain into the room. 'Whew. Put the wood in the hole, lad,' Jinna rebuked Hap as he lurched in. Obediently he shut the door behind him and latched it, and then stood dripping before it.

'It's wild and wet out there,' he told her. His smile was beatifically drunken, but his eyes were lit with more than wine. Infatuation shone there, as unmistakable as the rain slipping from his lank hair and running down his face. It took him a moment or two to realize that I was there, watching him. Then, 'Tom! Tom, you've finally come back!' He flung his arms wide in a drunkard's ebullience for the ordinary, and I laughed and stepped forward to accept his wet hug.

'Don't get water all over Jinna's floor!' I rebuked him.

'No, I shouldn't. Well. I won't then,' he declared, and dragged off his sodden coat. He hung it on a peg by the door and peeled off his wool cap to drip there as well. He tried to take his boots off standing, but lost his balance. He sat down on the floor and tugged them off. He leaned far to set them by the door under his wet coat and then sat up with a blissful smile. 'Tom. I've met a girl.'

'Have you? I thought you'd met a bottle from the smell of you.'

'Oh, yes,' he admitted unabashedly. 'That, too. But we had to drink the Prince's health, you know. And that of his intended. And to a happy marriage. And for many children. And for as much happiness for ourselves.' He gave me a wide and fatuous smile. 'She says she loves me. She likes my eyes.'

'Well. That's good.' How many times in his life had folk looked at his mismatched eyes, one brown and one blue, and made the sign against evil? It had to be balm to meet a girl who found them attractive.

And I suddenly knew that now was not the time to burden him with any grief of mine. I spoke gently but firmly. 'I think perhaps you should go to bed, son. Won't your master be expecting you in the morning?'

He looked as if I had slapped him with a fish. The smile faded from his face. 'Oh. Yes, yes that's true. He'll expect me. Old Gindast expects his apprentices to be there before his journeymen, and his journeymen to be well at work when he arrives.' He gathered himself and slowly stood up. 'Tom, this apprenticeship hasn't been what I expected at all. I sweep and carry boards and turn wood that is drying. I sharpen tools and clean tools and oil tools. Then I sweep again. I rub oil finishes into the completed pieces. But not a tool have I had in my hand to use, in all these days. It's all, "watch how this is done, boy," or "repeat back what I just told you" and "This isn't what I asked for. Take this back to the wood stock and bring me the fine-grained cherry. And be quick about it". And, Tom, they call me names. "Country boy" and "dullard".'

'Gindast calls all his apprentices names, Hap.' Jinna's placid voice was both calming and comforting, but it was still strange to have a third person include herself in our conversation. 'It's common knowledge. One even took the taunt with him when he went into business for himself. Now you pay a fine price for a Simpleton table.' Jinna had moved back to her chair. She had taken up her knitting but not resumed her seat. The cat still had it.

I tried not to show how much Hap's words distressed me. I had expected to hear that he loved his position and how grateful he was that I had been able to get it for him. I had believed that his apprenticeship would be the one thing that had gone right. 'Well, I warned you that you would have to work hard,' I attempted.

'And I was ready for that, Tom, truly I was. I'm ready to cut wood and fit it and shape it all day. But I didn't expect to be bored to death. Sweeping and rubbing and fetching . . . I might as well have stayed at home for all I'm learning here.'

Few things have such sharp edges as the careless words of a boy. His disdain for our old life, spoken so plainly, left me speechless.

He lifted his eyes to mine accusingly. 'And where have you been and why have you been gone so long? Didn't you know that I'd need you?' Then he squinted at me. 'What have you done to your hair?'

'I cut it,' I said. I ran a self-conscious hand over my mourning-shortened locks. I suddenly did not trust myself to say more than that. He was just a lad, I knew, and prone to see all things first in how they affected himself. But the very brevity of my reply alerted him that there was much I had not said.

His eyes wandered over my face. 'What's happened?' he demanded.

I took a breath. No help for it now. 'Nighteyes is dead,' I said quietly.

'But . . . is it my fault? He ran away from me, Tom, but I did look for him, I swear I did, Jinna will tell you—'

'It wasn't your fault. He followed and found me. I was with him when he died. It was nothing you did, Hap. He was just old. It was his time and he went from me.' Despite my efforts, my throat clenched down on the words.

The relief on the boy's face that he was not at fault was another arrow in my heart. Was being blameless more important to him than the wolf's death? But when he said, 'I can't believe he's gone,' I suddenly understood. He spoke the exact truth. It would take a day, perhaps several, before he realized the old wolf was never coming back. Nighteyes would never again sprawl beside him on the hearthstones, never nudge his hand to have his ears scratched, never walk at his side to hunt rabbits again. Tears rose in my eyes.

'You'll be all right. It will just take time,' I assured him thickly.

'Let's hope so,' he responded heavily.

'Go to bed. You can still get an hour or so of sleep before you must rise.'

'Yes,' he agreed. 'I suppose I'd better.' Then he took a step towards me. 'Tom. I'm so sorry,' he said, and his awkward hug took away much of the earlier hurt he had dealt me. Then he lifted his eyes to mine to ask earnestly, 'You'll come by tomorrow night, won't you? I need to talk to you. It's very important.'

'I'll come by tonight. If Jinna does not mind.' I looked past Hap's shoulder at her as I released him from my embrace.

'Jinna won't mind at all,' she assured me, and I hoped only I could hear the extra note of warmth in her voice.

'So. I'll see you tonight. When you're sober. Now to bed with you, boy.' I rumpled his wet hair, and he muttered a good night. He left the room to seek his bedchamber and I was suddenly alone with Jinna. A log collapsed in the fire and then the small crackling of its settling was the only sound in the room. 'Well. I must go. I thank you for letting me wait for Hap here.'

Jinna set down her knitting again. 'You are welcome, Tom Badgerlock.'

My cloak was on a peg by her door. I took it down and swirled it around my shoulders. She reached up suddenly to fasten it for me. She pulled the hood of it up over my shorn head, and then smiled as she tugged at the sides of the hood to pull my face down to hers. 'Good night,' she said breathlessly. She lifted her chin. I put my hands on her shoulders and kissed her. I wanted to, and yet I wondered that I allowed myself to do it. Where could it lead, this exchange of kisses, but to complications and trouble?

Did she sense my reservations? As I lifted my mouth from hers, she gave her head a small shake. She caught my hand in hers. 'You worry too much, Tom Badgerlock.' She lifted my hand to her mouth and put a warm kiss on the palm of it. 'Some things are far less complex than you think they are.'

I felt awkward, but I managed to say, 'If that were true, it would be a sweet thing.'

'Such a courtier's tongue.' Her words warmed me until she added, 'But gentle words won't keep Hap from running aground. You need to take a firm hand with that young man soon. Hap needs some lines drawn or you may lose him to Buckkeep Town. He wouldn't be the first good country lad to go bad in a town.'

'I think I know my own son,' I said a bit testily.

'Perhaps you know the boy. It's the young man I fear for.' Then she dared to laugh at my scowl and add, 'Save that look for Hap. Good night, Tom. I'll see you tomorrow.'

'Good night, Jinna.'

She let me out, then stood in her doorway watching me walk away. I glanced back at her, a woman watching me from a rectangle of warm yellow light. The wind stirred her curly hair, blowing it about her round face. She waved to me, and I waved back before she shut the door. Then I sighed and pulled my cloak more tightly around me. The worst of the rain had fallen, the storm decayed to swirling gusts that seemed to lurk in wait at the street corners. It had made merry with the festival trim of the town. The blustering gusts sent fallen garlands snaking down the street, and whipped banners to tatters. Usually the taverns had torches set in sconces to guide customers to their doors, but at this hour they were either burned out or taken down. Most of the taverns and inns had closed their door for the night. All the decent folk were long abed, and most of the indecent ones, too. I hurried through the cold dark streets, guided more by my sense of direction than my eyes. It would be even darker once I left the cliff-side town behind and began the winding climb through the forest towards Buckkeep Castle, but that was a road I had known since my childhood. My feet would lead me home.

I became aware of the men following me as I left the last scattered houses of Buckkeep Town behind. I knew that they were stalking me, not merely men on the same path as myself, for when I slowed my steps, they slowed theirs. Obviously they had no wish to catch up with me until I had left the houses of the town behind me. That did not bode well for their intentions. I had left the keep unarmed, my country habits telling against me. I had the belt knife that any man carries for the small tasks of the day, but nothing larger. My ugly, workaday sword in its battered sheath was hanging on the wall in my little chamber. I told myself it was likely that they were no more than common footpads, looking for easy prey. Doubtless they believed me drunk and unaware of them, and as soon as they fought back, they would flee.

It was thin solace. I had no wish to fight at all. I was sick of strife, and weary of being wary. I doubted they would care. So I halted where I was and turned in the dark road to face those who came after me. I drew my belt knife and balanced my weight and waited for them.

Behind me, all was silence save for the wind soughing through the whispering trees that arched over the road. Presently, I became aware of the waves crashing against the cliffs in the distance. I listened for the sounds of men moving through the brush, or the scuff of footsteps on the road, but heard nothing. I grew impatient. 'Come on, then!' I roared to the night. 'I've little enough for you to take, save my knife, and you won't get that hilt first. Let's get this done with!'

Silence flowed in after my words, and my shouting to the night suddenly seemed foolish. Just as I almost decided that I had imagined my pursuers, something ran across my foot. It was a small animal, lithe and swift, a rat or a weasel or perhaps even a squirrel. But it was no wild creature, for it snapped a bite at my leg as it passed. It unnerved me and I jumped back from it. Off to my right, I heard a smothered laugh. Even as I turned towards it, trying to peer through the gloom of the forest, a voice spoke from my left, closer than the laugh had been.

'Where's your wolf, Tom Badgerlock?'

Both mockery and challenge were in the words. Behind me, I heard claws on gravel, a larger animal, a dog perhaps, but when I spun about, the creature had melted back into the darkness. I turned again to the sound of muffled laughter. At least three men, I told myself, and two Wit-beasts. I tried to think only of the logistics of this immediate fight, and nothing beyond it. I would consider the full implications of this encounter later. I drew deep slow breaths, waiting for them. I opened my senses fully to the night, pushing away a sudden longing not just for Nighteyes' keener perception but for the comforting sensation of my wolf watching my back. This time I heard the scuttle as the smaller beast approached. I kicked at it, more wildly than

I had intended, but caught it only a glancing blow. It was gone again.

'I'll kill it!' I warned the crouching night, but only mocking laughter met my threat. Then, I shamed myself, shouting furiously, 'What do you want of me? Leave me alone!'

They let the echoes of that childish question and plea be carried off by the wind. The terrible silence that followed was the shadow of my aloneness.

'Where is your wolf, Tom Badgerlock?' a voice called, and this time it was a woman's, melodic with suppressed laughter. 'Do you miss him, renegade?'

The fear that had been flowing with my blood turned suddenly to the ice of fury. I would stand here and I would kill them all and leave their entrails smoking on the road. My fist that had been clenched on my knife haft suddenly loosened, and a relaxed readiness spread through me. Poised, I waited for them. It would come as a sudden rush from all directions, the animals coming in low, and the people attacking high, with weapons. I had only the knife. I'd have to wait until they were close. If I ran, I knew they'd take me from behind. Better to wait and force them to come to me. Then I would kill them, kill them all.

I truly don't know how long I stood there. That sort of readiness can make time stand still or run swift as wind. I heard a dawn bird call, and then another answered it, and still I waited. When light began to stain the night sky, I drew a deeper breath. I took a long look around myself, peering into the trees, but saw nothing. The only movement was the high flight of small birds as they flitted through the branches and the silver fall of the raindrops they shook loose. My stalkers were gone. The little creature that had snapped at me had left no trace of his passage on the wet stone of the road. The larger animal that had crossed behind me had left a single print in the mud at the road's edge. A small dog. And that was all.

I turned and resumed my walk up to Buckkeep Castle. As I strode along, I began to tremble, not with fear, but with the tension that was now leaving me, and the fury that replaced it.

What had they wanted? To scare me. To make me aware of them, to let me know that they knew what I was and where I denned. Well, they had done that, and more. I forced my thoughts into order and tried to coldly assess the full threat they presented. I extended it beyond myself. Did they know about Jinna? Had they followed me from her door, and if so, did they know about Hap as well?

I cursed my own stupidity and carelessness. How could I have ever imagined the Piebalds would leave me alone? The Piebalds knew that Lord Golden came from Buckkeep, and that his servant Tom Badgerlock was Witted. They knew Tom Badgerlock had lopped off Laudwine's arm and stolen their prince-hostage from them. The Piebalds would want revenge. They could have it as easily as posting one of their cowardly scrolls, denouncing me as practising the Wit, the despised beast magic. I would be hanged, quartered and burned for it. Had I supposed that Buckkeep Town or Castle would keep me safe from them?

I should have known that this would happen. Once I plunged back into Buckkeep's court and politics and intrigue, I had become vulnerable to all the plotting and schemes that power attracted. I *had* known this would happen, I admitted bitterly. And for some fifteen years that knowledge had kept me away from Buckkeep. Only Chade and his plea for help in recovering Prince Dutiful had lured me back. Cold reality seeped through me now. There were only two courses open to me. I either had to sever all ties and flee, as I had once before, or I had to plunge fully into the swirling intrigue that had always been the Farseer court at Buckkeep. If I stayed, I would have to start thinking like an assassin again, always aware of the risks and threats to myself, and how they affected those around me.

Then I wrenched my thoughts into a more truthful path. I'd have to *be* an assassin again, not just think like one. I'd have to be ready to kill when I encountered people that threatened my prince or me. For there was no avoiding the connection: those who came to taunt Tom Badgerlock about his Wit and the death of his wolf were folk who also knew that Prince Dutiful shared their despised beast magic. It was their handle on the Prince, the lever they would use not just to end the persecution of those with the Wit, but to gain power for themselves. It was no help to me that my sympathies were, in part, with them. In my own life, I had suffered from the taint of being

Witted. I had no desire to see anyone else labour under that burden. If they had not presented such a threat to my prince, I might have sided with them.

My furious striding carried me up to the sentries at the gate to Buckkeep. There was a guardhouse there, and from within came the sound of men's voices and the clatter of soldiers at food. One, a lad of about twenty, lounged by the door, bread and cheese in one hand and a mug of morning beer in the other. He glanced up at me, and then, mouth full, nodded me through the gates. I halted, anger coursing through me like a poison.

'Do you know who I am?' I demanded of him.

He startled, then peered at me more closely. Obviously he was afraid he had offended some minor noble, but a glance at my clothing reassured him.

'You're a servant in the Keep. Aren't you?'

'Whose servant?' I demanded. Foolishness, to call attention to myself this way, and yet I could not stop the words. Had others come this way before me last night, were they inside the keep even now? Had a careless sentry admitted folk bent on killing the Prince? It all seemed too possible.

'Well . . . I don't know!' the boy sputtered. He drew himself up straight, but still had to look up to glare at me. 'How am I supposed to know that? Why should I care?'

'Because, you damned fool, you are guarding the main entrance to Buckkeep Castle. Your queen and your prince depend on you to be alert, and to keep their enemies from walking in. That is why you are here. Isn't it?'

'Well. I—' The boy shook his head in angry frustration, then turned suddenly to the door of the guardhouse. 'Kespin! Can you come out here?'

Kespin was a taller man, and older. He moved like a swordsman, and his eyes were keen above his grizzled beard. They appraised me as a threat and dismissed me. 'What's the problem here?' he asked us both. His voice was not a warning, but an assurance that he could deal with either of us as we deserved.

The sentry waved his beer mug at me. 'He's angry because I don't know whose servant he is.'

'What?'

'I'm Lord Golden's servant,' I clarified. 'And I'm concerned that the sentries on this gate seem to do no more than watch folk go in and out of the keep. I've been walking in and out of Buckkeep Castle for over a fortnight now, and I've never been challenged once. It doesn't seem right to me. A score of years ago, when I visited, the sentries on duty here took their task seriously. There was a time when . . .'

'There was a time when that was needed,' Kespin interrupted me. 'During the Red Ship War. But we're at peace, man. And the keep and the town are full of Outislander folk and nobility from the other duchies for the Prince's betrothal. You can't expect us to know them all.'

I swallowed, wishing I hadn't started this, yet determined to follow it to the end. 'It only takes one mistake for our prince's life to be threatened.'

'Or one mistake to insult some Outislander noble. My orders come down from Queen Kettricken, and she said we were to be welcoming and hospitable. Not suspicious and nasty. Though I'd be willing to make an exception for you.' The grin he gave me somewhat modified his words, yet it was still clear he did not enjoy my questioning of his judgment.

I inclined my head to him. I was going about this all wrong. I should bother Chade about it, and see if he could not put the guards more on edge. 'I see,' I said conciliatingly. 'Well. I but wondered.'

'Well, next time you ride that tall black mare out of here, remember that a man doesn't have to say much to know a lot. And as long as you've made me wonder, what is your name?'

'Tom Badgerlock. Servant to Lord Golden.'

'Ah. His servant.' He smiled knowingly. 'And his bodyguard, right? Yeah, I'd heard some tale of that. And that isn't all that I heard about him. You're not what I expected he'd choose to keep by him.' He gave me an odd look as if I should make some reply to that, but I held my tongue, not knowing what he was implying. After a moment, he shrugged. 'Trust some foreigner to think he needs his own guard even while he lives in Buckkeep Castle. Well, go on with you, Tom Badgerlock.

We know you now, and I hope that helps you sleep better at night.'

So they passed me into Buckkeep Castle. I walked away from them, feeling both foolish and dissatisfied. I must speak with Kettricken, I decided, and convince her that the Piebalds were still a very real danger to Dutiful. Yet I doubted my queen would have even a moment to spare for me in the days to come. The betrothal ceremony was tonight. Her thoughts would be full of her Outisland negotiations.

The kitchens were well astir. Maids and pages were preparing ranks of teapots and rows of porridge tureens. The smells awoke my hunger. I paused to load a breakfast tray for Lord Golden. I stacked a platter with smoked ham and fresh morning rolls and a pot of butter and strawberry preserves. There was a basket of pears from the keep orchard, and I chose firm ones. As I left the kitchen, a garden maid with a tray of flowers on her arm greeted me. 'You're Lord Golden's man?' she asked, and at my nod, she motioned me to a halt so that she could add a bouquet of fresh-cut flowers and a tiny nosegay of sweet white buds to the tray I carried. 'For his lordship,' she told me needlessly, and then hastened on her way.

I climbed the stairs to Lord Golden's chambers, knocked and then entered. The door to his bedchamber was closed, but before I had finished setting out his breakfast things, he emerged fully dressed. His gleaming hair had been smoothed back from his brow and was secured at the nape of his neck with a blue silk ribbon. A blue jacket was slung over his arm. He wore a shirt of white silk, the chest puffed with lace, and blue leggings a shade darker than the jacket. With the gold of his hair and his amber eyes, the effect was like a summer sky. He smiled warmly at me. 'Good to see that you've realized your duties require you to arise early, Tom Badgerlock. Now if only your taste in clothing would likewise awaken.'

I bowed gravely to him and drew out his chair. I spoke softly, casually, as his friend rather than in my role as servant. 'The truth is that I have not been to bed. Hap did not come home until the dim hours of the morning. And on my walk home, I encountered some Piebalds who delayed me a bit longer.'

The smile melted from his face. He did not take his chair,

but seized my wrist in a cool grip. 'Are you hurt?' he asked
earnestly.

'No,' I assured him, and gestured him to the table. He sat down
reluctantly. I moved to the side of the table and uncovered the
dishes before him. 'That was not their intent. They just wanted
to let me know that they knew my name, where I lived, and that
I am Witted. And that my wolf is dead.'

I had to force out the last words. It was as if I could live with that
truth so long as I did not utter it aloud. I coughed and hastily took
up the cut flowers. I handed the nosegay to him and muttered, 'I'll
put these ones by your bedside.'

'Thank you,' he returned in a voice as muted as mine.

I found a vase in his room. Evidently even the garden-maid was
more familiar with Lord Golden's niceties than I was. I filled it
with water from his wash-pitcher and set the flowers on a small
table adjacent to his bed. When I returned, he had donned his
blue jacket and the white nosegay was pinned to the front of it.

'I need to speak to Chade as soon as I can,' I said as I poured
his tea. 'But I can't very well go and hammer on his door.'

He lifted the cup and sipped. 'Don't the secret passages offer you
access to his rooms?'

I gave Lord Golden a look. 'You know that old fox. His secrets
belong to him alone, and he will not risk anyone spying on him in
an unguarded moment. He must have access to the corridors, but
I don't know how. Was he up very late last night?'

Lord Golden winced. 'He was still dancing when I decided to
seek my bed. For an old man, he finds an amazing wealth of
energy when he wishes to enjoy himself. But I'll send a page
round with a message to him. I'll invite him to ride with me
this afternoon. Is that soon enough?' He had caught the anxiety
in my voice but was not asking questions. I was grateful for
that.

'It will do,' I assured him. 'It will probably be the soonest that
his mind is clear.' I rattled my own head as if it would settle my
thoughts. 'There is suddenly so much to think of, so many things
I must worry about. If these Piebalds know about me, then they
know about the Prince.'

'Did you recognize any of them? Were they from Laudwine's band?'

'It was dark. And they stayed well back from me. I heard a woman's voice and a man's, but I'm sure there were at least three of them. One was bonded with a dog, and another with a small, swift mammal – a rat or a weasel or a squirrel, perhaps.' I took a breath. 'I want the guards at Buckkeep's gates to be put on alert. And the Prince should have someone accompanying him at all times. "A tutor of the well-muscled sort", as Chade himself once suggested. And I need to make arrangements with Chade, for ways to contact him if I need his help or advice immediately. And the keep should be patrolled daily for rats, especially the Prince's chambers.' He took a breath to speak, then bit down on his questions. Instead, he said, 'I fear I must give you one more thing to think about. Prince Dutiful passed a note to me last night, demanding to know when you will begin his Skill lessons.'

'He wrote down those words?'

At Lord Golden's reluctant nod, I was horrified. I had been aware that the Prince missed me. Linked by the Skill as we were, I must be aware of such things. I had put up my own Skill-walls to keep my thoughts private from the young man, but he was not so adept. Several times I had felt his feeble efforts to reach towards me, but I had ignored them, promising myself that a better time would soon present itself. Evidently my prince was not so patient. 'Oh, the boy must be taught caution. Some things should never be committed to paper, and those—'

My tongue suddenly faltered. I must have gone pale, for Lord Golden stood up abruptly and became my friend the Fool as he offered me his chair. 'Are you all right, Fitz? Is it a seizure coming on?'

I dropped into the chair. My head was spinning as I pondered the depth of my folly. I could scarcely get the breath to admit my idiocy. 'Fool. All my scrolls, all my writings. I came so swiftly to Chade's summons, I left them there in my cottage. I told Hap to close up the house before he came to Buckkeep, but he would not have hidden them, only shut the door to my study. If the Piebalds are clever enough to connect me with Hap . . .'

I let the thought trail away. I needed to say no more to him. His eyes were huge. The Fool had read all that I had so recklessly committed to paper. Not only my own identity was bared there, but also many Farseer matters better left forgotten. And personal vulnerabilities also were exposed in those cursed scrolls. Molly, my lost love. Nettle, my bastard daughter. How could I have been so stupid as to set such thoughts to paper? How could I have let the false comfort of writing about such things lull me into exposing them? No secret was safe unless it was locked solely in a man's own mind. It should all have been burned, long ago.

'Please, Fool. See Chade for me. I have to go there. Now. Today.'

The Fool set a cautious hand to my shoulder. 'Fitz. If they are gone, it is already too late. If Tom Badgerlock goes racing off today, you will only stir curiosity and invite pursuit. You may lead the Piebalds straight to them. They will be expecting you to bolt after they threatened you. They'll be watching the gates out of Buckkeep. So, think coolly. It could be that your fears are groundless. How would they connect Tom Badgerlock to Hap, let alone know where the boy came from? Take no reckless action. See Chade first and tell him what you fear. And speak to Prince Dutiful. His betrothal is tonight. The lad holds himself well, but his is a thin and brittle façade. See him, reassure him.' Then he paused and ventured, 'Perhaps someone else could be dispatched to—'

'No.' I cut him off firmly. 'I must go myself. Some of what is there I will take, and the rest I will destroy.' My mind danced past the charging buck that the Fool had carved into my tabletop. FitzChivalry Farseer's emblem graced Tom Badgerlock's board. Even that seemed a threat to me now. Burn it, I decided. Burn the whole cottage to the ground. Leave no trace that I had ever lived there. Even the herbs growing in the garden told too much about me. I should never have left that shell of myself for anyone to nose through; I should never have allowed myself to leave my marks so plainly on anything.

The Fool patted me on the shoulder. 'Eat something,' he suggested. 'Then wash your face and change your clothes. Make no abrupt decisions. If we hold our course, we'll survive this, Fitz.'

'Badgerlock,' I reminded him, and hauled myself to my feet. The roles, I decided, must be adhered to sharply. 'I beg pardon, my lord. I felt a moment's faintness, but I am recovered now. I apologize for interrupting your breakfast.'

For an instant the Fool's sympathy for me shone naked in his eyes. Then, without a word, he resumed his seat at the table. I refilled his teacup, and he ate in pondering silence. I moved about the room, seeking tasks to busy myself, but his innate tidiness had left me little to do in my role as servant. I suddenly perceived that his neatness was a part of his privacy. He had schooled himself to leave no sign of himself save those that he wished to be seen. It was a discipline I would do well to adopt. 'Would my lord excuse me for a few moments?' I asked.

He set down his cup and thought for a moment. Then, 'Certainly. I expect to go out shortly, Badgerlock. See that you clear away the breakfast things, bring fresh water for the pitchers, tidy the hearth and bring wood for the fire. Then, I suggest you continue to sharpen your fighting skills with the guardsmen. I shall expect you to accompany me when I ride this afternoon. Please see that you are dressed appropriately.'

'Yes, my lord,' I agreed quietly. I left him eating and went into my own dim chamber. I considered it quickly. Nothing would I keep here, I decided, save the items appropriate to Tom Badgerlock. I washed my face and flattened my butchered hair. I donned my blue servant's garb. Then I gathered all my old clothing and saddlepack, the roll of lock-picks and tools that Chade had given me, and the few other items that I had brought from my cottage. In the course of my hasty sorting, I came across a salt-water-shrivelled purse with a lump in it. The leather strings had dried shut and stiff so that I had to cut them to get it open. When I shook out the contents, the lump was the odd figurine the Prince had picked up on the beach during our ill-fated Skill-adventure. I slid it back into the ruined purse to return to him later and put it on top of my bundle. Then I shut the door to my bedchamber and walked across the pitch-dark room to press on a different section of wall. It gave way noiselessly to my push. Tentative fingers of daylight overhead betrayed the slits that admitted light to the secret passages of the keep. I closed the door firmly behind myself and began the steep climb to Chade's tower.

TWO

Chade's Servant

Hoquin the White had a rabbit of which he was extremely fond. It lived in his garden, came at his beck, and would rest motionless on his lap for hours. Hoquin's Catalyst was a very young woman, little more than a child. Her name was Redda but Hoquin called her Wild-eye, for she had one eye that always peered off to one side. She did not like the rabbit, for whenever she seated herself near Hoquin the creature would try to drive her away by nipping her sharply. One day the rabbit died, and upon finding it dead in the garden, Redda gutted and skinned the creature and cut it up for the pot. It was only after Hoquin the White had eaten of it that he missed his pet. Redda delightedly told him he had dined upon it. Rebuked, the unchastened Catalyst replied, 'But master, you yourself foresaw this. Did not you write in your seventh scroll, "The Prophet hungered for the warmth of his flesh even as he knew it would mean his end?"'

Scribe Cateren, of the White Prophet Hoquin

I was about halfway to Chade's tower when I suddenly realized what I was really doing. I was fleeing, heading for a bolt hole, and secretly hoping that my old mentor would be there, to tell me exactly what I should do as he had in the days when I was his apprentice assassin.

My steps slowed. What is appropriate in a lad of seventeen ill becomes a man of thirty-five. It was time I began to find my own way in the world of court intrigues. Or time that I left it completely.

I was passing one of the small niches in the corridor that indicated a peephole. There was a small bench in it. I set my bundle of possessions on it and sat down to gather my thoughts. What, rationally, was my best course of action?

Kill them all.

It would have been a fine plan if I had known who they were. The second course of action was more complicated. I had to protect not just myself but also the Prince from the Piebalds. I set aside my concerns for my own safety to ponder the danger to the Prince. Their bludgeon was that at any time they could betray either of us as Witted. The dukes of the Six Duchies would not tolerate such taint in their monarch. It would destroy not just Kettricken's hope of a peaceful alliance with the Outislands, but very likely lead to a toppling of the Farseer throne. But such an extreme action would have no value that I could see to the Piebalds. Once Dutiful was flung down, their knowledge was no longer useful. Worse, they would have brought down a queen who was urging her people to have tolerance for the Witted. No. The threat to expose Dutiful was useful only so long as he remained in line for the throne. They would not seek to kill him, only to bend him to their will.

And what could that entail? What would they ask? Would they demand that the Queen strictly enforce the laws that prohibited Witted ones from being put to death simply for carrying the bloodlines for that magic? Would they want more? They'd be fools if they did not try to secure some power for themselves. If there were dukes or nobles who also were Old Blood, perhaps the Piebalds would endeavour to bring them into royal favour. I wondered if the Bresingas had come to court for the betrothal ceremony. That would be worth investigating. The mother and son were definitely Old Blood, and had co-operated with the Piebalds in luring the Prince away. Would they take a more active role now? And how would the Piebalds persuade Kettricken that their threats were in earnest? Who or what could they destroy in order to demonstrate their power?

Simple answer. Tom Badgerlock. I was but a playing piece on the board as far as they were concerned, a minor servant, but an unpleasant fellow who had already upset their plans and maimed one of their leaders. They'd showed themselves to me last night, confident that I would pass the 'message' to those actually in power in Buckkeep. And then, to prove to the Farseers that they were vulnerable, the Piebalds would pull me down as hounds pull down a stag. I would be the object lesson to Kettricken and Dutiful.

I lowered my face into my hands. My best course of action was to flee. Yet having returned to Buckkeep, even so briefly, I hated to leave again. This cold castle of stone had been my home once, and despite the illegitimacy of my birth, the Farseers were my family.

A whisper of sound caught my ear. I sat up straight, and then realized that it was a young girl's voice, penetrating the thick stone wall to reach me in my hidden spy-place. With a weary curiosity, I leaned forward to the peephole and peered through it. A bedchamber, lavishly furnished, greeted my gaze. A dark-haired girl stood with her back to me. Next to the hearth, a grizzled old warrior lounged in a chair. Some of the scarring on his face was deliberate – fine lacerations rubbed with ash, considered decorative by the Outislanders – but some of it was the track of an earnest blade. Grey streaked his hair and peppered his short beard. He was cleaning and cutting his nails with his belt knife while the girl practised a dance step before him.

'—And two to the side, one back, and turn,' she chanted breathlessly as her small feet followed her own instructions. As she spun lightly about in a whirl of embroidered skirts, I glimpsed her face for an instant. It was the Narcheska Elliania, Dutiful's intended. No doubt she was practising for their first dance together tonight.

'And again, two steps to the side, and two steps back and—'

'One step back, Elli,' the man corrected her. 'And then the turn. Try it again.'

She halted where she stood and said something quickly in her own language.

'Elliania, practise the farmers' tongue. It goes with their dance,' he replied implacably.

'I don't care to,' the girl announced petulantly. 'Their flat language is as insipid as this dance.' She dropped her hold on her skirts, clasped her elbows and folded her arms on her chest. 'It's stupid. All this stepping and twirling. It's like pigeons bobbing their heads up and down and pecking each other before they mate.'

'Yes. It is,' he agreed affably. 'And for exactly the same reason.

Now do it. And do it perfectly. If you can remember the steps of a sword exercise, you can master this. Or would you have these haughty farmers think that the God Runes have sent them a clumsy little boat-slave to wed their pretty prince?'

She showed her very white teeth to him in a grimace. Then she snatched up her skirts, held them scandalously high to reveal that she was barefoot and barelegged, and went through the steps in a frenzy. 'Two-steps-to-the-side-and-one-step-back-and-spin-and-two-steps-to-the-side-and-one-step-back-and-spin-and-two-steps-to-the-side—' Her furious chant changed the graceful dance to a frantic cavorting. The man grinned at her prancing, but did not intervene. *The God Runes*, I thought to myself, and unearthed the familiar ring of the words. It was what the Outislanders called the scattered isles that made up their domain. And the single Outislander chart that I had ever seen did impart a runic rendering to each of the small pieces of land that broke their icy waters.

'Enough!' the warrior snorted suddenly.

The girl's face was flushed with her efforts, her breath coming swift. But she did not stop until the man came suddenly to his feet and caught her up in an embrace. 'Enough, Elliania. Enough. You have shown me that you can do it, and do it perfectly. Let it go for now. But tonight you must be all grace and beauty and charm. Show yourself as the little spitfire that you are, and your pretty prince may decide to take a tamer bride. And you wouldn't want that.' He set her down on her feet and resumed his chair.

'Yes, I would.' Her response was instantaneous.

His reply was more measured. 'No. You wouldn't. Unless you'd like my belt across your backside as well?'

'No.' Her reply was so stiff that I immediately perceived his threat was not an idle one.

'No.' He made the word an agreement. 'And I would not relish doing it. But you are my sister's daughter, and I will not see the line of our mothers disgraced. Would you?'

'I don't want to disgrace my mothers' line.' The child held herself warrior-straight as she declared this. But then her shoulders began to shake as she went on, 'But I don't want to marry that prince. His mother looks like a snow harpy. He'll make me fat with babies, and they'll all be pale and cold as ice wraiths. Please, Peottre, take me home. I don't want to have to live in this great cold cave. I don't want that boy to do the thing to me that makes babies. I just want our mothers' low house, and to ride my pony out in the wind. And I want my own boat to scull across Sendalfjord, and my own skates of gear to set for fish. And when I am grown, my own bench in the mothers' house, and a man who knows that it is right to dwell in the house of his wife's mothers. All I want is what any other girl my age wants. That prince will tear me away from my mothers' line as a branch is torn from a vine, and I will grow brittle and dry here until I snap into tiny pieces!'

'Elliania, Elliania, dear heart, don't!' The man came to his feet with the fluid grace of a warrior, yet his body was stocky and thick, a typical Outislander. He caught the child up and she buried her face in his shoulder. Sobs shook her, and tears stood in the warrior's eyes as he held her. 'Hush, now. Hush. If we are clever, if you are strong and swift and dance like the swallows above the water, it will never come to that. Never. Tonight is but a betrothal, little shining one, not a wedding. Do you think Peottre would abandon you here? Foolish little fish! No one is going to make a baby with you tonight, or any other night, not for years yet! And even then, it will happen only if you want it to. That I promise you. Do you think I would shame our mothers' line by letting it be otherwise? This is but a dance we do. Nevertheless, we must tread it perfectly.' He set her back on her little bare feet. He tilted her chin up so she must look at him, and wiped the tears from her cheeks with the back of one scarred hand. 'There, now. There. Smile for me. And remember. The first dance you must give to the pretty prince. But the second one is for Peottre. So, show me now how we will dance together, this silly farmers' prancing.'

He began a tuneless humming that set a beat, and she gave her small hands into his. Together they stepped out a measure, she moving like thistledown and he like a swordsman. I watched them dance, the girl's eyes focused up at the man's, and the man staring off over her head into a distance only he could see.

A knock at the door halted their dance. 'Enter,' Peottre called, and a serving woman came in with a dress draped over her arm. Abruptly, Peottre and Elliania stepped apart and became still. They could not have been more wary if a serpent had slithered into the room. Yet the woman was garbed as an Outislander, one of their own.

Her manner was odd. She made no curtsey. She held the dress up for their inspection, giving it a shake to loosen the folds of the fabric. 'The Narcheska will wear this tonight.'

Peottre ran his eyes over it. I had never seen anything like it. It was a woman's dress, cut for a child. The fabric was a pale blue, swooping low at the neckline. A gush of lace on the front along with some clever gathers drew up the fabric. It would help the Narcheska pretend a bosom she did not yet possess. Elliania reddened as she stared at it. Peottre was more direct. He stepped between Elliania and the dress as if he would protect her from it. 'No. She will not.'

'Yes. She will. The Lady prefers it. The young prince will find it most attractive.' She offered not an opinion, but a directive.

'No. She will not. It is a mockery of who she is. That is not the garb of a God's Rune narcheska. For her to wear that is an insult to our mothers' house.' With a sudden step and a slash of his hand, Peottre knocked the dress from her hands to the floor.

I expected the woman to cower back from him or beg his pardon. Instead she just gave him a flat-eyed stare and after a brief pause said, 'The Lady says, "It has nothing to do with the God Runes. This is a dress that Six Duchies men will understand. She will wear it."' She paused again as if thinking, then added, 'For her not to wear it would present a danger to your mothers' house.' As if Peottre's action had been no more than a child's wilful display, she stooped and lifted the dress again.

Behind Peottre, Elliania gave a low cry. It sounded like pain. As he turned to her, I caught a quick glimpse of her face. It was set into a determined stillness, but sweat suddenly misted her brow and she had gone as pale as she had been flushed before.

'Stop it!' he said in a low voice, and I first thought that he spoke to the girl. Then he glanced over his shoulder. Yet when he spoke again, he did not appear to be addressing the servant at all. 'Stop it!' he repeated. 'Dressing her like a whore was not a part of our arrangement. We will not be driven into it. Stop it, or I will kill her, and you will lose your eyes and your ears here.' And he drew his belt knife and advancing upon the serving woman, he laid the edge of it along her throat. The woman did not blanch or shrink away. She stood still, her eyes glittering, almost smirking at his threat. She made no response to his words. Then suddenly Elliania drew a deeper, ragged breath and her shoulders sagged. A moment later, she squared them and stood upright. No tears escaped her.

In a fluid motion, Peottre snatched the dress from the woman's arm. His knife must have been honed to a razor's edge, for it slashed effortlessly down the front of the gown. He threw the fluttering ruins to the floor and trod upon them. 'Get out!' he told the woman.

'As you will, my lord, I am sure,' she muttered. But the words were a mockery as she turned and retired. She did not hurry, and he watched her leave until the door closed behind her. Then he turned back to Elliania. 'Are you much hurt, little fish?'

She shook her head, a quick gesture, chin up. A brave lie, for she looked as if she would faint.

I stood up silently. My forehead was gritty with dust from leaning against the wall as I spied on them. I wondered if Chade knew the Narcheska did not wish to wed our prince. I wondered if he knew that Peottre did not consider the betrothal to be a binding gesture. I wondered what illness ailed the Narcheska, and wondered, too, who 'the Lady' was and why the servant was so disrespectful. I tucked my bits of information away alongside my questions, gathered up my clothing and resumed my trek up to Chade's tower. At least my spying had made me forget my own concerns for a short time.

I climbed the last steep stair to the tiny room at the top, and pushed on the small door there. From some distant part of the castle, I caught a strain of music. Probably minstrels limbering their fingers and instruments for tonight's festivities. I stepped out from behind a rack of wine bottles into Chade's tower room. I caught my breath, then shouldered the rack silently back into place and set my bundle down beside it. The man bent over Chade's worktable was muttering to himself, a guttural singsong of complaints. The music came louder and clearer with his words. Five noiseless steps carried me in towards the corner of the hearth and Verity's sword. My hand just touched the hilt as he turned to me. He was the half-wit I had glimpsed in the stableyard a fortnight ago. He held a tray stacked with bowls, a pestle, and a teacup, and in his surprise he tipped it and all the crockery slid to one end. Hastily he set it down on the table. The music had stopped.

For a time, we stared at one another in mutual consternation. The set of his eyelids made him appear permanently sleepy. The end of his tongue was pushed out of his mouth against his upper lip. He had small ears that were snug to his head below his raggedly cropped hair. His clothing hung on him, the sleeves of his shirt and the legs of his pants sawed off, marking them as the cast-offs of a larger man. He was short and pudgy, and somehow all his differences alarmed me. A shiver of premonition ran over me. I knew he was not a threat, but I did not wish him near me. From the way he scowled, the feeling was mutual.

'Go away!' He spoke in a guttural, soft-mouthed way.

I took a breath and spoke evenly. 'I am permitted to be here. Are you?' I had already deduced that this must be Chade's servant, the boy who hauled his wood and water and tidied up behind the old man. But I did not know how deeply he was in Chade's confidence, and so I did not say Chade's name. Surely the old assassin could not be so careless as to entrust his secret ways to a half-wit.

YOU. GO AWAY. DON'T SEE ME!

The solid thrust of Skill-magic that he launched at me sent me staggering. If I had not already had my walls up, I am certain that I would have done as he told me, gone away and not seen him. As I slammed my Skill-walls tighter and thicker around me, I wondered fleetingly if he had done this to me before. Would I even recall it if he had?

LEAVE ME ALONE! DON'T HURT ME! GO AWAY, STINK DOG!

I was aware of his second blast, but less cowed by it. Even so, I did not lower my walls to Skill back at him. I spoke my words in a voice that shook despite my best effort to hold it steady. 'I won't hurt you. I never had any intention of hurting you. I'll leave you alone, if that is what you wish. But I won't go away. And I won't allow you to push me like that.' I tried for the firm tones of someone reprimanding a child for bad manners. He probably had no idea what he was doing; doubtless he was only using a weapon that had previously worked for him.

But instead of chagrin, his face flared with anger. And fear? His eyes, already small, nearly disappeared in his fat cheeks when he narrowed them. For a moment, his mouth hung ajar and his tongue stuck out even farther. Then he picked up his tray and slammed it back to the table so that the dishes on it jumped. '*Go away!*' His Skill echoed the angry commands of his mouth. '*You don't see me!*'

I groped my way into Chade's chair and sat down in it firmly. 'I do see you,' I replied evenly. 'And I'm not going away.' I crossed my arms on my chest. I hoped he could not see how rattled I was. 'You should just do your work and pretend that *you* don't see *me*. And when you are done, *you* should go away.'

I was not going to retreat from him; I could not. For me to leave would reveal to him how I had come, and if he did not already know that, I wasn't going to show him. I leaned back in my chair and tried to look as if I were relaxing there.

He glared at me, and the beat of his Skill-fury against my walls was daunting. He was strong. If he were this strong, untrained, what would his talent be if he could learn to master it? It was a frightening thought. I stared at the cold hearth, but watched him from the corner of my eye. Either he had finished his work, or decided not to do it. In any case, he picked up his tray, stalked across the room, and tugged at a scroll rack. This was the entry I had seen Chade once use. He vanished inside it, but as the rack swung into place behind him, both his voice and his Skill reached me again. '*You stink like dog poop. Chop you up and burn you.*'

His anger was like an ebbing tide that slowly left me stranded. After a time, I lifted my hands and pressed them to my temples. The stress of holding my walls so tight and solid was beginning to tell on me, but I dared not let them down just yet. If he could sense my lowering them, if he chose then to blast me with a Skill-command, I would be prey to it, just as Dutiful had been prey to my impulsive

Skill-command not to fight me. I feared that his mind still bore the stamp of that decree.

That was yet another worry that I must tend to. Did that order still restrain him? I made the resolution then that I must discover how to reverse my Skill-command. If I did not, I knew it would soon become a barrier to any true friendship between us. Then I wondered if the Prince were cognizant at all of what I had done to him. It had been an accident, I told myself, and then despised my lie. A burst of my temper had imprinted that command on my prince's mind. It shamed me that I had done so, and the sooner it was removed, the better for both of us.

Dimly I became aware of music again. I made a tentative connection. As I gradually lowered my walls, it became louder in my mind. Putting my hands over my ears did not affect it at all. Skilling music. I had never even imagined such a thing, yet the half-wit was doing it. When I drew my attention away from it, it faded into the shushing curtain of thoughts that stood always at the edges of my Skill. Most of it was formless whispering, the overheard thoughts of the folk who possessed just enough talent to let their most urgent thoughts float out onto the Skill. If I focused my abilities on them, I could sometimes pluck whole thoughts and images from their minds, but they lacked enough Skill to be aware of me, let alone reply. This half-wit was different. He was a roaring Skill-fire, his music the heat and smoke of his wild talent. He made no effort to hide it; possibly he had no idea how to hide it, or had any reason to do so.

I relaxed, keeping only the wall that ensured my private thoughts would remain hidden from Dutiful's budding Skill-talent. Then with a groan, I lowered my head into my hands as a Skill-headache thundered through my skull.

'Fitz?'

I was aware of Chade's presence an instant before he touched my shoulder. Even so, I startled as I awoke and raised my hands as if to ward off a blow.

'What ails you, boy?' he demanded of me, and then leaned closer to peer at me. 'Your eyes are full of blood! When did you last sleep?'

'Just now, I think.' I managed a feeble smile. I ran my hands through my chopped hair. It was sweated flat to my skull. I could recall only tatters of my fleeting nightmare. 'I met your servant,' I told him shakily.

'Thick? Ah. Well, not the brightest man in the keep, but he serves my purpose admirably. Hard for him to betray secrets when he hasn't the sense to recognize a secret if he fell over it. But enough of him. As soon as Lord Golden's message reached me, I came up here, hoping to catch you. What is this about Piebalds in Buckkeep Town?'

'He wrote that down in a message?' I was incensed.

'Not in so many words. Only I would have picked out the sense of it. Now tell me.'

'They followed me last night . . . this morning. To scare me and to let me know they knew me. That they could find me any time. Chade. Set that aside for a moment. Did you know your servant – what is his name? Thick? Did you know Thick is Skilled?'

'At what? Breaking teacups?' The old man snorted as if I had made a bad jest. He heaved a sigh and gestured at the cold fireplace in disgust. 'He's supposed to set a small fire in the hearth each day. Half the time he forgets to do that. What are you talking about?'

'Thick is Skilled. Strongly Skilled. He nearly dropped me in my tracks when I accidentally startled him here. If I had not been keeping up my walls to ward my mind from Dutiful, I think he would have blasted away every thought in my head. "Go away" he told me, and "Don't see me". And "Don't hurt me". And Chade, you know, I think he's done that before. To me, even. Once, in the stableyard, I saw some of the boys teasing him. And I heard, almost as if someone said it aloud, "Don't see me". And then the stableboys were all going about their business and after that, I don't recall that I *did* see him there. Any more, I mean.'

Chade slowly sank down into my chair. He reached out to take one of my hands in his as if that would make my words more comprehensible. Or perhaps he sought to feel if fever had taken me. 'Thick has the Skill-magic,' he said carefully. 'That's what you're telling me.'

'Yes. It's raw and untrained, but it burns in him like a bonfire. I've never encountered anything like it before.' I shut my eyes, put my palms flat to my temples and tried to push my skull back together. 'I feel like I've taken a beating.'

A moment later, Chade said gruffly, 'Here. Try this.'

I took the cold wet cloth he offered me and placed it across my eyes. I knew better than to ask him for anything stronger. The stubborn old man had made up his mind that my pain drugs would interfere with my ability to teach Dutiful to Skill. No good to long for the relief that elfbark could bring. If there were any left in Buckkeep Castle, he'd hidden it well.

'What am I going to do about this?' he muttered, and I lifted a corner of the cloth to peer at him.

'About what?'

'Thick and his Skill.'

'Do? What can you do? The half-wit has it.'

He resumed his seat. 'From what I've translated of the old Skill-scrolls, that makes him something of a threat to us. He's a wild talent, untaught and undisciplined. His Skilling can inadvertently disrupt Dutiful just as he is trying to learn. Angered, he can use his Skill against people; apparently, he has already done so. Worse, you say he is strong. Stronger than you?'

I lifted one hand in a futile gesture. 'I have no way of knowing. My talent has always been erratic, Chade. And I know no way of measuring it. But I have not felt so besieged since all of Galen's coterie turned their collective strength on me.'

'Mmh.' He leaned back in his chair and considered the ceiling. 'The most prudent course might simply be to put him down. Kindly, of course. It is not his fault he is a threat to us. Less radical would be to begin dosing him with elfbark to dampen or destroy his talent. But as your reckless abuse of that herb over the last decade has not completely scoured the Skill-ability from you, I have less faith in its efficacy than the writers of the Skill-scrolls did. Yet I tend towards a third path. More dangerous, perhaps. I wonder if that is not why it appeals to me, because the possibilities are as great as the hazard.'

'Teach him?' At Chade's tentative smile, I groaned. 'Chade, no. We don't know enough between the two of us to be certain that we can teach Dutiful safely, and he is a tractable boy with a bright mind. Thick is already hostile to me. His insults make me fear that somehow he has detected that I am Witted. And what he has learned on his own is potent enough to be dangerous to me if I try to teach him more.'

'Then you think we should kill him? Or cripple his talent?'

I didn't want that decision to be mine. I didn't even want to know that such a decision was being made, yet here I was again, neck deep in Farseer plotting. 'I don't think either of those things,' I muttered. 'Cannot we just send him very far away?'

'The weapon we throw away today is the one at our throats tomorrow,' Chade returned implacably. 'That is why King Shrewd chose, long ago, to have his bastard grandson close to hand. We must make the same sort of decision with Thick. Use him, or render him useless. There is no middle path.' He held one hand out towards me, palm up, and added, 'As we have seen with the Piebalds.'

I do not know if he intended it as a rebuke to me, but his words stung nonetheless. I leaned back in my chair and let the wet cloth fall over my eyes.

'What would you have had me do? Kill them all, not just the Piebalds who lured the Prince away but also the Old Blood elders who came to our aid? And then the Queen's own huntswoman? And then the Bresinga family? And Sydel, young Civil Bresinga's intended, and—'

'I know, I know,' he cut me off as I pointed out the widening circle of assassinations that still would not have completely protected our secret. 'And yet, there we are. They have shown us they are swift and competent. You have scarcely been back at Buckkeep for two days, and yet they were watching and ready for you. Am I correct in saying that last night was the first time you had ventured into town?' At my nod he continued, 'And they immediately located you. And made very sure that you knew they were aware of you. A deliberate gambit.' He took a deep breath and I saw him turning it over in his mind, trying to see what message they had intended to convey. 'They know the Prince is Witted. They know you are Witted. They can destroy either of you whenever they please.'

'We already knew that. I think this was intended in a different way.' I took a breath, put my thoughts in order, and gave him a skeletal account of my encounter. 'I see this in a new light now. They wanted me to be frightened, and to think what I could do to be safe from them. I can either be a threat to them, one they would eliminate, or I can be useful to them.' That wasn't exactly how I had seen it earlier, but the implications now seemed obvious. They had frightened me, and then let me go, to give me time to realize I could not possibly kill them all. Impossible to know how many now shared my secret. The only way I could survive was to become useful to them. What would they ask of me? 'Perhaps as a spy within Buckkeep Castle. Or as a weapon within the keep, someone they could turn against the Farseers from within.'

Chade had followed my thoughts effortlessly. 'Is that not what we could choose? Hmm. Yes. For a time at least, I counsel you to be wary. Yet open, too. Be ready for them to contact you again. See what they demand, and what they offer. If necessary, let them think you will betray the Prince.'

'Dangle myself like bait.' I sat up and lifted the cloth off my eyes.

A smile twitched at his mouth. 'Exactly.' He held out a hand and I gave him the wet cloth. He tilted his head and regarded me critically. 'You look terrible. Worse than a man coming off a weeklong drunk. Are you in much pain?'

'I can deal with it,' I replied gruffly.

He nodded to himself, pleased. 'I'm afraid you'll have to. But it grows less each time, doesn't it? Your body is learning to handle it. I think perhaps it is like a swordsman training his muscles to tolerate the hours of drill.'

I leaned forward with a sigh to rub my stinging eyes. 'I think it is more like a bastard learning to tolerate pain.'

'Well. Whatever it is, I am pleased.' His reply was brisk. I would get no sympathy from the old man. He stood. 'Go and get cleaned up, Fitz. Eat something. Be seen. Go armed, but casually so.' He paused. 'You recall where my poisons and tools are kept, I am sure. Take whatever you need, but leave me a list so I can have my apprentice replace the inventory.'

I didn't retort that I would take nothing, that I was no longer an assassin. I had already thought of one or two powders that might be useful if I found myself out-numbered as I had this morning. 'When will I meet his new apprentice of yours?' I asked casually.

'You have.' Chade smiled. 'When will you know my new apprentice? I am not sure that would be wise, or comfortable, for either of you. Or for me. Fitz, I am going to ask you to be honourable about this. Leave me this secret, and do not attempt to pry into it. Trust me that it is better left alone.'

'Speaking of prying, there is something else I should tell you about. I paused on my way up the stairs, and heard voices. I looked in on the Narcheska's room. There is some information I think I should share with you.'

He cocked his head at me. 'Tempting. Very tempting. But you failed to distract me completely. Your promise, Fitz, before you try to lure me into thinking of other things.'

I did not wish to give it, in truth. It was not just curiosity that burned in me, nor even jealousy of an odd sort. It went against all the training I had ever received from the old man. Discover as much as you can about all that is going on around you, he had taught me. You never know what might prove to be useful. His green eyes stared at me balefully until I lowered my gaze before his. I shook my head but I said the words. 'I promise I will not deliberately attempt to discover the identity of your new apprentice. But may I ask one thing? Is he aware of me, of what and who I was?'

'My boy, I do not give out secrets that are not mine to share.'

I gave a small sigh of relief. It would have been uncomfortable to imagine someone in the keep watching me, knowing who I was but shielded from my gaze. At least I was on an equal footing with this new apprentice.

'Now. The Narcheska?'

And so I reported to him, as I had never expected to do again. As I had when I was a boy, I spoke to him the exact words I had overheard, and afterwards he quizzed me as to what I had thought those words had meant. I spoke bluntly. 'I do not know the man's status in the Narcheska's offering to Queen Kettricken. But I do not think he feels bound by the betrothal, and his advice to the girl affirms to her that she need not feel bound.'

'I find that most interesting. It is a valuable titbit, Fitz, and no mistake. Their strange servant intrigues me as well. When your time permits, you could look in on them again, and let me know what you discover.'

'Cannot your new apprentice do that just as well?'

'You are prying again, and you know it. But this time, I will answer. No. My apprentice is no more privy to the network of spy passages in the castle than you were. That is not a matter for apprentices. They have enough to do with minding themselves and their own secrets without being entrusted with mine. But I think I shall have my apprentice pay special attention to the serving woman. That is the piece I fear most in this new puzzle you have handed me. But the spy tunnels and secret ways of Buckkeep remain ours alone. So,' and here a strange smile crooked his mouth, 'I suppose you could see yourself as having reached journeyman status. Not, of course, that you are an assassin any more. We both know that is not so.'

That jest prodded me in a tender place. I did not want to think about how deeply I had slipped back into my old roles as spy and assassin. I'd already killed again for Prince Dutiful, several times. That had been in the heat of anger, while defending myself and rescuing him. Would I kill again, in secret, by poison, in the cold knowledge of necessity, for the Farseers? The most disturbing part of that question was that I could not answer it. I reined my mind to more productive paths.

'Who is the man in the Narcheska's chamber? Besides being her Uncle Peottre, I mean.'

'Ah. Well, your question unwittingly gives you the answer. He is her uncle, her mother's brother. In the old ways of the Outislands, that was more significant than being her father. To them, the mother's lineage was the significant one. A woman's brothers were the important men in the lives of her children. Husbands joined the clans of their wives, and the children took on the clan symbol of their mothers.'

I nodded silently to his words. During the Red Ship War, I had read what scrolls about the Outislanders that the Buckkeep library held, trying to make sense of their war against us. I had also served alongside dissident Outisland warriors on the warship *Rurisk*, and from them learned something of their lands and customs. What he said now matched my recollections on the topic.

Chade tugged at his chin thoughtfully. 'When Arkon Bloodblade approached us with this offer of an alliance, he had the support of his hetgurd behind him. I accepted that, and accepted that as her father, he could arrange Elliania's marriage. I thought perhaps the Outislands had left their matriarchal ways behind them but now I wonder if perhaps Elliania's family clings to them still. But why, then, is there no female relative here, to speak on Elliania's behalf and negotiate the betrothal? Arkon Bloodblade seems to be the one doing the bargaining. Peottre Blackwater has been acting as the Narcheska's chaperone and bodyguard. But now I perceive that he is her advisor as well. Hmm. Perhaps our attentions to her father have been misplaced; I will see that Peottre is accorded more respect.' He furrowed his brow, hastily restructuring his concept of the marriage offer. 'I knew of the woman-servant. I thought she would be the Narcheska's confidante, perhaps her old nursemaid or a poor relative. Yet your spying seems to put her at odds with both Elliania and Peottre. Something is not right here, Fitz.' He sighed heavily, and reluctantly admitted his error. 'I thought we were negotiating this marriage with Bloodblade, Elliania's father. Perhaps it is Elliania's mother's family that I should know more about. But if they are truly the ones offering Elliania, then is Bloodblade a dupe or a puppet? Does he speak with any true authority at all?'

His forehead was graven deep with thoughtfulness as he pondered these things and I realized that the Piebald threat against me had been reduced to a minor concern, something that Chade expected I could largely manage on my own. I could not decide if his confidence in me flattered me, or diminished me to a lesser game-piece. An instant later he recalled me to myself.

'Well. I think we've resolved this as much as we can just now. Extend my regrets to your master, Tom Badgerlock. Let him know that a headache prevents me from enjoying the pleasures of his company this afternoon, but that my prince has been most happy to accept his invitation. That will give Dutiful the time with you that he has been pestering me for. I don't need to remind you to be discreet in your contact with the boy. We don't want to rouse any speculation. And I suggest that you keep your ride either to areas where your privacy is assured, or to very public areas where the Piebalds would have to be bold to seek a contact. In truth, I do not know which to offer as the wiser selection.' He took a breath and his tone changed. 'Fitz. Do not underestimate your influence on the Prince. In our private conversations, he speaks freely of you, with admiration. I am not sure you were wise to reveal your connection to me, but there, it is done. It is not just Skill-instruction he seeks from you, but a man's advice on all aspects of his life. Be careful. An incautious word from you could set our wilful prince's feet on a path where none of us could safely follow him. Please speak positively of his betrothal and encourage him to undertake his royal duties with a willing heart. And in the matter of the Piebalds threatening you . . . well, today might not be the best day to burden him with concerns for you. As it is, some may look askance that our prince chooses to go riding with a foreign noble and his bodyguard on such an important day in his life.' He paused suddenly. 'Not that I'm trying to dictate how you behave with our prince. I know that you have formed a relationship of your own.'

'That's correct,' I said, and tried to keep from sounding brusque. In truth, I had known a moment of anger as he started his long list of directives. Now I took a deep breath. 'Chade. As you have said, the boy is looking to me for a man's advice. I am not a courtier, nor an advisor. If I endeavoured to steer Dutiful merely to suit the goals of the Six Duchies . . .' I let my words drain away before I told him that such a course would be false to all of us. I cleared my throat. 'I wish always to be honest with Dutiful. If he asks for advice, I will tell him what I truly think. But I don't think you need to fear that much. Kettricken has shaped her son. I think he will be true to that training. As for me, well, I suspect the boy does not want to have someone talk to him so much as he wants someone to listen to him. Today I will listen. And regarding my encounter with the Piebalds this morning, I see little need for Dutiful to know about that right now. I may warn him that they are not to be entirely dismissed from his thoughts. They are definitely a force to be reckoned with.

Which brings me to a question of my own. Will the Bresingas be present for the Prince's betrothal ceremony?'

'I assume so. They have been invited, and are expected to arrive sometime today.'

I scratched the back of my neck. My headache was not fading, but it seemed to be changing to an ordinary one rather than one of the Skill variety. 'If you would share such information with me, I would like to know who accompanies them, as well as what horses they rode, the coursing beasts that journeyed with them, hawks, even pets. All in as much detail as can be discovered. Oh, and one other thing. I think we should acquire a ferret or rat-dog for these chambers; something small and light-footed to patrol for rats and other vermin. One of the Wit-beasts I encountered this morning was a rat, or perhaps a weasel or squirrel. Such a creature could be a versatile spy in the castle.'

Chade looked dismayed. 'I'll request a ferret, I think. They are more quiet than a rat-dog, and could accompany you through the corridors.' He cocked his head. 'Are you thinking of taking it as a bond-beast?'

I winced at the question. 'Chade. It doesn't work that way.' I tried to remind myself that he had asked the question out of ignorance, not callously. 'I feel like a newly-widowed man, Chade. I've no wish to bond with any creature just now.'

'I'm sorry, Fitz. It's a difficult thing for me to understand. The words may sound odd, but I meant no disrespect to his memory.'

I changed the subject. 'Well. I'd best tidy myself if I'm to ride with the Prince this afternoon. And we should both ponder what to do about this servant of yours.'

'I think I shall arrange a meeting for all three of us. But not today, nor tonight. Nor even tomorrow, perhaps. The betrothal is what must be managed right now. Nothing must go wrong with that. Do you think that the situation with Thick can wait?'

I shrugged. 'It will have to, I suppose. Good luck with the rest of it.' I rose to go, picking up the basin and wet cloth to tidy up in passage.

'Fitz.' His voice made me pause. 'You know, I have not said so directly, but you should treat these chambers as your own now. I know that a man in your position needs a private spot sometimes. If you wish things changed . . . the bed's position, the hangings, or if you wish food left out for you here, or a supply of brandy. Whatever . . . let me know.'

The offer put a chill down my back. I never wanted this assassin's workroom to belong to me. 'No. Thank you, but no. Let's just leave all as it is for now. Though I may keep some of my things up here. Verity's sword, private things.'

There was some secret regret in his eyes as he nodded. 'If that's all you wish, that's fine. For now,' he conceded. He looked at me critically, but his voice was very gentle as he added, 'I know you still grieve. But you should let me even your hair out for you, or let someone else do it. It draws attention to you, as it is now.'

'I'll see to it myself. Today. Oh. And there is something else.' Strange, how that first urgent concern had almost been driven from my mind by other fears. I took a breath. It seemed even more difficult to confess my carelessness to him now. 'I've been foolish, Chade. When I left my cottage, I did so expecting to return to it soon. I left things there . . . dangerous things, perhaps. Scrolls where I have written down my own thoughts, as well as a history of our waking of the dragons that is, perhaps, too accurate to bear sharing. I need to go back there, soon, to either put those scrolls into a safer place or to destroy them.'

His face had grown graver as I spoke. Now he blew out a long breath. 'Some things are better left unwritten,' he observed quietly. Mild as the rebuke was, it still stung. He stared at the wall but seemed to see into a distance. 'But I confess, I think it is valuable to have the truth recorded somewhere. Think what it would have saved Verity in his quest for the Elderlings if even one accurate scroll had been preserved. So gather your writings, boy, and bring them to safety here. I advise you to wait a day or so before you depart. The Piebalds may be expecting you to bolt. If you went now, likely you'd have some following you. Let me arrange a time and a way for you to go. Do you want me to send some trustworthy men with you? They'd not know who you were or what you went to retrieve, only that they were to aid you.'

I considered it, then shook my head. 'No. I've left too many edges of my secrets showing as it is. I'll take care of this myself, Chade. But there is one other concern I have. I think the guards on the gates of Buckkeep are entirely too relaxed. With Piebalds about and the Prince's betrothal and Outislanders visiting, I think they ought to be more vigilant.'

'I suppose I should see to that as well. Odd. I had thought that persuading you to come here would have eased some of my work onto you and left me more time to be an old man. Instead, you seem intent on giving me ever more to think about and to do. No, do not look at me like that . . . I suppose it is for the best. Work, the old people say, keeps a man young. But perhaps that is something old folk say just because they know they must go on working. Be off with you, Fitz. And try not to discover any more crises for me before the day is out.'

And so I left him sitting in his chair by his cold fireside, looking both thoughtful yet somehow pleased with himself.

THREE

Echoes

On the night that the dastardly Witted bastard murdered King Shrewd in his room, King-in-Waiting Verity's Mountain-born queen chose to flee the safety of Buckkeep Castle. Alone and gravid with child, she fled into the cold and inhospitable night. Some say that King Shrewd's jester, fearing for his own life, begged her protection and accompanied her, but this may be but castle legend to account for his disappearance that night. With the clandestine aid of those sympathetic to her cause, Queen Kettricken crossed the Six Duchies and returned to her childhood home in the Mountain Kingdom. There, she made efforts of her own to discover what had become of her husband, King-in-Waiting Verity. For if he lived, she reasoned, he was now the rightful King of the Six Duchies and their last hope against the depredations of the Red Ships.

She reached the Mountain Kingdom, but her king was not there. She was told that he had left Jhaampe and pressed on in his quest. Nothing had been heard from him since then. Only some few of his men had returned, their wits scattered and some injured as from battle. Her heart knew despair. For a time, she sheltered amongst her native people. One of the tragedies of her arduous journey was the stillbirth of the heir to the Six Duchies throne. It is said that this blow hardened her heart to the necessity of finding her king, for if she did not, his line would die with him and the throne pass to Regal the Pretender. Possessed of a copy of the same map that King Verity had hoped would take him to the land of the Elderlings, Queen Kettricken set out to follow him. Accompanied by the faithful minstrel Starling Birdsong and several servants, the Queen led her band ever deeper into the Mountain fastness. Trolls, pecksies and the mysterious magic of those forbidding lands were but a few of the obstacles *she faced. Nevertheless, eventually she won through to the land of the Elderlings.*

It was an arduous search, but eventually she came to the hidden castle of the Elderlings, a vast hall built all of black and silver stone. There she found that her king had persuaded the Dragon-King of the Elderlings to come to the aid of the Six Duchies. This same Dragon-King, recalling the ancient Elderling oath of alliance with the Six Duchies, bent his knee to Queen Kettricken and King Verity. On his back he carried home not only King Verity and Queen Kettricken but the loyal minstrel Starling Birdsong. King Verity saw his queen and her minstrel safely delivered to Buckkeep. Before his loyal subjects could greet him, before his people even knew he had returned, he left them again. Sword blazing in the sun, he bestrode the Elderling Dragon-King as together they rose into the sky to do battle against the Red Ships.

For the rest of that long and triumphantly bloody season, King Verity led his Elderling allies against the Red Ships. Whenever his folk saw the jewel-bright wings of the dragons in the sky, they knew their king was with them. As the King's forces struck the Red Ship strongholds and fleet, his loyal dukes rallied to his example. The few Red Ships that were not destroyed fled our shores to carry word of the Farseer wrath back to the Outislands. When our shores were cleared of marauding invaders and peace restored to the Six Duchies, King Verity kept his pledge to the Elderlings. The price of their aid was that he would reside with them in their distant land, never to return to the Six Duchies. Some say that our king took a deadly injury in the last days of the Red Ship War, and that it was but his body the Elderlings bore away. It is said by those ones that the body of King Verity lies in a vault of ebony and gleaming gold in a vast cave in their mountain keep. There the Elderlings honour forever the valiant man who sacrificed all to seek aid for his people. But others say that King Verity lives still, well-feasted and highly acclaimed in the Elderling kingdom, and that if ever again the Six Duchies is in need, he will return with his heroic allies to aid his people.

'The Brief Reign of Verity Farseer' Nolus the Scribe

I returned to the stuffy darkness of my little cell. Once I had closed the access to the secret passage, I opened the door to the Fool's chambers in the hopes of gaining at least some natural light. It didn't help much, but there was little I needed to do. I tidied my bedding and looked around my austere room. Safely anonymous. Anyone might live here. Or no one, I thought sarcastically. I buckled on my ugly sword, and made sure of the knife at my belt before I left the room.

The Fool had left a generous share of the food for me. Cold, it was not especially appetizing, but my hunger made up for it. I finished his breakfast and then, recalling his instructions to Tom Badgerlock, took the dishes down to the kitchen. On my return trip, I hauled wood for the hearth and water for the pitchers. I dumped and wiped the washing basins and did the other small and necessary chores of the room. I opened the window shutters wide to air the chamber. The view from his window showed me that we would have a fine if chill day. I closed them again before I left.

I had the hours until our afternoon ride to myself, I decided. I thought of going down to Buckkeep Town but swiftly decided against it. I needed to put my thoughts about Jinna in order before I saw her again and I wished to ponder her worries about young Hap. Nor would I risk that Piebalds might be spying on me. The less interest I took in Jinna or my son, the safer they were.

So I took myself down to the practice courts. Weaponsmaster Cresswell greeted me by name and asked if Delleree had been sufficient challenge to my skills. Even as I groaned appreciatively, I was somewhat surprised to be so well recalled. It was both welcoming and disconcerting. I had to remind myself that perhaps the best way to ensure I was never recognized as the FitzChivalry that had lived in Buckkeep Castle sixteen years ago was to make solid my recognition as Badgerlock. So I deliberately paused to talk with the man, and humbly admitted that Delleree had indeed been more than a match for me. I asked him to recommend a partner for this day's challenge, and he yelled across the courts to a man who moved with the centred ease of a veteran fighter.

Wim's beard was shot with streaks of grey and his waist thickened with his years. I guessed his age at forty-five, a good ten years older than my true age, yet he proved a good match for me. Both his wind and endurance were better than mine, but I knew a few tricks with a blade that made up for some of that. Even so, he was kind enough, after he had beaten me three times, to assure me that my proficiency and stamina would return with repeated practice. It was small solace. A man likes to think that he has kept his body in good trim, and in truth mine was hardened to the tasks of a small farm as well as to the skills of a frequent hunter. But the muscles and wind of a fighter are a different matter, and I would have to rebuild mine. I hoped I would not need those abilities, but sourly resigned myself to daily practice. Despite the chill day, my shirt was stuck to my back with sweat when I left the courts.

I knew they were the territory of the guards and stablehands, yet I made my way to the steams behind the barracks anyway. I reasoned that at this time of day, they would be little occupied, and that using them would be more in keeping with Tom Badgerlock's character than hauling water for a midday bath. The castle steams were in an old building of rough stone, built low and long. I shed my sweaty clothes in the outer chamber that fronted the steam and washing rooms, folding them onto a bench. I lifted Jinna's good-will charm necklace from around my neck and tucked it under my shirt. Naked, I went through the heavy wooden door that led to the steams. It took a moment for my eyes to adjust. The room was lined with tiered benches surrounding the squat stone firebox. The only light came from the deep red glow of the fire leaking from its stone dungeon. It had been well stoked. As I had suspected, the steams were mostly deserted, but there were three Outislanders there, guards from the Narcheska's contingent. They kept to themselves at one end of the clouded room, conversing low in their own hard-edged language. They gave me a single glance, then dismissed me. I was more than willing to yield them their privacy.

I took water from the cask in the corner and splashed it liberally onto the hot stones. A fresh curtain of mist went up, and I breathed it deeply. I stood as close to the steaming stones as I could stand until I felt my sweat break and run freely over my skin. It stung in the healing scratches on my neck and back. There was a box of coarse salt and some sea sponges, just as there had been when I was a boy. I scrubbed my body with the salt, wincing at the necessary pain, and then dashed it clean with the sponges. I had nearly finished when the door opened and a dozen guardsmen crowded in. The veterans in the group looked weary, while the younger men-at-arms were shouting and elbowing one another in good-natured horseplay, energized by returning home from the long patrol they had just finished. Two young men proceeded to stuff more wood into the firebox while another slopped more water on the stones. Steam rose in a wall, and the roar of competing conversations suddenly filled the room.

Two old men followed them into the room, moving more slowly, obviously not a part of the first group. Their scarred and gnarled bodies were testimony to their long years of service. They were deep in talk, some complaint about the beer in the guardroom. They greeted me and I grunted a reply before turning aside. I kept my head down and my face turned away from them. One of the older men had known me when I was just a lad. Blade was his name, and the old guardsman had been a true friend to me. I listened to his familiar oaths as he roundly cursed his stiff back. I would have given much to greet him honestly and share talk with him. Instead I smiled to myself to hear his abuse of the beer and wished him well with all my heart.

I watched surreptitiously to see how our Buckkeep guards would mingle with the Outislanders. Oddly, it was the young men who avoided them and gave them suspicious glances. The guards old enough to have fought in the Red Ship War seemed more at ease. Perhaps when one is a man-at-arms for long enough, war becomes a job and it is easier to recognize another man as a fellow warrior rather than a former enemy. Whatever the reason, it seemed to me that the Outislanders were more reluctant to socialize than the Buck guards. But perhaps that was only the natural caution of soldiers disarmed and surrounded by a group of strangers. Staying to watch for longer would have been interesting, but also dangerous. Blade had always had a sharp eye. I would not invite his recognition by lingering in his company.

But as I rose to go, a young guardsman shouldered into me. It was not an accident, or even a well-feigned one. It was but his excuse to loudly exclaim, 'Watch yourself, man! Who are you, anyway? Which guard company?' He was a sandy-haired fellow, perhaps of

Farrow stock, well-muscled and belligerent with youth. He looked about sixteen to me, a boy aching to prove himself before his more experienced fellows.

I gave him a glare of tolerant disgust, veteran to green soldier. To be too passive would only invite attack. I simply wanted to leave as swiftly as possible, attracting no more attention than necessary. 'Watch your own step, lad,' I warned him genially. I moved past him, only to have him shove me from behind. I turned to confront him, loose but not yet aggressive. He had his fists up ready to defend himself. I shook my head tolerantly at that, and several of his companions snickered. 'Let it be, lad,' I warned him.

'I asked you a question,' he snarled.

'So you did,' I agreed benignly. 'If you'd cared to favour me with your name before you demanded mine, I might have answered. That used to be the custom at Buckkeep.'

He narrowed his eyes at me. 'Charl of Bright's Guard. I've no need to be ashamed of my name or company.'

'Nor I,' I assured him. 'Tom Badgerlock, man to Lord Golden. Who expects me shortly. Good day.'

'Lord Golden's serving man. I might have known.' He gave a snort of disgust and turned to his fellows to confirm his superiority. 'You don't belong in here. This place is for the guardsmen. Not pages and lackeys and "special servants".'

'Is it?' I let a smile crook the corner of my mouth as I ran my gaze over him insultingly. 'No pages or lackeys. That surprises me.' All eyes on us now. Hopeless to avoid notice. I'd have to establish myself as Tom Badgerlock. He reddened to my insult, and then swung.

I leaned aside to let his blow go past, then took a step forward. He was ready for my fists, but instead I kicked his feet out from under him. It was a move more befitting a brawler than a noble's guardsman, and it obviously shocked him. I kicked him again as he went down, driving the air out of him. He fell gasping, to sprawl perilously near the firebox, and I stepped forward to place my foot on his bare chest, pinning him close by the firebox. I snarled down at him. 'Let it go, lad. Before it gets ugly.'

Two of his companions stepped forward, but 'Hold!' shouted Blade, and they halted. The old guardsman stepped forward, one hand pressed to the small of his back. 'Enough! I won't have it in here.' He glared at the man that was likely the guards' commander. 'Rufous, get that pup of yours under control. I came here to ease my back, not to be annoyed by an ill-trained braggart. Get that boy out of here. You, Badgerlock, take your foot off him.'

Despite his years, or perhaps because of them, old Blade still commanded universal respect from the guardsmen. As I stepped back, the boy came to his feet. He had both murder and chagrin in his eyes, but his commander barked, 'Out, Charl. We've all had enough of you today. And Fletch and Lowk, you can both go with him, for being fools enough to step forward for a fool.'

So the three of them went hulking past me, sauntering as if they didn't care. There was a surge of muttering among the guardsmen, but most of it seemed to be agreement that the young man was more churl than Charl. I sat back down, deciding that I'd give them the time to get dressed and be clear of the steams before I left. To my dismay, Blade walked stiffly over and sat down beside me. He offered me his hand, and when I gripped it, it was still the callused hand of a swordsman. 'Blade Havershawk,' he introduced himself gravely. 'And I know the scars of a man-at-arms when I see one, even if that pup didn't. You're welcome to use the steams; ignore the boy's wrangling. He's new to his company and still trying to overcome the fact that Rufous took him on as a favour to his mother.'

'Tom Badgerlock,' I replied. 'And many thanks to you. I could see he was trying to curry favour with his fellows by it, but I've no idea why he chose me. I'd no wish to fight the boy.'

'That much was plain, as plain as that it was lucky for him you did not. As for why, well, he's young and listens too much to gossip. It's no basis for judging a man. Do you hail from about here, Badgerlock?'

I gave a short laugh. 'Buck in general is where I hail from, I suppose.'

He gestured at the scratches on my throat and asked, 'And how did you come by those marks?'

'A she-cat,' I heard myself say, and he took it for a bawdy jest and laughed. And so for a time, we chatted, the old guardsman and myself. I looked into his seamed face, nodded and smiled at his old man's gossip, and saw no spark of recognition at all. I should have felt reassured, I suppose, that even an old friend like Blade did not recognize FitzChivalry Farseer. Instead, it unleashed a welling of gloom in me. Had I been that forgettable, that unremarkable to him? I found it hard to keep my mind on his words, and when I finally excused myself from his company, it was almost a relief to leave him, before I could give in to the irrational impulse to betray myself, to drop a word or a phrase that would hint to him that he had once known me before. It was a boy's impulse, a hunger to be recognized as significant, close kin to the impulse that had made young Charl attempt to spark a fight with me.

I left the steam room and walked through to the washing chamber, where I sluiced the last of the salt from my skin and towelled myself dry. Then I went back into the first room, dressed, and headed out, feeling clean but not renewed. A glance at the sun told me it was nearly time for Lord Golden's afternoon ride. I headed for the stables, but as I started to go in, I met a stablehand leading Myblack, Malta and an unfamiliar grey gelding. All the mounts were groomed to gleaming and already saddled. I explained to him I was Lord Golden's man, but he regarded me with suspicion until a woman's voice greeted me, with, 'Ho, Badgerlock? Do you ride with Lord Golden and our prince today?'

'Such is my good fortune, Mistress Laurel,' I greeted the Queen's Huntswoman. She was dressed in forest green, in the tunic and leggings of a hunter, but her figure gave them an entirely different air. Her hair was bundled out of the way in a most unfeminine way that somehow only made her more womanly. The stableman abruptly offered me a short bow and let me take the horses from him. When he was out of earshot, Laurel smiled at me and asked quietly, 'And how is our prince?'

'In good health, I am sure, Mistress Laurel.' I apologized with my eyes, and she did not seem to take my careful words amiss. Her glance flickered over the good-will charm at my throat. Jinna had used her hedge-witch magic to make it for me. It was supposed to make folk regard me kindly. Laurel's smile grew warmer. I casually turned up my collar to conceal more of the charm.

She glanced aside from me and then spoke with more formality, huntswoman to servingman. 'Well. I hope you enjoy your ride today. Please pass on my greetings to Lord Golden.'

'That I shall, mistress. A good day to you as well.' As she walked away, I grumbled to myself over the role that I must wear as a shirt to my back. I would have liked more talk with her, but in the middle of the stableyard was not the place for private conversation.

I led the horses around to the great front door of the hall and waited there.

And waited there.

The Prince's gelding seemed accustomed to such delays, but Malta was plainly put out, and Myblack tested my patience with tactics from a quick tug on her reins to a steady even pull. I'd need to put in more hours with her if I expected to make a good mount of her. I wondered where I would find those hours, cursed the time that was being wasted now, and then dismissed the thought. A servant's time belonged to his master; I had to behave as if I believed that. I was beginning to feel chilled as well as annoyed before a commotion alerted me to stand straight and put an obliging expression on my face.

A moment later, both the Prince and Lord Golden emerged, surrounded by well wishers and hangers-on. I did not see Dutiful's intended or any Outislanders among this party. I wondered if that was odd. There were several young women, including one pouting with disappointment. Doubtless she had hoped the Prince would invite her along for the ride. Several of his male companions also looked a bit disgruntled. Dutiful wore a pleasant expression, but the pinch at the corners of his mouth and eyes let me know that he held it in place with an effort. Civil Bresinga was there, on the outskirts of the circle of admirers. Chade had said he was expected to arrive today. He gave me one dark glance, and I perceived that he manoeuvred to stand closer to the Prince, but on the side away from Lord Golden. His presence sent a prickle of both irritation and fear up my spine. Would he leave this farewell and hasten to let others know that I had ridden out with the Prince? Did he spy for the Piebalds, or was he as innocent as had been claimed?

It was obvious to me that the Prince wished to make a swift departure, but even so we lingered some time longer, as he made individual farewells and promised his later time and attention to many of them. All of this he managed graciously and well. It came to me that it was the thread of Skill between us that made me aware of his impatience and irritation with all the finely-dressed nobility that surrounded them. As if he were a restive horse, I found myself sending thoughts of calm and patience to him. He glanced at me, but I could not be sure he was aware of my reaching towards him.

One of his companions took his horse's head from me, and held the animal while the Prince mounted. I held Malta for Lord Golden, and then at a nod from him mounted my own horse. There was yet another round of farewells and good wishes, as if we were setting off on a long journey rather than merely an afternoon ride. Finally, the Prince firmly reined his gelding to one side and touched heels to him. Lord Golden followed him and then I let Myblack go. A chorus of goodbyes rained down behind us.

Despite Chade's advice, I had little chance to suggest any route for our afternoon ride. The Prince led and we followed to the gates of Buckkeep, where again we had to pause to allow the guards formally to salute and then pass their young prince through the gate. The moment we cleared the gate, Dutiful put his heels to his horse. The pace he set precluded any conversation. He soon turned off the road onto a lesser-travelled trail, and then kicked his grey to a canter. We followed, and I felt Myblack's satisfaction in the chance to stretch her muscles. She was not so pleased that I held her back, for she knew that she could easily outdistance both Malta and the grey if given her head.

The Prince's route led us out onto the sunny hillsides. Once there had been forest here, and Verity had hunted deer and pheasant. Now sheep grudgingly ambled out of our way as we crossed open pasturage, and then ventured into the wilder hills beyond. And all this time, we rode in silence. When we left the flocks behind, Dutiful gave his grey a free head and we galloped through the hills as if fleeing an enemy. Myblack had lost a little of her edginess by the time the Prince finally pulled in his mount. Lord Golden moved up to ride behind him as the walking horses snorted and blew. I kept my place behind them until the Prince turned in his saddle and irritably waved me up beside him. I let

Myblack advance and the Prince greeted me coldly with, 'Where have you been? You promised me that you would teach me, and I haven't even seen you since we returned to Buckkeep Castle.'

I bit back my first response, reminding myself that he spoke as a prince speaks to a servant, not as a boy would address his father. Yet that brief moment of silence seemed to rebuke him as much as words would have done. Not that he looked chastened, but I recognized the stubborn flex of his lips. I took a breath. 'My prince, it has been scarcely two days since we returned. I had assumed that you would be very busy with the tasks of your reign. In the meantime, I resumed the chores of my own life. If it please my prince, I thought that you would summon me when you required me.'

'Why do you speak to me like this?' the Prince demanded angrily. 'My *prince* this and *my prince* that! You didn't address me in this fashion on our way home. What happened to our friendship?'

I saw the Fool's warning in Lord Golden's quick glance, but I ignored it. I kept my voice low and even as I answered. 'If you rebuke me as you would a servant, my prince, then I assume that I am to respond in a style appropriate to my station.'

'Stop that!' Dutiful hissed at me, as if I had mocked him. I suppose in truth that I had. The result was awful. For a moment, his face tightened as if he were on the verge of tears. He spurred ahead of us, and we let him go. Lord Golden gave me a minuscule shake of his head, and then nodded that I should catch up with the lad. I debated making the Prince pull in and wait for us, then decided that perhaps he could not bend so far. A boy's pride can be very stiff.

I let Myblack move alongside the trotting grey as she wished, but before I could speak to Dutiful, he addressed me. 'I've started this all wrong. I'm beleaguered and frustrated. These last two days have been horrible . . . just horrible. I've had to behave with perfect courtesy even when I wanted to shout, and smilingly accept flowery compliments on a situation I wish to flee. Everyone expects me to be happy and excited. I've heard enough ribald tales about wedding nights to gag a goat. No one knows or cares about my loss. No one even noticed my cat was gone. I have no one that I can speak to about it.' He suddenly choked. He pulled his horse abruptly to a halt and turned in his saddle to face me. He took a deep breath. 'I'm sorry. I apologize, Tom Badgerlock.'

The bluntness of his words and the honest offering of his hand were so like Verity that I knew it was truly his spirit that had fathered this boy. I felt humbled. I gripped the offered hand gravely, then pulled him close enough that I could set a hand upon his shoulder. 'It's too late to apologize,' I told him seriously. 'I've already forgiven you.' I took a breath as I released him. 'And I have felt as badgered, my lord, and it has shortened my own temper. So many tasks have fallen to me lately that I've scarcely had time to see my own boy. I'm sorry I did not seek you out sooner. I am not sure how we can arrange our meetings without making others aware that I teach you, but you are right. It must be done, and putting it off will not make it easier.'

The Prince's face had gone very still at my words. I sensed a sudden distancing in him but could not perceive the cause until he asked quietly, 'Your "own boy"?'

His inflection puzzled me. 'My foster son. Hap. He is apprenticed to a woodworker in Buckkeep Town.'

'Oh.' The single word seemed to fade into silence. Then, 'I did not know you had a son.'

The jealously was courteously masked but it rang green against my sense of him. I did not know how to react to it. I gave him the truth. 'I've had him since he was eight or so. His mother abandoned him and he had no other folk willing to take him in. He's a good lad.'

'But he is not truly your son,' the Prince pointed out.

I took a breath and replied firmly, 'In every way that matters, he is a son to me.'

Lord Golden sat his horse at the outskirts of our circle but I dared not glance to him for advice. After a time of silence, the Prince tightened his knees and his horse moved forward at a walk. I let Myblack pace him, the Fool dawdling along behind us. Just when I thought I must break the silence before it became a wall between us, Dutiful blurted out, 'Then what need have you of me, if you already have a son of your own?'

The hunger in his voice shocked me. I think he startled himself, for he suddenly kicked his horse into a trot and rode ahead of me again. I made no effort to catch up with him until the Fool at my side whispered, 'Go after him. Don't let him close himself off from you. You should know by now how easy it is to lose a person just by letting someone walk away from you.' Even so, I think it was more the prompting of my own heart that made me set my heels to Myblack and catch up with the boy. For boy he very much looked now, chin held firm, eyes straight ahead as he trotted along. He did not look at me as I came alongside him, but I knew he listened when I spoke.

'What need do I have of you? What need do you have of me? Friendship is not always based on need, Dutiful. But I will tell you plainly that I need you in my life. Because of who your father was to me, and because you are your mother's son. But mostly because you are you, and we have too much in common for me to walk away from you. I would not see you grow up as ignorant of your magics as I did. If I can save you that torment, then perhaps in some way I will have saved myself as well.'

I suddenly ran dry of words. Perhaps, like Prince Dutiful, I was surprised by my own thoughts. Truth can well out of a man like blood from a wound, and it can be just as disconcerting to look at.

'Tell me about my father.'

Perhaps for him the request logically followed what I had said, but it jolted me. I walked a line here. I felt I owed him whatever I could give him of Verity. Yet how could I tell him stories of his father without revealing my own identity? I had firmly resolved that he would know nothing of my true bloodlines. Now was not the time to reveal to him that I was FitzChivalry Farseer, the Witted Bastard, nor that my body had fathered his. To explain that Verity's spirit, by strength of his Skill-magic, had occupied my flesh for those hours was far too complicated an explanation for the boy. In truth, I could barely accept it myself.

So, much as Chade once had with me, I hedged, asking him, 'What would you know of him?'

'Anything. Everything.' He cleared his throat. 'No one has spoken to me much of him. Chade sometimes tells me stories of what he was like as a boy. I've read the official accounts of his reign, which become amazingly vague after he leaves on his quest. I've heard minstrels sing of him, but in those songs he is a legend, and none of them seem to agree on exactly how he saved the Six Duchies. When I ask about that, or what it was like to know him, everyone falls silent. As if they do not know. Or as if there were a shameful secret that everyone knows but me.'

'There is no shameful secret of any kind attached to your father. He was a good and honourable man. I cannot believe that you know so little of him. Not even your mother has told you of him?' I asked incredulously.

He took a breath and slowed his horse to a walk. Myblack tugged at her bit but I held her pace to match the Prince's mount. 'My mother speaks of her king. Occasionally, of her husband. When she does talk of him, I know that she still grieves for him. It makes me reluctant to pester her with questions. But I want to know about my father. Who he was as a person. As a man among men.'

'Ah.' Again, it rang in me, the similarities we shared. I had hungered for the same truths about my own father. All I had ever heard of was Chivalry the Abdicator, the King-in-Waiting who had been tumbled from his throne before he ever truly occupied it. He had been a brilliant tactician, a skilled negotiator. He had given it up to quiet the scandal of my existence. Not only had the noble prince sired a bastard, he had got me on a nameless Mountain woman. It only made his childless marriage the more stinging to an heirless kingdom. That was what I knew of my father. Not what foods he liked, or whether he laughed easily. I knew none of the things a son would know if he had grown up seeing his father daily.

'Tom?' Dutiful prodded me.

'I was thinking,' I replied honestly. I tried to think what I would like to know about my own father. Even as I pondered this, I scanned the hillside around us. We were following a game-path through a brushy meadow. I examined the trees that marked the beginning of the foothills, but saw and felt no sign of humans there. 'Verity. Well. He was a big man, near as tall as I am, but bull-chested with wide shoulders. In battle harness, he looked as much soldier as prince, and sometimes I think he would have preferred that more

61

active life. Not that he loved battle, but because he was a man who liked to be outdoors, moving and doing things. He loved to hunt. He had a wolfhound named Leon that shadowed him from room to room, and . . .'

'Was he Witted, then?' the Prince asked eagerly.

'No!' The question shocked me. 'He simply had a great fondness for his dog. And . . .'

'Then why am I Witted? They say it runs in families.'

I gave a half-hearted shrug. To me, it seemed the lad's mind leapt from topic to topic as a flea hops from dog to dog. I tried to follow it. 'I suppose the Wit is like the Skill. That is supposed to be the Farseer magic, yet a child born in a fisherman's cot may suddenly show the potential for it. No one knows why a child is born with or without magic.'

'Civil Bresinga says the Wit winds through the Farseer line. He says that perhaps the Piebald Prince got his Wit as much from his royal mother as his baseborn father. He says that sometimes it runs weak in two family lines, but when they cross, the magic shows itself. Like one kitten with a crooked tail when the rest of the litter is sound.'

'When did Civil say these things to you?' I demanded sharply.

The Prince gave me an odd look but answered. 'Early this morning, when he arrived from Galekeep.'

'In public?' I was horrified. I noticed that Lord Golden had edged his horse closer to us.

'No, of course not! It was very early this morning, before I had breakfasted. He came to the door of my bedchamber himself, urgently begging audience with me.'

'And you just let him in?'

Dutiful stared at me in silence for a moment. Then he said stiffly, 'He has been a friend to me. He gave me my cat, Tom. You know what she meant to me.'

'I know how that gift was intended, as do you! Civil Bresinga may be a dangerous traitor, my prince, one who has already conspired with the Piebalds to snatch you away from your throne and eventually from your own flesh. You must learn more caution!'

The Prince had gone pink about the ears at my rebuke. Yet he still managed to keep his voice level. 'He says he is not. And that they didn't. Conspire, that is. Do you think he would have come to me to explain if he had? He and his mother did not know about . . . the cat. They were not even aware I was Witted when they gave her to me. Oh, my little cat.' His voice suddenly faltered on his last words, and I knew how all his thoughts had diverted to the loss of his Wit-partner.

The chill grief of his loss blew through his words. It stirred my own loss of Nighteyes to a sharper ache. I felt as if I were probing a wound as I asked relentlessly, 'Then why did they do it? It must have seemed a strange request. Someone comes to them and gives them a hunting cat and says, "Here, give this to the Prince". And they've never said who gave it.' He took a breath, then stopped. 'Civil spoke to me in confidence. I don't know if I should break that trust.'

'Did you promise not to tell?' I demanded, dreading the answer. I needed to know what Civil had told him, but I would not ask him to break his promise.

An incredulous look came over Dutiful's face. 'Tom Badgerlock. A noble does not ask his prince to "promise not to tell". It would not be appropriate to our station.'

'And this conversation is,' the Fool observed wryly. His comment made the Prince laugh, easily dispersing a building tension between us that I had not been aware of until the Fool disarmed it. Strange, suddenly to recognize his gift for doing that, after all the years I had known him.

'I see your point,' the Prince conceded easily, and now the conversation included all of us as we rode three abreast. For a short time, the steady clopping of the horses' hooves and the whispering of the cool wind were the only sounds. Dutiful took a breath. 'He did not ask me to promise. But . . . Civil humbled himself to me. He knelt at my feet to offer his apology. And I think any man who does that has a right to expect it will be kept from the public gossip.'

'It would not become public gossip through me, my prince. Nor through the Fool. I promise. Please tell me what passed between you.'

'The fool?' Dutiful turned a delighted grin on Lord Golden.

Lord Golden snorted contemptuously. 'An old joke between old friends. One that is becoming far too worn to be humorous any more, Tom Badgerlock,' he added warningly to me. I ducked my head to his rebuke, but smirked also, hoping the Prince would accept the hasty explanation. Inside my chest, my heart sank down to the pit of my belly as I castigated myself for my carelessness. Did some part of me long to reveal myself to the Prince? I felt an old familiar twist in my gut. Guilt. Secrets withheld from ones who trusted me. Had not I once promised myself never to do that again? But what choice did I have? I guarded my own secret even as Lord Golden worked at prying the Prince's secret loose from him.

'But if you would tell us, I promise that my tongue will wag it no further. Like Tom, I am dubious of Civil Bresinga's loyalty to you, as friend or subject. I fear you may be in danger, my prince.'

'Civil is my friend,' the Prince announced in a voice that brooked no argument. His boyish confidence in his own judgement cut me. 'I know that in my heart. However,' and here a strange look flickered over Dutiful's face, 'he warned me to be wary of you, Lord Golden. He seems to regard you with . . . extreme distaste.'

'A small misunderstanding between us when I guested at his home,' Lord Golden demurred casually. 'I am sure we will soon resolve it.'

I rather doubted that myself but the Prince seemed to accept it. He pondered for a time, turning his horse to the west and skirting the edges of the forest. I manoeuvred Myblack to put myself between Dutiful and possible ambushers hiding amongst the trees. I tried to keep one eye on the woods and one on the Prince. When I spotted a crow in a nearby treetop, I wondered sourly if it were a Piebald spy. Little I could do if it were, I told myself. Neither of the others seemed to take notice of the bird. The Prince's words broke from him just as the bird rose cawing from the trees and flew away.

Dutiful's words came reluctantly. 'The Bresingas were threatened. By the Piebalds. Civil would not say how, only that it was very oblique. The cat was delivered to his mother with a note, directing her to give the cat to me as a gift. If she did not, well, reprisal was threatened, but Civil didn't tell me exactly what.'

'I can guess,' I said bluntly. The crow had disappeared from sight. It did not make me feel any more secure. 'If they didn't give the cat to you, one of them would be betrayed as Witted. Probably Civil.'

'I think that is likely,' Dutiful conceded.

'That doesn't excuse it. She had a duty to her prince.' Privately I resolved to find a way to spy on Bresinga's room. A quiet visit to it and a search through his possessions might also be a good idea. I wondered if he had brought his cat with him.

Dutiful gave me a very direct look and he seemed to speak with Verity's bluntness as he asked me, 'Could you put your duty to your monarch ahead of protecting a member of your own family? That is what I asked myself. If my mother were threatened, what could I be forced to do? Would I betray the Six Duchies for the sake of her life?'

Lord Golden shot me a Fool's glance, one that was well pleased with this boy. I nodded to it, but felt distracted. Dutiful's words itched at me. I suddenly felt as if there were something important I needed to remember but could not trace the thought any further. I could not think of an answer to Dutiful's question either, so the silence lengthened. At last I said, 'Be careful, my prince. I caution you against taking Civil Bresinga into your confidence, or making his friends your own.'

'There is little to fear there, Badgerlock. I've no time for friends right now; all is duty. It was hard for me to wrench this hour out of my schedule and say that I would go riding with only the two of you. I have been warned that it will look odd to the Dukes, whose support I must court. Far better had I ridden out with some of their sons accompanying me. But I needed this time with you. I've something important to ask you, Badgerlock.' He paused, then asked bluntly, 'Will you come to my betrothal ceremony tonight? If I must endure this, I'd like to have a true friend nearby.'

I immediately knew the answer, but I tried to look as if I were pondering it. 'I cannot, my prince. It would not be fitting to one of my station. It would look even odder than this riding out together.'

'Could not you be there as Lord Golden's bodyguard?'

Here Lord Golden himself intervened for me. 'That would appear as if I did not trust my prince's hospitality to protect me.'

The Prince pulled in his horse, a stubborn look coming over his face. 'I want you to be there. Find a way.'

This direct command set my teeth on edge. 'I'll consider it,' I replied stiffly. I was still not completely confident of my anonymity at Buckkeep. I wanted to settle more firmly into my role as Tom Badgerlock before I had any more chance confrontations with folk who might recall me from the past. There would be many of them at the betrothal ceremony tonight. 'But I wish to point out to my prince that even if I am present, conversing with you will be out of the question. Nor should you take any sort of an interest in me that might call undue attention to our connection.'

'I'm not a fool!' he retorted, very close to anger at my indirect refusal. 'I simply would like to have you there. To know I had one friend in the crowd of those watching me being sacrificed.'

'I think you are being overly dramatic,' I said quietly. I tried not to let it sound like an insult. 'Recall that your mother will be there. And Chade. And Lord Golden. All people with your best interests at heart.'

He reddened a bit as he glanced at Lord Golden. 'I do not discount your value as a friend, Lord Golden. Forgive me if my words were ill considered. As for my mother and Lord Chade, they are, like me, obliged to duty before love. They want what is best for me, that is true, but the largest facet of that is always what is best for my reign. They see the well-being of the Six Duchies as intrinsic to my own well-being.' He looked suddenly weary. 'And when I disagree, they say that when I have been King for a time, I will understand that what they obliged me to do was actually in my own best interests as well. That ruling a country that is prosperous and at peace will bring me far more satisfaction over the years than the choosing of my own bride.'

We rode for a time in silence. When Lord Golden broke the quiet, his voice was reluctant. 'My prince, I fear the sun does not wait for us. It is time to turn back towards Buckkeep Castle.'

'I know,' Dutiful replied dully. 'I know.'

I knew they were the wrong words to offer as comfort even as I said them, but the customs of society dictate strongly to all of us. I tried to make him content with what he must face. 'Elliania does not seem such a terrible choice for a bride. Young as she is, she is still lovely, with the potential for true beauty as she matures. Chade speaks of her as a queen in the bud and seems well pleased with the match the Outislanders have offered us.'

'Oh, she is that,' Dutiful agreed as he turned his grey. Myblack snorted as the other horse cut her path and seemed reluctant to turn and follow him. The hills and a longer gallop enticed her. 'She is a queen before she is a child or a woman. She has not said one incorrect word to me. Nor one word that might betray what goes on behind those bright black eyes. She offered me her gift quite correctly, a chain of silver fitted with the yellow diamonds of her land. I must wear it tonight. To her I gave the gift my mother and Chade had selected, a coronet of silver set with one hundred sapphires. The stones are small, but my mother favoured their intricate patterning over larger gems. The Narcheska curtseyed as she took it and told me in measured words how lovely she found it. Yet I could not help but notice how general her thanks were. She spoke of "my generous gift", never once saying a word of the designs or that she liked sapphires. It was as if she had memorized a speech that would suffice for any gift we gave her, and then recited it faultlessly.'

I was almost certain that was exactly what she had done. Yet I did not feel it was right to fault her for that. She was, after all, only eleven years old, with as little say in these proceedings as our prince had. I said as much to the Prince.

'I know, I know,' he conceded tiredly. 'Yet I tried to meet her eyes, and to let her see something of who I am. When first she stood beside me, Badgerlock, my heart truly went out to her. She seemed so young and small, and such a foreigner in our court. I felt for her as I would for any child snatched away from her home and forced to serve a purpose not her own. I had chosen a gift to give her that was from me, not the Six Duchies. It was in her room, awaiting her, when she first arrived. She has made no mention of it, not even a word.'

'What was it?' I asked.

'Something I would have liked, when I was eleven,' the young man replied. 'A set of puppets carved by Bluntner. They were dressed as if to tell the tale of the Girl and the Snow Steed. I was told it is a well-known tale in the OutIslands as well as the Six Duchies.'

Lord Golden's voice was neutral as he observed, 'Bluntner is a skilful carver. Is that the tale where the girl is borne far away from a cruel step-father by her magic steed, and carried off to a rich land where she weds a handsome prince?'

'Perhaps not the best tale in these circumstances,' I muttered.

The Prince looked startled. 'I never considered it in that light. Do you think I insulted her? Should I apologize?'

'The less said, the better,' Lord Golden suggested. 'Perhaps when you know her better you can discuss it with her.'

'Perhaps when ten years have passed,' the Prince conceded lightly, but I felt the thrumming of his anxiety across our Skill-bond. For the first time, I understood that one aspect of his dissatisfaction was that he did not feel he was doing well with the Narcheska. His next words echoed that knowledge.

'She makes me feel like a clumsy barbarian. She is the one from a log village near an ice shelf, but she makes me feel uncultured and awkward. She looks at me and her eyes are like mirrors. I see nothing of her in them, only how stupid and doltish I appear to her. I have been raised well, I am of good blood, but she makes me feel as if I am a grubby peasant that might soil her with my touch. I do not understand it!'

'There will be many differences you must resolve as you come to know one another. Understanding that each of you comes from a different, but no less valuable culture may be the first one,' Lord Golden suggested smoothly. 'Several years ago, I pursued my own interest in the Outislanders and studied them. They are matriarchal, you know, with their mother-clans indicated by the tattoos they wear. As I understand it, she has already done you great honour by coming to you rather than demanding that her suitor present himself at her motherhouse. It must feel awkward for her to face this courtship without the guidance of her mothers, sisters and aunts to sustain her.'

Dutiful nodded thoughtfully to Lord Golden's words, but my glimpse of the Narcheska made me suspect the Prince had measured her feelings for him accurately. I did not utter that thought. 'She has obviously studied our Six Duchies' ways. Have you given any consideration to learning about her land, and who her family is there?' Dutiful cast me a sidelong glance, a student who had skimmed his lesson but knew he had not studied it well. 'Chade gave me what scrolls we have, but he warned me that they are old and possibly out-dated. The Out Islands do not commit their history to writing, but entrust it to the memories of their bards. All we have is written from the view of the Six Duchies folk who have visited there. It betrays a certain intolerance for their differences. Most of the scrolls are traveller's accounts, expressing distaste for the food, for honey and grease seem to be the prized ingredients for any guest dish, and dismay at the housing, which is cold and draughty. The folk there do not offer hospitality to weary strangers, but seem to despise anyone foolish enough to get themselves into circumstances where they must ask for shelter or food rather than barter for it. The weak and the foolish deserve to die; that seems to be the main credo of the Out Islands. Even the god they have chosen is a harsh and unforgiving one. El of the sea they prefer, over the bountiful Eda of the fields.' The Prince heaved a sigh as he finished.

'Have you listened to any of their bards?' Lord Golden asked quietly.

'I've listened, but not understood. Chade urged me to learn the basics of their language, and I have tried. It shares many roots with our own. I can speak it well enough to make myself understood, though the Narcheska has already told me that she would rather speak to me in my own tongue than hear hers so twisted.' For an instant, he clenched his teeth to that insulting reproof. Then he went on, 'The bards are more difficult to understand. Evidently the rules of their language change for their poetry, and syllables can be stretched or shortened to make them fit a measure. Bard's Tongue, they call it, but add their windy music blasting past the words and it is difficult for me to get more than the basics of every tale. All seem to be about chopping down enemies and taking bits of their bodies as trophies. Like Echet Hairbed, who slept under a coverlet woven from the scalps of his enemies. Or Sixfinger, who fed his dogs from skull bowls of those he had defeated.'

'Nice folks,' I observed wryly. Lord Golden scowled at me.

'Our songs must sound as strange to her, especially the romantic tragedies of maidens who die for love of a man they cannot possess and such,' Lord Golden gently pointed out. 'These are barriers you must overcome together, my prince. Such misunderstandings yield most easily to casual conversation.'

'Ah, yes,' the Prince conceded sourly. 'Ten years from now, perhaps we'll have a casual conversation. For now, we are so ringed by her hangers-on and my well-wishers, that we speak to one another through a throng, in raised voices to reach one another. Every word we exchange is overheard and discussed. Not to mention dear Uncle Peottre, standing over her like a dog over a bone. Yesterday afternoon, when I attempted to stroll though the gardens with her, I felt more as if we were leading a horde to war. There were over a dozen people chattering and trampling along behind us. And when I did pluck a late flower to offer to her, her uncle stepped between us to take it from my hand and examine it before he passed it on to her. As if perhaps I were offering him something poisonous.'

I grinned in spite of myself, recalling the noxious herbs that Kettricken herself had once offered to me when she considered me a threat to her brother. 'Such treachery is not unknown, my prince, even in the best of families. Her uncle is doing no more than his duty. It has not been long since our lands warred against one another. Give time for old wounds to close and heal. It will happen.'

'But for now, my prince, I fear we must put our heels to our horses. Did not I hear you say that you had an afternoon appointment with your mother? I think we had best put a little haste into our pace.'

'I suppose,' the Prince replied listlessly to Lord Golden's words. Then he turned a commanding stare on me. 'So then, Tom Badgerlock. When will we next meet? I am most anxious to begin my lessons with you.'

I nodded, wishing I shared his enthusiasm. I felt obliged to add,

'The Skill is not always a kindly magic to deal with, my prince. You may find these lessons less than pleasant after we begin them.'

'I expect that to be so. My experiences of it to date have been both unsettling and confusing.' His gaze became clouded and distant as he said, 'When you took me . . . I know it had something to do with a pillar. We went to . . . somewhere. A beach. But now when I try to recall that passage, or the events that occurred there or immediately afterwards, it is like trying to recall a dream from childhood. The ends of it don't meet somehow, if you know what I mean. I thought I understood all that had happened to me. Then, when I tried to discuss it with Chade and my mother, it all fell to tatters. I felt like an idiot.' He lifted one hand to rub his wrinkled brow. 'I cannot make the pieces go in order to make a complete memory.' Then he fixed me with a direct stare and said, 'I cannot live with that, Tom Badgerlock. I have to resolve it. If this magic must be a part of me, then I must control it.'

His words were far more sensible than my reluctance to deal with it. I sighed. 'Tomorrow, dawn. In Verity's tower room,' I offered, expecting him to refuse me.

'Very well,' he replied easily. An odd smile curved his mouth. 'I thought only Chade called the Seawatch tower "Verity's tower". Interesting. You might have at least referred to my father as King Verity.'

'Your pardon, my prince,' was the best reply I could think of, and he merely snorted at it. Then he fixed me with a truly royal look and added, 'And you will make every attempt to be at my ceremony tonight, Tom Badgerlock.'

Before I could reply, he set his heels to his grey and rode back to Buckkeep like a man pursued by demons. We had little choice but to follow. He did not slow until we reached the gate, where we paused to be formally recognized and admitted. From there we walked our horses, but Dutiful was silent and I could think of nothing to say. When we arrived at the tall doors of the main hall, courtiers were already gathered to meet him. A groom hurried up to take his horse's head, and a stableboy took Malta's reins. I was left to fend for myself, for which I was grateful. Lord Golden thanked the Prince formally for the extreme pleasure of his exclusive company and the

Prince courteously replied. We sat our mounts, watching Dutiful as he was engulfed by his nobles and carried off. I swung off Myblack and stood awaiting my master.

'Well. A pleasant ride,' Lord Golden observed, and dismounted. As his boot lightly touched the ground, his foot seemed to fly out from under him and he fell badly. I had never seen the Fool so ungraceful. He sat up, lips pinched tight, then with a groan leaned forward to clutch at his booted ankle.

'Such a wrench!' he cried, and then, imperiously, 'No, no, stay back, see to my horse,' as he waved the stableboy away. Then, quite sharply to me, 'Well, don't stand there, you dolt! Give the stableboy your horse and help me up. Or do you propose that I shall hop up to my chambers?'

The Prince had already been borne away on a wave of chattering ladies and lords. I doubted that he was aware of Lord Golden's mishap. Some of the Prince's attendants looked our way, but most were intent on Dutiful. So I crouched and as Lord Golden put his arm across my shoulders, I asked quietly, 'How bad is it?'

'Bad enough!' he snapped sharply. 'I shall not be dancing tonight, and my new dancing slippers were just delivered yesterday. Oh, this is intolerable! Help me to my rooms, man.' At his irritated scolding, several lesser nobles hastened towards us. His manner changed instantly as he replied to their anxious queries with assurances that he was sure he would be fine, and that nothing could keep him from the betrothal festivities tonight. He leaned most of his weight on me, but one sympathetic young man took his arm, and a lady sent her maid scuttling off to order hot water and soaking herbs immediately taken to Lord Golden's chambers, and to fetch a healer as well. No less than two young men and three very lovely young ladies trailed us as we made our way into Buckkeep.

By the time we had lurched and hobbled our way up the stairs and corridors to Golden's chambers, he had sharply rebuked me for clumsiness a dozen times. We found the healer and the hot water awaiting us outside the door. The healer took Lord Golden out of my hands, and I was almost immediately sent off to fetch brandy to steady his shaken nerves and something from the kitchens to settle his stomach. As I left, I cringed in sympathy for his sharp cries of pain as the healer carefully freed his foot from his boot. By the time I returned with a tray of pastries and fruit from the kitchen, the healer had departed and Lord Golden was ensconced in his chair with his well-propped foot stretched out before him while his sympathizers filled the other chairs. I set out the food upon the table and carried brandy to him. Lady Calendula was sympathizing with him over the heartless and incompetent healer. What kind of a bumbler was he, to cause Lord Golden such pain and then declare that he could find very little indication of an injury? Young Lord Oaks told a long, detailed and plaintive story of how the healer at his father's house had nearly let him die of a stomach ailment under similar circumstances. When he was finally finished with his tale, Lord Golden begged their understanding that he needed to rest after his disaster. I concealed my relief as I bowed them all out the door.

I waited until the door was well closed behind them and the sound of their chattering voices and tapping feet had died away before I approached the Fool. He leaned back in his chair, a rose scented kerchief draped over his eyes.

'How bad is it?' I asked in a low voice.

'As bad as you wish it to be,' he replied, not taking the fabric from his face.

'What?'

He lifted the cloth and smiled up at me beatifically. 'Such a display, and all for your benefit. You might at least show your gratitude.'

'What are you talking about?'

He lowered his bound foot to the floor, stood up and strolled casually to the table where he picked through the leftover food there. He didn't even limp. 'Now Lord Golden has an excuse to have his man Tom Badgerlock at his side tonight. I shall lean on your arm when I walk, and you shall carry my little footstool and cushion about for me. And fetch for me and run my greetings and messages about the room for me. You'll be there for Dutiful to see, and I don't doubt that you'll find it a better vantage point for your spying than sneaking about through the walls.' He looked at me critically as I gaped. 'Luckily for us both, the new clothing I ordered for you was delivered this morning. Come. Sit down and I'll trim your hair now. You can't go to the ball looking like that.'

FOUR

The Betrothal

The use of intoxicants can be of benefit in testing an aspirant's aptitude for the Skill, but the master must use caution. Whereas a small amount of a suitable herb, such as Hebben's leaf, synxove, teriban bark or covaria may relax a candidate for Skill-testing and enable rudimentary Skilling, too much may render the student incapable of sufficient focus to display the talent. Although some few Skillmasters have reported success using a herb during the actual training of Skill students, it is the consensus of the Four Masters that more often such drugs become crutches. Students never properly learn how to place their minds into a receptive Skill-state without these herbs. There is also some indication that students trained with herbs never develop the capability for the deep Skill-states and the more complicated magic that can be worked there.

Four Masters Scroll – Translation, Chade Fallstar

'I never imagined I would wear stripes,' I muttered again.

'Stop complaining,' the Fool managed around the pins in his mouth. He removed them a pin at a time as he fastened the tiny pocket in place, and then swiftly began to make it permanent with his needle and thread. 'I've told you. It looks astounding on you and complements my garb perfectly.'

'I don't want to look astounding. I want to be nondescript.' I thrust a needle through the waistband of the trousers and into the meat of my thumb. That the Fool refrained from laughing as I cursed only made me more irritable.

He was already impeccably and extravagantly attired. He sat cross-legged in his chair, helping me hastily add assassin's pockets

75

to my new garb. He didn't even look up at me as he assured me, 'You will be nondescript. Folk will remember your clothing, not your face, if they remark you at all. You will be in close attendance upon me for most of the evening, and your clothing will obviously mark you as my serving man. It will conceal you, just as a servant's livery can make a lovely miss simply another lady's maid. Here. Try this now.'

I set down the trousers and put on the shirt. Three tiny vials from Chade's supply, fashioned from bird's bones, fitted neatly into the new pocket. Fastened, the cuff betrayed nothing. The other cuff already held several pellets of a powerful soporific. If afforded the chance, I would see that young Lord Bresinga slept well tonight while I had an opportunity to look through his chamber. I had already ascertained that he had not brought his hunting cat with him; or rather, I told myself, I had ascertained that it was not in his rooms or stabled with the other coursing beasts. It could very well be prowling the wooded lands that bordered Buckkeep. Lady Bresinga, Lord Golden had learned through court gossip, was not in attendance at Buckkeep Castle for the betrothal ceremony. She pleaded a painful spine following a bad fall from her horse during a hunting accident. If it was a sham, I wondered why she had chosen to stay home at Galekeep while she sent her son to represent her name. Did she think she had sent him out of danger? Or into it, to save herself?

I sighed. Speculation was useless without facts. While I had been tucking the vials of poison into my cuff pocket, the Fool had finished the stitching in the waistband of my trousers. That was a sturdier pocket, to hold a slender blade. No one would openly wear arms to the betrothal ceremony tonight. It would be a discourtesy to the hospitality of the Farseers. Such niceties did not bind assassins, however.

As if following my thoughts, the Fool asked as he handed me my striped trousers, 'Does Chade still bother with all this? Little pockets and hidden weapons and such?'

'I don't know,' I replied truthfully. Yet somehow I could not imagine him going without it. Intrigue came as naturally to him as breathing. I pulled up the trousers and sucked in a breath to fasten them. They fit more snugly than I liked. I reached behind my back, and with the end of a fingernail managed to snag the concealed blade's brief hilt. I slipped it out and inspected it. It had come from Chade's tower stores. The entire weapon was no longer than my finger, with only enough of a hilt to grasp between my finger and thumb. But it could cut a man's throat, or slip between the knobs of his spine in a trice. I slid it back into its hiding place.

'Does anything show?' I asked him, turning for his inspection.

He surveyed me with a smile and then assured me salaciously, 'Everything shows. But nothing that you're worried about showing. Here. Put on the doublet and let me see the entire effect.'

I took the garment from him reluctantly. 'Time was when a jerkin and leggings was good enough to wear anywhere in Buckkeep,' I observed resentfully.

'You deceive yourself,' the Fool replied implacably. 'You got away with such dress because you were little more than a boy, and Shrewd did not wish attention called to you. I seem to recall that once or twice Mistress Hasty had her way with your garments and dressed you stylishly.'

'Once or twice,' I conceded, cringing at the memory. 'But you know what I mean, Fool. When I was growing up, folk at Buckkeep dressed, well, like folk from Buck. There was none of this "Jamaillian style" or Farrow cloaks with tailed hoods that reach to the floor.'

He nodded. 'Buckkeep was a more provincial place when you were growing up. We had a war, and when a war demands your resources, there is less to spend on dress. Shrewd was a good king, but it suited him to keep the Six Duchies a backwater. Queen Kettricken has done all she can to open the duchies to trade, not just with her own Mountain Kingdom, but with the Jamaillians and Bingtowners and folk even farther away. It's bound to change Buckkeep. Change isn't a bad thing.'

'Buckkeep as it was wasn't a bad thing either,' I replied grumpily.

'But change proves that you are still alive. Change often measures our tolerance for folk different from ourselves. Can we accept their languages, their customs, their garments, and their foods into our own lives? If we can, then we form bonds, bonds that make wars less likely. If we cannot, if we believe that we must do things as we have always done them, then we must either fight to remain as we are, or die.'

'That's cheery.'

'It's true.' The Fool insisted. 'Bingtown just went through such an upheaval. Now they war with Chalced, mostly because Chalced refuses to recognize the need for change. And that war may spread to include the Six Duchies.'

'I doubt it. I don't really see where it has anything to do with us. Oh, our southern duchies will jump into the fray, but only because they have always relished the conflict with Chalced. It's a chance to carve away a bit more of their territory and make it ours. But as far as the whole Six Duchies engaging . . . I doubt it.'

I shrugged into the Jamaillian doublet and buttoned it. It had far more buttons than it needed. It fitted tightly to my waist, with skirt-like panels that reached nearly to my knees. 'I hate dressing in Jamaillian clothing. And how am I to reach my knife if I need it?'

'I know you. If you need it, you'll find a way to reach it. And I assure you, in Jamaillia you'd be at least three years out of date. In Jamaillia, they'd assume you were a provincial from Bingtown, attempting to dress like a Jamaillian. But it's enough. It reinforces the myth that I am a Jamaillian nobleman. If my clothing looks exotic enough, folk accept the rest of me as normal.' He stood up. His right foot wore an embroidered dancing slipper. The left was bound as if his ankle needed support. He took up a carved walking stick. I recognized it as the work of his own hands; to anyone else, it would seem extravagantly expensive.

Tonight, we were purple and white. Rather like turnips, I thought to myself savagely. Lord Golden's garments were far more elaborate and showy than mine were. The cuffs of my striped shirt were loose at the wrist, but his were dagged and extended past his hands. His shirt was white, but the purple Jamaillian doublet that snugged his chest had embroidered skirts that glittered with thousands of tiny jet beads. Rather than the trousers of a servant, he wore silk leggings. He had chosen to let his hair fall loose to his shoulders in long ringlets of gleaming gold. I had no idea what he had put on his hair to persuade it to such excess. And as I had heard some Jamaillian nobles did, he had painted his face, a scale-like pattern of blue above his brows and across the tops of his cheeks. He caught me staring at him. 'Well?' He demanded, almost uneasily.

'You're right. You're a very convincing Jamaillian lord.'

'Then let us descend. Bring my footstool and cushion. We'll use my injury as an excuse for arriving early in the Great Hall and watching the others come in.'

I picked up his stool in my right hand and tucked the cushion for it under my right arm. My left I offered to him as he affected a very convincing hobble. As always, he was a consummate actor. Perhaps because of the Skill-bond between us, I was aware of the keen pleasure he took in such dissembling. Certainly, it did not show in his demeanour as he grumbled and rebuked me for clumsiness all the way down the stairs.

A short distance from the immense doors that led to the Great Hall, we paused briefly. Lord Golden appeared to be catching his breath as he leaned heavily on my arm, but the Fool spoke closely by my ear. 'Don't forget you're a servant here now. Humility, Tom Badgerlock. Regardless of what you see, don't look at anyone in a challenging way. It wouldn't be proper. Ready?'

I nodded, thinking I scarcely needed his reminder, and tucked his cushion more firmly under my arm. We entered the Great Hall. And here, too, I encountered change. In my boyhood, the Great Hall had been the gathering place for all of Buckkeep. Near that hearth I had sat to recite my lessons to Fedwren the scribe. As often as not, there would have been other gatherings at the other hearths throughout the hall: men fletching arrows, women embroidering and chatting, minstrels rehearsing songs or composing new ones. Despite the roaring hearths and the serving boys who fetched wood for them, the Great Hall was always, in my memories, slightly chill and dank. The light never seemed to reach to the corners. In winter, the tapestries and banners that draped the walls retreated into dimness, a twilight interior night. For the most part, I recalled the cold flagged floor as being strewn with rushes, prone to mildew and damp. When the boards were set for meals, dogs sprawled beneath them or cruised amongst the benches like hungry sharks awaiting a tossed bone or dropped crust. It had been a lively place, noisy with the tales of warriors and guardsmen. King Shrewd's Buckkeep, I thought to myself, had been a rough and martial place, a castle and keep before it was a king's palace.

Was it time or Queen Kettricken that had changed it so?

It even smelled different, less of sweat and dogs, more of burning applewood and food. The dark that the hearth fires and candles had never been able to disperse had yielded, albeit grudgingly, to the overhead candelabra suspended by gilded chains over the long blue-clothed tables. The only dogs I saw were small ones, temporarily escaped from a lady's lap to challenge another feist or sniff about someone's boots. The reeds underfoot were clean and backed by a layer of sand. In the centre of the room a large section of the floor was bared sand, swept into elaborate designs that would soon fall prey to the dancers' tread. No one was seated at the tables, yet there were already bowls of ripe fruit and baskets of fresh bread upon them. Early guests stood in small groups or sat in chairs and on cushioned benches near the hearths, the hum of their conversations mingling with the soft music of a single harper on a dais near the main fire.

The entire room conveyed a carefully constructed sense of waiting. Rows of standing torches lit the tiered high dais. Their brightness drew the eye, the light as much as the height proclaiming the importance of those who would be seated there. On the highest level, there were throne-like chairs for Kettricken and Dutiful and Elliania and two others. The slightly humbler but still grand chairs of the second dais would be for the dukes and duchesses of the Six Duchies who had gathered to witness their prince's betrothal. A second dais of equal height had been provided for Elliania's nobles. The third dais would be for those who were high in the Queen's regard.

Almost as soon as we entered the Great Hall, several lovely women broke away from the young noblemen they had been talking to and converged on Lord Golden. It was rather like being mobbed by butterflies. Gauzy wraps seemed to be the fashion, an imported foolishness from Jamaillia that offered no sort of warmth in the permanent chill of the Great Hall. I studied the goosebumps on the arms of Lady Heliotrope as she sympathized with Lord Golden. I wondered when Buckkeep had become so avid for these foreign styles of dress and grudgingly admitted that I resented the changes I saw around me, not only because they eclipsed more and more of the Buckkeep I remembered from my childhood, but also because they made me feel stodgy and old. Cooing and clucking over his injured foot, the women escorted Lord Golden to a comfortable chair. I assisted him obediently there, set his footstool in place, the cushion upon it. Young Lord Oaks reappeared and with a firm, 'Let me do that, man,' insisted on helping Lord Golden position his foot upon it.

I stepped aside, lifted my eyes and seemed to glance past a group of Outislanders who had just entered. They moved almost as a phalanx of warriors might, entering the hall as a compact group. Once within the hall, they did not disperse but kept to their own. They reminded me of the Outisland warriors I had fought on Antler Island, so long ago. The men wore not only their furs and leather harness but some of the older men flaunted battle trophies: necklaces of fingerbones, or a braid dangling at the hip that was made from locks of hair taken from vanquished foes. The women among them moved as dauntlessly as their men. Their robes were woven of wool, richly dyed, and trimmed with white fur only: fox, ermine and tufts of ice-bear.

Outislander women were not likely to be warriors; they were the landowners among their folk. In a culture in which the men often wandered off to spend years as raiders, the women were more than the caretakers of the land. Houses and farmlands were passed from mothers to daughters, as was the family's wealth in the forms of jewellery and ornaments and tools. Men might come and go in the women's lives, but a daughter kept always her ties to her mother's house, and a man's connection to his mother's home was stronger and more permanent than his marriage bonds. The woman determined how binding the marriage yoke was. If a man was overly long away at his raiding, she might take another husband or a lover in his absence. As children belonged to the mother and the mother's family, it little mattered who had fathered them. I studied them, knowing they were not nobles and lords in the sense that we used those titles. More likely the women owned substantial land and the men had distinguished themselves in battle and raiding.

As I watched the Outislander delegation, I wondered if change had come to their lands as well. Their women had never been chattels of their men. The men might traffic in the women and youngsters dragged home as the trove of their raiding, but their own women were immune to such bargains. How strange was it, then, for a father to have the right to offer his daughter as a token to secure peace and trade? Did Elliania's father truly offer her? Or was her presence here a ploy of an older, more powerful family: her mother's kin? Yet if that were so, why hide it? Why let it appear that her father was offering her? Why was Peottre the sole representative of their motherhouse?

And all the while I was watching the Outislanders, I listened with half an ear to the chattering of the women who surrounded Lord Golden. Two, Lady Heliotrope and Lady Calendula had been in his rooms earlier. I now deduced they were sisters as well as rivals for his attention. The way that Lord Oaks constantly managed to stand between Lady Calendula and Lord Golden made me wonder if he did not desire her attention for himself. Lady Thrift was older than the other women, and perhaps older than I. I suspected she had a husband somewhere about Buckkeep. She sported the matronly aggression of a woman who was securely married yet still relished the thrill of the pursuit, rather like some foxhunters I have known. It was not that she had any need for her prey, but rather that she liked to prove she could unerringly bring it down even when pitted against the sharpest competition. Her gown bared more of her breasts than was seemly, but it did not seem as brazen as it might have in a younger woman. She had a way of setting her hand to Lord Golden's arm or shoulder that was almost possessive. Twice I saw him capture the hand touching him, pat it or give it a squeeze and then carefully release it. She probably felt flattered, but to my eye it looked more as if he plucked lint from his sleeve.

Lord Lalwick, a pleasant-faced man of middle years, drifted over to join those clustered about Lord Golden. He was a tidily-dressed man of gentle manner who made a point of introducing himself to me, a rare courtesy to show to a servant. I smiled as I bowed to his greeting. He bumped against me several times as he jockeyed to get closer to Lord Golden and the conversation, but it was easy to excuse his clumsiness. Each time I begged his pardon and stepped back only to have him smile and warmly assure me that it was entirely his own fault. The conversation centred upon poor Lord Golden's injured ankle and how rough the unsympathetic healer had been and how devastated they all were that he could not join them upon the dance floor. Here Lady Thrift stole a march upon her competitors, declaring as she took up Lord Golden's hand that she would keep him company while 'you girls dance with your suitors'. Lord Lalwick immediately declared that he would be happy to keep Lord Golden company, for he himself was a poor dancer. When Lord Golden assured him that he knew such a statement was false modesty and that he would never dream of depriving the Buckkeep ladies of such a graceful partner, the man looked torn between disappointment at his dismissal and gratitude for the compliment.

Before the rivalry amongst the ladies could escalate any further, the minstrel suddenly stopped his harping. A page-boy beside him had evidently cued him, for the minstrel arose and, in a trained voice that filled the Great Hall and overrode all conversation, announced the entrance of Queen Kettricken Farseer and Prince Dutiful, heir to the Farseer throne. At a gesture from Lord Golden, I offered him my arm to help him stand. A hush fell and all eyes turned towards the doors. The folk near the entry pressed back into the crowd to allow a walking space between the doors and the high dais.

Queen Kettricken entered with Prince Dutiful at her right hand. She had learned much in the years since I had last seen her make such an entrance. I was unprepared for the sudden tears that stung my eyes, and I struggled valiantly to control the triumphant smile that threatened to take over my face.

She was magnificent.

An elaborate gown would only have distracted from her. She wore Buck blue with a contrasting trim of sable. The simple lines of her dress emphasized both her slenderness and her height. Straight as a soldier was she, yet also as supple as a wind-blown reed. The gleaming gold of her hair had been gathered in a braid that wreathed her head, with the excess spilling down her back. Her queen's crown looked dull in comparison to those shining locks. No rings graced her fingers; no necklaces bound the pale column of her throat. She was queenly by virtue of who she was rather than what she wore.

Beside her, Dutiful was clad in a simple blue robe. It reminded me of how both Kettricken and Rurisk had been dressed the first time I had seen them. Then, I had mistaken the heirs of the Mountain Kingdom for serving people. I wondered if the Outislanders would see the plainness of Dutiful's garb as humility or lack of wealth. He wore a simple silver band on his unruly black curls, for he was not yet old enough to wear the coronet of the King-in-Waiting. Until he was seventeen, he was simply a prince even though he was the sole heir. His only other ornamentation was a chain of silver trimmed with yellow diamonds. His eyes were as dark as his mother's were pale. His looks were Farseer but the calm acceptance on his face was his mother's Mountain schooling.

Queen Kettricken's silent passage through her folk was both dignified and intimate, for the smile that lit her face as her eyes lingered on her assembled people was genuinely warm. Dutiful's expression was grave. Perhaps he knew he could not smile without looking stricken. He offered his mother his arm as she ascended the stairs to the dais and they took their places at the table but were not seated. In a gracious yet carrying voice, Kettricken spoke. 'Please, my people and friends, welcome to our Great Hall the Narcheska Elliania, a daughter of the Blackwater line of the God Runes Islands.'

I noted with approval that she gave Elliania not only the name of her mother's line, but called her home by their name for the Outislands. Also, I noted that our queen had chosen to announce her rather than giving this task to the minstrel. As she gestured towards the open door, all eyes turned that way. The minstrel repeated the names of not only Elliania but also of Arkon Bloodblade, her father and Peottre Blackwater, her 'mother's brother'. The way he spoke the last phrase made me suspect it was one word in the Outislands and that he strove to give it that flavour. Then the Outislanders entered.

Arkon Bloodblade led the way. He was an imposing figure, his size enhanced by a bearskin cloak flung back over one shoulder. It was the yellow-white fur of an ice bear. His clothing was of woven cloth, a jerkin and trousers, but a leather vest and broad leather belt gave him an armoured, martial air despite his lack of weapons. He glittered with gold and silver and gems. He wore them at his throat and wrists, across his brow, in his ears. He wore bands of silver on his left upper arm, and bands of gold on his right. Some were studded with gems. His brash posture transformed his display of wealth into bragging gaudiness. His gait combined a sailor's rolling stride with a warrior's arrogant strut. I suspected I would dislike him. He scanned the room with a wide grin, as if he could not believe his good fortune. His eyes travelled across the waiting tables and gathered nobles and then lifted to where Kettricken awaited his company on the dais. His smile widened as if he glimpsed unclaimed plunder. I then knew that I already disliked him.

Behind him walked the Narcheska. Peottre escorted her, a pace behind her and to her right. He was dressed as simply as a soldier, in fur and leather. He wore earrings and a heavy torc of gold, but he seemed unaware of his jewellery. I marked that he took not just a guard's place but also a guard's attitude. His eyes roved the crowd watchfully. If there had been any in the crowd who wished the Narcheska ill and dared to act on it, he would have been ready to kill the attacker. Yet he gave off an aura not of suspiciousness but of quiet competence. And the girl walked before him, serene in the safety of the hulking man behind her.

I wondered who had selected her garments. Her short tunic was of snowy white wool. An enamelled pin, a leaping narwhal, secured her cloak at one shoulder. A panelled skirt of blue fell nearly to the floor. Glimpses of her feet as she walked revealed little white fur slippers. Her sleek black hair was caught in a silver clasp at the back of her head. From there it flowed down her back, an inky river. At intervals, tiny silver bells glittered in its current. Upon her brow she wore the coronet of silver set with one hundred sapphires.

Elliania set her own pace, a step, then a pause, and another step. Her father, unmindful of this, or perhaps ignorant of it, strode up to the dais, mounted it, and then was forced to stand at Queen Kettricken's left, awaiting his daughter. Peottre matched the Narcheska's gait calmly. The girl did not look straight ahead as she approached the high table, but turned her head to left or to right with each step. She looked intently at the people who met her gaze, as if to memorize each one. The small smile that graced her lips seemed genuine. It was an unnerving poise to witness in a child so young. The little girl who had been on the verge of a petulant tantrum when I had last seen her had been replaced by a presence who was, indeed, a queen in the bud. When she was two steps away from the dais, Dutiful descended it to offer her his arm. Here was the only moment when I saw her uncertain. She glanced at her uncle out of the corner of her eye, as if imploring that he offer her support instead. I do not know how he conveyed that she must accept the Prince's gesture; I saw only her resignation as she carefully hovered her hand above his proffered arm. I doubted that she put a pressure equal to an alighting butterfly as she ascended the steps beside him. Peottre followed them, his tread heavy. He did not take a place before a chair, but rather stood behind the Narcheska's. After the others were seated, it took a gesture and a quiet verbal invitation from the queen before he took his seat.

Then the dukes and duchesses of the Six Duchies entered, each slowly crossing the hall and taking a place on the dais reserved for them. The Duchess of Bearns appeared first, her consort at her side. Faith of Bearns had grown into her title. I still recalled her as a slender maiden with a bloody sword in her hand, battling vainly to save her father's life from Red Ship raiders. She wore her dark hair as short and sleek as ever. The man at her side was taller than she was and grey-eyed, pacing her with a warrior's graceful stride. The bond between the two was a thing that could be felt, and I rejoiced that she had found happiness for herself.

Behind her came Duke Kelvar of Rippon, aged and crooked, one hand on a staff and one on his wife's shoulder. Lady Grace had matured into a well-rounded woman of middle years. Her hand on top of her husband's supported him in more ways than one. Both her gown and her jewels were simple, as if she finally felt confident of her stature as Duchess of Rippon. She matched her stride to his now-halting steps, her loyalty still strong to the man who had raised her from the peasantry to be his consort.

Duke Shemshy of Shoaks walked alone, widowed now. The last time I had seen him had been when he stood with Duke Brawndy of Bearns outside my cell in Regal's dungeons. He had not condemned me, but neither had he thrown me a cloak for warmth as Bearns had. He still had hawk's eyes and a slight stoop in his shoulders was his only concession to his years. He had entrusted his current war-making with Chalced to his daughter and heir while he took time to attend his prince's betrothal.

Behind him walked Duke Bright of Farrow. He had matured since the days when Regal had foisted the defence of Buckkeep Castle onto his callow shoulders. He looked a man now. I had never seen his duchess. She looked half of his forty years, a fair and slender young woman who smiled warmly as she met the gazes of the lesser nobles who watched her ascend the dais. Finally came the Duke and Duchess of Tilth. Both were unfamiliar to me; the blood-cough had passed through Tilth three years before, and carried off not only the old duke, but also both his elder sons. I rummaged my memory for the name of the daughter who had inherited. Duchess Flourish of Tilth, the minstrel announced a moment later, and her consort, Duke Jower. Her nervousness made her appear younger than she was, and Jower's hand over hers on his arm seemed to lead her as much as reassure her.

The dais reserved for the Outislander nobles and warriors who had accompanied the Narcheska awaited them. Grand entrances seemed a foreign custom to them, for they simply trooped up in a group and seated themselves as they pleased, with many exchanged grins and comments to one another. Arkon Bloodblade smiled down broadly upon them. The Narcheska seemed caught between loyalty to her folk and chagrin that they had not bothered to observe our customs. Peottre gazed out over their heads as if it did not concern him in the least. It was only as they were seated that I realized that these folk were Arkon's, not Peottre's. Each one bore, in some form or another, the image of a tusked boar. Arkon's was wrought in gold upon his breast. One of the women had a tattoo on the back of her hand, and one man wore his boar as a bone carving on his belt. The motif did not appear anywhere upon the Narcheska nor on Peottre. I recalled the leaping narwhal I had seen embroidered on the Narcheska's clothing the first time I had glimpsed her. This emblem secured her cloak again. A close study of Peottre's garments revealed that a narwhal fastened his belt. I decided that the stylistic tattoo on his face could be considered suggestive of a narwhal's horn. So, did we have two clans here, both offering the Narcheska? I decided that would bear looking into.

Those who filled the table at the foot of the high dais entered with less pageantry. Chade was among them, as was Laurel, the Queen's Huntswoman. She was gowned in scarlet, and I was pleased to see her so well seated. I did not recognize the others, save for a final two. Starling, I suspected, had deliberately chosen to be the last to enter the Great Hall. She was resplendent in a green gown that reminded me of a hummingbird's throat. She wore fine lacy gloves on her hands, as if to emphasize that tonight she was her Queen's guest rather than her minstrel. And one of those gloved hands rested on the muscular forearm of the man who escorted her. He was a fine-looking young fellow, fit of body and open of countenance. His pride in his wife was evident in his beaming smile and the way he escorted her. It seemed to me that he displayed her on his arm as a falconer might hold aloft a fine bird. I looked at the youngster I had unwittingly cuckolded, and felt shame enough for both Starling and myself. She was smiling, and as they passed before us, she deliberately met my gaze. I shifted my eyes and stared past her as if I knew her not at all. He knew nothing of me, and I wished to keep it that way. I did not even wish to know his name, but my traitor ears marked it anyway. Lord Fisher.

As these last two took their places and were seated, the folk in the hall flowed towards the tables to assume their places there. I scooped up Lord Golden's footstool and cushion and helped him hobble to his place at table and made him comfortable there. He was well seated, considering that he was a foreign noble and a recent arrival to court. I suspected he had contrived to be placed as he was, between two older married couples. The women left his side with many promises to return and keep him company during the dancing. As he turned to depart, Lord Lalwick contrived to jostle his buttocks against my hip a final time. He saw my shock as I finally realized that the contact was deliberate, for in addition to his small smile, one eyebrow lifted at me. Behind me, Lord Golden gave a small, amused cough. I scowled at the man, and he left more hastily.

As folk settled to their seats and the servants paraded into the hall, the buzz of conversation rose. Lord Golden made skilful and charming conversation with his table partners. I stood behind him within his beck and let my eyes drift over the gathered folk. When I glanced up at the high dais, Prince Dutiful's eyes met mine. Gratitude shone in his face. I looked away from his glance, and he followed my example, letting his eyes lift to look past me. The magic link between us trembled with his thankfulness and nervousness. It both humbled and frightened me to realize how important it was to him that I be present.

I tried not to let it distract me from my duties. I located Civil Bresinga. He was seated at a table of lesser nobility from the smallholdings of Buck and Farrow. I did not see Sydel, his intended, among the women at the table, and I wondered if their engagement had been broken. Lord Golden had flirted outrageously with her when we had guested at Galekeep, the Bresinga's manor. That discourtesy and his apparently equal interest in Civil Bresinga had led to the young man's intense dislike of him. It had all been a sham, but Civil would never discover that. I marked that at least two young men at his table seemed to know Civil well, and resolved to discover who they might be. In a gathering of this size, my Wit-sense was near overwhelmed by the life-presence of so many beings. Impossible for me to tell in that throng who might or might not be Witted. Doubtless if any here possessed the Wit, it was well masked tonight anyway.

No one had warned me that Lady Patience would be in attendance. When my eye fell on her at one of the higher tables, my heart leapt and then began to hammer. My father's widow was in lively conversation with a young man next to her. At least, she was speaking. He stared at her, his mouth slightly ajar, blinking his eyes. I did not blame him; I myself had never been able to keep up with her leaping fountain of observations, questions and opinions. I jerked my eyes away from them, as if my gaze might somehow make her aware of me. Over the next few minutes, I stole glimpses of her. She wore the rubies my father had given her, the ones she had once sold to gain coin to ease the suffering of the people of Buck. Her greying hair was garlanded with late flowers, a custom as outdated as the gown she wore, but to me her eccentricity was endearing and precious. I wished I could go to her, kneel by her chair and thank her for all she had done for me, not only during my life, but when she had supposed me dead. It was a selfish wish, in some ways.

In pulling my eyes away from her, I got my second great shock of the evening.

The Queen's ladies and maids were seated honourably at a side table almost adjacent to the high dais. This was a true mark of the Queen's favour that ignored rank. Some of the ladies I knew from of old. Lady Hopeful and Lady Modesty had been Kettricken's companions when last I lived in Buckkeep Castle. I was glad to see they still remained at her side. Of Lady Whiteheart I recalled only her name. The others were younger; doubtless they had been but children when I last attended my queen. But one looked more familiar than the others. I wondered, had I known her mother? And then, as she turned her round face and dipped her head to acknowledge some jest, I recognized her. Rosemary.

The plump little girl had grown into a buxom lady. She had been the Queen's little maid when last I had seen her, always tripping along at her heels, always present, an unusually placid and good-natured child. She had had a habit of drowsing off at Kettricken's feet when the Queen and I were conferring. Or so it had seemed. She had been Regal's spy upon Kettricken, not only reporting back to him, but later aiding him in his attempts on the Queen's life. I had not seen her commit any of her betrayals, but in retrospect both Chade and I had deduced that she must have been Regal's wee bird. Chade knew; Kettricken knew. How could it be that she lived still, how could it be that she laughed and dined so near the Queen, that now she lifted a glass in a toast to her? I tore my eyes away from her. I tried to still the tremor of fury that raced through me.

I looked at my feet for a time, drawing long, steadying breaths, willing away the colour in my face that my anger had brought.

Wrong?

The tiny thought rang in my mind like a dropped coin. I lifted my eyes and found Prince Dutiful's worried gaze fixed on me. I shrugged my shoulders to him, then tugged at my collar as if the tight fit of my jacket bothered me. I did not reach back to him with the Skill. It disturbed me that he had been able to reach me past my habitual walls. It disturbed me more that, as before, he used his Wit-sense of me to push the thought that he formed with the Skill. I did not wish him to use the Wit. I especially didn't want to encourage him to use those magics together. He might form habits he could never break. I waited a short time, then again met his anxious gaze and smiled briefly. I looked away from him again. I could sense his reluctance but he followed my example. It would not suit me at all for anyone to notice us and wonder why Prince Dutiful was exchanging significant glances with a serving man.

The meal was magnificent and lengthy, yet I noted that neither Dutiful nor Elliania ate much. But Arkon Bloodblade ate and drank enough to make up for the both of them. Watching him, I decided he was a hearty man, sharp of wit, but not the diplomat or tactician who had arranged this marriage. His personal interest in Kettricken was obvious, and perhaps by Outislander standards it was complimentary. My stolen glimpses of the high table showed me that Kettricken responded courteously to his conversation, yet seemed to attempt to address more of her words to the Narcheska. The girl's replies to her were brief, but pleasantly delivered. She was reserved rather than sulky. And midway through the meal, I noticed that Uncle Peottre seemed to be thawing towards Kettricken, perhaps despite himself. Doubtless Chade had advised the Queen that we would be wise to bestow more attention about the Narcheska's 'mother's brother'. Certainly Peottre seemed to respond to it. He began by adding some comments of his own to whatever Elliania replied, but soon he and Kettricken were conversing over her head. Admiration lit Kettricken's eyes, and she followed his words with genuine interest. Elliania seemed almost grateful to be able to pick at her food and nod to the words that flowed past her.

Dutiful, well-bred lad that he was, engaged Arkon Bloodblade in talk. The boy seemed to have mastered the knack of asking the naturally garrulous Bloodblade the best questions to keep him talking. From the waving of his implements, I deduced that Bloodblade was telling tales of his hunting and battle prowess. Dutiful looked suitably impressed, nodding and laughing at all the right moments.

The one time that Chade's eyes met mine, I glanced pointedly at Rosemary and scowled. But when I looked back for his reaction, he was once more chatting with the lady at his left. I growled to myself, but knew that clarification would come later.

As the end of the meal grew closer, I could feel Dutiful's tension mounting. The Prince's smile showed too much of teeth. When the Queen motioned to the minstrel and he called for silence, I saw Dutiful shut his eyes for an instant as if to steel himself to the challenge. Then I took my eyes from him and focused my attention on Elliania. I saw her moisten her lips, and then perhaps she clenched her jaws to still a trembling. The cant of Peottre's posture made me suspect that he clasped her hand under the table. In any case, she drew a deep breath and then sat up straighter.

It was a simple ceremony. I paid more attention to the faces of those witnessing it. All the participants moved to the front of the high dais. Kettricken stood next to Dutiful, and Arkon Bloodblade by his daughter. Unbidden, Peottre came to stand behind her. When Arkon set his daughter's hand in the Queen's, I noticed that Duchess Faith of Bearns narrowed her eyes and clamped her lips. Perhaps Bearns remembered too well how they had suffered in the Red Ship War. There was quite a different reaction from the Duke and Duchess of Tilth. They looked warmly into one another's eyes as if recalling the moment of their own pledge. Patience sat, still and solemn, her gaze distant. Young Civil Bresinga looked envious, and then turned his eyes away from the sight as if he could not bear to witness it. I saw no one who looked at the couple with malice, though some, like Faith, plainly had their own opinions about this alliance.

The couple's hands were not joined at this time; rather Elliania's hand was put in Kettricken's, and Dutiful and Arkon grasped wrists in the ancient greeting of warriors well met. All seemed a bit surprised when Arkon tugged a gold band from his wrist and clasped it onto Dutiful's. He guffawed in delight at how it hung on the boy's lesser-muscled arm, and Dutiful managed a good-natured laugh, and even held it aloft for others to admire. The Outislander delegation seemed to take this as a sign of good spirit in the Prince, for they hammered their table in approval. A slight smile tugged at the corner of Peottre's mouth. Was it because the bracelet that Arkon had bestowed on Dutiful had a boar scratched on it rather than a narwhal? Was the Prince binding himself to a clan that had no authority over the Narcheska?

Then came the only incident that seemed to mar the smoothness of the ceremony. Arkon gripped the Prince's wrist and turned it so that the Prince's hand was palm up. Dutiful tolerated this but I knew his uneasiness. Arkon seemed unaware of it as he asked the assemblage loudly, 'Shall we mingle their blood now, for sign of the children to come that share it?'

I saw the Narcheska's intake of breath. She did not step back into Peottre's shelter. Rather, the man stepped forward and in an unconscious show of possession, set a hand to the girl's shoulder. His words were unaccented and calm as he said, in apparent good-natured rebuke, 'It is not the time or the place for that, Bloodblade. The man's blood must fall on the hearthstones of her mother's house for that mingling to be auspicious. But you might offer some of your blood to the hearthstones of the Prince's mother, if you are so minded.'

I suspect there was a hidden challenge in those words, some custom we of the Six Duchies did not comprehend. For when Kettricken began to hold out her hand to say such an act was not necessary, Arkon thrust out his arm. He pushed his sleeve up out of the way, and then casually drew his belt knife and ran the blade down the inside of his arm. At first the thick blood merely welled in the gash. He clawed at the wound and then gave his arm a shake to encourage the flow. Kettricken wisely stood still, allowing the barbarian whatever gesture he thought he must make for the honour of his house. He displayed his arm to the assembly, and in the murmurous awe of all, we watched his cupped hand catch his own trickling blood. He suddenly flung it wide, a red benediction upon us all.

Many cried out as those crimson droplets spattered the faces and garments of the gathered nobility. Then silence fell as Arkon Bloodblade descended from the dais. He strode to the largest hearth in the Great Hall. There he again let his blood pool in his hand, then flung the cupped gore into the flames. Stooping, he smeared his palm across the hearth, and then stood, allowing his sleeve to fall over his injury. He opened his arms to the assembly, inviting a response. At the Outislander table, his people pounded the board and whooped in admiration. After a moment, applause and cheers also rose from the Six Duchies folk. Even Peottre Blackwater grinned, and when Arkon rejoined him on the dais, they grasped wrists before the assemblage.

As I watched them there, I suspected that their relationship was far more complicated than I had first imagined. Arkon was Elliania's father, yet I doubted that Peottre ceded him any respect on that account. But when they stood as they did now, as fellow warriors, I sensed between them the camaraderie of men who had fought alongside one another. So there was esteem, even if Peottre did not think Arkon had the right to offer Elliania as a treaty-affirming token.

It brought me back full circle to the central mystery. Why did Peottre allow it? Why did Elliania go along with it? If they stood to gain from this alliance, why did not her mothers' house stand proudly behind it and offer the girl?

I studied the Narcheska as Chade had taught me. Her father's gesture had caught her imagination. She smiled at him, proud of his valour and the show he had made for the Six Duchies nobles. Part of her enjoyed all this, the pageantry and ceremony, the clothing and the music and the gathered folk all looking up at her. She wanted all the excitement and glory but at the end of it she also wanted to return to what was safe and familiar, to live out the life she expected to live, in her mothers' house on her mothers' land. I asked myself, how could Dutiful use that to gain her favour? Were there any plans for him to present himself, with gifts and honours at her mothers' holding? Perhaps she would think better of him if his attention to her could be flaunted before her maternal relatives back home. Girls usually enjoyed that sort of elevation, didn't they? I stored up my insights to offer them to Dutiful tomorrow. I wondered if they were accurate, or would be of any use to him.

As I pondered, Queen Kettricken nodded towards her minstrel. He signalled the musicians to ready themselves. Queen Kettricken then smiled and said something to the other folk on the grand dais. Places were resumed and as the music began, Dutiful offered his hand to Elliania.

I pitied them both, so young and so publicly displayed, the wealth of two folks offered to one another as chattel for an alliance. The Narcheska's hand hovered above Dutiful's wrist as he escorted her down the steps of the dais to the swept sand of the dance floor. In a brief swell of Skill, I knew that his collar chafed against his sweaty neck, but none of that showed in his smile or in the gracious bow he offered his partner. He held out his arms for her, and she stepped just close enough for his fingertips to graze her waist. She did not put her hands to his shoulders in the traditional stance; rather she held out her skirts as if to better display both them and her lively feet. Then the music swirled around them and they both danced as perfectly as puppets directed by a master. They made a lovely spectacle, full of youth and grace and promise as they stepped and turned together.

I watched those who gazed upon them, and was surprised by the spectrum of emotions I saw in those mirroring faces. Chade beamed with satisfaction but Kettricken's face was more tentative, and I guessed her secret hope that Dutiful would find true affection as well as solid political advantage in his partner. Arkon Bloodblade crossed his arms on his chest and looked down on the two as if they were a personal testimonial to his power. Peottre, like me, was scanning the crowd, ever the bodyguard and watchman for his ward. He did not scowl, but neither did he smile. For a chance instant, his eyes met mine as I studied him. I dared not look aside, but stared through him with a dull expression as if I did not truly see him at all. His eyes left me to travel back to Elliania and the faintest shadow of a smile crossed his lips.

Drawn by his scrutiny, my gaze followed his. For that moment, I allowed myself to be caught in the spectacle. As they stepped and turned to the music, slippers and skirts swirled the brushed sand on the floor into a fresh pattern. Dutiful was taller than his partner; doubtless it was easier for him to look down into her upturned face than it was for her to gaze up at him and smile and keep the step. He looked as if his outstretched hands and arms framed the flight of a butterfly, so lightly did she move opposite him. A spark of approval kindled in me as well, and I thought I understood why Peottre had given that grudging smile of approval. My lad did not seek to grasp the girl; his touch sketched the window of her freedom as she danced. He did not claim nor attempt to restrain; rather he exhibited her grace and her liberty to those who watched. I wondered where Dutiful had learned such wisdom. Had Chade coaxed him in this, or was this the diplomatic instinct some Farseers seemed to possess? Then I decided it did not matter. He had pleased Peottre and I suspected that that would eventually be to his advantage.

The Prince and the Narcheska performed alone for the first dance. After that, others moved to join them on the dance floor, the dukes and duchesses of the Six Duchies and our Outislander guests. I noticed that Peottre was true to his word, claiming the Narcheska away from Dutiful for the second dance. That left the Prince standing alone, but he managed to appear graceful and at ease. Chade drifted over to speak with him until the Queen's advisor was claimed by a maiden of no more than twenty.

Arkon Bloodblade had the effrontery to offer his hand to Queen Kettricken. I saw the look that flickered over her face. She would have refused him, but decided it was not in the best interest of the Six Duchies to do so. So she descended with him to the dance floor. Bloodblade had none of Dutiful's nicety in the matter of a partner's preference. He seized the Queen boldly at her waist so that she had to set her hands on his shoulders to balance the man's lively stepping, or else find herself spinning out of control. Kettricken trod the measure gracefully and smiled upon her partner, but I do not think she truly enjoyed it.

The third measure was a slower dance. I was pleased to see Chade forsake his young partner, who sulked prettily. Instead he invited my Lady Patience out to the floor. She shook her fan at him and would have refused, but the old man insisted, and I knew that she was secretly pleased. She was as graceful as she had ever been – though never quite in step with the music, but Chade smiled down on her as he steered her safely around the floor and I found her dance both lovely and charming.

Peottre rescued Queen Kettricken from Bloodblade's attention, and he went off to dance with his daughter. Kettricken seemed more at ease with the old man-at-arms than she had with his brother-in-law. They spoke as they danced, and the lively interest in her eyes was genuine. Dutiful's eyes met mine for an instant. I knew how awkward he felt standing there, a lone stag, while his intended was whirled around the dance floor by her father. But at the end of the dance, I almost suspected that Bloodblade had known of it, and felt a sympathy for the young prince, for he firmly delivered his daughter's hand to Dutiful's for the fourth dance.

And so it went. For the most part, the Outislander nobles chose partners from among themselves, though one young woman dared to approach Lord Shemshy. To my surprise, the old man seemed flattered by the invitation, and danced not once with her, but thrice. When the partner dances were over, the patterns began, and the high nobles resumed their seats, ceding the floor to the lesser nobility. I stood silently and watched, for the most part. Several times my master sent me on errands to different parts of the room, usually to deliver his greetings to women and his heartfelt regrets that he could not ask them to dance due to the severity of his injury. Several came to cluster near him and commiserate with him. In all that long evening, I never once saw Civil Bresinga take to the dance floor. Lady Rosemary did, even dancing once with Chade. I watched them speak to one another, she looking up at him and smiling mischievously while his features remained neutral yet courteous. Lady Patience retired early from the festivities, as I had suspected she might. She had never truly felt at home in the pomp and society of court. I thought that Dutiful should feel honoured that she had troubled to come at all.

The music, the dancing, the eating and the drinking, all of it went on and on, past the depths of night and into the shallows of morning. I tried to contrive some way to get close to either Civil Bresinga's wine glass or his plate, but to no avail. The evening began to drag. My legs ached from standing and I thought regretfully of my dawn appointment with Prince Dutiful. I doubted that he would keep it, and yet I must still be there, in case he appeared. What had I been thinking? I would have been far wiser to put the boy off for a few more days, and use that time to visit my home.

Lord Golden, however, seemed indefatigable. As the evening progressed and the tables were pushed to one side to enlarge the dancing space, he found a comfortable place near a fireside and held his court there. Many and varied were the folk who came to greet him and lingered to talk. Yet again it was driven home to me that Lord Golden and the Fool were two very distinct people. Golden was witty and charming, but he never displayed the Fool's edged humour. He was also very Jamaillian, urbane and occasionally intolerant of what he bluntly referred to as 'the Six Duchies attitude' towards his morality and habits. He discussed dress and jewellery with his cohorts in a way that mercilessly shredded any outside the circle of his favour. He flirted outrageously with women, married or not, drank extravagantly and when offered Smoke, grandly declined on the grounds that 'any but the finest quality leaves me nauseous in the morning. I was spoiled at the Satrap's court, I suppose'. He chattered of doings in far-off Jamaillia in an intimate way that convinced even me that he had not only resided there, but been privy to the doings of their high court.

And as the evening deepened, censers of Smoke, made popular in Regal's time, began to appear. Smaller styles were in vogue now, little metal cages suspended from chains that held tiny pots of the burning drug. Younger lords and a few of the ladies carried their own little censers, fastened to their wrists. In a few places, diligent servants stood beside their masters, swinging the censers to wreathe their betters with the fumes.

I had never had any head for this intoxicant, and somehow my mental association of Smoke with Regal made it all the more distasteful to me. Yet even the Queen was indulging, moderately, for Smoke was known in the Mountains as well as the Six Duchies, though the herb they burned there was a different one. Different herb, same name, same effects, I thought woozily. The Queen had returned to the high dais, her eyes bright through the haze. She sat talking to Peottre. He smiled and spoke to her, but his eyes never left Elliania as Dutiful led her through a pattern dance. Arkon Bloodblade had also joined them on the floor and was working his way through a succession of dance partners. He had shed his cloak and opened his shirt. He was a lively dancer, not always in step with the music as the Smoke curled and the wine flowed.

I think it was out of mercy for me that Lord Golden announced that the pain in his ankle had wearied him and he must, he feared, retire. He was urged to stay on, and he appeared to consider it, but then decided he was in too much discomfort. Even so, it took an interminable amount of time for him to make his farewells. And when I did take up his footstool and cushion to escort him from the merry-making, we were halted at least four times by yet more folk wishing to bid him goodnight. By the time we had clambered slowly up the stairs and entered our apartments, I had a much clearer view of his popularity at court.

When the door was safely closed and latched behind us, I built up our dying fire. Then I poured myself a glass of his wine and dropped into a chair by the hearth while he sat down on the floor to unwind the wrappings from his foot.

'I did this too tight! Look at my poor foot, gone almost blue and cold.'

'Serves you right,' I observed without sympathy. My clothing reeked of Smoke. I blew a breath out through my nostrils, trying to clear the scent away. I looked down on him where he sat rubbing his bared toes and realized what a relief it was to have the Fool back. 'How did you ever come up with "Lord Golden"? I don't think I've ever encountered a more backbiting, conniving noble. If I had met you for the first time tonight, I would have despised you. You put me in mind of Regal.'

'Did I? Well, perhaps that reflects my belief that there is something to be learned from everyone that we meet.' He yawned immensely and then rolled his body forward until his brow touched his knees, and then back until his loosened hair swept the floor. With no apparent effort, he came back to a sitting position. He held out his hand to me where I sat and I offered him mine to pull him to his feet. He plopped down in the chair next to mine. 'There is a lot to be said for being nasty, if you want others to feel encouraged to parade their smallest and most vicious opinions for you.'

'I suppose. But why would anyone want that?'

He leaned over to pluck the wine glass from my fingers. 'Insolent churl. Stealing your master's wine. Get your own glass.' And as I did so, he replied, 'By mining such nastiness, I discover the ugliest rumours of the keep. Who is with child by someone else's lord? Who has run themselves into debt? Who has been indiscreet and with whom? And who is rumoured to be Witted, or to have ties to someone who is?'

I nearly spilled my wine. 'And what did you hear?'

'Only what we expected,' he said comfortingly. 'Of the Prince and his mother, not a word. Nor any gossip about you. An interesting rumour that Civil Bresinga broke off his engagement to Sydel Grayling because there is supposed to be Wit in her family. A Witted silversmith and his six children and wife were driven out of Buckkeep Town last week; Lady Esomal is quite annoyed, for she had just ordered two rings from him. Oh. And Lady Patience has on her estate three Witted goosegirls and she doesn't care who knows it. Someone accused one of them of putting a spell on his hawks, and Lady Patience told him that not only did the Wit not work that way, but that if he didn't stop setting his hawks on the turtledoves in her garden she'd have him horsewhipped, and she didn't care whose cousin he was.'

'Ah. Patience is as discreet and rational as ever,' I said, smiling, and the Fool nodded. I shook my head more soberly as I added, 'If the tide of feeling rises much higher against the Witted ones, Patience may find she has put herself in danger by taking their part. Sometimes I wish her caution was as great as her courage.'

'You miss her, don't you?' he asked softly.

I took a breath. 'Yes. I do.' Even admitting it squeezed my heart. It was more than missing her. I'd abandoned her. Tonight I'd seen her, a fading old woman alone save for her loyal, ageing servants.

'But you've never considered letting her know that you survived? That you live still?'

I shook my head. 'For the reasons I just mentioned. She has no caution. Not only would she proclaim it from the rooftops, but also she would probably threaten to horsewhip anyone who refused to rejoice with her. That would be after she got over being furious with me, of course.'

'Of course.'

We were both smiling, in that bittersweet way one does when imagining something that the heart longs for and the head would dread. The fire burned before us, tongues of flame lapping up the side of the fresh log. Outside the shuttered windows, a wind was blowing. Winter's herald. A twitch of old reflexes made me think of all the things I had not done to prepare for it. I'd left crops in my garden, and harvested no marsh grass for the pony's winter comfort. They were the cares of another man in another life. Here at Buckkeep, I need worry about none of that. I should have felt smug, but instead I felt divested.

'Do you think the Prince will meet me at dawn in Verity's tower?'

The Fool's eyes were closed but he rolled his head towards me. 'I don't know. He was still dancing when we left.'

'I suppose I should be there in case he does. I wish I hadn't said I would. I need to get back to my cabin and tidy myself out of there.'

He made a small sound between assent and a sigh. He drew his feet up and curled up in the chair like a child. His knees were practically under his chin.

'I'm going to bed,' I announced. 'You should, too.'

He made another sound. I groaned. I went to his bed, dragged off a coverlet, and brought it back to the fireside. I draped it over him. 'Good night, Fool.'

He sighed heavily in reply and pulled the blanket closer.

I blew out all the candles save one that I carried to my chamber with me. I set it down on my small clothing chest and sat down on the hard bed with a groan. My back ached all round my scar. Standing still had always irritated it far more than riding or working. The little room was both chill and close, the air too still and full of the same smells it had gathered for the last hundred years. I didn't want to sleep there. I thought of climbing all the steps to Chade's workroom and stretching out on the larger, softer bed there. That would have been good, if there had not been so many stairs between it and me.

I dragged off my fine clothes and made an effort at putting them away properly. As I burrowed beneath my single blanket, I resolved to get some money out of Chade and purchase at least one more blanket for myself, one that was not so aggressively itchy. And to check on Hap. And apologize to Jinna for not coming to see her this evening as I had said I would. And get rid of the scrolls in my cabin. And teach my horse some manners. And instruct the Prince in the Skill and the Wit.

I drew a very deep breath, sighed it and all my cares away, and sank into sleep.

Shadow Wolf.

It was not a strong call. It was drifting smoke on the wind. It was not my name. It was someone's name for me, but that did not mean I had to answer to it. I turned away from the summoning.

Shadow Wolf.

Shadow Wolf.

Shadow Wolf.

It reminded me of Hap tugging at my shirt-tail when he was small. Incessant and insistent. Nagging as a mosquito buzzing near your ear in the night.

Shadow Wolf.

Shadow Wolf.

It wasn't going to go away.

I'm sleeping. I suddenly knew that was so, in that odd way that dreamers do. I was asleep and this was a dream. Dreams didn't matter. Did they?

So am I. That's the only time I can reach you. Don't you know that?

My replying seemed to have strengthened her sending. It was almost as if she clung to me now. *No. I didn't know that.*

I looked idly around myself. I nearly recognized the shape of the land. It was spring and close by apple trees were in bloom. I could hear bees busy amongst the blossoms. There was soft green grass under my bare feet and a gentle air moved through my hair.

*I've come so often to your dreams, and watched what you did. I
thought I would invite you to one of mine. Do you like it?*

There was a woman beside me. No, a girl. Someone. It was hard
to tell. I could see her dress and her little leather shoes, and her
weather-browned hands but the rest of her was fogged. I could not
resolve her features. As for myself . . . it was strange. I could behold
myself, as if I stood outside myself, and yet it was not the me that
I saw when I looked in a mirror. I was a shaggy-haired man, much
taller than I truly am, and far more strong. My rough grey hair spilled
down my back and hung over my brow. The nails of my hands were
black, and my teeth were pointed in my mouth. Uneasiness nibbled
at me. Danger here, but not to me. Why couldn't I remember what
the danger was?

This isn't me. This isn't right.

She laughed fondly. *Well, if you won't let me see you as you are,
then you'll just have to be how I've always imagined you. Shadow Wolf,
why have you stayed away? I've missed you. And I've feared for you.
I felt your great pain, but I do not know what it was. Are you hurt?
There seems less of you than there was. And you seem tired and older.
I've missed you and your dreams. I was so scared you were dead, and
then you didn't come any more. It's taken me forever to discover that I
could reach out to you instead of waiting for you to come to me.*

She chattered like a child. A very real and wakeful dismay crept
through me. It was like a cold mist in my heart, and then I saw it,
a mist rising around me in the dream. Somehow, without knowing
how, I had summoned it. I willed it thicker and stronger around
me. I tried to warn her. *This isn't right. Or good. Stay back, stay
away from me.*

That isn't fair! She wailed as the mist became a wall between us.
Her thoughts reached me more faintly. *Look what you've done to my
dream. It was so hard to make and now you've spoiled it. Where are
you going? You are so rude!*

I twitched free of her failing grip on me, and found I could wake
up. In fact, I was already awake, and an instant later I was sitting on
the edge of my cot. My combing fingers stood up what was left of my
hair. I was almost ready for the Skill-pain when it lurched through
my belly and slammed against the cap of my skull. I took deep,

steadying breaths, resolved not to vomit. When some little time had passed, a minute or half a year, I could scarcely tell which, I painstakingly began to reinforce my Skill-walls. Had I been careless? Had weariness or my exposure to Smoke dropped them?

Or was my daughter simply strong enough to break through them?

FIVE

Shared Sorrows

A storm of gems they were.
Scaled wings jewel-like glittered.
Eyes flaming, wings fanning
The dragons came.

Too flashing bright for memory to hold.
The promise of a thousand songs fulfilled.
Claws shredding, jaws devouring
The King returned.
    Verity's Reckoning – Starling Birdsong

Air stirred against my cheek. I opened my eyes wearily. I had dozed off, despite the open window and chill morning. Before and below me stretched a vista of water. Waves tipped with white wrinkled under a grey sky. I got up from Verity's chair with a groan; two steps carried me to the tower window. From here, the view was wider, showing me the steep cliffs and the clinging forest below this aspect of Buckkeep castle. There was the taste of a storm in the air, and the wind was cutting its winter teeth. The sun was a hand's-breadth above the far horizon, dawn long fled. The Prince had not come.

I was not surprised. Dutiful was probably still deeply asleep after last night's festivities. No, it was no surprise that he should forget our meeting, or perhaps rouse just enough to decide it wasn't that important and roll back into sleep. Yet I felt some disappointment, and it was not just that my prince had found sleep more important than meeting me. He had said he would meet me here, and then hadn't. And had not even sent word to cancel the meeting and save me the time and trouble of being here. It was a trifling thing in a boy of his years, a bit of thoughtlessness. Yet what was minor in a boy was not so in a prince. I wanted to rebuke him for it, as Chade would have chastened me. Or Burrich. I grinned ruefully. In fairness, had I been any different at Dutiful's age? Burrich had never trusted me to keep dawn appointments. I could well recall how he would thunder at my door to be sure I did not miss a lesson with the axe. Well, perhaps if our roles had been different, I would have gone and pounded on the Prince's chamber door.

As it was, I contented myself with a message, drawn in the dust on the top of a small table beside the chair. 'I was here; you were not.' Brief and succinct, a rebuke if he chose to take it that way. And anonymous. It could just as easily have been a sulky page's note to a tardy chambermaid.

I closed the window shutters and let myself out by the way I had come, through a side panel in the decorative mantel around the hearth. It was a narrow squeeze and it was tricky to properly seat it closed behind me. My candle had gone out. I descended a long and gloomy stair, sparsely lit by tiny chinks in the outer wall that let in thin fingers of light and wind. There was a level section that I negotiated through pitch dark; it seemed far longer than I recalled, and I was glad when my groping foot found the next stair. I made a wrong turn at the bottom of it. The third time I walked into a faceful of cobwebs, I knew I was lost. I turned around and groped my way back. When, some time later, I emerged into Chade's chamber from behind the wine rack, I was dusty and irritable and sweaty. I was ill prepared for what met me there.

Chade started up from his seat before the hearth, setting down a teacup as he did so. 'There you are, FitzChivalry,' he exclaimed, even as a wave of Skill slammed into me.

Don't see me, stink dog man.

I staggered and then caught at the table to remain standing. I ignored Chade, who was scowling at me, to focus on Thick. The idiot serving-man, his face smudged with soot, stood by the work-hearth. His figure wavered before my eyes and I felt giddy. If

I had not reset my walls the night before to guard against Nettle's Skill tinkering, I think he would have been able to wipe all image of himself from my mind. As it was, I spoke through gritted teeth.

'I do see you. I will always see you. But that does not mean I will hurt you. Unless you try to hurt me. Or unless you are rude to me again.' I was sorely tempted to try the Wit on him, to *repel* at him with a burst of sheer animal energy, but I did not. I would not use the Skill. I would have had to open my walls to do so, and it would have revealed to him what my strength was. I was not yet ready for that. Remain calm, I told myself. You have to master yourself before you can master him.

'No, no, Thick! Stop that. He's good. He can be here. I say so.'

Chade spoke to him as if he were three years old. And while I recognized that the small eyes in the round face that glowered at me were not the eyes of a man my intellectual equal, I also saw a flash of resentment there at being thus addressed. I seized on it, keeping my gaze on Thick's face but speaking to Chade.

'You don't need to talk to him like that. He isn't stupid. He's . . .' I groped for a word to express what I suddenly was certain of. Thick's intelligence might be limited in some ways, but it was there. '. . . different,' I ended lamely. Different, I reflected, as a horse was different from a cat and they both were different from a man. But not lesser. Almost I could sense how his mind reached in another direction from mine, attaching significance to items I dismissed even as he dismissed whole areas that anchored my reality.

Thick scowled from me to Chade and back again. Then he took up his broom and a bucket of ash and cinders from the fireplace and scuttled from the room. After the scroll rack had swung back into place behind him, I caught the flung thought-fragment. *Dog-stinker.*

'He doesn't like me. He knows I'm Witted, too,' I complained to Chade as I dropped into the other chair. Almost sulkily, I added, 'Prince Dutiful didn't meet me in Verity's tower this morning. He had said he would.'

My remarks seemed to drift past the old man. 'The Queen wants to see you. Right away.' He was neatly if not elegantly attired in a

simple robe of blue this morning with soft fur slippers on his feet.
Did they ache from dancing?

'What about?' I asked as I rose and followed him. We went back
to the wine rack, and as we triggered the concealed door, I remarked,
'Thick didn't seem surprised to see me enter from here.'

Chade shrugged one shoulder. 'I do not think he is bright
enough to be surprised by something like that. I doubt that he
even noticed it.'

I considered and decided that it might be true. To him, it might
have no significance. 'And the Queen wanted to see me because?'

'Because she told me so,' he replied a bit testily.

After that I kept silent and followed him. I suspected his head
throbbed, as mine did. I knew he had an antidote to a night's
hard drinking, and knew also how difficult it was to compound.
Sometimes it was easier to put up with the throbbing headache
than to grind one's way through creating a cure.

We entered the Queen's private chambers as we had before.
Chade paused to peer and listen to be sure there were no witnesses,
then admitted us to a privy chamber, and from there to the Queen's
sitting room, where Kettricken awaited us. She looked up with a
weary smile as we entered. She was alone.

We both bowed formally. 'Good morning, my queen,' Chade
greeted her for us, and she held out her hands in welcome, gesturing
us in. The last time I had been here, an anxious Kettricken had
awaited us in an austere chamber, her thoughts centred solely on
her missing son. This time, the room displayed her handiwork. In
the middle of a small table, six golden leaves had been arranged on
a tray of gleaming river pebbles. Three tall candles burning there
gave off the scent of violets. Several rugs of wool eased the floor
against winter's oncoming chill, and the chairs were softened with
sheepskins. A day-fire burned in the hearth, and a kettle puffed
steam above it. It reminded me of her home in the Mountains. She
had also arranged a small table of food. Hot tea exhaled from a fat
pot. I noticed there were only two cups as Kettricken said, 'Thank
you for bringing FitzChivalry here, Lord Chade.'

It was a dismissal, smoothly done. Chade bowed again, perhaps
a bit more stiffly than he had the first time, and retreated by way

of the privy chamber. I was left standing alone before the Queen, wondering what all this was about. When the door closed behind Chade, she gave a sudden great sigh, sat down at the table and gestured at the other chair. 'Please, Fitz,' and her words were an invitation to drop all formality as well as to be seated.

As I took my place opposite her, I studied her. We were nearly of an age, but her years rode her far more graciously than mine did me. Where the passage of time had scarred me, it had brushed her, leaving a tracery of lines at the corners of her eyes and mouth. She wore a green gown today, and it set off the gold of her hair as well as carrying her eyes to the jade end of their spectrum. Her dress was simple, as was the plaiting of her hair; she wore no jewellery or cosmetics.

And she did not indulge in any kind of ceremony as she poured tea for me and set my cup before me. 'There are cakes, too, if you wish,' she said, and I did, for I had not yet broken my fast that day. Yet something in her voice, an edge of hoarseness, made me set down the cup I'd started to lift. She was looking aside from me, avoiding my eyes. I saw the frantic fluttering of her eyelashes, and then a tear brimmed over and splashed down her cheek.

'Kettricken?' I asked in alarm. What had gone awry that I did not know about? Had she discovered the Narcheska's reluctance to wed her son? Had there been another Wit-threat?

She caught her breath raggedly and suddenly looked me full in the face, 'Oh, Fitz, I did not call you here for this. I meant to keep this to myself. But . . . I am so sorry. For all of us. When first I heard, I already knew. I woke that dawn, feeling as if something had broken, something important.' She tried to clear her throat and could not. She croaked out her words, tears coursing down her face. 'I could not put my finger on the loss, but when Chade brought your tidings to me, I knew instantly. I felt him go, Fitz. I felt Nighteyes leave us.' And then a sob wracked her, and she dropped her face into her hands and wept like a devastated child.

I wanted to flee. I had almost succeeded in mastering my grief, and now she tore the wound afresh. For a time I sat woodenly, numbed by pain. Why couldn't she just leave it alone?

But she seemed not to notice my coldness. 'The years pass, but you never forget a friend like him.' She was speaking to herself, her head bowed into her hands. Her words came muffled and thick with tears. She rocked a little in her chair. 'I'd never felt so close to an animal, before we travelled together. But in the long hours of walking, he was always there, ranging ahead and coming back and then checking behind us. He was like a shield for me, for when he came trotting back, I always knew that he was satisfied no danger awaited us. Without his assurance, I am sure my own poor courage would have failed a hundred times. When we began our journey, he seemed just a part of you. But then I got to know him for himself. His bravery and tenacity, even his humour. There were times, especially at the quarry, when we went off to hunt and he alone seemed to understand my feelings. It was not just that I could hold tight to him and cry into his fur and know he would never betray my weakness. It was that he rejoiced in my strengths, too. When we hunted together and I made a kill, I could feel his approval like . . . like a fierceness that said I deserved to survive, that I had earned my place in this world.' She drew breath raggedly. 'I think I will always miss him. And I didn't even get to see him again before . . .'

My mind reeled. Truly, I had not known how close they had been. Nighteyes also had kept his secrets well. I had known that Queen Kettricken had a predilection for the Wit. I had sensed faint questing from her when she meditated. I had often suspected that her Mountain 'connection' with the natural world would have a less kindly name in the Six Duchies. But she and my wolf?

'He spoke to you? You heard Nighteyes in your mind?'

She shook her head, not lifting her face from her hands. Her fingers muffled her reply. 'No. But I felt him in my heart, when I was numb to all else.'

Slowly I rose. I walked around the small table. I had intended only to pat her bent shoulders, but when I touched her, she abruptly stood and stumbled into my embrace. I held her and let her weep against my shoulder. Whether I would or not, my own tears welled. Then her grief, not sympathy for me but true grief at Nighteyes' death gave permission to mine, and my mourning ripped free. All the anguish I had been trying to conceal from those who could not understand the depth of loss I felt suddenly demanded vent. I think I only realized that our roles had changed when she pushed me gently down into her chair. She offered me her tiny, useless handkerchief and then gently kissed my brow and both my cheeks. I could not stop crying. She stood by me, my head cradled against her breast, and stroked my hair and let me weep. She spoke brokenly of my wolf and all he had been to her, words I scarcely heard.

She did not try to stop my tears or tell me that everything would be all right. She knew it would not. But when my weeping finally had run its course, she stooped and kissed me on my mouth, a healing kiss. Her lips were salt with her own tears. Then she stood straight again.

She gave a sudden deep sigh as if setting aside a burden. 'Your poor hair,' she murmured, and smoothed it to my head. 'Oh, my dear Fitz. How hard we used you! Both of you. And I can never . . .' She seemed to feel the uselessness of words. 'But . . . well . . . drink your tea while it is still hot.' She moved apart from me, and after a moment I felt I again had control of myself. As she took my chair, I lifted her cup and drank from it. The tea was still steaming hot. Only a short time had elapsed, yet I felt as if I had passed some important turning point. When I took a breath, it seemed to fill my lungs more deeply than it had in days. She took up my cup. When I looked up at my queen, she gave me a small smile. Her tears had left her pale eyes outlined in red, and her nose was pink. She had never looked lovelier to me.

So we shared some time. The tea was a spice tea, friendly and enlivening. There were flaky rolls stuffed with sausage, and little cakes with tart fruit filling, and plain oatcakes, simple and hearty. I don't think either of us trusted our voices to speak, and we didn't have to. We ate in silence. I got up once to replenish the hot water in the teapot. When the herbs had steeped, I poured more tea for both of us. After a time of silence, she leaned back in her chair and said quietly, 'So, you see, this supposed "taint" in my son comes from me.'

She spoke it as if we were continuing a conversation. I had wondered if she would make the connection. Now that she did, I grieved for the guilt and chagrin I heard in her voice. 'There have been Witted Farseers before Dutiful,' I pointed out. 'Myself among them.'

'And you had a Mountain mother. It's possible that she was the source of your Wit. Perhaps Mountain blood carries it.'

I walked perilously close to the edge of the truth as I said, 'I consider it just as likely that Dutiful could have gotten the Wit from his father as his mother.'

'But—'

'But it matters little where it came from,' I interrupted the Queen ruthlessly. I wanted to divert this conversation. 'The boy has it, and that is what we must deal with. When he first asked me to teach him about it, I was horrified. Now I think his instincts were true. Better he know as much as I can teach him about both his magics.'

Her face lit up. 'Then you have agreed to teach him!'

Truly, I was out of practice at intrigue. Or perhaps, I reflected wryly, over the years my lady had learned that subtlety and gentleness could win her secrets that even Chade's deviousness had not pried from me. The accuracy with which she read my face seemed to support the second theory.

'I will say nothing of it to the Prince. If he wishes it to remain private between you, then so it shall be. When will you start?'

'At the Prince's earliest convenience,' I replied evasively. I would not tattle that he had already missed his first lesson.

She nodded at that, and seemed content to leave it to me. She cleared her throat. 'FitzChivalry. The reason I summoned you here was my intent to . . . make things right for you. As much as we can. In so many ways, I cannot treat you as you deserve. But whatever we can do for your comfort or pleasure, I desire that we do. You masquerade as Lord Golden's servant, and I understand all the reasons for this. Still, it chagrins me that a prince of your bloodlines should go unacknowledged amongst his own folk. So. What can we do? Would you like other chambers prepared for you, ones that you could reach privately and where you could have things arranged for your comfort?'

'No,' I replied quickly, and hearing the brusqueness of my reply, I added, 'I think things are best as they are now. I am as comfortable as I need to be.' I would live here but I could not make it a home. It was useless to try. That private thought jolted me. Home, I reflected, was a place shared. The loft over the stable with Burrich, or the cottage with Nighteyes and Hap. And the chambers that I now shared with the Fool? No. For there was too much caution in both of us, too much privacy preserved, too many constraints of roles.

'. . . arranged for a monthly allowance. After this, Chade will see you receive it, but I wanted you to have this today.'

And my queen was setting a purse before me, a little bag of cloth embroidered with stylized flowers. It clinked sturdily as she placed it on the table. I flushed in spite of myself, and could not hide it. I looked up to find her cheeks equally pink.

'It does feel awkward, doesn't it? Make no mistake in this, FitzChivalry. This is not pay for what you have done for me and mine. No coin could ever pay for that. But a man has expenses, and it is not fitting that you should have to ask for what you need.'

I understood her, but I could not forbear from saying, 'You and yours are also mine, my queen. And you are right. No amount of coin could buy what I do for them.'

Another woman might have taken it as a rebuke. But my words brought a gleam of fierce pride to Kettricken's eyes and she smiled at me. 'I rejoice in the kinship we share, FitzChivalry. Rurisk was my only brother. No one can ever replace him. But you have come as close to that as it is possible for anyone to do.'

And at that, I thought we understood each other very well indeed. It warmed me that she claimed me through our kinship, through the bloodlines I shared with her husband and her son. Long ago, King Shrewd had first made me his with a bargain and a silver pin to seal it. Both pin and king were long gone now. Did our bargain still remain? King Shrewd had chosen to invoke his claim on me as the right of my king rather than as my grandfather. Now Kettricken, my Queen, claimed me first as kin and second as brother. She struck no bargains. She would have scowled at the thought that any setting of terms to my loyalty was necessary.

'I wish to tell my son who you truly are.'

That jolted me from my brief complacency. 'Please, no, my queen. That knowledge is a danger and a burden. Why put it upon him?'

'Why deny that knowledge to the Farseer heir?'

A long moment of silence held between us. Then I said, 'Perhaps in time.'

I was relieved when she nodded. Then she took that from me when she said, 'I will know when the time is right.'

She reached across the table to take my hand. When I let her have it, she turned it palm up and set something in it. 'Long ago, you wore a small ruby-and-silver pin that King Shrewd gave you. One that marked you as his, and said that his door was always open to you. I would have you wear this now, in the same spirit.'

It was a tiny thing. A little silver fox with a winking green eye. It sat alertly, its brush curled around its feet. The image was fastened to a long pin. I studied it carefully. It was perfect.

'This is the work of your own hands.'

'I am flattered that you recall that I like working silver. Yes. It is. And the fox is that which you made my symbol here at Buckkeep.'

I unlaced my blue servant's shirt and opened it. While she watched, I thrust the pin into the facing of the shirt. From the outside, nothing showed, but when I fastened my shirt again, I could feel the tiny fox against my breast.

I cleared my throat. 'You honour me. And as you have said you hold me as close as your brother, then I shall ask a question that I am sure Rurisk would have asked you. I shall be so bold as to demand why you keep amongst your ladies one who once attempted to take your life. And that of your unborn child.'

Her glance was genuinely quizzical. Then, as if someone had poked her with a pin, she gave a small start, and 'Oh, you mean Lady Rosemary.'

'Yes, I do.'

'It has been so long . . . All of that was so very long ago, Fitz. You know, when I look at her, I do not even think of that. When Regal and his household returned here at the end of the Red Ship War, Rosemary was among the train. Her mother had died, and she had been . . . neglected. At first, I could not abide to have either her or Regal in my presence. But there were appearances to preserve, and his abject apologies and vows of loyalty to the unborn heir and me were . . . useful. It served to unite the Six Duchies, for with him he brought the nobility of Tilth and Farrow. And we needed that support, desperately. It would have been so easy for the Six

Duchies to follow the Red Ship War with a civil strife. There are so many differences among the duchies. But Regal's influence was enough to sway his nobles back to allegiance to me. Then Regal died, so strangely and so violently. It was unavoidable that there were mutterings that I had had him murdered in vengeance for old wrongs. Chade advised me strongly that I must make gestures among his nobles to bind them to me. So I did. I put Lady Patience in his place at Tradeford, for I felt I must have strong support there. But his other holdings I distributed judiciously amongst those that most needed quelling.'

'And Lord Bright's reaction to that?' I asked. This was all news to me. Bright had been Regal's heir, and was Duke of Farrow now. Much of what they had 'distributed' was doubtless his hereditary wealth.

'I recompensed him in other ways. After his dismal performance at defending Buck and Buckkeep, he was on shaky ground. He could not protest strongly, for he had not inherited Regal's influence with the nobles. Yet I strove to make him not only content with his lot, but a better ruler than he otherwise would have been. I saw to his schooling, in things other than fine wine and dress. Most of his years as Duke of Farrow have been spent right here in Buckkeep. Patience manages his Tradeford holdings for him, probably far better than he would have himself, for she has the common sense to appoint people who know what they are doing. And she sends reports to him monthly, far more detailed than he relishes, but I insist he go over them with one of my treasury men, not only to be sure he understands them, but also that he must profess he is satisfied with how they fare. And I think that now, he genuinely is.'

'I suspect his duchess has something to do with that,' I hazarded.

Kettricken had the grace to flush slightly. 'Chade thought he might be better content wedded. And it is time he got himself an heir. Left single, he was an invitation to discord at the court.'

'Who selected her?' I tried not to sound cold.

'Lord Chade suggested several young women of good family who had the . . . requisite qualities. After that, I saw that they were introduced. And that the families knew I would be pleased at the prospect of the Duke selecting one of their daughters. The competition spread rapidly amongst the chosen women. But Lord Bright selected his own bride from amongst them. I but saw that he had the opportunity to choose . . .'

'Someone who was tractable and not too ambitious. A daughter of someone loyal to the Queen.' I filled in the rest.

She met my eyes squarely. 'Yes.' She caught a small breath. 'Do you fault me, FitzChivalry? You, who were my first instructor in managing the intrigues of the court to my advantage?'

I smiled at her. 'No. In truth, I am proud of you. And from the look on Lord Bright's face at last-night's festivities, you chose well for him, in heart as well as in allegiance.'

She gave a sigh, almost of relief. 'Thank you. For I value your regard, FitzChivalry, as I ever have. I would not want to think I had shamed myself before you.'

'I doubt that you could,' I replied, truthfully as well as gallantly. Then, dragging the conversation back to my interest, 'And Rosemary?'

'After Regal died, most of his hangers-on dispersed to their family holdings, and some to inspect new holdings I had given them. No one claimed Rosemary. Her father had died before she was born. Her mother had his title, Lady Celeffa of Firwood, but the title was little more than words. Firwood is a tiny holding, a beggar's fiefdom. There is a manor house there, but I am told it has not been inhabited in some years. But for being in Prince Regal's favour, Lady Celeffa would never have come to court at all.' She sighed. 'So there was Rosemary, an orphan at eight, and not in favour with the Queen. I suspect you need little help to imagine how she was treated by the court.'

I had to wince. I could recall how I had been treated.

'I tried to ignore her. But Chade would not let it rest. Nor in truth could I.'

'She was a danger to you. A half-trained assassin, taught by Regal to hate you. She could not simply be left to wander about as she pleased.'

She was silent for a moment. Then, 'Now you sound like Chade. No. She was worse than that. She was a neglected child in my home, a little girl blamed by me for becoming what she was taught to be. A daily rebuke to me for my own neglect of her and my hardness of heart. If I had been all to her that a lady should be to her page, Regal could not have taken her heart from me.'

'Unless he had it before she ever came to you.'

'And even then, I should have known it. If I had not been so focused on my own life and problems.'

'She was your page, not your daughter!'

She was silent for a time. 'You forget, I was raised in the Mountains, to be Sacrifice to my people, Fitz. Not a queen, such as you expect. I demand more of myself.'

I stepped to the side of that argument. 'So it was your decision to keep her.'

'Chade said I must either keep her or be rid of her entirely. I was filled with horror at his words. Kill a child for doing what she had been taught? And then his words made me see all of it clearly. It would have been kinder to kill her outright than to torture and neglect her as I had been doing. So. That night I went to her chamber. Alone. She was terrified of me, and her room was cold and near bare, the bedding gone unwashed I don't know how long. She had outgrown her nightgown; it was torn at the shoulders and far too short for her. She curled up on the bed as far from me as she could get and just stared at me. Then I asked her which she would prefer, to be fostered out to Lady Patience or to be my page again.'

'And she chose to be your page.'

'And she burst into tears and threw herself to the floor and clung to my skirts and said she had thought I didn't like her any more. She sobbed so hard that before I could calm her, her hair was plastered flat to her skull with sweat and she was shaking all over. Fitz, I was ashamed to have been so cruel to a child, not by what I had done, but simply by ignoring her. Only Chade and I ever knew that we suspected her of trying to harm me. But my simple shunning of her had given the lesser folk of the keep permission to be cruel and callous to her. Her little slippers were all gone to tatters . . .' Her voice trailed off, and despite myself, I felt a stab of pity for Rosemary. Kettricken took a deep breath and resumed her tale. 'She begged to be allowed to serve me again. Fitz, she was not even seven years old when she did Regal's bidding. She never hated me, or understood what she did. To her, I am sure it was a game, to listen in secret and repeat all that she heard.'

I tried to be pragmatic and hard. 'And greasing the steps so you would fall?'

'Would she be told the why of it, or simply told to put the grease on the steps after I had gone up to the roof garden? To a child, it might have been framed as a prank.'

'Did you ask her?'

A pause. 'Some things are best left alone. Even if she knew the intent was to make me fall, I do not think she realized the full import of it. I think perhaps that I was two people to her, the woman that Regal wanted to bring down, and Kettricken whom she served every day. The one who should be blamed for her conduct is dead. And ever since I took her back to my side, she has been nothing but a loyal and diligent subject to me.' She sighed and stared past me as she went on, 'The past must be left in the past, Fitz. This is especially true for those who rule. I must wed my son to a daughter of an Outislander. I must promote trade and alliance with the folk who doomed my king to death. Shall I quibble about taking a little spy under my wing and turning her into a lady of my court?'

I took a deep breath. If in fifteen years she had not regretted her decision, no words of mine would change it now. Nor should they, perhaps. 'Well. I suppose I should have expected it. You did not quibble to take an assassin as your adviser when you came to court.'

'As my first friend here,' she corrected me gravely. She furrowed her forehead. When I had met her, she had not had those lines on her brow and between her eyes, but now use had set them there. 'I am not happy with this charade we must keep. I would have you at my side to advise me, and to teach my son. I would have you honoured as my friend as well as a Farseer.'

'It cannot be,' I told her firmly. 'And this is better. I am more use to you in this role, and less risk to you and the Prince.'

'And more risk to yourself. Chade has told me that Piebalds threatened you, right upon our doorstep in Buckkeep Town.'

I discovered that I hadn't wanted her to know that. 'It is a thing best handled by me. Perhaps I can tease them out into the open.'

'Well. Perhaps. But I am ashamed that you face such things seemingly alone. In truth, I hate that such bigotry still exists in the Six Duchies, and that our nobles turn a blind eye to it. I have done what I could for my Witted folk, but progress has been slow. When the Piebald postings first began to appear, they angered me. Chade urged me not to act in the heat of that anger. Now, I wonder if it would not have been wise to let my wrath be known. My second reaction was that I wished to let my Witted folk know that my justice was available to them. I wanted to send out a summons, inviting the leaders of the Witted to come to me, that together we might hammer out a shield for them against the cruelty of these Piebalds.' She shook her head.

'Again Chade intervened, telling me that the Witted had no recognized leaders, and that they would not trust the Farseers enough to come to such a meeting. We had no go-between that they would trust, and no sureties we could offer them that this was not a plan to lure them in and destroy them. He persuaded me to abandon the idea.' Her words seemed to come more reluctantly as she added, 'Chade is a good councillor, wise in politics and the ways of power. Yet I sometimes feel that he would steer us solely on the basis of what makes the Six Duchies most stable, with less thought for justice for all my people.' Her fair brow wrinkled as she added, 'He says that the greater the stability of the country, the more chance there is for justice to prosper. Perhaps he is right. But often and often I have longed for the way you and I used to discuss these things. There, too, I have missed you, FitzChivalry. I dislike that I cannot have you at my side when I wish it, but must send for you in secret. I wish that I could invite you to join Peottre and I for our game today, for I would value your opinion of him. He is a most intriguing man.'

'Your game with Peottre today?'

'I shared some talk with him last evening. In the course of discussing the chance that Dutiful and Elliania would be truly happy, other talk of 'chance' came up. And from there, we moved to games of chance. Do you recall a Mountain game played with cards and rune chips?'

I dredged through my memory. 'I think you spoke of it to me once. And yes, I recall reading a scroll about it, when I was recovering from Regal's first attempt on me.'

'There are cards or tablets, either painted on heavy paper or carved on thin slabs of wood. They have emblems from our old tales, such as Old Weaver Man and Hunter in Hiding. The rune chips have runes on them, for Stone, Water and Pasture.'

'Yes. I'm sure I've heard of it.'

'Well, Peottre wants me to teach him to play it. He was very interested when I spoke of it. He says that in the Outislands they have a game played with rune cubes, where they are shaken and tumbled out. Then the players set out their markers onto a cloth or board that is painted with minor godlings, such as Wind and Smoke and Tree. It sounds as if it might be a similar game, does it not?'

'Perhaps,' I conceded. But her face had brightened at the prospect of teaching Peottre this new game in a way that was out of proportion to the pleasure I expected her to take in it. Did my queen find this bluff Outislander warrior attractive? 'You must tell me more of this game later. I would like to hear if the runes on the dice are similar to the runes on your rune chips.'

'That would be intriguing, wouldn't it? If the runes resembled one another? Especially as some of the runes from my game were similar to the runes on the Skill-pillars.'

'Ah.' Kettricken was still capable of putting me off-balance. She had always seemed able to think along several lines at once, bringing oddly disparate facts together to make a pattern others missed. This had been how she had rediscovered the lost map to the kingdom of the Elderlings. I felt suddenly as if she had given me too much to think over.

I stood to excuse myself, bowed, and then wished I had words to thank her. An instant later it seemed a strange impulse, to thank someone for mourning someone you had loved. I made a fumbling effort, but she stopped me, coming to take both my hands in hers. 'And perhaps only you understood what I felt at Verity's loss. To see him transformed, to know he would triumph, and yet still to mourn selfishly that I would never again see him again as the man he had been. This is not the first tragedy we have shared, FitzChivalry. We both have walked alone through much of our lives.'

It was unmannerly, but I did it anyway. I enfolded her in my arms and held her tightly for a moment. 'He loved you so,' I said, and my voice choked on the words I spoke for my lost king.

She rested her forehead on my shoulder. 'I know that,' she said quietly. 'That love sustains me even now. Sometimes I think I can almost feel him still, at my shoulder, offering counsel when times are difficult. May Nighteyes be with you as Verity is with me.'

I held Verity's woman for a long moment. Things could have been so different. Yet her wish was a good wish, and healing. I released her with a sigh, and the Queen and the serving-man parted to their daily tasks.

SIX

Obliteration

. . . and it is almost certain that the Chalcedeans could have defeated the Bingtown Traders and claimed their territory for their own if only they could have maintained a solid blockade of Bingtown Bay.

Two magics hampered them in this regard, and magic it most certainly was, despite any who would dispute it, for the Bingtown Traders are merchants and not fighters, as all know. The first magic was that the Bingtown Traders possess Liveships, trading vessels that, by some arcane practice involving the sacrifice of three children or elderly family members, are brought to sentient life. Not only can the figureheads of these vessels move and speak, but they are also possessed of prodigious strength, enabling them to crush lesser vessels if once they grip them. Some of them are able to spit fire for a distance equal to three of their vessels' lengths.

The second magic is as likely to be disputed by the ignorant as the first, but as this traveller witnessed it, I defy those who call this a lie. A dragon, cunningly crafted of blue and silver gemstones and activated by a marvellous combination of magic and . . . (passage obscured by damage to parchment) . . . was hastily created by the Bingtown artisans for the defence of their harbour. This creature, named Tinnitgliat by her creators, rose from the smoking wreckage that the Chalcedeans had made of the Bingtown warehouse district and drove the enemy vessels from the harbour.

Winfroda's My Adventures as a World Traveller

I threaded my way back through the maze of corridors and emerged once more into my cell. I paused to peer into the darkness before entering it. Once within, I secured the secret door behind me. Then I paused, standing perfectly still in the darkness. Through the closed door that led to the Fool's apartment, voices reached me.

'Well, as I've no idea when he rose and left, nor why, I've no idea when he will return. It seemed such a charming concept at first, to have a strong and able man-at-arms, capable not only of defending me from street ruffians but also serving as my valet and seeing to my other needs as well. But he has proven most unreliable at daily tasks. Look at this! I've had to snatch a passing page from the corridor and have him tell a kitchen-boy to bring up my breakfast. And it isn't what I would have chosen at all! I'm tempted to let Badgerlock go entirely, except that with my ankle as it is, it is no time for me to be without a sturdy servant. Well. Perhaps I shall have to accept his limitations and acquire a page or two to see to my daily tasks. Look at the layer of dust on that mantle! Shameful. I can scarcely invite visitors to my chambers with them looking like this. It is almost fortunate that the pain in my ankle makes me tend towards solitary occupations just now.'

I froze where I was. I longed to know to whom he was speaking and why that person sought me, but I could scarcely make an entrance if Lord Golden had already insisted I was not here.

'Very well. May I leave a message for your man then, Lord Golden?'

The voice was Laurel's and the irritation level in it was unmasked. She had seen too much of us when she had accompanied us on our journey to be deceived by our charade. She would never again believe us to be merely master and man: we had bungled our roles too often. Yet I also understood why Lord Golden insisted on resuming the masquerade. To do otherwise would eventually have unravelled our deception of the court.

'Certainly. Or you would be welcome to return this evening, if you wish to take the chance that he may have recalled his duties and wandered home.'

If he had intended that to mollify her, it failed. 'A message will suffice, I am sure. In passing through the stable, I noticed something about his horse that made me concerned for her. If he will meet me there at noon today, I will point it out to him.'

'And if he does not return by noon . . . by Sa, how I detest this! That I should have to act as a secretary to my own serving-man!'

'Lord Golden.' Her quiet voice cut through his dramatics. 'My concern is a grave one. See that he meets me then, or arranges to speak to me about my concern. Good day.'

She shut the door very firmly behind her. I heard the thump, but even so I waited some minutes, to be completely certain that the Fool was alone. I eased the door open silently, but the Fool's preternatural awareness served him well. 'There you are,' he exclaimed with a sigh of relief. 'I was beginning to worry about you.' Then he looked more closely at me and a smile lit up his face. 'The Prince's first lesson must have gone very well.'

'The Prince chose not to attend his first lesson. And I am sorry to have put you out. I didn't think to arrange for Lord Golden's breakfast.'

He made a disparaging noise. 'I assure you, the last thing I would expect is that *you* would be a competent servant. I'm perfectly capable of arranging my own breakfast. It is required, however, that I raise a suitable fuss when I am forced to waylay a page for it. I've muttered and complained enough now that I can add a boy to my staff without exciting any comment.' He poured himself another cup of tea, sipped it and made a face. 'Cold.' He gestured at the remains of the repast. 'Hungry?'

'No. I ate with Kettricken.'

He nodded, unsurprised. 'The Prince sent me a message this morning. It now makes sense to me. He wrote, 'I was saddened to see that your injury prevented you from joining in the dancing at my betrothal festivities. Well do I know how frustrating it is when an unexpected inconvenience denies you a pleasure long anticipated. I heartily hope that you are soon able to resume your favourite activities.'

I nodded, somewhat pleased. 'Subtle, yet it conveys it. Our prince is becoming more sophisticated.'

'He has his father's wit,' he agreed, but when I glanced at him sharply, his expression was mild and benign. He continued, 'You have another message as well. From Laurel.'

'Yes. I overheard it.'

'I thought you might have.'

I shook my head. 'That one both puzzles and alarms me. From the way she spoke, I don't think this meeting has anything to do with my horse. Still, I'll meet her at noon and see what it is about. Then I'd like to go down to Buckkeep Town, to see Hap, and to apologize to Jinna.'

He lifted a pale eyebrow.

'I had said I would come by last night, to talk to Hap. As you know, I went to the betrothal festivities with you instead.'

He picked up a tiny nosegay of white flowers from his breakfast tray and sniffed it thoughtfully. 'So many people, all wanting a bit of your time.'

I sighed. 'It is hard for me. I don't quite know how to manage it. I'd grown used to my solitary life, with only Nighteyes and Hap making claims on me. I don't think I'm handling this very well. I can't imagine how Chade juggled all his tasks for so many years.'

He smiled. 'He's a spider. A web-weaver, with lines stringing out in all directions. He sits at the centre and interprets each tug.'

I smiled with him. 'Accurate. Not flattering, but accurate.'

He cocked his head at me suddenly. 'It was Kettricken, then, wasn't it? Not Chade.'

'I don't understand.'

He looked down at his hands, twiddling the little bouquet. 'There's a change in you. Your shoulders are squared again. Your eyes focus on me when I talk to you. I don't feel as if I should glance over my shoulder to see if a ghost is there.' He set the flowers down carefully on the table. 'Someone has lifted a part of your burden.'

'Kettricken,' I agreed with him after a moment. I cleared my throat. 'She was closer to Nighteyes than I realized. She mourns him, too.'

'As do I.'

I thought about my next words before I said them. I wondered if they were necessary, feared that they might hurt him. But I spoke them. 'In a different way. Kettricken mourns Nighteyes as I do, for himself, and for what he was to her. You . . .' I faltered, unsure how to put it.

'I loved him through you. Our link was how he became real to me. So, in a sense, I do not mourn Nighteyes as you do. I grieve for your grief.'

'You have always been better with words than I am.'

'Yes,' he agreed. Then he sighed and crossed his arms on his chest. 'Well. I am glad that someone could help you. Even as I envy Kettricken.'

That made no sense. 'You envy her, that she mourns?'

'I envy her, that she could comfort you.' Then, before I could even think of any reply, he added briskly, 'I'll leave it to you to clear the dishes away to the kitchen. Take care to be a bit surly when you return them, as if your master had just harshly rebuked you. Then you may be off to Laurel and Buckkeep Town. I plan to spend a quiet day today, in my own pursuits. I've let it out that my ankle pains me and that I wish to rest, without visitors. Later this afternoon, I am invited to gaming with the Queen's favoured. So if you do not find me here, look for me there. Will you be back in time to help me limp down to dinner?'

'I expect so.'

His spirits seemed suddenly dampened, as if he were truly in pain. He nodded gravely. 'Perhaps I will see you then.' He rose from the table and went to his private room. Without another word he opened the door, then shut it quietly but firmly behind him.

I gathered the dishes onto the tray. Despite his words about my incompetence as a servant, I took care to straighten the room. I returned the tray to the kitchens, and then fetched wood and water for our chambers. The door to the Fool's personal room remained shut. I wondered if he were ill. I might have ventured to tap at the door if noon had not been upon me. I went to my room and buckled on my ugly sword. I took some of the coins from the purse Kettricken had given me and put the rest under the corner of my mattress. I checked my hidden pockets, took my cloak from its hook and headed down to the stables.

With the influx of people for Prince Dutiful's betrothal, the regular stable was filled to capacity with our guests' horses. In these circumstances, the beasts of lesser folk like me had been moved to the 'Old Stables', the stables of my childhood. I was just as content with the arrangement. Far less chance that I might encounter Hands there or any who might recall a boy who had once dwelt with Stablemaster Burrich.

I found Laurel leaning against the gate of Myblack's stall, talking softly to her. Perhaps I had misinterpreted her message. My concern for the animal mounted and I hastened to her side. 'What's wrong with her?' I asked, and then, belatedly recalling my manners, 'Good day to you, Huntswoman Laurel. I am here as you requested.' Myblack benignly ignored both of us.

'Badgerlock, good day. Thank you for meeting me here.' She glanced about casually, and finding our corner of the stable deserted, she leaned still closer and whispered to me, 'I need a word with you. In private. Follow me.'

'As you wish, mistress.' She strode off and I followed at her heels. We walked past the rows of stalls to the back of the stables and then to my shock we began the climb up the now-rickety steps that had once led to Burrich's loft. When he was Stablemaster, he had claimed to prefer to live close to his charges rather than accept better quarters in the castle itself. When I had lived with him, I had believed that to be true. In the intervening years, I had decided that he had kept his humble residence there as much for the sake of keeping me out of the public eye as he did for his own privacy. Now, as I followed Laurel up the steep steps, I wondered how much she knew. Did she bring me here as a prelude to telling me that she knew who I really was?

The door at the top of the steps was not latched. She shouldered it open and it scraped across the floor. She stepped inside the dim chamber and motioned for me to follow. I ducked a dusty cobweb in the doorframe. The only light came from the cracked shutter over the little window at the end of the room. How small the space suddenly seemed. The sparse furnishings that had sufficed for Burrich and I were long gone, replaced by the clutter of a stable. Twisted bits of old harness, broken tools, moth-eaten blankets: all the horsey litter that folk set aside, thinking that perhaps one day they will mend it or that it might come in useful in a pinch, filled the chamber where I had spent my childhood.

How Burrich would have hated this! I thought to myself. I wondered that Hands allowed such clutter to gather, and then decided that he probably had more pressing matters to attend to. The stables were a larger and grander concern than they had been during the years of the Red Ship War. I doubted that Hands sat up at night greasing and mending old harness.

Laurel misinterpreted the look on my face. 'I know. It smells up here, but it's private. I would have seen you in your own room, but Lord Golden was too busy playing the grand noble.'

'He *is* a grand noble,' I pointed out, but the flashing look she gave me stilled my tongue. Belatedly it came to me that Lord Golden had bestowed much attention on Laurel during our journey, yet not a word had they exchanged last night. Oh.

'Be that as it may, or be you whom you may.' She dismissed her annoyance with us, obviously intent on graver matters. 'I received a message from my cousin. Deerkin didn't intend the warning for you; he intended it for me. I doubt that he would approve my passing it on to you, for he has ample reasons not to be fond of you. The Queen, however, seems to hold you in some regard. And it is the Queen I am sworn to.'

'As we both are,' I assured her. 'Have you shared these tidings with her as well?'

She looked at me. 'Not yet.' She admitted. 'It may be that there is no need to, that this is a matter you can handle yourself. And it is not as easy for me to manage a quiet moment with the Queen as it is for me to summon you.'

'And the warning?'

'He bade me flee. The Piebalds know who I am and where I live. I am twice a traitor, to their way of thinking. For by my family connection, they consider me Old Blood. And I serve the hated Farseer regime. They will kill me if they can.' Her voice betrayed no emotion as she recounted the threat to herself. But she lowered her tone and looked aside from me as she added, 'And the same is true of you.'

Silence floated between us. I watched dust particles dancing in the thin sunlight through the shutters and pondered. After a time, she spoke again.

'This is the gist of it. Laudwine still languishes, recovering from your chopping off his forearm. In the wake of our little adventure, many of his followers have abandoned him, to return to the true Old Blood ways. Old Blood families have put pressure on their sons and daughters to forsake the Piebalds' extreme politics. There is a feeling amongst many that the Queen genuinely intends to better the lot of the Old Blood folk. As it has become known that her own son is Witted, they have a kindlier feeling towards her. They are content to wait, for a short time at least, to see how she will treat us now.'

'And those who remain amongst the Piebalds?' I asked unwillingly.

Laurel shook her head. 'Those who remain with Laudwine are the ones most dangerous and least reasonable. He attracts those who desire to shed blood and wreak havoc. They desire revenge more than justice, and power more than peace. Some, like Laudwine, have seen family and friends put to death for the crime of being Witted. Others have hearts that pump more madness than blood. They are not many but as they place no limits on what they will do to attain their goals, they are as dangerous as a vast army.'

'Their goals?'

'Simple. Power for themselves. Punishment for those who have oppressed the Witted. They hate the Farseers. But even more, they hate you. Laudwine feeds their hatred. He wallows in hate and offers it to his followers as if it were gold. You have stirred their wrath against all Old Blood who "grovel before the Farseer oppressors". Laudwine's Piebalds bring reprisals against the Old Blood who came to your aid against the Piebalds. Some homes have been burned. Flocks have been scattered or stolen. Those sort of attacks are already happening, but worse is threatened. The Piebalds say they will expose any that will not side with them against the Farseers. It thrills them that we should be killed by the folk we will not rise against. The Piebalds say that all Old Blood must either stand with them or be purged from the community.' Her face had gone both grave and pale. I knew there was a real threat to her family, and it curdled my stomach to think that I was partially responsible for provoking it.

I took a breath. 'Only some of what you tell me is news to me. Only a few nights ago I was stalked on the road from

Buckkeep Town by Piebalds. I am only surprised that they let me live.'

She lifted one shoulder in a shrug that did not dismiss my danger, only the possibility of understanding the Piebalds. 'You are a special target for them. You struck Laudwine's hand from his arm. You are Old Blood, serving the Farseers and directly opposing the Piebalds.' She shook her head. 'Take no comfort that they have left you alive when they could have so easily killed you. It only means that they have some use for you that requires you to be alive. My cousin hinted as much, when he warned me, for he said that perhaps I had mixed myself with worse company than I thought. The Piebald rumour is that Lord Golden and Tom Badgerlock were not what they seemed to be – small surprise to me that was, but Deerkin seemed to think it portentous.'

She paused, as if to give me time to reply. I said nothing but thought much. Had someone firmly connected Tom Badgerlock to the Witted Bastard of song and legend? And if so, what use would they have for me that required me alive? If they had wanted to take me hostage and use me against the Farseers, they could have done so that night. But my thoughts were cut off as Laurel scowled at my silence and then resumed her talk.

'The raids and attacks against their own stir Old Blood against them, even amongst some who once called themselves Piebalds. Some raids, it seems, are carried out to settle old scores or for personal profit rather than for any "lofty" Piebald motives. No one restrains them. Laudwine is still too weak to resume full leadership. He is feverish and febrile from the loss of his arm. Those closest to him hate you doubly for that; they will be swift as wildfire to set their vengeance against you. Witness that you have been back in Buckkeep only a few days, and they have already located you.'

We stood silent in the dusty room for a time, both of us following thoughts too dark to share. At last, Laurel spoke reluctantly.

'You understand that Deerkin still has ties to those in the Piebalds. They try to lure him back. He must . . . pretend to side with them. To protect our family. He walks a thin and dangerous line. He hears things that are very dangerous for him to repeat, and yet he has sent word.' Her words trickled away. She stared at the obscured window as if she could truly see what was beyond it I knew what she was trying to express. 'You should speak to the Queen. Tell her that Deerkin must appear a traitor to the crown for the sake of keeping your family safe. Will you flee, as he bids you?'

She shook her head slowly. 'Flee where? To my family? Then I plunge them into more danger. Here, at least, the Piebalds must reach into danger's mouth to extract me. I will stay here and serve my queen.'

I wondered if Chade would be able to protect her, let alone her cousin.

Her voice was flat when she spoke again. 'Deerkin hears hints that the Piebalds are forming an alliance with outsiders. "Powerful folk who would be happy to destroy the Farseers and leave Laudwine's folk in power".' She gave me a worried glance. 'That sounds like a silly boast, doesn't it? It couldn't be real, could it?'

'Best tell the Queen,' I said, and hoped she could not hear that I did think it possible. I knew I would take the tale to Chade.

'And you?' She asked me. 'Will you flee? I think you should. For you would make a fine example of the Piebalds' power. Exposed, you would illustrate that there are Witted even within the walls of Buckkeep. Quartered and burned, you would be a fine example to other traitors to the Old Blood, that those who deny and betray their own kind are in turn betrayed by them.'

She was not herself Witted. Her cousin was. Even though the magic ran in her family blood, she had no love for the Wit or those who used their magic. Like most Six Duchies folk, she regarded my ability to sense animals and bond with a beast as a despicable magic. Perhaps her use of the word 'traitor' should have carried less sting because of that, yet the contempt of the message burned me.

'I am not a traitor to my Old Blood. I but keep my oath where it was sworn, to the Farseers. If Old Blood had not tried to harm the Prince, it would not have been necessary for me to wrest him back from them.'

Laurel spoke flatly. 'Those are the words of my cousin's message to me. Not mine. He sent me those words so that I might warn the queen, partly because he feels a debt to me. But also because she is the most tolerant of Old Blood of any recent Farseer reign we have known. He would not see her shamed and her influence lessened. I suspect he thinks she would rid herself of you if she knew you could be used against her. I know her better. She will not heed my warning and send you away from Buckkeep before you can be used against her.'

So. That was her real message for me. 'Then you think that would be best for all? If I simply removed myself, without her having to ask me to leave.'

She gazed past me, spoke past me. 'You suddenly appeared from nowhere. Perhaps it were best if you returned there.'

For an instant, I actually toyed with the notion. I could go downstairs, saddle Myblack and ride off. Hap was safely apprenticed, and Chade would see that he remained so. I had been reluctant to teach Dutiful the Skill, let alone what I knew of the Wit. Perhaps this was the simplest solution for all of us. I could disappear. But.

'I did not come to Buckkeep at my own desire. I came at my queen's behest. And so do I stay. Nor would my departure remove the danger to her. Laudwine and his followers know the Prince is Witted.'

'I thought you would say as much,' Laurel conceded. 'And for all I know, perhaps you are right. Yet I will still pass on my warning to the Queen.'

'You would be remiss if you did not. Yet I thank you for taking the time to seek me out and pass on this warning to me, as well. I know I gave Deerkin little reason to think well of me. I am willing to let all that occurred between us fade into the past. If you have the chance, I ask you to pass that message on to him. That I bear no ill will to him, or to any that follow the true Old Blood ways. But I must always put my service to the Farseers first.'

'As do I,' she responded grimly.

'You say nothing of Laudwine's intentions towards Prince Dutiful.'

'Because Deerkin's message said nothing of that. So my only answer is, I don't know.'

'I see.'

And there seemed nothing else to say to one another. I let her leave first so we would not be seen together. I lingered in the old rooms longer than I needed to. Beneath the dust on the windowsill, I could just glimpse the track of my boyhood's idle knife. I looked up at the slanting ceiling over the spot where my pallet had been. I could still see the owl shape in the twisted grain of the wood there. There was little left here of Burrich or of me. Time and other occupants had obliterated us from the room. I left it, dragging the door closed behind me.

I could have saddled Myblack and ridden down to Buckkeep Town, but I chose to walk despite the edged chill of the day. I have always believed it is harder to shadow a man on foot. I passed out of the gates without incident or comment. I strode off briskly, but once I was out of sight of the guards and any other travellers, I stepped aside from the road, to stand in the scrub-brush that banked it and look back to see if anyone were following me. I stood still and silent until the scar on my back began to ache. There was damp in the wind, rain or snow to come tonight. My ears and nose were cold. I decided that no one was shadowing me today. Nonetheless, I performed the same manoeuvre twice more on my walk into town.

I took a roundabout path through Buckkeep Town to Jinna's house. Part of this was caution, but part of it was dithering. I wanted to take her a gift, both as an apology for not visiting last night as I had said I would and as thanks for helping me with Hap, yet I could not think what it should be. Earrings seemed somehow too personal and too permanent. So did the brightly woven scarf that caught my eye in the weaver's stall. Fresh smoked redfish teased my appetite, yet seemed inappropriate. I was a man grown, yet I felt caught in a boy's dilemma. How did I express thanks, apology and interest in her without appearing too grateful, apologetic or interested? I wanted, I decided, a friendly gift, and resolved that I would choose something that I could as easily present to the Fool or Hap without feeling any awkwardness. I settled on a sack of sweet hevnuts, this year's plump and shining harvest, and a loaf of fresh spice bread. With these in hand, I felt almost confident as I tapped at the door with the palm-reader's sign on it.

'A moment!' came Jinna's voice, and then she opened the top half of the door, squinting in the sunlight. Behind her the room was dim, shutters closed, candles burning fragrantly on the table. 'Ah. Tom. I'm in the midst of a reading for a customer. Can you wait?'

'Of course.'

'Good.' And then she shut the door firmly and left me standing outside. It wasn't what I had expected, and yet I reflected it was no more than I deserved. So I waited humbly, watching the street and the folk passing by, and trying to look at ease in the biting wind. The hedge-witch's house was on a quiet street in Buckkeep Town, and yet there was a steady trickle of folk along it. Next door to her lived a potter. His door was closed to the wind, his wares stacked beside it, and I heard the thump of his wheel as he worked. Across the street lived a woman who seemed to have an impossible number of small children, several of whom seemed intent on wandering out into the muddy street despite the chill day. A little girl not much older than the toddlers patiently hauled them back onto the porch. From where I stood, I could just glimpse the doors of a tavern down the street. The hanging sign that welcomed guests showed a pig wedged in a fence. The trade seemed to be mostly the sort who took their beer home in small buckets.

I was just beginning to think of either leaving or tapping on the door again when it opened. A lavishly garbed matron and her two daughters emerged. The younger girl had tears in her eyes, but her sister looked bored. The mother thanked Jinna profusely for a very long time before she tartly ordered her girls to stop tarrying and come along. The glance she gave me as she led them off did not approve of me.

If I had thought Jinna's leaving me standing outside was a sort of retribution, the warm and weary look she gave me dispelled the notion. She wore a green robe. A wide yellow waist cinched her middle and lifted her breasts. It was very becoming. 'Come in, come in. Oh, such a morning. It's strange. Folk want to know what you see in their hands, but so often they don't want to believe it.'

She shut the door behind me, plunging us back into dimness.

'I'm sorry I didn't come to visit last night. My master had duties for me. I've brought you some fresh spice bread.'

'Oh. How lovely! I see you bought hevnuts at the market. I wish I had known that you liked them, for my niece's trees have borne so heavily this year that we can scarcely decide what to do with them all. A neighbour out near her farm may take some for pig fodder, but they have fallen so thick this year one fair wades through them.'

So much for that. But she took the spiced bread from me and set it on the table, exclaiming over how delicious it smelled, and telling me that Hap was, of course, at his master's. Her niece had borrowed the pony and cart to haul firewood in, did I mind? Hap had said she might, and said, too, that it was better for the pony to do the light work the old beast could handle than to stand idly stabled. I assured her that was fine. 'No Fennel?' I asked, wondering at the cat's absence.

'Fennel?' She seemed surprised I would ask. 'Oh, he's probably out and about his own business. You know how cats are.'

I set the sack of hevnuts on the floor by the door and hung my cloak above it. The little room was warm and my cold ears stung as they returned to life. As I turned to the table, she was setting down two steaming cups of tea. The rising warmth beckoned me. A dish of butter and some honey waited beside the bread. 'Are you hungry?' she asked me, smiling up at me.

'A bit,' I admitted. Her smile was contagious.

Her eyes moved over my face. 'I am, too,' she said. Then she stepped forward, and I found my arms around her, and her mouth rising up to mine. I had to stoop to kiss her. Her lips opened to mine, inviting, and she tasted of tea and spices. I felt suddenly dizzy.

She broke the kiss, and pressed her cheek to my chest. 'You're cold,' she said. 'I should not have made you wait outside so long.'

'I'm much warmer now,' I assured her.

She looked up at me and smiled. 'I know.' And as her lips found mine again, her hand dropped down to trace the proof of that. I jumped at the touch, but her hand on the back of my neck kept my mouth on hers.

She was the one who walked us sideways to her bedchamber, never breaking the kiss. She released me to shut the door firmly behind us, plunging us into near darkness save for the bits of light that fingered their way in through the shakes of the roof and past the open rafters of a small loft. The bed was plump with featherbeds. The chamber smelled of woman. I tried to take a breath and find my mind. 'This isn't wise,' I said. I could scarcely get the words out.

'No. It isn't.' Her fingers loosened the laces of my shirt and tightened my desire. She gave me a small push and I sat down on the edge of her bed.

As she pulled my shirt off over my head, my eyes fell on a small charm on a bedside table. A string of red and black beads were looped and wound around a framework of dead sticks. It was a dash of cold water, stilling my desire and infusing me with a sense of futility. As she unbuckled her waist, her eyes followed my glance. She studied my face, and smiling, shook her head. 'Well. Aren't you the sensitive one? Don't look at that. It's for me, not you.' And she casually covered it with the shirt she took from my hands.

I knew then a moment of sanity when I could have stopped what was happening. But she gave me no chance to surrender to my common sense, for her hands were at my belt, her fingers warm against my belly, and I stopped thinking entirely. I stood and lifted her robe over her head, and its passage left her curly hair standing out in a cloud around her face. For a time we stood, nuzzling one another. She made some approving comment about the charm that she had made for me. It was all I currently wore. When she asked me what had given me the fresh scratches on my neck and belly, I silenced her mouth with mine. I recall picking her easily off her feet and turning to set her on her bed. I knelt on the bed over her and beheld the wealth of her, her nipples standing out pink and eager, and the delicious scent of woman rising from her.

Without a word, I mounted her and then possessed her. Blind lust drove me, and she gasped, 'Tom!' shocked at my fierce ardour. My hands were cupped on her shoulders, my mouth covered hers, and she rose to meet me. A sudden terrible need for her overtook me. To touch, skin to skin, in closeness and passion, to share myself completely with another being, to leave behind the sense of being isolated in my own flesh. I held nothing back, and I thought I carried her with me.

Then, as I lay dizzied with completion, she said in a small voice, 'Well. You're a hasty man, Tom Badgerlock.'

My hoarse breathing as I lay on top of her made a hideous silence of its own. Shame drenched me. After a terrible stillness, she stirred under me. I heard her draw a breath. 'You *were* hungry!' Perhaps she regretted her words of disappointment, but that did not call them back. Her gentle attempt at making light of it brought the blood to my face and completed my humiliation. I dropped my forehead to the pillow beside hers. I listened to the wind outside in the streets. Some people tramped by in the street, just on the other side of the plank wall. A man's sudden shout of laughter made me wince. Up in the attic loft, I head a thump and a squeak. Then Jinna kissed the side of my neck and her hands moved gently down my back. Her voice was a soothing whisper. 'Tom. The first time is seldom the best. You've shown me your boy's passion. Shall we find your man's skills, now?'

So she gave me another chance to prove myself, and I was shamefacedly grateful. I proceeded in a workmanlike way that soon rekindled both of us. There were several things Starling had taught me and Jinna seemed pleased with my second performance. It was only at the very end, as we lay panting together, that her words stirred a misgiving in me. 'So, Badgerlock,' she said, and then drew breath beneath me. 'So that is what it is like for a she-wolf.'

Incredulous, I lifted myself a little from her so that I could look down into her eyes. She blinked up at me, an odd smile on her face. 'I've never been with a Witted one, before this,' she confided to me. She drew another deeper breath. 'I've heard other women speak of it. That such men are more . . .' She paused, seeking for a word.

'Animal?' I suggested. The word as I spoke it was an insult.

Her eyes widened, and then she laughed uncomfortably. 'That isn't what I was going to say, Tom. You shouldn't take insults to yourself where a compliment is intended. Untamed, was what I was going to say. Natural, as an animal is natural, with no thought of what any other may think of his ways.'

'Oh.' I could say no more than that. I wondered abruptly what I was to her. A novelty? A forbidden indulgence with something not quite fully human? It was unnerving to wonder if she saw me as bestial and strange. Did our magics set us so far apart in her mind?

Then she pulled me down upon her breasts again, and kissed

the side of my neck. 'Stop thinking,' she warned me, and I did.

Afterwards, she dozed briefly beside me, my arm around her and her head pillowed on my shoulder. I judged that I had acquitted myself well. But as I watched the sunlight's passage on the wall, I realized it had been a performance. Neither of us had spoken of love. It had simply been a thing we had done together, something that felt good, something I was reasonably competent at. Yet if our first coupling had left her unsatisfied, the later ones left me feeling incomplete in a deeper way. With a sharpness I had not felt in years, I suddenly longed for Molly, and how simple, good, and true it had been between us. This was not that, any more than my partnering with Starling had been. It wasn't even sharing a bed. At the heart of my discontent, I wanted to be in love with someone the way I had been that first time. I wanted someone I could touch and be held by, someone that made everything else in the world more significant simply by her existence.

This morning, Kettricken had touched me as a friend, and that had held more meaning and even more true passion than this had. I suddenly wanted to be gone from here, for none of this ever to have happened. Jinna and I had been on the path to becoming friends. I was just beginning to know her. What had I done to that? And Hap was stirred up in this stew as well. If Jinna wanted to carry on with this, how would I manage it? Openly flaunting yet again all the rules I had taught him, for how a man should conduct his life. Or in secret, hiding it from Hap, furtively coming and going from Jinna's bed?

I was deathly tired of secrets. They seemed to spawn all around me, to fasten to me and suck the life from me like cold leeches. I hungered for something real and true and open. Could I change my relationship with Jinna to that? I doubted it. Not only was there no foundation of deep and honest love between us, but once again I was enmeshed in the secret business of the Farseer intrigues. There would be secrets I must keep from her, secrets that would eventually endanger her.

I had not realized she was awake. Or perhaps my deep sigh stirred her past the edge of drowsing. She set her hand to my chest and patted me lightly. 'Don't be troubled, Tom. It wasn't all your failure. I had guessed there might be a problem when the charm by the bed near unmanned you. And now your spirits grow bleak and grim, do they not?'

I shrugged one shoulder. She sat up beside me in the bed. She reached across me, her flesh warm against mine, and lifted my shirt off the bedside charm. The sad little thing hunched there, forlorn and alone.

'It's a woman's charm. It's difficult to make, as it must be very finely tuned to the individual woman. To construct this sort of charm, you have to know the woman from the skin in. So a hedge-witch can make one for herself, but not for anyone else . . . at least, not one that is certain. This one is mine, tuned to me. It's a charm against conception. I should have guessed that it might affect you. Any man who wants children so desperately that he takes in a foundling to raise on his own has that longing down to his bones. You may deny it, but that little hope burns in you each time you lie with a woman. I suspect it is what must drive your passion, Tom. And this little charm took that idle dream away from you before you could even wish it. It told you our joining would be futile and barren. That's what you feel now, isn't it?'

Having something explained to you does not always solve it. I looked aside from her. 'Isn't it?' I asked, and then winced at the bitterness in my voice.

'Poor boy,' she said sympathetically. She kissed me on the forehead, where Kettricken had kissed me earlier. 'Of course not. It's what we make it.'

'I'm in no position to be a father to anyone. I didn't even come to see Hap last night, when he told me it was important. I've no wish to start another little life that I cannot protect.'

She shook her head over me. 'What the heart longs for, and what the mind knows are two different things. You forget I've seen your palms, sweet man. Perhaps I know more of your heart than you do yourself.'

'You said my true love would come back to me.' Again, despite myself, my words sounded accusing.

'No, Tom. That I did not. Well do I know that what I say to

a person is seldom what that person hears, but I'll tell you again what I saw. It's here.' She took my hand. She held the open palm close to her near-sighted eyes. Her bare breasts brushed my wrist as her fingers traced a line in my palm. 'There is a love that twines in and out of your days. Sometimes, it leaves, but when it does, it runs alongside you until it returns.' She lifted my hand closer to her face, studying it. Then she kissed my palm, and moved it back to her breast. 'That doesn't mean that you must be alone and idle while you wait for it to come back,' she suggested in a whisper.

Fennel saved us both the embarrassment of my declining. *Want a rat?* I glanced up. The orange cat crouched on the edge of the loft, his catch squirming in his jaws as he stared down at us. *It's still got a lot of play in it.*

No. Just kill it. I felt the red spark of the rat's agony. It had no hope of living, but the life in it would not surrender easily. Life never gives up willingly.

Fennel ignored my refusal. He launched from the edge of the loft, dropping down to land beside us on the bed, where he released his prey. The frantic rodent scuttled towards us, dragging a hind leg. Jinna exclaimed in disgust and leapt from the bed. I snatched up the rat. A pinch and a twist ended its torment.

You're fast! Fennel approved.

Here. Take it away. I offered him the dead rat.

He sniffed the dead body. *You broke it!* Fennel crouched on the bed, staring at me in round-eyed disapproval.

Take it away.

I don't want it. It's no fun any more. He growled low at me, then leapt from the bed. *You ended it too fast. You just don't know how to play.* He went immediately to the door and clawed the jamb, demanding to go out. Jinna, clutching her robe against her nakedness, opened the door and he sidled out. I was left sitting naked in her bed, a dead rat in my hands. Blood leaked from the battered rat's nose and mouth over my hands.

My trousers and drawers were still tangled together when Jinna tossed them to me. 'Don't get blood on my bedding,' she cautioned me, so I didn't set the rat down, but struggled into my trousers one-handed.

I threw the rat out onto a midden behind the house. When I came back in, she was pouring hot water over tea in the pot. She gave me a smile. 'The other tea seems to have gone cold, somehow.'

'Did it?' I tried to speak as lightly as she did. I went back to her bedroom for my shirt. After I put it on, I twitched the bedding straight. I avoided looking at the charm. When I came out, I ignored my own desire to leave and sat down at the table. We shared bread and butter and honey, and hot tea. Jinna chatted of the three women who had come to see her. She had read the younger daughter's hands, to see if an offer of marriage boded well for her. Then she had advised her to wait. It was a long involved story, full of detail, and I let it stream gently past me. Fennel came to my chair, stood up and dug his front claws into my leg, then hauled himself up onto my lap. From there, he surveyed the table.

Butter for the cat.

I have no reason to be nice to you.

Yes, you do. I am the cat.

He was so supremely self-confident that that was enough reason for me to butter a corner of a slice of bread and offered it to him. I had expected him to carry it off. Instead, he allowed me to hold it while he licked it clean of butter. *More.*

No.

'. . . or Hap may find himself in the same sort of difficulty.'

I tried to backtrack her words, but realized I had hopelessly lost the thread of her conversation. Fennel was perversely digging his claws into my thigh as I ignored him. 'Well, I intended to speak with him today,' I said, and hoped that the comment made some sort of sense.

'You should. Of course, there's no good your waiting for him here. Even if you had come last night, you'd have had to sit and wait for him. He comes in late each night, and leaves late for his work every morning.'

Concern prickled me. That didn't sound like Hap.

'So what do you suggest?'

She took a breath and sighed it out, a bit annoyed. I probably deserved it. 'What I just said. Go to the shop, and speak with his master. Ask for some time with Hap. Corner him, and set down some rules for him. Say that if he doesn't keep them, you'll insist that he board with his master like the other apprentices do. That would give him a chance to govern himself, or be governed. For if he moves into the apprentices' quarters there, he'll find that one evening off twice a month is all he'll get to himself.'

I was suddenly listening closely. 'Then all the other apprentices live with Master Gindast?'

She gave me a look of amazement. 'Of course they do! And he keeps them on a tight leash, which perhaps Hap would benefit from – but there, you are his father, I suppose you would know best about that.'

'He has never needed one before,' I observed mildly.

'Well, that was when you lived in the country. And there were no taverns nor young women about within hailing.'

'Well . . . yes. But I had not considered that he might be expected to live in his master's house.'

'The apprentices' quarters are behind Master Gindast's workshop. It makes it easy for them to rise, wash, eat, and be at work by dawn. Did you not board with your master?'

At that, I supposed that I had. I had just never perceived it that way. 'I was never formally apprenticed,' I lied casually. 'So all of this is new. I had assumed I had to provide Hap's room and board while he was taught. Which is why I brought this with me.' I opened my pouch and spilled coins on her table.

And there they lay in a heap between us, and suddenly I felt awkward. Would she think this was intended as payment for something else?

She stared at me silently for a moment, and then said, 'Tom, I've scarcely touched what you sent down before. How much do you think it costs to feed a boy?'

I managed an apologetic shrug. 'Another town thing that I don't know. At home, we raised what we needed, or hunted for it. I know Hap eats a great deal after a day's work. I had assumed it would be expensive to feed him.' Chade must have arranged for a purse to be sent to her. I had no idea how much it had contained.

'Well. When I need more, I'll tell you. The use of the pony and cart has meant a great deal to my niece. It's something she has always wanted but you know how hard it is to set aside coin for something like that.'

'You are more than welcome to that. As Hap told you, it is much better for Clover to move about than to be stabled constantly. Oh. Feed for the pony.'

'That's easy enough for us to come by, and it seems only fair that we provide for an animal we use.' She paused, and glanced about us. 'Then you'll see Hap today?'

'Of course. It's why I came to town today.' I began to stack the coins, preparatory to returning them to my pouch. It felt awkward.

'I see. So that was why you came here,' she observed, but she smiled teasingly as she said it. 'Well then. I'll let you be on your way.'

And it suddenly dawned on me that she was letting me know it was time for me to leave. I chinked the coins into my purse again and stood. 'Well. Thank you for the tea,' I said and then halted. She laughed aloud at me and my cheeks burned but I managed to smile. She made me feel young and foolish, at a disadvantage. I did not see why that should be so, but I knew I did not care for it. 'Well. I had best go see Hap.'

'You do that,' she agreed, and handed me my cloak. Then I had to stop and get my boots on. I had just finished that when there was a rap at her door. 'A moment!' Jinna called, and then I was exiting, nodding to her customer in passing. It was a young man with an anxious expression on his face. He sketched a bow to me and then hastened inside. The door shut on the sound of Jinna greeting him, and I was alone once more in the windy street.

I trudged off to Gindast's shop. The day grew colder as I walked, and I began to smell snow in the air. Summer had lingered late, but now winter would have her way. Looking up at the sky, I decided it would be a heavy fall. It woke mixed feelings in me. A few months ago, such a sight would have made me check my woodstack, and do a final, critical consideration of what I had gathered for the winter. Now the Farseer throne provided for me. I no longer had to consider my own well-being, only that of the reign. The harness still sat uncomfortably on my shoulders.

Gindast was well known in Buckkeep Town and I had no difficulty finding his shop. His signboard was elaborately carved and framed, as if to be sure his skill were properly displayed. The front of his building held a cosy sitting room, with comfortable chairs and a large table. A fire fuelled with scraps of well-dried wood burned hotly in the hearth. Several pieces of his finest work were displayed in the room for the perusal of potential customers. The fellow in charge of this room listened to my request, then waved me on through to the shop.

This was a barn of a structure, with a number of projects in various stages of completion. An immense bedstead squatted next to a series of fragrant cedar chests emblazoned with someone's owl sigil. A journeyman knelt, putting stain on the owls. Gindast was not in his shop. He had ridden out with three of his journeymen to Lord Scyther's manor, to take measurements and consult over the construction of an elaborate mantle, with chairs and tables to match. One of his senior journeymen, a man not much younger than myself, allowed that I could speak with Hap for a time. He also suggested gravely that I might wish to call again, to make an appointment with Master Gindast to discuss my boy's progress. The journeyman made such a meeting sound ominous.

I found Hap behind the shop with four other apprentices. All appeared younger and smaller than he was. They were engaged in moving a stack of drying wood, turning and shifting each timber in the process. The trampled earth told me this was the third such stack to be turned. The other two were draped with roped-down canvas. There was a scowl on Hap's face as if this mindless yet necessary task affronted him. I watched him for a time before he was aware of me, and what I saw troubled me. Hap had always been a willing worker when he toiled alongside me. Now I saw suppressed anger in the way he handled himself, and his impatience at working with lads younger and weaker than he was. I stood silently, watching him until he noticed me. He straightened from the plank he had just set down, said something to the other apprentices, and then stalked over to me. I watched him come, wondering how much of his manner was expression of what he truly felt and how much was show for the younger boys. I didn't much care for the disdain he expressed towards his current task.

'Hap,' I greeted him gravely, and 'Tom,' he responded. He clasped wrists with me, and then said in a low voice, 'You see now what I was talking about.'

'I see you turning wood so it dries well,' I responded. 'That seems a necessary task for a woodworker's shop.'

He sighed. 'I would not mind it so much, if it were an occasional thing. But every task they put me to demands a lot of my back and little of my brain.'

'And are the other apprentices treated differently?'

'No,' he replied begrudgingly. 'But as you can see, they are just boys.'

'Makes no difference, Hap,' I told him. 'It's not a matter of age, but of knowledge. Be patient. There's something to learn here, even if it's only how to stack the wood properly, and what you learn from seeing it at this stage. Besides, it's a thing that must be done. Who else should they put to doing it?'

He stared at the ground while I spoke, silent but unconvinced. I took a breath. 'Do you think you might do better if you lived here with the other apprentices, instead of with Jinna?'

He met my eyes suddenly with a look full of outrage and dismay. 'No! Why do you suggest such a thing?'

'Well, because I have learned it is customary. Perhaps if you lived here, close by your work, it would be easier. Not so far to go to be on time in the morning, and—'

'I'd go crazy if I had to live here as well as apprentice here! The other boys have told me what it is like. Every meal the same as the last one, and Gindast's wife counts the candles, to be sure they are not burning them late at night. They must air their bedding and wash their own blankets and small-clothes weekly, not to mention that he keeps them at extra chores after the day's work is done, shovelling sawdust to mulch his wife's rose garden and picking up scraps for the kindling heap and—'

'It does not sound so terrible to me,' I interrupted, for I could see he was but building himself to more heat. 'It sounds disciplined.

Rather like what a man-at-arms goes through in his training. It wouldn't hurt you, Hap.'

He flung his arms wide in an angry gesture. 'It wouldn't help me, either. If I had wanted to break heads for a living, then, yes, I'd expect to be trained like a dumb animal. But I didn't expect my apprenticeship to be like this.'

'Then you've decided that this isn't what you want?' I asked, and near held my breath awaiting the answer. For if he had changed his mind, I had no idea what I would do with him. I could not have him up at Buckkeep with me, nor send him back to the cabin alone.

His answer came grudgingly. 'No. I haven't changed my mind. This is what I want. But they had better start actually teaching me something soon, or . . .'

I waited for him to say, 'or what' but his words ran out. He, too, had no idea what he would do if he left Gindast. I decided to take that as a positive sign. 'I'm glad this is still what you want. Try to be humble, to be patient, to work well, and listen and learn. I think that if you do so, and show yourself a sharp lad, you will soon progress to more challenging tasks. And I'll try to meet you tonight, but I dare not make any promises. Lord Golden keeps me very busy, and it's been hard for me to get this much time free. Do you know where Three Sails Tavern is?'

'Yes, but don't meet me there. Come to the Stuck Pig instead. It's very near Jinna's.'

'And?' I pressed, knowing there was another reason.

'And you can meet Svanja, too. She lives nearby, and watches for me. If she can, she joins me there.'

'If she can sneak away from her home?'

'Well . . . somewhat. Her mother doesn't much mind, but her father hates me.'

'Not the best start for a courtship, Hap. What have you done to deserve his hatred?'

'Kissed his daughter.' Hap grinned a devil-may-care grin, and I smiled in spite of myself.

'Well. That is a thing we will discuss this evening as well. I think you are young to begin a courtship. Better to wait until you have some solid prospects and a way to keep a wife. Perhaps then her father would not mind a stolen kiss or two. If I can get free tonight, I will meet you there.'

Hap seemed somewhat mollified as he waved me a farewell and went back to his stacking work. But I walked away from him with a heavier heart that I had come with. Jinna was right. Town life was changing my boy, and in ways I had not foreseen. I did not feel that he had truly listened to my counsel, let alone that he would act on it. Well. Perhaps tonight I could take a firmer line with him.

As I walked back through the town, the first flakes of snow began to fall. When I reached the steeper road that wound its way up to Buckkeep Castle, it began to fall thick and soft. Several times I paused and stepped aside from the road, to watch back the way I had come but I saw no sign that anyone followed me. For the Piebalds to threaten me, and then vanish completely made no sense They should have either killed me or taken me hostage. I tried to put myself in their position, to imagine a reason to leave your prey walking freely about. I could think of nothing. By the time I reached the gates of the keep, there was a thick carpet of snow on the road, and the wind had begun to whistle in the treetops. The weather brought an early darkness. It was going to be a foul night. I would be glad to spend it inside.

I stamped the clinging wet snow from my feet outside the entrance to the hall that went past the kitchens and the guardroom. I smelled hot beef soup and fresh bread and wet wool as I went past. the guardroom. I was tired and wished I could enter and share their simple food and rough jokes and casual manners. Instead I straightened my shoulders and hastened past and up to Lord Golden's chambers. He was not there, and I recalled he said he might be gaming with the Queen's favoured. I supposed I should seek him there. I went into my chamber to be rid of my damp cloak and found a scrap of parchment on my bed. There was a single word on it. 'Up.'

A few moments later, I emerged in Chade's tower chamber. There was no one there. But on my chair waited a set of warm clothing, and a green cloak of heavy wool with an overlarge hood. The outside bore the otter badge, unfamiliar to me. An unusual feature of the cloak was that it reversed to plain homespun, in servant blue.

Beside it was a leather travel-bag with food and a flask of brandy in it. Beneath it, folded flat, was a leather scroll-case. This heap of gear was topped with a note in Chade's hand. 'Heffam's troop rides out on highway patrol tonight from the north gate at sunset. Join them and then divert to your own goal. I hope you will not mind missing the harvest feast. Return as swiftly as possible, please.'

I snorted at myself. Harvest Fest. I had so looked forward to it as a boy. Now I had not even recalled that it was nigh. Doubtless the Prince's betrothal ceremony had been intentionally scheduled to precede Buckkeep's celebration of plenty. Well, I had missed it for the last fifteen years. Once more would not bother me.

On the end of the worktable was a hearty meal of cold meat, cheese, bread and ale. I decided to trust that Chade had arranged my disappearance from Lord Golden's service. I had no time to seek him out and relay the information, nor did I feel comfortable leaving him a note of any kind. I thought regretfully of my delayed-again meeting with Hap, and decided that I'd already warned him I might not be there. And the sudden opportunity to take some action on my own appealed mightily to me. I wanted to banish the hanging suspicion that the Piebalds had located my den. Even to discover that they had would be better than wondering fearfully.

I ate, and changed clothes. By the time the sun was setting, I was mounted on Myblack and approaching the north gate. My hood was pulled well forward to exclude the biting wind and blinding snow. Other anonymous green-cloaked riders were gathering there, some complaining bitterly about drawing road patrol while the betrothal festivities and harvest celebration were at their height. I drew closer and then nodded silent commiseration to one talkative fellow who was regaling the night with his woes. He began a long tale of a woman, the warmest and most willing woman imaginable, who would wait in vain for him at a Buckkeep Town tavern tonight. I was content to sit my horse beside him and let him talk. Others congregated about us. In the gathering dark and swirling snow, indistinct riders huddled in their cloaks and hoods. Scarves and darkness swathed our faces.

The sun was down and the night dark before Heffam appeared. He seemed as disgruntled as his men, and announced brusquely that we'd ride swiftly to First Ford, relieve the guard there tonight, and begin our regular tour of patrol of the highways in the morning. His men seemed very familiar with this duty. We fell in behind him in two ragged lines. I took care to take a place well to the back. Then he led us out of the gate and into the night and storm. For a time, our road led us steeply downward. Then we turned and took the river road that would lead us east along the Buck River.

When we had left the lights of Buckkeep far behind us, I began to hold Myblack in. She was not pleased with the weather or the dark, and was just as glad to go more slowly. At one point I pulled her in completely and dismounted on the pretext of tightening a cinch. The patrol rode on without me into the cloaking storm. I mounted again and rejoined it, now the last man of the troop. As we travelled, I held my horse back, letting the distance between us and the rest of the troop gradually lengthen. When at last a bend in the road took them out of sight, I pulled Myblack to a halt. I dismounted and again began to fuss with saddle straps. I waited, hoping that my absence would go unnoticed in the foul weather. When no one returned to see why I tarried, I turned my cloak, remounted Myblack and headed her back the way we had come.

As Chade had bid me, I hastened, yet there were inevitable delays. I had to wait for the dawn ferry across the Buck River, and then the winds of the storm and the ice that coated the lines and the decks slowed our loading and passage. On the other side, I discovered that the road was wider and better tended, as well as more travelled, than I recalled. A prosperous little market town clustered alongside it, the taverns and houses built on pilings to be beyond the reach of both ordinary and storm tides. By midday I had left it far behind.

My journey back to my home was uneventful in the ordinary sense. I rested several times in smaller, nondescript inns along the way. At only one was my night's rest disturbed. At first the dream was peaceful. A warm fireside, the sounds of a family at their evening tasks.

'*Umph. Off my lap, girl. You're far too big to sit on me now.*'

'*I'll never be too big for my papa's lap.*' There was laughter in her voice. '*What are you making?*'

'I'm mending your mother's shoe. Or trying to. Here. Thread this
for me. The firelight makes the needle's eye dance until I cannot find
it. Younger eyes will do better.'

And that was what had awakened me. A sudden wash of dismay
that Papa was admitting his sight was failing. I tried not to think
of that as I fell back into a guarded sleep.

No one seemed to remark my passage. I had time with Myblack
to improve her manners; we tested each other's wills in any number
of small ways. The weather continued foul. The nights were blowing
snow and sleet. When the storm did let up briefly during the day, the
watery sun only melted enough snow to turn the roads into mud and
slush that became dirty treacherous ice by the next morning. It was
not pleasant travelling weather.

Yet part of the cold that assailed me through this journey had
nothing to do with the weather. No wolf ranged ahead of me to see
if the road was clear nor circled back to see if we were followed. My
own senses and my own sword were all I could rely on for protection.
I felt naked and incomplete.

The sun broke through the clouds on the afternoon when I
reached the lane to my cabin. The snow had paused, and the
day's brief warmth was turning the most recent fall into heavy
wet mush. Irregular 'thumps' from the forest were the sounds of
trees dropping their heaped burdens. The lane to my cottage was
smooth and undisturbed save with rabbit tracks and pits from fallen
loads of snow. I doubted that any had passed here since the snow
had begun falling. That was reassuring.

Yet when I reached my cabin, all of my uneasiness returned. It
was obvious that someone had been here, and recently. The door
stood open. Uneven lumps beneath the snow were the rounded
shapes of furniture and possessions thrown out into the yard in a
heap. Fragments of vellum thrust up from the snow that here was
trampled and uneven beneath the smoothness of the most recent
fall. The pole fence around the kitchen garden had been torn down,
as had Jinna's charm on its post. I sat my horse a time in silence,
trying to be impassive as my eyes and ears gathered information.
Then I dismounted silently and approached the cabin.

No one was inside. It was cold and dark. It reminded me of

something, and then a prickling of foreboding helped me seize the memory; it reminded me of when I had returned to a cabin that had been raided by Forged Ones. The failing daylight showed me the muddy tracks of a pig's trotters on the floor. Several curious animals had investigated the cabin. There were muddy boot-tracks as well, a criss-crossing passage that indicated someone had made many trips in and out.

Everything portable and useful had been taken. The blankets from the beds, the smoked and preserved foods from the rafters, the pots from the cooking hearth; all were gone. Some scrolls had been used to kindle a fire in the hearth. Someone had eaten here, probably enjoying the supplies Hap and I had laid in for the winter. There was a scatter of fish bones still on the hearth. I felt I knew who had come here. The pig tracks were my best clue.

My desk still remained; my unlettered neighbour would have little use for a writing desk. In my little study, inkpots had been overset, scrolls opened and then tossed aside. This gave me concern. In the current disorder, it was impossible for me to tell if any scrolls had been carried off. I could not tell if Piebalds had scavenged here as well as my pig-keeper neighbour. Verity's map still hung crookedly on the wall; I was shocked at how my heart leapt with relief to find it intact. I had not realized I valued it so. I took it down and rolled it up, carrying it about with me as I explored the plundering of my home. I forced myself to make a careful survey of each room, and the stable and chicken house as well, before I allowed myself to gather what I would take away with me.

The small store of grain and all the tools had been taken from the shed in the stable. My work-shed was a jumble of rejected plunder. It seemed unlikely that was the work of Piebalds. My suspicion of an unpleasant neighbour who lived in the next valley was all but certain now. He kept pigs, and had once accused me of stealing piglets from him. When I had so hastily left here, I had directed Hap to take our chickens to the man, not out of kindness to the neighbour but knowing that he would feed and keep them for the sake of the eggs. That had seemed a better course than letting predators slaughter them. But, of course, it would have let him know that we expected to be gone for an extended period. I stood

with my fists clenched, looking about the small stable. I doubted
that I would ever return here. Even if the tools had been here still,
I would have left without them. What use had I now for a mattock
or a hoe? But the theft was a violation that was hard to ignore. I
ached for revenge even as I told myself that I had no time for it,
that the thief had perhaps done me a favour in ransacking my home
before Piebalds could.

I put Myblack in the stable and gave her what poor hay had
been left. I hauled her a bucket of water as well. Then I began my
salvage and destruction.

The heap of possessions under the snow proved to be a bedstead,
my table and chairs and several shelves. Probably he intended to
come back with a cart for them. I'd burn them. I knocked some
of the snow from the heap, gazed regretfully on the charging buck
that the Fool had carved into my table for me, and then went into
the cabin for tinder to start the fire. The straw-stuffed mattress from
my bed, discarded inside, worked admirably. In a very short time, I
had a nice blaze going.

I tried to be methodical. While daylight served me, I painstakingly gathered every scattered scroll that had been flung into
the yard. Some were hopelessly ruined with damp, others torn
and trampled with muddy hooves, and some were no more than
fragments. Mindful of Chade's words, some I tried to smooth and
roll up, even when they were but fragments, but most I ruthlessly
consigned to the fire. I kicked through the snow until I was as
certain as I could possibly be that no writing of mine remained
in the yard.

Dusk was deep by then. Inside the cabin, I kindled a fire in the
hearth, for light as well as heat. I began on the inside of the cabin.
Most of my possessions went straight into the fire. Old work clothes,
my writing tools, my bootjack, and other clutter and possessions
burned in the hearth. I was kinder to Hap's things, knowing that a
spinning top, long outgrown as a plaything, could still have meaning
to him. I made a sack of an old cloak and filled it with those sorts
of items. Then I sat down by the flames and painstakingly went
through the scrolls from my rack. There were far more of them than I
had expected, and far more than I could have carried back with me.

I chose first to save those I had not written myself. Verity's map went into the case, of course, and was soon joined by scrolls I had acquired in my travels and some brought to me by Starling. A few of these were quite old and rare. I was grateful to find them intact and resolved to make copies of them when I returned to Buckkeep. But apart from those, my culling was fierce. Nothing that was the work of my pen was immune to my scrutiny. Scrolls of herbal knowledge with my meticulous illustrations fed the fire. That information was still in my head; if it was that important, I could write it down again. Into the bag, against my better judgment, went those scrolls that dealt not only with my time in the mountains, but with my personal musings on my own life. A swift perusal of some of those left my cheeks burning. Juvenile and mawkish, self-pitying and full of grand assumptions about my own significance and declarations of things that I would never do again were these treatises. I wondered who I had been when I wrote them.

My writing on the Skill and the Wit went into the bag, as did my lengthy account of our journey through the Mountain Kingdom and into the realm of the Elderlings and the rise of Verity-as-Dragon. My attempts at poetry about Molly went into the flames, to burn in a final burst of passion. Writing I had done to help Hap learn his letters and numbers went after them. I winnowed my writings, and still there were too many. They underwent a second, harsher culling, and finally the scroll case would close.

Then I stood, closed my eyes, and tried to think: were there any still unaccounted for? I told myself it was a hopeless task. Some scrolls I had had the sense to destroy within days of writing them. Others I had given Starling to carry back to Chade. I could not decide if any were missing. Let any man try to recall all he might have written down over fifteen years of his life, and there would doubtless be some gaps. Had I ever committed to paper an account of my time with Black Rolf and the Old Bloods? I was sure I had written of those months, but had they been in a separate scroll, or was I recalling bits that had interjected themselves into other writings? I wasn't sure. And I could not know what scrolls the pig-keeper had used to kindle his cookfire. I sighed. Surrender it. I had done as much as I could.

In the future, I would be far more careful of what I entrusted to letters.

I went back out into the yard, and flipped the ends of the burning furniture into the fire. The rising wind and falling snow would soon smother it, but the charging buck was scorched to obliteration. The rest of it little mattered. I walked again though the little cabin that had been my home for so many years. I had left intact no personal article of my own. My presence here was erased. I thought of burning the cabin itself, and decided against it. It had stood here before I had come; let it still stand after I was gone. Perhaps some other needy man might come to make use of it.

I saddled Myblack again and led her out of the paddock. I loaded onto her the scroll-case and Hap's bundled possessions. The last items I included were two tightly stoppered pots, one of ground elfbark and the other of carryme. Then I mounted and rode away from that piece of my life. The fire of my burning past sent odd shadows snaking ahead of us as we made our way into the storm's resurgence.

SEVEN

Lessons

In this manner are the best coteries formed. Let the Skillmaster assemble together those he would train. Let them be at least six in number, though a greater number is preferable if sufficient students are available. Let the Skillmaster bring them together daily, not just for lessons, but for meals and amusements, and even to a shared sleeping chamber, if he judge that will not be a cause for distraction and rivalries amongst them. Give them time together, let them form their own bonds, and at the end of the year, the coterie will have formed itself. Those who have not formed bonds, let them serve the King as Solos.

It may be difficult for some Skillmasters to restrain themselves from directing the formation of a coterie. It is tempting to put the best with the best, and dismiss those who seem slow or difficult of temperament. The wisest Skillmaster will refrain from this, for only a coterie can know what strengths it will take from each member. He who seems dull may provide steadiness and temper impulse with caution. The difficult member can also be the one who displays flashes of inspiration. Let each coterie find its own membership, and choose its own leader.

Treeknee's translation of Skillmaster Oklef's *Coteries*

'Where have you been?' Dutiful demanded as he strode into the tower room. He shut the door firmly behind himself and then came to the middle of the room, his arms crossed on his chest. I stood up slowly from Verity's chair. I had been watching the white tips of the waves. There was impatience and annoyance in my prince's voice and a scowl on his face. It did not seem the most auspicious beginning to our relationship as tutor and student. I took a breath. A light hand, first. I spoke in a pleasant, neutral voice.

'Good morning, Prince Dutiful.'

Just as a young colt might, he bridled. Then, I watched him gather himself. He took a breath and visibly began anew. 'Good morning, Tom Badgerlock. It has been some time since I last saw you.'

'Important business of my own took me away from Buckkeep for a time. It is settled now, and I fully expect that the rest of this winter, most of my time will be at your disposal.'

'Thank you.' Then, as if the last of his annoyance had to find vent somewhere, 'I do not suppose I can ask more than that of you.'

I suppressed a smile and told him, 'You could. But you would not get it.'

And then Verity's smile broke on the boy's face and he exclaimed, 'Where did you come from? No one else in this keep would dare speak to me so.'

I purposefully misunderstood his question. 'I had to spend a bit of time at my old home, packing up or disposing of my possessions. I hate to leave loose ends. It's settled now. I'm here at Buckkeep, and I'm to teach you. So. Where shall we begin?'

The question seemed to unnerve him. He glanced around the room. Chade had added furnishings and clutter to the Seawatch tower since Verity had manned it as his Skill-outpost against the Red Ship Raiders. This morning I had made my own contribution, in the form of Verity's map of the Six Duchies newly hung on the wall. In the centre of the room there was a large table of dark, heavy wood. Four massive chairs crouched around it. I pitied whatever men had had to haul them up the narrow, winding steps. Against one of the curved tower walls there was a scroll-rack stuffed with scrolls. I knew that Chade would claim they were in perfect order, but I had never been able to understand the logic behind how he grouped his scrolls. There were also several trunks, securely locked, that held a selection of Skillmistress Solicity's scrolls on the Skill. Both Chade and I had judged them too dangerous to be left where the curious might paw through them. Even now, a man stood watch at the bottom of the tower steps. Access to this room was limited to Councillor Chade, the

Prince and Queen. We would not chance losing control of this library again.

Long years ago, when Skillmistress Solicity had died, all these scrolls had passed into the control of Galen, her apprentice. He had claimed her post as Skillmaster, even though his training had been incomplete. He had supposedly 'completed' the training of both Prince Chivalry and Prince Verity, but Chade and I suspected that he had deliberately truncated their education in the Skill. Thereafter, he had trained no others, until the time when King Shrewd had demanded that he create a coterie. And during all Galen's time as Skillmaster, access to those scrolls had been denied to all. Eventually, he disputed that such a library had ever even existed. When he died, no trace of them had been found.

Somehow, they had passed to Regal the Pretender. Eventually, with Regal's death, they were recovered and had been returned to the Queen and thence into Chade's safekeeping. Both Chade and I suspected that once the library had been substantially larger. Chade had advanced the theory that many of the choicest scrolls that had to do with Skill, dragons and Elderlings had been sold off to Outisland traders in the early days of the Red Ship raids. Certainly neither Regal nor Galen had felt any great loyalty to the Coastal Duchies that suffered from the raiders. Perhaps they would not have scrupled to traffic with our tormentors, or their go-betweens. The scrolls would undoubtedly have brought a good sum of coin into Regal's hands. At a time when the Six Duchies treasury had come close to being depleted, Regal had never seemed to lack money with which to entertain himself and court the loyalty of the Inland dukes. And the Red Ship Raiders had gained their knowledge of the Skill and the possible uses of the black Skill-stone from somewhere. It was even possible that somewhere, in one of those straying scrolls, they had found the knowledge of how to Forge folk. But it was not likely that Chade or I would ever be able to prove it.

The Prince's voice pulled my straying attention back to the present. 'I thought you would have planned it all out. Where to begin and all.' The uncertainty in the boy's voice was wrenching. I longed to reassure him, but decided to be honest with him instead.

'Pull up a chair and join me here,' I suggested to him. I resumed Verity's old seat.

For a moment he stared at me as if puzzled. Then he crossed the room, seized one of the heavy chairs and lugged it over to place it beside mine. I said nothing as he sat in it. I had not forgotten our relative ranks, but I had already decided that within this room, I would treat him as my student rather than my prince. For an instant I hesitated, wondering if my candid words might not undermine my authority over him. Then I took a breath and spoke them.

'My prince, roughly a score of years ago I sat in this room on the floor by your father's feet. He sat here, in this chair, and he looked out over the water and Skilled. He used his talents mercilessly, against both the enemy and the health of his own body. From here, he used the strength of his mind to reach out, to find Red Ships and their crews before they could touch our shores, and confound them. He made the sea and the weather our ally against them, confusing navigators to send the enemy ships onto rocks, or persuading captains to a false confidence that bid them steer straight into storms.

'I am sure that you have heard of Skillmaster Galen. He was supposed to create and train a Skill-coterie, a unified group of Skill-users who would provide their strength and talent to aid King-in-Waiting Verity against the Red Ships. Well, he did create a coterie, but they were false, their loyalty bound to Regal, Verity's ambitious younger brother. Instead of aiding your father's efforts, they hindered him. They delayed messages, or failed to deliver them at all. They made your father look incompetent. For the sake of breaking the loyalty of his dukes to him, they delivered our people into the hands of the raiders, to be killed or Forged.'

The Prince's eyes were locked onto my face. I could not meet his earnest gaze. I stared past him, out of the tall windows and over the grey and billowing sea. Then I steeled myself and trod the precipice path between deadly truth and cowardly falsehood. 'I was one of Galen's students. Because of my illegitimate birth, he despised me. I learned what I could from him, but he was a cruel and unjust master to me, driving me away from the knowledge he did not wish to share with me. Under his brutal tutelage, I learned the basics of Skilling, but no more than that. I could not predictably master my talent, and so I failed. He sent me away with the other students who did not meet his standards.

'I continued to work as a servant here in the keep. When your father laboured most heavily here, he had his meals brought up to him. That was my task. And it was here that we discovered, most providentially, that even though I could not Skill on my own, he could draw Skill-strength from me. And later, in the brief times he was able to give me, he taught me what he could of Skilling.'

I turned to face Dutiful and waited. His dark eyes probed mine. 'When he left on his quest, did you go with him?'

I shook my head and answered truthfully. 'No. I was young and he forbade it.'

'And you didn't try to follow him later?' He was incredulous, his imagination fired with what he was sure he would himself have done in my place.

It was hard to say the next words. 'No one knew where he had gone, or by what paths.' I held my breath, hoping that would still his questions. I didn't want to lie to him.

He turned away from me and looked out over the sea. He was disappointed in me. 'I wonder how different things might have been if you had gone with him.'

I had often told myself that if I had, Queen Kettricken would never have survived Regal's reign at Buckkeep. But I said, 'I've often pondered that question myself, my prince. But there is no knowing what might have happened. I might have helped him, but looking back on those days, I think it just as likely I would have been a hindrance to him. I was very young, quick-tempered and impetuous.' I took a breath and steered the conversation as I wished it to go. 'I tell you these things to be sure you understand well that I am no Skillmaster. I have not studied all those scrolls . . . I have read only a few of them. So. In a sense we are both students here. I will do my best to educate myself from the scrolls, even as I teach you the basics of what I know. It is a hazardous path that we will tread together. Do you understand this?'

'I understand. And of the Wit?'

I had not wanted to discuss that today. 'Well. I came to my

Wit-magic much as you did yours, stumbling into it by chance when I bonded with a puppy. I was a man grown before I met anyone who tried to put my random knowledge of my magic into a coherent framework. Again, time was my enemy. I learned much from him, but not all there was to know . . . far short of that, to be truthful. So, again, I will teach you what I know. But you will be learning from a flawed instructor.'

'Your confidence is so inspiring,' Dutiful muttered darkly. Then, a moment later, he laughed. 'A fine pair we shall make, stumbling along together. Where do we begin?'

'I am afraid that we shall have to begin by first moving backwards. You must be untaught some of what you have learned by yourself. Are you aware that when you attempt to Skill, you are mingling the Wit with that magic?'

He stared at me blankly.

After a moment of discouragement, I said briskly, 'Well. Our first step will be to untangle your magics from one another.' As if I knew how. I was not even certain that my own magics operated independently of one another. I shoved the thought aside. 'I'd like to proceed with teaching you the basics of Skilling. We'll set aside the Wit for now, to avoid confusion.'

'Have you ever known any others like us?'

He had lost me again. 'Like us in what way?'

'With both the Wit and the Skill.'

I took a deep breath and let it out. Truth or lie. Truth. 'I think I once met one, but I did not recognize him as such at the time. I don't think he even knew what he doing. At the time, I thought he was just very strong in the Wit. Since then, I've sometimes wondered at how well he seemed to know what passed between my wolf and me. I suspect that he had both magics, but thought them the same thing, and thus used them together.'

'Who was he?'

I should never have begun to answer his questions. 'I told you, it was a long time ago. He was a man who tried to help me learn the Wit. Now. Let's focus on why we are here today.'

'Civil.'

'What?' The lad's mind hopped like a flea. He'd have to learn focus.

'Civil has been well instructed in the Wit, since he was a small child. Perhaps he would be willing to teach me. As he already knows I am witted, it is not spreading my secret about. And . . .'

I think the look on my face made him falter into silence. I waited until I trusted myself to speak. Then, I pretended to be a wiser man than I was. I tried to listen before I spoke to him. 'Tell me about Civil,' I suggested. Then, because I could not quite control my tongue, I added, 'Tell me why you think it is safe to trust him.'

I liked that he did not answer immediately. His brow furrowed, and then he spoke as if he were recounting events from a lifetime ago. 'I first met Civil when he presented me with my cat. As you know, she was a gift from the Bresingas. I think Lady Bresinga had come to Buckkeep Castle before, but I don't recall ever seeing Civil. There was something about the way he gave me the cat . . . I think it was that he obviously cared for her welfare; he did not present her to me as if she were a thing, but as if she were a friend. Perhaps that is because he is Witted, also. He told me that he would teach me how to hunt with her, and the very next morning, we went out together. We went alone, Tom, so there would be no distractions for her. And he truly taught me how to hunt with her, paying more attention to that than to the fact that he had time alone with Prince Dutiful.' Dutiful halted and a slight flush rose on his face.

'That may sound conceited to you, but it is a thing I must always deal with. I accept an invitation to something that sounds interesting, only to find that the person who invited me is more fixed on gaining my attention than on sharing something with me. Lady Wess invited me to a puppet show performed by masters of the art from Tilth. Then she sat beside me and chattered at me about a land dispute with her neighbour all the way through the play.

'Civil was not like that. He taught me how to hunt with a cat. Don't you think that if he had intended ill to me, he could have done it then? Hunting accidents are not that rare. He could have arranged a tumble down a cliff. But we hunted, not just that morning, but every dawn for the week he was in Buckkeep, and each day it was the same. Only better, as I became more skilled at it. And it became best of all when he brought his own cat along with us. I really thought I had finally discovered a true friend.'

Chade's old trick served me well. Silence asks the questions that are too awkward to phrase. It even asks the questions one does not know to ask.

'So. When I . . . when I thought I was falling in love with someone, when I thought I had to flee this betrothal, well, I went to Civil. I sent him a message; when we had parted, he told me that if ever there was anything he could do for me, I had but to ask. So I sent the message, and a reply came, telling me where to go and who would help me. But here's the odd thing, Tom. Civil says now that he never got any message from me, nor sent me a reply. Certainly I never saw him after I left Buckkeep. Even when I reached Galeton, even when I stayed there, I did not see Civil. Or Lady Bresinga. Only servants. They made a place for my cat in their cattery.'

He fell silent and this time I sensed he would not go on without a nudge.

'But you did stay in the manor?'

'Yes. The room had been made up fresh, but I do not think that wing of the house was used much. Everyone kept emphasizing the need for secrecy if I was to slip away. So my meals were brought to me, and when word reached us that . . . that you were coming, then it was decided I had to leave again. But the people who were supposed to take me hadn't arrived yet. The cat and I went out that night and . . . your wolf found me.' He halted again.

'I know the rest,' I said, out of pity for both of us. Yet I asked, to be certain, 'And now Civil says he did not even know you were there?'

'Neither he nor his mother knew. He swore it. He suspects a servant intercepted my message to him and passed it on to someone else, who replied to it and arranged all the rest.'

'And this servant?'

'Is long gone. He vanished the same night I left there. We counted back the days and so it seems.'

'It seems to me you and Civil have discussed this in depth.' I could not keep the disapproval out of my voice.

'When Laudwine revealed himself and his true intentions, I thought that Civil must have been part of it. I felt betrayed by him. That was a part of my despair. I had not only lost my cat, but also discovered that my friend had betrayed me. I can't tell you how wonderful it felt to learn that I was wrong.' Relief and earnest trust shone in his face.

So he trusted Civil Bresinga, even to the point of believing that Civil could teach him the illegal magic of the Wit and never betray him. Or lead him into danger with it. How much of that trust, I wondered, was based on his aching need for a real friend? I compared it to his willingness to trust me and winced. Certainly I had given him small reason to bond with me, and yet he had. It was as if he were so isolated that any close contact at all became a friendship in his mind.

I held my tongue. I sat in silent wonder that I could do it, even as cold resolve flowed through me. I would get to the core of this Civil Bresinga, and see for myself what lurked there. If he were wormy with treachery, he would pay for it. And if he had betrayed Dutiful and then lied about it to him, if he trafficked upon the Prince's trusting nature, he would pay doubly. But for now, I would not speak of my suspicions to the lad. So, 'I see,' I said gravely.

'He offered to teach me about the Wit . . . Old Blood, he calls it. I didn't ask him, he offered.'

That didn't reassure me, but again I kept the thought to myself. I replied truthfully, 'Prince Dutiful, I would prefer you did not begin any lessons about Old Blood just now. As I have told you, we need to separate these two magics from each other. I think it would be best if we let the Wit lie fallow for now and concentrated on developing your Skill.'

For a time he stared out over the sea. I knew that he had looked forward to Civil teaching him, that he had hungered for that sharing. But he took a breath and replied quietly, 'If that is what you think best, that is what you and I shall do.' Then he turned and met my eyes. There was no reluctance in his face. He accepted the discipline I offered him.

He was of good temperament, amiable and willing to be taught.

I looked into his open glance and hoped I could be an instructor worthy of him.

We began that day. I sat down across the table from him and asked him to close his eyes and relax. I asked him to lower all barriers between himself and the outside world, to try to be open to all things. I spoke to him quietly, calmingly as if he were a colt waiting to feel the first weight of harness. Then I sat, watching the stillness in his unlined face. He was ready. He was like a pool of clear water that I could dive into.

If I could force myself to make the leap.

My Skill-walls were a defensive habit. They had, perhaps, been worn thin by carelessness, but I had never completely forsaken them. Reaching out to the Prince was different from simply plunging myself into the Skill. There was a risk of exposure. I was out of practice at Skilling, one person to another. Would I reveal more of myself than I intended? Even as I wondered such things, I felt the protective barriers around my thoughts grow thicker. To lower them completely was more difficult than one might think. They had been my protection for so long, the reflex was difficult to overcome. It was like looking into bright sunlight and trying to command my eyes not to squint. Slowly I pushed my walls down, until I felt I stood naked before him. There was just the distance of the tabletop to travel. I knew I could reach his thoughts but still I hesitated. I did not wish to overwhelm him, as Verity had me the first time we touched minds. Slowly, then. Gently.

I took a breath and eased towards him.

He smiled, his eyes still closed. 'I hear music.'

It was a double revelation to me. To this boy, Skilling came as easily as being told that he could. And his sensitivity was great, far greater than mine. When I reached out wide all around us, I became aware of Thick's music. It was there, trickling like running water in the back of my mind. It was like the wind outside the window, a thing I had unwittingly trained myself to ignore, like all the other susurrus of thoughts that float on the ether like fallen leaves on the surface of a woodland stream. Yet, as I brushed my mind against Dutiful's, he heard Thick's music clear and sweet, like a minstrel's pure voice standing strong amidst a chorus. Thick was indeed strong.

And the Prince's talent was as great, for at my grazing touch of Skill, he turned his regard towards me, and I was aware of him. It was a moment of shared cognizance as we *saw* one another through the bond. I looked into his heart and found within it not a shard of deception nor guile. The openness he had to the Skill was the same clarity that he offered to his life. I felt both small and dark in his presence, for I myself stood masked and let him behold only that which I could share with him, the single facet of myself that was his teacher.

Before I even bade him reach to me, his thoughts mingled with mine. *Is the music how you test me? I hear it. It's lovely.* His thoughts came clear and strong to me, but I sensed a Wit-edge to them. It was how he chose me to receive his Skill. He used his Wit-awareness of me to single my thoughts out from all the tangled muttering of thoughts in Buckkeep and beyond. I wondered how I was going to break him of that. *I think I've heard that tune before, but I can't recall the name of it.* His musing brought me back to the moment. Drawn towards the music, it was as if he took one step away from his self.

That settled it. Chade had been right. Thick would either have to be taught, or done away with. I shielded the Prince from that dark thought. *Careful now, lad. Let's go slowly. That you can hear the music is clear proof that you can Skill. What you sense now, the music and the random thoughts, is rather like the debris that floats upon a stream. You have to learn to ignore it and find instead the clear empty water where you can send your thoughts as you will. The thoughts you hear, the bits of whispers and notes of emotions, they all come from folk who have a tiny ability to Skill. You have to learn to ignore those sounds. As for the music, that comes from one stronger in the Skill, but for now he, too, must be ignored.*

But the music is so lovely.

It is. But the music is not Skill. The music is but one man's sending. It's like a leaf floating on the river's current. It's lovely and graceful, but beneath it flows the cold force of the river. If you let the leaf distract you, you may forget the strength of the river and be swept away by it.

Fool that I was, I had called his attention to it. I should have known that his talent outran his control of it. He turned his regard to it, and before I could intervene, he focused on it. And as quickly as that, he was swept away from me.

It was like watching a child wading in the shallows suddenly caught and borne away on a current. I was at first transfixed with horror. Then I plunged into it after him, well aware of how difficult it would be to catch up with him.

Later, I tried to describe it to Chade. 'Imagine one of those large gatherings where many conversations are being held at once. You start out listening to one, but then a comment from someone behind you catches your interest. Then, a phrase from someone else. Suddenly you are lost and tumbling in everyone else's words. And you cannot recall who you first began listening to, nor can you find your own thought. Each phrase you hear captures your attention, and you cannot distinguish one as more important than another. They all exist at once, equally attractive, and each one tears a piece of you free and carries it off.'

The Skill is not a place where sight exists, or sounds, or touch. Only thought. One moment, the Prince had been beside me, strong and intact and only himself. The next, he had given too much of his attention to a strong thought not his own. As one may swiftly unravel a large piece of knitting simply by drawing one loose thread out of it, so the Prince began to come undone. Catching up the thread and rolling it up does not restore the garment. Yet as I plunged through the maelstrom of random thoughts, I reached for him, snatching at the threads of him, gathering and grasping them even as I sought frantically for their ever-diminishing heart and source.

I had been in far stronger Skill-currents than the ones I navigated now, and I held myself intact. But the Prince's experience was far more limited. He was being torn apart, shredding rapidly in the clawing flow of sentience. To call him back, I would have to risk myself, but as the fault was mine, it seemed only fair.

Dutiful! I flung the thought out, and opened my mind wide, inviting any response. What I received back was a hailstorm of confusion as folk that were mildly Skilled sensed the intrusion of my thought into their minds, and in turn wondered what I was. The weight of their sudden regard fell upon me and then tugged at me, a thousand hooks tearing at me at once.

It was a strange sensation, at once alarming and exhilarating. Perhaps strangest of all was how much clearer my perception of it was. Perhaps Chade had been right to deprive me of elfbark. But that thought passed fleetly as I focused on what I must do. I shook them off wildly as a wolf would shake water from his coat. I felt their brief amazement and confusion as they fell away and then I was centred again. *DUTIFUL!* My thought bellowed not his name, but his concept of himself, the shape I had so clearly seen when I had first brushed my thoughts against his. What I felt in return from him was like a questioning echo, as if he could barely recall who he had been but moments before.

I netted him out of the tangled flux, sieving the threads of him and keeping them whilst letting the others flow through my perception of him. *Dutiful. Dutiful. Dutiful.* The tapping of my thought was a heartbeat for him, and a confirmation. Then for a time I held him, steadying him, and finally felt him come back to himself. Swiftly he gathered to his centre threads that I had not perceived as being part of him. I was a stillness around him, helping to hold the thoughts of the world at bay while he reformed himself.

Tom? He queried me at last. The template he offered me was a fractured portion of myself, the single facet I had presented to him.

Yes, I confirmed for him. *Yes, Dutiful. And that is enough and more than enough for today. Come away from this now. Come back to yourself.*

Together we separated ourselves from the tantalizing flow, and then peeled apart and went to our own bodies. Yet as we departed from the Skill-river, it seemed to me that someone else almost spoke to me, in a distant echo of thought.

That was well done. But next time, be more careful, with yourself as well as with him.

The message was arrowed at me, a thought with me as its target. I do not think Dutiful was aware of it at all. As I opened my eyes at the table and saw how pale he was, I pushed all consideration of that foreign Skilling aside. He slumped in his chair, head canted to one side, eyes nearly closed. Drops of sweat had tracked down his face from his hair and his lips puffed as the breath moved in and out of them. My first lesson had nearly been his last.

I rounded the table and crouched down beside him. 'Dutiful. Can you hear me?'

He gasped in a small breath. *Yes.* A terrible smile flowed onto his slack face. *It was so beautiful. I want to go back, Tom.*

'No. Don't do that; don't even think about it right now. Stay here and now. Focus on staying in your own body.' I glanced around the room. There was nothing here to offer him, no water, and no wine. 'You'll recover in a few moments,' I told him, not at all sure that was true. Why hadn't I planned for this possibility? Why hadn't I warned him first of the dangers of the Skill? Because I had never expected that he could Skill so well on his very first lesson? I had not thought he would be adept enough to get himself into trouble. Well, now I knew better. Teaching the Prince was going to be more dangerous than I had thought.

I set a hand to his shoulder, intending to help him sit up straighter. Instead, it was as if we leapt into one another's minds. I had lowered my walls to teach him, and Dutiful had no walls. The elation of the Skill flooded me as our minds met and matched. With him, I could hear the muted roar of Skill-thoughts like the carousing of a flood river in the distance. *Come away from that* I counselled him, and somehow drew him back from that brink. It was unnerving to feel his fascination with it. Once, I too had felt that drawn to the great Skill-current. It still exerted a tremendous attraction on me, but I also knew its dangers, and that made a balance. The Prince was like a baby reaching towards a candle flame. I drew him back from it, put myself between it and him, and at last sensed him curtaining his mind against the Skill-murmur.

'Dutiful.' I spoke his name aloud at the same time I Skilled it. 'It's time to stop now. This is enough for one day, and far too much for the first lesson.'

'But . . . I want . . .' His spoken words were little more than a whisper, but I was pleased he said them aloud.

'Enough,' I said, and took my hand from his shoulder. He leaned back in his chair with a sigh, rolling his head back. I fought temptations of my own. Could I share strength with him, to help him recover? Could I set walls for him, to protect him until he was better able to navigate the Skill-currents? Could I remove the Skill-induced command I had given him not to fight me?

When I had first been offered the chance to learn to Skill, I had seen it as a double-edged blade. There was great opportunity to learn the magic, but matched against it was always the danger that Galen the Skillmaster might learn I was Witted and destroy me. I had never approached the Skill as openly and eagerly as Dutiful did. Very quickly danger and pain had blunted my curiosity about the royal magic. I had used it with reluctance, drawn to it by its addictive lure yet frightened at how it threatened to consume me. When I had discovered that drinking elfbark tea could deaden me to the Skill's call, I had not hesitated to use it despite the drug's evil reputation. Now, with that drug cleared from my body, the Prince's excitement and the access to the Skill-scrolls an enthusiasm that I had thought long dead was rekindled in me. As much as Dutiful did, I longed to plunge back into that intoxicating current. I steeled my will. I must not let him feel that from me.

A glance at the climbing sun told me that our time together was nearing an end. Dutiful had recovered much of his colour but his hair was flat with sweat.

'Come, lad, pull yourself together.'

'I'm tired. I feel as if I could sleep the rest of the day.'

I did not mention my burgeoning pain. 'That's to be expected, but it's probably not a good idea. I want you to stay awake. Go do something active. Ride, or practise with your blade. Above all, rein your thoughts away from this first lesson. Don't let the Skill tempt you to come near it again today. Until I've taught you to balance focusing on it with resisting it, it's a dangerous thing for you. The Skill is a useful magic, but it has the power to draw a man as honey draws a bee. Venture there alone, be distracted by it, and you'll be gone to a place from which no one, not even I, can recall you. Yet here your body must remain, as a great drooling babe that takes no notice of anything.'

I cautioned him repeatedly that he must not try to use the Skill without me, that all his experiments with it must be made in my company. I suppose I lectured overlong on this point, for he finally told me, almost angrily, that he, too, had been there and knew he was lucky to have returned in one piece.

I told him I was glad he realized that, and on that note we parted. Yet at the door, he lingered, turning back to look at me.

'What is it?' I asked him when his silence had grown too long.

He suddenly looked very awkward. 'I want to ask you something.'

I waited, but had to finally say, 'And what did you want to ask me?'

He bit his lower lip and turned his gaze to the tower window. 'About you and Lord Golden,' he said at last. And halted again.

'What about us?' I asked impatiently. The morning was wearing on, and I had things to do. Such as somehow dampening the headache that now assailed me full force.

'Do you . . . do you like working for him?'

I knew instantly it was not the question he wanted to ask. I wondered what was troubling him. Was he jealous of my friendship with the Fool? Did he feel excluded somehow? I made my voice gentle. 'He has been my friend for a long time. I told you that before, in the inn on our way home. The roles we play now, master and man, are only for convenience. They afford me an excuse to attend occasions where a man such as myself would not be expected. That's all.'

'Then you don't truly . . . serve him.'

I shrugged a shoulder. 'Only when it fits my role, or when it pleases me to do a favour for him. We've been friends a long time, Dutiful. There is very little I wouldn't do for him, or him for me.'

The look on his face told me I had not laid to rest whatever was troubling him but I was willing at that point to let it go. I could wait until he found words for whatever it was. He also seemed willing to let it rest, for he turned away from me to the door. But with his hand on the handle, he spoke again, his voice harsh, the words wrung from him against his will. 'Civil says that Lord Golden likes boys.' When I said nothing, he added painfully,

'For bedding.' He kept staring at the door. The back of his neck grew scarlet.

I suddenly felt very tired. 'Dutiful. Look at me, please.'

'I'm sorry,' he said as he turned, but he couldn't quite meet my eyes. 'I shouldn't have asked.'

I wished he hadn't. I wished I hadn't discovered that the gossip was widespread enough to have reached his ears. Time to lay it to rest. 'Dutiful. Lord Golden and I do not bed together. In truth, I have never known the man to bed anyone. His actions towards Civil were a ploy, to provoke Lady Bresinga into asking us to leave her hospitality. That was all. But you cannot, of course, let Civil know that. It remains between you and me.'

He drew a deep breath and sighed it out. 'I did not want to think it of you. But you seem so close. And Lord Golden is, of course, a Jamaillian, and all know that they care little about such things.'

I debated for an instant about telling him the truth of that. I decided there was such a thing as burdening him with too much knowledge. 'It would probably be for the best if you didn't discuss Lord Golden with Civil. If the topic comes up, turn the conversation. Can you do that?'

He gave me a crooked smile. 'I, too, have been Chade's student,' he pointed out.

'I had noticed that you had become cooler towards Lord Golden of late. If that was the reason behind it, well, you create a loss for yourself in not getting to know him better. Once he is your friend, no man can ask for a truer one.'

He nodded, but said nothing. I suspected I had not dispelled all his doubts, but I had done the best I could.

He left the tower by the door, and I heard him turn the key in the lock before he descended the long, spiralling stair. If asked, he would tell folk that he had chosen the tower as his new place for dawn meditation. It seemed unlikely any would ask. He, Chade and I were the only ones prone to come here.

I glanced about the room again, and resolved to stock it against dangers such as we had had this morning. A bottle of brandy, in case Dutiful needed restoration. And we'd need a supply of wood for the hearth as winter gained more bite. I did not hold with Galen's austere teaching that students must be uncomfortable in order to learn well. I'd talk to Chade about it.

I yawned hugely, wishing I could go back to bed. I had arrived back at Buckkeep only the previous evening. A hot bath and a long report to Chade had filled hours when I would rather have been sleeping. He had taken custody of the scrolls and writings I'd brought back. I was not enthusiastic about that, but there was little in any of them that he would not already have known or guessed. After my bath to take the chill from my bones, I had sat before Chade's hearth and talked long with him.

A young brown ferret had already taken up residence in the tower room. His name was Gilly and he was obsessed with his own youth, his new territory, and rumours of rodents. His interest in me was limited to sniffing my boots thoroughly and then rooting his way into my pack. His eagerly darting mind was a pleasant counterpoint to the gloom of the tower room. His opinion of me was that I was a creature too big to eat that shared his territory.

Chade's gossip had covered everything from the Duke of Tilth arming runaway Chalcedean slaves and teaching them military tactics to Kettricken being called on to mediate between Lord Carolsin of Ashlake, who claimed that Lord Dignity of Timbery had seduced and stolen his daughter. Lord Dignity countered that the girl had come to him of her own will and that as they were now married, any issue of seduction no longer mattered. Then there was the matter of the new docks that one Buckkeep merchant wanted to build. Two others claimed that the docks would cut water access to their warehouses. Somehow this trivial matter that the town council should have resolved had become a citywide issue to be debated before the Queen. Chade spoke of a dozen or more other boring and wearisome issues, and it recalled to me that the concerns he and Kettricken dealt with every day went both wide and deep.

When I observed as much to him, he replied, 'And that is why we are fortunate that you have returned to Buckkeep, with Prince Dutiful as your sole focus. Kettricken thinks the only way it could be better would be if you could accompany him openly, but I still feel that your ability to observe the court without being too directly connected to the Prince has advantages of its own.'

There had been no further stirring from the Piebalds that Chade had detected. No new postings exposing Witted ones, no clandestine notes, no threats to the Queen. 'But what of Laurel's warning to the Queen, of Deerkin's rumours?' I asked him.

For a moment he looked discomfited. 'So you know of that, do you? Well, I was speaking only of direct tidings from the Piebalds to the Queen. We have taken Laurel's information seriously and done what we could to protect her, in a subtle way. She is training a new huntsman now, her new assistant. He is quite brawny and very adept with a sword, and accompanies her almost everywhere. I have great faith in him. Other than that, I have instructed the guards on the gates to be more suspicious of strangers, especially if animals accompany them. Obviously, we are aware that the Piebalds and the Old Blood are at odds. My spies have brought me rumours of families massacred in their beds, and then the houses burned to destroy all sign. All the better, some might say. Let them chew on one another and leave us in peace for a time. Oh, don't scowl at me like that. Some might say, I said, not that I wished they would all kill one another off. What would you have me do? Turn out the guard? No one has come seeking the Queen's intervention. Shall we chase shadows that no one has accused of committing crimes? I need something solid, Fitz. A man or men, named by name, and accused of committing these murders. Until someone of Old Blood dares step forward and speak out, there is little I can do. If it is any comfort to you, the rumours alone put the Queen into a fury.' And then he turned his talk to other things.

Civil Bresinga was still at court, still seeing Dutiful daily, and still showing no overt signs of being a traitor or plotter. I was pleased that in my absence Chade had set other spies onto the boy. Harvest Fest had gone well. The Outislanders had seemed to enjoy it. Dutiful and Elliania's formal courtship continued under the watchful eyes of all. They walked together, rode together, dined together, danced together. Buckkeep minstrels sang of Elliania's beauty and grace. On the surface, everything was absolutely correct, but Chade suspected the young couple was less than enamoured of one another. Chade hoped they could remain on civil terms until the Narcheska departed for her own land. The negotiations with the traders who had accompanied the Narcheska's delegation were going very well indeed. Bearns uncertainty about the alliance had been somewhat mollified when the Queen had formally awarded Seal Bay permission to be the Six Duchies' exclusive trading port for furs, ivory and oil. From Buckkeep Town would ship the products of the Inland Duchies, the wines and brandy and grain. Shoaks and Rippon would claim the bulk of the trade in wool, cotton, leather and such.

'Do you think each duchy will respect the other's licence?' I had asked idly as I swirled brandy in my glass.

Chade snorted. 'Of course not. Smuggling is an old and honoured profession in every port town I've ever visited. But each duke has been given a bone to growl over, and each is already calculating the value that the alliance with the Outislands will bring to his home province. That is all we were truly after. To convince all of them that the entire Six Duchies would profit from this.' Then he had sighed and leaned back in his chair, rubbing the bridge of his nose. A moment later he shifted uncomfortably, and then said, 'Oh.'

From a fold in his robe, he brought out the figurine from the beach. She dangled from her chain, small and perfect. Her sleek black hair was crowned with a blue ornament. 'I found this on a pile of rags in the corner. Is it yours?'

'No. But that "pile of rags" was probably my old work-clothes. The necklace belongs to the Prince.' As Chade frowned at me in puzzlement, I added, 'I told you about it. The time we spent on that strange beach. He picked it up there. I ended up putting it in his purse for him. I should give it back to him.'

Chade had scowled then. 'When he told me his tale of his adventures, he had little to say about the journey through the Skill-pillars or his time on the beach. He certainly never mentioned this.'

'He wasn't trying to deceive you, Chade. Even for an experienced Skill-user, going through a pillar is an unsettling experience. I took him through to the beach without warning; he had no idea what had happened to him. And, to return, I took him through three pillars. I'm not surprised his memories of it are scrambled. I'm just glad he is sane; most of Regal's young Skill-users did not fare so well.'

A frown furrowed his brow. 'So. An inexperienced Skill-user cannot pass through a pillar on his own?'

'I don't know. The first time I went through one, it was purely accidental on my part. But I had spent that whole day in a sort of Skill-stupor, on an Elderling road . . . Chade. What are you thinking?'

His quizzical look was too innocent.

'Chade, stay away from those pillars. They are dangerous. Perhaps more dangerous to you, who may have traces of Skill-magic in your blood, than to ordinary folk.'

'What are you afraid of?' he asked me quietly. 'That I might discover that I possessed an aptitude for the Skill? That perhaps, if I had been taught as a boy, I too could wield it now?'

'Perhaps you could. But what I fear is that you will read some cracked and dusty old scroll and risk yourself in some experiment just when the Six Duchies needs you most.'

Chade made a disapproving grunt as he got up to place the figurine on his mantel. 'And that reminds me of another thing. The Queen sends you this.' He picked up a small scroll from the mantel and handed it to me. Unfurled, I immediately recognized Kettricken's squared hand. She had never become accustomed to the flowing script we used in the Six Duchies. Twelve careful runes were inked there, and by each one was a single word. 'Harbour, Beach, Glacier, Cave, Mountain, Motherhouse, Hunter, Warrior, Fisher, Allmother, Smith, Weaver.'

'It's from some game she was playing with Peottre. I see why she sent you this. Do you?'

I nodded. 'The runes look similar to the runes on the Skill-pillars. They are not the identical runes, but they look as if they might be from the same system of writing.'

'Very good. But one, at least, is almost identical. Here. These are the runes that marked the pillar that you and the Prince used. The one near the old mounds.'

Chade took up a second scroll from the table between us. It was obviously the work of a true scribe. It showed four carefully replicated symbols, with the orientation of each facet of the pillar marked, as well as notations on the size and placement of the originals. Chade had obviously sent his little bees out to gather information for him. 'Which one took you to the beach?' Chade asked me.

'This one.' It was similar to the one for 'Beach' on Kettricken's scroll, save for an extra tail or two.

'And did an identical one bring you back?'

I frowned. 'I had little time to note the appearance of the one that brought me back. I see you've been busy in my absence.'

He nodded. 'There are other stone pillars within the Six Duchies. I'll have information on them within the next few weeks. Obviously they were originally used by Skilled-ones, and somehow the knowledge of how they worked was lost for a time. But we have a chance to regain it.'

'Only at great danger. Chade, may I point out that our trip to the beach ended with Dutiful and me underwater? It could have been much worse. Imagine if one of the exit pillars was face down on the ground. Or shattered. What happens to the user then?'

Chade looked only mildly flustered as he said, 'Well, then I assumed you would see the way was blocked and come right back.'

'My assumption is that I would be expelled from the pillar into solid stone. It isn't like a doorway where you can halt and look out. It dumps you out, as if you'd stepped through a trapdoor.'

'Ah. I see. Well, then their use will have to be investigated much more carefully. But as we read the Skill-scrolls, we may be able to decipher what each rune means and at least establish where each "gate" originally opened. And thus, eventually, determine which ones are safe to use. And perhaps right or repair the others. What other Skill-users did in the past, we can reclaim.'

'Chade. I am not at all certain that those pillars were the work of Skill-users. Perhaps some have used them, but each time I've passed through one, the disorientation and the . . .' I groped for words. 'Foreignness,' I hazarded at last. 'The foreignness makes me wonder if Skill-users are the ones who built them. If they were built by humans at all.'

'Elderlings?' he had suggested after a moment.

'I don't know,' I had replied.

The conversation echoed through my mind as I gazed at the racked scrolls and the locked chests in the Skill-tower. The answers might be here, waiting for me.

I selected three scrolls from the rack from among the ones that looked most recent. I'd start with the ones in letters and languages that I knew well. I found none by Solicity, which struck me as odd. Certainly, our last Skillmistress must have committed something of her wisdom to paper; it was generally assumed that one who achieved Master status would have something unique to pass on to their followers. But if Solicity had ever written anything, it was not amongst these scrolls. The three I finally chose were by someone named Treeknee, and were labelled as a translation of an older manuscript by Skillmaster Oklef. The translations had been done at the behest of Skillmaster Barley. I had never heard of any of them. I tucked the three scrolls under my arm and departed by way of the false panel in the hearth mantel.

I intended to leave the scrolls in Chade's tower room. They did not belong in Tom Badgerlock's chamber. But before I went there, I made a brief detour through the hidden corridors until I reached an irregular crack in the wall. I approached it silently and peeped through it. Civil Bresinga's chamber was empty. This confirmed what Chade had told me last night, that young Civil would ride out with a party accompanying the Prince and his intended. Good. Perhaps I'd have the opportunity for a quick tour of his rooms, not that I expected it would yield much. Other than his clothes and the small daily possessions of a man, he kept nothing there. In the evenings, his chamber was either empty or he was alone in it. When he was there, his most common diversion was playing a small pipe, badly, or indulging in Smoke and staring out of the window. In all the spying I'd ever done, Civil was the most boring subject I'd ever had.

I headed up to Chade's tower room, but paused before triggering the hidden catch, to listen and then peep into the room. I heard a soft-mouthed muttering, the thud of firewood being unloaded. I nearly turned aside, thinking I could leave the scrolls in the corridor until later. Then I decided there were too many laters in my life, and that I was leaving too much up to Chade. Only I could do this, really. I took a slow and calming breath, focused myself, and then eased my walls down.

Please don't be startled. I'm coming into the room.

It didn't help. Almost as soon as I got through the door, the wave hit me. *Don't see me, stink dog! Don't hurt me! Go away!*

But my walls were up and I was braced.

'Stop that, Thick. By now you should know that it doesn't work on me, and that I have no intention of hurting you. Why are you so afraid of me?' I set the scrolls down on the worktable.

Thick had stood to meet me. At his feet was a hod of firewood. Half had been loaded into the box by the hearth. He squinted his sleepy-looking eyes at me. 'Not afraid. I just don't like you.'

There was an oddness to his voice, not a lisp, but an unfinished edge to his words, as if a very young child spoke them. Afterward, he stood glaring at me, the end of his tongue resting on his lower lip. I decided that despite his short stature and childish voice and ways, he was not a child. I would not speak to him as one.

'Really? I try to know people before I decide I don't like them. I don't think I've given you any reason to dislike me.'

He scowled at me, his brow furrowing. Then he gestured around the room. 'Lots of reasons. You make more work. Water for baths. Bring up the food, take away the dishes. A lot more work than the old man only.'

'Well, I can't deny that.' I hesitated, then asked, 'What would make it fair?'

'Fair?' He squinted at me suspiciously. Very cautiously, I lowered my guard and tried to sense what he was feeling. I needn't have bothered. It was obvious. All his life, he had been mocked and teased. He was sure this was more of it.

'I could give you money for the things you do for me.'

'Money?'

'Coins.' I had a few loose in my pouch. I lifted it and jingled it at him.

'NO. No coins. I don't want coins. He hit Thick, take the coins. Hit Thick, take the coins.' As he repeated himself, he mimed the motion, swinging a meaty fist on his short arm.

'Who does?'

He narrowed his eyes at me, then shook his head stubbornly. 'Someone. You don't know. I didn't tell no one. Hit Thick, take the coins.' He swung again, obviously caught up in remembered anger. His breath was beginning to come more quickly.

I tried to cut through it. 'Thick. Who hits you?'

'Hit Thick, take the coins.' He swung again, tongue and lower lip out now, eyes squinted nearly shut. I let the punch spend itself on the empty air, then stepped in. I set my hands on his shoulders, intending to calm him so I could speak to him. Instead he yelled loud, a wild wordless cry and sprang back from me. At the same moment, *DON'T SEE ME! DON'T HURT ME!*

I winced from the impact and recoiled. 'Thick. Don't hurt me!' I retorted. Then, catching my breath, I added, 'That doesn't always work, does it? Some people don't feel you push them away with that. But there are other ways, ways that I could stop them.'

So. Some of his fellow servants were either completely immune to his Skill-touch, or sensed it only enough to be angered by it. Interesting. As strongly Skilled as he was, I would have thought he could impose his will on almost anyone. I should tell Chade about this. I set the thought aside for later. His blow on top of the Skill-headache from earlier made me feel as if blood were running down the backs of my eyes. I forced my words past a slamming red pain in my skull. 'I can make them stop, Thick. I will make them stop.'

'What? Stop what?' he demanded suspiciously. 'Stop Thick?'

'No. The others. I will make them stop hitting Thick and taking his coins.'

'Humph.' He blew out his breath in a disbelieving snort. 'He said, "get a sweet". But then he took the coins. Hit Thick, take the coin.'

'Thick.' It was hard to break in past his fixation. 'Listen to me. If I make them stop hitting you, if I make them not take your sweets, will you stop hating me?'

He stood, saying nothing, but scowling. I decided that the two ideas were not connecting. I made it simpler. 'Thick. I can make them stop bothering you.'

He made his 'humph' again. Then, 'You don't know. I didn't tell you.' He dumped the rest of the firewood from his hod willy-nilly into the box and stumped off. When he was gone, I sank down for a time, clutching my head. It was all I could do to stagger over to the abandoned scrolls and put them on the bedside table. I sat down on the edge of the bed, and then lay down just for a moment. My head sank into the cool pillow. I fell asleep.

EIGHT

Ambitions

'Thus every magic has its space in the spectrum of magic, and together they make up the great circle of power. All magical lore is encompassed in the circle, from the skills of the humble hedge-wizard with his charms, the scryer with his bowl or crystal, the bestial magic of the Wit and the celestial magic of the Skill, and all the homely magics of hearth and heart. All can be placed as I have shown them, in a great spectrum, and it must be clear to any eye that a common thread runs through all of them.

But that is not to say that any user can or should attempt to master the full circle of magic. Such a wide sweep of the art is not given to any mortal, and with good reason. No one is meant to be master of all powers. A Skill-user may expand his expertise to scrying, and there have been tales of beast-magickers who had mastered some of the fire- magic- and water-finding skills of the hedge-wizards. As illustrated by the chart, each of these lesser arcs of magic are adjacent to the greater magics, and thus a mage can expand his powers to include these minor skills as well. But to have larger ambitions than these is a great error. For one who augurs through a crystal to attempt to master the bringing of fire is a mistake. These magics are not neighbouring magics, and the strains of supporting their differences may bring discord to his mind. For a Skill-user to demean himself with the beast-magic of the Wit is to invite the decay and debasement of his higher magic. Such a vile ambition should be condemned.'

Treeknee's translation of *The Circle of Magic* by Skillmaster Oklef

Looking back, I suspect that I learned more at Dutiful's first Skill lesson than he did. Fear and respect were what I learned. I had dared to set myself up as a teacher of something that I barely grasped myself. And so my days and nights became fuller than I had ever expected, for I must be both student and teacher, yet could not surrender my other roles as Lord Golden's servant or Hap's father or the Farseer's spy.

As winter shortened the days, my lessons with Dutiful began in the black of the morning. Usually we left Verity's tower before the true dawn lightened the sky. Both the boy and Chade were eager for us to press on, but I was determined to err on the side of caution after our near disaster.

In the same spirit, I had procrastinated against Chade's demands that I at least evaluate Thick's Skill-ability. I need not have bothered. Thick was as reluctant to have any contact with me as I was to teach him. Thrice, Chade had arranged for Thick to meet me in his chambers. Each time, the half-wit had not been there at the appointed hour. Nor had I lingered, hoping my wayward student was merely late. I arrived, noted his absence, and left. Each time, Thick had told Chade that he had 'forgotten' the appointment, but he could not hide his apprehension and distaste from Chade.

'What did you do to him, to create such aversion?' Chade had demanded of me. To which I had been able to honestly reply that I had done nothing. I knew of no reason that the half-wit would dread me. I was only glad that he did.

My lesson times with Dutiful were the exact opposite of that. The boy greeted me warmly and eagerly every time he arrived, and anticipated his lessons with eagerness. It amazed me. Sometimes I wondered wistfully what it would have been like if Prince Verity had been my first Skill-instructor. Would I have responded as readily as his son did to me? My own memories of Skillmaster Galen's lessons were painful in the extreme. I had seen no wisdom in emulating his set routines and mental exercises designed to prepare a student to Skill. In truth, Dutiful seemed not to need any of them. For the Prince, Skilling was an effortless spilling of his soul. I soon wondered if I had not benefited from my own early struggles to master the Skill. I had had to force my way out past my own walls; Dutiful could not seem to find any boundaries. He was as prone to share his upset stomach with me as he was to convey his thoughts. When he opened himself, it was as if he opened the floodgate to all of the scattered and wafting thought in the world. Standing witness and guard in his mind, it near overwhelmed me. It frightened and fascinated him, and both emotions kept him from achieving full concentration on what he was attempting. Worse, when he Skilled out to me, it was as if he tried to thread a needle with a rope. Verity had once told me that being Skilled to by my father Chivalry was like being trampled by a horse: he barged in, dropped his information, and fled. So it was with Dutiful.

'If he can master his talent, he will swiftly exceed his teacher,' I complained to Chade one very late night when he chanced to visit his old chambers. I sat at our old compounding table, surrounded by a welter of Skill-scrolls. 'I felt almost relief when I started teaching him Kettle's Stone game. He found it difficult to grasp at first, though he seems to be catching on to it now. I hope it will slow him down, and help him learn to look for deeper patterns in his magic. All else seems to come to him so easily. He Skills as a hound pup instinctively puts his nose to a trail. As if he is remembering how to do it, rather than being taught.'

'And that is bad?' the old assassin asked genially. He began to rummage amongst the tea herbs on the high shelves. Those shelves had always been reserved for his most dangerous and potent concoctions. I smiled briefly as he clambered up on a stool, and wondered if he still supposed them safely out of my reach.

'It could be dangerous. Once he surpasses me and begins to experiment with the Skill's other powers, he will be venturing where I have no experience. I will not even be able to warn him of the dangers, let alone protect him.' In disgust, I slid a Skill-scroll aside and pushed my awkward translation after it. There, too, Dutiful excelled me. The lad had Chade's gift for alphabets and languages. My translations were a plodding word-by-word puzzling out, while Dutiful read sentence by sentence and jotted the sense of them down in concise prose. Years of absence from such work had blunted my language abilities. I wondered if I envied my pupil's quickness. Would that make me a bad teacher?

'Perhaps he got it from you,' Chade observed thoughtfully
'Got what?'

'The Skill. We know that you touched minds with him from the time he was very small. Yet you say the Wit is not a magic that allows that. Therefore, it must have been the Skill. Therefore, perhaps you taught him to Skill when he was a tiny boy, or at least prepared his mind to be ready for it.'

I didn't like the trend of his thoughts. Nettle instantly sprang to my mind and a wave of guilt swept through me. Had I endangered her as well? 'You're just trying to make it my own fault.' I tried to make my tone light, as if that would chase away my sudden dread. I sighed and reluctantly pulled my translation work back in front of me. If I was to have any hope of continuing as Dutiful's teacher, I needed to learn more of the Skill myself. This was a scroll that suggested a series of exercises that a student should be given to improve his focus. I hoped it would be useful to me.

Chade came to look over my shoulder. 'Hmm. What did you think of the other scroll, the one on pain and the Skill?'

I glanced up at him, puzzled. 'What other scroll?'

He looked annoyed. 'You know the one. I left it out for you.'

I gave our littered table a meaningful glance. There were at least a dozen other scrolls and papers cluttering it. 'Which one?'

'It was one of these. I showed it to you, boy. I'm sure of it.'

I was equally certain he had not, but I held my tongue. Chade's memory was failing him. I knew it. So did he, but he would not admit it. I had also discovered that even a mention of that possibility would throw him into a fury that was more unsettling to me than the notion that my old mentor was not as sharp as he had been. So I silently watched him poke through the jumble of writings until he came to a scroll with a decorative blue edge. 'See. Here it is, right where I left it for you. You haven't studied it at all.'

'No. I haven't.' I admitted it easily, hoping to avoid the whole topic of whether or not he'd shown me the scroll. 'What did you say it's about?'

He gave me a disgusted glance. 'It's about pain related to Skilling. The sorts of headaches you have. It suggests some remedies, exercises as well as herbs, but it also says that in time you may simply stop having the headaches. But it's the note towards the end that interested me. Treeknee says that some Skillmasters used a pain barrier to keep their students from experimenting on their own. He doesn't say that it might be made strong enough to prevent a man from Skilling at all. It interested me for two reasons. I wondered if Galen had done it to you. And I wondered if it might be a way to control Thick.' I noticed he did not suggest it as a safety barrier for the Prince.

So we were back to Thick again. Well, the old man was right. Sooner or later, we'd have to deal with him. Still, 'I'd be reluctant to use pain as a curb on any creature. Thick Skills out his music near constantly. Give him pain for doing that, block him from it . . . I don't know what that would do to him.'

Chade made a dismissive noise. He had known I would not do it before he asked me. But I knew Galen would not have scrupled to hobble me in such a way. I wondered. Chade spread the scroll out before me, his gnarled fingers bracketing the passage in question. I read it over, but discovered little he had not already said. Then I leaned back in my chair. 'I'm trying to remember when Skilling first started to hurt. It always left me wearied. The first time Verity drew strength from me, I fainted dead away. Any real effort with it left me almost sick with fatigue. But I don't recall the Skill having an aftermath of pain until . . .' I pondered for a time, then shook my head. 'I can't draw a line. The first time I Skill-walked, by accident, I woke trembling with weakness. I used the elfbark for it, then and in the times that followed. And after a time, the weakness after I'd Skilled began to be pain as well.' I sighed. 'No. I don't think the pain is a barrier anyone put in me.'

Chade had wandered back to his shelves. He turned with two corked bottles in his hands. 'Could it be because you have the Wit? Much is said in the scrolls about the dangers of using both magics.'

Was the old man trying to remind me of everything I didn't know? I hated his questions. They were stark warnings that I was guiding my prince through unknown territory. I shook my head wearily. 'Again, Chade, I don't know. Perhaps if the Prince begins to have pain after Skilling, we can assume that.'

'I thought you were going to separate his Wit from his Skill.'

'I would if I knew how. All I can do is try to make him use the

Skill in ways that force him to use it independently of the Wit. I don't know how to make him separate the two magics any more than I know how to remove the Skill-command I set on him back when we were on the beach.'

He lifted one white eyebrow as he measured herbs into a teapot. 'The command not to fight you?'

I nodded.

'Well, it seems that should be a simple thing to me. Simply reverse it.'

I clenched my teeth. I did not say, 'it only seems simple to you because you have neither magic and don't know what you are talking about'. I was weary, I told myself, and frustrated. I should not take it out on the old man. 'I don't quite know how I burned the command into him, and so I don't quite know how to lift it. "Simply reverse it" is not simple at all. What would I command him? "Fight me?" Remember that Chivalry did the same thing to Skillmaster Galen. In anger, he burned a command into him. And he and Verity never puzzled out how to remove it.'

'But Dutiful is your prince and your student. Surely that puts you on a different footing.'

'I don't see what that has to do with it,' I told him, and tried not to sound short-tempered.

'Well. Only that I think he might help you remove it.' He shook a few drops of something into the teapot. He paused, then asked delicately, 'Is the Prince aware of what you did to him? Does he know you commanded him not to fight you?'

'No!' I did let my temper show on that word. Then I took a breath. 'No, and I'm ashamed I did it, and ashamed to admit to you that I'm afraid to tell him. In so many ways, I'm still getting to know him, Chade. I don't want to give him reason to distrust me.' I rubbed my brow. 'We did not meet one another under the best circumstances, you know.'

'I know, I know.' He came to pat me on the shoulder. 'So. What have you been doing with him?'

'Mostly getting to know him. We've been translating scrolls together. And I "borrowed" some practice blades from the weapons sheds, and we've tried one another that way. He's a good swordsman. If the number of bruises he has given me are a fair indication, then I think I lightened my Skill-command if not erased it.'

'But you aren't sure?'

'Not really. When we spar, we aren't truly trying to hurt one another. It's a game, just as it is when we wrestle. Still, I've never noticed that he holds back at all, or allows me to win more easily.'

'Well. You know, I think it's very good that he has you for those sorts of things. As well as the Skill lessons. I think he was missing that sort of rough companionship in his life.' Chade took the kettle from the hearth and poured hot water over his newest mixture of leaves. 'I suppose only time will tell. So. Do you Skill at all with him?'

I lifted a hand to my nose. The odour from the pot made my eyes water but Chade didn't seem to notice. 'Yes. We've been doing some exercises to help him focus his magic.'

'Focus?' Chade swirled the pot, then put the lid on it.

'Right now when he Skills he shouts from the top of the tower and anyone listening could hear him. We strive to narrow that shout, to make it a whisper only to me. And we work to have him convey only what he wishes to tell me, not all the information in his mind at that time. So we do set exercises. I have him try to reach my mind while he is at table and carrying on a conversation. Then we refine it; can he reach my mind, convey what he is eating, while keeping to himself who his companions are? After that, we set other goals. Can he wall me out of his mind? Can he set walls that I could not breach, even in the dead of night while he sleeps?'

Chade frowned to himself as he found a cup, and wiped it clean with one end of his trailing sleeve. I tried not to smile. Sometimes, when we were alone like this, he reverted from the grand noble to the intent old man who had taught me my first trade. 'Do you think that's wise? Teaching him how to close you out of his mind?'

'Well, he has to learn to do it, in case he ever encounters someone who doesn't have his best interests at heart. At the moment I'm the only other Skill-user he can practise with.'

'There's Thick,' Chade pointed out as he poured for himself. The hot liquid splashed, greenish-black, into his cup. He regarded it with distaste.

'I think one student is all I can deal with right now,' I demurred. 'Did you take any action on Thick's problem?'

'What problem?' Chade took his cup over in front of the fire.

I felt a moment's alarm and tried to conceal it by speaking casually. 'I thought I told you about it. He was having problems with the other servants hitting him and taking his money.'

'Oh. That.' He leaned back in his chair as if it were of no consequence. I breathed a silent sigh of relief. He hadn't forgotten our conversation. 'I found a reason for the cook to give him separate quarters. Ostensibly, that's where he works, you know. The kitchens. So now he has his own room near the pantries. It's small, but I gather it's the first time he's ever had any place all to himself. I think he likes it.'

'Well. That's good, then.' I paused for a moment. 'Did you ever consider sending him away from Buckkeep? Just until the Prince has a better grasp on the Skill? There are times when his wild Skilling is a bit distracting. It's like trying to work a complicated sum while near you someone else is counting out loud.'

Chade sipped from his revolting cup. He made a face, then swallowed determinedly. I winced sympathetically, and said nothing as he reached a long arm to seize my wine glass and wash away the taste. When he spoke, his voice was hoarse. 'As long as Thick remains the only other Skill candidate we have, I will not send him away. I want him where we can watch over him. And where you can try to win his regard. Have you made any efforts with him?'

'I haven't had the opportunity.' I got up and brought another glass back to the table and poured more wine for both of us. Chade came back to the table. He set the teacup and the wine glass side by side and eyed them dolorously. 'I don't know if he's avoiding me, or if his other duties for you simply have kept him out of my way.'

'He has had other tasks, of late.'

'Well, that explains his lack of care with his work here,' I observed sourly. 'Some days he remembers to replace the candle stubs with fresh tapers, some days he doesn't. Some days the hearth is cleared of ashes and wood laid for the fire, and sometimes the old ashes and coals remain. I think it's because he dislikes me so. He does as little as he possibly can.'

'He can't read, so I can't give him a list of tasks. Sometimes he remembers to do all I tell him, sometimes he doesn't. That only made him a poor servant, not a lazy or spiteful one.' Chade took another mouthful of his brew. This time, despite his efforts, he coughed, spraying the table. I snatched the scrolls out of harm's way. He wiped his mouth with his kerchief and then blotted the table. 'Beg pardon,' he said gravely, his eyes watering. He took a gulp of wine.

'What's in the tea?'

'Sylvleaf. Witch's butter. Seacrepe. And a few other herbs.' He took another mouthful of it and chased it down with more wine.

'What's it for?' A memory tickled at the back of my mind.

'Some problems I've been having,' he demurred, but I rose and began to shuffle through the scrolls on the table. I came up with the one I wanted almost immediately. The illustrations were still bright despite the years. I unrolled it and pointed to the sylvleaf drawing.

'Those herbs are named here as being helpful to open a candidate to the Skill.'

He gave me a flat look. 'So?'

'Chade. What are you doing, what are you trying?'

For a moment, he just looked at me. Then he asked coldly, 'Are you jealous? Do you also think my birthright should be forbidden me?'

'What?'

An odd sort of anger broke from him in a tumble of words. 'I was never even given the chance to be tested for the Skill. Bastards are not taught it. Not until you, when Shrewd made an exception. Yet I am as much Farseer as you are. And I've some of the lesser magics, as well you should know by now.'

He was upset, and I didn't know why. I nodded and said calmingly, 'Such as your scrying in water. It was how you knew of the Red Ship attack on Neatbay all those years ago.'

'Yes,' he said with satisfaction. He sat back in his chair, but his hands scuttled along the table's edge like spiders. I wondered if the drugs in the tea were affecting him. 'Yes, I have magics of my own. And perhaps, given the chance, I'd have the magic of my blood, the magic I've a right to. Don't try to deny it to me, Fitz. For all those years, my own brother forbade me even being tested. I was good enough to watch his back, good enough to teach his sons and his grandson. But I was never good enough to be given my rightful magic.'

I wondered how long the resentment had festered in him. Then I recalled his excitement when Shrewd allowed me to be taught, and his frustration when I seemed to fail and would not even discuss my lessons with him. This was a very old anger, unveiled to me for the first time.

'Why now?' I asked him conversationally. 'You've had the Skill scrolls for fifteen years. Why have you waited?' I thought I knew what the answer would be: that he had wanted me to be close by, to help him with it. Again, he surprised me.

'What makes you think I waited? But, yes, I've applied more effort to it of late, because my need for this magic become so desperate. We've spoken of this before. I knew you would not wish to help me.'

It was true. Yet if he had asked me just then, I would not have been able to say why. I avoided the question. 'What is your need now? The land is relatively peaceful. Why risk yourself?'

'Fitz. Look at me. Look at me! I'm getting old. Time has played me a treacherous trick. When I was young and able, I was locked up in these chambers, forced to remain hidden and powerless. Now, when I have a chance to set the Farseer throne on a firm foundation, when indeed my family needs me most, I am old and becoming feeble. My mind totters, my back aches, my memories cloud. Do you think I haven't seen the dread on your face whenever I tell you I must look through my journals to find you a titbit of information? Imagine then how I feel. Imagine how it is, Fitz, not to have your own memories at your beck and call any more. To grope for a name, suddenly to lose the thread of a conversation in the midst of a jest. As a boy, when you thought your body had betrayed you with your fits, you plunged into despair. Yet you always had your mind. I think I'm losing mine.'

It was a terrible revelation, as if I had discovered that the foundations of Buckkeep Castle itself were weakening and crumbling. Only recently had I begun to appreciate fully all that Chade juggled for Kettricken. The enmeshing net of social relationships that formed the politics of Buckkeep had snared me, and from within its folds, I struggled to comprehend it all. When I was a boy, Chade had interpreted for me all that went on in the castle, and I had been content to accept his word on it. Now I viewed things with a man's eyes, and found the level of complication astonishing.

And fascinating. It was like Kettle's Stone game, played on a grand scale. Markers moved, alliances changed and power shifted, sometimes all within a passage of hours. It made Chade's depth of knowledge all the more amazing, as he conducted Queen Kettricken's balancing act on the shifting loyalties of the nobility. I could not possibly keep up with it all, and yet it all was interconnected.

Since I had returned to Buckkeep, I had marvelled that he could integrate it all, and dreaded the coming of a day when he could not. None of this was as easy for him as it once had been. The presence of his journals, massive volumes of pages bound flat in the Jamaillian style, were an indication that he did not trust his own memory any more. There were six identical volumes, with covers of red, blue, green, yellow, purple and goldenrod, one for each of the Six Duchies. How he determined what information belonged in each was beyond my understanding. A seventh volume, white with the Farseer Buck on the front, was where he penned his day-to-day minutiae. This he referred to most often, leafing through it for scraps of gossip or the text of a conversation or the summary of a spy's report. Even within this secret volume hidden in the concealed chamber, he made his entries in his own cryptic words. He did not offer me access to his volumes and I did not ask it. I am sure there was much in them that I would not have wished to know. And it was safer so for the spies who toiled for the Six Duchies, for I could not accidentally betray the secrets I did not know. Yet knowing Chade feared the failing of his memory still did not explain to me what he did. 'I know things have been difficult for you lately. I've worried about you.

But why, then, would you tax yourself further with trying to learn the Skill?'

His hands became knotty fists on the table edge. 'Because of what I've read. Because of what you've told me you've done with it. The texts say a Skill-user can repair his own body, can extend his years. How old was that Kettle you journeyed with? Two hundred years, three hundred? And she was still spry enough to take on a Mountain winter. You yourself have told me that you reached into your wolf and with it made him whole again, at least for a time. If I could open myself to your Skill, could not you do that for me? Or, if you refused, as I think you might, could not I do it for myself?'

As if he needed to show his strength of resolve, he snatched up the cup and drained it in a manful draught. Then he choked and sputtered. His lips were wet with the dark potion as he seized his wine glass and gulped the contents. 'I notice you do not spring to offer me your aid,' he observed bitterly as he wiped his mouth.

I sighed deeply. 'Chade. I barely know the rudiments I strive to teach the Prince. How can I offer to teach you a magic I barely understand myself? What if I . . . .'

'That has been your greatest weakness, Fitz. All your life. Too much caution. Not enough ambition. Shrewd liked that in you. He never feared you, as he did me.'

As I gaped in pain at him, he spoke on, seeming unmindful of the blow he had just dealt me. 'I did not expect you to approve. Not that your approval is necessary. I think it is best I explore the edges of this magic on my own. Once I have the door open, well, then we shall see what you think of your old mentor. I think I will surprise you, Fitz. I think I have it, that perhaps I've always had it. You yourself gave me the hint of that, when you spoke of Thick's music. I've heard it. I think. On the edges of my mind, just as I start to fall asleep at night. I think I have the Skill.'

I could not think of a word to say to that. He was waiting for me to react to his claim to have the Skill. All I could think was that I did not feel I had ever lacked in ambition, only that my aspirations had not matched his goals for me. So the silence grew and became ever more awkward. And when he broke it, with a complete change of topic, it only made it worse.

'Well. I see you've nothing to say to me. So.' He forced a smile to his face and inquired, 'How is your boy doing at his apprenticeship?'

I stood up. 'Poorly. I suppose that, like his would-be father, he lacks ambition. Good night, Chade.'

And I left and went down to my servant's chambers for the rest of the night. I did not sleep. I dared not. Of late, I avoided my bed, surrendering to it only when complete exhaustion demanded it. It was not just that I needed to spend those dark hours in my studies of the Skill-scrolls, but because when I did close my eyes, I was besieged. Nightly I would set my Skill-walls before retiring, and near nightly, Nettle assaulted those walls. Her strength and her single-mindedness unsettled me. I did not want my daughter to Skill. There was no way I could bring her to Buckkeep to instruct her, and I feared for her, attempting these explorations on her own. I reasoned that to let her through would only encourage her in her pursuit of this magic. As long as she did not know that she Skilled, as long as she thought she was just reaching out to some dream companion, some other-worldly being she had imagined, perhaps I could keep her safe. And frustrated. If I had reached back to her even once, even to push her away, I feared she might somehow grasp who and where I was. Better to leave her in ignorance. Perhaps, after a time of failing to reach me, she might give it up. Perhaps she would find something else to distract her, a handsome neighbour lad or an interest in a trade. So I hoped. But I arose each morning near as haggard as I had gone to bed.

The rest of my personal life had become equally frustrating. My efforts to get time to speak to Hap alone were no more fruitful than Chade's arranged meetings with Thick. Either Hap never arrived, or when he did, he came with Svanja. He was completely besotted with the girl. Over a period of three weeks, I spent most of my free nights sitting in the Stuck Pig, waiting in vain for a chance to speak to Hap alone. The establishment's draughty common room and watery beer did little to extend my patience with my son. On the occasions when Hap actually met me there, he brought Svanja with him. She was a lovely young thing, all dark hair and huge eyes, slender and supple as a willow wand, yet conveying an air of toughness as well.

And she loved to talk, giving me little opportunity to get a word in, let alone address Hap privately. Hap sat beside her, basking in her approval and beauty, as she told me a very great deal about herself and her parents and her plans for her future, and what she thought of Hap, Buckkeep and life in general. I gathered that her mother was worn down by her daughter's wilful ways and was glad that she was seeing a young man with some prospects. Her father's opinion of Hap was not as charitable, but Svanja expected to bring him around to her way of thinking soon. Or not. If he could not accept that she would choose her own young man, then perhaps her father should stay out of her life. That seemed a fine sentiment for an independent young woman to fling boldly to the winds, save that I was a father, and I did not completely approve of this young woman that Hap had chosen. Svanja herself seemed to care little that I might not favour her attitude. I found myself liking her spirit, but disliking her disregard of my feelings.

Eventually, there came an evening when Hap arrived alone, but my only opportunity for private conversation with him proved less than satisfying. He was morose that Svanja was not with him, and complained bitterly that her father had become more stubborn about forcing her to stay in for the evenings. The man would not give him a chance. When I forcefully steered the conversation to his apprenticeship, he only repeated what he had already told me. He felt dissatisfied with how he was treated in his work. Gindast thought he was a dolt and mocked him before the journeymen. They assigned him the most boring tasks and gave him no opportunity to prove himself. Yet, when I pressed him for an example, those he gave made me see Gindast as a demanding but not unreasonable master.

Hap's complaints did not convince me he was ill-treated. I formed a different opinion from his talk. My boy was in love with Svanja, and she was the real focus of his thoughts. Many of his repeated mistakes and his late arrivals in the morning could be blamed on this feminine distraction. I felt certain that if Svanja did not exist, Hap would be more intent, and perhaps better satisfied with his lessons. A stricter father might have forbidden him to see the girl. I did not. Sometimes I thought it was because of how such restrictions had felt to me; at other times, I wondered if I feared that Hap would not obey such a command, and so I dared not give it.

I saw Jinna, too, but coward that I was, I attempted to visit her home only when the presence of the pony and wagon indicated that her niece was likely present. I wished to slow our headlong lust even as the simple warmth of her bed was a lure I could scarcely resist. I tried. Each time I called on her, I kept my visits brief, begging the excuse of pressing errands for my master. The first time Jinna seemed to accept that tale without question. The second time she asked when I might expect to have an afternoon free. Although she made the query in her niece's presence, her eyes conveyed a separate question to me. I evaded her, saying that my master was capricious, and would not give me a set time to go freely about my own errands. I couched it as a complaint, and she nodded her condolences.

The third time I visited her, her niece was not home. She had gone off to help a friend in Buckkeep Town who had experienced a difficult birth. Jinna told me this after she had greeted me with a warm embrace and a lingering kiss. In the face of her willing ardour, my resolve to be restrained melted like salt in the rain. With no other prelude, she latched the door behind me, took my hand and led me to her bedchamber. 'A moment,' she cautioned me at the threshold, and I halted there. 'Now come in,' she told me, and when I did, I saw the charm had been draped with a heavy scarf. She took a deep breath, like a hungry man anticipating a good meal, and suddenly all I could focus on was the surge of her breasts against the bodice of her gown. I told myself it was a foolish mistake, but nevertheless I made it. Several times. And when we both were spent and she was half-dozing against my shoulder, I made an even more foolish mistake.

'Jinna,' I asked her softly, 'do you think this is wise, what we do?'

'Foolish, wise,' she had sleepily responded. 'What does it matter? It harms no one.'

Her question was asked lightly, but I answered seriously. 'Yes. I think it does. Matter, that is. And perhaps does harm.'

She heaved a heavy sigh, and sat up, brushing her tousled curls from her face. She peered at me near-sightedly. 'Tom. Why are you always so determined to make this a complicated matter? We are both adults, neither of us is vowed to another, and I've promised you that you cannot get me with child. Why should not we take a simple, honest pleasure in one another while we may?'

'Perhaps for me, it feels neither simple nor honest.' I struggled to make my reasons sound sensible. 'I do what I have taught Hap is not right to do: to be with a woman I have not pledged myself to. Did he tell me today that he was doing with Svanja what we have just done, I would rebuke him severely, telling him he had no right to—'

'Tom,' she interrupted me. 'We give our children rules to protect them. When we are grown, we know the dangers, and choose for ourselves what risks we take. Neither you nor I are children. Neither of us is deceived about what is offered by the other. What danger do you fear here, Tom?'

'I . . . I dread what Hap would think of me, if he found out. And I do not like that I deceive him, doing that which I forbid him to do.' I looked aside from her as I added, 'And I would that there was more to this than just . . . adults taking a risk for pleasure.'

'I see. Well, perhaps in time, there may be,' she offered, but there was an edge of hurt in her voice. And I knew then that perhaps she had deceived herself as to what we shared.

What should I have replied? I don't know. I took the coward's part and said, 'Perhaps in time there will be,' but I did not believe my own words. We lingered a while longer in bed, and then rose to share a cup of tea by her fireside. When at last I told her I must go, and then lamely insisted that I could not tell her a specific night when I could call again, she looked aside and said quietly, 'Well, then, come when you've a mind to, Tom Badgerlock.'

And with those words she gave me a parting kiss. After her door closed behind me, I looked up at the bright stars of the winter night and sighed. I felt guilty as I began my long walk back to Buckkeep. I was cheating Jinna out of something, not by denying her a false avowal of love, but by accommodating our attraction. I doubted that I would ever feel for her anything more than I felt right now. Worst was that I could not promise myself I would not continue to see her, even though a lusty friendship was all I could ever offer her. I did not think well of myself, and felt worse as I forced myself to admit that Hap probably guessed that I now shared Jinna's bed from time to time. It was a poor example to set for my boy, and the road back to Buckkeep Castle seemed very black and cold that night.

NINE

Stone Wager

As a Skill-user advances in strength and sophistication, so also increases the lure of the Skill for him. A good instructor will be wary with his Skill candidates, strict with his trainees, and relentless with his journeymen. Far too many promising Skill-users have been lost to the Skill itself. The warning signs that a Skill student is being tempted by the Skill include distraction and irritability when he is about his normal daily tasks. When he Skills, he will exert more strength than is necessary for the task, for the pleasure of the power running through him, and spend more time in a Skilling state than is required for him to accomplish his business. The instructor should be aware of such students, and be quick to chastise them for such behaviour. Better to be cruel early, than to vainly wish one could call back a student who sits drooling and mumbling until his body perishes of hunger and thirst.

Treeknee's translation, Duties of a Skill Instructor

The days of winter came and went as relentlessly as the tides that rose and fell on the beaches of Buckkeep Town, and as monotonously. Winterfest approached, that celebration which heralds both the longest night and the gaining day that follows it. Once I would have looked forward to it with anticipation. But now I had too many tasks to do, and no time to do any of them well. During the mornings I was the Prince's instructor. During the meat of my day, I masqueraded as Lord Golden's servant. Lord Golden had hired two lackeys to tend his wardrobe and fetch his breakfast, but I was still expected to ride out with him and trail after him at social functions. Folk had become accustomed to seeing me at his side, and so I shadowed him even though his ankle was apparently well healed now. It was useful to me. There were times when Golden led conversations about to test a noble's opinion of trade with the Outislanders, or the way trading rights had been allocated. I was privy to many a casually expressed opinion, and gathered all such threads of information for Chade.

Lord Golden also professed an interest in the Wit, and asked about this strange magic. The virulence of the replies he received from some was shocking even to me. The acrimony against the magic ran deep, past all logic. When he asked what harm the magic did, he was told that Witted ones did everything from coupling with animals to gain their ability to speak their tongues to cursing their neighbours' flocks and herds. Supposedly Witted ones could take on the guise of animals to gain access to those they would seduce or worse, rape and murder in their beast forms. Some spoke out angrily against the Queen's leniency for the beast-magic, and told Lord Golden that the Six Duchies were a better place in the days when Witted ones could be dispatched easily. Oh, I learned more than I wished to know of the intolerance that my own people had for their neighbours in the evenings when I was occupied as Lord Golden's servants. In the hours he left free to me, I tried to further my own studies of the Skill-scrolls. More often than I like to admit, I left my studies and went instead to Buckkeep Town, and not to meet my boy. Sometimes I caught a brief glimpse of Hap as he left Jinna's home on his way to meet Svanja. Our conversations were limited to brief greetings, and his empty promise to come home early so that we might have a real visit. Often enough, I saw a speculative look pass over his face as he watched Jinna and me together, and just as often I was relieved that he did not come home as early as he had promised.

I was in danger of settling into a routine that was, if not comfortable, at least predictable. Despite my intentions to remain ever wary against the Piebalds, their continued silence and inactivity was lulling. I almost dared to hope that Laudwine had died of his injuries. Perhaps his followers had disbanded, and the threat was no more. Despite the way they had terrorized me that night on the road to Buckkeep Castle, it was difficult to maintain an ever-watchful stance when drowned by a constant wave of silence from them. Complacency threatened. Periodically, Chade would quiz me on my spying efforts, but I never had anything to report to him. As far as I could determine, the Piebalds had forgotten us.

I spied on Civil Bresinga regularly, but found nothing to justify my suspicions of him. He appeared to be no more than a lesser noble, come to court in a bid to increase his stature amongst the aristocracy. I found no sign of his cat in the stables. He rode out often accompanied by his groom, but on the few occasions when I shadowed him, he appeared to be doing no more than exercising his horse. I searched his room several times, but discovered nothing more interesting than a brief note from his mother assuring him that she was well and that she preferred he stay at court, for 'we are all so pleased that your friendship with Prince Dutiful is prospering'. And indeed, his friendship with the Prince did prosper, despite my frequent entreaties that Dutiful regard him with caution. It was something Chade and I had discussed. Both of us would prefer that the friendship be severed, but we wondered how the Old Blood folk would interpret that.

We had had no more direct communications from any of the Witted, neither the Old Bloods nor the Piebalds. Their continued silence was uncanny. 'We have kept our end of the bargain,' Chade once observed to me grumpily. 'Since the Prince was returned to us, there have been no executions of any Witted ones in Buck. Perhaps that was all they ever sought. As for what the Piebalds may do to their fellows, well, we cannot protect them from their own folk unless they bring complaint before us. It all seems to have died down, and yet in my heart I fear it is but the calm before the storm. Be wary, boy. Be wary.'

Chade was correct about the public executions. Queen Kettricken had accomplished this by the simple expedient of announcing that no criminal in Buck could be executed for any crime, save by royal decree, and that any such executions would take place only within Buckkeep. So far, no town had seen fit to petition for an execution. Paperwork is daunting to even the hottest quest for vengeance. Yet as time passed, and we heard nothing from the Piebalds, I felt not relief, but a sense of continued scrutiny. Even if the Piebalds ceased to trouble us, I could not forget that too many Old Bloods now knew our prince was Witted. It was a lever that could be used against us at any time. I regarded strange animals with suspicion and was glad of the little ferret Gilly on patrol within the walls of Buckkeep.

Then came a night that sharpened my wariness once more. I had gone down to Buckkeep Town. When I knocked at Jinna's door, her niece told me that Aunt Jinna had gone out to deliver several charms to a family whose goats had been plagued with a mange. Privately, I wondered if charms would have any efficacy against such a thing, but aloud I asked her niece to let Jinna know I had come calling. When I asked after Hap, she made a face of disapproval and said that perhaps I might find him at the Stuck Pig with 'that Hartshorn girl'. Her disparagement of my son's companion stung. As I made my way to the Stuck Pig through the crisp winter night, I pondered what steps I should take. Hap's passionate courtship of the girl was neither balanced nor appropriate. For those very reasons, I doubted he would listen to me advising him to temper his wooing.

Yet when I entered the Stuck Pig's draughty common room, I saw no sign of Hap or Svanja. I wondered briefly where they were, but was sharply distracted from that question when I saw Laurel sitting at one of the stained tables. The Queen's huntswoman drank alone. I scowled at that, for I well recalled that Chade had assigned a man to guard her. As I watched, the tavern boy came to fill her mug again. The reckless way she lofted it told me it had already been filled several times that night.

I bought myself a beer and studied the population of the common room. Two men and a woman at a corner table seemed positioned to watch the huntswoman. But just as I wondered if they had ill intentions, the obvious couple of the group rose, bid the lone man farewell, and sauntered out without a backward glance. The remaining man gestured a tavern maid to his table. To my glance, it appeared he was trying to purchase something warmer than beer from her. His loutish behaviour calmed my reservations.

I crossed the crowded common room. Laurel seemed startled as I set my mug down, then looked away miserably as I took a seat on the bench beside her. I spoke quietly.

'Not the sort of place where one would expect the Queen's Huntswoman to drink.' I glanced about the grubby tavern pointedly, and then asked, 'And where is your apprentice tonight?' I'd had a glimpse or two of Chade's man. The sheer muscle of him would have daunted any ambusher. I thought less of his intellect, especially at this moment. 'Doesn't it seem a bit unwise for you to visit Buckkeep Town without him?'

'Unwise? Where, then is your keeper? The danger to you is greater than the threat to me,' she rebuked me bitterly. Her eyes were red-rimmed, but from tears or drink, I could not tell.

I kept my voice low. 'Perhaps I am more accustomed to this sort of danger.'

'Well. That might be true. I know little enough of you to know what you are accustomed to. But as for me, I have no intention to becoming accustomed to it. Or limiting the choices in my life by walking in constant fear.' Laurel looked tired, and there were lines at the sides of her mouth and the corners of her eyes that I did not recall. She had been walking in constant fear despite her brave dismissal of it.

'Have there been any further threats?' I asked her quietly.

She smiled, a showing of teeth. 'Why? Isn't one enough for you?'

'What's happened?'

She shook her head at me and drank the rest of her ale. I signalled to the tavern boy to bring us more. After a moment, she said, 'The first was nothing that anyone else would have recognized as a threat. Just a sprig of laurel tied to the latch of my horse's stall. Hung by a little noose of twine.' Almost unwillingly, she added, 'There was a feather as well. Cut in four pieces and scorched.'

'A feather?'

It took her a long time to decide to answer. 'Someone I care about is bonded to a goose.'

For an instant, my heart was still. Then it started again with a jolt. 'So they show you that they can reach inside the walls of the keep,' I said quietly. She nodded as the boy replenished our mugs from a heavy pitcher. I gave him his coin and he turned away. Laurel picked her mug up immediately, and a small wave of ale slopped over the brim and onto her hand. She was slightly drunk.

'Did they ask anything of you? Or simply show that they could reach you where you live?'

'They asked quite clearly.'

'How?'

'A little scroll, left amongst the grooming gear for my horse. All in the stables know that I insisted on caring for Whitecap myself. It simply said that if I knew what was wise, I should leave your black horse and Lord Golden's Malta in the far paddock at night.'

Cold seemed to spread out from my belly and fill the rest of my body. 'You didn't do it?'

'Of course not. Instead, I assigned a groom that I trust to watch over them both last night.'

'So this is recent?'

'Oh, yes.' Her head wobbled slightly as she nodded.

'And you told the Queen?'

'No. I told no one.'

'But why not? How can we protect you if we don't know you are threatened?'

She was silent for a time. Then she said, 'I didn't want them to think that they could use me against the Queen. I wanted it to be that if they pulled me down, they pulled only me down. I should protect myself, Tom, not hide behind the Queen's skirts and let my fears spread to her.'

Brave. And foolish. I kept the thoughts to myself. 'And what happened?'

'To them? Nothing. But Whitecap was dead in her stall the next morning.'

For a moment, I couldn't speak. Whitecap was Laurel's horse, a willing and responsive creature that had been her pride. When I kept silent, she glared at me. 'I know what you're thinking.' She lowered her voice to an ugly, taunting whisper. 'She's not Witted. The horse was no more to her than a horse, just a thing she rode.'

'But that's not true. I raised Whitecap from a foal, and she was my friend as well as my beast. We didn't have to share a mind to share a heart.'

'I didn't think anything of the kind,' I said very quietly. 'I've numbered many animals as my friends, without sharing the special bond of the Wit with them. Anyone who had seen you with Whitecap knew that the horse worshipped you.' I shook my head. 'I feel sick that you protected our horses, and paid for it with your own.'

I don't know if she even heard me. She was staring at the scarred tabletop as she spoke. 'She . . . she died slowly. They gave her something, somehow, that lodged in her throat and choked her as it swelled. I think . . . no, I know. It was their ultimate mockery, that I came from an Old Blood family but did not have the magic in me. If I had, I would have known that she was in trouble. I would have come to her and saved her. When I found her, she was down, her muzzle and chest all soaked in saliva and blood . . . She died slowly, Tom, and I wasn't even there to ease it for her or say goodbye.'

Shock that a Witted person could do so cruel a thing froze me like an icy wave. It was evil past my imagining. I felt tainted that people who shared my magic could stoop to such wickedness. It gave substance to all the evil things said of the Witted.

She took a sudden gasping breath and turned to me blindly. Her face was panicky with a pain she did not want to admit. I lifted my arm and she put her face against my chest as I folded her in my embrace. 'I'm sorry,' I whispered by her ear. 'I'm so sorry, Laurel.' She didn't weep, but only took long, shuddering breaths as I held her. She was past weeping, and nearly past fear. I thought to myself that if the Piebalds succeeded in pushing her to fury, they might face a stronger foe than they had intended to create. If they didn't kill her first. I shifted in my chair. Habit had made me place my back to the wall. Now I deliberately sought a full view of the tavern and any who might have followed her here.

It was then that I saw Jinna. She had probably come to the tavern to look for me after speaking with her niece. She stood by the door she had just entered. For a fraction of an instant, our gazes met. She stared, stricken, at the woman I embraced. My eyes pleaded with her, but her face went cold. Then her gaze skated past me as if she had neither seen nor recognized me. She turned and departed, her stiff back speaking volumes to me.

Frustration squeezed my heart. I was doing nothing wrong, and yet Jinna's posture as she left the tavern told me how affronted she was. Nor could I leave Laurel sitting alone and inebriated to hurry after Jinna and explain to her, even if I had felt inclined to do so. So I sat stewing in my discomfort while Laurel took several more deep breaths and recovered herself. She sat up abruptly, almost pushing me away. I released her from my embrace. She rubbed her eyes and then picked up her mug and drained it off. I had scarcely touched mine.

'This is stupid of me,' Laurel suddenly announced. 'I came here because I'd heard a rumour that Witted ones congregated here. I came hoping someone would approach me so I could kill him. I'd probably just be killed. I don't know how to fight that way.'

I saw a disturbing thing in her eyes then. They had gone calculating and cold as she considered just how she did know how to fight. 'You should leave the fighting to those who—'

'They should have left my horse alone,' she broke in blackly, and I knew she would not hear anything else I said on that topic.

'Let's go home,' I offered.

She gave me a weary nod and we left the tavern. The cold streets were lit only by what lamplight leaked from the windows. As we left the houses behind and began the long walk up the dark road to the keep, I asked her unwillingly, 'What will you do? Will you leave Buckkeep?'

'And go where? Take this home to my family? I think not.' She drew a breath and sighed it out, steaming, in the cold night. 'Yet I think you are right. I cannot stay here. What will they do next? What is worse than killing my horse?'

We both knew several answers to that. The rest of the way, we walked in silence. Yet she was neither angry nor taciturn. I could sense her eyes straining through the uncertain moonlight, and her head turned to every small sound. My vigilance matched hers. I broke the silence once, to ask, 'Is it true, that Witted go to the Stuck Pig?'

She gave a shrug. 'So it is said of that tavern. Folk say it of many dives. "Fit for the Witted." Surely you've heard that phrase before.'

I hadn't, but I filed the information away. Perhaps in that slander lurked a germ of truth. Was there a tavern in Buckkeep Town where the Witted congregated? Who would know? What might I learn there?

Just past the gates of Buckkeep Castle, I saw her 'apprentice' hastening to meet us. He wore a worried expression. At the sight of me, it changed to a snarl. Laurel sighed and took her hand from my arm. She walked unsteadily towards him and he all but swooped her up. Despite whatever her soft words were, he glared at me suspiciously before escorting her to her chambers. Before I sought my own room for the night, I made a quick and quiet tour of the stables. Myblack greeted me with her usual warm show of indifference. I could scarcely blame the horse; I had not had much time for her lately. In truth, she was to me 'just a horse'. I rode her when Lord Golden rode Malta, but other than that, I trusted her care to the stablehands. It suddenly seemed a callous way to treat her, but I knew that I had no time to give her more. I wondered what the Piebalds had intended. If our horses had been left in the far paddock, would they have been stolen? Or worse?

Wit-sense straining, I strolled past every stall and scrutinized every drowsy stablehand there. I saw no one whom I recognized, and Laudwine was not lurking beneath the stairs or outside the door. Nonetheless, I did not feel at ease until I was in Chade's upper chambers that night. He was not there, but I left him a full written account.

We discussed it the next day, but came to no real conclusion. He would rebuke Laurel's bodyguard for letting her slip away alone. He could not think of any way to keep Laurel safer without confining her even more tightly. 'And she would not care for that. She does not like that I have a man beside her. Yet, what more can I do, Fitz? She is valuable to us, for it may be she will draw these Piebalds out of hiding.'

'At what cost?' I had asked him harshly.

'As little as we can make it,' he replied grimly.

'Why did they want my horse and Lord Golden's?'

Chade lifted a brow at me. 'You know more of Witted magic than I do. Could they ensorcel them to throw you, or somehow use them to listen in on your words?'

'The Wit doesn't work that way,' I said wearily. 'Why our horses? Why not Prince Dutiful's? It is almost as if the Fool and I were their targets rather than the Prince.'

Chade looked uncomfortable. Almost reluctantly, he suggested quietly, 'A cautious man might wish to follow that thought and see where it led.'

I stared at him, wondering what the old assassin was telling me in his obscure way. He folded his lips and shook his head at me, as if he regretted having spoken the words. Shortly after that, he made an excuse to leave. I sat pondering before the fire.

In the days that followed, I felt too uncomfortable to call on Jinna. I knew it was foolish, but there it was. I did not feel I owed her an explanation, but I was sure she would expect one. No convenient lie came to me to explain why I had been embracing Laurel in the Stuck Pig. I did not want to discuss Laurel with Jinna at all. It would lead her too close to dangerous topics. Hence, I did not visit Jinna at all.

On the occasions when I went down to Buckkeep Town, I sought Hap at his workplace. Our conversations there were brief and unsatisfactory. The boy seemed very aware of the other apprentices watching us talk, and spoke his words to me as if he were displaying to them his anger with his master. He was frustrated, too, with his stalled courtship of Svanja. Her father was making it hard for him to see her, and refused to speak with Hap on the streets. I sensed that some of Hap's anger was for me. He seemed to think I neglected him, yet when it came to finding time to meet with me in the evening, he preferred Svanja's company. I kept resolving that I would do better with Hap and make amends with Jinna, but somehow the days dribbled past and I could not find the time to accomplish either task.

Within Buckkeep, the festivities and trade negotiations of the Prince's betrothal continued. Winterfest came and went, grander than ever I had seen it in the castle. Our Outislander guests enjoyed it tremendously. In the time that followed there were trading discussions every day and aristocratic amusements every night. The puppeteers, minstrels, jugglers and other entertainers of the Six Duchies prospered. The Outislanders became a familiar sight in the halls of Buckkeep Castle. Some formed genuine friendships, both with the nobles staying at the keep and with the merchant-traders from Buckkeep Town. In the town below, our ancient trade with the Outislands began to revive. Trading vessels arrived, and goods were bartered. Messages were exchanged as well, and it was no longer socially unacceptable to admit to a cousin or two in the Outislands. Kettricken's plans seemed to be prospering.

The late nights of court gaiety showed me a Buckkeep I had never known. As a servant, I was almost as invisible as I had been when I was a nameless boy. The difference was that as Lord Golden's man, I attended him on socially lofty occasions when the nobility were gaming, dining and dancing. I saw them in their best clothes and worst behaviour. Drunk with wine or vapid with Smoke, besotted with lust or frantic to recover gaming losses ... if ever I had supposed that our lords and ladies were made of finer stuff than the fishers and tailors that crowded the Buckkeep Town taverns, I was disillusioned that winter.

Women, young and old, single and married, flocked to the Lord Golden's charms, as well as young men desirous of distinguishing themselves as 'the Jamaillian lord's friend'. It amused me somewhat that not even Starling and Lord Fisher were immune to Lord Golden's social allure. Often they joined him at the gaming table. Twice they even came to Lord Golden's chambers to sample fine Jamaillian brandies with his other guests. It was difficult for me to maintain my attitude of servitude and uninterest in her presence. Her husband was a physically affectionate man, often drawing her body close to his and boyishly stealing a kiss. Then she would gaily rebuke him for such unseemly public conduct, yet often enough manage to snatch at glance at me as she did so, as if to be sure I had noticed how passionately Lord Fisher still courted his wife. At times, it was all I could do to keep a stoic impression on my face. It was not that my heart or flesh burned for her. The pang that assaulted me at such a time was that she deliberately flaunted her happiness in a way calculated to remind me of how solitary a life I led. In the midst of the fine court with its merriment and elaborate entertainment, I stood, a silent servant, witness only to their pleasures.

In this way, the long dark of winter dawdled on. The constant whirl of activity took a toll on the young prince as well as myself. One early morning, we both arrived at the tower with absolutely no inclination for studies or tasks of any kind. The Prince had been up late the night before, gaming with Civil and the other young noblemen currently residing at the keep.

I had had the good sense to seek my own bed at a more reasonable hour, and had succeeded in several hours of deep sleep before Nettle has insinuated herself into my dreams. I was dreaming of catching river fish, sliding my hands into the water and abruptly flipping the lurking fish out onto the bank behind me. It was a good dream, a comforting dream. Unseen but felt, Nighteyes was with me. Then my groping fingers encountered a door handle under the chill water. I plunged my head under to look at it. As I stared at it through water-green light, it opened and pulled me in. Suddenly I stood, wet and dripping, in a small bedroom. I knew I was in the upper chambers of the house by the slanting ceiling. The house was silent around me, and only a guttering candle lighted the room. Wondering how I had arrived here, I turned back to the door. A girl stood there, her back pressed resolutely to the door, her arms spread wide to bar it from me. She wore a cotton nightdress and her dark hair hung in a single long braid over one shoulder. I stared at her in astonishment.

'If you will not let me into your dreams, then I will trap you in mine,' she observed triumphantly.

I stood very, very still and held my silence. On some level, I sensed that anything of myself I might give her, word or gesture or look, would only increase her hold on me. I took my gaze from her, for in recognizing her, I was entering into her dream more deeply. Instead, I forced my eyes down, to my own hands. With a curious elation, I realized they were not my own. She had trapped me here as she visualized me, not as I truly was. My fingers were short and stubby. The palms of my hand and the inside surface of my fingers

were black and coarse as a wolf's pads, and rough black hair coated
the backs of my hands and my wrists.

'This isn't me.' I spoke the words aloud, and they came out as a
queer growl. I lifted my hands to my face, found a muzzle there.

'Yes, it is!' she asserted, but already I was fading, drifting out
of the form she had thought would contain me. The trap was the
wrong shape to hold me. She leapt towards me and seized me by
one wrist, only to find she grasped an empty wolfskin.

'I'll catch you next time!' she declared angrily.

'No, Nettle. You won't.'

My use of her name froze her. Even as she struggled to mouth the
question, how did I know her name, I dissipated from her dream into
my own wakefulness. I shifted on my hard bed, and briefly opened
my eyes to the now-familiar blackness of my servant's chamber.
'No, Nettle. You won't.' I spoke the words aloud, reassuring myself
that they were true. But I had not slept well the rest of the night.

And so the two of us, Dutiful and I, faced one another blearily
over the table in the Skill tower the next dawn. It was dawn in
name only. The winter sky outside the tower window was black,
and the candles on our table reached vainly towards the darkness
in the corners of the room. I had kindled a fire in the hearth, but
it had not yet taken the edge off the chill. 'Is there anything so
miserable as being sleepy and cold at the same time?' I asked him
rhetorically.

He sighed, and I had the feeling he had not even heard my question. The one he asked me sent a different sort of chill up my back.
'Have you ever used the Skill to make someone forget something?'

'I . . . no. No, I've never done anything like that.' Then, dreading
the answer, 'Why do you ask?'

He heaved an even deeper sigh. 'Because if it could be used that
way, it could make my life much simpler right now. I fear that I . . .
I said something last night, to someone, never intending that . . .
I didn't even *mean* it that way, but she . . .' He faltered to a halt,
looking miserable.

'Start at the beginning,' I suggested.

He took a deep breath, then puffed it out, exasperated with
himself. 'Civil and I were playing Stones and—'

'Stones?' I interrupted him.

He sighed again. 'I made myself a game-cloth and playing pieces. I thought I could get better at it by playing against someone besides you.'

I strangled back an objection. Was there any reason why he should not introduce his friends to the game? None that I could think of. Yet it disgruntled me.

'I had played a game or two with Civil, which he lost. As he should and did expect to, for no one plays a game well the first few times one is shown it. But he had declared he had had enough of it for now, that it was not the sort of game he relished, and he got up from the table and went over to the hearth to talk to someone else. Well, Lady Vance had been watching us play earlier in the evening, and had said she wanted to learn, but we were in the midst of the game then, so there had been no place for her. But she had been standing by our table, watching us play, and when Civil left, instead of following him as I thought she would, for she had seemed very attentive to him, she sat down in his place. I had been putting the cloth and pieces away, but she reached over and seized my hand and commanded that I should set the game out afresh, for now it was her turn.'

'Lady Vance?'

'Oh, you wouldn't have met her. She's, let me see, about seventeen and she's quite nice. Her full name is Advantage, but she thinks it's too long. She's very friendly and tells funny stories and, well, I don't know, she's just more comfortable to be around than most girls. She doesn't always seem to be, you know, so aware that she is a girl. She acts just like anybody else. Lord Shemshy of Shoaks is her uncle.' He shrugged a shoulder, dismissing my concern over who she was. 'Anyway, she wanted to play, and even when I warned her that she'd likely lose the first few games, she said she didn't care, that in fact if I would play her five straight games, she'd wager she'd win at least two of them. One of her friends overheard that and came close to the table, and asked what the wager was on the bet. And Lady Vance said that if she won, she wanted me to go riding with her on the morrow – that's today – and that if I won, well, I could name my own stakes. And the way she said it was, well, daring me to make her bet something that might be a bit, well, improper or . . .'

'Like a kiss,' I suggested, my heart sinking. 'Or something of that sort.'

'You know I wouldn't go that far!'

'So how far did you go?' Did Chade know anything of this? Or Kettricken? How late last night had it happened? And how much wine had been involved?

'I said if she lost, she had to bring breakfast for Civil and me to Mirror Hall and serve it to us herself, owning up that what had been said earlier was true, that Stones is not a game that a girl can master.'

'What? Dutiful, this game was taught to me by a woman!'

'Well—' He had the grace to look uncomfortable. 'I didn't know that. You had said it was part of your Skill-training. I thought my father had taught it to you. So . . . wait. Then a woman helped train you in the Skill? I'd thought it had only been my father who taught you.'

I cursed my carelessness. 'Leave that,' I commanded him crossly. 'Finish your story.'

He snorted, and gave me a glance that promised he'd come back to his question later. 'Very well. And besides, it wasn't me who said that to Elliania, it was Civil, and—'

'Said what to Elliania?' Dread clutched at me.

'That it wasn't a game for a girl's mind. Civil said it to her. Civil and I were playing, and she came up and said that she'd like to learn. But . . . well, Civil doesn't like Elliania much. He says she is just like Sydel, that girl who insulted him and trampled his feelings, that Elliania is only interested in making a good match. So. He doesn't like her to stand near us when we talk or are playing games of chance.' He flinched before my scowl, and added grumpily, 'Well, she's not like Lady Vance. Elliania is always being a girl, she's always so aware of what are proper manners and what courtesies are due between folk. She's so correct that she's always wrong. If you see what I mean?'

'It sounds to me as if she is a foreigner at the court, intent on complying with our customs. But go on with the story.'

'Well. Civil knows that about her, that she always strives to be absolutely correct in her manners. So he knew that the fastest way to be rid of her was to tell her that in the Six Duchies, Stones was considered a man's occupation. He explained it to her in a way that seemed like he was being kind, but at the same time it was horribly funny, in a cruel sort of way, because she doesn't know our language or our customs well enough to realize how ridiculous his excuse was . . . Don't look at me like that, Tom. I didn't do it. And once he had begun to do it, there was no way I could put a stop to it without making it worse. So. Anyway. He had told her that the Stone game wasn't for girls, and Elliania had left us and gone off to stand near her uncle's shoulder. He was playing toss-bones with her father, at a table on the other side of the hall. So. She wasn't anywhere near us when Lady Vance sat down. Well. I set up the game and we began to play. The first two games went exactly as I had supposed they would. On the third game, I made a silly mistake, and she won. The fourth game, I won. And now – I think I deserve credit for this – halfway through the fifth game, I realized how it might be seen as improper when she lost if she actually did come to serve breakfast to Civil and me. I mean, even Duke Shemshy might see it as an insult, his niece acting as a servant to us, even if it didn't bother Elliania or mother. So. I decided it might be better to let her win. I'd still have to take her riding, but I could make sure there were others with us, perhaps even Elliania.'

'So you let her win.' I said the words heavily.

'Yes. I did. And by then, because she had been quite excited when she won the third game, laughing and shouting and calling out to all that she had bested me, well, by then there was quite a group of people gathered around us, watching us play. So, when she won the final game, she was crowing over her victory, and one of her friends said to me, "Well, my lord, it seems you were badly mistaken earlier when you said this was not a game a girl could master." And I said . . . "I only meant to be clever, Tom, I swear, not to offer insult." I said—'

'What did you say?' I asked harshly as he faltered.

'Only that no girl could master it, but perhaps a beautiful woman could. And everyone laughed, and lifted glasses to drink a toast to that. So we drank, and then it was cups down. And only then did I realize that Elliania was standing there, at the edge of the crowd. She hadn't drunk with us, and she didn't say a word. She just stared at me, with her face very still. Then she turned and walked away. I don't know what she said to her uncle, but he stood up immediately and gave over the game to her father, even through there was quite a stack of coins riding on the outcome. And the two of them left the gaming hall and went directly to their chambers.'

I leaned back in my chair, striving to think my way through it. Then I shook my head and asked, 'Does your lady mother know of this yet?'

He sighed. 'I do not think so. She excused herself early from the gaming last night.'

'Or Chade.'

He winced, already dreading the councillor's opinion of his rashness. 'No. He, too, left the tables early. He seems weary and distracted of late.'

Too well did I know that. I shook my head slowly. 'This is not something that can be solved with the Skill, lad. Wiser to take it immediately to those who know diplomacy the best. And then do whatever they say.'

'What do you think they will demand of me?' There was dread in his voice.

'I don't know. I think a direct apology might be a mistake; it would only confirm that you had insulted her. But . . . oh, I don't know, Dutiful. Diplomacy has never been my talent. But perhaps Chade will know something you can do. Some special attention from you to confirm that you do think Elliania is beautiful and a woman.'

'But I don't.'

I ignored his bitter little contradiction. 'And above all, do not go out riding alone with Lady Vance. I suspect you'd be wise to avoid her company entirely.'

He slapped his hand on the table in frustration. 'I can't back out of paying my wager!'

'Then go,' I snapped. 'But if I were you, I'd be sure that Elliania rode at my side, and that your conversation was with her. If Civil is as good a friend as you say he is, perhaps he can help you. Ask him to distract Lady Vance's attention from you, make it appear as if he is the one accompanying her on the ride.'

'What if I don't want her attention distracted from me?'

Now he sounded simply stubborn and contrary, as vexing as Hap the last time I had seen him. I simply looked at him, flat and level, until he cast his eyes aside. 'You'd best go now,' I told him.

'Will you go with me?' His voice was very soft. 'To speak to Mother and Chade?'

'You know I cannot. And even if I could, I think you'd best do this on your own.'

He cleared his throat. 'This morning, when we ride. Will you go with me then?'

I hesitated, then suggested, 'Invite Lord Golden. That isn't a promise to be there, only that I'll think it over.'

'And do what Chade thinks is best.'

'Probably. He's always been better than me at these niceties.'

'Niceties. Pah. I'm so sick of them, Tom. It's why Lady Vance is so much easier to be with. She's just herself.'

'I see,' I said, but I reserved judgment on that. I wondered if Lady Vance was just a woman who had set her cap at a prince, or someone else's playing piece, positioned to set Kettricken's game awry. Well. We'd all find out soon enough.

The Prince left me, locking the door behind him. I stood, silent and considering in the tower room, listening to the sound of his footsteps on the stone stairs fade away. I caught the raised voice of the guard's greeting at the bottom of the steps. I cast my eyes around the room, blew out the candle on the table and then left, carrying another taper to light my way.

I stopped at Chade's tower room on the way back to my servant's chamber. I stepped out of the secret door, then halted, surprised to find both Chade and Thick in the room. Chade had evidently been waiting for me. Thick looked sullen and sleepy, his heavy-lidded eyes even droopier than usual.

'Good morning,' I greeted them, and, 'Yes, it is,' Chade responded. His eyes were bright and he appeared well pleased about something. I waited for him to share it with me, but instead he said,

'I've asked Thick to be here early this morning. So we could all talk.'

'Oh.' I could think of no more to say than that. Now wasn't the time to tell Chade I'd wished he had warned me first. I would not talk over Thick's head in his presence. I remembered too well how I had once underestimated the cunning of a little girl and spoken too freely. Rosemary had been Regal's treacherous little pet. I doubted that Thick was anyone's spy, but what I didn't say in front of him, he could not repeat.

'How is the Prince this morning?' Chade asked suddenly.

'He's well,' I replied guardedly. 'But there is something he'll wish to see you about, something rather urgent. You might wish to be, uh, where you can easily be found. Soon.'

'Prince sad,' Thick confirmed dolorously. He shook his heavy head commiseratingly.

My heart sank, but I resolved to test him. 'No, Thick, the Prince isn't sad. He's merry. He has gone to have a fine breakfast with all his friends.'

Thick scowled at me. For an instant, his tongue stuck out even farther than usual, and his lower lip sagged pendulously. Then, 'No. Prince is a sad song today. Stupid girls. A sad song. La-la-la-le-lo-lo-lo-o.' The dimwit sang a mournful little dirge.

I glanced at Chade. He was watching our exchange closely. His eyes never left me as he asked Thick, 'And how is Nettle today?'

I kept my face expressionless. I tried hard to breathe normally, but suddenly I could not quite remember how.

'Nettle is worried. The dream man won't talk to her any more, and her father and brother argue. Yah, yah, yah, yah, her head hurts with it, and her song is sad. Na-na-na-na, na-na-na-na.' It was a different tune for Nettle's sadness, one fraught with tension and uneasiness. Then suddenly Thick stopped in mid-note. He looked at me and then jeered triumphantly, 'Dog-stink doesn't like this.'

'No. He doesn't,' I agreed flatly. I crossed my arms on my chest and moved my glare from Thick to Chade. 'This isn't fair,' I said. Then I clenched my jaw over how childish that sounded.

'Indeed, it isn't,' Chade agreed blandly. Then, 'Thick, you may go if you wish. I think you've finished your chores here.'

Thick pursed his lips thoughtfully. 'Bring the wood. Bring the water. Take the dishes. Bring the food. Fix the candles.' He picked his nose. 'Yes. Chores done.' He started to go.

'Thick,' I said, and when he halted, scowling, I asked, 'Do the other servants still hit Thick, take his coins? Or is it better now?'

He frowned at me, his brow wrinkling. 'The other servants?' He looked vaguely alarmed.

'The other servants. They used to "hit Thick, take his coins", remember?' I tried to copy his inflection and gesture. Instead of jogging his memory, it made him draw back from me in panic. 'Never mind,' I said hastily. My effort to remind him that perhaps he owed me a favour had instead worsened his opinion of me. Thrusting out his lower lip, he backed away from me.

'Thick. Don't forget the tray,' Chade reminded him gently.

The serving-man scowled, but he came back for a tray of dishes that held the remains of Chade's breakfast. He took it up and then crabbed hastily from the room as if I might attack him.

When the wine-rack swung back into place behind him, I sat down in my chair. 'So?' I asked Chade.

'So, indeed,' he replied agreeably. 'Were you ever going to tell me?'

'No.' I leaned back in my chair, and then decided there was nothing more to say about it. Instead, I settled on a distraction. 'Earlier I told you that Dutiful has something urgent to speak about with you. You should be available.'

'What is it?'

I gave him a look. 'I think what Dutiful wishes to tell you would come best directly from him.' I bit down on my tongue before I could add, 'of course, you could always ask Thick what it is about'.

'Then I'll go to my own chambers. Shortly. Fitz. Is Nettle in any danger?'

'I'm sure I don't know.'

I saw him rein in his temper. 'You know what I mean. She's Skilling, isn't she? Without guidance of any kind. Yet she seems to have found you. Or did you initiate that contact?'

Had I? I didn't know. Had I intruded on her dreams when she was younger, as I had on Dutiful's? Had I unwittingly laid the foundation for the Skill-bond that she sought to build now? I pondered it, but Chade took my silence for mulishness. 'Fitz, how can you be so short-sighted? In the name of protecting her, you're endangering here. Nettle should be here, at Buckkeep, where she can be properly taught to master her talent.'

'And she can be put into service for the Farseer throne.'

He regarded me levelly. 'Of course. If the magic is the gift of her bloodlines, then the service is her duty. The two go hand-in-hand. Or would you deny it to her because she, too, is a bastard?'

I strangled on sudden anger. When I could speak, I said quietly, 'I don't see it so. As denying her something. I'm trying to protect her.'

'You see it that way only because you are stubbornly focused on keeping her away from Buckkeep at all costs. What is the terrible threat to her if she comes here? That she could know music and poetry, dance and beauty in her life? That she might meet a young man of noble lineage, marry well, and live comfortably? That your grandchildren might grow up where you could see them?'

He made it all sound so rational on his part and so selfish on mine. I took a breath. 'Chade. Burrich has already said "no" to his daughter coming to Buckkeep. If you press him, or worse, force the issue, he will suspect there is a reason. And how can you reveal to Nettle that she is Skilled without leading her to ask, "where did this magic come from?" She knows Molly is her mother. That leaves only her father's lineage in question—'

'Sometimes children are found to have the Skill with no apparent link to the Farseer bloodline. She might have received it from Molly or Burrich.'

'Yet none of her brothers have it.' I pointed out.

Chade slapped the table in frustration. 'I have said it before. You are too cautious, Fitz. "What if this, what if that?" You hide from trouble that may never knock at our door. What if Nettle did discover that a Farseer had fathered her? Would that be so terrible?'

'If she came to court, and found herself not only a bastard, but the bastard of a Witted Farseer? Yes. What of her fine husband and genteel future then? What does it do to her brothers and to Molly and Burrich, to have to face that past? Nor can you have Nettle here without Burrich coming to see her, to be sure she is well. I know I have changed, but my scars are no disguise to Burrich, nor are my years. If he saw me, he'd know me, and it would destroy him. Or would you try to keep secrets from him, tell Nettle that she must never tell her mother and father that she is taught the Skill, let alone that she is taught by a man with a broken nose and a scar down his face? No, Chade. Better she stays where she is, weds a young farmer she loves, and lives a settled life.'

'That sounds very bucolic for her,' Chade observed heavily. 'I'm sure that any daughter of yours would be delighted with such a sedate and settled life.' Sarcasm dripped from his words until he demanded, 'But what of her duty to her prince? What of Dutiful's need for a coterie?'

'I'll find you someone else,' I promised recklessly. 'Someone just as strong as she is, but not related to me. Not tarnished with any complications.'

'Somehow I doubt that such candidates will be easy to find.' He scowled suddenly. 'Or have you encountered such others, and not seen fit to tell me of them?'

I noticed he did not offer himself. I let that sleeping dog lie. 'Chade, I swear to you, I know of no other Skill candidates. Only Thick.'

'Ah. Then he is the one you will train?'

Chade's question was flippant, an attempt to make me admit there were no other real candidates. I knew Chade expected a flat refusal from me. Thick hated and feared me, and was dim-witted besides. A less desirable Skill student I could not imagine. Except for Nettle. And perhaps one other. Desperation forced the next words from my tongue. 'There might be one other.'

'And you haven't told me?' He trembled at the edge of rage.

'I wasn't sure. I'm still not sure. I've only recently begun to wonder about him myself. I met him years ago. And he may be as dangerous to train as Thick, or even more so. For not only has he strong opinions of his own, but he is Witted.'

'His name?' It was a demand, not a request.

I took a breath and stepped off the precipice. 'Black Rolf.'

Chade scowled. He squinted, rummaging through the attics of his mind. 'The man who offered to teach you the Wit? You encountered him on the way to the Mountains?'

'Yes. That's the one.' Chade had been present when I had offered Kettricken my painfully complete account of my travels across the Six Duchies to find her. 'He used the Wit in ways I'd never seen it used. He alone seemed to almost know what Nighteyes and I said privately to one another. No other Witted one has shown me that ability. Some could tell when we used the Wit, if we were not extremely careful, but did not seem to understand what we said to one another. Rolf did. Even at the times when we tried to keep it secret from him, I always suspected that he knew more than he let on. He could have been using the Wit to find us, and the Skill to listen to my thoughts.'

'Wouldn't you have felt it?'

I shrugged. 'I didn't. So perhaps I am mistaken. Nor am I eager to seek out Rolf to discover the truth of it.'

'In any case, you could not. I'm sorry to tell you that he died three years ago. He took a fever, and his end was swift.'

I stood still, stunned as much by the news as by the fact that Chade knew it. I found my way to a chair and sat down. Grief did not flood me. My relationship with Black Rolf had always been a fractious one. But there was regret. He was gone. I wondered how Holly managed without him, and how Hilda his bear had endured his passing. For a time I stared at the wall, seeing a small house far away. 'How did you know?' I managed at last.

'Oh, come, Fitz. You reported about him to the Queen. And I'd heard his name from you before, when you were delirious and raving with fever from the infection in your back. I knew he was significant. I keep track of significant people.'

It was like the Stone game. He'd just set another piece on the board, one that revealed his old strategy. I filled in all he had not said. 'So you know that I returned there. That I studied with him for a time.'

He gave a half nod. 'I wasn't certain of it. But I suspected it was you. I received the news with joy. Prior to that, the last I had heard of you was what Starling and Kettricken reported when they left you at the quarry. To hear you were alive and well . . . For months, I half-expected you to turn up at my doorstep. I looked forward to hearing from your lips of what had happened after Verity-as-Dragon left the quarry. There was so much we did not know! I envisioned that reunion a hundred ways. Of course, you know that I waited in vain. And eventually, I realized you'd never come back to us of your own will.' He sighed, remembering old pain and disappointment. Then he added quietly, 'Still, I was glad to hear that you were alive.'

The words were not a rebuke. They were only his admission of pain. My choice had hurt him, but he had respected my right to make it. After my time with Rolf, he would have had spies watching for me. They would not know it was FitzChivalry Farseer they sought, but doubtless they had found me. Otherwise, how would Starling have found her way to my door, all those years ago? 'You've always had an eye on me, haven't you?'

He looked down at the table and said stubbornly, 'Another man might see it as a hand sheltering you. As I have just told you, Fitz. I always keep track of significant people.' He next spoke as if he could hear my thoughts. 'I tried to leave you alone, Fitz. To find what peace you could, even if it excluded me from your life.'

Ten years ago, I could not have understood the pain in his voice. I would only have seen him as interfering and calculating. Only now, with a son of my own intent on ignoring every bit of advice I'd ever given him, could I recognize what it had cost him to let me go my own way and make my own choices. He had probably felt as I did about Hap, that he was so obviously choosing the wrong course. But Chade had let me steer it.

In that instant, I made my decision. I pushed Chade off balance with it. 'Chade. If you wish, I could attempt . . . do you want me to try to teach you the Skill?'

His eyes were suddenly impenetrable. 'Ah. So you offer that now, do you? Interesting. But I think I am proceeding with my own studies well enough. No, Fitz. I don't wish you to teach me.'

I bowed my head. Perhaps I deserved his disdain. I took a breath. 'Then I'll do as you ask, this time. I'll train Thick. Somehow, I'll persuade him to let me teach him. As strong as he is, perhaps he will be all the coterie that Dutiful will need.'

Shock silenced him for a moment. Then, he smiled sourly, 'I doubt that, Fitz. And you don't doubt it; you don't believe it at all. Nevertheless, for the time being, we will leave it at that. You will begin Thick's training. In exchange, I will leave Nettle where she is. You have my thanks. And now I must go to see what mischief Dutiful had got himself into.' He rose as if his back and knees pained him. I watched him go but said no more.

TEN

Resolutions

By all accounts, both Kebal Rawbread and the Pale Woman perished in the last month. They set sail in the last White Ship for Hjolikej with a crew of their most stalwart followers. They were not seen again, nor was any wreckage of the ship ever found. The assumption is that, like so many other Outisland ships, the dragons overflew it, throwing the crew into a vacant-eyed stupor, and then destroyed it with the great wind and waves that their wings could stir. As the ship was heavily loaded with what translates from the Outislander tongue as 'dragonstone', it probably went down swiftly.
A report to Chade Fallstar, penned at the end of the Red Ship War

I made my slow descent to Lord Golden's chambers. I tried to focus on the Prince's difficulties, but could only wonder what larger problem I had created for myself. I could barely instruct the Prince, and he was an apt and amiable student. I'd be lucky if Thick didn't kill me when I attempted to teach him. But there was a worse shadow to it. Chade had tempted me well, as only one who knew me so deeply could. Nettle, here at Buckkeep, where I could see her daily and watch her blossom into womanhood, and perhaps chart for her an easier life than the one Burrich and Molly could give her. I tried to tear that idea from my mind. It was a selfish yearning.

On my trip through Chade's secret corridors, I made a brief detour to one of the spy-posts. I stood for a time beside it, hesitating. It would be the first time I had deliberately come to spy and listen. Then I sat down silently on the dusty bench and peered into the Narcheska's chambers.

Fortune was with me. Their breakfast was still set out on the table between Peottre and the girl, though it did not look as if either one had eaten much. Her uncle was already dressed in his riding leathers. Elliania was in a pretty little frock, blue and white, with much lace on the cuffs and throat. Peottre was shaking his heavy head at her. 'No, little one. As with a fish on a line, you must first set the hook before you can play him. Flaunt your displeasure with him now and he will avoid that bitter taste, to follow instead the bright feathers of someone else's lure. You cannot show him what you feel, Elli. Set aside the insult; behave as if you did not notice it.'

She clacked her spoon back onto the tray, so that a tiny glop of porridge leapt from it. 'I cannot. I have pretended as much calmness as I could muster, last night. Right now, I could not show him what I truly feel about him with less than a knife's edge, Uncle.'

'Ah. How well *that* would benefit your mother and little sister.' He spoke the words quietly, but Elliania's face grew very still, as if he spoke of death and disease in the next chamber. She tucked her proud little chin, bowing her head before him with lowered lashes. I sensed the strength of will she used to rein herself in and suddenly saw the changes that her months at Buckkeep had wrought in her. Peottre might call her his 'little fish' still, but this was a different girl from the one I had first spied on. The last vestiges of child had been hammered from her by the pounding of Buckkeep society. She spoke now with a woman's determination.

'I will do what I must, Uncle, for our mothers' house. You know that. Whatever I must, to "hook" this fish.' When she looked up at him, her mouth was set and flat in determination, but tears stood in her eyes.

'Not that,' he said quietly. 'Not yet, and perhaps never at all. So I hope.' He sighed suddenly. 'But you must be warm to him, Elli. You cannot show him your anger. It tears my heart to say that to you, that you must appear untroubled by his insult. Smile upon him. Behave as if it never happened.'

'She must do more than that.' I could not see who spoke, but I recognized the serving-maid's voice. She walked into view. I studied her more closely than I had previously. She appeared to be about my age, dressed simply as if she were a servant. Yet she bore herself as if she were in charge. Her hair and eyes were black, her cheeks wide, and nose small. She shook her head at both of them. 'She must appear humble and willing.'

She paused, and I saw the muscles of Peottre's face bunch as he clenched his jaws. It made the woman smile. She went on with evident relish. 'And you must make him think it is possible that you will . . . yield yourself to him.' Then she spoke in a deeper voice. 'Bring the farmer-prince to heel, Elliania, and keep him there. He must not look at another, he must not even consider anyone else as someone to bed before he is wed. He must be yours alone. Somehow, you must claim him, heart and flesh. You have heard the Lady's warning. If you fail in this, if he strays, and gets a child with another, you and yours are all doomed.'

'I cannot do it!' she burst out. She mistook her uncle's horrified look for a rebuke, for she continued desperately, 'I have tried, Uncle Peottre. I have. I have danced for him, and thanked him for his gifts, and tried to look entranced by his boring talk in his farmer's tongue. But it is all useless, for he thinks I am a little girl. He disdains me as a child, an offering from my father simply for the making of a treaty.'

Her uncle leaned back in his chair, pushing his untouched dish away from him. He sighed heavily, then glared at the serving-woman. 'You hear her, Henja. She has already tried your disgusting little tactic. He does not want her. He is a boy with no fire in his blood. I do not know what more we can do.'

Elliania suddenly sat up straight. 'I do.' Her chin had come up again, as had the fire in her black, black eyes.

He shook his head at her. 'Elliania, you are only—'

'I am not a child, nor a mere girl! I have not been a girl since this duty was laid upon me. Uncle. You cannot treat me as a child and expect others to see me as a woman. You cannot dress me like a doll, and bid me be sweet and tractable as some doting auntie's little treasure, and expect me to attract the Prince. He has been raised in this court, among all these females as sweet as spoiling fish. If I am but one more of them, he will not even see me. Let me do what I must. For we both know that if I continue as I have, we will fail. So. Let me try it my way. If I fail on that path, also, what will we have lost?'

For a time he sat staring at her. She cast her gaze aside from his piercing eyes, and busied herself with topping the cups of untouched tea before them. Then she lifted hers and sipped from it, all the while avoiding meeting his glance. When he spoke, dread was in his voice. 'What do you propose, child?'

She set down her cup. 'Not what Henja suggests, if that is what you fear. No. This woman proposes that you tell him my age. Today. In his farmer's years, rather than my God's Rune years. And that, for this day at least, you let me dress and behave as one of the daughters of our mothers' house would, insulted as he has insulted me, to prefer another woman's beauty to my own, and announce it to all. Let me bring him to heel, as you have commanded. But not with cloying sweets, but with a whip, as a dog such as he deserves.'

'Elliania. No. I forbid it.' The serving-woman spoke with the snap of command.

But it was Peottre who replied to her. He surged to his feet, his broad hand lifted high. 'Get out, woman! Get out of my sight, or you will be dead. I swear it, Lady. If she doesn't leave now, I kill your servant!'

'You will regret this!' Henja snarled, but she scuttled from the room. I heard the door close behind her.

When Peottre spoke again, it was slowly and heavily, as if his words could fence Elliania from some precipice. 'She had no right to speak to you so. But I do, Narcheska. I forbid this.'

'Do you?' she asked levelly, and I knew Peottre had lost.

A knock at the chamber door was her father. He came in and greeted them both, and Elliania almost immediately excused herself, saying she must dress appropriately to go out riding with the Prince by midmorning. As soon as she left the room, her father launched into some discussion of a shipload of trading goods that was overdue. Peottre answered him, but his eyes lingered on the door where Elliania had vanished.

A short time later, I emerged cautiously into my own servant cell, and thence even more cautiously into Lord Golden's warm and spacious chambers. He was alone, at table, finishing his share of the ample breakfast he commanded daily for us. All at court must wonder at the suppleness of his waist given the substantial morning appetite he professed to.

His golden glance assessed me as I silently entered his room. 'Hmm. Sit down, Fitz. I'll not wish you a good morning, for it's plainly too late for that. Care to share what has overshadowed you with gloom?'

Useless to lie. I took a chair opposite him at the table and picked food off the serving plate while I confided Dutiful's social stumble to him. There was little point in doing otherwise. There had been enough spectators that I was sure the tale would reach him soon enough, if he had not witnessed it himself. Of Nettle, I said nothing. Did I fear he would concur with Chade? I am not sure, I only knew that I wished to keep it to myself. Nor did I speak of what I had seen through my peephole. I needed time to sort it out before I shared it with anyone.

When I had finished my tale, he nodded. 'I was not at the gaming tables last night, preferring to listen instead to one of the Outisland minstrels who have recently arrived. But the tale reached me last night before I retired. I've already been invited to ride out with the Prince this morning. Do you want to come along?' When I nodded, the Fool smiled. Then Lord Golden patted his lips with his napkin. 'Dear, dear, this is a most unfortunate social stumble. The gossip will be delectable. I wonder how the Queen and her Councillor will manage to juggle it back into balance?'

There were no easy answers to that. I knew he would use the turmoil stirred by this to dig into where loyalties truly lay. Between us, we cleared the breakfast platters of food. I took them down to the kitchen, where I lingered briefly. Yes, the servants were already gossiping of it, and speculating that there was more between Lady Vance and the Prince than a mere game of Stones. Someone already claimed to have seen them walking alone in the snowy gardens several evenings ago. Another maid said that Duke Shemshy was said to be pleased, and quoted him as saying he saw no real obstacle to the match. My heart sank. Duke Shemshy was powerful. If he began to solicit support among the nobles for a match between his niece and the Prince, he could possibly put an end to both betrothal and alliance.

One other thing I saw while I was there that caused me suspicion. The Narcheska's maid, whom I had last seen quarrelling with Peottre, hurried past the doors of the kitchen and out into the courtyard. She was dressed warmly, in a heavy cloak and boots, as if for a long walk on this cold day. I supposed it was possible that her mistress had sent her off on some task into Buckkeep Town, but she carried no market basket. Nor did she seem the type of serving-woman who would be chosen for such an errand. It both puzzled and concerned me. If I had not all but promised the Prince that I would be there for his ride, I would have shadowed her. Instead, I hurried up the stairs to dress for the morning ride.

When I re-entered Lord Golden's chamber, I found him putting the finishing touches to his own costume. For a moment, I wondered if Jamaillian nobles truly dressed in such a gaudy fashion. Layer upon layer of rich fabric cloaked his slender form. A heavy fur cloak flung across a chair awaited him. The Fool had never had any great tolerance for cold, and Lord Golden apparently shared that weakness. He was turning up a fur collar to his satisfaction. One long narrow hand waved me on to my own chamber, bidding me hurry, while he continued to peruse himself in the mirror.

I glanced inside my room at the garments laid out on my bed and then protested, 'But I'm already dressed.'

'Not as I wish you to be. It has come to my attention that several of the other young lords of the court have also furnished themselves with bodyguard-servants, in a pale imitation of my style. It is time to show them than an imitation cannot equal the original. Garb yourself, Tom Badgerlock.'

I snarled at him, and he smiled sweetly in return.

The garments were servant's blue, and of excellent quality. I recognized Scrandon's tailoring. I supposed that now that he had my measurements, Lord Golden could inflict stylish clothing on me at will. It was fine fabric, very warm, and in that I recognized the Fool's concern for my comfort. He had been kind enough to have it cut and sewn so that I could move freely. But stretching out an arm of the oddly-tailored shirt revealed pleated insets in varying shades of blue, with an effect like a bird's wing opening to reveal the different colours of its plumage. I noticed as I donned it that a number of clever pockets had been fitted into interesting places. I approved of the pockets even as I winced at Lord Golden instructing the tailor to add them. I would rather that no one else had known of my need for concealed pockets.

As if he had sensed my concern, Lord Golden spoke from the other room. 'You will note that I had Scrandon add pockets to permit you to carry a number of small but necessary items for me, such as my smelling salts, my digestive herbs, my grooming aids and my extra kerchiefs. I gave him most precise measurements for those.'

'Yes, my lord,' I responded gravely, and proceeded to fill those pockets as my own needs dictated. When I lifted the winter cloak, it revealed the final addition to my garb. The guard of the blade and the scabbard were so gaudily adorned that I winced. But when I drew the blade, it whispered death as it came free from the sheath and balanced like a bird on my fingers. I sighed and looked up to find the Fool standing framed in my door. The look on my face pleased him well. He grinned at my astonishment. I shook my head. 'My skill doesn't deserve a blade like this.'

'You deserve to be able to carry Verity's sword openly. That one is a pale compensation.'

It was too large a thing to offer thanks for. He watched me buckle the sword-belt and seemed to take as much pleasure in that as I did to wear it.

When we assembled in the courtyard to await the Prince, the gathering was larger than I had expected. A few nobles already awaited Dutiful. Young Civil Bresinga was there, deep in conversation with Lady Vance. Did she look displeased as she gestured at the waiting horses, a far larger party than she had obviously wagered on? Two other young women, her close friends by the way they stood, commiserated with her. They all greeted Lord Golden warmly as he joined them. It struck me that he looked only a few years older than they, a handsome, wealthy and exotic foreign nobleman in his early twenties. All the women drew closer to him, talking, while three young noblemen, one of them a Shemshy kinsman from his strong resemblance to the Duke, also lingered nearby. Lady Vance was obviously already the centre of her own tiny court. If she did manage to win the Prince, these newly-loyal courtiers would rise with her.

Servants held the bridles of their horses. The padded perch for Civil's cat was empty behind his saddle. Privately, I doubted that he had left his cat at Galekeep as it was said; no Witted one would willingly be parted from his partner that long. Probably the beast was roaming the hills around Buckkeep. Civil must visit it regularly. I resolved to spy on one of those assignations. Perhaps a little confrontation with him and his cat would shake me out a bit more information about the Old Blood community, and his ties to the Piebalds.

I did not have time to ponder this for long. I took Myblack and Malta from a waiting stable-boy and then stood holding their reins as Lord Golden mingled with the others gathered to accompany the Prince. I could not courteously stare at the nobles, but I could study their horses and deduce who would join us. One mare was so richly caparisoned that she must have been awaiting the Queen herself. I recognized Chade's horse as well. In addition to the Prince's horse there were three other richly-decked mounts; so it seemed that Arkon Bloodblade and Uncle Peottre would be part of the gathering as well. The bay mare with bells in her mane would be for the Narcheska.

Then there came a burst of conversation and laughter near the door and the main party arrived. The Prince was dazzlingly attired in Buckkeep blue trimmed with the white fox of his mother's colours. The Queen had chosen blue and white as well, accented with goldenrod stripes on her mantle. Yet despite the brightness of the colours that echoed so well the blue and white of the winter day, the lines of her garb were simple in contrast to the extravagant clothing of her court. Chade was elegant in shades of blue, trimmed with black, and all the jewellery he wore was silver. The Prince was smiling, but I knew he was chastened by the way he lingered at the top of the steps, conversing with his mother and Chade rather than joining his younger companions. He acknowledged to no one that this ride was supposed payment for an ill-considered wager. By dismissing it, perhaps he hoped it would be devalued in the eyes of the others as well. Lady Vance stood smiling up at him and, for a moment, caught his eyes. He nodded courteously, but then his gaze wandered to Civil. The nod he gave him was equal to the first. Were Lady Vance's cheeks a bit pinker than they were before? He descended only when Chade and the Queen did, and still he remained beside his mother.

Several Outislander merchant nobles next appeared with Arkon Bloodblade. They had adopted all the most extravagant fashions of Buckkeep. Lace and ribbons fluttered from them like pennants, and the heavy furs of their homeland had been replaced with rich fabrics from Bingtown and Jamaillia and even more distant ports. Kettricken, Chade and Dutiful greeted them effusively. Pleasantries were exchanged, comments made on the fine weather, compliments on clothing and other civilities were bandied about as all awaited the Narcheska and Peottre.

And we all waited.

It was a ruse calculated to set us all on edge. Kettricken's eyes kept darting to the door. Dutiful's laughter at Chade's pleasantries sounded forced. Arkon scowled and spoke gruffly to a man at his side. The delay was long enough that the thought came to all of us: this will be how she displays her displeasure with Dutiful. She will humiliate him before all of his friends and family by leaving him standing. If she embarrassed her father before the Queen, would it create friction there as well? Just as I saw Chade and Kettricken conferring as to whether a servant should be sent to ask if the Narcheska would join them, Peottre appeared.

In contrast to the other Outislanders, he had reverted completely to his native garb, yet the effect was not that of barbarism, but of purity. His trousers were leather, his cloak of rich fur. His jewellery was ivory and gold and jade. The simplicity of line suggested he would be ready to ride, hunt, travel or fight, and not be encumbered by frippery. He emerged onto the steps above us, and stood there, as if he had taken the centre of a stage. He did not look happy to be there, but determined. As he stood silently, his arms crossed on his chest, the entire gathering fell silent. All eyes fixed on him. When he saw it was so, he spoke quietly, in a voice that was affable but would brook no disagreement.

'The Narcheska desires me to make it known that ages are reckoned differently in the God Runes. She fears an ignorance of this may have led people to misunderstand her status among our folk. She is not a child by our standards, nor even by yours, I suspect. In our islands, where life is harsher than in your gentle, pleasant land, we think it bad luck to count a child a member of the family during those first twelve months when tiny lives may so easily wither. Nor do we give a child a name until that first crucial year is past. By our God Runes reckoning, then, the Narcheska is only eleven years old, nearly twelve. But by your reckoning, she is twelve, verging on thirteen. Nearly the same age as Prince Dutiful.'

The door opened behind him. No servant held it; the Narcheska shut it firmly behind herself. She emerged to stand beside Peottre, dressed in the same fashion as he was. She had discarded her Buckkeep finery. Her trousers were of spotted sealskin, her vest of red fox. The cloak that draped her from her shoulders to her knees was of white ermine, the tiny black tails swinging tassels. She pulled up her hood as she smiled coolly down upon us. The ruff was made of wolf. As she looked out of its depths, she observed, 'Yes, I am nearly the same age as Prince Dutiful. Ages are accounted differently in our land. As are our ranks. For, although I was not named nor my days numbered until I was a year old, I was still the Narcheska. But Prince Dutiful, I understand, will not be a king; no, not even the King-in-Waiting for his crown, until he is seventeen. This is correct?'

She asked this of Kettricken as if she were uncertain, standing above the queen at the top of the steps. My queen was unflustered as she looked up and replied, 'In this you are correct, Narcheska. My son will not be accounted ready for that title until he has reached his seventeenth year.'

'I see. An interesting difference from the customs of my home. Perhaps in my land we believe more in the strength of the lineage: that a babe is already who she will be, and hence worthy of her title from her first breath. While you, in your farmers' world, wait to see if the line has bred true. I see.'

It could not be construed as an insult, quite. With her foreign accent and her odd placement of words, it could have been merely an unfortunate phrasing of thought. But I was sure it was not. Just as I was sure that her quiet, clear words spoken to Peottre as she descended the steps to his side were intended to be overheard. 'Perhaps, then, I should not wed him until we are sure he will truly become the King? Many a man hopes to ride a throne, but is tumbled from it before he ascends to it. Perhaps the marriage should be postponed until his own people judge him worthy?'

Kettricken's smile did not fade but it grew fixed. Chade's eyes narrowed briefly. But Dutiful could not control the flush that seared his face. He stood silent, beaming his humiliation at her slight. I thought she had accomplished her revenge quite tidily; he had been humbled much as she had, and before much the same company. But if I thought she was finished with him, I was wrong.

When the Prince approached her courteously to assist her in her mount, she waved him away, saying, 'Allow my uncle to help me. He is a man of experience, with both horses and women. If I require assistance, I shall be safest in his hands.' And yet when Peottre approached her, she smiled and assured him that she was certain she could mount on her own, 'For I am not a child, you know.' And she did, though I was certain the tall horse was much larger than the tough little ponies the Outislanders used.

Astride, she moved her horse forward to ride at Kettricken's side and converse with the Queen. The two, clad richly yet simply, presented a contrast to the sumptuous and extravagant dress of the others. Somehow, their clothing made it seem as if they not only belonged together, but also were the only two who shared a sensible attitude to a pleasure ride on a winter's day. Either of them, if faced with a lamed horse, could easily have trekked home through the snow. Without an obvious intent, they had made the coifed and decorated nobles appear silly and frivolous. I wrinkled my brow as the thought came to me. By complementing Kettricken's simple attire, yet remaining true to the customs of her own folk, the Narcheska claimed an equal footing with our queen.

Prince Dutiful glanced at his youthful friends. I saw his eyes meet Civil's, and Civil's brows rise in a query. But constrained by his mother's rebuking glance, the Prince rode at the Narcheska's left side. She scarcely noticed him and when she did occasionally turn in her saddle to address a remark to Dutiful, it was with the air of someone who politely strives to include an outsider in the conversation. He could contribute little more to the talk than a nod and a smile before she dismissed him again.

Immediately behind them, Chade rode between Arkon Blood-blade and Peottre Blackwater. Lord Golden insinuated himself amongst the Prince's young friends, and I trailed behind them. They rode together, in a chattering knot. I am certain Prince Dutiful was well aware of their eyes upon his back and that they discussed how his betrothed had snubbed him. Lord Golden was adroitly transparent to the conversation, encouraging it with his interest but contributing no remarks of his own that might have deflected its course. I noted that while Lady Vance was merry to her friends and attentive to Lord Civil, her eyes wandered often and speculatively to the Prince. I wondered if her ambitions were her own or those of her uncle, Lord Shemshy.

I knew one disconcerting moment, when Dutiful abruptly crashed through my barriers and into my thoughts. *I don't deserve this! It was an accidental remark, but she behaves as if I deliberately humiliated her. I almost wish I had!*

The jolt of his thought was shock enough, but worse was to see Lord Golden flinch to it. He glanced back at me, one eyebrow raised, almost as if he thought I had spoken to him. Now was he alone, though his reaction was the most extreme. Several other riders in our party glanced off abruptly in different directions, as if they had heard a distant shout. I took a breath, narrowed my focus to a pin's head, and Skilled back to the lad.

Silence. Master your emotions, and do not do that again. Elliania has no way to know that you did not deliberately humiliate her. And she is not the only one who may believe that of you. Consider the attitudes of the young women who ride with Civil. But for now, ponder this to yourself. Your Skill control is not good when you are emotional. Refrain from using it at such times.

The Prince lowered his head at my stern reprimand. I saw him draw a long breath, then he squared his shoulders and sat straighter in his saddle. Then he glanced about as if enjoying the beauty of the day.

I relented and offered him a bit of comfort. *I know you don't deserve this. But sometimes a prince, or any man, must endure what he did not deserve. Just as Elliania did last night. School yourself to patience, and submit to it.*

He nodded as if to himself, and replied to one of the Narcheska's brief comments.

It was not a long ride through the snowy fields, but I am sure it seemed so to Dutiful. He took his punishment manfully, but when it was time to dismount our eyes met for an instant and I saw the relief in his eyes. There. It was over. He had atoned for his gaffe of the night before, and now all would return to the way it had been.

I could have told him that is never so.

There was an entertainment planned for the afternoon, a play acted out by costumed individuals in the Jamaillian fashion rather than using puppets. I did not see how it could be done effectively, but Lord Golden had assured me that he had seen many such plays in the southern cities, and many clever things could be done to distract the watchers from the flaws. He had seemed quite pleased at the prospect of this diversion, and even more pleased at the arrival of the ship bringing the actors. Bingtown's continuing war with Chalced was disrupting shipping and travel badly. Chalced's fleet evidently had been temporarily beaten back, for two ships from the south had docked today, with rumours of others following. I had seen Lord Golden's face light up at that news. Lord Golden dismissed the war to his friends as an inconvenience that interrupted his supply of apricot brandy but I noticed that the ships that did evade Chalced's patrols often brought packets of letters for him as well as brandy, and these the Fool took into his private room immediately. I suspected that far more than his supply of brandy and money concerned him. But he said nothing of what the missives contained, and I knew better than to ask. Evincing curiosity on any topic had always been the swiftest way to make the Fool cut off the flow of information.

So I spent the afternoon standing at his shoulder in a darkened hall. The story was very Jamaillian, all about priests and nobles and intrigues, and at the end their dual-faced deity appeared to restore order and mete out justice. The play more befuddled than amused me. I could not adjust to people playing different roles. A puppet has no life of its own, save the story for which it is intended. It was disconcerting to recognize that the man now playing a servant had been one of the acolytes earlier in the play. It was difficult for me to concentrate on the story, and not just because of my confusion, but because the Prince's misery spread out like a miasma that lapped against me in the dimmed hall. He did not deliberately Skill it; it leaked from him like moisture seeping from a waterskin. On the stage, actors gestured and shouted and struck poses. But the Prince sat beside his mother, alone and miserable in his social discomfort. In the last month or so, the renewed gaiety of Buckkeep Castle had exposed him to many folk his own age. Through Civil, he had begun to explore camaraderie and flirtation. Now all that must be curtailed for the sake of the political alliance his mother strove to forge. I could feel him pondering both the unfairness and the necessity of it. It was not sufficient that he be bound in marriage to the Narcheska Elliania. He must make it appear it was his choice to be so bound.

Yet it was not.

Later in the evening, Lord Golden granted me a few hours of my own. I changed back into comfortable clothes and made my way to Buckkeep Town and the Stuck Pig. In light of what I had witnessed at the keep, I was disposed to be more tolerant of Hap's wayward courtship. Perhaps, I reflected as I strode through falling snow on my way to town, it struck some greater balance in the wide world, that Hap could freely indulge in what was completely denied to the Prince.

The Stuck Pig was quiet. I had been here often enough that I could recognize the tavern's regular customers. They were there, but there were few others. Doubtless the blowing snow and rising storm were keeping many indoors tonight. I glanced about but saw no sign of Hap. My heart lifted a trifle; perhaps he was at home, already abed. Perhaps the novelty of life in town was wearing thin, and he was learning to order his life more sensibly. I sat in the corner that Hap and Svanja favoured and a boy brought me a beer.

My musing was brought to a swift close when a red-faced man of middle years came in the door. He wore no cloak or coat of any kind and his head was bare, his dark hair spangled with snowflakes. He gave his head an angry shake to clear both snow and water droplets from his hair and beard, and then glared at my corner of the tavern. He seemed surprised to see me sitting there; he turned and confronted the tavern keeper, asking him something angrily in a low voice. The man shrugged. When the newcomer clenched his fists and made a second demand, the tavern-keeper gestured hastily at me, speaking in a low voice.

The man turned and stared at me, eyes narrowed, and then strode angrily towards me. I came to my feet as he drew near, but prudently kept the table between us. He thudded his fists on the scarred wood, and then demanded, 'Where are they?'

'Who?' I asked, but with a sinking heart I knew to whom he referred. Svanja had her father's brow.

'You know who. The keeper says you've met them here before. My daughter Svanja and that demon-eyed country whelp who has lured her away from her parents' hearth. Your son, is what the keeper says.' Master Hartshorn made the words an accusation.

'He has a name. Hap. And yes, he is my son.' I was instantly angry, but it was a cold anger, clear as ice. I shifted my weight very slightly, clearing my hip. If he came across the table at me, my knife would meet him.

'Your son.' He spoke the word with contempt. 'I'd be shamed to admit it. Where are they?'

I suddenly heard the desperation as well as the fury in his voice. So. Svanja wasn't at home, and neither she nor Hap was here. Where could they be on a snowy, dark night like this? Little question of what they were doing. My heart sank, but I spoke quietly. 'I don't know where they are. But I feel no shame to claim Hap as my son. Nor do I think he "lured" your daughter into anything. If anything, it is the reverse, with your Svanja teaching my son town ways.'

'How dare you!' he roared and drew back a meaty fist.

'Lower your voice and your hand,' I suggested icily. 'The first to spare your daughter's reputation. The second to spare your life.'

My posture drew his eyes to my ugly sword at my hip. His anger did not die, but I saw it tempered with caution. 'Sit down,' I invited him, but it was as much command as suggestion. 'Take control of yourself. And let us speak of what concerns us both, as fathers.'

Slowly he drew out a chair, his eyes never leaving me. I was as slow to resume my seat. I made a gesture at the innkeeper. I did not like the eyes of the other customers fixed on us, but there was little I could do. A few moments later, a boy scuttled over to our table, clapped down a mug of beer before Master Hartshorn and then scurried away. Svanja's father glanced at the beer contemptuously. 'Do you really think I will sit here and drink with you? I need to find my daughter, as swiftly as possible.'

'Then she is not at home with your wife,' I concluded.

'No.' He folded his lips. The next words he spoke were barbed, with bits of his pride torn free with them. 'Svanja said she was going up to her bed in the loft. Some time later, I noticed a task she had left undone. I called to her to come back down and finish her work. When she did not reply, I climbed the ladder. She is not there.' The words seemed to disarm his anger, leaving only a father's disappointment and fear. 'I came here directly.'

'Without even a hat or cloak. I see. Is there nowhere else she might be? A grandmother's house, a friend's home?'

'We have no kin in Buckkeep Town. We only arrived here last spring. And Svanja is not the kind of girl who makes friends with other girls.' With every word, he seemed to have less fury and more despair.

I suspected then that Hap was not the first young man to claim her fancy, nor that this was the first time her father had sought for her after dark. I kept the observation to myself. Instead, I picked up my beer and drained it off. 'I know of only one other place to seek them. Come. We'll go there together. It's where my son boards while I work up at the keep.'

He left his beer untouched, but rose as I did. Eyes followed us as we left the tavern together. Outside in the darkness, snow had begun to swirl more swiftly. He hunched his shoulders and crossed his arms on his chest. I spoke through the wind, asking the question I dreaded but must. 'You completely oppose Hap's courtship of your daughter?'

I could not see his face in the dimness but his voice was bright with outrage. 'Oppose? Of course I do! He has not even had the courage to come to me, to say his name to me and declare his intent! And even if he did, I would oppose it. He tells her he is an apprentice . . . well then, why does not he live at his master's house, if that is true? And if it is true, what is he thinking, to court a woman before he can even make his own living? He has no right. He is completely unsuitable for Svanja.'

He did not need to mention Hap's mismatched eyes. Nothing Hap could do would overcome Hartshorn's dislike of him.

It was a short walk to Jinna's door. I knocked, dreading encountering her as much as I dreaded finding that Hap and Svanja were not there. It took a moment before Jinna called through the closed door, 'Who's there?'

'Tom Badgerlock,' I replied. 'And Svanja's father. We're looking for Hap and Svanja.'

Jinna opened only the top half of her door, a clear indication of how far I had fallen in her regard. She looked at Master Hartshorn more than me. 'They're not here,' she said briskly. 'Nor have I ever permitted them to spend time in each other's company here, though there's little I can do to stop Svanja from knocking at my door and asking for Hap.' She swung her reproachful gaze to me. 'I haven't seen Hap at all this evening.' She crossed her arms on her chest. She didn't need to say she had warned me it would come to this. The flat accusation was there in her eyes. Suddenly I could not meet her stare. I'd avoided seeing her since the night she had glimpsed Laurel in my arms. That I had never offered her the courtesy of an explanation shamed me. It was an act both cowardly and juvenile.

'I'd best go look for him, then,' I muttered. I'd hurt Jinna and tonight I had to face that. The truth speared me. It hadn't been for any lofty moral reasons, but because I was afraid, because I had known she would become a facet of my life that I could not control. Just as Hap was now.

'Damn him! Damn him for ruining my girl!' Hartshorn suddenly raged. He turned and stumbled away into the swirling snowfall. At the edge of the light from Jinna's door, he looked back to shake a fist at me. 'You keep him away from her! Keep your demon-blasted son away from my Svanja!' Then he turned. In a few steps, he was beyond the range of the light from Jinna's door, vanished into blackness and despair. I longed to follow him, but I felt caught in the light.

I took a deep breath. 'Jinna, I need to find Hap tonight. But I think—'

'Well. We both know you won't find him. Or Svanja. I doubt they want to be found this night.' She paused, but before I could even draw breath, she said evenly, 'And I think Rory Hartshorn is right. You should keep Hap away from Svanja. For all our sakes. But how you're going to do it, I don't know. Better you had never let your son run wild like this, Tom Badgerlock. I hope it isn't too late for him.'

'He's a good boy,' I heard myself say. It sounded feeble, the excuse of a man who has neglected his son.

'He is. That is why he deserves better from you. Good night, Tom Badgerlock.'

She shut the door, shutting away her light and warmth. I stood in the dark, with the cold sweeping past me. Snowflakes were finding their way down my collar.

Something warm bumped my ankles. *Open the door. The cat wants to go in.*

I stooped to stroke him. Cold snow spangled his coat but the warmth of his body leaked through it. *You'll have to find your own way in, Fennel. That door doesn't open for me any more. Farewell.*

Stupid. You just have to ask. Like this. He stood up on his hind legs and clawed diligently at the wood as he yowled.

The sound of his demands followed me as I strode off into the darkness and cold. Behind me, I heard the door open for an instant and knew he had been admitted. I walked back up to Buckkeep Castle, envying a cat.

ELEVEN

Tidings from Bingtown

'Past Chalced, keep your sails spread.' This old saying is based on sound observations. Once your ship is past the Chalcedean ports and their cities, old as evil itself, spread sail and move swiftly. Aptly named are the Cursed Shores to the south of Chalced. Water from the Rain River will rot your casks and burn your crew's throats. Fruit from those lands scalds the mouth and breaks sores on the hands. Beyond the Rain River, take on no water that comes from inland. In a day it will go green, and in three it seethes with slimy vermin. It will foul your casks so they can never be used again. Better to keep the crew on short rations than to put ashore there for any reason. Not even to weather a storm or take a day's rest at anchor in an inviting cove is safe. Dreams and visions will poison your sailors' minds, and your ship will be plagued with murder, suicide and senseless mutiny. A bay that beckons you to safe harbour may seethe with savage sea serpents before the night is over. Water-maidens come to the top of the waves, to beckon with bare breasts and sweet voices, but the sailor that plunges in for that pleasure is dragged under to be food for their sharp-toothed mates hiding below the water.

The only safe harbour along all that stretch is the city of Bingtown. The anchorage is good there, but beware of their docks where ensorcelled ships may call down curses on your own vessels of honest wood. Best to avoid their docks. Drop your hook in Trader Bay and row in, and likewise have goods brought out to your ship. Water and food from this port can be trusted, though some of the wares from their shops are uncanny and may bring ill luck to a voyage. In Bingtown, all manner of goods may be bought and sold, and the trade goods from there are unlike any others in the wide world. Yet keep your crew close by your vessel, and let only the master and mate go ashore and amongst the townsfolk.

Better for common ignorant sailors not to touch foot to that soil, for it can entrance men of lesser mind and intellect. Truly is it said of Bingtown, 'if a man can imagine it, he can find it for sale there'. Not all that a man can imagine is wholesome to a man, and much is sold there that is not. Beware, too, of the secret people of that land, sometimes seen by night. It brings on the foulest of bad luck should one of the Veiled Folk of that place cross a captain's path when he is returning to his ship. Better to spend that night on shore, and return to your ship the next day than to sail immediately after such an ill omen.

Beyond Bingtown, leave the safety of the inner passage and take your ship out Wildside. Better to brave the storms and harsh weather than to tempt the pirates, serpents, sea-maidens and Others of those waters, to say nothing of the shifting bottoms and treacherous currents. Make your next stop corrupt Jamaillia with its many raucous ports. Again, keep a tight hand on your crew, for they are known to steal sailors there.

Captain Banrop's Advice to Merchant Mariners

I left Prince Dutiful a note on the table in the Skill-tower. It said only, 'Tomorrow'. Before the dawn watch had changed, I was standing outside Master Gindast's establishment. The lamplight from the windows sliced across the snowy yard. In that dimness, apprentices crunched along the footpaths, hauling water and firewood for both the master's home and his workshop and clearing snow from the canvassed tops of the wood stockpiles and the pathways. I looked in vain for any sign of Hap amongst them.

Light had brought colour to the day when he finally appeared. I could tell at a glance how he had spent his night. There was a gleam of wonder in his eyes still, as if he could not grasp his own good fortune, and an almost drunken swagger to his walk. Had I shone like that the first morning after Molly had shared herself with me? I tried to harden my heart as I lifted my voice and called out, 'Hap! A word with you.'

He was smiling as he came to meet me. 'It will have to be a short one then, Tom, for I'm already late.'

The day was blue and white around us, the air crisp with chill, and my son stood grinning up at me. I felt a traitor to all of it as

I said, 'And I know why you're late. As does Svanja's father. We were looking for you last night.'

I had expected him to be abashed. He only grinned wider, a knowing smile between men. 'Well. I'm glad you didn't find us.'

I felt an irrational urge to strike him, to wipe that expression from his face. It was as if he stood within a burning barn and rejoiced at the heat, unmindful of the peril to himself and Svanja. That, I suddenly knew, was what infuriated me, that he seemed completely unaware of how he endangered her. An edge of my anger crept into my voice.

'So. I take it Master Hartshorn didn't find you either. But I imagine he'll be waiting for Svanja when she gets home.'

If I had hoped to dampen his reckless spirit, I didn't succeed. 'She knew he would be,' he said quietly. 'And she decided it was worth it. Don't look so serious, Tom. She knows how to handle her father. It will be fine.'

'It may be any number of things, but I doubt "fine" will be one of them.' My voice grated past my anger. How could he be so cavalier about this? 'You're not thinking, boy. What will this do to her family, to their day-to-day life, to know their daughter has made this choice? And what will you do, if you get her with child?'

The smile finally faded from his face, but he still stood straight and faced me. 'I think that's for me to worry about, Tom. I'm old enough now to take charge of my own life. But, to put your mind at rest, she told me that there are ways women know to keep such a thing from happening. At least, until we are ready for it, until I can make her my wife.'

Perhaps the gods punish us by bringing us face to face with our own foolish mistakes, condemning us to watch our children fall into the same traps that crippled us. For all the sweetness of the secret hours I had shared with Molly, there had been a price. At the time, I had thought that we shared it, that the only cost was keeping our love secret. Molly had known better, I am sure. She had been the one to pay it, far more than I had. If Burrich had not existed to shelter and shield them both, my daughter would have paid it as well. Perhaps she still would, in her differences, in the dangers of being a cuckoo's nestling, unlike her brothers. I wondered if I could warn Hap, if he would listen to me, as I had not listened to Burrich or Verity. I pushed my anger aside and spoke out of my fears for them both.

'Hap. Please hear me. There are no safe and certain ways for a woman to avoid conceiving. All of them have a risk and a price to her. Every time she lies with you, she must wonder, "will I conceive from this? Will I bring shame to my family?" You know I would not cast you from my household for any mistake you made, but Svanja's life is not so certain. You should protect her, not expose her to danger. You are asking her to risk all, for the pleasure of being with you, with no guarantees. What will you do if her father turns her out? Or beats her? What will you do if she suddenly finds herself ostracized and condemned by her friends? How can you be responsible for that?'

A scowl darkened his face. His stubbornness, so rarely woken, mastered him now. He took several breaths, each deeper than the last, and then the words exploded from him. 'If he throws her out, I'll take her in, and do whatever I must to support her. If he beats her, I'll kill him. And if her friends turn on her, then they were never truly her friends anyway. Don't worry about it, Tom Badgerlock. It's *my* consideration now.' He bit off each of his final words, as if somehow I had betrayed him just by stating my concerns. He turned away from me. 'I'm a man now. I can make my own decisions and my own way. And now, if you'll excuse me, I must get to my work. I'm sure Master Gindast is waiting for his turn to lecture me on responsibility.'

'Hap.' I spoke the word sharply. When the boy turned back to me, startled at the harshness in my tone, I forced out the rest of what I knew I had to say. 'Making love to a girl does not make you a man. You have no right to do that; not until you both can declare yourself partners publicly, and provide for any children that come along. You should not see her again, Hap. Not like that. If you don't go soon to meet her father and face him squarely, you'll never be able to stand before him as a man in his eyes. And—'

He was walking away. Halfway through my speech he turned and walked away from me. I stood stunned, watching him go. I kept thinking he would stop and come back to ask my forgiveness and help in putting his life to rights. Instead, he strode into Master Gindast's shop without a backward glance.

I stood a time longer in the snow. I was not calm. On the contrary, an anger flamed in me that seemed enough to warm all winter away from the land. My fists were clenched at my sides. I think it was the first time I had ever felt deeply furious with Hap, to the point at which I longed to beat some sense into him if he would not listen to reason. I pictured myself barging into the shop and dragging him out, forcing him to confront what he was doing.

Then I turned and stalked away. Would I have listened to reason at his age? No. I had not, not even when Patience had explained to me, over and over and over, why I must stay away from Molly. Yet such a realization did not decrease my anger with Hap, nor my belated contempt for my boyhood self. Instead it gave me a sense of futility, that I must witness my foster son committing the same foolish and selfish acts that I had performed myself. Just as I had, he believed that their love justified the risks they took, without ever considering that the child might come to pay the price for their intemperance. It could all happen again, and I could not stop it. I think I grasped then, fleetingly, the passion that powered the Fool. He believed in the terrible strength of the White Prophet and the Catalyst, to shoulder the future from the rut of the present and into some better pathway. He believed that some act of ours could prevent others from repeating the mistakes of the past.

By the time I reached Buckkeep and had ascended to the Skill-tower, I had walked away the fierceness of my anger. Yet the sick, dull weight of it lingered, poisoning my day. I was almost relieved to find that Dutiful had given up on me and left. Only a simple underlining of the word had altered my note. The boy was learning to be subtle. Perhaps at least with this young man I could succeed in turning him aside from the errors of the past. That errant thought only made me feel cowardly. Was I surrendering Hap then, abandoning him to his own poor judgement? No, I decided, I was not. But that decision put me no closer to knowing what to do about it.

I returned to Lord Golden's chambers and was in time to join the Fool for his breakfast. As I entered, however, he was not eating.

Rather he sat at table, bemusedly twirling a tiny bouquet of flowers between his forefinger and thumb. It was an unusual token, for the blossoms were made of white lace and black ribbon. It seemed a clever subterfuge for a season without flowers, and it put me in mind of his old fool's motley for this season. He saw me looking at the posy, smiled at my bemusement, and then carefully pinned it to his breast. It was the Fool who gestured at the spread of food before him and said, 'Sit down and eat quickly. We are summoned. A ship docked at dawn with an ambassadorial contingent from Bingtown. And not just any ship, but one of their liveships, with a talking, moving figurehead. *Goldendown*, I believe his name is. I don't think one has ever ventured into Buck waters before. Aboard was an emissary mission from the Bingtown Council of Traders. They have applied with great urgency to see Queen Kettricken at her earliest convenience.'

The news startled me. Usually Six Duchies contacts with Bingtown were contacts between individual merchants and traders, not their ruling council treating with the Farseers. I tried to recall if the city-state had ever sent us ambassadors when Shrewd was king, then gave it up. I had not been privy to such matters when I was a lad. I took a seat at the table. 'And you are to be there?'

'At Councillor Chade's suggestion, we will both be there. Not visibly, of course. You are to take me there through Chade's labyrinth. He himself came to tell me so. I'm quite excited to see it, I admit. Save for my brief glimpse of it on the night Kettricken and I fled the castle and Regal, I've never glimpsed it.'

I was shocked. It was inevitable that he knew of the spy passages' existence, but I had not thought Chade would ever offer him access to them. 'Does the Queen concur in this?' I asked, trying to be delicate.

'She does, but reluctantly.' Then, dropping the aristocratic air, he added, 'As I have spent some time in Bingtown and know something of how their council operates, Chade hopes my evaluation of their words may give him a deeper understanding. And you, of course, provide an extra pair of eyes and ears for him, to catch any nuances that might otherwise be missed.' As he spoke, he served us adroitly, adapting a platter to be my plate. He was generous with smoked fish, soft cheese and fresh bread and butter. A pot of tea steamed in the middle of the table. I went to my room to fetch my cup. As I returned with it, I asked, 'Why could not the Queen simply invite you to be present when she receives them?'

The Fool shrugged one shoulder as he took a forkful of smoked fish. After a moment, he observed, 'Don't you think the Bingtown ambassadors might look askance at the Queen of the Six Duchies inviting a foreign noble to attend her first meeting with them?'

'They might, but then they might not. I believe it has been decades since the Bingtown Council has sent a formal declaration to the Six Duchies court. And we have a Mountain queen now, a woman from a realm completely outside their ken. Did she greet them by slaughtering chickens in their honour or scattering roses before them, it would be all one to them. Whatever she does, they will assume it is her custom, and they will attempt to receive it politely.' I took a sip of tea and then added pointedly, 'Including inviting foreign nobles to her first reception of them.'

'Perhaps.' Then, grudgingly he admitted, 'But I have reasons of my own for not wishing to be visibly present.'

'Such as?'

He took his time cutting a bite of food and then eating it. After he had followed it with a sip of tea, he admitted, 'Perhaps they would recognize that I bear no resemblance to any Jamaillian noble family that they have ever encountered. The traders of Bingtown have far more commerce with Jamaillia than any Six Duchies venture. They would see through my sham and spoil it.'

I accepted that, but reserved my opinion as to whether it was the complete reason. I did not ask if he feared he would be recognized. He had told me that he had spent some time in Bingtown. Even dressed as a nobleman, the Fool's appearance was sufficiently unique that he might be recognized by any that had seen him there. He was looking more uncomfortable than I had seen him in a long time. I changed the subject.

'Who else will be "visibly present" at the ambassadors' initial reception by the Queen?'

'I don't know. Whoever represents each of the Six Duchies and is currently at court, I imagine.' He took another bite, chewed thoughtfully, swallowed and added, 'We shall see. It may be a delicate situation. I understand that there have been messages exchanged, but erratically. This delegation was actually expected to arrive months ago, but the Chalcedeans intensified the war. The Bingtown war with Chalced has disrupted shipping woefully to all points south of Shoaks. I gather that the Queen and Chade had given up all expectations until today.'

'Messages?' All of this was news to me.

'Bingtown has approached the Queen, proposing an alliance to quell Chalced once and for all. To entice her, they have offered trade advantages in Bingtown, and a new closeness between the realms. Kettricken has rightly seen it as an empty offer. There can be no free trade until Chalced gives over its harassment of the ships in and out of Bingtown. Once Chalced is battered into submission, then Bingtown will be open for trade again, whether or not the Six Duchies took any part in subjugating Chalced. Bingtown lives on trade. It cannot even feed itself. So. A cold evaluation is that the Six Duchies risked inflaming its own disagreements with Chalced, with very little to gain by it. That being so, Kettricken has graciously declined their invitation to join their war. But now the Bingtown Councils hint that they have something else to offer, something so stupendous and so secret that word of it cannot be entrusted to a scroll. Hence, these envoys. A clever ploy, to play on the curiosity of the Queen and her nobles. They will have a rapt audience. Shall we eat and go?'

We dispatched the food swiftly between us, and then I cleared the breakfast tray away to the kitchens. All was in a hubbub there. The unexpected delegation demanded an amazing luncheon and an extraordinary feast in their honour. Old Cook Sara had actually descended into the thick of the culinary skirmish in progress, proclaiming that she would do it all herself, that those Bingtowners would never be able to say that the Six Duchies lacked in any sort of food. I retreated hastily from the commotion and hurried back to Lord Golden's chambers.

I found the door latched. At my knock and quiet call, it was opened. I stepped through and shut it behind me, and then stood in shock. The Fool stood before me. Not the Fool in Lord Golden's garb, but the Fool very nearly as I had known him when we were both boys. It was the garment he wore, close-fitting hose and a full tunic of solid black. His only ornaments were the earring and the tiny black and white posy. Even his slippers were black. Only his stature and colouring seemed changed from those days. I half-expected him to shake a rat's-head sceptre at me or turn a flip. At my raised brows, he said, almost abashedly, 'I did not wish to risk any of Lord Golden's wardrobe in your dusty warren. And I can move most quietly in simple garments.'

I made no reply to that, but kindled a candle, and handed him two extra ones. I led him into my chamber. Closing the outer door, I triggered the entry to the concealed corridors and led him into Chade's labyrinth. 'Where is Queen Kettricken receiving them?' I belatedly thought to ask.

'In the West Reception Hall. Chade said to tell you the access is actually in the outer wall there.'

'Directions on how to get there would have been more helpful. But never mind, we'll find it.'

My optimism was not justified. It was an area of the castle's internal maze that I had not explored before. I frustrated us both by finding the chamber above the audience hall, and one next to it before I deduced that I had to go to a lower level and then make my way up into the outer wall. The corridor had one very narrow bend in it, one I barely squeezed through. By the time we reached our spy post, we were both festooned with cobwebs. The sole peephole proved to be a narrow, horizontal slit. I hooded the candle flame and then moved the leather flap that concealed it from our side. Standing crouched side-by-side, we could each just put one eye to it. The Fool's breathing by my ear seemed loud. I had to concentrate to pick out the words that dimly penetrated our hiding place.

We were late. The ambassadors had already been greeted. I could not see Kettricken or Chade. I imagined that Kettricken occupied the high seat, with Dutiful to one side and Chade standing on a lower step of the dais. Our vantage was such that we looked out over the hall, probably over the heads of the Queen and Prince. In the back of the audience chamber were seated the dukes and duchesses of the Six Duchies, or those representing them at court. Starling was there, of course. No gathering of significance could happen at court without a minstrel as witness. She was finely dressed, yet her expression was more solemn than alight with interest as I would have expected. She seemed distracted and pensive. I wondered what might be troubling her, and then resolutely fixed my gaze and attention where it belonged.

Central to our view were the four ambassadors from Bingtown. As befitted that wealthy trading town, these were merchants rather than dukes and lords. Nonetheless, the richness of their attire made them seem the equal of any noble. Their clothing glittered with jewels, and in the dimness of the audience chamber, some of the gems seemed to gleam with their own light. One short woman was robed in fabric that flowed over her form like water, so supple and fine was it woven. On the shoulder of one of the men perched a bird, its plumage every shade of red and orange, save for its head, which was of wrinkled white skin. It had an enormous blue-black beak.

Behind these impressive merchants stood a second row of folk, most likely servants despite their elegant dress. They bore the caskets and chests of good-will gifts. Two stood out in their rank. One was a woman, her face heavily tattooed. There was no art to the marking, no balance, no discernible design, only a succession of ink scrawls that crawled across her cheeks. I knew it meant she had been a slave, and each tattoo was the sigil of an owner. I wondered what she had done, to be bought and sold so often. The other strange servant was hooded and veiled. The fabric of his drapery was rich and elaborate, the veil across his face of fine yet heavy lace. I could not see his features, and even his hands were gloved, as if to be sure that no part of his skin showed. It made me uneasy and I resolved to watch him most closely.

We were just in time for the presentation of the gifts. There were five gifts in all, and each more entrancing than the last. They were offered with flowery compliments and elegant titles, as if our queen's favour could be bought with parsed words and flattery. I mistrusted the speeches, but the gifts fascinated me. The first was a tall glass vial containing a perfume. As the tattooed servant approached to offer it to Queen Kettricken, a tall woman explained that the fragrance would bring sweet dreams to even the most restless sleeper. I could not vouch for the dreams, but unstoppered for just a moment, the fragrance spread to fill the hall, reaching even to the Fool and me in our concealment. It was not a heady fragrance, but more like the wind-blown breath of a summer garden. Even so, I saw the expressions change on the faces of the nobles in the back of the hall as that rare essence reached them. Smiles grew wider and furrowed brows relaxed. Even I felt a lessening of my wariness.

'A drug?' I breathed to the Fool.

'No. Only a perfume, a scent from a kindlier place.' A faint smile played over his face. 'I knew that scent of old, when I was a child. They traded far for that.'

The next servant approached, and opened his cask at the Queen's feet. From it he lifted a simple set of dangling chimes, such as any garden might hold, save that these seemed to me made of scaled glass rather than metal. He kept them stilled with his hand until, at a signal from the parrot-man, he shook them, a delicate shiver that still set them to swinging and ringing. Each tone was sweet, and their random pattern swiftly fell into a rippling song. Abruptly the servant muted them, far too soon for me. But then he gave them another tiny shake, and again a shimmering melody burst forth, as different from the first as the crackling of a fire is from the muttering of a brook. He let them play for a time, and they showed no sign of stilling themselves. When the servant muted them again, the parrot-man spoke. 'Fair Queen Kettricken, most noble lady of both the Mountains and the Six Duchies, we hope this sound pleases you. No one is certain how many tunes these chimes hold. Each time they are freed, they seem to spell a different song. As vast and great as your lands are, and as sophisticated as your tastes must no doubt be, we hope you will deem this humble gift worthy of you.'

Kettricken must have made some sign of acceptance, for the chimes were restored to their chest and brought forward to her.

The third gift was a length of fabric, similar in kind but not in hue to the one the woman wore. This was lifted from a small chest, but when the small woman and the parrot man moved forward to take it from the servant, the cloth unfolded again, and yet again, and yet again, until the swathe of it was enough to cloth a long table in the great hall and drape still to the floor. It shimmered when they shook it, moving through shades of blue from deep violet to pale summer sky. And they folded it effortlessly to a compact square that they restored to its chest. This, too, was set before our Queen. The fourth gift was a set of bells, arranged in a scale. The tone was good but no more than that. What was amazing about them was that the metal they were made of shimmered with light as each bell rang. 'This is jidzin, most gracious Queen Kettricken, ruler of the Six Duchies and heir to the Mountain Throne,' the short woman told her. 'This is one treasure that can come from Bingtown alone. We are certain that you are worthy of no less than the very best we can offer you. Jidzin is among our most unique treasures. As are these.' She waved a hand at the hooded man and he came forward. 'Flame-jewels, fair Queen Kettricken. Rarest of the rare, for a rare queen.'

My muscles tightened as the veiled man approached the dais where Kettricken and Dutiful were seated. Chade was there, I reminded myself, even as my stomach clenched in apprehension. The old assassin would be as wary as I; he would let no harm come to the Queen or Prince. Even so, I sent a tiny Skill-thought to Dutiful.

Be wary.

I shall.

I had not expected the Prince to reply to my warning. His was a thought flung wide rather than a careful channelling. All the hair on the back of my neck stood up as I saw the veiled man twitch as if poked. For an instant, he stood very still. I sensed something from him, a reaching I had no name for.

Ssh, I cautioned Dutiful in a thread of thought. *Be very still.*

I desperately longed to see the veiled man's expression. Did he stare at my prince? Did he glance about the chamber seeking me?

Whoever he was, his control was masterful. He made his abrupt halt a ceremonial pause. Then he bowed low, and presented his gift, setting the cask on the floor before him. At a stroke of his hand, it seemed to open by itself. He reached in and took out a smaller box. This he opened to reveal a torc of gold set with gems. He displayed it to the Queen, and then held it aloft so the gathered nobles might see it. While it was still raised, the bearer gave the ornament a shake. All of the jewels suddenly flared to life, glowing an unearthly blue in the dim hall. As he turned back toward the Queen, offering it for her regard, I heard the Fool give a quiet gasp at the beauty of the thing. The veiled man spoke clearly despite his muffling veils, and his voice was young, almost a boy's. 'The blues are the rarest of the flame-jewels, most gracious queen. They were chosen for you, in the colour of Buck Duchy. And for each noble and gracious ruler of each of your noble and gracious Duchies . . .'

There were gasps from the back of the hall as the gift-bearer lifted from the cask five additional boxes. He opened each in turn, to show neckpieces of narrow silver rather than wide gold. Each of these bore a single jewel, but they were nonetheless breath-taking. Someone had studied the Six Duchies well, for each gem was the proper colour for the duchy it was intended for, even to distinguishing between the pale yellow of the Bearns flower sigil to the deeper gold of Farrow. After the Queen had accepted her collar, the hooded servant moved to the gathered nobles, to bow gravely to each and then proffer the Bingtown gift. Despite the man's unusual garb, I noticed that no one hesitated to accept his offering.

As this was going on, I watched the other Bingtown emissaries closely. 'Who is their leader?' I muttered to myself, for none seemed to give precedence to any of the others. The Fool took it as a query.

'Do you see the woman with green eyes, the taller of the two?' The Fool barely breathed the words by my ear. 'I believe her name is Serilla. She was originally from Jamaillia and a companion to their satrap. That is, she was an advisor to the ruler of all Jamaillia, an expert within her chosen area. Hers was Bingtown and the surrounding area. She came to Bingtown under very odd circumstances, and has since remained there. Gossip had it that she had fallen into deep disfavour with the ruling satrap, and that he all but exiled her to Bingtown. Some say she had made an attempt to seize power from him. But instead of taking her exile as a punishment she has made Bingtown her home and has risen to the status of a professional negotiator for the Traders. Despite her bad blood with the Satrap, her intimate knowledge of both Bingtown and Jamaillia have given Bingtown an edge in its dealings with Jamaillia.'

'Ssh,' I hushed him hastily. I wondered how he knew all that, and wanted to hear more, but for now I must be aware of every nuance of all that was said. He subsided, but I could sense his ferment. His cool cheek was pressed against mine as we stared side by side through the narrow slit. He rested a hand on my shoulder to steady himself, but I could feel the tension of his suppressed excitement. Obviously, this meeting had a deeper significance to him. Later, I would ask him who the others were. For now, I was engrossed with the scene before me. I only wished I could see the Queen, Chade and Prince Dutiful as I watched this encounter unfold.

I listened as the Queen offered thanks for the gifts and extended welcome to the emissaries. Her words were simple. She did not reply with extravagant compliments and embroidered titles, but instead offered them sincerity in honest phrases. She was thrilled by the surprise of their long-expected visit. She hoped they would enjoy their stay in Buckkeep, and that this delegation represented a future of more open communication between the Six Duchies and Bingtown. The tall woman, Serilla, stood serenely, listening intently to the Queen's words. The tattooed woman folded her lips as Kettricken spoke, plainly holding back some response. The man at her side cast her an anxious glance. He was a broad-shouldered, bluff man, his hair cropped short and curly above his weathered face. He was obviously accustomed to physical work, and to getting things accomplished rather than wading through protocol and courtesies. As he waited for the Queen to finish speaking, his fists knotted and unknotted themselves reflexively. The bird on his shoulder shifted restlessly. The other man, a narrow, bookish sort of fellow, seemed more of Serilla's cast. He would let Kettricken set the pace for this encounter.

Serilla was the one who spoke when Kettricken's voice fell silent. She, in turn, thanked the Queen and all the Six Duchies for such a gracious welcome. She told them that all of them would welcome the chance to rest in our peaceful land, far from the horrors of the war that Chalced had forced upon them. She spoke some little time on what they had been enduring; the random attacks on their ships that disrupted all commerce, the very lifeblood of Bingtown, and the hardships this created for a city that relied on trade to feed its population. She spoke of Chalcedean raids on outlying Bingtown settlements.

'I didn't think they had any outlying settlements,' I breathed in an aside to the Fool.

'Not many. But as their population has swelled with freed slaves, folk have been attempting to find arable land.'

'Freed slaves?'

'Sshh,' the Fool responded. He was right. I needed to listen now, and ask my questions later. I leaned my forehead against the cold stone of the wall.

Serilla was swiftly reviewing Bingtown's current list of grievances with Chalced. Most of them were ones I was very familiar with, and many were the same quarrels that the Six Duchies had with our grasping neighbour to the south. Chalcedean raiders, border disputes, harassment and piracy of passing trade vessels, ridiculous taxes on those merchants that did attempt to trade with them: all of these were familiar rants. But then she launched into an account of how Bingtown had risen up against corrupt Chalcedean influence to free all the slaves within its borders and to offer them a chance to become full citizens of Bingtown. Bingtown would no longer allow slave-ships to stop in its port, regardless of whether they were bound north to Chalced or south to Jamaillia. By an agreement with Bingtown's new allies in the so-called Pirate Isles, slave-ships that put into Bingtown were boarded, the cargoes seized and the slaves offered freedom.

This disruption of the Chalcedean slave-trade was a major area of conflict. It had brought into new prominence the old disagreement over where the Chalcedean-Bingtown border actually lay. In both of these areas, Serilla hoped that the Six Duchies would recognize the legitimacy of Bingtown's position. She knew that Shoaks Duchy welcomed escaped slaves to their lands as free men, and that Shoaks had also suffered from Chalced's efforts to claim lands not rightfully part of that dukedom. Could she, perhaps, hope that the Six Duchies would grant what their previous envoys

had proposed to the most gracious and royal Queen Kettricken –
an alliance, and support for the war against Chalced? In return,
Bingtown and her ally had much to offer the Six Duchies. Open
trade with Bingtown, and a share in Bingtown's favourable trade
agreements with the so-called Pirate Isles could be of great benefit
to all. The gifts bestowed today represented but a small part of the
spectrum of goods that would become available to the people of
the Six Duchies.

Queen Kettricken heard her out gravely. But at the end of
Serilla's speech, she had offered nothing new to us. It was Chade,
in his role as Councillor, who gravely pointed this out. The wonders
of their trade-goods were well known, and justifiably so. But not
even for such wonders could the Six Duchies consider moving
into war. He concluded his remarks with, 'Our most gracious
Queen Kettricken must always consider first the well-being of
our own folk. You know that our relations with Chalced are at
best uneasy. Our grievances with them are many, and yet we
have held our hands back from waging a full war with them on
our own accounts. All know the saying, "Sooner or later, there
is always war with Chalced." They are a contentious folk. But
war is expensive and disruptive. War later is almost always better
than war now. Why should we risk provoking their full wrath on
Bingtown's behalf?' Chade let the question hang for a moment, and
then made it even plainer. 'What do you offer the Six Duchies that
will not eventually come to us, regardless of the outcome of this
war of yours?'

Several dukes in the back nodded sagely. All knew this was the
Trader way. All they understood was bargaining and trade. They
expected Chade to haggle, and haggle he would.

'Most gracious Queen, noble Prince, wise Councillor and lordly
Dukes and Duchesses, we offer you . . .' Serilla halted, obviously
flustered by the directness of Chade's question. 'Our offer is a
delicate one, perhaps best reviewed in private contemplation before
you seek the agreement of your nobles. Perhaps it would be
better . . .' Serilla did not glance toward the nobles in the back
of the room, but her pause was plain.

'Please, Serilla of Bingtown. Speak plainly. Put your proposal before all of us, so that my nobles and my councillors and I may discuss it freely together.'

Serilla's eyes widened, almost in shock. I wondered what sort of place Jamaillia was, that she was so surprised by my queen's forthright answer. While she floundered, the man with the parrot on his shoulder suddenly cleared his throat. Serilla shot him a warning look, but the man stepped forward anyway. 'Most gracious Queen, if I may presume to address you directly?'

Kettricken's response was almost puzzled. 'Of course. You are Trader Jorban, I believe?'

He nodded gravely. 'That is correct. Most gracious Queen Kettricken, ruler of all the Six Duchies and heir to the Mountain Throne.' I felt uncomfortable for the young man as he strung the titles awkwardly together. Obviously such flowery address was new to him, but despite Serilla's angry glance, he was determined to forge ahead with it. 'I believe you are a person, a queen, that is, who can appreciate directness. I have chafed under this delay. But now, hearing today that you have as little love for Chalced as we do, I dare to hope that you will be in favour of our proposition as soon as you hear it.' He cleared his throat, then plunged on. 'We come to you seeking to forge an alliance against a common enemy. We have had three years of war with Chalced. It has drained us, and our early hopes to a swift end to the conflict have faded. The Chalcedeans are a stubborn folk. Every defeat we deal them only seems to make them more determined to injure us. They thrive on war; they love raiding and destruction, as we do not. Bingtown needs peace to prosper, peace and free seas. We depend on trade, not just for our livelihoods, but for our most basic needs. Magic and wonders we may possess in Bingtown, and yet we cannot feed our children on that alone. We have no vast fields to grow grain and pasture cattle. Chalced would overrun us, out of simple greed. They would kill us all, to possess what we have, with no understanding of what that possessing requires of us. They will destroy what they seek, in the very act of trying to possess it. What we have cannot be taken from us, and still exist. It is . . .' The man's words shuddered to a halt, like a ship run aground on a sand-bar.

Kettricken waited for a time, as if offering him a chance to find his tongue, but the man only spread his hands open, wide and helpless. 'I'm a trader and a sailor, ma'am. Most gracious Queen.' He appended the honorific as if he had suddenly recalled it. 'I speak out of our need, and yet I do not explain myself well.'

'What do you ask, Trader Jorban?' Queen Kettricken's question was simple yet polite.

Hope gleamed suddenly in the man's eyes, as if her directness reassured him. 'We know that the folk of your Shoaks Duchy hold a hard border with Chalced. You contain them, and your vigilance demands much of their attention.' He turned suddenly, to sweep a wide bow to the nobles in the back of the chamber. 'For this, we thank you.'

The Duke acknowledged his thanks with a grave nod. Trader Jorban turned back to the Queen. 'But we must ask more than this. We ask your warships and warriors to pressure Chalced from your side. To harry and sink the ships that interfere in our trade with you. We would . . . put an end to the generations of strife Chalced has forced on all of us.' He drew a sudden breath. 'We would subjugate that land completely, and end this ancient strife. If they will not abide as our neighbour, then let them accept our rule instead.'

Serilla the Jamaillian suddenly interrupted. 'Trader Jorban, you go too far! Fair and gracious Queen Kettricken, we come but to make suggestions, not to propose a conquest.'

Jorban set his jaw and dived in as soon as Serilla fell silent. 'I do not make a suggestion. I come to bargain with potential allies. I seek for an end to Chalced's endless war against us. I will speak plainly what is in many Traders' hearts.' His blue eyes glinted as he met Kettricken's gaze. He spoke honestly, with passion. 'Let us subjugate the Chalcedean states completely, dividing their territory between us. All would gain. Bingtown would have arable land, and an end to Chalcedean harassment. The Duke of Shoaks could expand his holdings and have, not an enemy at his back, but an ally and trading partner. Trade to the south would open wide for the Six Duchies.'

'Subjugate Chalced completely?' I could tell from Kettricken's voice that she had never even considered it, that such a conquering ran counter to all her Mountain ways. But in the back of the room,

the Duke of Shoaks was grinning broadly. This was a war he would
relish, a meal of vengeance long in the simmering for him. He
overstepped himself, perhaps, when he lifted a fist and suggested,
'Let us include the Duke of Farrow in this partitioning. And perhaps
your lord father, King Eyod of the Mountains, would like a share of
this, my queen. He, too, shares a boundary with Chalced, and from
all accounts has never been too fond of them.'

'Peace, Shoaks,' she rebuked him, but it was a gentler shushing
than I would have expected. Perhaps there was history there I did
not know. Just how bitterly did the Mountain Kingdom dispute its
own border with Chalced? Did Kettricken bring an older rancour to
this conflict than I knew? Yet there was reserve as she replied to the
Bingtown delegation. 'You offer us a share of your war, as if it were
trade goods we should covet. We do not. We have had a war, and
even now we seek to make those former enemies our friends. Your
war does not tempt us. You offer us Chalced's lands, if we defeat
them. That is a distant and uncertain victory. Holding that territory
might be more of a burden than an advantage. A conquered people
are seldom content to accept foreign rule. You offer us free trade to
the south, if we achieve that victory. Yet Bingtown has ever courted
open trade with us; I do not see that as a new gain. Again, I ask you.
Why should we even consider this?'

I watched the Bingtown envoys exchange glances, and smiled
small to myself. So. A proposal to divide Chalced's territory was
not the limit of their offer. But whatever it was that they held back,
they would not part with it unless forced to it. I felt no sympathy.
They should not have provoked Chade's curiosity as to how deep
their purse might be. Trader Jorban made a small gesture with his
hand, palm up, as if inviting someone else to succeed where he had
failed in his bargaining.

Then, as if by accord, the Bingtown merchants stepped aside,
parting to let the shrouded man stand directly before the Queen.
Some unspoken agreement had been reached amongst them.

I swiftly revised my opinion of the hooded man. He was no
servant. Perhaps none of them were, not even the woman with
the slave tattoos. As the veiled man stepped suddenly forward, I
winced, expecting some sort of attack, but all he did was to throw

back his hood. His lace veil, attached to it, was swept away with it. I gasped at what was revealed, but others, Chade amongst them, were less subtle.

'Eda, mercy!' I heard the old assassin exclaim, and from the back of the hall there were exclamations of both horror and shock.

The envoy was young, younger than Dutiful and Hap, though he was as tall. Scales rimmed his eyes and framed his mouth. They were not cosmetic. A fringe of shaggy growths depended from his jaw. He drew himself up very straight. I had thought his hood exaggerated his height. Instead I saw now that the bones of his arms and legs were unnaturally long, yet somehow he still managed to convey grace rather than awkwardness. He looked directly at Kettricken, uncowed by her position, and spoke in a boy's clear tenor.

'My name is Selden Vestrit, of the Bingtown Trader Vestrits, fostered by the Khuprus family of the Rain Wild Traders.' The second part of his introduction made no sense to me. No one lived in the Rain Wilds. The lands adjacent to the river were all swamp and bog and morass. It was one reason that the boundary between Chalced and Bingtown had never been firmly set. The river and its swampy shores defied them both. But what the boy said next was even more outrageous. 'You have heard Serilla, who speaks for the Council of Bingtown. There are others here who can speak for the Tattooed, those once slaves and Bingtown citizens, and for the Bingtown Traders and for our liveships. I speak for the Rain Wild Traders. But I also speak for Tintaglia, the last true dragon, sworn to aid Bingtown in our time of need. Her words do I bear.'

A shiver ran over me at the dragon's name. I did not know why.

'She is tired of Chalced's constant wrangling with her Bingtown folk. It distracts them and hinders them from another, greater work that she has in mind for them. This war Chalced is intent on waging imperils a far greater destiny.' He spoke as if he were not a man, with a contempt that dismissed petty human concerns. It was both chilling and inspiring. He swept us all with his eyes. I realized then that I had not imagined the faint bluish glow from his gaze. 'Aid Bingtown in destroying Chalced and putting this war to an end, and Tintaglia will bestow on you her favour. And not only her favour, but also the favour of her offspring, rapidly growing in size, beauty and wisdom. Aid us, and one day the Six Duchies legends of dragons rising to protect them will be replaced by the reality of a dragon ally.'

A stunned silence followed his words. I am sure they all misinterpreted it. Trader Jorban rashly grinned at what must have been the shock on Kettricken's face, and dared to add, 'I do not blame you for doubting us. But Tintaglia is real, as real as I am. But for her need to tend her offspring, she would have made a swift end to Chalced's harassment of us years ago. Have not you heard rumours of the battle of Trader Bay, and how a Bingtown dragon, silver and blue, swept forth to drive the Chalcedeans from our shore? I was there that day, fighting to free our harbour of Chalcedeans. Those rumours are neither fanciful exaggerations nor wild tales, but simplest truth. Bingtown possesses a rare and marvellous ally, the last true dragon in the world. Aid us in subduing Chalced, and she could be your ally as well.'

I do not think he expected his words to be spark to Kettricken's tinder. I doubt he could understand how deeply her feelings for our Six Duchies dragons went.

'The last true dragon!' she exclaimed. I heard the rustle of her gown as she shot to her feet. She strode down the steps, to confront the Bingtown upstarts, stopping but one riser above them. My rational, gracious queen's voice grated with fury. It rose to fill the hall. 'How dare you speak so! How dare you dismiss the Elderling dragons as legends! I have seen the skies jewelled with not one, but a horde of dragons that rose to the defence of the Six Duchies. I myself bestrode a dragon, the truest of them all, when he bore me back to Buckkeep Castle. There is not a grown person in this chamber who did not witness their wide wings over our waters, scattering the Red Ships that had harried us so long. Do you insinuate our dragons were false somehow, in heart or deed? The boy may plead the excuse of his youth and inexperience, not just in that he probably was not even born when we fought our war, but that he has had little training in the respect due to such creatures. You can plead only your ignorance of our history. The last true dragon, indeed!'

I doubt that any insult to our queen's person would have provoked such an outraged reaction. No one there could know that it was her king, Verity, her love, whose honour she upheld. Even some of our own nobles looked startled to see their usually placid queen rebuke an envoy so sharply, but their surprise did not mean they disagreed with her. Heads nodded at her words. Several of her dukes and duchesses came to their feet, and she who represented Bearns set a hand to her sword. The scaled boy glanced around, mouth ajar with dismay as Serilla rolled her eyes at his gaffe. The Bingtown contingent instinctively drew closer to one another.

The scaled lad advanced a step closer to the Queen. Chade made a motion to forbid it, but the boy merely dropped to one knee. He looked up at her as he spoke. 'I beg forgiveness if I have given offence. I speak only of what I know. As you have said, I am young. But it is Tintaglia who has told us, with great sadness, that she is the last true dragon in the world. If it were otherwise, I would rejoice to bring her these tidings. Please. Let me see your dragons, let me speak to them. I will explain to them her need.'

Kettricken's shoulders were still rising and falling with the strength of her passion. She drew a quieter breath at last, and when she spoke, she was herself again. 'I bear no resentment against you for speaking of what you knew not. As for speaking to our dragons, it is out of the question. They are Six Duchies dragons, for the Six Duchies alone. Young sir, you presume too much. But you are young, and on that basis I forgive you.'

The boy remained as he was, on one knee but not at all subservient as he gazed up doubtfully at our queen.

It was up to Chade to calm the room. He stepped forward to confront the Bingtown delegation. 'It is, perhaps, natural that you appear to doubt our queen's word, even as we doubt yours. The last true dragon, you say, but then you speak of her offspring. It sets my mind a puzzle; why do you not consider them "true dragons"? If your dragon exists, why has not she come with you, to show herself and give impetus to our decision to side with you?' He swept them with his hard green gaze. 'My friends, there is something very peculiar about your offer. There is much you are not saying. Doubtless, you believe your reasons for doing so are sound. But keeping your secrets may lose you not only an alliance, but also our respect. Weigh that bargain well.'

Even looking at his back, I knew that Chade pulled now at his chin, considering. He glanced over at the Queen. Whatever he saw on her face made up his mind. 'Lords and ladies, I suggest we end this audience for the time being. Let our fair and gracious queen discuss your offer with her nobles. Chambers have been prepared for you. Enjoy our hospitality.' I could hear the faint smile that came into his voice as he added, 'Any of the minstrels we have provided will be happy to enlighten you, in song or story, about the dragons of the Six Duchies. Perhaps when next we meet, all our tempers will be evened with song and rest.'

Dismissed so firmly, the Bingtown envoys could do little but withdraw. The Queen and Prince Dutiful departed next. Chade lingered amongst the nobles; he seemed to be arranging a time for all to sit down and discuss the Bingtown proposal. The Duke of Shoaks was striding about, visibly excited, while the Duchess of Bearns stood, tall and silent, her arms crossed before her breast as if denying any interest at all. I leaned back from the peephole, letting the flap of leather fall. 'Let us go,' I whispered to the Fool, and he nodded in silent agreement.

I took up our candle again, and we negotiated the narrow warren of rat-runs that threaded Buckkeep's walls. I did not take him directly back to my chamber, but instead stopped at Chade's old tower room. Immediately inside the room, the Fool halted. He closed his eyes for a moment, and then took a deep breath. 'It has not changed much since the last time I was here,' he said in a choked voice.

I used my candle to kindle the waiting ones on the table. I added another piece of wood to the coals on the hearth. 'I imagine Chade brought you here the night King Shrewd was murdered.'

He nodded slowly. 'I had encountered Chade before, and conversed with him over the years. The first time I met him was shortly after I came to King Shrewd. Chade would come by night, to speak with the King. Sometimes they played dice together; did you know that? Mostly they sat by the fire and drank fine brandy and talked of whatever danger was currently confronting the kingdom. That was how I first heard of your existence. In a fireside conversation between those two. My heart pounded until I thought I would faint as I understood what their words meant to me. They scarcely noticed me listening. They thought me but a child, perhaps lacking in true wit and I had taken care initially to appear to have little mastery of your language.' He shook his head to himself. 'Such a strange time in my life. So significant and portentous, and yet, sheltered by King Shrewd, it was the closest I ever came to having a true childhood.'

I found two cups and Chade's current bottle of brandy. I set them out at the table and poured for us. The Fool lifted an eye to that. 'This early in the day?'

I shrugged. 'It seems later to me than it is, perhaps. My day started early. With Hap.' I sat down heavily as that particular worry weighed my heart again. 'Fool. Do you ever long to go back in your life and do something differently?'

He took his seat but did not touch the glass. 'All men do. It's a foolish game we play. What troubles you, Fitz?'

And I told him, pouring out my heart as if I were a child, giving him all my fears and disappointments to sort, as if somehow he could make sense of them for me. 'I look back, Fool, and sometimes it seems that the times when I was most certain I was doing the right thing was when I made my gravest errors. Hunting down Justin and Serene and killing them before the assembled dukes after they had assassinated my king. Look what that did to us, the cascade of events that followed.'

He nodded to that. 'And?' he prompted me as I poured more brandy for myself.

I drank it off. 'And bedding with Molly,' I said. I sighed, but felt no easing. 'It seemed so right. So sweet and true and precious. The only thing in my world that belonged completely to me. But if I had not . . .'

He waited for me.

'If I had not, if I had not got her with child, she would not have left Buckkeep to hide her pregnancy. Even when I made my other stupid mistake, she would have been able to take care of herself. Burrich would not have felt that he had to go to her, to watch over her until her child was born. They would not have fallen in love; they would not have married. When . . . After the dragons, I could have come back to her. I could have something, now.'

I wasn't weeping. This was pain past weeping. The only thing new about this was admitting it aloud, to myself. 'I brought it all down on myself. It was all my own doing.'

He leaned across the table to set his long cool hand atop mine. 'It's a foolish game, Fitz,' he said softly. 'And you attribute too much power to yourself, and too little to the sweep of events. And to Molly. If you could go back and erase those decisions, who knows what others would take their places? Give it over, Fitz. Let it go. What Hap does now is not a punishment for what you did in the past. You didn't cause him to make this choice. But that doesn't free you from your duties as a father, to try to turn him aside from that path. Do you think because you made that same decision it disqualifies you from telling him it was a mistake?' He took a breath, then asked, 'Have you ever considered telling him about Molly and Nettle?'

'I . . . no. I can't.'

'Oh, Fitz. Secrets and things held back . . .' His voice trailed away sorrowfully.

'Such as Bingtown's dragons,' I said levelly.

He lifted his hand from mine. 'What?'

'We were drinking that night, and you told me a story. About serpents that went into butterfly cocoons and came out as dragons. But for some reason they came out small and sickly. You thought somehow it was your fault.'

He leaned back in his chair. He looked more sallow than golden. 'We had been drinking. A lot.'

'Yes. We had. You were drunk enough to talk. But I was still sober enough to listen.' I waited, but he just sat quietly looking at me. 'Well?' I demanded at last.

'What do you want to know?' he asked in a low voice.

'Tell me about Bingtown's dragons. Are they real?'

I sat and watched him reach some decision. Then he sat up and poured more brandy for us both. He drank. 'Yes. As real as the Six Duchies dragons were, but in a different way.'

'How?'

He took a breath. 'Long, long ago, we argued this. Remember? I said that at one time there had to have been dragons of flesh and bone, to inspire Skill-coteries to create dragons of stone and memory.'

'That was years ago. I barely recall the conversation.'

'You don't need to. All you need to know is that I was right.' A smile flickered across his face. 'Once, Fitz, there were real dragons. The dragons that inspired the Elderlings.'

'The dragons were the Elderlings,' I contradicted him.

He smiled. 'You are right, Fitz, but not in the way you think you mean those words. I think. It is a shattered mirror I am still reassembling. The dragons you and I awoke, the Six Duchies dragons ... they were created things. Carved by coteries or Elderlings, the memory-stone took on the shapes they gave it, and came to life. As dragons. Or as winged boars. Or flying stags. Or as a Girl-On-A-Dragon.'

He was putting it together almost too swiftly for me to follow. I nodded nonetheless. 'Go on.'

'Why did Elderlings make those stone dragons and store their lives in them? Because they were inspired by real dragons. Dragons that, like butterflies, have two stages to their lives. They hatch from eggs into sea serpents. They roam the seas, growing to a vast size. And when the time is right, when enough years have passed that they have attained dragon size, they migrate back to the home of their ancestors. The adult dragons would welcome them and escort them up the rivers. There, they spin their cocoons of sand – sand that is ground memory-stone – and their own saliva. In times past, adult dragons helped them spin those cases. And with the saliva of the adult dragons went their memories, to aid in the formation of the young dragons. For a full winter, they slumbered and changed, as the grown dragons watched over them to protect them from predators. In the hot sunlight of summer, they hatched, absorbing much of their cocoon casing as they did so. Absorbing, too, the memories stored in it. Young dragons emerged, full-formed and strong, ready to fend for themselves, to eat and hunt and fight for mates. And eventually to lay eggs on a distant island. The island of the Others. Eggs that would hatch into serpents.'

As he spoke, I could almost see it. Perhaps my dreams had primed me to it. How often in my sleep had I imagined what it would be to be a dragon as Verity had become, to fly the skies, to hunt and to feed? Something in his words reached those dreams, and they suddenly seemed true memories of my own rather than the imaginings of sleep. He had fallen silent.

'Tell the rest,' I prodded him.

He leaned back in his chair and sighed. 'Something killed them. Long ago. I don't know exactly what. Some great cataclysm of the earth, that buried whole cities in a matter of days. It sank the coast, drowning harbour towns, and changed the courses of rivers. It wiped out the dragons, and I think it killed the Elderlings as well. All of that is a surmise, Fitz. Not just from what I have seen and heard, but from what you have told me and from what I have read in your journals. That empty, riven city you visited, your own vision there of a dragon landing in the river, and of a strangely-formed folk who greeted it. Once, those people and dragons lived alongside one another. When the disaster came that ended them both, the folk tried to save some of the cocooned dragons. They dragged them into their buildings. The dragon cocoons and the people were buried alive together. The people perished. But inside the cocoons, untouched by the light and warmth that would signal a time of awakening, the half-formed dragons lingered on.'

Rapt as a child, I listened to his wild tale.

'Eventually, another folk found them. The Rain Wild Traders, an offshoot of the Bingtown Traders, dug into the ancient buried cities, seeking treasure. Much did they find there. Much of what you saw today, offered as gifts to Kettricken, the flame-gems, the jidzin, even the fabric, is the trove of those Elderling dwellings. They also found the cocooned dragons. They had no idea that was what they were, of course. They thought . . . who knows what they thought at first? Perhaps they seemed like massive sections of tree trunks. So they refer to it: wizardwood. They cut them up and used the cases as lumber, discarding the half-formed dragons within. That is the material they made their liveships from, and those strange vessels have the roots of their vitality in the dragons they would have been. Most of the half-formed dragons were dead, I suspect, long before their cocoons were cut up. But one, at least, was not. And a chain of events that I am not fully privy to exposed that dragon-cocoon to sunlight. It hatched. Tintaglia emerged.'

'Weak and badly formed.' I was trying to connect this tale with what he had told me previously.

'No. Hale and hearty, and as arrogant a creature as you would ever wish to encounter. She went searching for others of her own kind. Eventually she gave up looking for dragons. Instead, she found serpents. They were old and immense, for – and again, I speculate, Fitz – for whatever cataclysm that had destroyed the adult dragons had changed the world enough to prevent the serpents from returning to their cocooning grounds. Decade after decade, perhaps century after century, they had made periodic attempts to return, only to have many of their number perish. But this time, with Tintaglia to guide them, and the folk of Bingtown to dredge the rivers so they could pass, some of the serpents survived their migration. In the midst of winter, they made their cases. They were old and weakened and sickly, and had but one dragon to shepherd them and help them spin their cases. Many perished on their journey up the river; others sank into dormancy in their cases, never to revive. When summer came, those that hatched in the strength of the sunlight emerged as weaklings. Perhaps the serpents were too old, perhaps they did not spend enough time in their cocoons, perhaps they were not in good enough condition when they began their time of change. They are pitiable creatures. They cannot fly, nor hunt for themselves. They drive Tintaglia to distraction, for the dragon way is to despise weakness, to let perish those not strong enough to survive. But if she lets them die, then she will be completely alone, forever, the last of her kind, with no hope of rekindling her race. So Tintaglia spends all her time and energy in hunting for them and bringing kills back to them. She believes that if she can feed them sufficiently, they may yet mature to full dragons. She wishes, nay, she *demands* that the Rain Wild Traders aid her in this. But they have young of their own to feed, and a war that hinders them in their trading. So, they all struggle.

So it was when last I was on the Rain Wild River, two years ago. So I suspect it remains.'

I sat for a time not speaking, trying to fit his exotic tale into my mind. I could not doubt him; he had told me far too many other strange things in our years together. And yet, believing him made so many of my own experiences suddenly take on new shapes and significance. I tried to focus on what his tale meant to Bingtown and the Six Duchies now.

'Do Chade and Kettricken know any of what you've told me?' Slowly he shook his head. 'At least, not from me. Perhaps Chade has other sources. But I've never spoken of this to him.'

'Eda and El, why not? They treat with the Bingtowners blindly, Fool.' A worse thought struck me. 'Did you tell any of them about our dragons? Do the Bingtown Traders know the true nature of the Six Duchies dragons?'

Again he shook his head.

'Thank Eda for that. But why haven't you spoken of these things to Chade? Why have you concealed them from everyone?'

He sat looking at me silently for so long that I thought he would not answer. When he did speak, it was reluctantly. 'I am the White Prophet. My purpose in this life is to set the world into a better path. Yet . . . I am not the Catalyst, not the one who makes changes. That is you, Fitz. Telling what I know to Chade would most definitely change the direction of his treating with the Bingtowners. I cannot tell if that change would aid me or hinder me in what I must do. I am, right now, more uncertain of my path than I have ever been.'

He stopped speaking and waited, as if he hoped I would say something helpful. I knew nothing to say. Silence stretched between us. The Fool folded his hands in his lap and looked down at them. 'I think that I may have made a mistake. In Bingtown. And I fear that in my years in Bingtown and . . . other places, that I did not fulfil my destiny correctly. I fear I went awry, and that hence all I do now will be warped.' He suddenly sighed. 'Fitz, I feel my way forward through time. Not a step at a time, but from moment to moment. What feels truest? Up until now it has not felt right to speak of these things to Chade. So I have not. Today, now, it felt as if it was time you knew these things. So I have told them to you. To you, I have passed on the decision. To tell or not to tell, Changer. That is up to you.'

It felt odd to have Nighteyes' name for me spoken aloud by a human voice. It prodded me uncomfortably. 'Is this how you always have made these crucial decisions? By how you "feel"?' My tone was sharper than I intended, but he did not flinch.

Instead he regarded me levelly and asked, 'And how else would I do it?'

'By your knowing. By omens and signs, portentous dreams, by your own prophecies . . . I don't know. But something more than simply by how you feel. El's balls, man, it could be no more than a bad serving of fish that you're "feeling".' I lowered my face into my hands and pondered. He had passed the decision on to me. What would I do? It suddenly seemed a more difficult decision than when I had been rebuking the Fool for not telling. How would knowing these things affect Chade's attitude toward Bingtown and a possible alliance? Real dragons. Was a share of a real dragon worth a war? What would it mean not to ally, if the Bingtowners prevailed, and then had a phalanx of dragons at their command? Tell Kettricken? Then there were the same questions, but very different answers were likely. A sigh blasted out of me. 'Why did you give this decision to me?'

I felt his hand on my shoulder and looked up to find his odd half-smile. 'Because you have handled it well before, when I've previously done it to you. Ever since I went hunting for a boy out in the gardens and told him, "Fitz fixes a feist's fits. Fat suffices".'

I goggled at him. 'But you'd told me you'd had a dream, and so come to tell me it.'

He smiled enigmatically. 'I did have a dream. And I wrote it down. When I was eight years old. And when the time felt right, I told it to you. And you knew what to do with it, to be my Catalyst, even then. As I trust you will now.' He sat back in his chair.

'I had no idea of what I was doing, then. No concept of how far the consequences would reach.'

'And now that you do?'

'I wish I didn't. It makes it harder to decide.'

He leaned back in his chair with a supercilious smile. 'See.' Then he leaned forward suddenly. 'How did you decide how to act back then, in the garden? On what you would do?'

I shook my head slowly. 'I didn't decide. There was a course of action and I took it. If anything decided me, it was based on what I thought would be best for the Six Duchies. I never thought beyond that.'

I turned my head an instant before the wine-rack moved, revealing the passage behind it. Chade entered. He looked out of breath and harassed. His eyes fell on the brandy. Without a word, he walked to the table, lifted my glass and drained it. Then he took a breath and spoke. 'I thought I might find you two hiding out here.'

'Scarcely hiding,' I objected. 'We were having a quiet discussion where we were sure things would remain private.' I got up from my chair and he sank into it gratefully. Evidently he had hastened up the secret steps into the tower.

'Would that Kettricken and I had kept our audience with the Bingtown Traders similarly private. Folk are already talking and the kettle already simmering.'

'About whether or not to ally with them and join their war with Chalced. Let me guess. Shoaks is willing to launch the warships tomorrow.'

'Shoaks I could deal with,' Chade replied irritably. 'No. It's more awkward than that. Scarcely had Kettricken returned to her chambers, scarcely had we begun to sort out between us what Bingtown is really asking and offering than a page knocked at the door. Peottre Blackwater and the Narcheska required an immediate meeting with us. Not requested: required.' He paused to let us ponder that. 'The message was conveyed most urgently. So, what could we do but comply? The Queen feared that the Narcheska had taken some new offence at something Dutiful had done or said. But when they were admitted to her private audience chamber, Peottre informed us that he and the Narcheska were most distressed that the Six Duchies was receiving the ambassadors from the Bingtown Traders. They both seemed extremely agitated. But the most interesting part was when Peottre declared firmly that if the Six Duchies entered into any sort of alliance with "those dragon-breeders", he would terminate the entire betrothal.'

'Peottre Blackwater and the Narcheska came to you about this, not Arkon Bloodblade?' I clarified.

At almost the same moment, the Fool asked with intense interest, 'Dragon-breeders? Blackwater called them "dragon-breeders"?'

Chade glanced from one to the other of us. 'Bloodblade wasn't there,' he replied to me, and to the Fool, 'Actually, it was the Narcheska who used that term.'

'What did the Queen say?' I asked.

Chade took in a long breath. 'I had hoped she would say that we needed a moment to confer. But evidently Kettricken felt more short-tempered about the previous day's humiliation of Prince Dutiful than I thought. Sometimes I forget she is a mother as well as a queen. She rather stiffly told the Narcheska and her uncle that the Six Duchies arrangements with the Bingtown Traders will be determined by the Six Duchies' best interests, not by threats. From anyone.'

'And?'

'And they left the audience chamber. The Narcheska seemed in high dudgeon, walking stiff-backed as a soldier. Blackwater hunched like a man heavily burdened.'

'They're scheduled to return to the Outislands soon, aren't they?'

Chade nodded heavily. 'A few days from now. All of this happens just in time to leave everything out of balance. If the Queen does not return an answer to the Bingtowners soon, then when the Narcheska departs, the whole betrothal will be left in uncertainty. All of that work to solidify our relations gone to waste or worse. Yet I feel there must be no haste in returning an answer to the Bingtown Traders. This whole offer must be considered carefully. This talk of dragons . . . is this a threat? A mockery of our dragons? A wild offer to us, of something that doesn't even exist, because they need our help so desperately? I need to make sense of that. I need to send spies and buy information. We dare not return an answer until we have our own sources of facts.'

The Fool and I exchanged a glance.

'What?' Chade demanded.

I took a deep breath and threw caution to the wind. 'I need to speak with you and the Queen. And perhaps Dutiful should be present as well.'

TWELVE

Jek

I am no coward. I have always accepted the will of the god-born. More than a dozen times has my life been put at the feet of Duke Sidder, for the good of glorious Chalced. None of those risks do I regret. But when the most gracious and divinely just Duke Sidder finds fault with us for failing to hold Bingtown Harbour, he is unfortunately basing his judgement on the reports of men who were not there. Hence, our most gracious and divinely just duke cannot be faulted in any way for coming to flawed conclusions. Herewith, I endeavour to correct those reports.

Scribe Wertin wrote that '. . . a fleet of seasoned battleships was defeated and driven away by slaves and fishermen.' This is not the case. Slaves and fishermen were, indeed, responsible for much treachery against our ships, done in secret and under cover of darkness rather than in true battle. But as our captains had not been given warning that the Bingtown Traders might have such organized forces at their disposal, why would we be expected to be on guard against them? I think the fault here lies not with our captains, but with those Bingtown emissaries, scribes and accountants, not warriors, who neglected to keep us well informed. Hanging is too kind for them. Many brave warriors died unworthy deaths due to their laxity in reporting.

Scribe Wertin also suggests that perhaps treasure was loaded from the warehouses before they were destroyed, and that individual captains kept it for themselves following our defeat. This is most emphatically not true. The warehouses, stuffed with the spoils our assiduous treasure collecting had gathered for you, were burned to the ground with all their contents by Bingtown fanatics. Why is this so hard for scribes to believe? There were also reports of Bingtown folk who killed their kinfolk and themselves rather than face our raiders. In consideration of our reputations, I think this can be taken as fact.

But Scribe Wertin's gravest and most unjust error is his denial of the existence of the dragon. May I ask, most courteously and humbly, on what he bases this report? Every captain who returned to our shores reported sightings of a blue-and-silver dragon. Every captain. Why are their words dismissed as cowardly excuses, while the tales of a soft eunuch are heralded as truth? There was, indeed, a dragon. We took disastrous damage from it. Your scribe fatuously states that there is no proof of this, that the reports of the dragons are 'the excuses of cowards for fleeing a certain victory, and perhaps a subterfuge for keeping treasure and tribute from Duke Sidder.' What proof, I ask, could be sought that is more telling than those hundreds of men who never returned home?

Captain Slyke's rebuttal of his Execution Verdict,
Chade Fallstar's translation from the Chalcedean

It was hours later when I wearily climbed the stairs back to Lord Golden's room. I had had a long audience with the Queen and Chade. Chade had declined to summon Prince Dutiful to attend it. 'He knows that we know one another, you and I, of old. But I don't think we would be wise to strengthen that connection in his mind. Not just yet.'

On reflection, I decided that perhaps I agreed with him. Chade was technically my great-uncle, though I had never related to him that way. Always he had been my mentor. Old as he was and scarred as I was, we still shared some family resemblance. Dutiful had already voiced his suspicions that I was related to him. Best that he did not see us together, and gain strength for any of his theories.

My session with Chade and the Queen had been long. Chade had never before had the opportunity to have both of us in the same room while he questioned us about the true nature of the Six Duchies dragons. He sipped one of his foul tisanes and took copious notes until his bony hand wearied. After that, he passed the pen to me and commanded me to write as we spoke. As ever, his questions were concise and thoughtful. What was new in his demeanour was his obvious enthusiasm and fervour. For him the wonder of the stone dragons, brought to life with blood, Skill and Wit, were a manifestation of the extended powers of the Skill. I saw hunger in his eyes, as he speculated that perhaps men seeking to avoid death's cold jaws had first worked this magic.

Kettricken frowned at that. I surmised that she preferred to believe that the stone dragons had been created by Skill-coteries in the hope of serving the Six Duchies some day. She probably believed that the older dragons had likewise been carved for some loftier goal. When I countered this with the concept that a Skill-addiction led one to the creation, they both scowled at me.

I had been scowled at a great deal. My relaying of the information about the Bingtown dragons was treated first with scepticism, and then annoyance that I had not spoken sooner. Why I shielded the Fool from their disapproval, I could not have said. I did not lie directly; Chade had trained me too well for that. Instead, I let them think that he had told me his tales of Bingtown dragons when first he came to visit me. I took upon myself the responsibility that I had not passed the knowledge on to them. I shrugged, and said carelessly that I had not thought such tales could affect us here in Buckkeep. I did not have to add that it seemed a wild story to me then. Both of them were still teetering on whether they accepted it.

'It puts our own dragons into a new light,' Kettricken mused softly.

'And makes the veiled man's remarks a bit less offensive,' I ventured to add.

'Perhaps. Though I still feel affront that he dared to doubt our dragons were real.'

Chade cleared his throat. 'We must let that pass, for now, my dear. Last year I came into possession of some papers that spoke of a dragon defending Bingtown from the Chalcedean fleet. It seemed but a wild battle tale to me, such as men often use to excuse defeat. I surmised that the rumours of our real dragons had led the Chalcedeans to pretend themselves defeated by a Bingtown dragon rather than simple strategy. Perhaps I should have heeded it; I will see what other information I can purchase. But for now, let us consider our own resources.' He cleared his throat and stared at me as if he suspected me of withholding vital information. 'The buried cities the Fool told you about . . . could they be related to the abandoned city that you visited?' Chade pushed the question in as if it were more important than the Queen's comment about affront.

I shrugged. 'I have no way of knowing. The city I visited was not buried. Some great cataclysm had riven it, true. It was like a cake chopped with an axe. And the water of the river had flowed in to fill the chasm.'

'What cracks the earth in one city could have precipitated a sinking of the ground in another,' Chade speculated aloud.

'Or wakened a mountain to wrath,' Kettricken put in. 'We have many such tales in the Mountain Kingdom. The earth quakes, and one of the fire mountains awakes to pour forth lava and ash, sometimes darkening the sky and filling the air with choking smoke. Sometimes it is only a slurry of water and muck and stones that cascade down, filling valleys to the brim and spreading out across plains. There are also tales, not that old, of a town in a valley near a deep lake. The day before the earthquake, all was well there. It bustled with life. Travellers arriving there two days after the quake found folk dead in the street, yes, and their beasts beside them. None of the bodies bore any marks. It was as if they had simply dropped where they stood.'

A silence had followed her words. Then Chade had made me recite yet again all the Fool had told me of the Bingtown dragons. He had asked me a number of questions about the Six Duchies dragons, most of which I did not know the answers to. Could there be serpent-born dragons among the dragons I woke? If Bingtown's serpent-born dragons rose against the Six Duchies, did I think our own dragons could be persuaded to rise and protect us again? Or would they side with their scaly kin? And speaking of scales, what of the lizardish boy? Did the Fool know aught of people of that kind?

When finally they dismissed me so that they might deliberate together, I felt sure that several meals must have passed me by. I left Kettricken's private chambers by secret ways, emerged from my own room to find Lord Golden absent from his chambers, and went down to scavenge the kitchens for whatever I could find. The bustle and clatter was intense, and I found myself firmly refused entrance. I retreated, and then made a foray into the guardsmen's hall, where I secured bread, meat, cheese and ale, which were all I really needed to content my soul anyway.

As I climbed the stairs, I was wondering if I could steal a moment or two of sleep while Lord Golden and the rest of the Buckkeep nobility were at dinner with the Bingtown contingent. I knew I should dress and descend, to stand at his shoulder and watch how the evening proceeded, but I felt I had already taken in as much information as my mind could hold. I had passed on the information to Kettricken and Chade; let them deal with it. My dilemma with Hap still impaled my heart. I could think of no course of action that would better it.

Sleep, I told myself firmly. Sleep would shield me for a time from all of it, and upon waking perhaps some aspect of it would have come clear.

I tapped at Lord Golden's chamber door and entered. As I did so, a young woman stood up from one of the hearthside chairs. I glanced about the room, assuming that Lord Golden must have admitted her, but saw no sign of him. Perhaps he was in one of his other chambers, though it seemed unlike him to leave a guest unattended. Nor did I see food or wine set out, as he certainly would have done.

She was a striking woman. It was not just her extravagant garb; it was the sheer scale of her. She was at least my height, with long blonde hair and light brown eyes, and a warrior's muscling in her arms and shoulders. Her clothing was chosen to emphasize that last feature. Her black boots came to her knees, and she wore leggings rather than skirts. Her shirt was of ivory linen, and her fancifully decorated vest of soft doeskin. The sleeves of the shirt were pleated, and there was lace at the cuff, but not enough to get in her way. The cut of the garments was simple, but the extravagance of the fabrics was only exceeded by the embroidery that graced them. She wore several earrings in each ear, some of wood and some of gold. In the spiralling wooden ones, I recognized the Fool's handiwork. There was gold at her throat and on her wrists as well, but it was simple gold, and I would wager she wore it more for her own pleasure than for show. She bore a plain sword on one hip, and a practical knife on the other.

In the first moment of mutual surprise, her gaze met mine. Then her stare wandered over me in a way that was overly familiar. When her eyes came back to mine, she grinned disarmingly. Her teeth were very white.

'You must be Lord Golden.' She extended a hand to me as she strode toward me. Despite her foreign dress, her accent was Shoaks Duchy. 'I'm Jek. Perhaps Amber has spoken of me.'

I took her hand by reflex. 'I'm sorry, my lady, but you are mistaken. I am Lord Golden's serving-man, Tom Badgerlock.' Her grip was firm, her hand calloused and strong. 'I am sorry I was not here to admit you when you first arrived. I had not realized Lord Golden was expecting a visitor. May I bring you anything?'

She gave a shrug and released my hand as she walked back to the chair. 'Lord Golden isn't exactly expecting me. I came looking for him and a servant directed me here. I knocked, no answer, so I came in to wait.' She seated herself, crossed her legs at the knee and then asked with a knowing grin, 'So. How is Amber?'

Something was not right here. I glanced at the other closed doors. 'I know no one named Amber. How did you get in?' I stood between her and the door. She looked formidable, but her clothing and hair were unruffled. If she had done any damage to the Fool, she'd likely show some signs of a struggle. Nor was anything in the room awry.

'I opened the door and walked in. It wasn't locked.'

'That door is always locked.' I tried to make my contradiction pleasant, but I was becoming more and more worried.

'Well, it wasn't today, Tom, and I have important business with Lord Golden. As I am well known to him, I doubt he would mind me entering his rooms. I've conducted a lot of business on his behalf in the last year or so, with Amber as the go-between.' She tilted her head and rolled her eyes at me. 'And I don't believe for a minute that you don't know Amber.' She cocked her head the other way and stared at me discriminatingly. Then she grinned. 'You know, I like you better with brown eyes. Much more becoming than the blue ones Paragon has.' As I stared at her in consternation, her grin grew wider. It was like being stalked by a large, overly-friendly cat. I sensed no animosity from her. Rather it was as if she suppressed mirth and deliberately strove to make me uncomfortable, but in a friendly, teasing way. I could make no sense of her. I tried to decide if it would be better to eject her from the room or detain her here until Lord Golden returned. More and more, I longed to open the door to his bedchamber and privy, to be sure that no treachery had befallen him in my absence.

With sudden relief, I heard his key in the lock. I strode to the door, and opened it for him, proclaiming before he stepped in, 'Lord Golden, a visitor awaits you. A Lady Jek. She says this is a—'

Before I could get any further in my warning speech, he pushed past me in a most uncharacteristic hurry. He shut the door behind him as if Lady Jek were a puppy that might race out into the corridor, and latched it before he turned towards her. His face was as pale as I'd seen it in years as he confronted his unexpected guest.

'Lord Golden?' Jek exclaimed. For a long moment she stared. Then she burst into hearty laughter, pounding a doubled fist against her thigh. 'But, of course. Lord *Golden!* How could I not have guessed? I should have seen through it from the start!' She advanced on him, completely confident of a warm welcome, to hug him heartily and then step back. As she gripped him by the shoulders, her delighted gaze wandered over his face and hair. To me, he looked dazed, but her grin didn't fade. 'It's marvellous. If I didn't know, I never would have guessed. But I don't understand. Why is this ruse necessary? Doesn't it make it difficult for the two of you to be together?' She glanced from him to me, and it was apparent the question was addressed to both of us. Her implication was obvious, although I could not fathom her reference to a 'ruse'. I felt the rush of heat and colour to my face. I waited for Lord Golden to make some clarifying remark to her but he held his silence. The look I wore must have shocked her, for she turned her gaze back to Lord Golden. She spoke uncertainly. 'Amber, my friend. Aren't you glad to see me?'

Lord Golden's face seemed immobilized. His jaws moved and then he finally spoke. His voice was low and calm but still seemed somewhat breathless. 'Tom Badgerlock, I have no further need of your services today. You are dismissed.'

Never had it been harder for me to remain in my role, but I sensed desperation in his retreat into formality, so I clenched my teeth and bowed stiffly, containing my seething affront at Jek's obvious assumption about us. My own voice was icy as I answered him.

'As you will, my lord. I will take the opportunity to rest.' I turned and retreated to my own chamber. As I passed the table, I took a candle. I opened my door, went into my room and shut the door behind me. Almost.

I am not proud of what I did next. Shall I blame it on Chade's early training of me? I could, but that would not be honest. I burned with indignation. Jek obviously believed Lord Golden and I were lovers. He had not bothered to correct her misconception; her words and manner told me that he was the source of it. To some end of his own, he allowed her to continue in that belief.

It was the way Jek had looked at me, as if she knew far more about me than I knew of her. Obviously, she knew Lord Golden, but from another place and by another name. I was sure I had never seen her before. So, whatever she knew of me, she knew from the Fool. I justified my spying on the grounds that I had the right to know what he had said about me to strangers. Especially when it made a stranger look from him to me and smile in a way so knowing and so offensive. What things had he said about me to her, to make her assume such a thing? Why? Why would he? Outrage struggled to blossom in me, but I suppressed it. There would be a reason, some driving purpose behind such talk. There had to be. I would trust my friend, but I had a right to know what it was. I set the candle on my table, sat down on my bed and gripped my hands in my lap, forcing myself to discard all emotion. And no matter how distasteful my situation, I would be rational in my judgement. I listened. Their conversation came faintly to my straining ears.

'What are you doing here? Why didn't you let me know you were coming?' There was more than surprise or annoyance in the Fool's voice. It was almost despair.

'How could I let you know?' Jek demanded cheerfully. 'The Chalcedeans keep sinking all the ships that head this way. From the few letters I've received from you, it's obvious that half my own have gone awry.' Then, 'So, admit it. You are Lord Golden?'

'Yes.' He sounded exasperated. 'And it is the only name I am known by in Buckkeep. So I would thank you to bear that in mind at all times.'

'But you told me that you went to visit your old friend, Lord Golden, and that all my correspondence to you must be sent through him. And what of all the transactions I've made in Bingtown and Jamaillia? All the inquiries I've made and the information I've sent you? Were all of those actually for you, as well?'

He spoke tightly. 'If you must know, yes.' And then, pleading, 'Jek, you look at me as if I've betrayed you. I haven't. You are my friend, and I was not pleased to deceive you. But it was necessary. This ruse, as you put it, all of this, is necessary. And I cannot explain why to you, nor can I tell you the whole of it. I can only repeat to you, it is necessary. You hold my life in your hands. Tell this tale in a tavern some night, and you might as well have slit my throat now.'

I heard the sound of Jek's body dropping into a chair. When she spoke, there was a trace of hurt in her voice. 'You deceived me. And now you insult me. After all we've been through, do you really doubt my ability to hold my tongue?'

'I did not set out to do either,' said someone. And the hair on the back of my neck rose, for the voice was neither Lord Golden's nor the Fool's. This voice was lighter and devoid of any Jamaillian accent. *Amber's voice*, I surmised. Yet another façade for the person I thought I knew. 'It is just . . . you have taken me by surprise, and frightened me badly. I entered this room and there you were, grinning as if it were a fine joke, when actually you . . . Ah, Jek, I cannot explain it. I simply must trust to our friendship, and to all we have been through together, all we have been to one another. You have stumbled into my play, and now I fear you must take up a role in it. For the duration of your visit, you must speak to me as if I am truly Lord Golden, and as if you are my agent in Bingtown and Jamaillia.'

'That's easy enough for me to do, for such I have been. And you speak truly when you say we are friends. It hurts me still that you thought any of this deception was needed between us. Still, I suppose I can forgive it. But I wish I understood it. When your man, this . . . Tom Badgerlock, when he came in and I recognized his face, I was filled with joy for you. I watched you carve that figurehead. Don't deny to me what you feel for him. "They are reunited at last," I thought to myself. But then you bark at him and send him off as if he were a servant . . . Lord Golden's serving-man, in fact, is what he told me he was. Why the masquerade, when it must be so difficult for both of you?'

A long silence followed. I heard no sound of footsteps, but I recognized the chink of a bottle's neck against a glass's lip. I guessed that he poured wine for both of them as Jek and I awaited his answer.

'It is difficult for me,' the Fool replied in Amber's voice. 'It is not so difficult for him, because he knows little of it. There. Fool that I am and have been, truly, to have ever let that secret have breath to anyone, let alone shape. Such a monstrous vanity on my part.'

'Monstrous? Immense! You carved a ship's figurehead in his likeness, and hoped no one would ever guess what he meant to you? Ah, my friend. You manage everyone's lives and secrets so well and then when it comes to your own . . . Well. And he doesn't even know that you love him?'

'I think he chooses not to. Perhaps he suspects . . . well, after chatting with you, I am certain that he suspects now. But he leaves it alone. He is like that.'

'Then he's a damned fool. A handsome damned fool, though. Despite the broken nose. I'll wager he was even prettier before that happened. Who spoiled his face?'

A small sound, a little cough of laughter. 'My dear Jek, you've seen him. No one could spoil his face. Not for me.' A pretty little sigh. 'But come. I'd rather not talk of it, if you don't mind. Tell me of other things. How is Paragon?'

'Paragon. The ship or the pirate princeling?'

'Both. Please.'

'Well, of the heir to the Pirate Islands throne, I know little more than what is common gossip. He's a lively, lusty boy, the image of King Kennit, and his mother's delight. The whole Raven fleet's delight and darling, actually. That's his middle name, you know. Prince Paragon Raven Ludluck.'

'And the ship?'

'Moody as ever. But in a different way. It's not that dangerous melancholy he used to sink into, more like the angst of a young man who fancies himself a poet. For that reason, I find it much more annoying to be around him when he's moping. Of course, it's not entirely his fault. Althea's pregnant, and the ship obsesses about the child.'

'Althea's pregnant?'

This 'Amber' took a woman's delight in such tidings.

'Yes,' Jek confirmed. 'And she's absolutely furious about it, despite Brashen walking on air and choosing a new name for the child every other day. In fact, I think that's half of why she's so irritable. They were wed in the Rain Wild Traders Concourse ... I wrote to you about that, didn't I? I think it was more to placate Malta, who seemed humiliated by her sister's cavalier attitude toward her arrangement with Brashen than for any desire on Althea's part to be married. And now she's with child, and puking her guts up every dawn, and spitting at Brashen whenever he gets solicitous.'

'She must have known that eventually she'd get with child?'

'I doubt it. They're slow to conceive, those Traders, and half the time they can't carry the calf to term. Her sister Malta's lost two already. I think that's part of Althea's anger; that if she knew she'd have a baby to show for all the puking and cramps, she might accept it gracefully, even welcome it. But her mother wants her to come home to have it, and the ship insists the babe will be born on his decks and Brashen would let her give birth in a tree, so long as he had a baby to dandle and brag over afterwards. The constant stream of advice and suggestions just leaves her spitting mad. That's what I told Brashen. "Just stop talking to her about it," I said to him. "Pretend you don't notice and treat her as you always have." And he said, "How am I to do that, when I'm watching her belly rub the lines when she tries to run the rigging?" But of course, she was just around the corner when he said that, and she overheard, and like to burn his ears off with the names she called him.'

And so they went on, gossiping together like goodwives at a

market. They discussed who was pregnant, and who was not but wished to be, doings at the Jamaillian harbours and courts, politics of the Pirate Islands and Bingtown's war with Chalced. If I had not known who was in the other room, I would not have guessed. Amber bore no resemblance to Lord Golden or the Fool. The change was that complete.

And that was the second thing that scalded me that evening. Not just that he had spoken of me to strangers, in such detail that Jek could recognize me and believe I was his lover, but that there still remained a life or lives of his about which I had no knowledge. Strange, how being left out of a secret always feels like a betrayal of trust.

I sat alone by the light of my candle and wondered who, in truth, the Fool was. I scraped together in a small heap all the tiny hints and clues that I had gathered over the years and considered them. I'd put my life in his hands any number of times. He'd read all my journals, demanded a full report of all my travels, and I'd given such to him. And what had he offered to me in return? Riddles and mysteries and bits of himself.

And like cooling tar, my feelings for the Fool hardened as they grew colder. The injury grew in me as I thought about it. He had excluded me. The heart knows but one reaction to that. I would now exclude him. I stood and then walked to the door of my room. I shut it completely, not loudly, but not caring if he noticed it that it had been ajar. I triggered the secret door, then crossed the room to open it and entered the spy labyrinth. I wished that I could close that door and leave that part of my life behind me. I tried. I walked away from it.

There are few things so tender as a man's dignity. The affront I felt was a thing both painful and angry, a weight that grew in my chest as I climbed the stairs. I fingered all my grievances, numbering them to myself.

How dared he put me in this position? He had compromised his own reputation when we visited Galekeep in search of Prince Dutiful. He had kissed young Civil Bresinga, deliberately setting off a social flap that misled Lady Bresinga as to the purpose of our visit at the same time that it got us expelled from her home. Even now, Civil avoided him with distaste, and I knew that his act had inspired a squall of excited gossip and speculation about his personal preferences at Buckkeep. I thought I had managed to hold myself aloof from those rumours. Now I reconsidered. There had been Prince Dutiful's question. And suddenly my confrontation with the guardsmen in the steams took on a new connotation. Blood burned my face. Would Jek, despite her assurances of a still tongue, become a source of even more humiliating talk? According to her words, the Fool had carved my countenance onto a ship's figurehead. I felt violated that he would do such a thing without my consent. And what had he said to folk while he was carving it, to lead to Jek's assumption?

I could not fit what he had done with either what I knew of the Fool or what I knew of Lord Golden. It was the act of this Amber, a person I knew not at all.

Hence I did not truly know him at all. And never had.

And with that, I unwillingly knew I had worked my way down to the deepest source of my injury. To discover that the truest friend I had ever had was actually a stranger was like a knife in my heart. He was another abandonment, a missed step in the dark, and a false promise of warmth and companionship. I shook my head to myself. 'Idiot,' I said quietly. 'You are alone. Best get used to it.' But without thinking, I reached toward where there had once been comfort.

And in the next instant, I missed Nighteyes with a terrible physical clenching in my chest. I squeezed my eyes shut, and then walked two more steps and sat down on the little bench outside the spyhole to the Narcheska's apartments. I blinked, denying the stinging boy's tears that clung to my eyelashes. Alone. It always came back to alone. It was like a contagion that had clung to me since my mother had lacked the courage to defy her father and keep me, and since my father had abandoned his crown and holdings rather than own up to me.

I leaned my forehead against the cold stone, forcing control onto myself. I steadied my breathing, and then became aware of faint voices through the wall. I sighed deeply. Then, as much to retreat from my own life as for any other reason, I set my eye to the spyhole and listened.

The Narcheska sat on a low stool in the middle of the room. She was weeping silently, clasping her elbows and rocking back and forth. Tears had tracked down her face and dripped from her chin and they still squeezed out from her closed eyes. A wet blanket shawled her shoulders. She held herself in such silence amidst her pain that I wondered if she had just endured some punishment from her father or Peottre.

But even as I wondered, Peottre came hurrying into the room. A tight little whimper burst from her at the sight of him. His jaw was clenched and at the sound, his face went tighter and whiter. He carried his cloak, but it was bundled to serve as a sack. He hurried to Elliania's side and set the laden cloak on the floor before her. Kneeling, he took her by the shoulders to get her attention. 'Which one is it?' he asked her in a low voice.

She gasped in a breath, and spoke with an effort. 'The green serpent. I think.' Another breath. 'I cannot tell. When he burns, he burns so hot that the others seem to burn, too.' And then she lifted her hand to her mouth and bit down on the meat on her thumb. Hard.

'No!' Peottre exclaimed. He caught up the dripping hem of the blanket, folded it twice, and offered it to her. He had to shake her hand free of her jaws. Then, eyes closed, she clamped her teeth on the blanket edge. I saw the clearly demarcated prints of her teeth on her hand as it fell away to her side. 'I am sorry I took so long. I had to go secretly, so no one would notice what I did and ask questions. And I wanted it fresh and clean. Come, turn this way, into the light,' he told her. Taking her by the shoulders, he turned her so that her back was towards me. She let the wet blanket fall from her shoulders.

She was stripped to the waist above doeskin trousers. From shoulder to waist, she was tattooed. That was shocking enough to me, but the markings were like none I had ever seen. I knew that the Outislanders tattooed themselves, to show clan and claim victories and even to show the status of a woman, with marks for marriages and for children. But those were like the clan tattoo on Peottre's brow, a simple pattern of blue marks.

Elliania's tattoos were nothing like that. I'd never seen anything to compare to them. They were beautiful, the colours brilliant, the designs sharp and clear. The colours had a sparkling metallic quality to them, reflecting the lamplight like a polished blade. The creatures that sprawled and twined on her shoulders and spine and down her ribs gleamed and glistened. And one, an exquisite green serpent that began at the nape of her neck and meandered down her back amongst the others, stood out puffily, like a fresh burn blister. It was oddly lovely, for it gave the impression that the creature was trapped just below her skin, like a butterfly trying to break free from its chrysalis. At the sight of it, Peottre gave a sharp exclamation of sympathy. He opened the bundled cloak at his feet to reveal a mound of fresh, white snow. Cupping a handful of it, he held it to the serpent's head. To my horror, I heard a sizzling like a quenched blade. The snow melted immediately, to run down her spine in a narrow rivulet. Elliania cried out at the touch, but it was a cry of both shock and relief.

'Here,' Peottre said gruffly. 'A moment.' He spread his cloak out and then pushed the snow out into an even layer on it. 'Lie down here,' he instructed her, and helped her from the stool. He eased her back onto the bed of snow and she whimpered as it quenched the burning. I could see her face now, and the sweat that ran from her brow as well as the tears that still flowed down her face. She lay still, eyes closed, her new breasts rising and falling with each ragged breath she took. After a few moments, she began to shiver, but she did not roll away. Peottre had taken the discarded blanket and was wetting it fresh with water from a pitcher. He brought it back to her and set it by her side. 'I'm going out for more snow,' he told her. 'If that melts and stops soothing your back, try this blanket. I'll be back as soon as I can.'

She unclenched her jaws and wet her lips. 'Hurry,' she pleaded in a gasp.

'I will, little one. I will.' He stood up, and then said gravely, each word solemn, 'Our mothers bless you for what you endure. Damn these Farseers and their stiff-necked ways. And damn those dragon-breeders.'

The Narcheska rolled her head back and forth on the snow-bed.

'I just . . . I just wish I knew what she wanted. What she expected me to do about it, past what we have done.'

Peottre had begun moving about the room, looking for something to carry snow in. He had picked up the Narcheska's cloak. 'We both know what she expects,' he said harshly.

'I am not a woman yet,' she said quietly. 'It is against the mothers' law.'

'It is against *my* law,' Peottre clarified, as if his will was the only one that mattered in this. 'I will not see you used that way. There must be another path.' Unwillingly, he asked, 'Has Henja come to you? Has she said why you are tormented like this?'

Her nod was a jerk of her head. 'She insists I must bind him to me. Open my legs to him to be sure of him before I leave. It is the only path she believes in.' Elliania spoke through gritted teeth. 'I slapped her and she left. And then the pain became fourfold.'

Anger froze his features. 'Where is she?'

'She is not here. She took her cloak and left. Perhaps it is to avoid your temper, but I think she has gone into the town again, to further her cause there.' Elliania's teeth clenched in a smile. 'Just as well. Our position here is difficult enough without having to explain why you've killed my maid in a fury.'

I think her words recalled him to practicality, even if they did not calm him.

'It is well that slut is out of my reach. But aren't you a bit late to counsel me to restraint? My little warrior, you have inherited your uncle's temper. Your act was not wise, but I cannot find it in me to rebuke you for it. That empty-souled whore. She truly believes that is the only way a man can be bound to a woman.'

Unbelievably, the Narcheska gave a small laugh. 'It is the only one she believes in, Uncle. I did not say it was the only one I knew. Pride may bind a man, even where there is no love. That is the thought I cling to now.' Then her brow clenched in pain. 'Fetch more snow, please,' she gasped, and he nodded sharply and went out.

I watched him go. Then she sat up slowly. She scraped the melting snow into a narrower pallet. The tattoos on her back stood out as glowingly as ever. Around them, her bared flesh was bright red from cold. Gingerly she lay back down on her snow couch. She took a breath and lifted the backs of her hands to her brows. I recalled that one scroll had said that was how Outislanders prayed. But the only words she said were, 'My Mother. My Sister. For you. My Mother. My Sister. For you.' It soon became a toneless chant in time with her breathing.

I sat back on my stool. I was trembling, as much with awe at her courage as pity for what she suffered. I wondered what I had just witnessed and what was the significance of it. My candle had burned down to half its length. I took it up and slowly climbed the rest of the stairs to Chade's tower room. I was exhausted and downhearted and sought familiar comfort somewhere. But when I reached there, the room was empty and the fire gone out. A sticky wine glass stood empty on the table by the chairs. I cleaned the ashes from the hearth, muttering to myself at Thick's neglect of his duties, and built a fresh fire.

Then I took paper and ink and wrote down what I had witnessed. I coupled it to the previous interplay I had witnessed between Elliania, Peottre and the serving woman Henja. Plainly the last one was a woman to be watched. I sanded the fresh ink, tapped it off and left the paper on Chade's chair. I hoped he would come up to the rooms tonight. I reflected again, bitterly, on the stupidity that he refused to let me have a way of contacting him directly. I knew what I had witnessed was important; I hoped he would know why.

Then I reluctantly went back down the stairs to my own chamber. There I stood for a time, in silence, listening. I heard nothing. If Jek and Lord Golden were still there, they were either sitting silently or they were in his bedchamber. After what she had implied about me, that did not seem likely. After a time, I eased the door open a crack. The room was darkened, the fire banked on the hearth. Good. I had no wish to confront either of them just now. I had, I decided, words to say to both of them, but I was not yet calm enough to say them.

Instead I took my cloak from its hook and left Lord Golden's chamber. I would go out, I decided. I needed to be away from the castle for a time, away from all the interconnecting webs of intrigue and deceit. I felt I was drowning in lies.

I made my way down the stairs and toward the servants' entrance. But as I walked down the main hall, I felt a sudden shiver in the Wit. I lifted my eyes. Coming towards me from the opposite end of the hall was the veiled Bingtown youth. His veil was over his face, but through the lace that obscured his features I caught the faint blue glow of his eyes. It tightened the flesh on the nape of my neck. I wanted to turn aside, or even turn around and walk away, anything to avoid him. But such an action would have looked very strange. I steeled myself and resolutely walked towards him. I averted my eyes, but then when I dared to glance up at him, I felt his gaze on me. He slowed as we approached one another. When he was very close, I bobbed my head, a servant's gesture of acknowledgment. But before I could pass him, he stopped and stood still. 'Hello,' he greeted me.

I stiffened and became a correct Buckkeep servant. I bowed from the waist. 'Good evening, sir. May I be of service?'

'I . . . Yes . . . Perhaps you could.' He lifted his veil and pushed back his hood as he spoke, baring his scaled face. I could not help but gawk at him. Up close, his visage was even more remarkable than what I had glimpsed earlier. I had over-estimated his age. He was years younger than Hap or Dutiful, though I could not guess his exact age. His height made his boyish face incongruous. The silvery gleam in the scaling on his cheekbones and brow reminded me of the Narcheska's glimmering tattoos. Abruptly, I recognized that this scaling was what the Jamaillian make-up Lord Golden sometimes wore mimicked. It was an odd little insight, one I stored away with all the other significant things that the Fool had never bothered to explain to me. Doubtless, when it suited his purpose, he would reveal it to me. Doubtless. Bitterness welled in me like blood from a fresh wound. But the Bingtowner was beckoning me closer, even as he backed away from me. I followed him unwillingly. He glanced into a small sitting room and then gestured me into it. He was making me nervous. I repeated my question like a good servant. 'How may I be of service?'

'I . . . that is . . . I feel as if I should know you.' He peered at me closely. When I only stared at him as if puzzled, he tried again.

'Do you understand what I speak about?' He seemed to be trying to help me begin a conversation.

'I beg your pardon, sir? You are in need of help?' It was all I could think of to say.

He glanced over his shoulder and then spoke to me more urgently. 'I serve the dragon Tintaglia. I am here with the ambassadors from Bingtown and the representatives from the Rain Wild. They are my people, and my kin. But I serve the dragon Tintaglia, and her concerns are my first ones.' He spoke the words as if they should convey some deep message to me.

I hoped that what I felt did not show on my face. It was confusion, not at his strange words, but at the odd feeling that rang through me at that name. *Tintaglia*. I had heard the name before, but when he spoke it, it was the sharp tip of a dream breaking through into the waking world. I felt again the sweep of wind under my wings, tasted dawn's soft fogs in my mouth. Then that blink of memory was gone, and left behind only the uncomfortable feeling of having been someone other than myself for a sliced instant of my life. I said the only words I could think of. 'Sir? And how can I assist you?'

He stared at me intently, and I'm afraid I returned that scrutiny. The dangles along his jawline were serrated tissue. The fleshy fringe was too regular to be a scar or unnatural growth. It looked as if it belonged there as rightfully as his nose or lips. He sighed, and as he did so, I clearly saw him close his nostrils for a moment. He evidently decided to begin anew, for he smiled at me and asked gently, 'Have you ever dreamed of dragons? Of flying like a dragon or of . . . being a dragon?'

That was too close a hit. I nodded eagerly, a servant flattered at conversing with his betters. 'Oh, haven't we all, sir? We Six Duchies folk, I mean. I'm old enough to have seen the dragons that came to defend the Six Duchies, sir. I suppose it's natural that I've dreamed of them, sometimes. Magnificent they were, sir. Terrifying and dangerous, too, but that's not what stays with a man who has seen them. It's their greatness that stays in my mind, sir.'

He smiled at me. 'Exactly. Magnificence. Greatness. Perhaps that is what I sensed in you.' He peered at me, and I felt the bluish gleam in his eyes was more probing than the eyes themselves. I tried to retreat from that scrutiny.

I glanced aside from him. 'I'm not alone in that, sir. There are many in the Six Duchies who saw our dragons on the wing. And some that saw far more than I did, for I lived far from Buckkeep then, out on my father's farm. We grew oats, there. Grew oats and raised pigs. Others could tell you far better tales than I could. Yet even a single glimpse of the dragons were enough to set a man's soul on fire. Sir.'

He made a small dismissive gesture with his hand. 'I don't doubt that they were. But I speak of another thing, now. I speak of real dragons. Dragons that breathe, that eat and grow and breed just as any other creature does. Have you ever dreamed of a dragon like that? One named Tintaglia?'

I shook my head at him. 'I don't dream much, sir.' I left a little pause there and let it grow just long enough to be slightly uncomfortable. Then I bobbed a bow to him again and asked, 'And how can I be of service to you, sir?'

He stared past me for so long that I thought he had forgotten me entirely. I thought of simply leaving him there and slipping away, except that I seemed to feel something in the air. Does magic hum? No, that is not quite the way of it, but it is a similar wordless vibration that one feels, not with the body but with that part of a man that does magic or receives it. The Wit whispers and the Skill sings. This was something like to both of them, and yet its own. It crept along my nerves and stood up the hair on the back of my neck. Suddenly his eyes snapped back to me. 'She says you are lying,' he accused me.

'Sir!' I was as affronted as I could manage for the terror I felt. Something groped at me angrily. I felt as if swiping claws passed through me. Some instinct warned me to leave my Skill walls as they stood, that any effort to reinforce them now would only display me to her. For it was unmistakably a 'she' that sought to seize me. I took a breath. I was a servant, I reminded myself. Yet any servant of Buckkeep would have taken righteous offence at such words from a foreigner. I stood a bit straighter. 'Our Queen keeps a good cellar, sir, as all in the Six Duchies know. Perhaps it has been too good a cellar for your sensibilities. It is known to happen to foreigners here. Perhaps you should retire to your chamber for a time.'

'You have to help us. You have to make them help us.' He did not seem to hear my words. Desperation tinged his own. 'She is stricken to the heart over this. Day after day, she strives to feed them but there is only one of her. She cannot feed so many, and they cannot hunt for themselves. She herself grows thin and weary with the task. She despairs that they will ever grow to proper size and strength. Do not doom her to being the last of her kind. If these Six Duchies dragons of yours are any kind of true dragons, then they will come to her aid. In any case, the least you can do is persuade your queen that she must ally with us. Help us put an end to the Chalcedean threat. Tintaglia is true to her word; she keeps their ships out of the Rain Wild River, but she can do no more than that. She dares not range further to protect us, for then the young dragons would die. Please, sir! If you have a heart in you, speak to your queen. Do not let dragons pass away from this world because men could not stop their bitter squabbling long enough to aid them.'

He stepped forward and tried to catch at my hand. I hastily retreated from him. 'Sir, I fear you have taken too much to drink. You have mistaken me for someone of influence. I am not. I am but a servant here in Buckkeep Castle. And now I must be about my master's errands for me. Good evening, sir. Good evening.'

And as he stared after me, I backed hastily from the room, bobbing and bowing as if my head were on a string. Once I was in the hall, I turned and strode hastily away. I know he came to the doorway and looked after me, for I felt his blue gaze on my back. I was glad to turn the corner to the kitchen wing, and gladder still to put a door between him and me.

Outside it was snowing, huge white flakes wafting down with the nightfall. I left the keep, barely nodding to the guards on duty at the gate, and began the long walk down to town. I had no set destination in mind, only a desire to be away from the castle. I hiked down through the gathering darkness and thickening snowfall. I had too much to think about: Elliania's tattoos and what they meant, the Fool and Jek and what she believed of me because of something he had said, dragons and boys with scales and what Chade and Kettricken would say to the Bingtowners and to the Outislanders. Yet the closer I came to town, the more Hap pushed into my mind. I was failing the boy I considered my son. No matter how serious the events up at Buckkeep Castle were, I couldn't let them displace him. I tried to think how I could turn him around, make him return to his apprenticeship with a willing heart and eager hands, make him set aside Svanja until he could make an honest offer for her hand, make him take up residence with his master . . . make him live a tidy life, abiding by all the rules that could keep him safe but never ensure him success or happiness.

I thrust that last traitor thought aside. It angered me and I turned the anger on my boy. I should do as Jinna had suggested. I should take a firm line with him, punish him for disobeying my wishes for him. Take away both money and security until he agreed to do as I wished. Turn him out of Jinna's and tell him he must live with his master or fend for himself. Force him to toe the line. I scowled to myself. Oh, yes, that would have worked so well on me at that age. Yet something must be done. Somehow, I had to make him see sense.

My thoughts were interrupted by the hoofbeats of a horse on the road behind me. Instantly, Laurel's warning leapt foremost in my mind. I moved to one side as the horse and rider came abreast of me and set my hand lightly to my knife. I expected them to pass me without comment. It wasn't until the horse was reined in that I recognized Starling in the saddle. For a moment, she just looked down on me. Then she smiled. 'Get up behind me, Fitz. I'll give you a ride down to Buckkeep Town.'

The heart will flee anywhere when it is seeking comfort. I knew that and kept a rein on mine. 'Thank you, but no. This road can be treacherous in the dark. You'd be risking your horse.'

'Then I'll lead him and walk beside you. It has been so long since we talked, and I could use a friendly ear tonight.'

'I think I would prefer to be alone tonight, Starling.'

She was silent for a moment. The horse jigged restlessly and she pulled him in too tightly. When she spoke, she did not hide her irritation. 'Tonight? Why do you say tonight when you mean, "I'd always prefer to be alone rather than with you." Why do you make excuses? Why don't you just say that you haven't forgiven me, that you'll never forgive me?'

It was true. I hadn't. But that would have been a stupid thing to tell her. 'Can't we just let it go? It doesn't matter any more,' I said, and that was true as well.

She snorted. 'Ah. I see. It doesn't matter. *I* don't matter. I make one mistake, I fail to tell you one thing that doesn't really concern you at all, and you decide you can not only never forgive me, but that you will never speak to me again?' Her fury was building in an astounding way. I stood looking up at her as she ranted. The failing light touched her face indistinctly. She looked older and wearier than I had ever seen her. And angrier. I stood stunned in the flow of her wrath. 'And why is that, I ask myself? Why does "Tom Badgerlock" dispose of me so easily? Because perhaps I never mattered at all to you, save for one thing. One convenient little thing that I brought right to your door for you, one thing that I thought we shared in friendship and fondness and yes, even love. But you decided you don't want that from me any more, so you throw all of me aside. You make that the whole of what we shared, and discard me with it. And why? I confess, I've given much more thought to it than I should. And I think I've found the answer. Is it because you've found another place to quench your lusts? Has your new master taught you his Jamaillian ways? Or was I wrong, all those years ago? Perhaps the Fool was truly a man, and you've simply gone back to what you preferred all along.' She jerked her horse's head again. 'You disgust me, Fitz, and you shame the Farseer name. I'm glad you've given it up. Now that I know what you are, I wish I had never bedded with you. Whose face did you see, all those times when you closed your eyes?'

'Molly's, you stupid bitch. Always Molly's.' It was not true. I had not played that cheat on her or myself. But it was the most hurtful reply I could think of to insult her. She did not, perhaps, deserve it. And it shamed me that I would use Molly's name that way. But my festering anger had finally found a target this evening.

She took several deep breaths, as if I had doused her with cold water. Then she laughed shrilly. 'And no doubt you mouth her name into your pillow as your Lord Golden mounts you. Oh, yes, that I can imagine well. You're pathetic, Fitz. Pathetic.'

She gave me no chance to strike back, but spurred her horse cruelly and galloped off into the snowy night. For a savage instant, I hoped the beast would stumble and that she would break her neck.

Then, just when I needed that fury most, it deserted me. I was left feeling sick and sad and sorry, alone on the night road. Why had the Fool done this to me? Why? I resumed my trudge down the road.

Yet I did not go to the Stuck Pig. I knew I wouldn't find Hap or Svanja there. Instead I went to the Dog and Whistle, an ancient tavern I had once frequented with Molly. I sat in the corner and watched patrons come and go and drank two tankards of ale. It was good ale, far better than I'd been able to afford when Molly and I last sat here. I drank and I remembered her. She, at least, had loved me true. Yet comfort in those memories trickled away. I tried to remember what it was to be fifteen years old and in love and so terribly certain that love conveyed wisdom and shaped fate. I recalled it too well, and my thoughts spun aside to Hap's situation. I asked myself, once I had lain with Molly, could anyone have said anything to persuade me that it was not both my right and my destiny to do so? I doubted it. The best thing, I concluded a tankard later, would have been not to have allowed Hap to meet Svanja in the first place. And Jinna had warned me of that, and I hadn't paid attention. Just as Burrich and Patience had once warned me not to begin with Molly. They'd been right. I should have admitted that a long time ago. I would have told them that, that very minute, if I could have.

And the wisdom of three tankards of ale after a sleepless night and a long day of unsettling news persuaded me that the best thing to do would be to go to Jinna and tell her that she had been right. Somehow, that would make things better. The fuzziness of why that would be so did not dissuade me. I set out for her door through the quiet night.

The snow had stopped falling. It was a clean blanket, mostly smooth, over Buckkeep Town. It draped eaves and gentled the rutted streets, hiding all sins. My boots scrunched through it as I walked the quiet streets. I nearly came to my senses when I reached Jinna's door, but I knocked anyway. Perhaps I just needed a friend, any kind of a friend, that badly.

I heard the thud of the cat leaping from her lap, and then her footsteps. She peered out of the top half of her door. 'Who's there?'

'It's me. Tom Badgerlock.'

She shut the top half of the door. It seemed like a long time before she unlatched the whole door and opened it to me. 'Come in,' she said, but her voice sounded as if she didn't care if I did or didn't.

I stood outside in the snow. 'I don't need to come in. I just wanted to tell you that you were right.'

She peered at me. 'And you are drunk. Come in, Tom Badgerlock. I've no wish to let the night cold into my house.'

And so I went in instead. Fennel had already claimed her warm spot in her chair, but he sat up to look at me disapprovingly. *Fish?*

No fish. Sorry.

'Sorry' is not fish. What good is 'sorry'? He curled up again, and hid his face in his tail.

I admitted it. 'Sorry isn't much good, but it's all I have to offer.'

Jinna looked at me grimly. 'Well, it's far more than anything else you've given me lately.'

I stood with the snow from my boots melting on her floor. The fire crackled. 'You were right about Hap. I should have intervened a lot sooner and I didn't. I should have listened to you.'

After a time longer she said, 'Do you want to sit down for a while? I don't think you should try to walk back to the castle just now.'

'I don't think I'm *that* drunk!' I scoffed.

'I don't think you're sober enough to know how drunk you are,' she replied. And while I was trying to unravel that, she said, 'Take your cloak off and sit down.' Then she had to move her knitting off one chair and the cat off the other, and then we both sat down.

For a short time we both just looked into her fire. Then she said, 'There's something you should know about Svanja's father.'

I met her eyes unwillingly.

'He's a lot like you,' she said quietly. 'It takes some time for him to get his temper up. Right now, he just feels grief over what his daughter is doing. But as it becomes common talk in town, there will be men who will goad him about it. Grief will change to shame, and not long after that, to fury. But it won't be against Svanja that he vents it. He'll go after Hap, as the culprit who has deceived and seduced his daughter. By then, he'll be righteous as well as angry. And he is strong as a bull.'

When I sat silent, she added, 'I told Hap this.' Fennel came to her and wafted up into her lap, displacing her knitting. She petted him absently.

'What did Hap say?'

She made a disgusted sound. 'That he wasn't afraid. I told him that had nothing to do with it. And that sometimes being stupid and being not afraid were two twigs of the same bush.'

'That pleased him, no doubt.'

'He went out. I haven't seen him since.'

I sighed. I was just starting to get warm. 'How long ago?'

She shook her head at me. 'It's no use your going after him. It was hours ago, before sundown.'

'I wouldn't know where to look for him anyway,' I admitted. 'I couldn't find him last night, and wherever they were then is where they probably are now.'

'Probably,' she agreed quietly. 'Well, at least Rory Hartshorn didn't find them last night, either. So they're probably safe for now.'

'Why can't he just keep his daughter in at night? Then no one would have a problem.'

She narrowed her eyes at me. 'No one would have a problem if you could just keep your son in at night, Tom Badgerlock.'

'I know, I know,' I admitted resignedly. And a moment later I added, 'You really shouldn't have to deal with any of this.'

A few moments later, the rest of that thought forced its way to the front of my mind. 'When Svanja's father decides to look for Hap, he'll look for him here.' I squeezed my brows together. 'I never meant to bring all this trouble to your door, Jinna. I started out just wanting a friend. And now everything is a mess, and it's all my fault.' I considered the conclusion of that. 'I suppose I'd best go face up to Rory Hartshorn.'

'Wallow in it, Tom Badgerlock,' she said in disgust. 'What on earth would you say to the man? Why must you take full credit for everything that goes wrong in the world? As I recall, I met Hap and befriended him long before I knew you. And Svanja has been trouble looking for a place to sprout since her family came to Buckkeep Town, if not before. And she has two parents of her own. Nor is Hap the blundering innocent in this. You've not been dallying with Hartshorn's daughter, Hap has. So stop bemoaning what a mess you've made, and start demanding that Hap take responsibility for himself.' She settled herself deeper into her chair. As if to herself, she added, 'You've quite enough messes of your own to clean up, without claiming responsibility for everyone else's.'

I stared at her in amazement.

'It's simple,' she said quietly. 'Hap needs to discover consequences. As long as you claim that it's all your fault for being a bad parent, Hap doesn't have to admit that a good share of this is his own fault. Of course, he doesn't think it's a problem yet, but when he suddenly perceives that it is, he's going to come running to you to see if you can fix it. And you'll try, because you think it's your fault.'

I sat still, soaking up the words and trying to find the sense in them. 'So what should I do?' I demanded at last.

She gave a helpless laugh. 'I don't know, Tom Badgerlock. But telling Hap this is all your fault is certainly something you should not do.' She lifted up the cat and set him back on the floor. 'However, there is something I should do as well.' She went into her bedroom. A few moments later, she came back with a purse. She held it out to me. When I didn't move to take it, she shook it at me. 'Take it. This is the coin I haven't spent on Hap's keep. I'm giving it back to you. Tonight, when he comes back, I'm telling him that I'm turning him out of my house, because I don't want trouble to come calling at my door.' She laughed aloud at the look on my face. 'It's called a consequence, Tom. Hap should feel more of them. And when he comes moaning to you, I think you should let him deal with it on his own.'

I thought of the last conversation we'd had. 'I doubt that he'll come moaning to me,' I said sombrely.

'All the better,' she said tartly. 'Let him handle it himself. He's used to sleeping indoors. It won't take him long to realize that he'd best settle himself in at the apprentices' hall. And I think you might be wise enough to leave it up to him to have to ask Master Gindast to let him.' The cat had reinstated himself on her lap. She shook out her knitting over him and tugged more yarn free. It slid through Fennel's lazy clasp.

I winced at the thought of how much pride Hap was going to have to swallow. A moment later, I felt an odd sense of relief. Hap could do that for himself. I didn't have to humble myself on his behalf. I think she saw it on my face.

'Not every problem in the world belongs to you alone, Badgerlock. Let others have their share.'

I thought about it for a time longer. Then I said gratefully, 'Jinna, you're a true friend.'

She gave me a sideways look. 'So. You've worked that out, have you?'

I winced at her tone, but nodded. 'You're a true friend. But you're still angry at how I've behaved.'

She nodded as if to herself. 'And some problems do belong to you, Tom Badgerlock. Entirely.' She stared at me expectantly.

I took a breath and steeled myself to it. I'd lie as little as possible, I comforted myself. It was thin comfort.

'That woman, in the Stuck Pig that night. Well, we aren't . . . that is, she is just a friend. I don't bed with her.' The words clattered awkwardly out of me like dropped crockery, and lay between us, all sharp shards.

A long silence followed. Jinna looked at me, then into the fire, and then back at me. Tiny glints of anger and hurt still danced in her eyes, but a very tiny smile played around the corners of her lips as well. 'I see. Well, that is good to know, I suppose. And now you have *two* friends that you don't bed with.'

Her meaning was unmistakable. That comfort would not be

offered to me tonight, and perhaps never again. I will not pretend I didn't feel disappointment. But there was relief as well. Had it been offered, I would have had to refuse it. I'd already been through the consequences of refusing a woman once tonight. I nodded slowly to her words.

'The water in the kettle is hot,' she pointed out. 'If you wanted to stay, you could make tea for us.' It was not forgiveness. It was a second chance to be friends. I was happy to accept it. I got up to find the pot and cups.

THIRTEEN

Challenges

Now this is the way it must be for the ones who construct the maps and charts. A map of land must be made from the hide of a land beast, and it should show no more than can be helped of the sea. A chart can only be drawn on a sea-creature's hide, and though land must be marked on it, it is sin to show the features of that land on a chart that is devoted to the sea. To do otherwise is to offend the god who made the world as it is.

Our islands are as the god made them. Thus he wrote on the seas of the world, long ago. They are his runes, and so when they are drawn within the chart of the great seas, they must be drawn in the blood of a land beast. And if you would make a mark for good harbour or plentiful fish or hidden shoals or any other feature that belongs to the seas, these marks must be made with the blood of a sea creature. For this is how the god made the world, and who is a man to try to draw it otherwise?

Our islands are the runes of the god. Not all is made clear to us, for we are but men and it is not for us to know every rune the god can write, nor what it is he has spelled across the face of the sea. Some islands he cloaks in ice from us, and this we are to respect. Draw then the ice that cloaks the rune, and this must be drawn in the blood of a creature of that ice, but not one that flies. The blood of a seal is good for this, but the blood of a white bear best of all.

If one wishes to draw the sky's face, then is the time to use the blood of a bird for ink, and draw but lightly on the skin of a gull.

These are very old laws. Every woman with a good mother knows them already. I write them down only because our sons' sons and their offspring are grown foolish and unwary of the god's will. They will bring disaster on us all if we do not remind them that we have been taught better, and that these laws are from the god's own lips.

The Making of Guides – Chade Fallstar's translation of an Outisland scroll

I was relieved to be on better terms with Jinna again. We spent no time in her bed that night, nor did I kiss her goodbye. But both those things were a relief to my mind if not to my clamouring body. When I left her that night, I resolved to treat our patched friendship gently and to keep it within bounds I felt I could deal with. I think she still felt this was untrusting on my part, but, so I have ever been. At least, so Chade has often told me.

There followed a trying three days for me. The rest of my life remained unsettled. I didn't hear from Hap. I dreaded that my lad was sleeping out in the snow somewhere, even as I disgustedly told myself he was a sharper boy than that. The Queen and Chade were meeting daily with the leaders of the Six Duchies, in deep discussion about Bingtown's offer of an alliance. They did not summon me to share their thoughts. The Bingtown delegation was very visible within Buckkeep Castle, assiduously courting the individual dukes and duchesses with gifts and attentions of every kind. On our part, the banquets and entertainment proceeded with an eye to soothing the ruffled feelings of the Outislanders and to being gracious to our Bingtown guests. The success of those evenings was mixed. Strangely enough, Arkon Bloodblade and his Outisland traders seemed fascinated with the Bingtown folk, and openly talked with them about expanding trade alliances based on the betrothal between Prince Dutiful and their Narcheska. Yet both Elliania and Peottre Blackwater were largely absent from the festivities. On the few occasions when Elliania did make an appearance, she was grave and quiet.

Both the Narcheska and Peottre carefully avoided the Bingtown Traders in every way that they could. She exhibited a marked aversion to the scaled boy, Selden Vestrit of the Rain Wild Traders. Once I saw her physically recoil as he walked past her. But I was not certain that it was her choice, for afterwards she sat very stiff in her chair while the beads of sweat broke out on her brow. It was not long after that both she and Peottre excused themselves from attending a puppet play on the grounds that the Narcheska was weary and Peottre must attend to their packing. This was a scarcely-veiled reminder of the imminent departure of the Outisland contingent. The Bingtown Traders and their offer could hardly have arrived at a worse time for us.

'A week later, and they would have been gone when the Bingtown folk arrived. Yes, and I don't doubt that we could have mended the Prince's little stumble with the Narcheska, and sent them off happy. Now it appears that we stack our refusal to break off talk with Bingtown on top of the Prince's slighting of the Narcheska. It throws everything into doubt.'

This was Chade's curmudgeonly observation as we sat over wine one evening. He was out of sorts for a number of reasons. Starling had tried to give him a note to pass to me. She had done it privately, but even so, it was indiscreet in the extreme for her to acknowledge that she knew he and I were connected. Somehow, that was my fault. When he had refused, she had said, 'Then just tell him that I'm sorry. I'd quarrelled with my husband, and I wanted the comfort of his friendship. I'd been drinking at the keep before I started down to town to finish my drink. I know I shouldn't have said those things.'

While I was still gaping, he'd asked delicately if Starling and I had any sort of 'an arrangement' and when I angrily replied that it was no one else's business if we did, but we didn't, he had surprised me by saying that only a foolish man would deliberately provoke a minstrel to anger.

'I didn't provoke her to anger. All of this is because I've refused to have her in my bed since I discovered she was married. I think I have a right to decide with whom I'll sleep. Don't you?'

I'd expected him to be shocked at this revelation. Almost, I hoped that it would be enough to embarrass him and make him resolve not to pry into my personal affairs any more. He only slapped his forehead. 'Of course. Well, she should have expected you to shake her out of your sheets once you discovered she was married, but . . . Fitz, do you understand what it means to her? Think.'

Had he not been so intent on teaching me something, I think I would have been offended. Yet his air was so familiar I could not accept his question as anything other than the opening to a lesson. Thus he had often spoken to me when trying to teach me to see all the possible motivations for a man to do something, rather than just the first ones that sprang to mind. 'She is ashamed because my finding out she was married and yet still sleeping with me has lowered my opinion of her?'

'No. Think, boy. Did it really lower your opinion of her?'

Reluctantly, I shook my head. 'I only felt stupid. Chade, in some way I was not even surprised. Starling has always allowed herself to do such things. I've known that since I first met her. I didn't expect her to change her minstrel ways. I simply didn't want to be a party to it.'

He sighed. 'Fitz, Fitz. Your biggest blind spot is that you cannot imagine anyone seeing you in a different way from how you see yourself. What are you, *who* are you to Starling?'

I shrugged a shoulder. 'Fitz. The bastard. Someone she has known for fifteen years.'

A very small smile played across his face. He spoke softly. 'No. You are FitzChivalry Farseer. The unacknowledged prince. She'd made a song about you before she'd even met you. Why? Because you'd captured her imagination. The bastard Farseer. Had Chivalry acknowledged you, you'd have had a chance at the throne. Denied and ignored by your father, you were still loyal, still the hero of the battle at Antler Island Tower. You died in ignominy in Regal's dungeons, and rose as a vengeful ghost to plague Regal through his days as a pretender. She accompanied you on a quest to save your King, and though it did not come out as any of us intended, still there was triumph at the end. And she not only witnessed it, she was a part of it.'

'It seems a fine tale, to hear you tell it that way, with none of the dirt and pain and misfortune.'

'It is a fine tale, even with the dirt and pain and misfortune. A fine and glorious tale, one that would make any minstrel's reputation for life, did she ever sing it. Yet it is one Starling can never sing. Because it has been forbidden to her. Her great adventure, her wonderful song, locked up as a secret. Still, at least she knew she was a part of it, and she was a part of the royal bastard's life. She became his lover, a party to his secrets. I think she expected that when you returned to Buckkeep some day you would again be at the centre of intrigue and wondrous events. And she expected to be part of that also, to turn heads and bask in that shared glory. The Witted Bastard's minstrel mistress. If she could not sing the song herself, at least she was guaranteed a place in that tale, if it should ever be told. And don't doubt that she has composed it somewhere, as a song or a poem. She saw herself as a part of your tale, touched by your wild glory. Then, you took that from her. You not only walked away from her, you returned to Buckkeep as an ignominious servant. You are not only ending your tale on a disappointing note; you are making her of no consequence by doing it. She is a minstrel, Fitz. How did you think she'd react to that? Gracefully?'

I saw her suddenly in a different light. Her cruelty to Hap, her offence at me. 'I don't think of myself like that, Chade.'

'I know you don't,' he said more gently. 'But do you see that she could? And that you crashed her dreams down around her?'

I nodded slowly. 'But there's nothing I can do about it. I won't take a married woman into my bed. And I can't come back as FitzChivalry Farseer. I'd still face a noose around my neck if I did.'

'That's most likely true. I agree that you cannot be known as FitzChivalry again. As to the other . . . well. Let me remind you that Starling knows a great many things. We are all vulnerable to her. I expect you to maintain her goodwill towards us.'

Before I could think of a reply to that, he demanded to know why I had cancelled all of the Prince's Skill lessons until after the Bingtown representatives had left. The Prince had already asked that question. I said to Chade what I'd told Dutiful: that I feared the scaled boy in the Bingtown party had some sensitivity to the Skill, and that until the Traders departed, we would limit our lessons to translating scrolls together. The Prince was not patient with these more mundane studies. My suspicion of the veiled Trader intrigued both him and Chade. Thrice Chade had chewed over Selden Vestrit's conversation with me. Neither of us could find any meat in it. I was learning that sometimes it was easier to keep Chade uninformed than to give him bits of information he could not confirm. Such as telling him of the Narcheska's tattoos.

I know he spent some hours of his own time at the spyhole without glimpsing her tattoos. As she had not made any complaint about her health, he could not send the healer to her rooms to confirm what I had seen. Elliania had pointedly refused several invitations to ride or game with the Prince, so Dutiful could make no observations on whether or not she seemed to be in pain. And the Queen dared not make too many pressing invitations lest it appear that the Six Duchies desired the betrothal to proceed more than the Outislands did. In the end, all they had was my account of what I had seen. It baffled all of us, as did her handmaid, Henja.

The woman remained a complete cipher to us. Her references to a Lady were unclear, unless she referred to an older female relative with authority over Elliania. Discreet inquiries in that area availed us nothing. Chade's spies had failed us as well. Twice Henja had been followed down into Buckkeep Town. Each time she had vanished from their scrutiny, once in a market crowd, and once simply by turning a corner. We had no idea who she saw there, or even if it was of any significance. The arcane punishment of the searing tattoos bespoke a magic that neither of us knew. Perhaps we should have felt glad of an unseen power urging the Narcheska to make strong her betrothal to the Prince. Instead, we both were dismayed by the dark cruelty of it. 'Are you sure Lord Golden could not cast some light on this?' Chade demanded abruptly. 'I recall him telling several people at a dinner that he had once made quite a hobby of studying the Outisland history and culture.'

I shrugged eloquently.

Chade snorted. 'Have you asked him yet?'

'No,' I replied shortly. Then, as he lowered his brows at me, I added, 'I told you. He has taken to his bed and scarcely comes out. Even his meals are taken in to him. He has the curtains drawn, both across his windows and about his bed.'

'But you don't think he is ill?'

'He hasn't said he is ill, but that is the impression he lets his serving-boy chatter about the keep. Sometimes I think that was half his reason for taking Char on, so that the boy could be fed the rumours he wishes to spread. I think that the truth is that he wishes to avoid any public appearances until after the Bingtown folk have departed. He lived there for some time, and while he was there he was certainly not known as the Fool, nor as Lord Golden.

I think he fears that if one of them recognized them, it could cause difficulties for him at court.'

'Well. I suppose that's sensible then. But it's damned inconvenient for me. Look, Fitz, can't you just go in and talk to him? See if he has any ideas about this Selden Vestrit being Skilled?'

'As he has no Skill himself, I don't think he could possibly have detected that aura from Vestrit.'

Chade set down his wine cup. 'But you haven't asked him, have you?'

I lifted my cup and drank from it to gain a moment. 'No,' I said as I set it down. 'I haven't.'

He peered at me. After a moment, he said in amazement, 'You two have had a falling out of some sort, haven't you?'

'I'd rather not discuss it,' I said stiffly.

'Hmph. Wonderful timing on everyone's part. Let's mix the Bingtown Traders with the Outislanders, and in the midst of it you can offend the Queen's favourite minstrel, and then have some silly squabble with the Fool that renders you both all but useless.' He leaned back in his chair in disgust as if we had done it solely to inconvenience him.

'I doubt he would have any insights on this,' I replied. I had not been able to bring myself to say more than a dozen words to him in the last three days, but I was not going to share that with Chade. If the Fool had noticed my coldness, he had ignored it. He had given Tom Badgerlock an order to turn away all guests at the door until he was feeling more like himself, and so I had. I spent as little time in the chambers we shared as possible. Yet several times when I returned to the room I saw small signs that someone had called while I was gone, and it was not just Char tidying things. I recognized Jek's spicy perfume lingering in our chambers.

'Well. That's as may be.' He scowled at me. 'Whatever it is, you'd best patch it up soon. You're not worth a tinker's damn when something like this has your back up.'

I took a breath to keep my temper down. 'It's not the only thing I've had on my mind lately,' I excused myself.

'No. We've all had far too much on our minds. What did your

boy want, the other day when he came up to the castle? Is all well with him?'

'Not exactly.' I had been shocked when one of the kitchen boys had tapped at the door to tell me that a young man was asking for me in the kitchen yard. I hastened down to find Hap standing outside in the courtyard, looking both angry and sheepish. He wouldn't come in, even to the guards' room, though I assured him none of them would mind. They'd become accustomed to seeing me there of late. He didn't want to take much of my time, for he knew I was occupied with tasks of my own. And at that my guilt began to build, for I had been busy of late, often too busy to see him when I knew I should have. By the time he worked up the courage to tell me that Jinna had turned him out and why, my resolve was already wavering.

He looked past my shoulder as he spoke to the lowering sky. 'So, with no coin of my own, I've been sleeping wherever I could find a bit of shelter the last two nights. But I can't do that the rest of winter. So I've no choice save to move into the apprentice house with the others. Only . . . it seems so awkward for me to ask after Master Gindast has suggested it so often and I've always refused it.'

This was news to me. 'He has suggested it? Why? Seems he saves himself a bit of money, not having to give you your breakfast nor supper.'

Hap squirmed unhappily. He took a breath. 'He suggests it whenever my work is poor. He says if I slept a proper night and rose with the others, if I were on time to work and on time to bed, I would do better.' He glanced away. There was a gruff pride as he added, 'He says he can see that I could do better, far better at my work, if I weren't so sleepy in the mornings. I've always insisted I could manage my own hours. And I have. Oh, I've been late a time or two, but I've been there every day since I came to Buckkeep Town. I have.'

He said this as if I might doubt it. I kept to myself that I had wondered if he had been faithful to his master's hours.

I had let some little time lag. 'So, then? What is the difficulty now? It seems that as he has asked you several times, he'd be pleased to see you take his suggestion.'

Hap was silent. He went a bit pinker about the ears. I waited. Then he steeled himself to it. 'I wonder if perhaps you couldn't go by and tell him you had decided it was best for me. It just seems simpler that way. Less awkward.'

I had spoken slowly, wondering if the words were wise. 'Less like you knuckling under to his suggestion, perhaps? Or less like Jinna turning you out because she didn't want trouble on her doorstep?'

Hap flushed a deep scarlet and I knew I had struck true. He started to turn away. I put a hand on his shoulder and when he tried to shrug it off, I tightened my grip. He startled when he could not twist free of it. So my daily practices on the weapons court had counted for something. I could hold a squirming lad against his will now. Such an accomplishment. I waited until he stopped struggling. He hadn't tried to hit me, but neither had he turned back to face me. I spoke quietly, for his ears only, not for those who had turned to stare at our little contest. 'Go to Gindast yourself, son. You might save face with the other apprentices by saying your father had forced you to move in with them. But in the long run, Gindast will respect you more if you go to him and say you've thought it over and decided it would be for the best if you lived there. And you might recall that Jinna has been kind, not just to you but to both of us, far beyond what any coin would buy and far beyond what either of us deserves from her. Don't shun her because she wanted no trouble in her home. Trouble shouldn't be the price of her being our friend.'

Then I had loosened my hold and allowed him to shrug free of me and stalk off. I didn't know what he had done. I hadn't gone to check on him. I had to let him sort that much of his life out for himself. He had food and shelter if he chose to accept them on the terms offered. More than that I could not do for him. I dragged my thoughts back to my conversation with Chade.

'Hap's had some difficulties adjusting to life in town,' I admitted to the old assassin. 'On our holding, he was used to setting his own hours, as long as his chores were done. It was a simpler life. Less of a daily grind, and more choices for him.'

'Less beer and fewer girls, too, I imagine,' Chade added, and I suspected that, as usual, he knew far more about everything than he was letting on. But he smiled as he said it, and I let it pass. Not only because he meant no insult to Hap or me by it, but because it was a relief to me to see the old man as sharp as he had ever been. It seemed that the thicker the intrigue in Buckkeep Castle, the more Chade throve on it. 'Well. I hope you know that whatever your Hap gets into, you can turn to me for help. If it's needed. Without a price on it.'

'I know that,' I had replied, if a bit gruffly, and he had let me go. We both had to prepare ourselves for the afternoon's event. Chade had to dress appropriately for the formal farewell ceremony for the Outislanders. He was hoping desperately that tonight's honours and gifts would heal the cracks and rifts, and that they would depart on the morrow with the betrothal confirmed. As for me, I had to gather my supplies and make my way to my spy-post to watch from that vantage and store up any titbits that might escape Chade's eyes.

He departed to his chambers to make himself ready. My own preparations were far different. I gathered a supply of candles, a pillow from his bed and a blanket, a bottle of wine and some victuals. I expected to crouch in my hiding place for several hours, and I was determined that this time I would be comfortable. Winter had clenched its grip on the castle over the last few days, and the hidden tunnels and corridors were chill and comfortless.

I bundled it all together, removing Gilly several times from my efforts. The ferret had become a social little fellow of late, greeting me with whiskers twitching and sniffing whenever we encountered one another in the hidden network. As much as he enjoyed his hunting and despite the numerous trophies he left about to demonstrate his prowess, he surprised me often by begging for raisins or bits of bread. These he seemed to relish hiding behind the scroll-rack or under the chairs more than he did eating them. His mind darted like a hummingbird, inquisitive and restless. Like most animals, he was completely uninterested in bonding with a human. Our Wit-sense of one another brushed often but never engaged. Still, he was companionably intrigued in what I did, and followed me curiously as I made my way through the cramped passages.

I arrived in plenty of time to witness the farewell banquet. I set my cushion upon a rickety stool that I had gathered on the way, put my food on the dusty floor beside me and my candle and extra tapers beyond it. I seated myself, wrapped the blanket about my shoulders and settled myself by the peephole. This one offered a good vantage, I decided with approval. From here, I could see the high dais and almost a third of the hall.

The winter finery of the Great Hall had been renewed. Evergreen boughs and garlands trimmed the entrances and hearths, and the minstrels played softly as folk entered and sought their places. All in all it reminded me very much of the Betrothal Ceremony, witnessed from a different angle. Embroidered cloths covered the long tables, and bread and fruit preserves and wine glasses awaited the guests. Southern incense, a gift from the Bingtown Traders, sweetened the air of the hall. There was a bit less ceremony as the dukes and duchesses entered this time. I suspected that even the nobility had become a bit weary of all the festivities and pomp of late. The Bingtown delegation, I noted with interest, came in with the lesser aristocrats and was seated well away from the Outislanders' dais. I wondered if the distance would be enough to prevent sparks flying.

What I had begun to think of as Arkon Bloodblade's contingent entered next. They seemed in high spirits, and were once more decked in their extravagant versions of Buckkeep garb. Heavy furs had been replaced with satin and velvet, lace had been used indiscriminately and the colours seemed to favour the red and orange section of the spectrum. Strange to say, it suited them well, both the men and the women. The barbaric excess in adopting our modes of dress made them the Outislanders' own style. And that they had chosen to emulate some of our ways indicated to me that the doors would soon open wide to trade of all sorts. If Arkon Bloodblade had his way.

Peottre Blackwater and Elliania were not with them.

They still had not entered by the time the Queen and the Prince made their way to the high dais, with Chade trailing demurely behind them. I saw the Queen's eyes widen with dismay, but she did not let it reach her smile. Prince Dutiful kept a lordly reserve, apparently not noticing that his intended had not yet seen fit to join the ceremony designed to honour her departure. When the Farseers had assumed their places, an awkward little delay ensued.

Ordinarily, the Queen would have ordered the servants to pour the wine and begun with a toast to her honoured guests. It had just reached the point at which folk had begun to mutter when Peottre Blackwater appeared at the entrance to the hall. He had retained his Outisland skins and chains but the richness of the furs and the gold that weighted his forearms bespoke his very best. He stood in the doorway until the startled murmur at his appearance had stilled. Then he stepped silently aside and the Narcheska entered. The narwhal symbol of her matriarchal line was picked out in ivory beads on her leather vest. It was trimmed with white fur, probably snowfox. She wore a sealskin skirt and slippers. Her arms and fingers were innocent of all jewellery. Her hair flowed unfettered as night down her back, and upon her head she wore a curious blue ornament, almost like a crown. It reminded me of something but I could not quite recall what.

She stood for a moment in the entrance. Her gaze met Kettricken's and held it. Head up, she paced the length of the room towards the high dais with Peottre Blackwater coming slowly behind her. He let her lead him by enough that his presence did not distract from hers, but as always, he was close enough to protect her should any seek to do her harm. Never once did she look away from the Queen as she trod the length of the hall. Even when she ascended the steps to the dais, their gazes remained locked. When finally she stood before Kettricken, she made her a solemn curtsey, yet she did not bow her head nor avert her gaze as she did so.

'I am so pleased you have joined us,' Kettricken said graciously in a low voice. There was genuine welcome in her tone.

I thought for a moment that I saw a flicker of doubt pass over the Narcheska's face. But then her resolve seemed to harden. When she spoke, her young voice was clear, her enunciation crisp and her voice pitched to carry. They were not private words she spoke. 'I am here, Queen Kettricken of the Six Duchies. But I fear I have begun to have doubts that I will ever truly join you, as wife to your son.' She turned then, and her gaze slowly swept the assembly. Her father was sitting very straight. I surmised that her words were a surprise to him, one he sought to cover. The initial look of shock on the Queen's face had been replaced with a cold and courteous mask.

'Your words disappoint me, Narcheska Elliania Blackwater of the God Runes.' That was all Kettricken said. She spoke no question that would have invited a reply. I saw Elliania hesitate, fumbling for a way to begin her planned speech. I suspected she had expected more of a reaction; a demand for an explanation. Lacking that introduction, she had no choice but to tone her words to meet the Queen's attitude of polite regret.

'I find that this betrothal does not meet my expectations, which are those of my mothers' house. I was told that I would come here to promise my hand to a king. Instead I find my hand offered to a youngster who is but a prince, not even the King-in-Waiting, as you term one who learns the duties of his crown. This is not to my satisfaction.'

Kettricken did not reply immediately. She let the girl's words die away. When she did speak, it was with simplicity, as if she were explaining something to a child who might be too young to understand it. The effect was that of a mature and patient woman addressing a wayward young girl. 'It is unfortunate that you were not taught our customs in this manner, Narcheska Elliania. Prince Dutiful must be at least seventeen before he may be declared the King-in-Waiting. After that, it is up to his dukes to decide when he may be crowned as a full king. I do not expect it will take long for him to earn that responsibility.' She lifted her eyes and scanned her dukes and duchesses as she spoke. She honoured them when she acknowledged their role and they were sensible of that. Most of them nodded sagely to her words. It was smoothly done.

I think Elliania sensed her moment slipping away from her. Her voice was just the least bit shrill and she spoke perhaps a second too soon when she said, 'Nevertheless. If I accept my betrothal to Prince Dutiful now, none can deny that I am taking the chance of binding my fate to a prince who may never be declared King.'

As she drew breath, Kettricken quietly interjected, 'That is most unlikely, Narcheska Elliania.'

I felt, almost as if it were my own, Dutiful's prodded pride. A Farseer temper lurked behind his cool Mountain exterior. The Skill-link between us throbbed with his rising anger.

Steady. Let the Queen handle this. I kept my thread of suggestion small and tight between us.

I suppose I must, he replied recklessly. *However little I like it. Just as I must tolerate this arranged marriage at all.*

In the heat of his provocation, his control was more absent than sloppy. I winced at it and glanced towards the veiled Bingtown Trader. Selden Vestrit sat very straight, and perhaps his intentness was only the interest in the proceedings that he shared with all the other Bingtown Traders. Yet he seemed entirely too still, as if he listened with every pore of his body. I feared him.

'Nevertheless!' the Narcheska said again, and this time her accent flawed the word more sharply. I could see her losing her aplomb, but she ploughed ahead stubbornly. Doubtless this speech had been practised endlessly in her room, but now it was delivered without finesse or gestures. It was only words, pebbles hurled in desperation. Doubtless many thought it was to save herself from the betrothal. My suspicions were different.

'Nevertheless, if I am to accept this custom of yours as good, and give my promise of marriage to a prince who may never become a king, then it seems to me fair and good that in return I ask him to honour a custom of my land and people.'

There were too many faces to watch for responses from everyone. One I made sure of was Arkon Bloodblade. I was certain that his daughter's speech was a complete surprise to him. Yet at her naming this condition, he seemed pleased. But then, I reflected, he was obviously a man who enjoyed a challenge and a gamble, as well as putting on a show. He was content to let her stir the pot while he waited to see what would bob to the top. Perhaps it would be to his advantage. Several of the people seated alongside him did not look so sanguine. They exchanged apprehensive glances, fearing the girl's effrontery would endanger the betrothal and cripple their trade negotiations.

The blood had started to rise in Prince Dutiful's face. I could see and feel him fighting to maintain a serene demeanour. Kettricken held her calm almost effortlessly.

'Perhaps that might be acceptable,' she said quietly, and again it sounded as if she were indulging a child. 'Would you care to explain this custom to us?'

Narcheska Elliania seemed to know that she was not showing well. She pulled herself straighter, and took a breath before she spoke. 'In my land, in the God Runes, it is customary that if a man seeks to marry a woman, and the woman's mothers are uncertain of his blood or his character, then the mothers may propose a challenge to him whereby he can prove himself worthy.'

And there it was. Insult bald enough that no duchy would have blamed their queen if she had immediately voided the betrothal and alliance. No, they would not have blamed her, yet in the faces of more than one pride warred with the possible loss of trade profits. Eyes flickered as dukes and duchesses silently conferred with one another, faces set in stillness, mouths flat. But before the Queen could even draw breath to compose a reply, the Narcheska added to her words.

'As I stand before you without the benefit of my mothers to speak for me, I would myself propose a challenge that would prove the Prince worthy of me.'

I had known Kettricken in the days when she was the daughter of the Mountain Sacrifice, before she was Queen of the Six Duchies. I had known her in the days when she was transforming herself from a girl barely a woman into both woman and queen. Others might have been at her side longer, or spent more recent years with her, but I think my early knowledge of her let me read her as no one else could. I saw in the tiny movement of her lips how disappointed she was. All the months of effort spent crawling toward an alliance between the Six Duchies and the Outislands were erased in the rush of an impetuous girl's words. For Kettricken could not allow the worthiness of her son to be questioned. When Elliania looked askance at Dutiful, she looked askance at the entire Kingdom of the Six Duchies. It could not be tolerated, not because of maternal pride, but because of the danger of debasing the value of the Six Duchies alliance. I held my breath, waiting to hear how Kettricken would sever the negotiations. So focused was I on the Queen's face that I only caught from the tail of my eye the furtive grab that Chade made at the young prince's shoulder as Dutiful surged to his feet.

'I will accept your challenge.' The Prince's voice rang out, young and strong. Violating all protocol he stepped clear of his chair and moved to face the Narcheska as if this were truly a confrontation between lovers. His action seemed to exclude the Queen, as if she had no say in the matter at all. 'I will do it, not to prove myself worthy of your hand, Narcheska. I will not do it to prove anything about myself to you, or to anyone else. But I will do it because I would not see the days of negotiation towards a peace between our peoples put into jeopardy over a prideful girl's doubts of me.'

She was equal to his scalded pride. 'It matters little to me why you do it,' she said, and suddenly her crisp diction and precise pronunciation were back. 'So long as the task is performed.'

'And the task?' he demanded.

'Prince Dutiful,' said the Queen. Any son would have recognized the meaning of those words. In the naming of his name, she commanded him to be silent and step back. But the Prince did not seem even to hear them. His entire attention was focused on the girl who had humiliated him and then spurned his efforts at apology.

Elliania took a breath. When she spoke again I recognized plainly the polished diction of a prepared speech. Like a courser who finds solid ground beneath her feet, she sprang to the chase.

'You know little of our God Runes, Prince, and less of our legends. For legend many will term the dragon Icefyre, though I assure you he is real. As real as your Six Duchies dragons were, when they flew over our villages, snatching memories and sense from those who lived there.'

Bitter words that could only wake bitter memories in the Six Duchies folk who heard them. How dared she complain of what our dragons had done to her people, after the years of raids and Forging had provoked us to it? She walked on very thin ice, black water seeping up in her footprints. I think that only the sheer drama of the moment saved her. She would have been shouted down, had not all ardently wished to know what this Icefyre was. Even the Bingtown Traders had suddenly come to a more pointed attention.

'Our "legend" is that Icefyre, the black dragon of the God Runes, sleeps deep in the heart of a glacier on Aslevjal Isle. His slumber is a magic one, preserving the fires of his life until some deep need of the God Runes folk awakens him. Then, he will rip himself free of the glacier and come to our aid.' She paused and slowly scanned the whole room. Her voice was cool and emotionless when she observed, 'Surely, he should have done so when your dragons flew over us? Surely that was an hour of great need for us. Yet our hero failed to arise. And, for that, as for any hero who forsakes his duty, he deserves to die.' She turned back to Dutiful. 'Bring me Icefyre's head. Then I will know that, unlike him, you are a worthy hero. And I will wed you and be your wife in all ways, even if you never become the King of the Six Duchies.'

I felt Dutiful's instantaneous reaction. *NO* I forbade him, and for the first time since I had accidentally Skill-imprinted on him the command not to fight me, I hoped with all my heart that it was well and truly still in place.

And it was. I felt him hit that barrier like a rabbit finding the length of the snare. Like a rabbit, he struggled against the choking restriction of my command. But unlike a rabbit, I felt him, even in his panic and outrage, consider the type of stricture it was. He acted as swift as thought. He lifted his head, and almost like a tracing finger, I felt him follow the noose back to me.

He severed it. Not easily. In the moment before I lost my contact with him, I could feel the sweat burst from his skin. For me, it was like being slammed brow-first onto an anvil. I reeled with the impact, but had no time for considering the pain. For I was suddenly aware that the veiled Trader's pale blue eye-light was visible through his lacy veil. And he stared, not at the Prince, but at the peephole where I cowered, out of sight. I would have given much to see his expression just then. Even as I prayed it was some bizarre coincidence, I longed to huddle down, to shut my own eyes and hide until his gaze had swept past me.

But I could not. I had a duty, not just as a Farseer but as Chade's extra eyes. I kept my gaze fixed on the room. My head pounded with pain, and Selden Vestrit continued to stare at the wall that should have shielded me. Then Dutiful spoke.

His voice boomed forth, Verity's voice, a man's voice. 'I accept the challenge!'

So swift it all had happened. I heard Kettricken's gasp. She had not had time to think of nor phrase a refusal. A stunned silence followed Dutiful's words. Outislanders, including Arkon

Bloodblade, exchanged worried glances at the thought of a Six Duchies prince slaying their dragon. At the Six Duchies tables, the palpable thought was that Dutiful did not need to meet this foreign challenge. I saw Chade wince. Yet a moment later, the old assassin's eyes opened wide and I saw hope gleam in them. For cheers erupted, not just from the Six Duchies tables but from the Outislanders as well. The enthusiasm for a young man roaring like a bull that he would meet a challenge overpowered every shred of common sense that any man in the room might have held. Even I felt a surge of pride in my chest for this young Farseer prince. He could have refused the challenge, and rightfully so, with no loss to his honour. But he instead had stepped up to it, to defy the Outislanders' slighting assumption that he was less than worthy of their Narcheska's hand. At the Outislander table, I suspected that wagers were already being laid that the boy would fail. But even if he failed, his willingness to step up to Elliania's challenge to him had increased their regard for him. Perhaps they were not marrying their Narcheska off to a farmer prince at all. Perhaps there was a bit of hot blood in his veins.

And for the first time I noted the looks of consternation, even horror, amongst the Bingtown Traders. The veiled Trader was no longer staring at my wall. Selden Vestrit gestured frantically, speaking urgently to the others at his table, trying to make himself heard through the roar of sound that filled the Great Hall.

I caught a glimpse of Starling Birdsong. She had leapt to a table top, and her head pivoted like a beleaguered wind-vane as she tried to take in every aspect of the scene, mark every man's reaction and harvest every comment. There would be a song to be made from all this, and it would be hers.

'And!' Prince Dutiful shouted into the din. Something in the set of the lines around his eyes warned me.

'Eda, mercy,' I prayed, but knew no god or goddess would stop him. There was a wild and stubborn gleam in his eyes, and I feared whatever it was he was about to say. At his shout, the uproar in the Great Hall quieted abruptly. When he spoke again, his words were pitched for the Narcheska. Nonetheless, in the brimming silence in the room, they carried clearly.

'And I've a challenge of my own. For if I must prove myself worthy to wed the Narcheska Elliania, who has no prospects of being Queen of anything, save that she give her hand to me, then I think she must first prove herself worthy of being a queen of the Six Duchies.'

Now it was Peottre's turn to startle and then grow pale, for the words were scarcely out of the Prince's mouth before Elliania replied, 'Call me this challenge, then!'

'I shall!' The Prince took a breath. The eyes of the two youngsters were locked. They might have stood in the midst of a desert for all the care they took for the rest of us. The glance between them was not fixed, but alive, as if for the first time they saw one another as they clinched in this battle of wills. 'My father, as you may know, was "only" the King-in-Waiting when he embarked on a quest to save the Six Duchies. With little more than his own courage to guide him, he set forth to find the Elderlings that would rise to our aid and end the war your people had forced upon us.' The Prince paused, almost, I think, to see if his words had struck home, but Elliania remained icily silent in her stern contemplation of him. He cut on. 'When months passed and no word was heard from him, my mother, who by then was the besieged but rightful Queen of the Six Duchies, set out after him. With but a handful of companions she sought and found my father, and aided him in waking the dragons of the Six Duchies.' Again, that pause. Again, Elliania refused to put words in it. 'It seems fitting to me, that as she proved herself by joining my father's quest to wake the dragons, so you should play a similar role in my quest to slay your country's dragon. Go with me, Narcheska Elliania. Share the hardship and witness the deed you have laid upon me. And if, in truth, there be no dragon to slay, witness that.' Dutiful spun suddenly to the room and shouted, 'Let no man here ever say it was the will of the Six Duchies alone that slew Icefyre. Let your Narcheska who has commanded this deed see it through beside me.' He turned back to her and his voice dropped to a sugary whisper. 'If she dares.'

Her lip curled in disdain. 'I dare.'

If she had said more, the words would have gone unheard, for the hall erupted in noise. Peottre stood as pale and still as if he had been turned to ice, but every other Outislander, including Elliania's father, was pounding on the table. A sudden rhythmic chant in their own tongue burst from them, a song of determination and blood-lust more fit to the rowers on a raiding ship than to treaty negotiators in a foreign hall. The lords and ladies of the Six Duchies shouted as they attempted to be heard. The comments seemed to run the gauntlet that the Narcheska deserved the Prince's scornful challenge to that she had responded bravely and perhaps there was indeed a worthy queen inside the Outislander girl.

Amidst it all, my queen stood still and tall, silently regarding her son. I saw Chade's mouth move as if he offered some quiet bit of counsel to her. She sighed. I suspected I knew what he had said. Too late to change it; the Six Duchies must follow through on the Prince's thrust. To one side of them, Peottre was struggling to mask his deep dismay. And before them the Prince and the Narcheska still stood, their eyes locked in duel.

The Queen spoke, her voice low, the first words intended only to quell the sound in the hall. 'My guests and my lords and ladies. Hear me, please.'

The uproar died slowly, ending with the thumping at the Outislander table that gradually slowed and ceased. Kettricken took a deep breath and I saw resolve firm her features. She turned, not to Arkon Bloodblade and his table, but to where she knew the true power resided now. She looked toward the Narcheska, but I knew her focus was actually on Peottre Blackwater. 'It seems we now have a firm agreement. Prince Dutiful is hereby affianced to the Narcheska Elliania Blackwater of the God Runes. Providing that Prince Dutiful can bring to her the head of the black dragon Icefyre. And providing that Narcheska Elliania accompany him to witness the doing of this task.'

'BE IT SO!' roared out Arkon Bloodblade, unaware that the decision had never been his to make.

Peottre nodded twice, grave and silent. And to my queen, the Narcheska Elliania turned and lifted her chin. 'Be it so,' she agreed quietly, and the deed was done.

'Bring in the food and wine!' the Queen commanded suddenly. It was not at all the proper way the meal should have been commanded, but I suspected she needed to sit down, and that a glass of wine to fortify her would be welcome. I was trembling myself, not just in fear of what must eventually come of this but from the thundering pain that Dutiful had inflicted on me in the course of severing my power over him. The minstrels struck up suddenly at a signal from Chade as the serving-folk flooded into the hall. All resumed their seats, even Starling the Minstrel, stepping gracefully from the tabletop into her husband's waiting arms. He swung her to the floor, infected with the court's heady elation. It seemed whatever their quarrel had been, it was mended now.

As if Dutiful sensed me wondering at how he had freed himself of my Skill-command, the Prince swept suddenly into my skull. *Tom Badgerlock. You will answer to me later for this.* As abruptly, he was gone. When I falteringly reached after him, he was simply unavailable to me. I knew he was there, but I could not find a handle to open his mind to mine. I drew a deep breath. This did not bode well. He was angry with me, and quite likely the trust between us was badly damaged. It would not make teaching him any easier. I pulled my blanket more tightly around my shoulders.

Below, in the hall, only the Bingtown Traders were subdued. Their talk was quiet and confined to their own group. Even so, it did not prevent them from filling their plates and their glasses generously. Alone amongst them, Selden Vestrit sat, seemingly in deep thought. His plate and his glass were empty and he seemed to stare at nothing.

But at every other table, the talk was lively and the eating as ravenous as if they were men-at-arms fresh returned from battle. The excitement in the hall was palpable, as was the sense of triumph. It was done. For now, at least, the Six Duchies and the Outislands had a firm understanding with one another. The Queen had done it, well, yes, and the Prince, and the glances that were tossed his way seemed more appraising of him than previously. Obviously, this lad was proving himself spirited, to both his lords and ladies, and to the Outislander folk.

The guests in the hall settled down to their meat and drink. A minstrel struck up a lively tune, and the talk subsided as folk began to eat. I opened the bottle of wine I had brought with me. From my folded napkin, I took bread and meat and cheese. The ferret miraculously appeared at my elbow, his tiny paws on my knee. I broke off a piece of meat for him.

'A toast!' someone shouted in the hall. 'To the Prince and the Narcheska!'

A lusty cheer followed the words.

I raised my bottle, grinned grimly, and drank.

FOURTEEN

Scrolls

Owan, a fisherman, lived on the rune island called Fedois. His wife's mothers' house was of wood and stone and stood well above the tide line, for tides can run both exceeding high and very low in that place. It was a good place. There were clams on the beach to the north, and enough pasturage below the glacier that his wife could keep three goats of her own in a flock of many, even though she was a younger daughter. She bore for them two sons and a daughter, and all helped him fish. They had enough and it should have been enough for him. But it was not.

From Fedois, on a clear day, a keen-eyed man can see Aslevjal with its heart glacier glinting blue beneath the azure sky. Now all know that when the lowest tide of the winter season comes, a boat can venture under the glacier's skirts and find a way to the heart of the island. There, as all know, the dragon sleeps with a hoard of treasure scattered about him. Some say a bold man can go there and ask a favour of Icefyre as he sleeps locked in the glacier's cold, and some say it is only a man both greedy and foolish who would do such a thing. For it is told that Icefyre will give such a man not only what he asks, but what he deserves, and that is not always good luck and gold. To visit Icefyre by that path, a man must go swift, waiting for the tide to lower away from the ice, and then darting under it as soon as his boat will slide between the water and the icy roof. Once in that cold sapphire place, he must count the beats of his own pulse, for if he tarries too long, the tide will return to grind him and his boat between the water and the ice. And that is not the worst thing that can befall a man who ventures there. Few are there who tell the tale of visiting that place, and even fewer are truthful men.

Owan knew this well, for his mother had told him, and so had his wife and his wife's mother. 'No call have you to go begging at the dragon's

*door,' they warned him. 'For you will get no better of Icefyre than would
an impudent beggar that came to our own door.' Even his younger son
knew this was so, and he was a lad of only six winters. But his older son
had seventeen years, and his heart and his loins burned hot for Gedrena,
daughter of Sindre of the Linsfall mothers. She was a rich bride, high above
choosing the son of a fisherman for her mate. So his older son buzzed in
Owan's ear like a gnat by night, whining and humming that if they had
the courage to visit Icefyre, they both could be the richer for it.*

Outislander Scroll, Icefyre's Lair

The following morning the Outislanders departed, sailing with the
dawn tide. I didn't envy them their trip. The day was rough and
cold, spray flying from the tips of the waves. Yet they seemed to
make little of the harsh weather, accepting it as routine. I heard
that there was a procession down to the docks, and a formal farewell
as Elliania boarded the ship that would carry her back to the God
Runes. Dutiful bent over her hand and kissed it. She curtseyed to
him and to the Queen. Then Bloodblade made his formal farewells,
followed by his nobles. Peottre was the last to bid goodbye to the
Farseers. He was also the one who escorted the Narcheska aboard
the ship. They all stood on the deck to wave as the ship was pulled
out of the harbour. I think the folk who went to witness it were
disappointed that there were no last-minute dramatics. Almost, it
was a calm following a storm. Perhaps Elliania was still too dazed
from the previous evening's late night and cataclysmic agreements
to present any last-minute hurdles.

I knew that a quiet meeting between the Queen, Chade, Blackwater and Bloodblade had followed the formal banquet. It had
been arranged hastily and lasted into the early hours of the
morning. The behaviour of the Prince and Narcheska had doubtless
been discussed, but more importantly, the Prince's quest had now
metamorphosed into but one element of an extended visit to the
Outislands. Chade told me later that the slaying of the questionable
dragon had not been discussed so much as the time-table for the
Prince to meet not only the Hetgurd of the Outislands but to visit
the Motherhouse of Elliania's family. The Hetgurd was a loose

alliance of head men and tribal chiefs who functioned more as a trade clearinghouse than any sort of a government. Elliania's Motherhouse was a different matter. Chade told me later that Peottre had seemed very uneasy when Blackwater had calmly assumed that it must be a part of Dutiful's visit to the Outislands, almost as if he would have refused it if he could. The Prince and his entourage would depart for the Outislands in spring. My private response to that was that it gave Chade precious little time for his information gathering.

I was not a witness to that hastily-convened negotiation, nor to any of the farewell events. Lord Golden, much to Chade's annoyance, still begged off of any public appearances, citing his health. I was just as glad not to go. I was cramped and stiff from an evening spent wedged in a wall peering through a spyhole. A nice stormy ride down to Buckkeep Town and back was not alluring.

In the wake of the departure of the Outislanders, many of the lesser lords and ladies of the Six Duchies began to leave the court also. The festivities and occasions of the Prince's betrothal were over, and they had many stories to share with those at home. Buckkeep Castle emptied out like an upended bottle. The stables and servants' quarters suddenly became roomier, and life settled into a quieter winter routine.

To my dismay, the Bingtown Traders lingered on. This meant that Lord Golden continued to keep to his rooms lest he be recognized, and that at any hour I might encounter Jek visiting him. Propriety meant nothing to her. She had grown up rough, the daughter of fisherfolk, and had kept the carefree ways of that people. Several times I met her in the halls of the castle. Always she grinned at me and gave me a jovial good day. Once, when our steps were carrying us in the same direction, she thumped me on the arm and told me not to be so sombre all the time. I made some neutral reply to that, but before I could get away, she clamped her hand on my forearm and drew me to one side.

She glanced all about us to be sure the hall was deserted and then spoke in a low voice. 'I suppose this will get me into trouble, but I can't stand to see the two of you like this. I refuse to believe you don't know "Lord Golden's" secret. And knowing it—' She paused for a moment, then said quietly and urgently, 'Open your eyes, man and see what could be yours. Don't wait. Love such as you could have doesn't—'

I cut her off before she could say anything more. 'Perhaps "Lord Golden's secret" is not what you think it is. Or perhaps you have lived among Jamaillians for too long,' I suggested, offended.

At my sour look, she had only laughed. 'Look,' she said, 'You might as well trust me. "Lord Golden" has, for years now. Believe in my friendship for both of you, and know that, like you, I can keep a friend's secrets when they deserve to be kept.' She turned her head and regarded me as a bird looks at a worm. 'But some secrets beg to be betrayed. The secret of undeclared love is like that. Amber is a fool not to voice her feelings for you. It does neither of you any good to ignore such a secret.' She stared into my eyes earnestly, her hand still gripping my wrist.

'I don't know what secret you refer to,' I replied stiffly, even as I wondered uneasily just how many of my secrets the Fool had shared with her. At that moment, two serving maids appeared at the end of the hall and continued towards us, gossiping merrily.

She had dropped my wrist, sighed for me and shook her head in mock pity. 'Of course you don't,' she replied, 'and you won't even see what is put right on the table before you. Men. If it was raining soup, you'd be out there with a fork.' She slapped me on the back, and then our ways parted, much to my relief.

After that, I began to long to have things out with the Fool. Like an aching tooth, I jiggled over and over what I would say to him. The frustration was that he excluded me from his bedchamber, even as he seemed to welcome Jek in for private talks. Not that I rapped at his door and demanded entrance. I had been maintaining a sullen silence towards him, waiting hungrily for him to demand just what ailed me. The problem was that he did not. He seemed focused elsewhere; it was as if he did not notice my silence or my surliness. Is there anything more provoking than waiting for someone to open the lowering quarrel? My mood became ever darker. That Jek believed the Fool was some woman named Amber did nothing to soothe my irritation. It only made the situation ever more bizarre.

In vain, I tried to distract myself with other mysteries. Laurel was gone. In the dwindling days of winter, I had noticed her absence. My discreet inquiries as to where the Huntswoman was had led me to rumours that she had gone to visit her family. Under the circumstances, I doubted that. When asked bluntly, Chade informed me that it was not my concern if the Queen had decided to send her huntswoman out of harm's way. When I asked where, he gave me a scathing look. 'What you don't know is less danger for you and for her.'

'And is there more danger, then, that I should know of?'

He considered for a moment before replying, then sighed heavily. 'I don't know. She begged a private audience with the Queen. What was said there, I don't know, for Kettricken refuses to tell me. She gave some foolish promise to the Huntswoman that it would remain a secret between the two of them. Then, Laurel was gone. I don't know if the Queen sent her away, or if she asked permission to leave, or if she simply fled. I have told Kettricken that it is not wise to leave me uninformed about this. But she will not budge from her promise.'

I thought of Laurel as I had last seen her. I suspected she had gone forth to fight the Piebalds in her own way. What that could be, I had no idea. But I feared for her. 'Have we had any word about Laudwine and his followers?'

'Nothing that we know is absolutely true. But three rumours might as well be the truth, as the saying goes. And there are plentiful rumours that Laudwine has recovered from the injury you dealt him, and that he will once more take up the reins of power over the Piebalds. The closest we have to good news is that some may dispute his right to lead them. We can only hope that he has problems of his own.'

And so I hoped, fervently, but in my heart I did not believe it.

There was little to lighten my life elsewhere. The Prince had not come to the Skill tower on the morning of the Narcheska's departure. I thought little of that. He had had a late night, and his presence was demanded early on the docks. But on the two mornings since then, I had waited in vain for him. I had arrived at our appointed hour, and waited, labouring over some scroll translations alone, and then I left. He sent me no word of explanation. After simmering in my own anger through the second morning, I made a firm decision that I would not contact him. It was, I told myself firmly, not my place. I tried to put myself in the Prince's skin. How would I have felt if I had found that Verity had given me a Skill-command to be loyal? I knew too well how I felt about Skillmaster Galen fogging my mind and masking my Skill-talent from me. Dutiful had a right to both his anger and his royal contempt of me. I'd let them run their course. When he was ready, I'd give him the only explanation I could: the truth. I had not meant to bind him to obey me, only to stop him from attempting to kill me. I sighed at the thought and bent over my work again.

It was evening and I was sitting up in Chade's tower. I had been there since afternoon, waiting for Thick. It was yet another meeting that he had missed. As I had pointed out to Chade, there was little he or I could do if the half-wit would not voluntarily come to meet me. Still, I had not wasted my time. In addition to several of the older and more obscure Skill-scrolls that we were deciphering piecemeal, Chade had given me two old scrolls that dealt with Icefyre, the God Runes' dragon. They both dealt with legends, but he hoped I could sift whatever seed of truth had begun them. He had already dispatched spies to the Outislands. One had sailed secretly aboard the Narcheska's vessel, ostensibly working his way across to visit relatives there. His true mission was to reach Aslevjal, or at least to discover as much about that isle as could be learned, and to report back to Chade with it. The old man feared that having committed himself to the quest, Dutiful must actually go. But he was determined the Prince would go well prepared and well accompanied. 'I myself may go with him,' Chade had informed me at our last-chance encounter in the tower. I had groaned, but managed to keep it a silent one. He was too old for such a trip. By an amazing effort of will, I managed to keep those words to myself also. For I knew what would follow any protest: 'Who, then, do you think I should send?' I was no more in favour of visiting Aslevjal myself than I was for Chade going. Or Prince Dutiful, for that matter.

I pushed the Icefyre scroll to one side and rubbed my eyes. It was interesting, but I doubted that anything there was going to prepare the Prince for his quest. From what I knew of our stone dragons, even from what the Fool had told me of the Bingtown dragons, it seemed highly unlikely to me that there was a dragon asleep in a glacier on an Outislander isle. Far more likely that a 'slumbering dragon' was fancifully blamed for earthquakes and glaciers calving. Besides, I'd had enough of dragons for a time. The more I worked on the scroll, the more troubling thoughts of the veiled Bingtowner menaced my sleep. Yet I could wish those were my only concerns.

My eyes fell on a heavy pottery bowl, upside down on the corner of the table. There was a dead rat under it. Well, there was most of a dead rat under. I'd taken it from the ferret last night. From a sound sleep, a Wit-scream of hideous pain had awakened me. It was not the ordinary snuffing of a small creature's life. Anyone with the Wit had to become inured to those constant ripples. Usually, little creatures went like popping bubbles. Among animals, death is a daily chance one takes in the course of living. Only a human bonded to a creature could have given such a roar of dismay, outrage and sorrow over a creature's death.

Once jolted awake by it, I had given up all hope of going back to sleep. It was as if my wound of losing Nighteyes had suddenly been torn afresh. I had arisen and, loath to awaken the Fool, had instead come up to the tower. On the way I had encountered the ferret dragging the rat. It had been the largest, most glossily healthy rat I had ever seen. After a chase and a tussle, the ferret had surrendered it to me. There was no way I could prove that this dead rat had been someone's Wit-beast, but my suspicions were strong. I had saved it to show it to Chade. I knew we had a spy sneaking about within the keep's walls. Laurel's lynched sprig of laurel was proof enough of that. Now it seemed possible that the rat and his Wit-partner had not only penetrated to the royal residence, but knew something of our hidden lairs. I hoped the old man would come to the tower this evening.

I now turned to the two old Skill-scrolls we'd been piecing together. They were more challenging than the Icefyre vellums, and yet more satisfying to work on. Chade believed the two were part of the same work, based on the apparent age of the vellum and the style of lettering used. I believed they were two separate works, based on the choice of words and the illustrations. Both were faded and cracked, with portions of words or whole sentences unreadable. Both were in an archaic lettering that gave me headaches. Beside each scroll was a clean piece of vellum, with Chade's and my line-for-line translations of the two. Looking at them, I realized that my handwriting predominated now. I glanced at Chade's latest contribution. It was a sentence that began, 'The use of elfbark'. I frowned at that, and found the corresponding line in the old scroll. The illustration beside it was faded, but it was definitely not elfbark. The word Chade had translated as 'elfbark' was partially obscured by a stain. But squinting at it, I had to agree that 'elfbark' did seem the most likely configuration of the letters. Well, that made no sense. Unless the illustration did not pertain to that part of the text. In which case, the piece I had translated might be all wrong. I sighed.

The wine rack swung open. Chade entered, followed by Thick bearing a tray of food and drink. 'Good evening,' I greeted them, and carefully set my work to one side.

'Good evening, Tom,' Chade greeted me.

'Evening, master,' *Dogstink*. Thick echoed him.

Don't call me that. 'Good evening, Thick. I thought you and I were going to meet here earlier today.'

The half-wit set the tray down on the table and scratched himself. 'Forgot,' he said with a shrug, but his little eyes narrowed as he said it.

I gave Chade a glance of resignation. I had tried, but the old man's surly stare seemed to say I had not tried hard enough. I tried to think of a way to be rid of Thick so I could discuss the rat with Chade.

'Thick? Next time you bring up wood for the fire, could you bring an extra load? Sometimes in the evening, it gets quite cold up here.' I gestured at the dwindling flames. I'd had to let it die down as there was no more wood to fuel it.

Cold dogstink. The thought reached me clearly but he simply stood and stared at me slackly as if he had not understood my words.

'Thick? Two loads of firewood tonight. All right?' Chade spoke to him, a bit more loudly than was needed and saying each word clearly. Could he not sense how much that annoyed Thick? The man was simple, but not deaf. Nor stupid, really.

Thick nodded slowly. 'Two loads.'

'You could go get it right now,' Chade told him.

'Now,' Thick agreed. As he turned to go, he gave me a brief glance from the corner of his eyes. *Dogstink. More work.*

I waited until he had gone before I spoke to Chade. He had set the tray on the table opposite the scrolls. 'He doesn't try to assault me with the Skill any more. But he uses it to insult me, privately. He knows you cannot hear him. I don't know why he dislikes me so much. I've done nothing to him.'

Chade lifted one shoulder. 'Well, you will both just have to get past that and work together. And you must begin soon. The Prince must have some sort of Skill-coterie to accompany him on this quest, even if it's only a serving-man he can draw strength from. Court Thick, Fitz, and win him. We need him.' When I met his words with silence, he sighed. Glancing about, he offered, 'Wine?'

I indicated my cup on the table. 'No, thank you. I've been drinking hot tea this evening.'

'Oh. Very good.' Chade walked around the table to see what I was working on. 'Oh. Did you finish the Icefyre scrolls?'

I shook my head. 'Not yet. I don't think we're going to find anything useful in them. They seem to be very vague about the actual dragon. Mostly accounts of earthquakes that proved that the dragon would punish someone if he didn't do what was just, and so the man realizes that he had best behave in a righteous way.'

'Nevertheless, you should finish reading them. There might be something in there, some hidden mention of a detail that could be useful.'

'I doubt it. Chade, do you think there even is a dragon? Or might not this be Elliania's ploy to delay her marriage, by sending the Prince off to slay something that doesn't exist?'

'I am satisfied that some sort of creature is encased in ice on Aslevjal Isle. There are a number of passing mentions of it being visible in some of the very old scrolls. A few winters of very deep snowfalls and an avalanche seem to have obscured it. But for a time travellers in that area would go far out of their way to stare into the glacier and speculate on what they were seeing inside it.'

I leaned back in my chair. 'Oh, good. Perhaps this will be more a task for shovels and ice saws than for a prince and a sword.'

A smile flickered briefly over Chade's face. 'Well, if it comes to moving ice and snow swiftly, I think I've come up with a better technique. But it still needs refinement.'

'So. That was you on the beach last month?' I had heard rumours of another lightning blast, this one witnessed by several ships out in the harbour. The explosion had happened in the deep of night during a snowstorm. It befuddled all who spoke of it. No one had seen lightning streak through the sky, nor would expect to on such a night. But no one could deny hearing the blast. A sizeable amount of stone and sand had been moved by it.

'On the beach?' Chade asked me as if mystified.

'Let it go,' I conceded, almost with relief. I had no wish to be included in his experiments with his exploding powder.

'As we must,' Chade agreed, 'For we have other things to discuss, things of much greater importance. How is the Prince progressing with his Skill lessons?'

I winced. I had not informed Chade that the Prince had not been coming to them. I hedged at first, reminding him, 'I've been reluctant to let him do any actual Skilling while the scaled Bingtowner is still here. So we had only been studying the scrolls—'

Then I suddenly saw little sense in withholding the truth, and no future at all in lying to Chade. 'Actually, he hasn't come to any of his lessons since the farewell banquet. I think he's still angry at discovering I'd placed a Skill-command on him.'

Chade scowled at the news. 'Well. I'll take steps to correct him. Regardless of how ruffled his feathers are, he had best put himself to that task. Tomorrow, he will be there. I will arrange that he will be able to spend an extra hour with you each morning and not be missed. Now. As to Thick. You must get to the task of teaching him, Fitz, or at least getting him to obey you. I leave how you do that to you, but I suggest that bribes will work better than threats or punishments. Now. On to our next task: how do you propose that we begin looking for other Skill candidates?'

I sat down and crossed my arms on my chest. I tried to hold in my anger as I asked, 'Then you've found a Skillmaster to teach other candidates if you find them?'

He knit his brows at me. 'We have you.'

I shook my head. 'No. I teach the Prince at his request. And you've coerced me into trying to teach Thick. But I am not a Skillmaster. Even if I had the knowledge to be one, I would not be one. I cannot. You are asking me for a lifetime commitment. You're asking me to take on an apprentice who would eventually assume the duties of Skillmaster when I died. There is no possible way I could take on a class of students and instruct them in the Skill without revealing to all of them who I am. I won't do that.'

Chade stared at me, mouth slightly ajar at my contained anger. It seemed to give my words momentum.

'Furthermore, I'd prefer that you let me settle my quarrel with the Prince in my own way. It will go better so. It's a personal matter, between him and me. As for when and where I will be able to teach Thick? Never and nowhere,' I said shortly. 'He doesn't like me. He's unpleasant, ill-mannered and smelly. And, if you haven't noticed before, he's a half-wit. A bit dangerous to trust him with the Farseer magic. But even if he weren't all those things, he has rejected all my efforts to teach him anything.' That was true, I defended it to myself. He had quickly terminated all of my half-hearted attempts at conversation, leaving me in a cloud of Skilled insults. 'And he's strong. If I push him, he may take that dislike of me to a violent level. Frankly, he scares me.' If I had thought to provoke Chade to anger, I failed. He slowly sat down across from me and took a sip from his wine glass. He regarded me silently for a moment, then shook his head. 'This won't do, Fitz,' he said in a low voice. 'I know that you doubt you can instruct the Prince and create a coterie for him in the time we have, but as it is something we must do, I have faith you will find a way.'

'*You* are convinced the Prince needs a coterie at his side before he undertakes this quest. I'm not even sure this is a real quest, let alone that a coterie will be able to assist him better than a troop of soldiers with shovels.'

'Nevertheless, sooner or later the Prince will need a coterie. You might as well begin to create one now.' He leaned back in his chair and crossed his arms on his chest. 'I've an idea of how to find likely candidates.'

I stared at him silently. He blithely ignored my refusal to be Skillmaster. His next words incensed me.

'I could simply ask Thick. He located Nettle easily. Perhaps if he put his mind to it and was rewarded for each success, he could find others.'

'I really want nothing to do with Thick,' I said quietly.

'A shame,' Chade replied as softly. 'For I'm afraid this is no longer a matter for discussion between you and me. Let me say this plainly: it is THE Queen's command for us. We met for several hours this morning, discussing Dutiful and his quest. She shares my opinion that he must have a coterie to accompany him. She asked what candidates we had. I told her Thick and Nettle. She wishes their training to begin at once.'

I crossed my arms on my chest and held my silence in. I was shocked, and not just by Nettle being included. I knew that in the Mountain Kingdom babes such as Thick were usually exposed shortly after birth. I had surmised that she would be dismayed at the thought of such a man serving her son. In fact, I had been relying on her to refuse him. Once more, Kettricken had surprised me.

When I was sure I could speak in a steady voice, I asked, 'Has she sent for Nettle yet?'

'Not yet. The Queen wishes to handle this matter herself, with great tact. We know that if she requests this, Burrich may refuse again. If she commands it, well, neither of us can decide what response he might make to that. She wishes both Burrich and the girl to agree to this. And thus the precise way to phrase the summons will demand thought, but right now, the Bingtown delegation takes every spare moment she has. When they have departed, she will invite both Burrich and Nettle here to explain the need to both of them. And perhaps Molly as well.' Very carefully he added, 'Unless, of course, you would like to broach the matter to them for the Queen. Then Nettle could begin her lessons sooner.'

I took a breath. 'No. I would not. And Kettricken should not waste her time considering how to approach them. Because I won't teach Nettle to Skill.'

'I thought you might feel that way. But feelings no longer have anything to do with it, Fitz. It is our queen's command. We have no choice except to obey.'

I slid down in my chair. Defeat rose like bile in the back of my throat. So. There it was. The command of my queen was that my daughter be sacrificed to the need of the Farseer heir. Her peaceful life and the security of her home were as nothing before the needs of the Farseer throne. I'd stood here before. Once, I would have believed I had no choice except to obey. But that had been a younger Fitz.

I took a moment and considered it. Kettricken, my friend, the wife of my uncle Verity was a Farseer by virtue of marriage. The vows I had sworn as a child and a youth and as a young man bound me to the Farseers, to serve as they commanded me, even to giving up my life. To Chade, my duty seemed clear. But what was a vow? Words said aloud with good intentions of keeping them. To some, they were no more than that, words that could be discarded when the situation or the heart changed. Men and women who had vowed faithfulness to one another dallied with others or simply abandoned their mates. Soldiers under oath to a lord deserted in the cold and lean winters. Noblemen vowed to one cause cast off their obligations when another side offered them more advantage. So. Truly, was I bound to obey her? I found that my hand had strayed to the little fox pin inside my shirt.

There were a hundred reasons I did not wish to obey her, reasons that had nothing to do with Nettle. The Skill, I had told Chade before, was a magic better left dead. Yet I had allowed myself to be persuaded to teach Dutiful. Reading the Skill-scrolls had not made me more secure in my decision to teach him. The scope of the Skill that I had glimpsed from these forgotten scrolls was vaster than anything Verity had ever dared imagine. Worse, the more I read, the more I realized that what we had was not the Skill library, but only the remaining fragments of it. We had the scrolls that spoke of the duties of instructors, and the scrolls that delineated the most sophisticated uses of the Skills. There must have been other Scrolls, ones that spoke of the basics and how a Skill-user could build his abilities and control to the level demanded for the most advanced purposes. But we did not have those ones. El alone knew what had become of them. The bits and pieces of Skill-knowledge that I had glimpsed had convinced me that the magic offered abilities almost on a footing with the powers of the gods. With the Skill, one could injure or heal, blind or enlighten, encourage or crush. I did not think I was wise enough to wield such authority, let alone decide who should inherit it. The more Chade read, the more eager and avid he became for the magic that had been denied to him by his illegitimate birth. He frightened me, often, with his enthusiasm for all the Skill seemed to offer. It frightened me in a different way that he insisted on venturing into the magic alone. That he had lately said nothing made me hope he had had no success.

Yet I dared not hope that left the decision in my hands. I could refuse, I could flee, but even without me, Chade would pursue the magic. His will was strong, as was his desire for the Skill. He would try to teach, not only himself but also Dutiful and Thick. And Nettle, I realized. Because Chade saw the Skill not as dangerous, but as desirable. He felt he was entitled to it. He was a Farseer, and the Farseer magic was rightfully his; but his birthright had been denied him, because he was a bastard Farseer. Just as my daughter was.

I suddenly put my finger on a sore that had festered in me for years. The Farseer magic. That was what the Skill was. Supposedly, the Farseers had a 'right' to this magic. And with that assumption went the notions that a Farseer had the wisdom to deploy such a magic within the world. Chade, born on the wrong side of the sheets, had been judged unworthy and callously denied any education in the Skill. Perhaps he had never had any talent for it; perhaps it had withered away, unnourished. But the unfairness of being denied the opportunity still ate at the old man, after all these years. I was certain that his thwarted ambition was behind his consuming desire to restore the Skill to use. Did he see me as depriving Nettle in the same way he had been denied? I looked at him. Had not Verity and Chade and Patience intervened for me, I might be as he was.

'You're very quiet,' Chade said softly.

'I'm thinking,' I replied.

He frowned. 'Fitz. It is the Queen's command. Not a request to think about. An order to obey.'

Not a request to think about. In my youth, there had been so many things that I hadn't thought about. I'd simply done my duty. But I had been a boy then. Now I was a man. And I teetered, not between duty and not duty, but between right and wrong. I took a step back from the question. Was it right to teach another generation the Skill and preserve it in our world? Was it right to let that knowledge fail and pass beyond humanity's reach? If there would always be some who could not have it, was it more righteous to deny it to all? Was the guarded possession of magic like the hoarding of wealth, or was it simply a talent one did or did not have, like the ability to shoot a bow well or sing each note of a song perfectly?

I felt besieged by the questions whirling in my head. In my heart, another question clamoured at me. Was there no way to preserve Nettle from this? For I could not bear it. I could not bear to see all I had sacrificed made useless as the secrets of her birth and of my survival were suddenly revealed to those most vulnerable to them. I could refuse to teach the Skill, but that would not preserve her peace. I could steal her from her home and flee, but then I would have been every bit as destructive as what I feared.

When Kettle had taught me the Stone game, I had had a sudden shift in perception one day. The wolf had been with me then. I had seen the little stones set in their places on the crossing lines of the gamecloth not as a fixed situation but as only one point in a spreading flow of possibilities. I could not win Chade's game by saying 'no'. But what if I said 'yes'?

You always chose to be bound by who you are. Now choose to be freed by who you are.

I caught my breath as that thought floated unbidden into my mind. *Nighteyes?* I reached after it but it was as sourceless as the wind. I was not sure if the Skill had carried the thought to me from some other person, or if the conviction had welled from some place deep within me. Whence ever it had come, it rang with truth. I handled the conviction delicately, fearing it might cut me. So I was bound by who I was. I was a Farseer. But in a strange, detached way that freed me.

'I want a promise,' I said slowly.

Chade sensed the sea change in me. Carefully, he set down his wine glass. 'You want a promise?'

'It always went both ways between King Shrewd and me. I was his. And in exchange for that, he provided for me and saw that I was taught. He provided for me very well, something that I have only realized the fullness of since I have been a man. I would ask a similar promise now.'

Chade knit his brows at me. 'Are you lacking anything? Well, I know your present quarters leave much to be desired, but as I have told you, this chamber may be modified however you please to suit your needs. Your present mount seems a good one, but if you prefer a better horse, I could arrange . . .'

'Nettle,' I said quietly.

'You wish Nettle provided for? It could most easily be done if we brought her here, to be educated and offered the opportunity to meet young men of good position and—'

'No. I do not wish her provided for. I wish for her to be left alone.'

He shook his head slowly. 'Fitz, Fitz. You know I cannot give you that. The Queen commands that she be brought here and taught.'

'I don't ask it of you. I ask it of my queen. If I agree to become her Skillmaster, then she must agree to let me teach in my own way, whom I choose, in secret. And she must promise to leave my daughter in peace. Forever.'

A terrible expression crossed his face. His eyes lit with the wild hope that I would step into the role of Skillmaster. But the price I had set upon it made him quail. 'You would ask a promise of your queen? Do you not think you presume too much?'

I set my jaw. 'Perhaps. But perhaps for a long time, the Farseers have presumed too much of me.'

He took in a long breath through his nose. I knew he bottled his anger with his hope. His words were icily formal. 'I shall present your proposal to Her Majesty and relay to you her reply.'

'Please,' I replied in a low and courteous voice.

He rose stiffly and without another word to me he departed. I realized in that silence that his anger went deeper than I had supposed. It took me a moment to put my finger on it. I was not as he was, neither as a Farseer nor as an assassin. I was not sure that made me a better man. I longed to let him leave just then, but I knew there were other matters we had to discuss.

'Chade. Before you go, there is something else I must tell you. I think we've had a spy in our secret corridors.'

He set his anger aside, almost visibly drawing himself back from it. As he turned, I lifted the bowl to reveal the rat. 'The ferret killed this last night. I felt someone grieve for its death. I think this was the Wit-beast of someone within Buckkeep. It could be the same one I encountered on the road the night before the Prince's betrothal.'

Grimacing with distaste, Chade bent over the rat and poked at it. 'Is there any way to know whose?'

I shook my head. 'Not absolutely. But this will have distressed someone greatly. I suspect they would need a day or so at least to recover. So, if anyone vanishes from the social whirl of court for a day or so, you might want to pay a call on them, to see what ails them.'

'I'll make inquiries. You think our spy is a noble, then?'

'That's the difficult part. It could be a man or a woman, noble or servant or bard. It could be someone who has lived here all his life, or someone who has been here only since the betrothal festivities began.'

'Is there anyone you suspect?'

I frowned for a moment. 'We might look most closely at the Bresinga group. But only because we know at least some of them are Witted and sympathetic to others with the Wit.'

'That's a small group. Civil Bresinga is here, with a manservant, a page, and I think a groom for his horse. I'll make inquiries about them.'

'It interests me that he remains when so many other nobles have returned to their own holdings. Could we discreetly find out why?'

'He has become a close friend of the Prince. It is in the best interests of his family that he exploit that connection. But I will quietly ask how things are at Galekeep. I have a person there, you know.'

I nodded gravely.

'She has said that the household seems to be declining in the last month or so. Old servants have left, and the new ones seem unmannered and undisciplined. She said there was an incident of some new cook's assistants who helped themselves to the wine cellar. The cook was quite upset to find them drunk, and even more distressed to discover that the pilferage had been going on for some time. When Lady Bresinga did not send the guilty parties packing, the cook left, and she had been with the household for some years. And it seems there is a change in the guests entertained there. In place of the landed gentry and the lesser nobles who used to guest there, Lady Bresinga has hosted several hunting parties who seemed to my person to be rather unsophisticated, even boorish.'

'What do you think it means?'

'That perhaps Lady Bresinga is forming new alliances. I suspect her new friends are at best Witted, and at worst, Piebalds. Yet it may not be with the Lady's willing consent. My person there says that Lady Bresinga spends more and more time alone in her own chambers, even when her "guests" are dining.'

'Have we intercepted any letters between her and Civil?'

Chade shook his head. 'Not in the last two months. There don't seem to be any.'

I shook my head. 'I find that exceedingly curious. Something is going on there. We should watch young Civil more closely than ever.' I sighed. 'This rat is the first evidence of Piebald activity that we've had since Laurel's lynched twig. I had hoped that their restlessness had settled.'

Chade drew a deep breath and let it out slowly. He came back to the table and sat down. 'There have been other signs,' he said quietly. 'But like this one, they have not been obvious ones.'

This was news to me. 'Oh?'

He cleared his throat. 'The Queen has managed to quell executions of Witted ones in Buck. At least, public ones. I suspect that in the smaller towns and villages, it could happen and no word of it reaches us. Or it could be done under the pretence of punishment for some other crime. But in place of the executions, there have been murders. Are these citizens killing Witted? Or Piebalds moving against their own to force compliance with them. We can't tell. Only that the deaths go on.'

'We have discussed that before. As you said, there is little Queen Kettricken can do about that,' I said neutrally.

Chade made a small sound in his throat. 'It would be most helpful to me if you could convince our queen of that. It bothers her a great deal, Fitz. And not just because her son is Witted.'

I bowed my head in acknowledgement of her concern for me. 'And outside Buck?' I asked quietly.

'It is more difficult. The duchies have always resented the crown taking too deep an interest in what they regard as "personal" questions of power and justice. To demand that Farrow or Tilth cease executing people for the Wit is like demanding that Shoaks cease all harassment along their border with Chalced.'

'Shoaks has always wrangled with Chalced about the border they share.'

'And Farrow and Tilth have always executed Witted ones.'

'That's not completely true.' I leaned back in my chair. I had enjoyed having access to Chade's scroll collection and the Buckkeep library. 'Prior to the time of the Piebald Prince, the Wit was regarded in the same light as hedge magics. Not particularly powerful magic, but if a man had it, he had it. It did not make him evil and disgusting.'

'Well,' Chade conceded. 'That's so. But the attitude of the people is so set now that it is near impossible to root it out. Lady Patience had done her best in Farrow. When she has not been able to prevent an execution, she has most assiduously punished those involved afterward. No one can accuse her of not trying.' He chewed his upper lip again. 'Last week, the Queen received an anonymous message.'

'Why wasn't I told?' I instantly demanded.

'Why should you be told?' he demanded in reply. Then, at my scowl, he softened his tone. 'There was little to tell. It made no demands or threats. It simply listed by name those who had been executed in the Six Duchies for the Wit in the last six months.' He sighed. 'It was a sizeable list. Forty-seven names.' He cocked his head at me. 'It was not marked with the Piebald horse. So, we think this comes from a different faction of Witted.'

I pondered this for a time. 'I think the Witted know they have the Queen's ear. I think they are letting her know what is happening, to see what she will do. To take no action would be a mistake, Chade.'

He nodded at me, grudgingly pleased. 'So I saw it also. The Queen says it shows we are making progress in gaining the trust of the Witted. They would not send such a list to her unless they thought there was something she could do. We are making an effort to find kin of the executed ones. Then each duchy will be informed by the Queen that they must pay blood-gold to them.'

'I doubt you will have much success finding kin. Folk are not comfortable admitting they are related to anyone with the Wit.'

Again he nodded. 'We have found a few, however. And the blood-gold for the others will be held here at Buckkeep by the Queen's counting-man. Where she cannot find kin, she will command that notices be posted, informing that those related to the executed can come to Buck for compensation.'

I pondered a bit. 'For the most part, they'll be afraid to come. And gold may be seen as a cold thing. Some nobles may even think it is worth the price to rid their realms of Witted ones. Like a fee paid to a rat-catcher.'

Chade bent his head down and rubbed his temples. When he lifted his face and looked at me, his face was weary. 'We do the best we can, FitzChivalry. Have you any better suggestions?'

I thought a bit. 'Not really. But I should like to see the scrolls they have sent. This one listing the names, and any earlier ones. Especially the one that came right before the Prince was taken.'

'If you wish to see them, then you shall.'

There was something in his voice. The hair on the back of my neck stood up. I spoke carefully. 'I've already said that I wished to see them. Several times. I do wish to see them, Chade. When can I look at them?'

He gave me a look from under lowered brows. Then he got up and with ponderously slow steps walked to his scroll-rack. 'I suppose that eventually all of my secrets must pass to you,' he observed reluctantly. Then, by a means I did not discern, he did something to release a catch. The decorative crown-piece on top of the scroll-rack folded down. He reached inside, and after a moment he drew out three scrolls. They were all small and rolled tight into cylinders which could have been concealed in a man's closed fist. I stood, but he shut the rack-front before I could see what else might be concealed there.

'How did you open that?' I demanded.

His smile was very small. 'I said "eventually", Fitz. Not "today".' His tone was that of my erstwhile mentor. He seemed to have had set aside his earlier annoyance with me. He came back to me and offered me the three rolled scrolls on his outstretched palms. 'Kettricken and I had our reasons. I hope you will think them good enough.'

I took the scrolls, but before I could open even one, the scroll-rack swung to one side again and Thick entered. I flipped all three scrolls up my sleeve with a move so practised it was almost instinctive. 'And now I must be going, FitzChivalry.' He turned from me to Thick. 'Thick. You were to meet Tom earlier. Now that you are both here, I want you to spend some time together. I want you to be friends.' The old assassin gave me a final withering look. 'I'm sure that you'll have a pleasant chat now. Good night to both of you.'

And with that he left us. Did he sound relieved to leave? He hastened out before the rack could even close behind Thick. The half-wit carried a double load of wood in a canvas sling over one shoulder. He looked around, perhaps surprised to see Chade leave so swiftly. 'Wood,' he told me. He dumped his burden to the floor, straightened up, and turned to go.

'Thick.' My voice stopped him. Chade was right. I should at

least teach the man to obey me. 'You know that is not what you are supposed to do. Stack the wood in the holder by the hearth.'

He glared at me, flexing his shoulders and rubbing his stubby hands together. Then he seized one end of the sling and dragged the wood towards the hearth, spilling logs, bits of bark and dirt as he went. I said nothing. He crouched down beside it and, with a great deal more vehemence and noise than was required, began to stack the wood. He looked over his shoulder at me frequently as he worked, but I could not decipher if his squint was antagonism or fear. I poured myself a glass of wine and tried to ignore him. There had to be a way out of dealing with Thick each day. I did not want him around me, let alone to teach him. In truth, I found his malformed body and dim ways somewhat revolting.

As Galen had me. Just as Galen had not wanted to teach me.

That thought nudged me in a bruised place that had never quite healed. I felt a moment of shame as I watched him labour sullenly. He hadn't asked to become a tool for the Farseer crown, any more than I had. Like me, the duty had fallen upon him. Nor had he chosen to be born malformed and dim-witted. It grew in my mind that there was a question that no one had asked yet, one that suddenly seemed important to me. One that might put the entire question of a coterie for Dutiful in a different light.

'Thick,' I said.

He grunted. I said nothing more until he stopped in his wood tantrum and turned to glare at me. It was, perhaps, not the best time to ask him anything. But I doubted that there would ever be a favourable time for Thick and me to have this conversation. When I was sure he was paying attention, his small eyes beetling at me, I spoke again. 'Thick. Would you like me to teach you to Skill?'

'What?' He looked suspicious, as if he expected me to make him the butt of a joke.

I took a breath. 'You have an ability.' His scowl deepened. I clarified. 'A thing you can do that others can't. Sometimes you use it to make people "not see" you. Sometimes you use it to call me names, names that Chade can't hear. Like "dogstink".' That made him smirk. I ignored it. 'Would you like me to teach you to use it in other ways? In good ways that could help you serve your prince?'

He didn't even think about it. 'No.' He turned back and resumed thunking the wood chunks onto the pile.

The swiftness of his reply surprised me a bit. 'Why not?'

He rocked back on his heels and looked over at me. 'I got enough work.' He glared meaningfully from me to the firewood. *Dogstink.*

Don't do that. 'Well. We all have work we have to do. That's life.'

He made no reply of either kind, just kept on deliberately clunking each log into place. I took a breath and resolved not to react to that. I wondered what it would take to make him even a little more agreeable. For I suddenly wanted to teach him. I could make a start with him, as a sign to the Queen of my commitment. Could Thick be bribed to try to learn to Skill, as Chade as suggested? Could I buy my daughter's safety by enticing him? 'Thick,' I asked him. 'What do you want?'

That made him pause. He turned to look at me and his brow wrinkled. 'What?'

'What do you want? What would make you happy? What do you want out of life?'

'What do I want?' He squinted at me, as if by seeing better he could understand my words. 'You mean, to have? My own?'

At each query, I nodded. He stood slowly, and scratched at the back of his neck. His lips pushed out as he thought, his tongue sticking out with them. 'I want . . . I want that red scarf that Rowdy has.' He stopped and stared at me sullenly. I think he expected me to tell him that he could not have it. I didn't even know who Rowdy was.

'A red scarf. I think I could get that for you. What else?'

For minutes he just stared at me. 'And a pink sugar cake, to eat it all. Not a burnt one. And . . . and a whole lot of raisins.' He stopped, and then looked at me challengingly.

'And what else?' I asked him. None of those things sounded too difficult.

He peered at me, coming closer. He thought I was mocking him. I made my voice gentle as I asked, 'If you had all those things, right now, what else would you want?'

'If I . . . raisins *and* a cake?'

'Raisins *and* a cake, *and* a red scarf. Then what else?'

His mouth worked, his small eyes squinting. I don't think he'd ever considered the possibility of wanting more than those things. I'd have to teach him to be hungry if I were going to use bribery. At the same time, the simplicity of the things that this man longed for as unattainable cut to my heart. He wasn't asking for better wages or more time to himself. Just the small things, the little pleasures that made a hard life tolerable.

'I want . . . a knife like you got. And one of those feathers, those big feathers with the eyes in them. And a whistle. A red one. I used to have one – my mam gave me a red whistle, a red whistle on a green string.' He scowled more deeply, pondering. 'But they took it and broke it.' For an instant he said no more, breathing hoarsely as he remembered. I wondered how long ago it had happened. His little eyes were squinted nearly shut with the effort of the recall. I had thought him too stupid to have memories that went back to his childhood. I was rapidly revising my image of just who Thick was. His mind certainly did not work as mine or Chade's did, but work it did. Then he blinked his small eyes several times and took a long shuddering breath. The next words came out on a sob. His words, blunted at the best of times, were barely understandable now. 'They didn't even want to blow it. I said, "you can blow it. But then give it back." But they didn't even blow it. They just broke it. And laughed at me. My red whistle that my mam gave me.'

Perhaps there was an element of humour in the tubby little man with the jutting tongue weeping for the loss of his whistle. I've known many men who would have laughed aloud. As for me, I caught my breath. Pain radiated off him like heat from a fire, and it ignited boyhood memories of my own, long buried. The way Regal would give me a casual push as he passed me in the hallway, or trample through my playthings as I sat in one of my private games on the floor in the corner of the Lesser Hall. It broke something in me, some wall I had held between Thick and myself because of all the differences I perceived between us. After all, he was slow-witted and fat, awkward-bodied and ill-made, rude. Ragged and smelly and ill-mannered. And as much an outcast in this castle of wealth and pleasure as I had been when I was Nameless the dog-boy. It did not matter than he had a man's years to him. The boy was suddenly who I saw, the boy who could never be a man, could never say that such hurts were a part of his past when he was vulnerable. Thick would always be vulnerable.

I had intended to bribe him. I had intended to find out what he wanted, and then hold it over him to get him to do what I wanted. Not in a cruel way, but to barter with him for obedience to my will. It would not have been so different from how my grandfather once bought me. King Shrewd had given me a pin and a promise of an education. He had never offered me his love, though I believe he had eventually come to care for me as I had for him. Yet I had always wished that his compassion had been the first thing he had offered me, instead of the last. Towards the end, I had suspected that he shared that vain wish.

And so I found myself speaking words aloud before I knew I had thought them. 'Oh, Thick. We haven't done well by you, have we? But we will do better. That I promise you. We will do better by you before I ask you again to learn this thing for me.'

FIFTEEN

Quarrel

In the Outislands, there are but three places worthy of a traveller's time. The first of these is the Ice Boneyard on Perilous Island. This is a place where the Outislanders have for centuries interred their greatest warriors. Women are customarily buried within the confines of their own family's lands. Mingling one's blood, flesh and bones with the poor soil most holdings farm is considered to be the last sharing offered to their families. Men, on the other hand, are customarily offered to the sea. Only the very greatest of their heroes are interred within the glacier field on Perilous Island. The monuments that cover each grave are of sculpted ice. The oldest ones are weathered past recall, though from time to time they seem to be renewed by the folk of the island. In an effort to stave off the inevitable polishing away of the ice, the monuments are carved many times life-size. The creatures depicted are usually the hero's clan sign. Thus the visitor will discover here immense bears, looming seals, gigantic otters and a fish that would fill an oxcart.

The second place worthy of a visit is the Cave of the Winds. Here resides the Oracle of the Outislanders. Some say she is a young and nubile maid who walks forth naked despite the icy winds. Others say she is a crone, aged beyond imagining, and always clothed in a heavy garment of bird skins. Still others say she is one and the same. She does not venture forth to greet every traveller who comes to her door. Indeed, this one had no sight of her. The ground all around the cave's mouth for several acres is littered with offerings to the Oracle. Even to stoop to touch one is rumoured to bring death.

The third place worth the traveller's effort is the immense ice island of Aslevjal. Whereas many of the isles of the Outislands are saddled with glaciers, Aslevjal is immersed in one. It can only be approached at a low *tide that bares a hem of black and rocky beach on the east side of the island. From there, one must ascend the flank of the glacier with rope and axe. Guides to assist one in doing so can be hired at Island Rogeon. They are expensive, but greatly lessen the risk of the climb. The path to the Glacier Monster is a treacherous one. What appears solid ice may be but snowflakes blown across a crevasse to form a deceptive crust. Yet despite the cold, hardship and danger, it is worth the risk to confront the Monster trapped within the ice. Upon arrival, expect your assistants to spend some time sweeping the latest layer of snow from the icy window on the beast. Once cleared, the traveller can gape his fill. Although little more than the creature's back, shoulder and wings are visible, and the view is hazy, the size of the Monster cannot be disputed it. As each year the ice hazes more, this strange site will eventually vanish from all but man's memory.*

Travels in the North Lands – Cron Hevcoldwell

For perhaps an hour after Thick had gone, I sat staring into the freshly-fuelled fire. My conversation with the man had left me heavy of heart. He bore such a burden of sadness, all for the cruelty of folk who could not tolerate his difference. A whistle. A red whistle. Well, I would do my best to see that he got one, regardless of whether it made him more receptive to learning to Skill.

I sat for a time longer, wondering what the Queen would say to Chade when he offered my bargain. I regretted it now: not that I had decided to ask for it, but that I had not told him I would make the request myself. It seemed cowardly to send the old man in my stead, as if I feared to stand before her. Well. It could not be changed now.

After a time of brooding on that, I recalled the little scrolls I had tucked into my cuff. One by one, I tugged them out. They were written on bark-paper, crisp and stiff as it aged, and already reluctant to unfurl. I coaxed one carefully open on the table and weighted it flat. Then I had to bring a branch of candles near it before I could make out the crabbed and faded handwriting. The first one I opened was one Chade had not mentioned to me. It simply said, 'Grim Lendhorn and his wife Geln of Buckkeep Town are both Witted. He keeps a hound and she has a terrier.' This was signed only with the sketch of a piebald horse. There was nothing to indicate when it had been sent. I wondered if it had been sent directly to the Queen, or if this were an example of the sort of betrayals they posted to expose Old Bloods who did not wish to ally themselves with the Piebalds. I'd have to ask Chade.

The second scroll I managed to unfurl was the one he had mentioned to me that day. It was the freshest, and not as reluctant to uncoil. It simply said, 'The Queen says that to be Witted is no crime. For what, then, were these folk executed?' And there followed the list of names. I read them, noticing at least two family groups who had died together. I clenched my teeth and hoped they were not children, though how such a death might be easier for a grown man or an oldster, I could not say. There was only one name on the list that I thought I recognized, and even then I told myself I was not certain it was the same woman. Relditha Cane might not be the same as Rellie Cane. There had been a woman of that name among the Old Blood folk who lived near Crowsneck. I had met her several times at Black Rolf's house. I had suspected that Rolf's wife Holly had thought that Rellie and I might fancy one another, but Rellie had never been more than coolly courteous to me. It probably wasn't her, I lied to myself, and tried not to imagine her curly brown hair shrivelling when the flames touched it. There was no signature or symbol of any kind on the scroll.

The last scroll was rolled so tight it seemed almost solid. Likely it was the oldest. As I forced it open it broke in pieces: two, three, and eventually five. I regretted doing it, but it was the only way to read it. If it had stayed coiled much longer, it would have crumbled into bits, never to be read again.

After I had read it, I wondered if that had not been Chade's hope and intention.

This had been the scroll that had come before the Prince vanished. This was the message that had precipitated Chade sending a rider to my door with the urgent demand that I come to Buckkeep at once. He had told me what the unsigned threat had said. Now I read the words for myself. 'Do what is right and no one else ever need know. Ignore this warning, and we will take action of our own.'

What Chade had left out were the words that preceded those ones. The ink had soaked into the bark paper unevenly and the curled surface made it hard to read. Stubbornly, I pieced it together. Then I sat back and tried to remember how to breathe.

'The Witted Bastard lives. You know it and so do we. He lives and you shield him from harm, because he has served you. You protect him even as you let honest men and women die simply because they have the Old Blood. They are our wives, our husbands, our sons, our daughters, our sisters, and our brothers. Perhaps you will stop the slaughter when we show you what it is like to lose one of your own. How close must the cut be to you before you bleed as we do? We know much of what the minstrels do not sing. The Wit runs still in the Farseer bloodline. Do what is right, and no one else ever need know. Ignore this warning and we will take action of our own.' There was no signature of any kind.

Very slowly I came back to myself. I pondered all that Chade had wrought, and why he had deliberately withheld this threat to me from my knowledge. The moment the Prince vanished, the moment he knew the threat was serious, he had sent for me. He had led me to believe that the Piebalds had sent a note threatening the Prince before his disappearance. Certainly, this scroll could be read that way. But the more overt threat was to me. Had he called me close to protect me, or to shield the Farseer reign from scandal? Then I pushed Chade's actions from my thoughts and leaned forward once again to peruse the faded ink on the bark. Who had sent this? The Piebalds seemed to take delight in signing their missives with their stallion emblem. This was unsigned, as was the one that listed the dead. I put them side by side. Some of the letters were similar. The same hand could have written them. The one signed by the Piebalds was written boldly, in larger letters and more flourishes. A different person could have written it, yet that would prove little. The choice of paper for all was the same. Not surprising: good paper was expensive, but anyone could strip bark paper from a birch. It did not mean the notes came from only one source, or even two. I tried theories against one another. Even before the Prince was taken, had there been two factions of the Witted striving to put an end to the persecution of their fellows? Or did I think so only because

I so longed for it to be true? Bad enough that Black Rolf and his friends had suspected who I was, and therefore surmised that the Witted Bastard hadn't died in Regal's dungeon. I did not want the Piebalds to know the FitzChivalry lived.

I looked again at the list of the dead. There was one other name on there, Nat of the Fens. He might have been someone I had met once when I was staying with Black Rolf. I could not be sure. I drummed my fingers on the table, wondering if I dared visit the Witted community near Crowsneck. To do what? Ask them if they had sent the Queen a note threatening my life? That didn't seem the best strategy. Perhaps it had only been a bluff. If I went there and they saw me, it would confirm to them that I did still live, even after all the years. At the very least, I'd be a valuable hostage to them, an embarrassment to the Farseers whether I was displayed dead or alive. No. This was not a time for confrontations. Perhaps in truth Chade had taken the best action. He had removed me from where I had been, whilst outwardly behaving as if the threat had no teeth in it. My annoyance with him faded. Nonetheless, I must convince him that this withholding of truth from me was a poor idea. What had he feared? That I would not come to the Prince's aid, that I would flee the country to begin life elsewhere? Was that what he thought of me?

I shook my head to myself. Plainly it was time I had it out with Chade. He needed to accept that I was a man now, in full control of my own life and capable of making my own decisions. And with Kettricken. I'd have Chade arrange a meeting with her, so that I could tell her myself my fears for my daughter, and ask her promise that Nettle be left alone. And the Fool. Best to settle that festering as well. Those were my thoughts as I left Chade's tower and sought my bed for the night.

I did not sleep well. Nettle battered at my dreams like a moth trying to destroy itself in a lantern's flame. I slept, but it was the rest of a man who sleeps with his back braced against a besieged door. I was aware of her. At first she was determined, then angry. Towards morning, she became desperate. Her pleas then were the hardest to hold my walls against. 'Please. Please.' That was all she said. But her Skill made it a sweeping wind of pleading against my senses.

I awoke with my head pounding dully. All my senses felt abraded. The yellow candlelight in my room seemed too bright, and any sound too loud. The guilt that gnawed me for ignoring her didn't improve any of it. It was definitely a morning that deserved a bit of elfbark, and with or without Chade's approval, I wasn't going to begin the day without it. I rose, splashed my face and dressed. The shock of the cold water on my face and the necessity of bending down to fasten my shoes seemed as battering as a beating.

I left our chambers. Slowly I descended to the kitchens. On my way down, I met Lord Golden's serving-boy. I dismissed Char for the morning, telling him that I would fetch the lord's breakfast that day. His delighted grin and repeated thanks reminded me that once I had been a boy who could have easily filled any free hour with a dozen activities. It made me feel old and his heartfelt thanks gave me a moment of shame. I wanted to eat alone in our rooms, and fetching Lord Golden's breakfast was my best pretence for doing so.

The clatter and steam and shouting in the kitchen did nothing for my headache. I filled the tray, including a generous pot of hot water, and headed back up the stairs. I was halfway up the second landing when a panting woman over took me. 'You've forgotten Lord Golden's flowers,' she told me.

'But it's winter,' I grumbled as I reluctantly halted. 'There are no flowers to be found anywhere.'

'Nevertheless,' she replied with a warm smile that made her a maid again. 'There will always be flowers for Lord Golden.' I shook my head at the Fool's curious particulars. She set a small nosegay on the tray, a confection of stark black twigs with white ribbon stitched into tiny buds on them. The creation was finished with two narrow bows, one white and one black. I thanked her dutifully, but she assured me that it was her pleasure before she went off about her other duties.

When I carried the tray into our chambers, I was surprised to see the Fool up and sitting in a chair by the hearth. He wore one of Lord Golden's elaborate dressing gowns, but his hair was in loose disarray down to his shoulders. He was not posing as the nobleman right now. It put me off balance. I'd planned on taking food into my room and then rapping on his door to let him know there was food on the table for him. Well, at least Jek was not here. Perhaps I'd finally be able to have private words with him. He turned his head slowly as I came in. 'There you are,' he said languidly. He looked as if he'd had a late night.

'Yes,' I agreed shortly. I thunked the tray on the table and went back to latch the door. Then I went to my room for the dishes I'd been gradually purloining from the kitchens, and set up breakfast for both of us at the table. Now that the moment had come to confront him, I couldn't find a place to begin. I hungered to have this over with. Yet, the first words out of my mouth were, 'I need a red whistle. On a green string. Do you think you could make one for me?'

He rose, a pleased but puzzled smile on his face. He came slowly to the table. 'I suppose so. Do you need it soon?'

'As soon as possible.' My voice sounded flat and hard, even to my own ears. As if it hurt me to ask him this favour. 'It isn't for me. It's for Thick. He had one once, but someone took it from him and broke it. Evidently just to cause him pain. He's never forgotten it.'

'Thick,' he said, and then, 'He's a odd one, isn't he?'

'I suppose so,' I conceded stiffly. He seemed not to notice my reserve.

'Whenever I encounter him, he stares at me. But if I look back at him at all, he scuttles away like a whipped dog.'

I shrugged. 'Lord Golden is not the kindliest noble in the keep, as far as the servants are concerned.'

He took a small breath and sighed it out. 'True. A necessary deception, but it pains me to see the man react to it. A red whistle on a green string. As soon as possible, then,' the Fool promised

'Thank you.' My reply was crisp. His words had reminded me yet again that Lord Golden was only a role he played. I already wished I hadn't asked anything of him. Asking a favour is a poor way to begin a quarrel. I refused to meet his puzzled gaze. I carried my cup to my room. I shook a measure of elfbark into the bottom of it and then returned to the table. When I got there, the Fool was bemusedly turning his posy in his fingers, his mouth twisted in a small smile. I poured the hot water over my elfbark and over the tea herbs in the waiting pot. As he watched, the smile ran away from his face and eyes.

'What are you doing?' he asked softly.

I groaned, then spoke briskly. 'Headache. Nettle was rattling my shutters all last night. It's getting harder and harder to keep her out.' I lifted my cup and swirled the water. Inky black tendrils were rising from the steeping elfbark. The brew darkened and I sipped at it. Bitter. But the throbbing in my head quieted almost immediately.

'Should you be doing that?' the Fool asked me evenly.

'If I didn't think so, I wouldn't be doing it,' I pointed out pleasantly.

'But Chade—'

'Chade has not the Skill, and does not know the pains of it, nor understand the remedies for those pains.' I spoke more sharply than I intended, from a well of unexpected annoyance. I realized then that I was still angry with Chade for withholding from me the full content of the note. As he always had, he was still trying to control my life. It is strange to find that an emotion you thought you had set aside is still simmering under the surface. I took a second mouthful of the bitter brew. As elfbark always did, it would plunge my spirits into a low even as it fired me with restlessness. It was a bad combination, but better than trying to wade through the day with a Skill headache hammering through my skull.

The Fool sat deathly still for several long moments. Then, with his eyes on the teapot as he lifted it and delicately filled his cup, he asked, 'Will not the elfbark interfere with your teaching Prince Dutiful to Skill?'

'The Prince himself has already interfered with that by not coming to his lessons for the last several days. Elfbark or no, I cannot teach a student who does not come to me.' Again, I felt a small twinge of surprise to find how much I was upset by that. Somehow, the act of sitting down at table with my old friend, knowing I intended to confront him, was making all these odd and painful truths bubble out of me. As if somehow they were all his fault for holding himself so aloof from me for the past week, while allowing his friend to believe falsehoods about us.

The Fool leaned back in his chair, the cup of tea cradled between his long and graceful hands. He looked past me. 'Well. It seems as if that is a matter to take up with the Prince.'

'It is. But there is also a matter that I must take up with you.' I heard how my voice dropped accusingly as I said those words, but could not control it.

A long silence held between us. For a moment the Fool folded his lips, as if holding in words. Then he took a sip of his tea. He lifted his eyes to meet mine, and I was surprised by the weariness on his face. 'Is there?' he asked unwillingly.

Reluctance tugged at me but I forced the word out. 'Yes. There is. I want to know what you have said to that Jek woman to make her think that I, that we, that—' I hated that I could not form the words. It was as if I feared to express the thought, that by speaking it aloud it would gain some sort of reality.

An odd expression fleeted over the Fool's face. He shook his head. 'I've said nothing to her, Fitz. "That Jek woman" as you name her, is capable of concocting her own theories on just about anything. She is one of those people you never need lie to; simply withhold information, and she makes up her own stories. Some, wildly inaccurate, as you have seen. Rather like Starling, in some ways.'

I didn't need to hear that name right then. She was another one who had believed that my bond with the Fool went beyond friendship. I recognized now that he had led her to believe that by the same technique he had used with Jek. No denials of it, leading remarks and witticisms, all encouraging her to form a mistaken opinion. At one time it had seemed a trifle uncomfortable but humorous all the same, to watch her labouring under her delusion. Now it seemed humiliating and deceitful that he had led her to believe that.

He set his teacup down on the table. 'I thought I was feeling stronger, but I am not,' he said in Golden's aristocratic tones. 'I think I shall retire to my room. No visitors, Tom Badgerlock.' He started to rise.

'Sit down,' I said. 'We need to talk.'

He stood. 'I think not.'

'I insist.'

'I refuse.' He looked past me, into a distance I could not see. He lifted his chin.

I stood. 'I need to know, Fool. You look at me sometimes, you say things, apparently in jest, but . . . you let both Starling and Jek believe that we could be lovers.' The word came out harshly, like an epithet. 'Perhaps you deem it of little importance that Jek believes you are a woman and in love with me. I cannot be so blithe about such assumptions. I've already had to deal with rumours of your taste in bed partners. Even Prince Dutiful has asked me. I know that Civil Bresinga suspects it. And I hate it. I hate that people in the keep look at us, and wonder what you do to your servant at night.'

At my harsh words, he shuddered and then swayed, like a sapling that feels the first blow of the axe. When he spoke, his words were faint. 'We know what is real between us, Fitz. What others may wonder about should remain their issue, not ours.' Slowly he turned from me, ending the discussion.

I almost let him go. It was such a long habit with me, to accept the Fool's decisions on such things. But suddenly it did matter to me what others in the keep gossiped about, what Hap might overhear as a crude jest in a Buckkeep Town inn. 'I want to know!' I suddenly roared at him. 'It does matter, and I want to know, once and for all. Who are you? What are you? I've seen the Fool, I've seen Lord Golden, and I heard you speak to that Jek in a woman's voice. Amber. I confess that baffles me most of all. Why would you live as a woman in Bingtown? Why do you allow Jek to go on believing you are a woman and in love with me?'

He did not look at me. I thought he would let my questions go unanswered, as he so often had before. Then, he took a breath and spoke quietly. 'I became Amber because she most suited my purpose and needs in Bingtown. I walked amongst them as a foreigner and a woman, unthreatening and without power. In that guise, all felt free to speak to me, slave and Trader, man and woman. That role suited my needs, Fitz. Just as Lord Golden fulfils them now.'

His words cut right to my heart. I spoke coldly what injured me most. 'Then the Fool, too, was only a role? Someone you became because it "suited your purpose"? And what was your purpose? To gain a doddering king's trust? To befriend a royal bastard? Did you become what we most needed in order to get close to us?'

He still was not looking at me, but as I gazed at his still profile, he closed his eyes. Then he spoke. 'Of course I did. Make of that what you will.'

His words were like spurs to my fury. 'I see. None of it was real. I've never known you at all, have I?' I expected no answer as for an instant I strangled silently on my anger and insult.

Then, 'Yes. You have. You more than anyone in my life.' He looked down now and stillness seemed to grow around him.

'If that is true, then I think you owe me the truth about yourself. What is the reality, Fool, not what you jest about or allow others to suspect? Who and what are you? What is it you feel for me?'

He looked at me at last. His eyes were stricken. But as I continued to gaze at him, demanding this knowledge, I saw his own anger come to life there. He suddenly stood straight and gave a small huff of disdain, as if unbelieving that I could ask. He shook his head then drew a deep breath. The words rushed out of him in a torrent. 'You know who I am. I have even given you my true name. As for what I am, you know that, too. You seek a false comfort when you demand that I define myself for you with words. Words do not contain or define any person. A heart can, if it is willing. But I fear yours is not. You know more of the whole of me than any other person who breathes, yet you persist in insisting that all of that cannot be me. What would you have me cut off and leave behind? And why must I truncate myself in order to please you? I would never ask that of you. And by those words, admit another truth. You know what I feel for you. You have known it for years. Let us not, you and I, alone here, pretend that you don't. You know I love you. I always have. I always will.' He spoke the words levelly. He said them as if they were inevitable. There was no trace of either shame or triumph in his voice. Then he waited. Words such as that always demand an answer.

I took a deep breath and managed the elfbark's black mood. I spoke honestly and bluntly. 'And you know that I love you, Fool. As a man loves his dearest friend. I feel no shame in that. But to let

Jek or Starling or anyone think that we take it beyond friendship's bound, that you would want to lie with me is—' I paused. I waited for his agreement. It did not come. Instead, he met my eyes with his open amber gaze. There was no denial in them.

'I love you,' he said quietly. 'I set no boundaries on my love. None at all. Do you understand me?'

'Only too well, I fear!' I replied, and my voice shook. I took a deep breath and my words grated out. 'I would never . . . do you understand me? I could never desire you as a bed partner. Never.'

He glanced aside from me. A faint rose came to his cheeks, not of shame, but of some other deep passion. He spoke quietly in a controlled voice. 'And that, too, is a thing that we both have known for years. A thing that never needed speaking, those words that I must now carry with me for the rest of my life.' He turned to look at me, but his eyes seemed blinded. 'We could have gone all our lives and never had this conversation. Now you have doomed us both to recall it forever.'

He turned and began to walk slowly toward his bedchamber. His pace was measured, as if he truly were ill. Then he stopped and looked back at me. Anger gleamed in his eyes and it shocked me that he could look at me so. 'Did you ever truly believe I might seek from you something that you did not share my desire for? Well do I know how distasteful you would find that. Well do I know that seeking that from you would irreparably damage all else that we have shared. So I have always avoided this very discussion that you have forced upon our friendship. It was ill done, Fitz. Ill done and unnecessary.'

He went another halting step or two, like a man who walks dazed after a blow. Then again he halted. Hesitatingly, from the pocket of his dressing gown, he took the black and white posy. 'This isn't from you, is it?' he asked. His voice was suddenly husky. He did not look at me.

'Of course not.'

'Then whom?' His voice trembled.

I shrugged, irritated by the strange question in the midst of a serious discussion. 'The garden woman. She puts one on your tray every morning.'

He drew a deeper breath and closed his eyes for a moment. 'Of course. They were never from you, not any of them.' A long pause. He closed his eyes and from the set of his face I suddenly thought he might faint. Then he spoke softly. 'Of course. There would be one who saw past my semblances, and if there was one, it would be she.' He opened his eyes again. 'The garden woman. She is about your age. Freckles on her face and arms. Hair the colour of clean straw.'

I called the woman's image back into my mind. 'Freckles, yes. Her hair is light brown, not gold.'

He clenched his eyes shut. 'Then it must have darkened as she grew older. Garetha was a garden girl here, when you were just a boy.'

I nodded. 'I recall her, though I had forgotten her name. You're right. So?'

He gave a short laugh, almost bitterly. 'So. So love and hope blind us all. I thought the flowers were from you, Fitz. A fatuous notion. Instead they are from someone who, long ago, was infatuated with the King's fool. Infatuated, I thought. But like me, she loves where love is not returned. Yet she remained true enough of heart to recognize me, despite all other changes. True enough of heart to keep my secret, yet let me know privately that she knew it.' He held the posy up again. 'Black and white. My winter colours, Fitz, back when I was the King's jester. Garetha knows who I am. And she still harbours some fondness for me.'

'You thought I was bringing you flowers?' I was incredulous at his fancy.

He looked aside from me suddenly, and I perceived that my words and tone had shamed him. Head bowed, he walked slowly towards his bedchamber. He made no reply to my words and I felt a sudden rush of sympathy for him. As my friend, I loved him. I could not change my feelings about his unnatural desires, but I had no wish to see him shamed or hurt. So of course I made it worse as I blundered in with, 'Fool, why do you not let your desires go where they would be welcome? Garetha is a fairly attractive woman. Perhaps, if you gladly received her attention—'

He rounded on me suddenly, and the true anger that flared up in his eyes lit them to a deep gold. His face flushed darker with the emotion as he demanded caustically, 'Then? Then what? Then I could be like you, sate myself with whoever was available merely because it was offered to me? That, I would find "distasteful". I would never use Garetha or any person that way. Unlike some we both know.' He weighted those last two words for me. He took two more steps toward his room, then rounded on me again. A terrible, bitter smile was on his face. 'Wait. I see. You imagine that I have never known intimacy of that sort. That I have been "saving myself" for you.' He gave a contemptuous snort. 'Don't flatter yourself, FitzChivalry. I doubt you would have been worth the wait.'

I felt as if he had struck me, yet he was the one who suddenly rolled up his eyes and collapsed limply on the floor. For a moment, I stood frozen with both fury and terror. As only friends can do, we had found each other's most tender spots to wound. The worst part of me bade me let him lie where he had fallen; I owed him nothing. But in less than a moment I went down on one knee by his side. His eyes were nearly closed, showing only a slit of white. His breath puffed in and out as if he had just run a race. 'Fool?' I said, and my pride forced annoyance into my voice. 'Now what is wrong with you?' Hesitantly I touched his face.

His skin was warm.

So he had not been feigning illness these last few days. I knew that ordinarily the Fool's body was cool, much cooler than an ordinary man's, so this mild warmth in him now was as a raging fever would be to me. I hoped it was no more than one of those strange times that came on him occasionally, when he was febrile and weakened. My experience of them was that in a day or two he recovered, with much peeling of skin to reveal a darker complexion beneath. Perhaps this fainting was only that weakness. Yet even as I stooped to slide my arms under him and lift him, my heart pinched with the fear that perhaps he was seriously ill. Truly, I had picked the worst possible time for my little confrontation with him. With him feverish and me dosed with elfbark, no wonder all our words to one another had gone awry.

I lifted him and carried him to his room, kicking the door open.

The room smelled heavy and oppressive. The bedding was rucked about as if he had tossed restlessly all night. What sort of a senseless clod was I, not even to have wondered if he could have been truly ill? I set his limp body down on the bed. I shook a pillow fat again and awkwardly slid it under his head, then tried to tug the bedding straight around him. What was I going to do? I knew better than to run for the healer. The Fool had never allowed any healer to touch him in all his years at Buckkeep. Occasionally he had gone to Burrich for some remedy or other when Burrich was the Stablemaster, but that help was far beyond my reach now. I patted his cheek lightly but he showed no sign of waking.

I went to the windows. I pushed the heavy curtains aside, and then unfastened the shutters and pushed them open to the cold winter day. Clean, chill air flowed into the room. I found one of Lord Golden's kerchiefs, and gathered snow from the windowsill into it. I folded it into a compress and carried it back to the bed. I sat down on the bed beside him and pressed the kerchief gently to the Fool's forehead. He stirred slightly, and when I pressed it to the side of his neck he suddenly revived with a frightening alacrity. 'Don't touch me!' he snarled, thrusting my hands aside.

His rejection of my concern ignited my anxiety into anger. 'As you wish.' I jerked away from him and slapped the compress down onto the bedside table.

'Please leave,' he replied in a voice that rendered the courtesy an empty word.

And I did.

In a sort of frenzy, I put the other chamber to rights, clattering the dishes back onto the tray. Neither of us had eaten anything. So be it. My appetite had fled anyway. I took the tray back to the kitchens and cleared it there. Then I hauled water and wood for our chambers. When I came back upstairs with my load, I found the door to the Fool's bedchamber closed. Even as I stood there, I heard the window shutters inside it slammed shut. I knocked loudly on his door. 'Lord Golden, I've firewood and water for your room.'

He made no reply, so I replenished the main room's hearth and my wash water. I left the remaining supplies outside the door of his room. Anger and pain simmered in my heart. A great deal of my anger was for me. Why hadn't I realized he was truly ill? Why had I insisted on pursuing this discussion over all his objections? Above all, why had not I trusted the instincts of our own friendship over the gossip of know-nothings? And the pain that ate at me was the pain of knowing what Chade had told me so often; that saying I was sorry could not always mend everything. I greatly feared that the damage I had done today was not something I could repair; that, as the Fool had warned me, today's conversation was something that we both must carry to the very end of our days. I could only hope that the sharp-edged memory of my words would eventually dull with time. His still sliced me like razors.

I recall the next three or four days as a time foggy with misery. I did not see the Fool at all. He still admitted his young serving-boy to his bedchamber, but as far as I was aware, he himself did not emerge at all. Evidently Jek saw him at least one more time before the Bingtown delegation departed, for she stopped me once on the stairs. With icy courtesy, she said that Lord Golden had completely cleared from her mind any erroneous opinions she might have formed about my relationship to my master. She begged my pardon if her assumptions had in any way distressed me. Then, in a low hiss, she added that I was the stupidest and cruellest person she had ever met. Those were the last words she said to me. The Bingtown delegation departed the next day. The Queen and her dukes had not given them any firm answer on an alliance, but had accepted from them a dozen messenger birds, and given into their care as many Bingtown pigeons. Those negotiations would continue.

On the heels of their departure, there was an uproar in the keep when the Queen herself rode out with a company of her guards late that night. Chade told me that even he had found her action rather extreme. Evidently her dukes found it even more so. The purpose of her ride was to halt an execution in Bidwell, a small hamlet near Buck's border with Rippon. They rode out in the deep of night, evidently in response to some spy's report that a woman was to be hanged and burned the following morning. Torches streaming and the horses' breath smoking, they had departed in haste. The Queen, dressed in her purple cloak and white fox tunic, had ridden in their midst. I had stood at the window and impotently wished that I were riding at her stirrup. My role as Lord Golden's servant always seemed to condemn me to be where I least wished to be.

They had returned the following evening. A battered woman, swaying in her saddle, rode with them. Evidently they had arrived at the last possible moment, literally plucking the rope from her neck. The lynch throng had made no physical resistance to the armed and mounted guardsmen. Kettricken had not been content with gathering the town elders for several hours of stern royal reprimand. She had commanded that every citizen of every cot be rousted out to stand in the town's tiny square and attend to her. She herself had stood before them, to read aloud to them her royal proclamation that forbade the execution of folk solely for being Witted. Afterwards, every soul down to the smallest child that could hold a pen was required to make a sign on that copy of the proclamation, attesting that they had been present, had heard the royal command and would abide by it. As they lacked a town hall, Kettricken further decreed that the signed proclamation must be continuously displayed over the hearth of the sole tavern in the town. She assured the folk that her road guards would drop by often to be sure that it was still in place and intact. She also assured them that if any of the signers ever again participated in such an attempt against a Witted, he would forfeit all property and be banished, not just from Buck, but from the entire Six Duchies.

On the Queen's return, the accused woman was taken to the guards' infirmary and treated for her injuries. Her village had not been gentle with her. She was a newcomer there with few ties. She had come to visit her cousin, who had been the one to accuse her to the elders when she supposedly caught the woman conversing with pigeons. There was some talk of an inheritance dispute which left me wondering if the accused were Witted at all, or merely a threat to her cousin's holdings. As soon as the woman was well enough to travel, Queen Kettricken furnished her with funds, a horse, and some said a deed to a bit of land far away from her cousin's village. In any case, the woman took herself well away from Buck as soon as she could travel.

The incident became the centre of a swirl of controversy. Some said the Queen had overstepped her bounds, that Bidwell actually

straddled the border of Buck and Rippon and that she should not
have taken action without at least consulting the Duke of Rippon.
The Duke seemed to take her personal intervention as a criticism
and an affront. Although he himself did not utter such words, it
was gossiped about that perhaps the Mountain queen was too eager
to make ties with foreigners such as Outislanders and Bingtown
Traders while not giving enough respect to the dukes of the Six
Duchies. Did she not trust her own nobility to manage their own
domestic affairs? From there, the rumours and grumbling wandered
farther afield. Did she not think a Six Duchies bride would be good
enough for her half-Mountain son? And even more insidious, the
gossip that the bloodlines of Duke Shemshy had been slighted, for
the Prince had shown an obvious interest in Lady Vance until
his lady mother had crushed it. Why did she court the disdainful
Outislander Narcheska when even the young prince could see that
there was a worthier lady closer to hand?

Because no such complaints were ever officially uttered, it was
difficult for Kettricken to make any response to them. Yet she knew
they could not be completely ignored, for that would feed the fires
of Rippon's and Shoak's discontent and encourage its spread to
her other dukes. Kettricken's solution was to command that her
dukes each send a representative to a council, with the objective
of creating solutions to end the persecution of the Witted. That
yielded her only the results I could have predicted; they suggested
that all Witted enter their names on a roll, to be sure they were
not unfairly persecuted. A second suggestion was that the Witted be
removed to certain villages and encouraged to live only within their
boundaries, for their own protection. And most generous of all, a
proposal that any person found to be Witted should be given passage
to either Chalced or Bingtown, where they would undoubtedly be
more welcome than in the Six Duchies.

I knew my own reaction to such suggestions. The dullest could
perceive that such a registration and resettlement within the Six
Duchies could easily be a prelude to a wide-scale massacre. As
for 'passage' to Chalced or Bingtown it was little different from
banishment. The Queen tartly told these councillors that their
solutions lacked imagination and bade them try again. This was

when a young man from Tilth inadvertently gave the Queen a great advantage. He suggested facetiously that the executions of Witted ones 'trouble most folks not at all. In truth, those who practise the beast-magic bring these disasters upon themselves. As it is only the Witted they bother; perhaps you should seek your solution from them'.

The Queen seized on his suggestion with alacrity. The smirk faded from his face and the chuckles of the other councillors died away as she announced, 'Now this, at least, is a suggestion with both imagination and merit. As my councillors have suggested to me, so I will do in this matter.' Perhaps only Chade and I knew it was an idea she had long cherished. She wrote up a royal proclamation and ordered couriers to bear it throughout the Six Duchies, where it was not only to be announced in the towns and cities but also to be posted prominently. The Queen invited the Witted ones, also known as those of Old Blood, to form a delegation to meet her, to discuss ways in which their unlawful persecution and murder might be ended. The Queen chose her words deliberately, despite Chade's beseeching that she be more circumspect. Many a noble was incensed by her indirect accusation that they sanctioned murder within their holdings. Yet I appreciated the stance she took, and surmised that other Witted would as well, even as I doubted that any Witted delegation would ever come to speak out on their own behalf. Why would they risk their lives by becoming known?

After my disastrous attempt to confront my differences with the Fool, I at least gained the wisdom to be more circumspect with Chade, the Queen, and the Prince. I left the bits of scroll where Chade must see them, on our worktable. A chance encounter in the tower gave me the opportunity to ask him, calmly, what had been his reason for keeping such knowledge from me. His assassin's answer was one that I had not expected. 'Under the circumstances, it was too personal a thing for you to know. I needed you to help me discover the Prince's whereabouts and return him safely to Buckkeep. If I had shown you this, that would never have been your focus. Instead you would have devoted all your energies to discovering who had sent this note, even though we could not absolutely connect it to Dutiful's disappearance. I needed you to have a cool head for that, Fitz. I could not help but recall your temper of old, and how it had often led you to wild actions. So, I withheld what I feared might distract you from the most important part of our task.'

It did not mollify me completely, but it made me realize that Chade often brought a very different perspective to a problem than what I had expected. I think my calm acceptance of his reasoning almost rattled him. He had expected the confrontation I had so recently planned. He was almost shamefaced as he, without prompting from me, assured me that he now knew I had matured and that it had been incorrect of him to keep the full missive to himself.

'And if I turn my attention to it now?' I asked quietly.

'It would be useful to us, to know who sent it,' he admitted. 'But not at the price of losing or distracting the Prince's Skillmaster. I have not been lax in pursuing all tracks that might lead us back to them. Yet they seem to vanish like mist. I have not forgotten about the rat, but despite all my queries, I have not found a single trace of a Wit spy. You know that our observations of Civil have yielded nothing.' He sighed. 'I beg you, Fitz, trust me to pursue this thread, and let me use you where you are most important to us.'

'Then you have spoken to the Queen. She agreed to my terms.'

His green eyes hardened to the colour of copper ore. 'No. I haven't. I had hoped you would reconsider.'

'Actually, I have,' I said, and tried not to enjoy the shock on his face. Then, before he could think I had capitulated completely, I added, 'I've decided this is a thing I must discuss with her myself.'

'Well.' He sought for words. 'In that we concur. I will ask her to make time to speak with you today.' And so we parted, having disagreed but not quarrelled. He gave me a strange look as he left, as if I still puzzled him. It left me feeling pleased with myself, and wishing I had learned this lesson earlier.

So when he notified me of my appointed rendezvous with the Queen, I again approached my encounter calmly. Kettricken had set out a small table of wine and cakes for us. I had schooled myself to equanimity before I entered. Perhaps that was what allowed me to see Kettricken's wariness.

My queen sat tall and poised as I entered, but I recognized her stillness as her armour. She, too, expected hot words and outrage from me. Her guarded attitude almost provoked me to express my injured feelings at her obvious opinion of my temperament. Instead, I took a deep breath and quelled that rising tide of affront. I forced myself to make my courtesy to her calmly, to wait until she had invited me to be seated at the table with her, and even then to exchange some small pleasantries about the weather and the state of her health before I approached my true concern. Even so, I marked the small narrowing at the corners of her eyes that plainly said she held herself in readiness for a tirade. When had all those who knew me best decided that I was such an unreasonable, ill-tempered man? And then I reined aside from even considering who might be at fault for that. Instead, I met my queen's gaze and asked quietly, 'What are we going to do about Nettle?'

For an instant, I saw her blue-green eyes widen almost in shock. Then she recovered herself. She leaned back in her chair and for a moment she considered me. 'What has Chade told you about this?' she countered.

Despite myself, I grinned. For a moment, all my concerns for my daughter fled. I heard myself reply, 'Chade has told me to beware of women who answer a question with a question.'

For a moment, I thought my sally had overstepped our bounds. Then an answering smile woke on her face. Sadly, with the dawning of that smile, she lowered her guard to me. I suddenly perceived that behind my queen's placid façade of calm, she was weary and troubled. Too many concerns snapped at her like yapping feists. The Prince's betrothal to the unpredictable Narcheska and his ridiculous 'quest', the problem of the Witted, the political unrest of the Piebalds, her contentious nobles and even Bingtown with its war and dragons all vied for her attention. As an errant gust of wind may kindle a faded ember to a glow, so her beleaguered expression woke in me a distant echo of the love Verity had borne for this woman. The Skill-link I had once shared with my king had occasionally made me privy to his feelings. Still, it was strange to feel that remote rippling of his love for her. For his sake, as well as for my own fondness for her, I felt a sudden and compelling concern for her. As she leaned back in her chair, obviously relieved that I did not intend to clash with her, I felt a moment of shame. In the welter of my own concerns, I too often forgot that other people had burdens just as heavy.

She released a pent-up breath. 'Fitz, I am glad that you have come yourself to discuss this with me. Chade is a wise councillor, tried and true to the Farseer throne. On his good days, he sees clearly in affairs of state. He is wise also in the ways of the hearts of my people. His advice is sage and solid. But when he speaks to me of Nettle, he speaks always as a councillor to the Farseer throne.' She reached across the table and set her gracile hand upon my rough one. 'I would rather speak to her father, as his friend.'

It seemed a very good time to hold my silence.

The Queen's hand did not move from mine as she spoke simply. 'Fitz, Nettle should be trained in the Skill. You know that, in your heart. Not only to protect her from the dangers of that magic in untrained hands – yes, I have read something of those scrolls, when deciding how to deal with Dutiful's potential – but also because of who she is. The potential Farseer heir.'

Her words knocked the wind out of me. I had expected to debate the wisdom of teaching Nettle to Skill, not to come back to that older, graver threat to her. I could not find words to express my dismay, but it was just as well. My queen was not finished speaking.

'We cannot change who we are. Ever, I am Verity's queen. Your are Chivalry's son, illegitimate but a Farseer nonetheless. Yet you are also dead to our people, and Chade is both elderly and unacknowledged as a Farseer. August, as we both know, never fully recovered his wits after Verity reached through him to me. My king, I am sure, never intended to do the damage he did to his cousin, and yet again, there it is. We cannot change who we are, and August, though his name makes him a Farseer, is a wandering old man before his time. He cannot seriously be considered a likely heir to the throne in the event that Verity's line should fail.'

Her careful construction of logic drew me in. I found myself forced to nod in agreement with her, even as I saw where the chain of her thoughts inexorably led.

'Yet there must be, there must always be, one who stands in reserve, ready to assume the throne should all else fail.' She looked past me. 'Your daughter, invisible as she is to her people, is nonetheless next in line. We cannot change who Nettle is. No amount of wishing on anyone's part can make her any less a Farseer. Should the need arise, FitzChivalry Farseer, your daughter must serve. So we arranged it, all those years ago. I know you opposed it then, when we drew up those documents in Jhaampe. I know you oppose it still. But she is a Farseer acknowledged, by you her father, by me as Queen, and a minstrel to whom you had told the truth witnessed all this. The written document still exists, Fitz, as it must. Even should you and I and Chade and Starling Birdsong die all at once, still in the treasury will be found that document, with a codicil that spells out where she can be found. This must be, Fitz. We cannot change her bloodlines; we cannot undo her birth. Would you ever truly desire to? I think not. Even to wish such a thing is an affront to the gods.'

And then it happened again. I suddenly saw with another's eyes. It gutted my anger, this sudden insight into my queen's reasoning. Kettricken saw as unchangeable that Nettle had a place in the line of heirs to the throne. To her, it was not a matter of what I wished or what she wished. It simply was, and we could not tamper with that. Nettle was not a bargaining point for her. She could not agree to release her from a duty she had been born to: that was how Kettricken saw it.

I took a deep breath, but she lifted a finger, asking me to let her finish speaking her thoughts. 'I know that you dread the thought of Nettle becoming Sacrifice. I, too, pray it will never come to pass. Think what it would mean for me: that my only son was dead, or somehow unfit to serve. As a mother, I put such a possibility furthest from my mind, even as you beseech fate that Nettle never be burdened with a crown. Yet even as we both hope such a thing never comes to pass, we must prepare that if it should happen, she would be ready to serve her people well. She should be trained, not only in the Skill, but educated in languages, in the history of her land and people, and in the courtesy and traditions that go with the throne. It is negligent of us both that she has gone uninstructed in such things, and unforgivably negligent of us that she remains unenlightened of her own bloodlines. If a time ever arrives when she must serve, do you think she will thank either of us for letting her remain ignorant?'

And that was yet another blow to my conviction. The world twisted around me, and suddenly I questioned every decision I had made for Nettle. I felt sickened as the truth came to me. I spoke it aloud. 'She would probably hate me for letting her remain ignorant. Yet, I do not see how I can change that at this late time, without doing even more damage.' I sagged back in my chair. 'Kettricken, neglectful as it must seem to you, I still implore you. Let her continue as she is. If you will say "yes" to that, then I promise you that I will bend all my efforts, with a willing heart, to make certain that she must never serve as Sacrifice.' I swallowed, and then bound myself anew. Yet again, I stood before a Farseer monarch and ceded my life. This time, I did it as a man. 'Willingly will I try to craft a coterie for Dutiful. I will serve as Skillmaster.'

The Queen regarded me steadily. After a moment she asked, 'And how is this a new offer from you, FitzChivalry? Or a new request to me?'

There was a rebuke in those questions. I bowed my head and accepted it. 'Perhaps because now I will be honestly willing in my efforts.'

'And will you also accept your queen's word, and not ask to have it reaffirmed to you again? I will speak it to you clearly. I will allow your daughter, Nettle Farseer, to remain where she is, fostered to Burrich, for as long as it is safe for us to do so. Will you accept that I will abide by my words to you?'

Another rebuke. Had I injured her feelings with my repeated demand that Nettle be left in peace? Perhaps. 'I will,' I said quietly.

'Good,' she said, and the tension that had been between us eased. For a time longer we sat at the table, in silence, as if silence between us completed the affirmation. Then, without a word, she poured wine for me and set a little spiced cake before me. For a time, we ate and talked, but only of inconsequential things. I did not mention to her that Dutiful was snubbing me. That I would settle with the Prince himself. Somehow.

When I rose to go, she looked up at me and smiled. 'It seems a shame, FitzChivalry, that I am so seldom able to speak to you. I regret the shams we must make, for they keep us apart. I miss you, my friend.'

I departed from her, but when I went, I carried those words with me like a blessing.

SIXTEEN

Fathers

If a merchant captain has sufficiently strong contacts in Jamaillia, it is entirely possible that he can fill his holds there with valuable goods from many a far and foreign port. He will get the advantage of having these exotic stuffs to sell without having to face the risks to both crew and vessel that a deep sea voyage always presents. He will, of course, pay in coin for what he saves in worry, but that is ever the trade that a wise merchant must face.

Jamaillia is not only the northernmost port that Spice Island traders regularly visit, it is the only port on our shores visited by the Great Sail fleet. These ships come as a fleet to visit Jamaillia (which they call, in their barbarous way, West Port) but one year out of three. The hazards of the crossing that they make can well be seen by their tattered canvas and weary sailors. The goods that they bring are both exotic and expensive. These ships are the only source for redspice and sedgum. As their entire stocks of these items are always bought by the Satrap's palace, with very little released back to the market, we can safely dismiss them as out of the reach of ordinary merchants. But other items they bring may be available to the sagacious merchant who is both lucky and wise enough to time a Jamaillia visit to the arrival of the Great Sail fleet.

Captain Banrop's Advice to Merchant Mariners

Another handful of days came and went. Lord Golden emerged from his bedchamber, polished and sophisticated as ever, to announce to all and sundry that he once more enjoyed perfect health. His Jamaillian make-up, applied carefully every morning, had become even more extravagant. Sometimes he wore the scaling even by daylight. I suspected he did it to distract any attention away from the darkening of his skin. It must have succeeded, for no one mentioned it. The court greeted his return to health with enthusiasm, and his popularity was undiminished.

I once again took up my duties as his servant. Sometimes Lord Golden entertained in his rooms in the afternoon, with games of chance or hired minstrels. The young nobility, both youths and maidens, vied to be invited. On those occasions, I remained at his beck within my own little chamber, or was dismissed entirely. I still accompanied him on his pleasure rides with other members of the nobility, and I still stood behind his chair at elaborate dinners. Such events were rarer now. With the departure of both the Outislanders and the Bingtown Traders, the population of Buckkeep Castle had thinned and returned to a more normal routine as the Six Duchies nobility also returned to their holdings. There were fewer gaming sessions and puppet shows and other amusements. The evenings became longer and quieter. If I was given an hour to myself in the evening, I often spent it in the Great Hall. Once more, the children of the keep studied their lessons by the hearths, while weavers wove and fletchers shaped arrows. Gossip and tales were spun alongside yarn. Shadows draped the corners of the room, and if I tried, I could pretend this was my Buckkeep from the days of my boyhood.

But of the Fool, I saw nothing at all. By no word or sign to me did Lord Golden ever indicate that we were anything other than what Buckkeep believed us to be: master and servant. At no time did he address any words to me that would have been out of character for Lord Golden to speak. And if I vouchsafed some pleasantry that strayed outside the limit of those roles, he ignored it.

The gulf that opened inside my soul at this isolation surprised me. Wider it yawned each day. When I returned one day from my weapons training session with Wim, I found a small packet on my bed. Within the fabric pouch, I found a red whistle threaded onto a green string. 'For Thick,' read the note in the Fool's plain hand. I had hoped it was some sort of peace offering, but when I dared thank Lord Golden, he looked up from the herbery he was perusing with a glance at once distracted and irritated. 'I have no idea what you are thanking me for, Tom Badgerlock. I do not recall giving you any gift, let alone a red whistle. Preposterous. Find some other vagary to occupy yourself, man. I am reading.'

And I withdrew from his presence, recognizing that the whistle had not been created as a favour to me, but as a sincere gift to Thick, from someone who knew well what is was to be ignored or mocked. Truly, it had nothing to do with me. And with that thought, my heart sagged a notch lower in my chest.

Worst was that there was no one I could confide my misery to, unless I wanted to share the full depth of my stupidity with Chade. So I bore it silently and did my best to conceal it from all.

On the day the Fool gave me the whistle, I decided I was ready to take my errant students in hand. It was time to do as I had promised my queen.

I visited first Chade's tower and then clambered up to the Skill-tower. When, as had become usual, Dutiful did not arrive, I opened the shutters wide to the chill and dark of the winter morn. I seated myself in Verity's chair and stared bleakly out into that blackness. I knew that Chade had directed Dutiful to come to me, and had even arranged the Prince's social schedule to allow him more time with me. It had made no difference. Since he had discovered the Skill-command and broken it, he had not come to me once for a lesson. I had let Dutiful go much longer in his errant behaviour than Verity would ever have tolerated in me. Left to himself, the Prince would not come back to me. I dismissed my doubts as to the wisdom of my actions. I took several deep, slow breaths of the cold sea air and closed my eyes. I narrowed my Skill to a fine and demanding point.

Dutiful. Come to me now.

I felt no response. Either he had not made one or he was ignoring me. I expanded my awareness of him. It was difficult to grasp him. I concluded he was deliberately blocking me, having set his Skill-walls against me. I leaned on them, and became fairly certain that he was sleeping. I tested the strength of his walls. I knew that I could punch past them, if I chose to do so. I took a breath, summoning the strength to do just that. Then, abruptly, I shifted my strategy. Instead I leaned on his walls, an insidious pressure. Distantly, I felt a thin smile stretch my lips. The Nettle technique, I thought to myself as I slipped through his wall and into his sleeping mind.

If he was dreaming, I could not sense it. Only the stillness of his unaware mind spread around me like a quiet pool. I dropped into it like a pebble. *Dutiful.*

He twitched into awareness of me. His instant reaction was outrage. *Get out!* He tried to thrust me from his mind, but I was already inside his defences. I offered a quiet resistance to him, displaying no aggression but simply refusing to be banished. Just as he had the first time we had wrestled, he threw himself against me in a fury without strategy. I maintained my resistance, accepting the mental pummelling as he wore himself out against me. When he was all but stunned with exhaustion, I spoke again.

Dutiful. Please come to the tower.

You lied to me. I hate you.

I did not lie to you. Without intending to, I did you a wrong. I attempted to undo it; I believed I had undone it. Then, at the worst possible moment, we both discovered I had not.

You've been restraining me. Forcing me to do your will, ever since we met. You probably forced me to like you.

Search your memories, Dutiful. You will discover that is not so. But I will no longer discuss this matter in this manner. Come to the Skill-tower. Please.

I won't.

I'll be waiting.

And with that I withdrew from his mind.

For a time I sat still, gathering both my strength and my thoughts. A headache pressed against my skull, demanding attention. I pushed it to one side. I took a deep breath, and once more reached out.

Finding Thick was easy. Music was spilling from his mind, a music uniquely his own, for it was music without sound. When I let it flow unimpeded into my mind, it became even stranger, for it was not composed of notes from a flute or harp. For a moment, I became caught in it. On one level, the 'notes' of his song were bits of ordinary noises from everyday life. The clop of a hoof, the clack of a plate on a table, the sound of wind slipping past a chimney, the ring of a dropped coin on a cobblestone. It was a music made of the sounds of life. Then I slipped deeper into it, and discovered it was not music on this new level, but was instead a pattern. The sounds were separated from one another by different degrees of pitch, but there was a pattern to that as well as to how they were repeated. It was rather like approaching a tapestry. One sees first the whole picture that is formed, then a closer inspection reveals the material used to make up the images. A deeper study reveals the individual stitches, the different colours and textures of the threads.

With difficulty I disentangled myself from Thick's song. I wondered at how so simple a mind could conceive of so convoluted and intricate a music. And in the next moment, I grasped an understanding of him. This embroidery of music was the framework of his thoughts and world. It was what he paid attention to, putting each sound he heard into its proper place in the vast scheme of sound. Little wonder, then, that he had so little thought or focus to spare for the petty concerns of the world Chade and I perceived. How much consideration did I give to the sound of water trickling or the ringing of a blade against a sharpening stone?

I came to myself sitting in Verity's chair. I felt as if my mind were a sponge that had been dipped into a water of music. I had to let Thick's song drain away from me before I could recall my own thoughts and intents. After a time, I once more drew breath into my lungs, settled my mind and reached out.

This time I made sure I only brushed against the edges of his music. I hesitated there, trying to decide how to make him aware of me without startling him. As gently as I could, I made contact. *Thick?*

I felt the impact of his fear and anger like a fist in the belly. It was like poking a sleeping cat. He fled, but not before he had clawed me. Shaken, I opened my eyes to the tower's view of rolling waves. Even so, it was hard to settle myself into my body again and persuade myself I belonged there. Nausea roiled through me. Well, that first effort had gone well, I thought sourly. I sat for a time in discouragement. Dutiful was not coming and Thick was not going to accept any sort of training from me. To that linked chain of defeat, I added the thought that I had heard nothing from Hap since I had bade him make his own peace with his master. I marvelled at my knack for sowing disillusion and discontent among those I most cherished. Then once more I collected myself.

One more effort, I promised myself. Then I would return to my dismal chamber, and from thence announce to Lord Golden that his lowly servant was taking the day off. I'd go down to Buckkeep Town and make some sort of contact with Hap. That was my frame of mind as I once more settled myself into my chair. I took out the red whistle and considered it. The Fool had outdone himself. It was much fancier than any penny whistle I'd ever seen before. It was decorated with tiny birds. I set it to my lips and tried a few notes on it. When I was a youth, Patience had tried to teach me to play several musical instruments. I'd had little success with any of them. Still, I could pick out the notes of a simple child's song. I played it several times, trying in vain to smooth out the roughness. Then I leaned back, the whistle still set to my lips. As I played, I reached out to Thick, trying to send him only the piping notes of the whistle rather than any thoughts or hints of my presence. It broke in on his own music, and for a time we jangled discordantly together. Then his notes died away as he focused on mine.

What's that?

The thought was not intended for me. He merely reached out to see where the sound was coming from. I tried to make the thought I sent him very delicate. I did not stop playing as I told him, *It's a red whistle. On a green string. It's yours, if you want to come and get it.*

A long moment of guarded thought. Then, *Where?*

That gave me a moment of thought. There was a guard on duty at the base of the Skill-tower steps. I couldn't tell Thick to come that way. He'd be turned back. Chade had trusted him with at least some of the labyrinth of passages of the keep. I knew I should consult Chade before I revealed more to him, but this was too good of an opportunity to miss. I wanted to see if I could guide Thick through the passages via our mind-link. Not only would it test the current limits of our ability to Skill to one another, but also it would give me an insight into what he was capable of. I refused to spend too much time in hesitation. *Come to me this way.* I showed him a mental image of Chade's tower room. Then I showed him, step by step, the passages he must use to come to the Skill-tower. I did not rush through them, but neither did I linger. I finished with, *If you get lost, reach out to me. I will help you.*

Then I gently broke the link between us. I leaned back in the chair, and considered the whistle in my hand. I hoped it would be bait enough. I set it down on the table, and beside it I placed the figurine of a woman. It was the one the Prince had found on the beach that the Skill-stones had taken us, too. Without any clear idea why, I had brought it from Chade's tower, to give it back to Dutiful. With a sudden lurch of my heart, I thought of the feathers I had found on the same beach. I had never shared that discovery with the Fool. The time had never seemed right. Now I wondered if I ever would. I pushed the thought from my mind. I had to focus on what I did now.

I wiped away the sweat on my brow. I found I was a bit shaky when I stood. This morning's exercise was more Skill than I had used in quite some time. The headache was proportionately larger, rather too big for my skull. If I'd had a kettle, cup, water and elfbark, I probably would have indulged. Instead I had to settle for pouring myself a measure of brandy and leaning out of the window for a while.

When I heard the scuff of footsteps coming up the tower stairs, I thought it was the guard. I took the bottle and my glass, retreated to a dim corner of the room and stood very still. I heard the key turn slowly in the lock, and the door opened. Then Dutiful entered. He shut the door firmly behind himself and then glanced about the apparently empty room. His irritation was plain on his face. He crossed to the table and once more looked about him. A slow realization came to me. Witted the Prince might be, but not as strongly as I was. Even in the room with me, he remained unaware of my presence. This was a new idea to me: that, just as with the Skill, men could possess the Wit-magic in various strengths.

'Here.' When I spoke, he jumped, and then became aware of me as I stepped from the shadows, bottle and glass in hand. He glared at me as I advanced to the table and set the glass down. 'Good morning, my prince.'

He spoke firmly, with great disdain. 'Tom Badgerlock, you are dismissed. I no longer wish to have you teach me anything. I will be speaking to my mother to have you removed from Buckkeep entirely.'

I kept my calm. 'As you wish, my prince. Undoubtedly, that would be the easiest route for me as well.'

'This is not about what is "easiest" for me. This is about treachery and betrayal. You have used the Skill against me, your rightful prince. I could ask for your banishment. Even your execution.'

'You could, my prince. Or, you could ask for my explanation.'

'No explanation could excuse what you did.'

'I did not say you could ask for my excuse. I said you could ask for my explanation.'

And there the conversation stopped. I refused to lower my eyes. I met his gaze steadily. I was determined that he would ask, courteously, for my explanation before he would hear another word from me. He seemed equally determined that he would cow me with his princely stare until I decided to beg his pardon.

Suspense was on my side.

'An explanation is long overdue.'

'Perhaps it is,' I conceded, and waited again.

'Explain yourself, Tom Badgerlock.'

A 'please' would have been nice, but I sensed he had bent as far as he could. A boy's pride can be a brittle thing.

I walked back over to the table and refilled my glass. I lifted the bottle questioningly toward him, but he shook his head, an abrupt refusal to share drink with such as me. I sighed. 'How much do you recall of the beach? The one that we fled to through the standing stone?'

His face clouded a bit and he looked wary. 'I . . .' He came very close to lying. Then, 'I recall parts of it. It fades, like a dream, and then sometimes bits of it come back to me bright and clear. I know you used the Skill-magic to take us there. It weakened and confused me somehow. I imagine that is when you cast your power-spell over me.'

I sighed. This was going to be even more difficult than I had feared. 'Do you remember a time by the fire, when you attacked me? Attacked me with every intent of killing me?'

He looked aside briefly, then nodded as if surprised that he did recall such a thing. 'But that was not entirely of my own will. You know that! Peladine was striving even then to control my body. And I did not know you, then. I thought you were my enemy!'

'Nor did I know you. Not as I do now. Yet already we were bound by a Skill-link, for I had had to go after your soul once before, and haul it back to your body.' I hesitated, then decided I would not speak of that other being I had encountered, the great being that had aided us both to return. That memory remained hazy even for me. Best not to bring up what I could not explain. I took a breath. 'I knew Peladine was within you. And that she would stop at nothing to kill me, even if she had to damage you in the process. It frightened me. And then, in my anger and fear for my life, I commanded you, "Dutiful, stop fighting me." It was a Skill-command. One that printed itself onto your mind with far more force than I intended. I never meant to do it, Dutiful. It was an accident, one I have regretted, and one I have tried to amend. I thought I had amended it.' I felt an unwanted smile twist my mouth. 'I thought I had lifted it from you, right up until the very moment when I tried to keep you from your foolish declaration in the hall. Only then did I perceive that some final shadow of it remained, and only when you broke it.'

'Yes. I broke it.' He spoke with satisfaction. Then he glared at me again. 'But knowing that it existed, knowing that you can do such a thing to me, how can I ever trust you again?'

I was still pondering an answer to that when Thick pushed the mantel-side door open. The entry was an even tighter fit for the stout-bodied man than for me, and he was festooned with cobwebs and powdered with dust. For a moment he stood blinking his sleepy-looking eyes at the startled Prince and me. His jaw was thrust forward, his tongue protruding thoughtfully. Then he spoke. 'I come for my whistle.'

'And you shall have it,' I said. I scooped it up from the table and held it out to him, dangling by its green string. Gently, I added, 'And that was good Skilling, Thick. You followed my directions and here you are.'

He shuffled forward suspiciously. I doubt that he recognized Prince Dutiful, out of context of his throne and robes of state.

He included him in his scowl as he said, 'You made me come a long way.' Then he snatched the whistle and held it close to his peering little eyes. Then he frowned. 'This isn't my whistle!'

'It is now,' I told him. 'It's a new one, made especially for you. Did you see the birds on it?'

He turned it in his hands, then grudgingly admitted, 'I like birds.' Then he turned to go, the whistle clutched to his chest.

The Prince was staring at him in dismay bordering on disgust. I knew the Mountain way for babes such as Thick had been; he would have been exposed to a swift and perhaps merciful death, much as Burrich would have drowned a deformed puppy. But Queen Kettricken had commanded that I train this man. Would Mountain ethics prevent Dutiful from accepting Thick? I tried not to hope that the Prince would refuse him as a coterie member. I wanted to delay Thick's leaving. 'Aren't you even going to try it, Thick?'

'No.' Thick was shuffling toward the door.

'Try that tune you Skill to yourself. The one that goes la-da-da-da-de—' Even as I tried to mimic back to him the music I had come to know by heart, Thick spun around to face me. Outrage glittered in his little eyes.

'Mine!' He roared. 'My song! My Mum's song!' He came at me with murder in his eyes. He lifted the whistle as if it were a knife that he could plunge into my heart.

'I'm sorry, Thick. I didn't realize that was private.' But I should have, I suddenly knew. I gave ground before him. His body was thick, his limbs short and awkward, his belly pudgy. I knew that in a physical struggle, I could master him. I also knew it would involve hurting him, because that would be the only way to defeat him. I didn't want to do that. I needed his goodwill. I darted behind the table.

'My song!' Thick repeated. 'Dog poop stink stealer!'

An unwilling bubble of laughter burst from the Prince's lips. I think he was both horrified and fascinated by the spectacle of the dimwit attacking me over a song. Then a sudden frown divided his brow. Even as I circled the table, trying to keep it between Thick and me until I could find a way to calm him, the Prince suddenly exclaimed, 'I know that song!' He hummed a short bit of it, making Thick's scowl deepen. 'It's the first thing that I always hear when I try to Skill. It comes from you?' His question was incredulous.

'My song!' Thick asserted again. 'My Mum's song! You can't hear it. Only me!' He diverted his steps and suddenly charged the Prince in a wild run. As he went, he caught up the brandy bottle, lifting it like a club heedless of the liquor that galloped out of it and down his arm. The Prince's eyes went wide, but he was too foolishly proud to retreat before Thick's onslaught. He stood his ground, dropping into the fighter's crouch I'd taught him. His hand moved to his belt knife. In response, I felt Thick's mind-numbing cloud of *Don't see me, don't see me, don't see me* even as he closed on the Prince. I saw Dutiful struggle against the little man's Skill and felt him begin to mount a blast of his own to thrust through it.

'No!' I roared in dismay. 'Don't hurt each other!'

And my command shimmered with an edge of Skill. I saw them both flinch at it, saw them both spin to confront me, arms upraised as if that would ward off the magic. I could almost see it rebound from them, but just for an instant it dizzied them both. The backwash of my command as they instinctively repulsed it giddied me, but I recovered faster than they did. The Prince staggered back a step, while Thick lifted his pudgy hands to cover his eyes. I was horrified at what I had done, yet when they stood still and for a moment docile, I added, 'That's enough. You must never attack one another that way. Not if you are going to work together to master the Skill.' I was proud that I kept my voice from shaking.

Dutiful shook his head and then spoke in a dazed voice. 'You did it again! You dared to use the Skill against me!'

'That I did,' I admitted, and then demanded, 'What else would you have me do? Watch you blast the sense from one another? Have you ever met your cousin August, Dutiful? That drooling, doddering old man? What happened to him was an accident. Yet there have been instances of Skill-users maiming one another in a battle such as you both nearly engaged in. Yes, and there have been deaths as well, deaths that seared the ones who wrought them almost as severely as the ones that died.'

Dutiful leaned against the table. Thick lowered his hands from his eyes slowly. He'd bitten his tongue and it dripped blood. Dutiful spoke to both of us. 'I am your prince. You are sworn to me. How dare you attack me?'

I took a breath and reluctantly stepped up to the task Chade had laid upon me. 'Not here.' I said quietly. 'It is true that I am sworn to the Farseers. I serve them, as best I may. And to serve them best in this, know this well, Dutiful. In this room, you are not my prince, but my student. And just as your swordmaster deals you bruises with a blunt blade to teach you, so will I use whatever force is necessary.' I swung my eyes to Thick, who was pouting sourly at us both. 'In this room, Thick is not a servant. Here, he is my student.' I looked from one to another and buckled them into the harness they must share. 'Here you are equals. Students. I will respect you as such, and I will demand that you respect each other as such. But make no mistake. Within this chamber, during the hours of our lessons, my authority is absolute.' I looked from one to the other. 'Do you both understand this?'

The Prince looked stubborn, and Thick suspicious. 'Not a servant?' he asked slowly.

'Not if you choose to be a student here. To learn what I have to teach. So that, eventually, you can help the Prince.'

He scowled, working through it slowly. 'Help the Prince. Work for him. Servant. More work for Thick.' His little eyes glittered maliciously as he exposed what he thought was my hidden intention.

I shook my head again. 'No. Help the Prince. As his coterie. His friend.'

'Oh, please,' Dutiful groaned disdainfully.

'Not a servant.' This obviously pleased Thick. It gave me yet another insight into him. I would have thought him too dull to care what his position was in the world. Yet plainly, he would prefer not to be a servant.

'Yes. But only if you are a student. If you do not come here, every day, and try to learn what I teach, then you are not a student. Thick is the servant again. Haul the wood, fetch the water.'

He set the empty bottle down on the table. Hastily he looped the string of the whistle around his neck. 'I'm keeping the whistle,' he insisted, as if that were an important part of the bargain.

'Servant or student, the whistle belongs to Thick,' I told him. This seemed to set back his understanding of the situation. His fat little tongue pushed farther out of his mouth as he considered it.

'You cannot be serious,' the Prince said in an undertone. '*That* is to be a member of my coterie?'

I knew both an instant of sympathy for him and a strong irritation with his disdain for Thick. I spoke levelly. 'He is the best candidate that Chade and I have discovered so far. Unless, of course, you have encountered others with his natural predilection for the Skill?'

He stood silent, then shook his head unwillingly. In some corner of my mind, I was amused that he was more distressed at the idea of Thick being his fellow student than he was by my declaration that I would treat them both the same during our lessons. I decided to take advantage of his temporary distraction. 'Good. That's settled, then. And I believe we've all learned enough for one morning. I shall expect you both to be on time tomorrow. For now, you are dismissed.'

Thick was just as happy to leave. Still clutching his whistle, he scuttled for the mantel door. As he shut it behind him, the Prince asked in a low voice, 'Why are you doing this to me?'

'Because I am sworn to the Farseer reign. To serve it as best I can. And you, Dutiful, are now dismissed.'

I hoped he would turn toward the door, but he did not. Not until there was a sharp rap at it. We both startled. I glanced at the Prince, who called out loudly, 'What is it?'

The voice of a young page reached us through the stout timbers of the door. 'A message for you, Prince Dutiful, sir, from Councillor Chade. He bade me beg your pardon, but also said to let you know it was urgent.'

'A moment.'

I faded back to a corner of the room as the Prince went to the door, unlatched it, opened it a crack and accepted a small, sealed scroll. As I watched him, I reflected sourly that despite all else Skillmaster Galen had been he had been right in several areas. No students of his would ever have dared attack one another, let alone question his authority over them. He had immediately reduced all his students to a harsh equality, though I had been the exception to that; all had known that he regarded me as beneath them. As much as it choked me, I needed to emulate at least some of his attitudes, even as I refused his harsh techniques. Discipline is not the same as punishment, I thought, and recognized it as an echo of some old words of Burrich's.

The Prince had shut the door behind him and picked the wax off the scroll. Then he frowned as he unrolled it to reveal a second, sealed scroll within it. 'I think this must be for you,' he said uneasily. In a script I would never have recognized as Chade's, the word 'teacher' was written on the outside of the scroll. At the sight of my own charging Farseer buck impressed in the wax, I took the scroll from Dutiful's hand.

'It is,' I agreed shortly. I turned aside from him, broke the wax, and read the single sentence. Then as he watched, I consigned it to the fire.

'What was it?' the Prince demanded.

'A summons,' I said shortly. 'I must go now. But I expect to see you on time tomorrow, and ready to learn. Good day, my prince.'

His stunned silence followed me as I squeezed behind the fireplace mantel and shut and latched the little door behind me. Once within the narrow passageway, I hurried as much as I could. Silently I cursed the low ceilings, the corners I must squeeze past and the labyrinthine wandering of the burrows when I wished to run as fast as I could in the straightest possible line.

When I arrived at my peephole outside the Queen's private audience chamber, my mouth was parched and I was panting like a hound. I took several deep breaths, forced myself to stand still until my breathing was steady and silent again. Then I flung myself down on the little stool and applied my eye to the tiny peephole. I was late. Chade and Queen Kettricken were already there, the Queen seated while the councillor stood at her shoulder. Their backs were to me. A gangly boy of perhaps ten years stood before them. His dark curls were sweated to his skull, and the hem of his cloak dripped muddy snow-water on the floor. The low shoes he wore had never been intended for winter travel. Caked snow was still melting on his leggings and feet. Wherever he had come from, he must have walked all night. His dark eyes were immense but he met his Queen's gaze steadily. 'I see,' she said quietly.

Her answer seemed to embolden him. I wished I had heard the entire conversation. 'Yes, ma'am,' he agreed. 'And so, hearing that you would not tolerate what was being done to the Witted, I came to you. Maybe here in Buckkeep I can just be what I am and not get beaten for it. I promise I'll never use it to any low end. I will vow myself to the Farseers and serve you well in any way you ask of me.' He lifted his eyes to meet the Queen's, not a bold stare but an honest, direct look from a boy confident that he had chosen the right path. I stared at Burrich's son, seeing Molly mingled in the boy's cheekbones and lashes.

'And your father approved of this?' Chade asked, stern but gentle.

The boy looked away. When he spoke, his voice was softer. 'My father doesn't know, sir. I just left when I knew that I couldn't take it any more. I won't be missed. You saw our home. He has other sons, good sons who are not Witted.'

'That does not mean he won't miss you, Nim.'

For the first time, the boy looked annoyed. 'I'm not Nim. Nimble doesn't have the Wit. I'm Swift, the other twin. See, that's another reason that my father won't miss me. He already has one of me that's perfect.'

A shocked silence followed his words. I am sure he mistook the cause of it. When Kettricken spoke, she tried to mend it.

'I knew Burrich, years ago. However much he may have changed, I am still certain that, Witted or no, he will miss you.'

Chade added, 'When I spoke with Burrich, he seemed very fond and proud of all his children.'

For a moment, I thought the boy would break. Then he took a breath and said matter-of-factly, 'Well, yes, but that was before.' Chade must have looked at him blankly, for the boy elaborated painfully, 'Before the taint come out in me. Before he knew I had the Wit.'

I saw the Queen and Chade turn to one another and confer silently. After a moment, Kettricken said softly, 'Then, Swift, Burrich's son, I say this to you. I am willing to take you into my service. But I think it best that I do so with your father's consent. He must be told of your whereabouts. It is unfair to let your parents fear that you have come to a bad end.'

Even as she spoke, we all became aware of raised voices in the corridor outside the chamber. There was a light knock at the door, and before they could respond, a hasty and heavier one. Kettricken nodded to a little page at her side, who went to answer it. When the door was opened, a guard stood before it, ready to relay a message. Behind him hulked Burrich, dark and scowling, and despite all the years that had passed, I quailed before that look. His black eyes glowered as he peered past the sentry into the room. Plainly dismissing the man as inconsequential, Burrich called out, 'Chade. A word with you, please.'

It was Queen Kettricken who replied. 'Burrich. Please, come in. Page, you are dismissed. Close the door behind you. No, Guardsmen Senna, I assure you, all is well. We have no need of your service just now. Close the door.'

Even as Burrich strode angrily into the chamber, the quiet courtesy of her words and her calm air as she received him took much of the wind from his sails. He walked with a swing to one leg where that joint did not bend well.

He went down on one knee before her, despite her, 'Oh, Burrich, that is hardly necessary. Please. Get up.'

It cost him to haul himself back to his feet, yet he did. When he lifted his eyes to hers, I saw something that smote me. The palest of cataracts, the barest beginning of a creeping cloud, hazed his dark glance. 'My queen. Lord Chade,' he greeted them formally. Then, as if there was no more to say to them, he turned to Swift and said, 'Boy. Get home. Now.' When the lad dared to glance at the Queen for confirmation, Burrich growled, 'I said, get home! Do you forget who your father is?'

'No, sir. I do not. But how . . . how did you find me?' Swift demanded in dismay.

Burrich snorted contemptuously. 'Easily enough. You asked the smith in Trura which road led to Buckkeep. Now I've had a long, cold ride and you've annoyed these people enough. I'm taking you home now.'

I admired Swift then, for he stood his ground gamely before his father's rising wrath. 'I have asked asylum of the Queen. And if she grants it to me, I intend to stay.'

'You're talking nonsense. You need no asylum. You've worried your mother to hysteria and had your sister in tears for two nights. Now you'll come home, and settle back into your place and do your duties. Without complaint.'

'Sir,' Swift replied. It was not assent, only a confirmation that he had heard Burrich's words. Silently he lifted his dark eyes to the Queen. It was a strange sight, Burrich, older and grayer, and beside him, his son mirroring the stubborn gaze of his father.

'If I might offer a suggestion –' Chade began, but Kettricken cut in with, 'Swift, you have come far and quickly. I know you are wet, cold and tired. Tell the guardsman at the door to take you down to the kitchens and see you are fed, and then to let you stand before the hearth and get warm and dry. I wish to speak to your father.'

The boy hesitated, and Burrich's scowl deepened. 'Obey her, boy!' he snapped at the lad. 'That is your queen. If you cannot show the filial piety to obey your father, at least show you've the upbringing to obey your rightful queen. Make your bow, and then go as you were told.'

I saw the boy's hopes die. He bowed stiffly but correctly and left. Even then, Swift did not scuttle from the room, but strode out, with dignity, as if to his own execution. When the door had closed behind him, Burrich swung his glance back to Kettricken. 'I beg my queen's pardon that you have been troubled with this. He's a good enough lad, ordinarily. He's just at . . . a difficult age.'

'He has not troubled us. Truth to tell, I would willingly be so troubled, if that is what it takes to bring you to visit us. Will you sit down, Burrich?' She gestured at an empty chair, one of several in a row before her.

Burrich held himself stiffly erect. 'You are kind to offer it, but I have not the time to linger, my lady. I promised my wife I would return to her, with the boy, as swiftly as I could and –'

'Must I command you to sit down, my stubborn old friend? Your good lady will forgive you the delay to rest yourself for a moment, I am sure.'

He was silent. Then, like a dog commanded to sit and stay, he walked to one of the chairs and sat down in it. Again, he waited.

After a pause, Kettricken recommenced. 'After all these years, this is an awkward way for all of us to come together again. And yet, no matter how awkwardly it came about, I am glad to see your face once more. Yes, and to see that you have a son with his father's proud spirit.'

Another man might have warmed to that paternal compliment, but Burrich only glanced down and tempered it with, 'And I fear he has many of his father's faults as well, my lady.'

Kettricken did not waste words or time. 'The Wit, you mean.'

Burrich twitched to that as if she had cursed at him.

'Swift told us, Burrich. I do not see it as a shameful thing. He told me he had come to me as I have forbidden men to persecute those with the Wit. He asked to take service with me. In truth, I would be glad to have such a stout-hearted lad to page for me. But I told him it must be with his father's consent.'

He shook his head as he refused her. 'I do not give it, my lady. Swift is far too young to live amongst strangers. To be raised so quickly and so far above his natural station could spoil him. He needs to remain at my side for some years yet, until he learns to control his boyish impulses.'

'Until you've extinguished the Wit in him,' Chade filled it in.

Burrich considered, then frowned. 'I don't believe that can be done. I've tried for many years to wipe it from myself. Still, it lingers. But if it cannot be purged from a man, he can nevertheless be taught to refuse it. Just as a man must learn to refuse all sorts of other vices.'

'And you are so certain that it is a vice, and something to despise?' Kettricken's voice was gentle. 'But for your possession of the Wit, I would have died at Regal's hands, all those years ago. But for your Wit, Fitz would have perished in Regal's dungeons.'

Burrich took a short breath. It seemed to catch in his throat, and he took another one, as a man who fights for control of himself. He looked up, blinking, and it wrung me to see that his lashes were wet with unshed tears. 'You can speak his name,' he said huskily. 'And yet do not perceive that he is why I take the stand I do? Lady Queen, but for the Wit, Fitz would have learned the Skill well. But for the Wit, he could never have been thrown into Regal's dungeons. But for the Wit, he might even now be alive. The Wit doomed him to die, and not even as a man. As a beast.' He dragged in a shuddering breath. His voice rasped but he held himself straight and retained command of himself. 'Every day I live, I live with my failure. My prince, Prince Chivalry, entrusted me with his only child, with the sole command that I raise him well. I failed my prince. I failed Fitz and I failed myself. Because I was weak. Because I had not the strength of will to be harsh with the boy where harshness was needed. And so he fell into the way of that vile magic, and he practised it, and it brought about his downfall. He paid the price for my misplaced tenderness. He died, horribly, and alone, and as a beast.

'My lady, I loved Fitz, first as my friend's son, and then as my friend. I loved him just as I love my own son now. And I will not lose another boy to that low magic. I will not.' Only on the last words did his deep voice begin to shake. His hands knotted and unknotted and then clenched into fists at his side. He regarded them both through his misted eyes.

'Burrich. Old friend.' Chade's voice was thick. 'Long ago, you sent me word Fitz had perished. I doubted it then. I still do. How can you be sure of his death? Remember what he said to both of us. That he intended to go south, to Chalced and beyond Chalced. Perhaps he did as he said he would and –'

'No. He did not.' Burrich's hands went slowly to his throat. He unfolded his collar, and then from beneath it, he drew a small and shining thing. My heart turned over in my chest and tears flooded my eyes. He showed it to both of them, gleaming on his calloused palm. 'Do you recognize it? It's the pin King Shrewd gave him, when he claimed the boy as his own.' He sniffed loudly, and cleared his throat. 'When I found his body, Fitz was long dead. Many a creature had gnawed on him. But this was still there, in the collar of the shirt he died in. He died as an animal, fighting with beasts almost like himself. He was the son of a prince, the son of the finest man I ever knew and he died like a dog.' He abruptly closed his hand around the stickpin. He spoke not a word as he refastened it into his collar.

I sat in the dark, behind the wall, my hand tight over my own mouth. I tried not to choke on my tears and betray myself. I must keep my secret. I must remain dead to him. Never had I thought what his assumption of my death might mean to him. I had little considered how much grief and guilt he might bear over how he supposed I had died. Burrich still believed that I had succumbed to the Wit, had reverted to an animalistic lifestyle, a beastman living in the woods until the Forged ones attacked and killed me. It was not so far from the truth. For a time I *had* retreated into being a wolf in a man's body. But I had dragged myself up and out of that refuge, and forced myself to become a man again. When the Forged ones had raided my home and attacked me, I had fled. Days passed before I realized that I had left my precious pin behind. Burrich had found the body of a Forged one I had killed. The shirt with the pin thrust into the collar had been on that body. And so he had assumed it was mine. For all these years, it had suited my purposes to leave him in ignorance of my survival. I had thought it the kindest thing for all of us. He and Molly had found a love and a life together. To discover I still lived could only damage that bond between them. It must remain so. It must. In a numbed stillness, I stood and peered at the man who felt responsible for my death. He must continue to carry that guilt. I could not change it.

'Burrich. I do not think you failed anyone.' Kettricken spoke softly. 'And I do not see the Wit as a flaw in your son. Leave him here with me. Please.'

Burrich shook his head slowly and heavily. 'You would not say that if he were your son. If he walked daily in danger of folk discovering what he was.'

I saw Kettricken's shoulders rise as she drew breath and knew she was about to tell him that her own son was Witted. Chade realized the danger as well, for he cut in smoothly with, 'I see your point, Burrich. I do not agree with it, but I see it.' He paused, then asked, 'What will you do to the boy?'

Burrich stared at him. Then he gave a brief bark of laughter. 'What? Do you fear I'll tan the hide off him? No. I'll take him home, and keep him well away from animals, and work him daily until he is so tired that he falls asleep before he gets into his bed at night. No worse than that. His mother's tongue will probably flay him worse than a cane ever could. Nor will his sister easily forgive him for the worry he's given us.' Then suddenly he scowled more blackly than ever. 'Did the lad tell you he was in fear of life or limb from me? For that's a lie, and he knows it, and for that he might get the back of my hand.'

'He said nothing of the kind,' Kettricken said quietly. 'Only that he could not stand it any more, to live at home and be forbidden the Wit.'

Burrich snorted. 'No one dies from being forbidden the Wit. There's a loneliness to giving it up, and well do I know that. But no one dies from avoiding the Wit. Using the Wit is how one dies from it.' Burrich rose abruptly from his chair. I heard his bad knee crack as he rose and saw him wince. 'My lady, forgive me, but if I sit too long, I'll stiffen, and this day's ride home will be all the harder for me.'

'Then take a day here, Burrich. Go to the steams to ease that leg of injuries twice taken in defending a Farseer's life. Eat well, and sleep in a soft bed tonight. Tomorrow is soon enough for your journey home.'

'I cannot, my lady.'

'You can. Must I command this comfort to you, also?' The Queen's voice was fond.

Burrich met her gaze squarely. 'My queen, would you command me to break my word to my own lady?'

Kettricken gravely bowed her head to him. 'Good man, your honour is the only thing as stiff as your stubbornness. No, Burrich, I would never command you to break your word. Too often has my own life depended upon it. I will let you go then, as you please. But you shall delay long enough to allow me to pack such gifts as I wish you to take back to your family. And while I do so, you may as well eat a hot meal and warm yourself at the hearth.'

Burrich was silent for a moment. Then, 'As you wish, my lady.' Again, he went ponderously and painfully down upon one knee.

When he rose and waited her permission, Kettricken sighed. 'You may go, my friend.'

When the door had closed behind him, Kettricken and Chade sat silently for a time. They were the only people left in the chamber. Then Chade turned and looked toward my peephole. He spoke softly. 'You have a little time while he eats. Think hard. Shall I summon him back to this chamber? You could be alone here with him. You could put his heart at ease.' He paused. 'This is your decision, my boy. Neither I nor Kettricken will make it for you. But . . .' His words died away. Perhaps he knew just how much I did not want his advice on this. In a soft voice, he added, 'If you wish me to ask Burrich to come back to this chamber, tell Lord Golden to send me a message. If you do not, then . . . do nothing.'

Then the Queen arose, and Chade escorted her from the audience chamber. She gave one pleading backward glance at my wall before she left the room.

I don't know how long I sat there in the dust and dimness. When my candle began to drown in its own wax, I rose and made my way back to my own small chamber. The corridor seemed long and dreary. I walked unseen, through dust and cobwebs and mouse-droppings. Like a ghost, I smiled stiffly to myself. Just as I walked through my life.

In my room, I took my cloak from its hook. I listened for a moment at the door, then stepped out into the central chamber of Lord Golden's apartments. He sat alone at the table. He had pushed his breakfast tray aside. He did not appear to be doing anything. He gave me no greeting. I spoke without preamble.

'Burrich is here. He followed his son Swift, Nimble's twin. Swift is Witted, and sought asylum in the Queen's service. Burrich refused to let her have the boy. He's taking him home with him, to teach him not to use the Wit. He still thinks the Wit is evil. He blames it for my death. He also blames himself, that he did not beat it out of me.'

After a moment, Lord Golden turned his head indolently to look at me. 'An interesting bit of gossip. This Burrich, he was Stablemaster here at one time, was he not? I don't believe I've ever met him.'

For a time, I just looked at him. He returned my stare with a gaze devoid of interest. 'I'm going down to Buckkeep Town today,' I announced flatly.

He turned back to his contemplation of the tabletop. 'As you will,

Tom Badgerlock. I've no need of your services today. But be ready to ride out tomorrow at noon. Lady Thrift and her niece have offered to take me out hawking. I don't care to keep a bird of my own, you know. Their talons spoil the sleeves of my coats. But perhaps I shall be able to add some feathers to my collection.'

My hand was on the door latch before he had finished his hateful charade. I shut it firmly behind me and went briskly down the stairs. I dared myself and fate. If I ran into Burrich in the hallway, he would know me. Let the gods decide for themselves if he should walk in guilty ignorance or pain-wracked truth. But I did not encounter him in the halls of Buckkeep, nor even glimpse him as I went past the guards' dining hall. Then I snorted at my own foolish fancy. Doubtless they would take the Queen's guest to the main hall, and there feed him well, alongside his wayward son. I did not let myself pause to consider any other temptations. I went out into the courtyard, and soon was striding down the road to Buckkeep Town.

The day was fine, clear and cold. It bit the tops of my cheeks and the tips of my ears, but my pace kept the rest of me warm. I played a dozen scenes in my head of how it might go were I to confront Burrich. He would embrace me. He would strike me and curse me. He would not recognize me. He would faint with shock. In some of these visions he welcomed me warmly with tears of joy, and in others he cursed me for all the years I had let him live in guilt. But in none of those scenes could I imagine how we would speak of Molly and Nettle, nor what would come after. If Burrich discovered that I was alive, could he keep it from Molly? Would he? Sometimes his honour operated on such a lofty scale that what was unthinkable for any other man became the only correct option for him.

I broke from my thoughts to find myself in the centre of Buckkeep Town. Men and women alike gave me a wide berth, and I realized I was scowling darkly and probably muttering to myself. I tried to find a more pleasant expression, but my face could not seem to recall how to form one. Nor could I decide where I wished to be. I went by the woodjoiner's shop where Hap was apprenticed. I lingered outside until I caught a glimpse of him within. There were tools in his hands. I wondered if that meant he was being given more responsibility, or if it only meant he was fetching them for someone. Well, at least he was where he was supposed to be. I would not trouble him today.

I next wandered by Jinna's shop, but found it closed up tight. A quick check of her shed showed that the pony and cart were gone. Something must have called her away today. I was not sure if I felt relief or disappointment. To quench my loneliness in her company would not have eased me, but if she had been home, I would probably have given myself over to the temptation.

So I made the next most foolish decision that I could make, which was to go to the Stuck Pig. A tavern fit for the Witted Bastard. I entered, and as I stood in the doorway with the bright winter sunlight flowing in from behind me, I decided it was one of those places that always looked better by lamplight. Daylight revealed, not just the weariness of the leaning tables and the damp straw that begged pardon on the floor, but the dreariness of the folk who came to such a tavern on a bright winter afternoon. People such as myself, I surmised sourly. A gaffer and a man with a twisted leg and only one arm sat together at a table near the hearth, some game bones between them. At another table, a man with a badly bruised face sat nursing a tankard and muttering to himself. A woman looked up as I came in. When she raised one brow inquiringly, I shook my head. She scowled at me and returned to staring at the hearthfire. A boy with a bucket and rag was scrubbing tables and benches. When I sat down, he wiped his hands on his trouser legs and came over to me.

'Beer,' I said, not because I wanted it, but because I was there and I had to order something. He bobbed acknowledgement, took my coin, brought me a mug, and went back to his tasks. I took a sip of it and tried to remember why I had walked down to Buckkeep Town. I decided it had simply been the need to be moving. But now I was sitting still. Stupid.

I was still sitting still when Svanja's father walked in. I don't think he saw me at first, coming into the dim tavern from the bright winter day. When I recognized him, I looked down at the tabletop, as if by not looking at him, I could make myself invisible. It didn't work. I heard his heavy boots on the sodden straw, and then he dragged out a chair and sat down across from me. I nodded at him guardedly. He stared at me blearily. His eyes were red-rimmed, but whether from weeping, lack of sleep or drink, I could not tell. His dark hair had been brushed that morning, but he had not shaved. I wondered that he was not at his trade. The tavern boy soon scurried over with a mug of ale for him. He took the man's coin and went back to his scrubbing. Hartshorn took a drink of his ale, scratched his whiskery cheek and said, 'Well.'

'Well,' I agreed mildly and drank from my beer. I wished so intensely to be somewhere else that it seemed unbelievable that my body remained where it was.

'Your boy.' Hartshorn shifted in his chair. 'Does he intend to marry my girl, or just ruin her?' His face remained calm as he spoke, but I could see both anger and pain bubbling up in him like vapours from the bottom of a stagnant pond. I think I knew then that we would come to blows. I realized it as a sort of enlightenment. The man had to do something to regain some self-respect, and I presented the first opportunity. Both the gaffer and the maimed man had lost interest in their game and were watching us. They knew what was coming as well as I did. They'd be Hartshorn's witnesses.

There wasn't a way out of what was to come, but I tried to find one. My voice was low and steady and earnest. I tried to reach him, father to father. 'Hap tells me that he loves Svanja. So there is no intent there to ruin her, or to use her and cast her aside. They are both very young. But, yes, there is a danger of ruining, and for my son as well as your daughter.'

I made a mistake when I paused then. I think if I had kept speaking, he would have stayed seated and paid some attention to my words. I had intended to ask him what he thought that we, as parents, could do to curb our children until their passions found some sort of foundation in planning for a future. Perhaps if I had not been thinking so earnestly of what to say to him, and what we actually could do, I would have noticed that he was earnestly thinking of the best way to give me a beating.

He surged suddenly to his feet. His mug was in his hand and desperate fury flamed in his eyes. 'Your son's fucking her! My little girl, my Svanja! And you think that isn't ruin for her?'

I was coming to my feet when the heavy mug hit me in the face.

A miscalculation, some part of me observed. I had thought he would club me with it, and I thought I'd leaned back out of his range. When he let it fly, that small distance was not enough. It hit my left cheekbone with a crack I heard, and white pain spider-webbed out from the impact.

Sharp pain makes some men retreat and paralyses others. My time under Regal's torture had branded in me a different reaction. *Attack now, before it gets any worse, before your attacker can overcome you and torment you at his leisure.* I had launched myself over the table at him before the thrown mug even thudded to the floor. The pain in my face reached its zenith at about the same time my fist slammed into his mouth. His teeth cut my knuckles and my left hand slammed into his breastbone, above my intended target.

Jinna's warning about him had been valid. He did not go down, but roared his fury at me. I had one of my knees on the tabletop. I got my other leg under me and pushed off from there, my hands going for his throat as the weight of my body bore him down to the dirty floor. The bench behind his knees helped me knock him down, but I clipped my own shins against it painfully as I landed on top of him.

He was stronger than he looked, and he fought without restraint, without concern for his own body. His entire aim was to hurt me, with no concern for himself and as we rolled and grappled, I heard his knuckles crack as his fist met my skull. I had not made good my grip on his throat, and the benches and tables that crowded the tavern added obstacles to our struggle. At one point he was on top of me, but we were under a table, and I was able to surge up against him and slam his head against the underside of the board. That stunned him for a moment and I rolled clear of his grasp. I scuttled clear of the table and came to my feet. He snarled at me from under the table, showing no sign of relenting in his anger.

Fights are simultaneous things: in one moment, I readied myself to kick him as he came out from under the table, the tavern keeper roared, 'I've called for the guard! Take your fight outside,' while the gaffer at the game-table shouted in a cracked voice, 'Watch out, Rory! He's gonna kick you, watch out!' But the voice that broke my concentration was Hap's crying, 'Tom! Don't hurt Svanja's father!'

Rory Hartshorn seemed to have no compunction about hurting Hap's father. He delivered a strong kick to my ankle that unbalanced me as he rolled out from under the table. I fell, but I fell on him. I grabbed his throat, but he tucked his chin, trying to defeat my strangle while his fists pounded my ribs.

'City Guard!' A bass voice bellowed in warning. As one we were plucked from the floor by two brawny armsmen. They didn't waste time trying to break our clinch, but dragged us bodily to the door and tumbled us out into the snowy street. A circle of men surrounded us as I still strove to clench my fingers into Rory's throat. He gripped my hair, forcing my head back as his fingers clawed at my eyes. 'Kick them apart!' bellowed a sergeant and my determination suddenly seemed foolish. I let go my grip and twisted myself off Rory's body. I left a scant handful of my hair in his fist as I did so. Someone grabbed my arm and hauled me to my feet. Whoever it was, he gripped both my wrists and hauled them expertly up behind my back. I gritted my teeth and concentrated all my will on not resisting him. As I stood panting and docile, I felt his grip ease slightly.

Rory Hartshorn was not thinking as clearly. He struggled as a guard dragged him to his feet, and was soundly thumped with her truncheon several times for it. When he was finally still, he was on his knees. Blood from his mouth dripped from his chin. He glared at me malevolently.

'Penalty for brawling in a tavern is six silvers. Each. Pay it now and part peacefully, or go to the lock-up, and pay twice as much to get out of there. Tavernkeeper. Any damages within?'

I didn't hear the man's reply because Hap hissed suddenly by my ear, 'Tom Badgerlock, how could you?'

I turned to look at my boy. He recoiled from my face. I wasn't surprised. Even in the cold of the winter day, my cheek burned hot. I could feel it puffing. 'He started it.' I meant it by way of an explanation, but it sounded like a boy's sulky excuse.

The guard who held me gave me a shake. 'You! Pay attention. Sergeant asked you if you got the six? Do you?'

'I've got it. Give me a hand free to reach for my purse.' I noted that the tavernkeeper had not tallied up any damages against us. Perhaps that was a benefit of being a regular customer there.

The guardsman released both my hands, warning me, 'No stupid tricks, now.'

'I've already done my stupid trick for the day,' I muttered, and was rewarded with a grudging chuckle from him. My hands were starting to swell. It hurt to tug my purse strings open and count out the coins for them. Now there was my queen's largesse well spent. My guard took the coins from me and walked away to hand them to his sergeant, who counted them and then slid them into a town bag at his belt. Rory Hartshorn, still gripped by a guard on either side, shook his head sullenly. 'I don't have it,' he said mushily.

One of the guard snorted. 'The way you've been spending coin on drink the last few days, it's a wonder you had any money to buy beer today.'

'To the lock-up,' the sergeant decreed stonily.

'I've got it,' Hap said suddenly. I had almost forgotten he was there until I saw him tug at the sergeant's sleeve.

'Got what?' the sergeant asked in surprise.

'His fine. I'll pay Hartshorn's fine for him. Please don't lock him up.'

'Don't want your money! Don' wan nothin' from him.' Rory Hartshorn was starting to sag between the men that held him. Bereft of his fury, pain was taking him over. Then, horribly, he began to weep. 'Ruined my daughter. Ruined our family. Don' take his dirty money.'

Hap went white. The sergeant looked him up and down coldly. Hap's voice cracked as he said, 'Please, don't lock him up. It's bad enough, isn't it?' The purse he lifted and tugged open was clearly marked with the sigil of his master, Gindast. Hap scooped coins out of it and proffered them to the guard. 'Please,' he said again.

The sergeant turned away from him abruptly. 'Take Hartshorn to his home. Fine suspended.' He turned coldly away from my boy, who reeled as if he had been struck. Shame burned his face scarlet. The two guardsmen holding Hartshorn hustled him away, but it was now plain that they were aiding him to walk rather than restraining him. The rest of the city patrol moved off on their regular rounds. Suddenly Hap and I were alone in the middle of the cold street. I blinked and my own hurts began clamouring to make themselves known. The worst was my cheekbone where the heavy mug had connected. My vision in that eye was blurred. I felt a moment of selfish gratitude that Hap was there to help me. But when he turned to look at me, he did not seem to see me at all.

'It's all ruined now,' he said helplessly. 'I'll never be able to make this right. Never.' He turned to stare after the retreating Hartshorn. Then his swung his gaze back to me. 'Tom, why?' he demanded heartbrokenly. 'Why did you do this to me? I went to live with Gindast like you told me to. I was getting everything sorted out. Now you've ruined it.' He stared after the departing men. 'I'll never make peace with Svanja's family now.'

'Hartshorn started the fight,' I said stupidly, and then cursed my own pathetic excuse.

'Couldn't you have walked away?' he asked self-righteously. 'You've always told me that's the best choice in a fight. To walk away if you can.'

'He didn't give me that opportunity,' I said. My anger was starting to swell worse than my face. I walked to the edge of the street, and reached up to take a handful of somewhat clean snow from an eave edge. I held it to my face. 'I don't see how you can blame me for any of this,' I added sullenly. 'You're the one who set it all in motion. You had to rush her into bed.'

For an instant he looked as if I had struck him. But even before I could feel regret for my words, he shifted into anger. 'You speak as if I had a choice,' he said coldly. 'But that's to be expected, I suppose, from a man's who has never known real love in his life. You think all women are like Starling. They're not. Svanja is my true love forever, and true love should not be made to wait. You and her father and mother would have us hold back from completing our love, as if tomorrow were a certainty for any of us. But we won't. Love demands that we grasp it all, today.'

His words enflamed my anger. I was certain that they were not his own, but had been harvested from some tavern minstrel. 'If you think I've never known love, then you don't know anything about me,' I retorted. 'As for you and Svanja, she's the first girl you've ever said more than "hello", and you tumble into her bed and proclaim it love. Love is more than bedding, boy. If love doesn't come first and linger after, if love can't wait and endure disappointment and separation, then it's not love. Love doesn't require bedding to make it true. It doesn't even demand day to day contact. I know this because I have known love, many kinds of loves, and among them, I've known what I felt for you.'

'Tom!' he barked in rebuke. He glanced behind his shoulder at a passing couple.

'You fear they will misunderstand what I say?' I sneered. At the anger in my voice, the man took the woman's arm and hurried her past us. I must have looked a madman. I didn't care. 'I fear you've misunderstood it all along. You came to Buckkeep Town and forgot everything that I ever tried to teach you. I don't even know how to talk to you any more.' I went back to the eaves for another scoop of snow. I glanced back at Hap, but he was staring stonily into the distance. In that instant, my heart gave him up. He was gone from me, following his own path, and there was nothing I could do. This arguing with him was as useless as all the words Burrich and Patience had spent on me. He'd go his own way, make his own mistakes, and maybe, when he was my age, learn his own lessons from them. Wasn't that what I had done? 'I'll still finish paying for your apprenticeship,' I said quietly. I spoke as much to myself as to him, telling myself that there it would end. That it had already ended save keeping that bargain with myself.

I turned and began the long walk back up to Buckkeep Castle. Breathing the cold air made my battered ribs ache. Not much choice about that. My hands were starting to swell, too. There was a sick familiarity to the pain of my puffing knuckles. I wondered dully when was I going to be old enough and wise enough to stop getting into physical fights. And I wondered at the curious disconnection in my chest, the gap where Hap had been in my life but moments before. It felt like a mortal injury.

When I heard running footsteps behind me, I spun to confront them, fearing another attack. Hap skidded to a halt at sight of my battle grimace. For a frozen instant, we just stood and regarded one another. Then he reached out and clutched at my sleeve, saying, 'Tom, I hate this. I'm trying hard, and I'm doing and saying all the wrong things. Svanja's parents are angry with her all the time, and when she complained to me about it and I said perhaps I should meet them and promise to go more slowly, she got angry at me. And she's angry at me for living at Gindast's and having to stay in most nights. But I did go to Gindast, on my own, and ask to move in. And he made me eat dirt, but I kept my head down and took it, and I'm there now, doing it his way, like you said. I hate how early we get up, and how he rations how many candles we can burn at night, and how I can't go out at all most nights. But I'm doing it. And today, for the first time, he sent me on an errand, to pick up some brass fittings over on the smiths' street. And now I'm going to be late getting back with them, and I'll have to bow my head to that when he scolds me. But I can't let you walk away and think I've forgotten everything you taught me. I haven't. But I have to find my own life here, and sometimes the things you taught me just don't seem to fit with how everyone else thinks. Sometimes the things you taught me don't seem to work here. But I'm trying, Tom. I'm trying.'

The words tumbled out from him in a rush. When they had cascaded away and silence threatened to fill in, I put my arm across his shoulders and hugged him despite the pain in my ribs. 'Hurry on your errand,' I said by his ear. I tried to think of other words to add, but couldn't find any. I couldn't tell him it would come out right, because I wasn't sure it would. I couldn't tell him that I'd trust his judgment, because I didn't. Then Hap found the words for both of us.

'I love you, Tom. I'll keep trying.'

I sighed in relief. 'Me, too. I love you, and I'll keep trying. Hurry, now. You're long-legged and swift. Perhaps you won't be late if you run.'

He gave me a fleeting smile, and turning, raced off toward the smiths' street. I envied him the easy movement of his body. I turned back towards Buckkeep Castle.

Halfway up the hill road to the Castle, I met Burrich coming down. Swift rode behind him, his hands clutching his father's waist. Burrich's game leg stuck out awkwardly. He'd modified the stirrup for it. For one instant, I stared at him. Swift gaped at me, but doubtless my purpling face was a sight. I damped my Wit to an ember, kept my head down and trudged past them without another glance. My heart strained to look back at them after they had passed, but I refused it. I feared too terribly that Burrich would be looking back at me.

The rest of the walk to Buckkeep Castle seemed cold and dreary. I went to the steams. The guardsmen, coming and going, left me alone. I had hoped the moist heat would ease some of my aches, but it didn't. The long climb up to our chambers hurt, and I knew that if I sat still, I would stiffen, but all I could think of was my bed. The day had been a wretched waste, I told myself. I doubted that even my efforts with Dutiful and Thick would bear fruit.

As I approached the door to our chambers, it opened. The garden maid came out of it. Garetha bore a basket of dried flowers. As I gazed at her, startled, she glanced up and her eyes met mine. She suddenly flushed a scarlet that all but obscured her freckles. Then she looked away from me and rushed off down the hall, but not before I had caught sight of the necklace she wore. It was a single charm on a leather strand. The little carved rose was painted white, with a stem inked black. I knew the Fool's work when I saw it. Had he taken my ill-conceived advice? Inexplicably, my heart sank in my chest. I tapped cautiously at the door and announced myself before I entered. As I shut the door behind me and looked round, I found a perfectly poised Lord Golden ensconced in the cushioned chair before the hearth. For an instant, his amber eyes widened at the sight of my bruises, but just as swiftly he had control of myself.

'I thought you were going out for the day, Tom Badgerlock,' he observed convivially.

'I did,' I said, and I thought that was all I was going to say. But I found myself rooted to the spot, regarding him as he sat looking back at me, so carefully contained. 'I had a conversation with Hap. I told him that loving someone and bedding someone were two different things.'

Lord Golden blinked slowly. Then he asked, 'And did he believe you?'

I took a breath. 'I don't think he completely understood me. But in time, I expect he will.'

'Many things take time,' he observed. He swung his gaze back to the fire, and my hopes, that had leapt high but a moment before, moderated themselves. I nodded a silent agreement to his words and went into my room.

I stripped off my clothes and lay down on my narrow bed. I closed my eyes.

The day had taken more from me than I realized. I slept, not just that afternoon, but into the night. Deep and dreamless was my rest, until in the dark of night I found myself nudged from that blissfully empty sleep into that hovering place that is between sleep and waking. What had roused me, I wondered, and then became aware of it. Outside my Skill-walls, Nettle wept. She no longer assaulted those walls or entreated me angrily. She simply stood outside them and mourned. Endlessly.

I lifted my hands and covered my eyes as if that would hold her at bay. Then, I drew a deep breath and let my walls collapse. A single step carried my thoughts to hers. I wrapped her in comfort and told her, *You worry needlessly, my dear. Both your father and your brother are on their way home to you. They are safe. I promise you this is true. Now. Stop your fretting and rest.*

But . . . how can you know this?

Because I do. And I offered her my absolute certainty, and my brief glimpse of Burrich and Swift riding double on a horse.

For a moment, she collapsed into formlessness, so great was her relief. I began to withdraw, but she clutched at me suddenly. *It has been so horrid here. First Swift disappeared, and we thought something awful had befallen him. Then the smith in town told Papa that he had asked him which roads led to Buckkeep Castle. Then Papa was furious and rode off in a temper, and Mama has done nothing but either weep or rant since then. She says that of all places in the world, Buckkeep is the most dangerous for Swift. But she will not say why. It frightens me when she is like this. Sometimes she looks at me, and her eyes don't even see me. Then she either shouts at me to make myself useful or she starts weeping and cannot stop. None of it makes sense. We all have been creeping about the house like mice. And Nim feels as if half of himself is missing, and somehow it is his fault.*

I interrupted her cascading words. *Listen to me. It is going to be all right.*

I believe you. But how can I make them know that?

I pondered. Should she tell Molly she had a dream? No. *You can't. I'm afraid they must endure. So, be strong for them, knowing all will be well. Help your mother, care for your little brothers, and wait. If I know your father at all, he will be at your side as soon as his horse can bear them there.*

You know my father?

Such a question. *Very well indeed.* And then I knew I had gone too far, that I had given her words that were dangerous to both of us. So I Skill-suggested to her, more gently than a willow leaf moves in a breeze, that she would sleep now, truly sleep, and wake refreshed in the morning. Her grip on me weakened and I slipped away from her, back behind the safety of my walls. I opened my eyes to the dark of my own chamber. I took a deep breath, rolled over, and shouldered deeper into my bedding. I was hungry, but morning and breakfast would come soon enough.

A fumbling thought intruded, wafting on music. The Skilling was hesitant, not with lack of ability but with a squeamish reluctance to touch his mind to mine. *You made her stop crying at last. Now Thick can sleep, too.*

His touch vanished from my mind, leaving me to stare restlessly at my ceiling. But even as I re-centred my mind and tried to convince myself that Thick's Skilling to me should be viewed as a positive step, not an invasion, another mind touched mine. It was distant and immense, and impossibly foreign. There was nothing human to the way her thoughts moved as she observed with bitter amusement, Now perhaps you will learn not to dream so loud. He is not the only one it bothers. Nor is he the only one you reveal yourself to, little man. What are you? What do you mean to me?

Then her thoughts abandoned me as a retreating wave leaves a drowned man on a beach. I rolled to the edge of my bed and retched dryly, more battered by that prodigious mind contact than by the beating I'd taken from Rory. The foreignness of the being which had pressed against my mind disrupted me, gagging my thoughts as if I had tried to breathe oil or drink flame. Panting in the dark, I felt the sweat slide down my brow and back and wondered what my errant Skilling had awakened in the world.

SEVENTEEN

Explosions

'. . . And overheard a conversation between Erikska and the captain. He complained that the wind battled the ship, as if El himself begrudged bearing their home-coming. Erikska laughed at him, and mocked him for believing in "such old gods. They have grown feeble of muscle and wit. It is the Pale Lady who commands the winds now. As she is displeased with the Narcheska, she makes all of you suffer". At her words, the captain turned aside from her. His face was angry, as an Outislander looks angry because he hates to show fear.'

Of the handmaid you bid me especially watch, I have seen no sign. Either she has remained within the Narcheska's cabin for this entire voyage, or she is not aboard this vessel. I think the second is likelier.
Unsigned report to Chade Fallstar on the Narcheska's journey home

Sleep was gone. I ended up rising, dressing, and ascending to my tower. It was cold up there, and dark save for a few coals in the fireplace. I lit candles from the embers on the hearth and restored the fire. I damped a cloth in water and held it to my aching face. For a time I just stared into the fire. Then, in a useless effort to distract myself from all the questions I could not answer, I sat down at the table and tried to study the current set of scrolls that Chade had left out on the tabletop. These were the Outislander dragon legends, but there were two there that were new, the ink clean and black on the pale cream vellum. He would not have left them there if he had not wanted me to see them. One dealt with a report of a silver-blue dragon seen over Bingtown Harbour during a decisive battle between the Bingtown Traders and the Chalcedeans. The other looked like a child's practise of the alphabet, the letters sprawling and malformed. But long ago he had taught me several ciphers by which we could leave messages for one another, and this parchment rapidly gave way to my efforts to decode it. Indeed, so simple was the secret of it that I scowled, wondering if Chade were losing his grip on our need for secrecy or if the quality of spies he retained had somehow lessened. For that is what it proved to be, an early report from the spy he had sent off to the Outislands. It was mostly an account of gossip, rumours and overheard conversations on the Narcheska's ship during the voyage to the Outislands. I found little that was immediately useful there, though a reference to a Pale Woman did disturb me. It was as if an old shadow out of my previous life had reached out toward me, with claws instead of insubstantial fingers.

I was making myself tea when Chade arrived. He thrust the scroll-rack door open and staggered in. His cheeks and nose were red, and for a shocked moment, I thought the old man was drunk. He clutched at the table edge and seated himself in my chair and said plaintively, 'Fitz?'

'What's happened?' I asked him as I went to him.

He stared at me, and then said over-loudly, 'I can't hear you.'

'What's happened to you?' I asked again, more loudly.

I don't think he heard those words either, but he explained, 'It blew up. I was working on that same mix, the one I showed you at your cottage. This time it worked too well. It blew up!' He lifted his hands to his face, patting at his cheeks and brow. His face was tragic. I immediately knew what troubled him. I went and got him a looking-glass. He stared into it while I fetched a fresh basin of water and a cloth. I wet it for him, and he held it against his face for a moment. When he took it away, some of the flush had gone from his skin, but most of his eyebrows had, also.

'It looks as if a great flash of fire hit you. Part of your hair is singed, too.'

'What?'

I motioned to him to lower his voice.

'I can't hear you,' he repeated plaintively. 'My ears are ringing as if my stepfather had boxed them for me. Gods, I hated that man!'

That he spoke of him at all was a measure of his distress. Chade had never told me much about his childhood. He lifted his hands and fingered his ears as if to be sure they were still there, and then plugged and unplugged them with his fingers. 'I can't hear,' he repeated yet again. 'But my face isn't too bad, is it? I'm not going to be scarred, am I?'

I shook my head at him. 'Your eyebrows will grow back. This—' I touched his cheek lightly, 'seems no worse than a sunburn or wind-scald. It will go away. And I think your deafness will pass, also.' I had no basis for saying the last, save that I hoped it so devoutly.

'I can't hear you,' he agonized.

I patted his shoulder comfortingly and put my cup of tea in front of him. I touched my mouth to draw his attention to my lips and then said carefully, 'Is your apprentice all right?' Well I knew he would not be conducting such experiments alone at such an hour.

He watched my mouth move, and after a moment he seemed to comprehend my words because he said, 'Don't worry about that. I took care of her.' Then, at my shocked look at his use of the feminine pronoun, he exclaimed angrily, 'Mind your own business, Fitz!'

His irritation was directed more at himself than at me, and if I had not been so worried about him, I would have laughed. Her. So I'd been replaced with a girl. I reined my mind away from considering who she was, or why Chade had chosen her, to giving Chade what comfort I could. After a time, I ascertained that Chade could hear me, but not well. I tried to convey to him that I hoped his hearing would recover. He nodded and waved a hand dismissively, but I could see the haunting worry in his eyes. If his deafness remained, it would severely compromise his ability to counsel the Queen.

Nevertheless, he bravely tried to ignore his injury, asking me loudly if I'd seen the scrolls on the table, and then asking me what on earth I'd done to my face. To keep him from shouting more questions, I wrote down brief answers to his questions. I dismissed my injuries as the result of getting accidentally involved in a random tavern brawl. He was too preoccupied with his own problems to question that. Next he wrote on the scrap of paper we were using, 'Did you speak with Burrich?'

'I judged it best not to,' I inked in reply. He pursed his lips, sighed, and said nothing, but I could tell that there was much he wished to say. He'd save it for later when conversation might be easier. Then we went over the spy-scrolls, pointing out interesting bits to one another even as we agreed that there was nothing there that was immediately useful. Chade wrote that he was hoping to hear soon from a spy that he'd sent out to Aslevjal Isle, to see if there was any scrap of truth to the legend.

I wanted to discuss my progress with Thick and Dutiful, but deferred that not only on account of his dampened hearing but because I was still trying to sort out how well I was doing. I'd already decided that I'd take my efforts with Thick further tomorrow.

It was then that I realized tomorrow was nearly upon us. Chade seemed to realize the same thing. He told me that he would seek his own bed, and plead a stomach affliction when the servant came to wake him.

I had no such luxury of bed rest. Instead, I retreated to my room to put on fresh clothing before I made the trek to Verity's tower to await my students. I am sure I dreaded the day's lesson more than either of them, for my head still pounded. I clenched my brow against it as I built a fire in the tower hearth and kindled some candles on the table. Sometimes I could not recall the last time I had been completely free of Skill-pain. I considered going back to my room for elfbark. When I rejected the notion, it was not because I feared it would damage my ability to Skill. It was that I connected the drug too strongly with my stupid quarrel with the Fool. No. No more of that.

I heard Dutiful's footfall on the stair outside the door, and there was no time to ponder such things any more. He shut the door firmly behind him and came to the table. I sighed silently. His posture plainly said that he had not completely forgiven me. The first words out of his mouth were, 'I don't want to learn the Skill with a half-wit as my partner. There must be someone else.' Then he stared at me. 'What happened to you?'

'I got in a fight.' I made the reply short, to let him know that was as much as I would say. 'And as far as Thick working with you on the Skill, I know of no other suitable candidates. He's our only choice.'

'Oh, he can't be. Have you made an organized search for ones?'

'No.'

Then, before I could say anything further, he picked up the little figurine from the table. The chain dangled from it. 'What's this?' he asked.

'It's yours. You found it on that beach where we encountered an Other. Don't you remember it?'

'No.' He stared at it with dread. Then, unwillingly, 'Yes. Yes, I do.' He swayed in his chair, looking at it. 'It's Elliania, isn't it? What does it mean, Tom? That I found it there, before I'd ever even met her?'

'What?' I held out my hand for it, but he didn't seem to notice. Instead he just sat, staring at it. I got up and walked around the table. When I looked at the small face and the coils of black hair, and bared breasts and the black, black eyes, I suddenly saw he was right. It was Elliania. Not as she was now, but as she would be, when she was a woman grown. The blue ornament carved in the woman's hair was identical to the one that the Narcheska had worn. I drew a deep breath. 'I don't know what it means.'

The Prince spoke as a man does when he dreams. He looked down into the doll's face. 'That place where we were, that beach . . . it was like a vortex. Like a whirlpool that draws magic to itself. All sorts of magic.' He closed his eyes for an instant. He still clutched the carved figurine in his hand. 'I nearly died there, didn't I? The Skill sucked me in and pulled me to pieces. But you came after me and . . . someone helped you. Someone—' He groped helplessly for a word. 'Someone great. Someone bigger than the sky.'

It was not how I would have expressed it, but I knew what he meant. I suddenly recognized how reluctant I had been to discuss the events on the beach or even think about them. There was a nimbus around the hours we had spent there, a light that obscured rather than illuminated. It filled me with dread. It was why I hadn't shown the feathers to the Fool or discussed them with anyone. They were a vulnerability. They were a door to the unknown. When I picked them up, I had set something larger in motion, something that was beyond anyone's controlling. Even now, my mind cringed away, as if by refusing to remember, I could undo those events.

'What was that? Who was it, that we encountered there?'

'I don't know,' I said shortly.

A deep enthusiasm suddenly kindled in the Prince's eyes. 'We have to find out.'

'No. We don't.' I took a breath. 'In fact, I think we should be very careful to avoid finding out.'

He stared at me in consternation. 'But why? Don't you remember what it felt like? How wonderful it was?'

I remembered only too well, especially now that we spoke of it together. I shook my head, and suddenly wished I'd kept the figurine hidden. The sight of her was pulling all the memories back into my mind, just as a familiar perfume or the few notes of a song will suddenly recall all of an evening's foolishness. 'Yes. It was wonderful. And it was dangerous. I didn't want to come back from there, Dutiful. Neither did you. She made us.'

'She? It wasn't a she. It was like ... like a father. Strong and safe. Caring.'

'I don't think it was either of those things,' I said unwillingly. 'I think that we each shaped it into what we wanted it to be.'

'You think we each made it up?'

'No. No, I think we encountered something that was bigger than we could grasp. And we set it into a familiar shape so that we could behold it. So that our minds could encompass it.'

'What makes you think that? Something you read in the Skill-scrolls?'

I answered reluctantly. 'No. I've found nothing in the Skill-scrolls about anything like that. I just think that because ... because I do.'

He stared at me and I shrugged hopelessly, because I had no better explanation for the boy or myself. Only a stirring anticipation at the memory of the creature we had encountered, backed by an ominous dread.

The mantel door scraping open saved me. Thick entered, sneezing. He wore the whistle outside his shirt. The contrast between the shiny paint on the whistle and the ragged, grimy garment suddenly made me see him anew. I was appalled. His lank hair was flat to his head, and the flesh that showed through his rent garments was grimy. Suddenly I perceived him as Dutiful did, and realized that the Prince's abhorrence went past the man's physical deformity and mental limits. Dutiful literally drew back as Thick came closer, his nose wrinkling. My years with the wolf had led me to accept that certain things smelled certain ways. But the reek of Thick's unwashed body was not simply a part of him as intrinsic as the ferret's musk. It could be changed, and it would have to be changed if I expected the Prince to work with him.

For now, 'Thick, would you sit here?' I invited him, and drew out the chair farthest from the Prince. Thick looked at me suspiciously. Then he dragged it out, looked at the seat as if there might be some trick to it, and then plopped down into it. He began to scratch at something behind his left ear. When I glanced at Dutiful, he seemed transfixed with a horrified fascination. 'Well. Here we all are,' I announced, and then wondered what I was going to do with them.

Thick's eyes wandered to me. 'That girl's crying again,' he informed me, as if it were my fault.

'Well. I'll attend to that later,' I told him firmly as my heart gave a lurch.

'What girl?' The Prince demanded instantly.

'It's nothing to worry about.' *Thick, let's not talk about the girl just now. We're here to do lessons.*

Slowly, Thick stopped scratching. He dropped his hand to the tabletop and stared at me earnestly. 'Why you do that? Talk in my head like that?'

'To see if I could make you hear me.'

He sniffed thoughtfully. 'I heard you.' *Dogstink.*

Don't do that to me.

'Are you Skilling to each other?' the Prince asked with earnest curiosity.

'Yes.'

'Then why can't I hear it?'

'Because we are selecting only one another to Skill to.'

Dutiful's brow furrowed. 'How did he learn to do that when I cannot?'

'I don't know,' I had to admit. 'Thick seems to have developed his Skill-abilities on his own. I don't really know all he can and can't do with them.'

'Can he stop making that music all the time?'

I unfolded my own Skill-awareness. I hadn't realized that I had been straining Thick's thoughts free of the music that surrounded them. I turned to him now. 'Thick, can you stop making the music? Can you think only the thoughts to me, without the music?'

He looked at me blankly. 'Music?'

'Your mother-song. Can you make it be quiet?'

He considered this for a time, chewing on his fat little tongue. 'No,' he decided abruptly.

'Why can't you stop the music?' the Prince demanded. He had been sitting quietly. I suspected he had been trying to sort through the music and see if he could pick out Thick and me Skilling to one another. He sounded frustrated. Frustrated, and jealous.

Thick looked at him, a look both dull and uncaring. 'I don't want to.' He looked away from the Prince and went back to scratching behind his ear.

Dutiful looked shocked. He took a breath. 'And if, as your prince, I command it?' There was suppressed fury in his voice.

Thick looked at him. Then he swung his gaze to me. His tongue thrust out a bit farther as he pondered something. Then he asked me, 'Both students here?'

I had not expected that from Thick. I hadn't expected him to hold tenaciously to that idea, let alone apply it. It gave me both new hopes and new fears. 'Both students here,' I confirmed for him. He sagged back in his chair and crossed his stubby arms on his chest.

'And I am the teacher,' I continued. 'And students obey the teacher. Thick. Can you stop your music?'

He looked at me for a time. 'Don't want to,' he said, but in a different tone.

'Perhaps not. But I am the teacher and you are the student. The student obeys the teacher.'

'Students obey, like servants?' He stood up to go.

It was hopeless but I tried anyway. 'Students obey like students. So that they can learn. So that everyone can learn. If Thick obeys, then Thick is still a student. If Thick won't obey, then Thick is not a student. Then we send Thick away, to be a servant instead.'

He stood for a time, silent. I could not tell if he was thinking. I could not tell if he had understood what I said at all. Dutiful sat slumped in his chair, chin sunk to his chest and arms crossed, glowering. He plainly hoped that Thick would leave. But after a moment, the little man sat down again. 'Stop the music,' he said. He closed his eyes. Then he opened them again and squinting at me, said, 'There.'

I had not realized how his steady Skilling had been battering my walls. In the stillness that followed, I felt an immense sense of relief. It was like the pause in the storm, when suddenly the winds cease howling and silence flows in. I gave a great sigh of relief and Dutiful suddenly sat up straight. He rubbed at his ears, looking puzzled, then looked at me. 'All of that was him?'

I nodded slowly, still recovering myself.

A great uncertainty dawned over Dutiful's face. 'But I thought . . . I thought that was the Skill itself. The great river you speak about . . .' He looked at Thick again, but his attitude towards the little man had changed. It wasn't respect, but it was wariness, which often precedes respect.

Then, like a sudden curtain of rain, the music swept to life again around my thoughts, separating me from Dutiful like hunters fogged from one another by mist. I glanced at Thick. His face had fallen back into its normal lax lines. The realization came to me that Skilling was to him, the natural state. Not Skilling was what required his effort. And where had he learned that?

Did your mother talk to you, like this?

No.

Then how did you learn to do this?

He frowned. *She sang to me. We sang together. And she made the bad boys not see me.*

Excitement filled me. *Thick. Where is your mother? Do you have brothers or—*

'Stop that! It isn't fair!' The Prince sounded as petulant as a child.

It startled me from my thoughts. 'What isn't fair?'

'You two Skilling to each other where I can't hear. It's rude. It's like whispering behind someone's back.'

I heard the jealousy in his voice as well. Thick, the half-wit, was doing something that the Prince of all the Six Duchies could not. And I was obviously enthused about it. I'd have to go carefully here. I suspected that Skillmaster Galen would have created a rivalry between them, to urge each to try harder. But that was not my goal. Instead, these two must be hammered into a unit.

'I'm sorry. You're right, that was not courteous. Thick just told me that his mother used the Skill to sing to him, and that they sang together. And that sometimes she used it to make bad boys not see him.'

'Then his mother has the Skill? Is she a half-wit, also?'

I saw Thick wince at the words, as I had once cowered from the word 'bastard'. That cut me. I wanted to correct the Prince, sharply, but knew that was hypocrisy. Was not that how I thought of Thick, as 'the half-wit'? For now, I would let it pass, but I would make sure that Thick never again heard that epithet from our lips.

'Thick, where is your mother?'

For a time, he just stared at me. Then, with the inflection of a wounded child, he said slowly, 'She di-ed.' His voice drew out the word. He looked around himself as if he had lost something.

'Can you tell me about it?'

He scowled in thought. 'We come to town with the others. For the crowd time, for the Springfest. Yes.' He nodded at having recalled the right name for it. 'Then, one morning, she didn't wake up. And the others took my stuff and said I didn't travel with them any more.' He scratched the side of his face miserably. 'Then, it was all done, all gone, and I was here. And then . . . I was here.'

It was not a very satisfactory account, but I doubted I would get more from him. It was Dutiful who asked gently, 'What did your mother and the others do when they travelled?'

Thick took a deep breath, as if aggrieved. 'Oh, you know. Find the big crowd. Mother sings and Prokie drums and Jimu dances. And Mother goes "don't see him, don't see him" while I go about and get the purses with my little silver scissors. Only Prokie took them, and my tassel hat and my blanket.'

'You were a cut-purse?' Dutiful asked incredulously.

What a use for the Skill – to hide your son while he cut purses, I thought silently.

Thick nodded, more to himself than to us. 'And if I do good, I get my own penny, to buy a sweet. Every day.'

'Had you any brothers or sisters, Thick?'

He scowled, pondering. 'Mother was old, too old for babies. So I was born stupid. Prokie said so.'

'My, Prokie sounds charming,' the Prince muttered sarcastically. Thick swung a suspicious glare to him.

I clarified it for him. 'The Prince is saying that he thinks Prokie was cruel to you.'

Thick sucked at his upper lip for a moment, then nodded as he warned us, 'Don't call Prokie "Papa". Not ever.'

'Not ever,' Dutiful agreed whole-heartedly. And I think that moment was when Dutiful's feelings towards Thick changed. He cocked his head as he regarded the grimy, misshapen little man. 'Thick. Can you Skill to me? So that only I can hear, not Tom?'

'Why?' Thick demanded.

'To be a student here, Thick,' I intervened. 'To be a student and not a servant.'

For a time, Thick sat silent. The end of his tongue curled over his upper lip. Then the Prince laughed aloud. 'Dogstink? Why do you call him dogstink?'

Thick made a face and then rolled one shoulder as if he didn't know. And in the moment I sensed a secret. It wasn't that he didn't know why. He held something back. Did he fear something?

I feigned a laugh I didn't feel. 'It's okay, Thick. Go ahead and tell him, if you want.'

For a moment, it seemed to confuse him. Had someone told him that I must not be told something? Chade? He had a small frown on his brow as he regarded Dutiful. Then he spoke. I expected him to reveal to the Prince that he knew I had the Wit, and that somehow he had sensed that my Wit-beast had been a wolf. Instead, he said words that made me sick with fear. 'S'what they call him when they ask me about him. The town ones that give me pennies for nuts and sweets. "Stinking dog of a traitor".' He turned to me, smirking and I forced my rictus grin wide. I chuckled.

'They do, do they? Those rascals!' *Smile, Dutiful. Laugh aloud, but do not Skill back to me.* I kept the sending as small and tight as I could. Even so, I saw Thick's gaze flicker from me to the Prince. Dutiful's face was white, but he laughed aloud, a stark 'ha-ha-ha' that sounded more like a man retching than laughter. I took a last chance. 'That would be the one-armed man that says it most, isn't it?'

Thick's smile grew uncertain. I thought I had guessed wrong, but then he said, 'No. Not him. He's new. He hardly talks. But when I tell, and they give me pennies, then he says, sometimes, "Watch that bastard. Watch him well". And I say, I do. I do.'

'Well. And a fine job you do, Thick. A fine job and you earn your pennies well.'

He rocked back and forth in his chair, pleased with himself. 'I watch the gold man, too. He's got a pretty little horse. And a hat, with eye feathers in it.'

'Yes, he does,' I admitted, my mouth dry. 'Like the eye feather you wanted.'

'I can have it, when he's gone,' Thick told me complacently. 'The town ones said so.'

I felt I could not find air to breathe. Thick sat there, nodding and pleased. Chade's dim servant, too dim to know a secret if it bit him, had sold us for pennies. What had he seen, and to whom had he told it? And all because I was too dim to see that he who walks unknowingly among one man's secrets may still carry other secrets of his own. 'Lessons are over for today,' I managed to say. I hoped he would just go, but he sat still, musing.

'I do a fine job. I do. Not my fault the rat died. I didn't want him anyway. He said, "the rat will be your friend", and I said no, I got bit by a rat once, but they said "take him anyway, this rat is nice. Bring him food and bring him back to visit us each week". So I did. Then he died, under the bowl. I think the bowl fell on him.'

'Probably so, Thick. Probably so. But that's not your fault. Not at all.' I wanted to race through the corridors of Buckkeep and find Chade. But the slow, cold truth was rising up around me. Chade hadn't seen this. Chade hadn't known about this. Chade could no longer protect his apprentice. It was time I learned to fend for myself. I lifted a finger as if I had suddenly recalled something. 'Oh, Thick. Today isn't the day you go to see them, is it?'

Thick looked at me as if I were stupid. 'No. Not on the bread-making day. On the washing day. When the sheets hang to dry. Then I go, and I get my pennies.'

'On the washing day. Of course. That's tomorrow. That's good, then. Because I didn't forget about the pink sugar cake. I wanted to give it to you today. Could you wait for me in Chade's room for a while? I might not be fast, but I want to bring it to you.'

'A pink sugar cake.' I watched him search his mind. I don't think he even recalled that I had promised him one. I tried to remember what else he had asked for. A scarf like Rowdy's. A red one. Raisins. My mind raced. It was like one of Chade's old games for me. What else? A knife. And a peacock feather. And pennies for sweets, or the sweets themselves. I'd have to get them all before tomorrow.

'Yes. A pink sugar cake. Not a burned one. I know you like them.' I prayed there would be such a thing in the kitchens.

'Yes!' His little eyes lit with an expression I'd never seen on his face before. Joyful anticipation. 'Yes. I'll wait. You'll bring it soon.'

'Well, not very soon. Not very fast. But today. You will wait for me there, and not go anywhere else?'

He had frowned when I said 'not fast', but he nodded grudgingly.

'That's good, Thick. You're a very good student. You go there now, and wait for me.'

As soon as the mantel door swung shut behind him, Dutiful opened his mouth to speak. I made a hand motion to silence him. I waited until I was sure that even Thick's plodding pace would have carried him far out of hearing. Then I sank down onto a chair.

'Laudwine,' Dutiful said in a shocked whisper.

I nodded. I wasn't ready to speak yet. Laudwine had called me 'bastard'. *A bastard* or *the Bastard*? I wondered.

'What shall we do?'

I lifted my eyes and looked at my prince. His dark eyes were large in his paled face. Chade's walls and spies had failed us. Suddenly I felt that I alone stood between him and the Piebalds. Perhaps I always had. I was selfishly glad that Laurel was gone, out of Laudwine's reach. At least I didn't have to worry about her. 'You must do nothing. Nothing!' I emphasized the word as he opened his mouth to protest it. 'You must not do anything out of the ordinary, anything that would let anyone know that we suspect a plot. Today must be like any other day. But you must stay within the walls of Buckkeep.'

He was silent for a breath. Then, 'I promised Civil Bresinga that I'd go out riding with him. Just he and I. We were going to slip off on our own, to hunt with his cat this afternoon. He came to my room, very late last night, to ask me.' He drew a breath and I watched him look at Civil's invitation in a different light. His voice was lower as he said, 'He seemed agitated. And he looked as if he had been weeping. When I asked him if he were feeling well, he assured me that the problem he had was one of his own making, and nothing a friend could help with. I assumed it had to do with a girl.' I absorbed that information and then asked, 'His cat is here?'

The Prince nodded shamefacedly. 'He pays an old woman for the use of a shed, at the edge of the woods down near the river landing. She feeds the cat, but lets it come and go as it wishes. And Civil visits with her as often as he can.' He took a breath and admitted, 'I've been there with him before. Once. Late at night.'

I bit back everything I wanted to say. It was no time for angry rebukes. Most of my anger was for myself. I'd failed there, too. 'Well. You're not going today. You're developing a boil on your arse. That's why you can't go with him. Tell him why when you excuse yourself from it.'

'I don't want . . . I won't say that. That's embarrassing. I'll say I have a headache. Tom, I don't think Civil is a traitor. I don't think he'd betray me.'

'You will say that, and exactly that, because it is embarrassing. A headache sounds like a ploy. A boil on your arse doesn't.' I took a breath, and hedged around what I suspected. 'Maybe Civil isn't a traitor to you. But it could be that someone else is using him to get you out and away from Buckkeep's walls. Or it could be that someone has threatened him, saying, oh, saying that they'll expose his mother as Witted if he doesn't deliver you. So. Whether or not you trust Civil is not the question. Buy me time. Go make your excuses. And take care to walk gingerly, and avoid anything that you would avoid if you really had a boil.'

He scowled but he nodded. It gave me a small measure of relief. But then he added, 'It's not going to be easy to beg off. He said he needed to ask a special favour of me today.'

'What was it?'

'I'm not sure. Something to do with his cat, I think.'

'All the more reason to avoid being out with him.' I tried to think of all the possible ramifications. Another thought intruded. 'Has Civil brought you any other animals? Has he tried to offer you a Wit-partner?'

'Do you think I'd be stupid enough to trust him if he did?' The Prince was both flustered and angered by my question. 'I'm not an idiot, Tom. No. In fact, Civil has told me that I must not bond with any creature until at least a year has passed. That is the Old Blood custom. There is a set time of mourning. It is to be sure that when the human next takes a partner, it is based on a true attraction between them, not as a replacement for one who has been lost.'

'It sounds to me as if Civil has been telling you a great deal about the Old Blood ways.'

For a moment, Prince Dutiful was silent. Then he said coldly, 'You declined to teach me, Tom. Yet I knew, in my guts, that this was something I had to know. Not just to protect myself, but to master my own magic. I will not be ashamed of my Wit, Tom. Conceal it I must, because of the unjust hatred many bear for it. But I will not be ashamed nor walk away from it.'

There seemed very little I could do or say about that. A traitor thought whispered that the boy was right. How much better would it have been for Nighteyes and me if I had been educated in my magic before I took up with him? Eventually, I replied stiffly, 'I am sure that my prince will do as he thinks best then.'

'Yes. I will,' he agreed. And then, as if he had won some point, he shifted his tactic and asked me suddenly, 'So I will pretend that I know nothing. And what will you do? For I fear you are in as great a danger as I am. No, greater. My name will protect me, to some extent. They would have to prove me Witted before they could move against me. But you, I fear, you could be bludgeoned in an alley in Buckkeep Town and folk might think it just another incident. You have no name to protect you, Tom.'

I nearly smiled. The very fact that my name was unknown was what protected me, and it was that shield I must strive to maintain. 'I have to go seek Chade. Right away. If you wish to do anything to aid me today, you might let the kitchen know that you've a fancy for pink sugar cakes.'

He nodded gravely. 'Is there no other way I can help?'

The offer was sincere, and that moved me. He was my prince, and yet he offered to serve me. I could have refused him. But I think he valued it more when I said, 'Actually, yes, you can. Besides the pink sugar cake, I need a large bunch of nice raisins, a red neck scarf, a good sheath knife and a peacock feather.' As the Prince's eyes grew round at this odd list, I impetuously added, 'A bowl of nuts and some sweets would also be a good idea. If you can bring them here with no one noticing, that would be very helpful. From here, I can take them to Chade's den.'

'They are all for Thick? You will buy his loyalty?' He sounded outraged.

'Yes. They are for Thick. But not to buy him. At least, not exactly. I need to win him to us, Dutiful. We will start with gifts and attentions. I think that the attentions will be more important, eventually, than the gifts. You heard from him what his life has been like. Why should he feel any loyalty to anyone? Let me tell you something from experience, my prince. Anyone, even a king, can begin to buy a man with gifts. And at first it may seem no more than that between them. But eventually, loyalty and even deep regard can spring up. For when we are cared for by someone, or when we care for someone, that is the beginning of the bond.' My mind wandered for an instant, not just to King Shrewd and myself, but to what Hap and I shared, and on to what had grown between Burrich and me, and then Chade and myself. 'So. We begin with the simple gifts that might ease a simple heart.'

'A bath wouldn't hurt him, either. And some whole clothes.' Dutiful spoke thoughtfully, not sarcastically.

'You're right,' I said quietly. I doubt that he knew how I meant my words. Let him be the one who puzzled out how to win Thick's heart. For in the end, the bond I sought to forge must be between these two. I suddenly shared Chade's conviction that the prince must have a coterie. There might come a time when 'Don't see him, don't see him' would keep a rope away from his neck.

We parted to our separate tasks. I hurried through the labyrinth of corridors to emerge in my bedchamber. From thence, I went straight through the Fool's rooms without even pausing to see if he was awake. A few moments later, I was striding up the stairs to the part of the castle where the Queen's most favoured councillor had his chambers. I wished there was a more subtle way for me to contact him, but I had resolved that if anyone stopped me, I would simply lie and say I was delivering a message from Lord Golden.

Despite all that had happened, it was still early morning. Most of the folk moving quietly within Buckkeep were servants, busy with the tasks that would make their masters mornings go more smoothly. Some hauled buckets of wash water, and others carried breakfast trays. A healer carrying a tray of lint and pots of salve hastened past my long-legged stride. The little woman was trotting doggedly, her cheeks red, as if hurry were of the utmost importance. I surmised she might be going to Chade's chambers to treat his burns. When she suddenly halted in front of me, I nearly stumbled over her. I caught my balance by clapping a hand to the wall, and then apologized.

'No need, no need. Just open this door for me, please.'

It wasn't Chade's door. I had long ago made certain that I knew where his chamber was. But my curiosity was piqued, so as I set my hand to the door, I earnestly exclaimed, 'I do hope Lady Modesty is not badly injured. You carry many supplies.'

The healer shook her head irritably. 'This is not Lady Modesty's chamber. Lady Rosemary is the one who needs my services. A fall of soot in her chimney last night ignited right in her face, poor thing. She has burned both her hands, and quite scorched her beautiful hair. Open the door, man.'

I gawked as I did so, and then risked a hasty glance inside before I pulled it shut. Lady Rosemary's cheeks and brow were as red as Chade's had been. She was garbed in a yellow wrapper and sat in a chair near the window as a maid busily snipped the singed ends from her hair. She held her hands on front of her, draped in wet cloths, as if they pained her. Then the door closed, shutting off my glimpse.

I swayed slightly where I stood as I put it together. I'd uncovered one too many secrets this morning. Lady Rosemary was Chade's new apprentice. Well, and why not? Regal had given little Rosemary her basic assassin's training years ago. Why waste a trained spy? Somehow the very practicality of it saddened me. Yet I had heard more than one Farseer say it: the weapon you discard today can be used against you tomorrow. Better to keep Lady Rosemary well in hand than to chance someone else might use her against us.

I walked more slowly as I went on to Chade's room. What I had discovered did not give my present mission any less urgency, yet I felt my mind was crowded with too many thoughts to follow any of them clearly. I knocked and a lad of about ten opened the door to me. I spoke in a loud and jovial tone. 'Good morn, young sirruh! Tom Badgerlock, servant to Lord Golden I am, with a message to deliver to Councillor Chade.'

The boy blinked up at me. He had not been awake for long. 'My master is not well today,' he said at last. 'He will see no one.'

I smiled at him affably. 'Oh, I need not see him, young master. He only needs to hear me for me to pass the message. May I not speak to him?'

'I'm afraid not. I can take the message from you if you wish.'

'Oh, he didn't write it down, young master. He just trusted me to repeat his words.' I boomed out the message, heedless of the quiet of the corridors behind me and the silence of the dim and shuttered chamber. The boy cast a glance towards a closed door behind him. That would be Chade's bedroom then. My heart sank. The old man could well have gone back to bed after his injury. And if he slept behind a closed door, his hearing damped by his mishap, I had small chance of him hearing my voice and coming out.

'And that message would be?' the young page asked me firmly. He smiled pleasantly but stood solidly in the doorway, barring my access. Obviously I was like many a man-at-arms around Buckkeep: not very bright to begin with, and not improved by a few blows to the head over the years.

I cleared my throat, and bobbed a bow in his direction. 'Lord Golden of Jamaillia invites Lord Chade of Buckkeep, chief councillor to Queen Kettricken of the Six Duchies, this morning for breakfast and to share a most amusing game of risk. It is a game he has only recently learned, and believes the Councillor will find it most intriguing. "Laudwine" they call it, in its place of origin. Each player receives a single hand of markers, and his entire fate depends on beating the other players at taking chances before the time runs out. There's been some word of it being played down in Buckkeep Town, though my master has not heard exactly where.'

The little page's jaw was beginning to hang open. He had been well schooled, I am sure, in relaying verbal messages exactly, but not ones of this length. I kept smiling and pitching my voice to carry through the closed doors. 'But the most intriguing part of this game is that it was traditionally played only on Wash-days. Fancy that! Now it can be played on almost any day, but the stakes wagered are always the highest on Wash-day.'

'I'll tell him,' the page interrupted. 'That he is invited to play a game of Laudwine in Lord Golden's chambers. But I fear he will decline. As I have told you, he is not feeling well today.'

'Well, that's not up to you and me, now is it? We're only the ones who have to be sure the messages are passed on. Thank you now and good morning to you.'

I turned and went off down the hall humming to myself. I tried not to look as if I were in a hurry. I went to the kitchens and loaded a very ample meal onto a tray. To keep up the pretence that Lord Golden would be entertaining Councillor Chade in his chambers, I took extra plates and cups as well, and then carried it up to his chamber. I reached the door of the room just in time to intercept Chade's page. The lad had come bringing Chade's apologies that he could not attend, due to a terrible headache. I promised to pass his regrets on to my master. I had scarcely entered the room and latched the door behind me and set the tray down on the table before Chade stepped out of my bedroom. 'What's this about Laudwine?' he demanded.

He looked, if anything, worse. The reddened skin on his brow and cheeks was peeling now, giving him a leprous look. At least he was speaking in closer to normal tones. I tested him, asking, 'Is your hearing coming back?' in a low voice.

He scowled at me. 'It's somewhat better, but I'll still need you to speak up for me to hear you clearly. Enough of that. What is this about Laudwine?'

At that moment, Lord Golden emerged from his chamber, still tying the belt of his morning robe. 'Ah. Good morning, Councillor Chade. This is an unexpected pleasure, but I see that my servant has greeted you and supplied breakfast for both of us. Please, be seated.'

Chade glowered at him, and then transferred the scowl to me. 'Enough! I don't care what your grievances with one another are right now. This is a threat to the Farseer throne, and I won't tolerate any nonsense. Fool, keep quiet. FitzChivalry, report.'

The Fool shrugged and dropped into the chair opposite Chade. Without any ceremony, he began dishing up food for my old mentor. It stung me that he would revert to being his old self for Chade, but not for me. I sat down at table with them. The Fool had left my plate empty. I served myself as I spoke. I reported the morning thoroughly. Chade's expression grew more alarmed as I progressed, but he did not interrupt. To pay the Fool back in kind, I didn't even glance at him as I spoke. When I finished at last, I poured tea for Chade and myself and attacked my food, discovering I was ravenous.

After a long moment of silence, Chade asked me, 'Have you planned an action?'

I shrugged with a casualness I didn't feel. 'It seems obvious. Keep Thick close so he can't give the game away. Keep the Prince safe within doors today and tomorrow. Find out from Thick where he's been going to report. Investigate the place. Go in and kill as many as possible, making sure that Laudwine dies this time.' I kept my voice steady, yet I felt a sudden revulsion for my own words. *So it begins again*, I thought. Not the killing in battle or under attack, but the quietly planned assassinations for the Farseers. Had I said I was not an assassin, would never be one again? I wondered if I had been a liar or an idiot to voice such words.

'Stop showing off for the Fool. He isn't impressed,' Chade responded gruffly.

If he had not hit the mark so neatly, I would not have been so chagrined. Yes. I had been posturing. I didn't even dare glance at the Fool to see how he had reacted to Chade's remark. I shovelled another mouthful of food in so that I did not have to say anything.

Chade's next remark shocked me. 'No killing, Fitz. And you stay away from all of them. I don't like their spying, and I'm ashamed at how neat a ruse they used against me. But we cannot risk killing any Witted ones without compromising our Queen's word. You are aware that Kettricken offered to entertain a delegation from the Old Blood community, to work on solving the issue of unjust persecution?' At my nod, he continued, 'Well, she has received messages in the last two days taking her up on her proposal. I suspect Laurel has a hand in these arrangements. Don't you?'

The old man shot the question and his grim look at me simultaneously. But if he had hoped to surprise a secret out of me, he failed. After a moment's consideration, I nodded. 'It does seem possible. Then they do this . . . this is being arranged without your guidance?' It was the most tactful way I could think of to say it.

Chade nodded, grimmer than ever. 'Not only without my guidance but against my counsel. We scarcely need another diplomatic worry to deal with now. Nonetheless, I suppose we will have one. The Queen seems to be leaving all the details of the meeting's time and place up to the Witted to determine. They have specified that to protect themselves, we must maintain secrecy. There will be no announcement of this convocation until they tell us they are ready. I think they fear what our nobles would do if they knew this was planned. As do I!' He took a breath and recovered his aplomb. 'An exact date has not been set, but they have promised us "soon". It may very well be that Laudwine is an emissary for the Witted ones. To kill him in his lodgings before he can meet with the Queen would be . . . politically unwise.'

'Not to mention rude,' the Fool interjected between bites of bread. He wagged a remonstrating finger at Chade.

'So I'm to do nothing?' I asked coldly.

'Not exactly,' Chade said mildly. 'You were wise to do what you have done. Keep Thick confined. Don't let him report back to them. See what other information you can wangle out of him. And you were correct to tell Dutiful not to be alone with Civil Bresinga. It may have been an innocent invitation, but it might also have been a ploy to give them a hostage. I have still not been able to determine how deeply the Bresingas were involved in the last kidnapping. The reports I get back from Galekeep are odd. For a time, I suspected that Lady Bresinga herself was in danger or some sort of hostage. Her movements were so limited and her life so restrained. Then I became to wonder if it were not merely a financial difficulty. Reports are now that she drinks far more than she used to. She retires early to bed and rises late. So.' He sighed. 'I've made no decision there. And with the Queen's efforts to befriend the Witted faction, I dared not take action against the Bresingas. I still don't know if they are threat or ally.' He fell silent, scowling, and then added, 'It is damnable bad luck that I have done this to my face just when I most need to get out and about and speak to people. Yet I cannot afford to excite comment. Some might make unwarranted connections.'

The Fool rose quietly from the table and went to his bedchamber. When he returned, he had a small pot of cosmetic. He set it on the table near Chade's elbow. When the old assassin glanced curiously at it, he spoke quietly. 'This is most efficacious for the skin peeling. There is a bit of colour in it to lighten the skin, as well. If the colour is too much, let me know. I can change it.' I noticed that he did not ask Chade what had happened to him, nor did Chade volunteer anything. The Fool added cautiously, 'If you wish, I can show you how to apply it. We might be able to restore some of your eyebrows as well.'

'Please,' Chade said after a moment. And so a place was cleared at the corner of the breakfast table, and the Fool brought out his paints and powders and went to work. It was, in a way, fascinating to watch him at his task. Chade appeared uncomfortable at first, but soon became involved in the task, studying himself in a looking-glass as the Fool restored his appearance. When the Fool was finished, Chade nodded, well pleased, and observed, 'Would that I had had paint and artifice of this quality when I was playing Lady Thyme. I would not have had to wear so many veils, nor smell so foul to make folk keep their distance.'

The memories that aroused made me grin. At the same time, I knew a moment's unease. It was unlike Chade to speak so carelessly his secrets, no matter how old they were. Did he assume I had told the Fool all there was to know of us? Or did he trust the man that completely? He raised a hand to pat his cheek, but the Fool made a cautioning gesture. 'Touch your face as little as possible. Take these pots with you, and make an excuse to be alone with a looking-glass after meals. That will be when you will most likely need to make repairs to it. And if you need my aid, simply send me a note inviting me to visit you. I'll come to your chambers.'

'Tell your page you have a question on how the game of Laudwine is played,' I interjected. Without looking at the Fool directly, I explained, 'That was my pretext for visiting Chade's chambers this morning. That you had invited him here for breakfast and to show him a new wagering game.'

'An invitation I declined, due to poor health,' Chade added. The Fool nodded gravely. 'And now, I must go. Carry on as you have been, Fitz. Have Lord Golden pass me a message with the word "horse" in it if you wish me to meet with you. If you can find out from Thick where Laudwine is staying, let me know quickly. I'll send a man round to snuff about.'

'I think I could do that myself,' I said quietly.

'No, Fitz. He knows your face. He may know from Thick that you are mine. Better you stay well away from him.' He lifted his napkin to wipe his mouth. At a warning look from the Fool, he just patted his lips instead. He rose to leave, and then suddenly turned back to me. 'The figurine from the Others' Beach, Fitz. You said the Prince believes it to be the Narcheska? Do you think such a thing is possible?'

I opened my hands and shrugged. 'That beach seemed a very odd place to me. When I think back on all that happened there, my memories seem vague and fogged.'

'That could have been from passing through the Skill-pillars, you said.'

I took a breath. 'Perhaps. And yet, I think there is more to it. Perhaps the Others or some other being maintain a bewitchment on that place. When I look back, Chade, my decisions make no sense to me. Why didn't I attempt to follow the path towards the forest? I remember looking at it and thinking that someone must have made it. Yet I had no inclination to even go look at it. No, it was even stronger than that. The woods seemed threatening to me, as no forest has ever seemed unwelcoming before.' I shook my head. 'I think that place has its own magic, neither Wit nor Skill. And it is one I would not willingly experience again. The Skill seemed exceptionally enticing there as well. And . . .' I let the thought trail away. I was still not ready to speak of whatever-it-was that had plucked both Dutiful and myself from the Skill current and reassembled us. The experience was both too large and too personal.

'A magic that could present the Prince with a figurine of his bride-to-be, not as she is but as she will be?'

I shrugged. 'Once Dutiful said it, it did seem right to me. I know I've seen the Narcheska wear a blue ornament like the one the figurine has. But I've never seen her dressed that way, nor has she breasts yet.'

'I seem to recall reading that there is some Outislander ceremony in which a girl presents herself thus to demand recognition of her womanhood.'

It sounded barbaric to me. I said so, and then added, 'There is a resemblance to the Narcheska, but perhaps it is merely the resemblance that all Outislander women have to one another. I don't think we should give it great consideration right now.'

Chade sighed. 'There is too much of the Outislanders that we do not know. Well. I must hasten away. I have much to report to the

Queen, and a number of questions that I must ask of other folk. Fitz, as soon as you know anything definite from Thick, get back to me. Send me a message from the Fool with the word "lavender" in it.'

My heart jolted in my chest. 'I thought you said the word to use was "horse".' I said.

Chade paused at the door of my room. I knew I had rattled him, yet he tried to cover it. 'Did I? But that seems too common a word, you know. Lavender suits me better. You're far less likely to write that to me by accident. Farewell.'

And he was gone, shutting my bedroom door behind him. I turned back to see if the Fool was as dismayed as I was by the old man's lapse, but he was gone. He had ghosted out of the room, taking his paints and powders with him. I sighed to myself and went about the tasks of gathering up the breakfast things. The brief interlude with him in the morning made me more aware than ever of how much I missed him. It cut me deeply that he would be himself to humour Chade, but not me.

If, I reminded myself sourly, the Fool was indeed who he truly was.

EIGHTEEN

Pink Sugar Cake

Have the student lie on his back. He should not be on a comfortable bed nor on a bare surface. Either is a distraction. A blanket folded on the floor suffices. Have the student remove or loosen any clothing that binds. Some students will perform the exercise best if naked and undistracted by clothing touching them. Others will be too distracted by the vulnerability of their nakedness. Let each student decide what is best for him, without comment.

Emphasize that the only movement of the body should be steady breathing. The eyes should be closed. Then, without moving any part of his body, ask the student to be aware of his body. He may need to be guided in this at first. Tell him to seek awareness of his middle toes without touching or moving them. Then have him think of his knees, but not flexing them. Proceed with the skin of his breast, of his forehead, the backs of his hands and continue as long as is necessary to name the boundaries of his flesh, until the student has been invited to truly consider the physical confines of the body he lives within. Thus prepared, ask him then to find the edges of his thoughts. Do they stop at the flesh of his brow? Can he feel them encased in his skull or trapped in his chest?

All but the dullest students will swiftly realize that the body does not confine thoughts. They extend outside our flesh, even as our vision, hearing, touch, smelling and even taste are senses that link us to the outside world while remaining functions of the physical body. So our thoughts reach out, unbound by distance or even time. Ask the student, 'Cannot you smell the wine that is opened across the room? Hear the shouts of sailors at work across the water? Then do not refuse to believe you can hear the thoughts of the man in the field that waft toward you.'

Treeknee's translation of *Preparing the Students*

I went first to Verity's tower to see what luck the Prince had had in filling Thick's list. I was surprised to find that not only had Dutiful obtained every item, but that he himself was waiting for me.

'Won't your friends remark on your absence?' I asked as I surveyed the trove on the table.

He shook his head. 'I made excuses. Sometimes my reputation for being slightly odd serves me well. No one questions that I have sudden needs for solitude.'

I nodded to myself as I sorted the items. I folded the red scarf and set it aside. 'I've seen you wearing this. If I remark it, then others will also. If Thick were seen wearing it, people would assume that he had stolen it. Or that he had some special connection to you. Either would be bad for us. The same goes for this knife. I appreciate your willingness to part with it, but such a well-crafted blade would only raise questions for him.' I set the knife on the folded scarf.

The little pink frosted cake was still slightly warm from the oven. A rich waft of almond rose from it. The peacock feather was long and nodded gracefully when I picked it up. There was an earthenware bowl full of plump raisins. Shelled nutmeats dipped in syrup and set aside to harden glistened among the raisins. 'This is wonderful. Thank you.'

'Thank you, Tom Badgerlock.' Dutiful took a deeper breath and then asked, 'Do you think Laudwine has come to kill you?'

'I think that is possible. But Chade seems to think he might be part of a Witted delegation sent to treat with the Queen. So I've been ordered to keep my hands off until I'm given further directions.'

'So you'll do nothing for now.'

'Oh, I'll do a lot of things,' I muttered. 'I just won't go out and immediately kill Laudwine.'

The Prince laughed aloud, and I suddenly realized how carelessly I had spoken before him. I was fortunate that he had assumed that I was joking. I forced a smile to my face. 'I'll take these things up to Thick and see what else he has to tell me. And you must remember to go about your day as normally as possible.'

He did not look pleased at that, but he conceded the necessity of it. I departed by way of the mantel door. As I climbed the uneven stairs and negotiated the narrow passages, I tried to think through for myself the significance of Laudwine's presence in Buckkeep Town. Kettricken had called for the Witted to negotiate with her. As the head of the Piebald faction, it made sense that he would come forward to present their views. But as a man that had all but kidnapped the Prince, hoping to take over his life, I was amazed that he dared to stand before Kettricken. She might not hang him for being Witted, but he certainly deserved to die for how he had plotted against the Farseers. And yet, there was the rub. She could level no charges against him without revealing that her son was Witted. All the events around Dutiful's disappearance had been hushed up or explained away. The nobles of his court believed he had simply gone away from them for a time to meditate. I wondered if Laudwine intended to use all those circumstances as a club against the Farseers. I sighed, and hoped there would be other, more moderate Old Blood folk who would also step forward. Laudwine, I felt, represented the worst and most extreme of our kind. His sort had made us hated and feared. If he stepped forward alone, claiming to represent all the Witted, that reputation would live on.

I pushed such thoughts aside as I reached Chade's chamber. I entered to find Thick sitting disconsolately on the hearthstones before the dwindling fire. He stared into the flames, his tongue protruding from his mouth. 'Did you think I'd forgotten?' I asked him as I came in.

He turned to me and as his eyes lifted and he beheld the items I carried, a terrible wave of gratitude rushed out from him and enveloped me. He stood up, literally trembling with excitement. 'Let's put these things on the table,' I suggested. He seemed struck dumb. He wiggled like an eager puppy as I pushed scrolls and inkpots carefully out of my way and set down the items one by one. 'Prince Dutiful helped me get these things for you,' I told him. 'See, here is the pink sugar cake. It's still warm from the oven. Here is a bowl of raisins for you, and candied nuts. He thought you might like to try the nuts. And the peacock feather, the feather with the eye in it. All for you.'

He didn't try to touch any of it. He stood, staring, his hands clasping one another on top of his rounded belly. His mouth worked as he thought through what I had said. 'Prince Dutiful?' he said at last.

I pulled out a chair for him. 'Sit down, Thick. Your prince sends you these things for you to enjoy.'

He sank slowly into the chair. His hands crept onto the table, and finally one finger dared to touch the edge of the feather. 'My prince. Prince Dutiful.'

'That's right,' I said.

I had expected him immediately to stuff his mouth with cake and raisins. Instead, he sat for a time with his one stubby finger just touching the shaft of the feather. Then he picked up the pink sugar cake and turned it over, looking at it from every angle. He set it carefully back on the table. Then he drew the bowl of raisins toward him. He took one raisin, looked at it, sniffed it, and then put it in his mouth. He chewed it very slowly, and swallowed it before he took another. I could feel the focus he put into this activity. It was as if he Skilled each raisin, comprehending completely what it was before he ate it.

I had plenty of time. Even so, the task of hauling water to the Fool's chambers and then up into Chade's room was laborious. Before I was done, the scar on my back ached abominably, and I well understood Thick's distaste for the task. I poured the last bucket into the copper and set it to heat while I set up the washtub. Thick paid no attention to me. He was still consuming the raisins one at a time. The pink sugar cake sat on the table in front of him, untouched. His concentration was absolute. As I idly watched him eat, I realized that his teeth gave him problems. Chewing seemed difficult: as he ate the nuts, it became even more evident. I left him alone as he worked his slow way through them. When he had finished, I thought he would finally eat the sugar cake. Instead, he set it in front of himself and admired it. After some time had passed and the hot water began to steam, I asked him gently, 'Aren't you going to eat your cake, Thick?'

He frowned thoughtfully. 'Eat it, and it's gone. Like the raisins.'

I nodded slowly. 'But you could get another one, perhaps. From the Prince.'

His gaze had reverted to a suspicious glare. 'From the Prince?'

'Of course. If you do good things that help your prince, he will probably give you good things in return.' I let him ponder that for a time, and then asked, 'Thick, do you have any other clothes?'

'Other clothes?'

'Different clothes from what you are wearing. Extra shirt and trousers.'

He shook his head. 'Just these.'

Even I had never been so poorly provided for. I hoped it wasn't true. 'What do you wear when those clothes are being washed?' I poured hot water into the tub.

'Washed?'

I gave it up. I really didn't want to know any more. 'Thick, I brought you water and heated it for a bath.' I went to a shelf and took down Chade's sewing supplies. At least I could stitch up some of the worst rents.

'A bath? Like, wash in the river?'

'Sort of. But with hot water. And soap.'

He thought about it for a moment. Then, 'I don't do that.' He went back to his contemplation of the sugar cake.

'You might like to try it. It feels nice to be clean.' I splashed my hand invitingly in the tub.

For a time he sat still, staring at me. Then he pushed back his chair and came over to the tub. He looked into the water. I splashed my hand in it again. Slowly he knelt down next to the tub. Holding tightly to the edge of the tub with one hand, he splashed with the other. He gave a grunt of amusement, and then said, 'It's warm.'

'It's nice to sit in it and be warm all over. And to smell nice afterwards.'

He made a sound, neither agreement nor denial. He thrust his hand deeper into the water. It soaked the ragged cuff of his shirt.

I stood up and walked away, leaving him alone by the water. It took him quite a while to investigate the water completely. When his sleeves were both soaking wet, I suggested that he should take his shirt off. The water had cooled substantially before he decided he would risk taking off his shoes and trousers and getting into the tub. He had no smallclothes. He was very suspicious when I tried to add more hot water, but after thinking it over, he allowed it. He played with the soap and washing cloth. As the warm water reached him, he gradually relaxed. Persuading him not only to wash his face, but also to rub soap in his hair and then rinse it out was not an easy task.

In scraps of conversation, I learned he had not washed at all since Springfest. No one told him to after his mother died. It made me realize how recent his bereavement was. When I asked him how he had come to work in the castle, he could not really tell me. I suspected he had wandered in one day, and with the general influx of people for Springfest and the betrothal ceremony, the folk of the keep had simply assumed he had belonged to someone. I would have to ask Chade how he had come to be his personal servant, I decided.

As Thick experimented with the water and soap, I hastily stitched up what I could of his clothing. Where seams had given out, the work was fairly easy despite the grime crusted onto the fabric. He had simply worn through his clothes at the knees and elbows, and with nothing to use for a patch, I had to leave them as they were.

When his fingers began to wrinkle, I found him a towel and told him to stand before the fire. I tossed his clothes into the silty water and gave them a quick scrubbing. When I wrung them out and hung them on the chair backs, they were not clean, but they were better than they had been.

Persuading him to sit down and let me work the knots out of his hair was just as difficult as coaxing him into the bath had been. He was suspicious of the comb, even when I let him hold the looking glass and watch what I was doing. I had not had such a demanding task since I had first taken Hap in and emphasized that nits and lice were not an ordinary part of one's hair.

Scrubbed and dried, his hair combed, Thick sat lethargically before the fire wrapped in one of Chade's quilts. I think the warm bath had worn him out. I turned one of his cracked shoes in my hand. This was something I knew how to do from Burrich's tutelage. 'I can make you some new shoes as soon as I go to town and buy some leather,' I told him. He nodded sleepily, no longer shocked by this largesse. I moved his clothing closer to the hearth to dry. 'I don't know what we're going to do about clothes for you right now. My sewing skills are limited to repair rather than construction. But we'll think of something.' He nodded again. I thought for a time, then went to Chade's old wardrobe in the corner of the chamber. A number of his old wool workrobes were still in it. One was scorched, and almost all the others had blotches and stains of various kinds on them. I doubted that he had worn any of them in recent years. Even so, they were cleaner and in better repair than Thick's rags. I took one out, held it up to gauge the length of it, marked it, and then ruthlessly sheared it off short. 'This will give you something to wear until we can get more clothes made for you.' He barely nodded as he stared, half-dozing, into the fire. As he relaxed, the music of his spilling Skill became more expansive. I started to firm my walls against it. Then, instead of that, I opened myself to it.

I settled myself, robe, needle and thread in the other chair. Thick looked almost asleep. I threaded the needle and began a new hem for the robe as I asked him, very quietly, 'So. They call me a stinking dog, do they?'

'Erhm.' The music changed slightly. Sharper notes. The ringing of a smith's hammer on hot iron. The slamming of a door. Somewhere a goat bleated and another answered it. I let his music into my mind, and let it carry my thoughts with it as I watched my needle dive into and then surface from the fabric of the robe.

'Thick. Do you remember the first time you met them? The ones who call me "stinking dog"?' *Please, show me.* I let the Skill-request float with my quiet words and the rhythmic motion of my needle. I listened to the quiet rip of the thread as it moved through the fabric, and the soft crackling of the fire, making those small sounds one with my request.

For a time Thick was silent save for the Skill-music that flowed from him. Then, I heard the sounds of my needle and the fire creep into his music.

'*He said, "Put down that bucket and come with me".*'

'Who said?' I asked too avidly.

Thick's music stopped. He spoke aloud. 'I'm not to talk about him. Or he'll kill me. Kill me dead with a big knife. Cut open my belly and my guts fall in the dust.' In his mind he stood and watched his own entrails unwind into the grit of a Buckkeep Town street. 'Like pig guts.'

'I won't let that happen to you,' I promised.

He shook his head stubbornly. He began to take short breaths through his nose. 'He said, "No one could stop me. I'd kill you." If I tell about him, he'll kill me. If I don't watch the gold man and the old man and you, he'll kill me. If I don't peep at the door and listen and tell him, he'll kill me. All my guts in the dust.'

And in our joining, I knew that Thick believed this down to his bones. I'd have to leave it alone for now. 'Very well,' I said mildly. I leaned back in my chair and once more focused my mind on my work. 'Don't think about him,' I suggested. 'Only the others. The ones you went to meet.'

He nodded his heavy head ponderously as he stared into the flames. After a time, his music seeped back. I set my breathing to its rhythm, and then my work as well. Gradually, I eased my mind closer and then let it brush Thick's.

I scarcely dared to breathe. I pushed my needle in and out of the fabric, and drew the long thread rippling after it. Thick was breathing slowly through his nose as he stared into the fire. I asked no questions but let his Skill flow through me. He hadn't liked that first meeting, not at all, nor the long trot from the castle down to the town, nor the way his companion kept a grip on his sleeve all that long and weary distance. He was taller than Thick, the one who clutched him as they walked and it made Thick walk crooked and too fast. His legs ached and his mouth was dry. In his memory, the man who gripped his sleeve shook him until Thick answered each question that the people in the room asked him.

Thick's memories were not vague. If anything, they were too detailed. He recalled as much of the blister on his heel as he did of the man's words. The sounds of a goat bleating somewhere and the creaking of wagons lumbering down the street were weighted as heavily as voice of his interrogator. Thick was repeatedly shaken to rattle loose an answer, and he well recalled both his fear and his confusion at why he was treated so.

Thick's answers to the questions were vague as much due to his lack of knowledge as to his odd sense of priorities. He told them about his work in the kitchen. They asked him which nobles he served. Thick wasn't sure of their names. They were impatient and muttering at first, and one cursed the man who had brought him for wasting their time. Then Thick complained of his extra work, up all the stairs, for the tall old man with the spotted face. 'Chade, Lord Chade, the Queen's councillor' someone hissed. And they all drew closer to him.

Thus they had learned that Chade wanted the firewood stacked with little logs to one side and bigger pieces on the other side, and that Thick had to wipe up any water he spilled on the stairs. *Never touch Chade's scrolls. Don't spill the ashes on the floor. Don't open the little door if anyone else can see you.* Only the last fact seemed to interest them, but when their other questions yielded them little, Thick recognized the displeasure in their voices. He had cringed from it, but the man who had brought him insisted that this was only the first time, that the dummy could be taught what to watch for. Then someone had given him other targets to watch: 'A *fancy Jamaillian noble, with yellow hair and tanned skin. He rides a white horse. And he keeps a stinking dog of a servant, with a crooked nose and a scar down his face.*'

Thick had not known Lord Golden nor me. But the man who gripped Thick's sleeve had recognized us from that description, and promised to point me out to Thick. That was when they had put gold into the man's outstretched hand, thick gold that clinked. And a man had given coins to Thick, also, three little silver coins that tinkled as he dropped them on Thick's flat palm. And he had warned both Thick and the faceless servant who gripped him that they should be wary of '*that stinking, traitorous dog. He'll kill you as soon as look at you if he thinks you're watching him*'.

I felt the man's black eyes boring into mine. Floating in the Skill amongst Thick's memories, I tried to see his face, but all Thick recalled were those piercing eyes. '*That stinking dog cut the arm right off a man, last time I saw him. Chop! Like a sausage on the table. And he'll do worse to you if he finds out you're watching him. So you be careful, dummy. Don't let him see you.*' Those words and the bleating goat and the rumbling of the wagons mixed in

Thick's mind with the blustery winter wind from the street outside. Blacksmith hammers rang somewhere, setting a clanging cadence.

And as they walked back up to Buckkeep, the other servant had warned Thick again to be careful not to get caught by *'that stinking dog he warned you about. You're to watch him, but not let him see you. You hear me, boy? Give us away, and you won't only be dead, I'll be out of a job. So you be careful. Don't let him see you. Hear me? Hear me?'*

And as Thick had cowered from him, muttering that he heard, the servant had demanded the coins that he had been given. *'You don't even know what to do with them, dummy. Give them to me.'*

'They're mine. To buy a sweet, he said. A sugar cake.'

But the other servant had struck Thick and taken his coins.

I floated in the flow of Thick's Skill, experiencing it again with him. As the servant slapped him, an open-handed blow that left his ear ringing, the Skill-wave leapt and nearly overwhelmed me. Useless to try to see the servant. Thick avoided looking at him, cowering away, squinting his eyes shut before the descending fist.

Look at him, Thick. Please, let me see him, I begged. But Thick's recalled agitation as much as my surge of hatred for the man blasted us both out of the Skill-reverie we had been sharing. Thick gave a wordless cry and recoiled from the remembered blow, falling from the chair to roll perilously close the fire. I leapt to my feet, head spinning from the sudden break in our contact. When I seized his blanket-wrapped body to pull him away from the hearth, he must have thought I was attacking him, for he abruptly struck back.

No, Dog-stink man, no! Don't see me, don't hurt me, don't see me, don't see me!

I went down as if axed. I had been so open to him that for a time I saw absolutely nothing, and I swear that I thought I smelled the clinging scent of a mangy hound.

In a little while, my vision came back to me. Getting my Skill-walls up took every bit of my concentration. A bit more time, and I got to my hands and knees. I ran my hands through my hair, expecting blood, for the pain was so great. Then I shakily sat up and looked around the room. Thick was fighting with his wet pants, making frantic grunts of fear and frustration as he struggled

443

to put them on. I took a deep breath and croaked, 'Thick. It's all right. No one is going to hurt you.'

He paid me no mind but kept struggling. I dragged myself up by the chair. I picked up the robe I had been working on. 'Wait a moment, Thick. I'll have this finished for you. It's dry and warm.' I sat down carefully. Well. Now I knew. I knew why I was the dog-stink man, to be hated and feared, and I knew why he had commanded me not to see him. Even the story of someone hitting him and taking his coins made more sense now. Thick had never tried to hide his secrets from us. We had simply been too foolish to notice them in front of us. Focusing my eyes on the needle was difficult, but I did it. Another dozen looping stitches and I was finished. I knotted the thread, bit it off and held up the robe. 'Put this on for now. Until your own clothes dry.'

He dropped his wet trousers to the floor but came no closer. 'You're angry with me. You'll hit me. Maybe chop my arm off.'

'No, Thick. You hurt me, but you were scared. I'm not angry with you and I won't ever chop your arm off. I don't want to hit you.'

'The one-arm man said . . .'

'The one-arm man lies. So do his friends. A lot. Think about it. Do I smell like dog poop?'

A grudging moment of silence. Then, 'No.'

'Do I hit you or chop your arms off? Here, come take this robe. You look cold.'

He approached me cautiously. 'No.' He looked at the robe suspiciously. 'Why are you giving me this?'

'Because it's like a pink cake or raisins or a feather. Your prince wants you to have better clothes. This will keep you warm until your old clothes dry. And soon, the Prince will have new clothes made for Thick.'

Walls up, I took a cautious step towards him. I held the neck-hole of the robe open, looked at him through it, then slipped it over his head. It was still too long. It fell to the floor around him, and even after he had found the sleeves, the cuffs hung past his hands. I helped him fold them back. I used a piece from the cut-off length of robe to make a makeshift tie for the robe. With the robe belted up, he could walk without tripping. He hugged it against himself. 'It's soft.'

'Well. Softer than your old clothes, perhaps. Mainly because it's cleaner.' I walked back to my chair and sank down in it. The headache was already abating. Perhaps Chade had been right about Skill-pain. My body was still smarting from my fall to the floor; it had wakened the bruises and lumps that Svanja's father had dealt me. I sighed heavily. 'Thick. How many times have you been to see them?'

He stood, tongue out, considering. Then, 'Washing days.'

'I know. You go on washing days. But how often? How many times?'

His tongue curled up over his upper lip while he thought. Then he nodded and said emphatically, 'Every washing day.'

That was as good as I was going to get. 'Do you go alone to see him?'

That brought a scowl to his face. 'No. I could, but he don't let me.'

'Because he wants the coins they give him. And the coins they give you.'

His scowl darkened. 'Hit Thick, take the coins. Then one-arm got mad. I told him. Now he takes the coins, but gives me back some pennies. For sweets.'

'Who does?'

He stood for a while. 'I'm not to talk about him.' I caught an echo of his dread as his Skill-music surged, full of goat-bleats and jangling harness. He scratched his head, then pulled his hair around to where he could see it. 'Are you going to cut my hair? My mother used to cut my hair, sometimes, after I washed.'

'Actually, yes, that's a good idea. Let's cut your hair.' I stood creakily. I must have hit my knee when I went down. It hurt. I was frustrated, but trying to force information from Thick would only bury it under his fear. 'Sit at the table, Thick, while I find the scissors. Is there anything you can tell me about them? Can you tell me about the one-arm man? Where does he live?'

Thick didn't answer. He went back to the table and sat down. Almost immediately, he picked up the pink cake and examined it closely. As he turned it in his hands, he seemed to forget all else. I brought the shears to the table. 'Thick. What does the one-arm man talk to you about?'

Thick didn't look at me; he spoke to the cake. 'Not supposed to talk about him. To anyone. Or they'll kill me, and my guts will fall in the dirt.' With both hands he patted his round belly, as if comforting himself that it was still whole.

I found the comb and smoothed his hair flat again. It calmed him and he went back to his contemplation of the cake. 'I'll cut your hair to chin-length. That way it will still keep your ears and the back of your neck warm.'

'Yes,' he agreed softly, lost in pink sugar musing.

Cutting Thick's hair again put me in mind of Hap. I suddenly and acutely missed him being a little boy. When Hap had been ten, it had been so much easier to know that I was doing the right things for him. Feed him well, teach him to fish, see that he had clean clothes and slept well at night. That was most of what a boy needed. A young man was a different animal entirely. Perhaps I could get away to check on him this evening. The silver blades snicked and uneven hanks of Thick's hair fell to the floor around the chair. I thought of another approach. 'I know you can't tell me about the one-arm man. I know you are not to talk about that. So we won't. I won't even ask him what he asks you. But you can tell me what you told him, can't you? They never said not to say that, did they?'

'No-o,' he said in slow consideration. He sighed deeply, relaxing under my touch. Then, 'The one-armed man,' he said softly, and an image of Laudwine rippled into my mind with his music. He was gaunter than I recalled him, but the loss of a limb and the fever that follows will do that to a man. He was looking down at me, and for a moment it disoriented me, and then I accepted Thick's viewpoint of the towering man. Even so, the image was vague. Thick recalled more sound than sight; what he saw in his mind's eyes was far more indistinct than what he heard. I listened to Laudwine's voice rippling through Thick's memory and cowered with him at the disapproval. '*This is your source of information? What were you thinking, Padget? Is this how you take charge of my* most important concerns? He won't do at all. He doesn't have the sense to remember his own name, let alone anything else.'

'He'll be fine for you,' someone said. I suspected it was the one called Padget. 'He's told us a lot already, haven't you, dummy? The old man's taken a liking to him. Hasn't he, Thick? Don't you work for Lord Chade himself now? Tell him about Lord Chade and his special room.' And then, obviously speaking to Laudwine and not Thick, 'This was sheer good fortune. When the stable-boy first dragged him down here, I thought as you do, that he'd be useless. But up at the keep, they let this moron wander wherever he wishes. He knows things, Laudwine. You just have to know how to drag them out of him.' I could not see Padget through Thick's eyes, but I felt him. A large man, wide rather than tall, threatening, who could make pain with his hands without hitting.

Then another voice spoke, a woman's voice. 'He's worked well for us, horseman. Don't try to change . . . what is your saying? To change horses in the middle of the stream? Yes. If you wish what we have to offer, then do not disrupt what is working well for us.'

I'd heard her voice before, I thought. I pummelled my memories, trying to place it, but could only decide that she was someone from inside the keep. I kept the thought tiny and to myself, fearful of breaking the unwinding thread of Thick's memories. He had been confused and frightened that day, overshadowed by the arrival of the tall man with one arm, and intimidated by the way they all spoke over and past him. Yet never once did the man who gripped his arm let him go.

Laudwine's voice was the hammering of a smith's blows. 'I don't care what is working well for you, woman, nor do I care for your offer. My vengeance belongs to me, and I won't sell it to you for your foreign gold. I care nothing about this Chade. I want Lord Golden's head, yes, and the bloody arm of that dog that works for him. Or have you forgotten that, Padget, in your quest to sell the Piebalds out? That Lord Golden owes me a life, and his traitorous servant an arm?'

'I haven't forgotten, Laudwine. I was with you, man!' Padget's voice was the low rumble of a rolling wagon-wheel, grinding out anger and rebuke. 'Do you forget it was me who rode double with you that day, to keep you from falling from your saddle? When she made her offer, I only thought, well, what do we care how they die? Let her have them, and let us use her gold for our cause, to bring the Farseer's false throne down.' Now his voice rose with self-righteousness, but it merged with the distant bleat of a goat in Thick's mind.

'*Shut up!*' Laudwine's voice was hot and heavy, ringing like hammers on red iron. '*I care how they die! Their deaths belong to me! And my blood vengeance is not for sale. "Our" cause will wait until my cause has been satisfied. I told you what I wanted, Padget. I want to know when they rise and where they eat, when they ride and where they sleep. I want to know when and where I can kill them. That's what I want to know. Can your half-wit give us that?*' Each word fell like a sledge blow, and they shaped Padget's anger.

'*Yes. He can. And he's already given us a lot more than that, if you'd only listen to me. This Lord Chade and what the dummy knows of him, that is important knowledge. But if all you want is revenge, with no thought of what more we can have, well you can have that. If you ask him right. Tell him, dummy. Tell him about the stinking traitor dog who chopped his arm off, and what the old man calls him. Then maybe he'll realize I've done better for the Piebalds while he was healing then he ever did for them when he had two hands.*'

And then Thick recalled the sound of a hand striking meaty flesh, and Laudwine's voice following it, a trifle out of breath at the effort. '*Remember your place, Padget. Or lose it.*'

Thick made a sharp movement, rocking forward, his hands clasped over his head. He made small animal sounds to himself as he rocked briefly, agitated at recalling the witnessed violence. 'Na, na, na,' he begged, and for a time I let him be. I held scissors and comb aloft from him and waited for him to calm himself. There was cruelty in what I did, forcing the stubby little man to relive his fear. I had no taste for it, and yet do it I must. So I waited until he quieted and as subtly as I knew, used the Skill to soothe him and take him back again to that room. 'It's all right to think about it,' I suggested. 'You're safe now, here. They can't find you here or hurt you here. You're safe.' Through our Skill-link, I felt him scowl. He resisted. I pushed gently, and suddenly his memories flowed again.

Thick took a long breath and sighed it out. I resumed my

grooming of him. I think the stroking of the comb and the tickling of the falling hair had half-stupefied him. I doubted that anyone touched him much, and seldom with gentleness. His muscles were loosening like a stroked puppy. He made an affirmative noise.

'So. After all that. What did you tell him about?' I kept my voice very soft.

'Oh, nothing. Only about the old man. How to stack his wood. Not to shake the wine bottles when I bring them to him. To take away the dirty dishes and old food every morning. Not to move his papers, even though he lets you move his papers. That he says I have to do what you say, even though I don't want to come to you. About you want to talk to me. And they said, "don't go! Say you forgot!" About how you talk at night sometimes.'

'Who talks? Chade and I?' I drew the comb slowly through his hair and trimmed the hair below it. The damp black points fell to the floor as my heart rose hammering in my throat at his next words.

'Yeah. That you talk about Skill and Old Blood. That he calls you a different name. Fizshovly. That you don't like me to know about the girl who cries.'

The sharp fear from his mangled naming of me was swallowed in his mention of 'the girl'. 'What girl?' I asked dully, longing for him to say only, 'that girl' or 'I don't know.' My guts were water inside me.

'She cries and cries,' Thick said softly.

'Who does?' I asked again with a sinking heart.

'That girl. That Nettle that whimpers at night and won't stop.' He cocked his head, making my scissors take too deep a cut. 'She cries right now.'

That stretched the bowstring of my fear tighter. 'Does she?' I asked. Gingerly, I lowered my walls. I opened myself to Nettle, but felt nothing. 'No. She's quiet now,' I observed.

'She cries to herself. In a different place.'

'I don't know what you mean.'

'In the empty place.'

'I don't know what you mean,' I repeated with a growing sense of alarm.

He frowned intently for a moment, then suddenly his face eased. 'Never mind. She stopped.'

'Just like that?' I asked incredulously. I set my scissors and comb down.

'Yeah.' His finger casually investigated his nose. 'I'm going now,' he announced suddenly. He stood up and glanced around the room. 'Don't eat my cake!' he warned me abruptly.

'I won't. Are you sure you won't stay and eat it?' A kind of shock had left me immune to all feeling. Had Laudwine untangled my true name from Thick's maiming of it? He definitely knew my daughter's name. Danger yawned below us, and I spoke to a half-wit about sugar cakes.

'If I eat it, then it would be gone.'

'There might be another.'

'There might not,' he pointed out with incontrovertible logic.

'I've an idea.' I went to one of Chade's less cluttered shelves and began to move things. 'We'll make a spot for you, here. And we'll put Thick's things on this shelf. So they'll always be where you can find them.'

For some reason, this seemed a difficult idea for him to master. I explained it several ways, and then had him put both the sugar cake and the feather on the shelf. Hesitantly, he picked up the bowl that had held the raisins and nuts. Only a handful of the sugared nuts remained. 'You can put that there, too,' I told him. 'And I will try to put more nice things to eat in it.' So he did, and then stood and admired it for a time.

'Going to go now,' he abruptly announced again.

'Thick,' I began carefully. 'Tomorrow, on washing day. Will a man come to take you to One-arm?'

'Don't talk about him.' He was adamant. Adamant and scared. I could hear the roiling of his Skill-music.

'Do you want to go, Thick? To see the one-arm man?'

'I have to go.'

'No, you don't. Not any more. Do you want to go?'

This seemed to require a lot of thought. Then, 'I want the pennies. To buy the sweet.'

'If you told me where One-arm is, I could go for you. And get the pennies for you, and bring you the sweet.'

He scowled and shook his head. 'I get my pennies for myself.

I like to buy it myself.' He was suspicious again, edging away from me.

I took a breath and counselled myself to patience. 'I'll see you tomorrow, for our lessons, then.'

He nodded sombrely and left Chade's chambers. I went over and picked up his wet trousers from the floor. I hung them on the chair back again. I doubted that anyone would wonder about the robe Thick now wore. It was a style long out-dated for Buckkeep Castle, and servants, especially the lowest level of servants, were often dressed in their master's cast-offs. I sighed and sat down in the chair and stared into the fire. What was I going to do?

I wished I could make Thick tell me where Laudwine was, or at least who took him to the Piebald leader. I couldn't force the information out of him without frightening him and shattering the fragile trust we'd built today. I could shadow Thick into Buckkeep Town tomorrow, but I was reluctant to do so; I'd be putting the little man into danger if Laudwine or anyone else recognized me following him. If I followed him and he met with Laudwine, what would I do then? Charge in, betraying myself to Laudwine or allow Laudwine to question the little man again, and gain still more knowledge of us? I considered watching Thick until the Buckkeep man came to take him down to town, then capture the go-between. I suspected I could wring Laudwine's location out of him, but when he didn't keep the rendezvous, Laudwine would be alerted. I didn't want to do anything that might startle that bird into flying before my nets were ready. My last available tactic seemed the simplest: find a ploy to keep Thick from going down to Buckkeep tomorrow. Distract him with toys, or simply busy him where no one could take him away without being noticed. Yet that would not put me one step closer to having a line on Laudwine. And I desperately wanted to have that man in my power.

I ached to kill him. No enemy, I knew, is more to be feared than the one you have grievously injured. And I had taken not just Laudwine's arm, but his sister's stunted life, and ended their vain grasp for power. Perhaps at one time he had dreamed of building power for his Piebald group; now I suspected he was driven more by hatred of me and a lust for revenge on the Farseers. Would any revenge he could take against me be too cruel to consider? I doubted it.

I crossed my arms on my chest and leaned back, scowling at the fire. Perhaps I had it all wrong. Perhaps Laudwine had come to town only to be an emissary from the Witted to Kettricken. Perhaps his spying was only caution. But I doubted it. I doubted it deeply.

I did not want to discuss it with Chade. Mine was the name Laudwine knew, mine was the child he threatened. What to do about him was my decision now. Later, perhaps, Chade would rant and scold at me. But he could do that later, when Nettle and Dutiful were no longer in any danger.

The more I pondered the situation, the greater my frustration with it. I left Chade's chambers and went down the stairs and through my room. Neither the Fool nor Lord Golden was there. That did not lessen my exasperation. I needed to think, yet I could not keep still. I went down to the snowy practice courts. I took my old ugly blade. The fine sword that the Fool had given me remained hanging on the wall, a mute and unforgiving reminder of my own foolishness.

Luck favoured me and Wim was there. I did my limbering up with my real blade, soon warming myself despite the chill day. Wim and I switched to dulled practice weapons for our more intent work. Wim seemed to sense that I only wanted to move my weapon and my body, not my tongue, nor engage my mind at all beyond the work of my body. I pushed all my concerns aside and focused only on attempting to kill him. When Wim abruptly stepped back and announced, 'Enough!' I thought he intended for us to pause and breathe. Instead, he lowered the tip of his blade to touch the ground and announced, 'I think that you have come back to what you used to be. Whatever that was, Tom.'

'I don't understand,' I said after a moment of watching him blowing.

He dragged in a deeper breath. 'When first we began to whet our blades on one another, I felt you were a fighter trying to recall what it was to be a fighter. Now you simply are. You've stepped back into your old skin, Tom Badgerlock. I can keep up with you, but only that. And full glad will I be to continue to sharpen my skills against you. But if you want a true challenge to your skills, or someone to teach you something new, you'll have to look beyond Wim now.'

And then he transferred his blade to his left hand and stepped forward to clasp hands with me. I felt a surge of warmth throughout my whole body. It had been years since I had felt a glow of pride such as that, and yet it was not for myself, but that this veteran fighter saw fit to honour me with such words. I went from the practice courts still bearing every problem that I had brought there with me, but buoyed with the idea that perhaps I possessed the wherewithal to face them.

I went through the steams, still carefully not thinking about what I would do next. I emerged cleansed, my will firmed and my mind clear. I went down to Buckkeep Town.

I had specific errands, I told myself. To see Hap. To buy a knife and a red scarf. And perhaps to discover a busy street where a goat might bleat while blacksmith hammers rang in the distance.

NINETEEN

Laudwine

Now King Shield was a merry man, as all well knew, fond of wine and jest. The Skillmistress of his reign was Solem, and often he made a jest of her name, saying she was as solemn as she was called. For her part, she found him overly given to banter and humour. He came to be King when she was all of seventy summers, and with his crown he inherited the coterie that she had trained for Queen Perceptive. They had served his mother full well before him, but like their Skillmistress, their years far outnumbered the King's. Oft he complained that both Skillmistress and coterie treated him as a child, and Solem, secure in her years, would disdainfully reply that it was because he so often behaved childishly.

To escape his ageing court and advisors, King Shield would sometimes by stealth leave Buckkeep, to travel the roads in disguise. Dressed as a roving tinker, it pleased him to mix with his common folk in inns and taverns of the ruder sort, where it was his pleasure to tell bawdy stories and sing comical songs for the entertainment of the folk who frequented such places. It was on one such evening when he was well in his cups that he began to tell his stories and ribald riddles. Now there was a youth working in the tavern, a lad of no more than eleven and unschooled in everything save how to draw a mug of ale and wipe a table. Yet as the King posed each riddle, this boy spoke the answers, not only correctly but also in the King's own well-rehearsed words. At first the King was not pleased to have his acclaim thus stolen. But soon he perceived that his irritation with the lad's too-swift answers was affording his audiences as much pleasures as the jests themselves. Before he left the inn that evening, he called the boy to his side and asked him, quietly, how it was that he knew the answers to so many riddles. The lad professed surprise. 'Were not you yourself whispering them to me, even as you told the riddle?' he asked.

Now the King was as perceptive as he was merry. That very night he took the boy back with him to Buckkeep and delivered him over to the Skillmistress, saying, 'This merry lad comes to you well started on the Skill-path. Find others like him, and train for me a coterie that can laugh as well as Skill.' And so the boy became known as Merry and the coterie that formed around him was Merry's Coterie.

Slek's *Histories*

It was a crisp, cold day. Packed snow squeaked under my boots as I strode down to Buckkeep Town. When I heard hoof-beats on the road behind me, I stepped aside to let horse and rider pass. I settled my hand on my sword hilt as I did so. Instead, Starling reined in and paced me with her mount. I glanced up at her and said nothing. She was almost the last person I wished to see today. She spoke to me anyway. 'Did Chade give you my message?'

I nodded and kept walking.

'And?'

'And I don't think I have anything to say to it.'

She reined in her horse so sharply that he snorted in protest. Then she jumped off him and ran around to stand in front of me. I stopped walking. 'What is the matter with you? What do you want from me?' she demanded. 'What can you possibly expect from me that I haven't already given you?' Her voice shook and to my astonishment, tears stood in her eyes.

'I . . . nothing. I don't . . . What do you want from me?'

'What we had before. Friendship. Talking to each other. Being someone the other person can count on.'

'But . . . Starling, you're married.'

'So you can't even talk to me any more? Can't even smile when you see me in the Great Hall? You act as if I don't even exist. Fifteen years, Fitz. We've known each other damn near fifteen years, and you discover I'm married and suddenly you can't even say hello to me?'

I gaped at her. Starling has often had that effect on me, but I've never become accustomed to it. My astonishment lasted too long. She attacked again.

'Last time I saw you . . . I needed a friend. And you thrust me aside. I was a friend to you when you needed one, for many years. Damn you, Fitz, I shared your bed for seven years! But you couldn't even be bothered to ask how I had been. And you refused to ride with me, as if I carried some disease you feared to catch!'

'Starling!' I shouted at her to break into her tirade. I didn't mean it as harshness, but she gasped suddenly and then burst into tears. And the reflexes of seven years put my arms around her and pulled her close to my chest. 'I didn't mean to hurt you,' I said by her ear. Her silky hair tangled against my chest, and the old familiar scent of her filled my nostrils. And I suddenly felt I had to explain what she already knew. 'You hurt me, when I discovered that I wasn't the only man in your life. Perhaps I was foolish ever to imagine that I was. You never told me I was. I know I deceived myself. But it did hurt me.'

She only sobbed harder, clinging to me. Her horse shifted restlessly and stepped on his reins. One arm still around Starling, I managed to step sideways and catch hold of them. *Calmness. Wait.* I told him, and he lowered his head a trifle.

I held her, thinking she would stop crying soon, but still she wept. I had thought her heartless. Careless was a better word for her, like a child who takes what she wants with no thoughts for the consequences. I knew more than she about consequences, and I should have behaved better. I spoke quietly, and as I had hoped, her sobbing softened so she could hear my words. 'I want you to know the truth about something. What I said last time, about thinking of Molly when you were in my arms. That wasn't true. Never. It was an unworthy thing for me to say, belittling to both of you. When you were in my arms, you filled my senses. I'm sorry that I tried to hurt you with a lie.' Her tears still did not calm. 'Starling. Talk to me. What's wrong?'

'It's not . . . it's not all from you being cruel to me. It's—' She took a shuddering breath. 'I think . . . I suspect my husband is . . . That night, he had said he had never realized how much he might want a child. Even though he cannot inherit and needs no heir of his own, he said that. And . . . and I think he is, or might be . . .' Her voice trailed off, unable to form the words of her greatest dread.

'Has he taken a mistress?' I asked quietly.

'I think so!' she wailed suddenly. 'When first we were wed, he wanted me every night! Well, I knew that would not last forever, but when his heat cooled, he still . . . but lately, he hardly seems to notice me. Even when I have been away from him for a few days, he no longer seems full of desire for me. He stays up late gaming with his friends, and comes to bed drunk. Dresses, jewellery, perfume, no matter how I adorn myself, he pays no heed.' Her words came out in a flood with her tears. Her sleeve smeared her wet face without drying it. I found a handkerchief and offered it to her.

'Thank you.' She wiped her face again. She took a sudden deep breath that lifted her shoulders and exhaled it again. 'I think he is tired of me. That he looks at me and sees an old woman. I stand before my glass, and I look at my breasts and my belly and the lines in my face . . . Fitz, have I aged that much? Do you think he regrets marrying a woman so many years older than he?'

I had no way of knowing the answers to her questions. I put my arm around her. 'It's cold here. Let's keep walking,' I said to gain a few moments to think. She kept her arm around my waist as we set off, her horse trailing us. For a time we both walked silently.

Then she said quietly, 'I married him to be safe, you know. Finally safe. He did not need children, he had wealth, he was comely, and he found me exciting. I overheard him once, telling a friend what a keen pleasure it was that he never needed to introduce me as other than his wife. That my name as the Queen's minstrel was known to all. He took such satisfaction in my fame that it gave me new pride in it. When he asked me to marry him and always be his, it was . . . it was like coming into safe harbour, Fitz. After all the years of wondering what would become of me when my voice faded or if I fell out of favour with the Queen. I never thought that to have him I must lose you. Then, when you insisted that was so, well . . . I was angry with you. I had come to think of our times together as a thing *we* owned. It shocked me that you could take them away from me, whether I would or not. But even so, I still had my Lord Fisher. And I told myself that losing you was a small price to pay for security when I was old.'

She fell silent for a time and the wind blew between us. I thought she had finished and then she said, 'But if he takes a mistress and gets her with child, or merely finds her more interesting than me . . . then I will have lost you for nothing, and still come up with my nets empty.'

'Starling. How can you imagine that Queen Kettricken and Chade would ever let you lack for anything? You know you will always be provided for.'

She sighed and suddenly looked older. 'A bed and food and clothes to my back. Those things, I suppose, I shall be sure of. But a time will come when my voice fails and my lungs cannot hold the notes long. A time will come when no one finds me comely or desirable. And then all regard for me will fade and Starling the Minstrel will become Starling the Crone in the Corner. And I will not be important to anyone. No one will hold me high in regard. I will still, in the end, be alone.'

I saw Starling from a new perspective. Perhaps it had always been the only perspective she had. Starling operated solely out of her own needs. She was a good musician, even excellent, but she did not have the brilliance that led to eternal fame. She was also a woman who could not bear children, and thus would always fear losing her man to another woman's charms and fertility. And as she aged and her beauty began to fade, that fear would only increase. With no children to bind her husband to her, she feared to lose him when the excitement of her bed palled. Perhaps that had been a great part of my charm for her; that I had always found her desirable, that I had never wearied of her body. In addition, I had been something that she had possessed, a powerful secret that she was privy to, as well as a lover and a man who never asked more of her than what she so casually offered. Bereft of my unquestioning enthusiasm for her body, and faced with her husband's fading ardour, she had begun to wonder if her desirability was fading. Yet I could neither sweep her into an hour of lovemaking to prove to her that she was still womanly, nor assure her that her husband still loved her. I tried to think of something that I could offer her.

I stopped her suddenly, turned and held her at arm's length. I pretended to appraise both her face and her body, as if making a judgement about her. In truth, I could only see her as

Starling, not as another might. But I managed a grin and told her, 'If your husband does not find you desirable, then he is a fool. I am sure that any number of men at Buckkeep would be very willing to share your bed. Myself among them, were circumstances different.' I tried to look thoughtful. 'Shall I tell him so?'

'No!' she exclaimed, and then managed to laugh, although it was a fragile thing. I took her hand to keep her at a more appropriate distance from me and we walked a bit farther down the road. 'Fitz,' she asked in a small voice some time later. 'Do you still care for me, at all?'

I knew I could not let that question hang unanswered for long. And, in fact, the truth was right before me. 'Yes. I do.' I met her eyes as we walked. 'You've hurt me sometimes. You've said some cruel things to me, and acted in ways I don't approve of. And I've done the same to you. But, it's as you said, Starling: fifteen years. When people have that much history together, they tend to take everything for granted. We accept as given the faults as well as the graces. How many songs have you sung before my hearth, for me alone? How many meals have I cooked for you? Fifteen years of knowing one another goes past likes and dislikes, into simple being. We've been careless of one another's feelings, even as Chade and I are careless of one another. Because we trust that what we are and what we know from all the years are more important than words flung in anger.'

'I deceived you,' she said after a time, quietly.

'Yes. You did.' I found I could speak without rancour. 'And I disappointed you. And just as I felt I had the right to decide what I would do with my life, regardless of what you thought about it, so did you. You married. I chose obscurity. Both those decisions came between us. Not just yours. But let me assure you of one thing. No matter how the years may pass for us, even though we never share a bed again, when we are old I will still hold you high in my regard. Always.'

Did I completely believe all I said to her? No. But, despite all, she was a friend, and she needed. The words I gave her eased that need, and cost me nothing. A small smile twisted my mouth. She had bedded me for the very reasons that I now gave her the small lies she needed to hear.

She nodded, and no more tears flowed. After a time of walking, she asked me, 'What should I do about my husband?'

I shook my head to that. 'I don't know, Starling. Do you still love him? Want him?'

She nodded stiffly to both my questions.

'Well, then. I think you should tell him that.'

'That's all?'

I shrugged. 'I think you are asking the wrong man for advice about this. Someone more successful in love might be able to give you better advice.'

'Like Chade, perhaps.'

'Chade?' I was both appalled and amused, but the temptation was too great. I kept a straight face. 'Chade's the ideal man to consult.' I wished I could be present at that discussion.

'I think you are right. He always manages to keep his lovers both satisfied and discreet. Even when he chooses to let one go,' she mused, and then laughed at the shocked look on my face. 'I see. Not even you know of his affairs. Ah, well, you are right, he is the man to ask. I've never heard of a woman turning him out of her bed; it's always the opposite. And he is not exactly the most youthful of men. Well. I shall discuss it with him when I report to him tonight.'

Her last words sparked a sudden suspicion. I risked it. 'Then you think you'll discover where the one-armed man is staying?'

She gave me a sideways look, as if awarding me a point in a game. 'Sooner than you will. And he asked me, when I overtook you, to let you know that he expects you to stay well away from Laudwine. Not that the man is known by that name in Buckkeep Town, or Chade would have him by now. So. I have passed on his wishes to you. He assures you that in this, he still knows best.'

'Or at least, he believes he does,' I returned coolly. I was putting together that this was no chance meeting. Chade had somehow discovered that I had left the castle and had sent Starling to intercept me and deflect me from Laudwine. Providing me with the opportunity to apologize to the ruffled minstrel was likely a part of his plan. How that old man loved pulling the strings! I found a smile and plastered it onto my face. 'Well, you'd best mount up then and be on your way, if you're to discover Laudwine before I do.'

She gave me a quizzical look. 'Are you still going down to Buckkeep Town?'

'Yes. I have other business down there.'

'Such as?'

'Hap.'

'He's in Buckkeep Town? I thought he would have stayed at your cabin.'

So Starling did not know everything that Chade knew. That was a small comfort. 'No. Part of my reason for returning to Buckkeep, a large part of it, was to make it possible for Hap to get a good apprenticeship. He's apprenticed to Gindast.'

'Is he? And is he doing well?'

By all the gods, I longed to lie to her and tell her that he was excelling. 'It hasn't been easy for him to adapt to city life,' I hedged. 'But I think he is beginning to master it now.'

'I shall have to go and see him. Gindast is a great admirer of mine. My expressing an interest in Hap cannot hurt him there.' There was an innocence to her assumption of fame and importance that made it impossible for me to take offence at it. Then she paused abruptly, and, as if the thought surprised her, asked, 'The boy is not still angry with me, is he?'

She gave injury so carelessly; perhaps she expected others to forgive it as easily. Perhaps that was the curse of a minstrel's tongue; to be gifted at wounding with words. At my hesitation, she filled in, 'He *is* still angry, isn't he?'

'I really have no idea,' I said hastily. 'You did injure his feelings rather deeply. But he's had so much on his mind, as I have, also. I've never discussed it with him.'

'Well. I suppose I must make amends with him, then. If I get a chance, I'll steal him for an afternoon. I know Gindast will let me have him. I'll take him out for a fine meal and show him the parts of Buckkeep Town an apprentice isn't likely to see. Don't frown like that. Hap's just a boy; I'll soon soothe his ruffled feathers. Now, as you say, I must be hastening along. Fitz, I'm glad things are better between us. I've missed you.'

'I've missed you, too,' I said, abandoning all attempts at honesty. I wondered how Hap would react to her invitation, and if she would even recognize how much he had grown and changed. In truth, I wished she would just leave him alone, but I didn't know how to ask that without offending her again. Evidently Chade wanted her well-disposed toward me. I'd corner him on the whys of that later. For now, I assisted her into the saddle, and smiled up at her as she looked down on me. When her smile answered me, I discovered that, yes, I had missed her. And that I preferred this to her festering anger at me. Then she nearly ruined it by quirking the smile to a grin and saying, 'So. Tell me true and take the sting from my last insult to you. Does Lord Golden prefer boys to girls? Is that why the ladies have had so little success with him?'

I managed to hold my smile in place. 'So far as I know, he prefers to sleep alone. For all the wild flirtations I've witnessed, I've never had to shake anyone out of his sheets in the morning.' I paused, then added in a lower voice, hating myself, 'I suspect the man is extremely discreet. I'm just his bodyguard, Starling. You can't expect me to know all his secrets.'

'Oh,' she replied, clearly disappointed at my lack of gossip. Minstrels are ever hungry for scraps of scandal. She had often told me that the best songs are found at the end of a trail of rumours. I thought she would ride off, but she surprised me again. 'Well, then. And yourself, these days?'

I sighed heavily. 'I've been emulating my master. I sleep alone, thank you.'

'You don't have to,' she offered, one eyebrow lifting archly.

'Starling,' I warned her.

'Oh, very well,' she laughed, and I saw that in some strange way my answer had reassured her. She had not been replaced. In refusing her offer, I forced myself to go without. I supposed that pleased her. She blew me a kiss as she rode off. I shook my head as I watched her go and then resumed my trudge down the hill.

A few minutes later, Civil Bresinga passed me, headed towards Buckkeep Town at a good clip despite the steep and snowy road.

He did not slow his horse and scarcely gave me a glance. I doubt that he recognized me or would have cared if he did. But he rode gloveless and bareheaded, his cloak fluttering behind him, as if he had left the castle in a very great hurry. Did it have something to do with the Prince refusing to ride out with him this morning? Did he have to notify someone of a failed plan? I muttered a curse to myself and hurried after him through the snow, but he was already out of sight.

I halted, out of breath and panting. Calm, I counselled myself. Calm. I had no way of knowing what was going on with Civil. I would stay with my original idea, and search for Laudwine. In that process, I suspected I might discover where Civil had gone.

My first stop in Buckkeep was the weekly market. I bought a red scarf and a serviceable belt-knife, and all the while I made casual inquiries as to where I might get fresh goat-flesh for a Jamaillian dish my master suddenly desired. I received a number of suggestions, but most were for goatherds who lived in the hills behind Buckkeep. There were only two suggested who lived in Buckkeep Town, and only one of them was near Smithy Row.

The short wintry day was ending as I headed toward Smithy Row. The fading of the light was fine with me. The recommended goat-keeper kept only a few beasts, more for milk than for flesh. I located his home as much from the smell as from my directions. In the dusk, I moved quietly closer to it. Through a window, I glimpsed a family with three young children settling in for the evening. In the shed behind their house were a dozen goats. Cheeses were stored in the rafters. The most nefarious creature around was a sullen old billy with evil yellow eyes. I left as quietly as I had come, wondering if I had tricked myself. Perhaps the sounds I had heard when I Skill-shared memories with Thick had nothing to do with where Laudwine was now. Perhaps it had been a temporary meeting place, not where the Piebald leader stayed.

I ghosted three more cottages nearby, discovering only families retiring for the night. Between a neglected shed and the next cottage, I discovered Civil's horse. He was tethered there, saddled still and steaming. Had he been put between the house and the shed to be less obvious? I stood very still. If I were approaching

Laudwine's hiding place, then there were certainly Witted on watch, beasts as well as men. It was possible they were already aware of me. That thought broke a sweat on my back. In the next instant, I knew there was nothing I could do about it. I drifted closer, trying to muffle my tread in the unpacked snow between the buildings.

As I crouched there, I heard a horse approach in the street. There are few riding horses in Buckkeep Town. The steep, cobbled streets are unsuited to them, and they are expensive to keep in a town where they are virtually useless. This was a large and heavy beast by the sound of him. There, at the front of the cottage, the sounds of his hoofbeats stilled. Almost immediately, I heard the door open. Someone heavy came out onto the porch and greeted the rider with, 'It's not my fault. I don't know why he came here and he won't say anything to me. Says he'll only speak to you.' I knew the voice from Thick's Skill-memory. This was the first man he had been taken to see.

'I'll take care of it, Padget.' Laudwine's voice. His tone cut off the man's attempt at explanation. I heard him dismount. I crouched down behind Civil's horse. 'Hammer, go with him,' Laudwine told the horse and I saw a passing shadow as a stout man led his chief's wit-beast past the alley mouth and towards the ramshackle shed. At a glance, I recalled him: I had first seen him riding at Laudwine's stirrup. Laudwine entered the cottage, shutting the door heavily behind him. A few moments later, Padget returned from tending the horse and followed him in.

The house was well constructed, the gaps in the walls properly chinked, and the windows tightly shuttered against night's chill. I could not see in, but the sound of raised voices leaked through to me. I could not make out the words. I crouched in the deep shadows between the buildings, pressed my ear tightly to the wall, and listened.

'Why were you so stupid as to come here? You were told never to come to me, never to seek any contact at all.' Laudwine's voice was deep with anger.

'I came to tell you that our agreement is over!' I thought I recognized Civil's voice, but it was shrill with fear.

'Do you think so?' This was Laudwine again, and the hair stood up on the back of my neck at the threat in his tone.

Civil made a low-voiced reply. He must have been defiant, for Laudwine laughed and said, 'Well, you think wrong. I will tell you when our agreement is over. And when our agreement is over, it will be because you have ceased to be useful to me. And you will know when you have ceased to be useful to me, because you will cease to be alive. Do you take my hint, Civil Bresinga? Be useful, boy. For your mother's sake, if not for your own. What titbits do you have for me?'

'For my mother's sake, I have nothing for you. Nor ever will again.' Civil's voice shook with both fear and determination.

Laudwine was a direct man, as I well recalled. He seemed to have learned to use his left hand well. I heard Civil's body hit the wall. Then he asked, pleasantly, 'And why is that, boy?'

There was no answer. I wondered if the powerful blow had killed the lad. 'Pick him up,' Laudwine ordered someone. I heard the sound of a chair dragged across the floor, probably to receive Civil. A moment later, Laudwine continued, 'I asked you a question, boy. Why are you suddenly turning traitor on me?'

Civil's voice was muffled. He'd probably been hit in the mouth or jaw. 'Not a traitor. Don't owe you anything.'

'Don't you?' Laudwine laughed. 'Your mother is still alive. Don't you owe me for that? You are still alive. Doesn't she owe me for that? Don't be a fool, lad. Do you believe the Mountain Queen's false promises? That she wants to listen to us, to make things better for us? Faugh! She wants to lure us in, like rats coming to poisoned grain. You think I'm a threat to you, that I could end your lives by betraying you. And so I could. But only if you betray me first. For now, I hold you in the palm of my hand, and I protect you. I am far more reasonable to deal with than some of the Piebalds that follow me. Be grateful that I keep them reined in. So let's have no more foolishness. You and I, we share too much to oppose one another.' His tone changed to one of genial inquiry. 'What brought this on, anyway?'

Civil hissed out an accusation I could not hear.

Laudwine laughed. 'So. She is a woman, boy, and one of our

own. I know it's hard for a lad to think of his own mother as a woman, but so she is, and a comely one as well. She should take it as a compliment, and as a reminder. She has lived too long apart from us, denying what she was, consorting with "the nobility" as if they, or she, were better than we are. It's going to come full circle, Bresinga. Consider yourselves fortunate that we accepted you as part of us again. For when we come to power, those of Old Blood who have denied their magic and turned their backs on their kin and even betrayed us to the Farseer filth . . . all of them will die. They'll die in their own King's Circle, just as that bastard Regal killed so many of us. And for what? Why did so many of our parents and their animal partners die in those circles? For the sake of creating a Witted turncoat, one that would hunt down the Witted Bastard for him. Full time and past due that the Farseers paid for that.'

And, ear pressed against the cold wood, I knew a familiar sickness in my bones as I crouched in the gathering cold and dark of the night. Ah yes. Once again the Farseers' past had returned to haunt us. For what Laudwine spoke was true. Regal had so hated and feared me that he had decided the only way to bring me down was to find one of the Witted who would help him. Many a man and woman died under Regal's torture before he found one who would hunt Old Blood for him. The painful scar in the centre of my back came from that man's arrow. Yet what I had always thought of as Regal's wrongdoing against the Witted would still be totted up against the Farseer family account.

Civil's voice was low but clear as he said, 'She does not take it as a "compliment" but as insult and assault most vile. You have forced me to live in Buckkeep, to spy for you here, leaving her alone and vulnerable. You have driven from her side every trusted servant and true friend she has ever known. And now your folk have dishonoured her, all in the name of taking her back into your "Piebald" legacy. Well, she does not want it, and neither do I. If this is what you mean when you speak of the fellowship of Old Blood, then I'd rather not be one of you.'

Laudwine's voice was almost lazy as he said, 'Well, boy, either you are foolish or you do not listen well. Answer me this. What are you if you are not one of us?'

'Free,' Civil snarled.

'Wrong. Dead. Kill him, Padget.'

It was a bluff. I was sure it was a bluff, but I was also certain the Civil would believe it. They would terrorize him back into obedience. Nor did I have any compelling reason to protect him from them, regardless of whether they only beat him or killed him. Save, perhaps, that he was a boy, coerced and cornered by circumstance. So it was that my belly was cold and my teeth gritted against what must next befall him.

Then the Skill-onslaught from Dutiful nearly dropped me to my knees. *Find Civil Bresinga. He is in great danger. Please, Tom, go now. I think he's down in Buckkeep Town.* The Prince sent the urgent demand out like a flood. Somewhere, I was dimly aware that Thick's music stopped in astonishment.

I found my wits and channelled a thought back to him. *I am not far from him. He is in danger, but it is not as great as you think. How did you know?*

An agonized outpouring of thought trampled my brain. *His cat told me. Civil brought him to me tied in a sack and asked me to keep him in my room and not let him out, no matter what. That was the favour he wanted earlier. He said he had to do something where he could not take the cat with him. Tom, don't wait. The cat says the danger is real, very real. They'll kill him.*

I'll protect him. I made the promise and then slammed my Skill-walls up to keep him out. Then I was off and running, circling the small house. Odd, how one's perceptions change in an instant. Civil had gone into this confrontation expecting to die. He had planned it. That was why he had taken his Wit-beast to Dutiful, to save the small cat's life lest he go down fighting for his partner. My ugly sword was in my hand as I shouldered the cottage door open. A man went down, his entrails spilling out between his fingers. He had not been armed or threatening me, merely in my way. I blocked against the rebounding pain of his injury as I charged into the room.

In a single glance, I knew Civil was right. Laudwine sat at the table, a glass of wine before him, watching Padget strangle the boy. Padget was enjoying it. He was a powerful enough man to have made a quick end of the boy if he had so desired. Instead he gripped Civil's throat from behind him, and held the boy off the ground, feet kicking, as he slowly squeezed. Civil's face was bright red, his eyes standing out as his fingernails tore hopelessly at Padget's leather-bound forearms. A nasty little dog, a shorthaired feist of some kind, was jigging merrily around them, snapping at Civil's dangling feet. The sight woke the red rage of battle in me. In an instant, I felt my chest swell with it and heard the thunder of my own heart. All other considerations fled. I'd kill them both.

Laudwine was leaning back in his chair, watching the performance, as I made my abrupt entrance. With no panic in his voice, he ordered Padget tersely to 'Finish him' and rose, drawing a short sword in one smooth motion to meet my attack. Then he recognized me and his face changed. From the corner of my eye, I saw Padget's fingers clamp in the flesh of the boy's throat.

I could have deflected Laudwine's sword-lunge or saved Civil's life, but not both. The table was between Civil and me. I took a running stride, pushed off, and landed on top of the table on one knee. I shoved my bloodied blade past Civil and deep into Padget's chest. Simultaneously, I felt the bite of Laudwine's sword. It went into the muscles on the right side of my back between my hip and my ribs. I screamed and rolled away from it, tearing my flesh from his blade. I struck back at him, but there was no strength to my blow. I wallowed off the table, my right leg folding under me. It was fortuitous, for it meant that Laudwine's follow-up thrust was high and missed me. I took breath and shrieked, 'Run!' at Civil. The boy had folded bonelessly to the floor when Padget let go of him to clutch at his chest. Civil still sprawled there, clutching at his neck and whistling frantic breaths into his lungs. Padget had gone to his knees, clutching at the flow of bright blood from his chest while his Wit-beast yipped brainlessly around him.

Laudwine towered over me as he stepped around the table, sword in his left hand. I rolled under the table, yelping when my injury hit the floor. On the other side, I scrabbled to my feet. The table was between us, but Laudwine was a tall man and had a long reach even with the short sword. I leaned back to avoid the first pass of

his blade. 'I'm going to kill you, you traitor bastard,' he promised
with savage satisfaction.

The words woke the wolf in me. The pain was not banished;
it simply became unimportant. *Kill first; lick your wounds later.
And make your snarl larger than his.* 'I won't kill you,' I promised
pleasantly. 'I'm just going to lop off your other hand and let you
live.' The look of horror that flickered through his eyes told me that
my words had bitten to the bone. I caught the edge of the table and
flipped it up on its end, then shoved it into him. The tabletop leaned
against him and I slammed against it. He stumbled backwards over
something, Padget or his yapping Wit-dog. He would have to drop
his sword to break his fall. Foolishly, though, he held onto it as he
went down. I pressed my advantage, shoving the table onto him
so that his legs were trapped under it as he fell.

On his back, with Padget's body under his, he swung his sword
at me, but the cut had no strength behind it. I avoided it and his
backslash, then jumped on top of the table and pinned him to the
floor with it. With a two-handed grip, I shoved my sword down into
his chest. He screamed, and I heard the battle-scream of a war-horse
echo him. The sword slipped and then twisted as I leaned my body
weight on it, sliding it between his ribs and into his vitals. He was
still yelling, so I pulled it out and stabbed him again. This time I
put it in his throat.

Outside in the street, I heard people shouting questions and
something like distant thunder. A horse neighed furiously. Someone
cried out, 'That horse has gone crazy!' and someone else yelled, 'Call
the city guard!' From the sounds, I decided that Laudwine's horse
was kicking the wall out of the shed in an attempt to get loose and
reach Laudwine's side. He was dying on the floor, his heart still
pumping his life's blood out of his throat, his eyes still full of fury
and fear. I had a sudden flash of insight. I turned to Civil. 'No time
to help you. Get up and get out, through the back. Avoid the guard
and get back to Buckkeep. Tell Dutiful everything. Everything, you
understand?'

The boy's eyes were wide and running tears, but whether from
fear, shock, or his recent strangulation, I could not tell. Padget's
feist came after me as I headed towards the door. I steeled my heart,

turned, and crushed the little animal with a stamp of my foot. It yelped sharply and was still. Did Padget depart with its death? I wasn't sure. But as I staggered into the street, I saw Laudwine's war-horse lunge against the framework of the shed that trapped it. Across the narrow street, the goatherd's children were clustered in his open doorway, staring. The horse's huge shod hooves had splintered the planks in his fury to escape. It had weakened the structure of the old shed, so that it was now collapsing sideways around him, actually making it more difficult for the horse to fight his way through the wall.

But he wasn't just a horse. Not any more. My Wit-sense of him was confusing, a sensation of both man and horse embodied in one. I saw the stallion pull back from the opening he had made and suddenly appraise his situation with a man's intelligence. I couldn't give him time to work out an escape. I ignored the people gawking in the street and ran towards the horse, yelling wordlessly. The war-horse tried to rear up and bring his deadly front hooves into use, but the shed was low-roofed, never intended to stable an animal of that size. The action only exposed his chest and I braced the hilt of my weapon against my own chest as I thrust it into him and rammed it as deep as I could make it go.

The animal screamed and a wash of Wit-fury and hatred near breached my walls, *repelling* me. I was flung backwards, leaving my blade trapped in his chest. He surged forward against the splintered walls, screaming his fury. But for the shed entrapping him, I know he would have killed me before he died. As it was, he collapsed at last, blood coursing from his mouth and nostrils as the city guard arrived. Their torches streamed in the winter night and sent confusing shadows leaping over me like springing wolves.

'What's going on here?' the sergeant demanded, and then as we recognized one another, he snarled, 'This is the second time you've caused trouble in my streets. I don't like it.'

I tried to think of an explanation, but my right leg abruptly folded under me and I collapsed into the trampled snow. 'There's two dead in here!' someone shouted. I rolled my head to see a white-faced girl in a guard's uniform emerge from Laudwine's cottage. I blinked and strained to see through the darkened streets. Civil's horse had gone.

Either it had bolted, or the boy had made his escape. I tried to move, and was suddenly aware of the hot, wet flow of blood down my side. I clutched at my injury.

'Get up!' the sergeant barked at me.

'I can't,' I managed to gasp. I lifted my hands and showed him the blood on them. 'I'm hurt.'

He shook his head in angry frustration, and I knew he longed to add to my injuries. He was a man who took his duties personally. 'What happened here?'

I gasped for breath, and blessed the goatherd's son who ran barefoot out of his door, shouting confusedly that the horse went crazy and tried to kick his way out of the shed and then I came out and killed it. The snow grew wet and warm under my back and I felt the night closing in from the edges of my vision.

Tom? The Prince's frantic Skill trickled through my crumbling walls. *Tom, are you hurt?*

Go away!

The sergeant leaned over me, demanding, 'What went on in there?'

I couldn't think of a lie. I told the truth. 'The horse went crazy. I had to kill it.'

'Yes, we know that. But what happened to the men in the house?'

Tom? Are you hurt?

I tried to Skill back to Dutiful, but pain was running over me in pounding waves now. I tried to move away from it, but a great spike of it nailed me down to the snowy street. A crowd was gathering around us. I scanned their faces, looking in vain for someone who would help me. They all just stared, eyes and mouths wide as they pointed and shouted explanations to one another. Then I glimpsed a face I did know. For just an instant, she stepped closer to me, and the look on her face seemed genuinely concerned. Henja, the Narcheska's servant, scowled down at me. Then, as my eyes met hers, she turned away suddenly from me and melted back into the crowd.

Chade! She's still here, she's here in Buckkeep Town. For an instant I knew how important that was. It was essential that Chade know it. Then pain washed all other concerns away from me. I was dying.

Stop. Make it stop. You're ruining the music. Thick's distress pounded me like a surf on a beach.

'Answer me!'

No lies left, no truth left. I looked up at the sergeant and tried to speak. Then I was slipping, sliding away from them all into the dark. *Keep watch, Nighteyes,* I begged him, but there was no answer and no wolf stood over me.

TWENTY

Coterie

The people of the Six Duchies have always been an independent folk.
The very fact that the Kingdom remains divided into six separate duchies,
all loyal to the Farseer monarchy but presided over by their own nobles,
speaks to that autonomous spirit. Each duchy represents the separate
annexation of a piece of territory, usually by warfare. In many instances,
the Farseer conqueror was wise enough to leave some of the indigenous
nobility in place. This is particularly true of both Farrow and Bearns.
An advantage to this system is that laws are adapted to the particular
situation of each duchy, as well as to the long-standing custom of the
inhabitants. One example of this concession to self-rule is that the larger
cities and towns frequently have not only their own city guards to keep
order, but finance this militia by a system of taxes on commerce and
punitive fines on lawbreakers.

Fedwren's Six Duchies Governance

Tom.

  Tom.

  Tom.

  At first it didn't bother me. I was down so deep that the sea itself could not reach me. All was dark and as long as I stayed still, the pain couldn't find me. Then the word crept slowly into the forefront of my mind. It was like a hammer thudding dully in my skull.

  Not Tom. I told it in annoyance. *Go away.*

  Not Tom? And the avid interest in Dutiful's thought pushed me to the edge of wakefulness. Reflexively I slammed up my walls against the boy's curiosity. An instant later, extreme discomfort drained away all my will and strength for Skilling. I was lying on my belly on what was supposed to be a straw mattress. There wasn't enough straw in it to matter. The cold of the stone floor seeped up through it. I was stiff and cold everywhere except on the small of my back. That burned. And when I tried to move, the pain savaged me. I groaned weakly and heard the scuff of footsteps.

'You awake?'

I moved a hand vaguely and opened my eyes to slits. Even the dim light seemed like an assault. I peered at the man above me. A short man, dressed in scruffy clothes with his hair wild about his face stared down at me. His nose and cheeks were the red of the perpetual drinker.

'Healer sewed you up. He said to tell you, don't move any more than you have to.' I grunted an assent and the man grinned and said, 'Hardly needed to tell you that, right?'

I grunted again. Now that I was fully awake, the extent of my pain was making itself known. I wondered what my situation was, but my mouth was too dry to speak. The chatty fellow seemed affable; perhaps he was the healer's assistant? I moved my mouth and when I could, took a deep breath and croaked out, 'Water?'

'I'll see what I can do,' he said. He went to the door. I followed him with my eyes. I noticed now that the small window in the stout door was barred. He shouted through it, 'Hey! The hurt fellow is awake. He wants water!'

If anyone replied, I didn't hear. He came away from the window and sat down on a stool beside my pallet. I became gradually more aware of my surroundings. Stone walls. A pot in the corner. A scattering of straw on the floor. Aha. My friend was my fellow prisoner. Before I could follow that thought any further, he began talking again. 'Well. You killed three men and a horse, eh? Pretty good fight, I bet. Wish I could have seen it. Me, I got in a fight last night, too. But I didn't kill no one. Got in a fight with a tall skinny guy, all scarred like the Pocked Man. Wasn't no fault of mine. I was talking, perhaps a bit loud, and you know what he said to me? He said, "Shut your mouth and don't say nothing. That's always the best advice for a fellow like you. Fellow like you talks and thinks he's explaining things, but he's just making a mess of it. He should leave the talking to his friends." Then he hit me, and I hit him back. And the guards came and arrested me and here I am, in the same predicament as you.'

I managed to nod that I understood his message. He was one of Chade's little birds. Chade wanted me to keep my mouth shut and wait. I wondered if he knew how badly hurt I was. I wondered if Civil had gone back to Buckkeep Castle. Then it occurred to me that I didn't need to wonder. I let my eyes sag shut, gathered my pitiful strength and reached out feebly. *Dutiful?*

Tom! Are you all right? His Skilling wavered through my mind like words inked on wet paper. The thought ran and faded even as I tried to grip it.

I tried to take a deep breath and centre myself. Pain jabbed deep. I breathed more shallowly and reached out hesitantly. *No. Laudwine stabbed me in the back, and I'm in jail. I killed him and someone named Padget. And, this is important. Tell Chade I saw Henja in the crowd. She's still in Buckkeep Town.*

Yes, he knows that. I told him. It was the last thing you Skilled out, that Henja was there. Why is that important?

I pushed his question aside. I didn't know the answer to it, and I had more pressing questions of my own. *What is going on? Why am I still here? Did Civil come back to you?*

Yes, yes he did. Listen, now, and don't interrupt me. The boy's excitement and fear were rattling him. His Skilling clattered at me like hooves on cobblestones. I knew he feared I'd lose consciousness again. *Chade says, 'say nothing'. He's working out a story for you. The whole town and the castle are buzzing about what happened in Buckkeep Town. There hasn't been a triple murder in Buckkeep Town in years, if ever, and that is how people are gossiping about it. So many people saw you kill the horse that, well, that it's going to be impossible to say you didn't kill Laudwine and his man. So, well, Chade's working on a reason why it wouldn't be murder. But he can't just come and get you out of there. You see why, don't you?*

I see why. There must be no connection between Chade and a bodyguard who committed a triple murder, no link between the Queen and the man who killed the Old Blood delegates, no bond between the Prince and the assassin who had done his bidding. I saw. I had always seen. *Don't worry about me.* The thought was cold.

I could tell Dutiful was trying to control his fear, but it stained his Skilling with dread. His worries whispered past his guard: what if Chade couldn't think of a tale, what if I died of a septic wound, sweet Eda, he killed them all, men and beast, who is Tom Badgerlock, really, who was he, to kill like that. To shut off his fears I closed my walls to him. I was too weary to Skill anyway, and he'd told me all I needed to know just now. I felt myself separating, not just from Dutiful, but from all of them. I sealed myself up inside my own skin. I was Tom Badgerlock, a servant at Buckkeep, in jail, guilty of murdering three people and killing a fine horse. That was all I was.

The guard came to the window, warned my fellow prisoner back from the door, and then ventured inside with a bucket and a dipper. He set it down by my pallet. I looked at his boots through my lowered eyelashes. 'He doesn't look like he's awake.'

'Well, he was for a minute there. Didn't say much, only "water".'

'If he wakes up again, you call out. Sergeant wants to talk to him.'

'To be sure, I will. But hasn't my wife come yet to pay my fine? You sent a boy to tell her, didn't you?'

'I told you we did. Yesterday. If she comes with the coin, you'll be out.'

'Any chance of some food here?'

'You've been fed. This isn't an inn.'

The guard went out, slamming the door behind him. I heard several bolts shot into place. My friend went to the door and watched the guard depart down the hallway. Then he came back to my side. 'Think you can drink?'

I didn't answer but I managed to wobble my head up off the straw. He held the brimming ladle near my mouth and I carefully sucked in a mouthful. He was patient, crouching there and holding the ladle steady as I drank. I had to go slow. I'd never realized that the muscles in my back could be involved in sucking water into my mouth and holding my head up. After a time, I let my head sag back down and he took the water away. I lay panting softly. Blackness hovered at the edges of my vision, then gradually receded. 'Is it night?'

'It's always night in these places,' he answered mournfully, and for a moment I glimpsed the real man, one who had spent far too much time in situations such as this. I wondered how long he'd been Chade's, then doubted that he knew anything of who employed him this way. He pulled his stool closer and spoke quietly. 'It's afternoon. You've been in here two days now. When they first brought me in, the healer was working on you. I thought you were awake then. Don't you remember it?'

'No.' Perhaps I could have, if I had tried, but I was suddenly queasily certain I didn't want to recall that. Two days. My heart sank. If Chade were going to get me out of here swiftly, he would have done so by now. That two days had already passed could indicate that I should expect to be here for a time. A sudden jab of pain broke that chain of thought. I tried to focus my mind again. 'No one has come to see me, or offered to pay my fine?'

He goggled at me. 'Fine? Man, you murdered three people. There's no fine for that.' Then he abruptly gentled his voice. I was still absorbing that I could die on a gallows when he added, 'There was a man who came after the healer got done with you. Some high lord, dressed all fancy and foreign. You were unconscious and they wouldn't let him come in here. He demanded to know what had become of a purse you were carrying for him. The guards said they didn't know anything about it. He got really angry then, and told them to think well what they were saying, that if his property was not restored to him intact, he would take extreme measures. He said you had a little red purse, embroidered with a bird, a, um, a pheasant on it. He wouldn't say what was in it, only that it was very valuable and it was his and he wanted it back.'

'Lord Golden?' I asked softly.

'Yes, that was his name.'

I had no idea what the Fool had been talking about. 'I don't remember the purse,' I said. The pain was rising like an engulfing tide. I tried to hold onto my thoughts but could not. I pushed back my fear and discovered that it cloaked my anger. I didn't deserve this. Why had they left me here? I could die here.

I could feel Dutiful fumbling at the edges of my mind. 'I'm so tired,' I said, meaning to Skill it but saying it instead. The pain from my wound was thudding down my leg, making my hip and knee ache. My right arm had no strength in it. I closed my eyes, centred myself and tried to reach out to the Prince. Instead, I plunged into blackness.

The next several days passed for me like images glimpsed by lightning during a thunderstorm. The few memories I have are starkly and strongly etched, yet they are so momentary as to be nearly meaningless. A man I suspect was a healer looked into a basin of my blood and proclaimed it too dark. My cellmate complained bitterly to someone at the door-grate that the stench was enough to choke a goat. I stared at an odd pattern of straw on the floor and listened to Hap scream obscenities at someone. I desperately wanted him to be quiet, lest they decide to hurt him, too. To be conscious was to be afraid. Sick, hurt and afraid. Alone. They'd left me alone here to die, so I would not embarrass them. Sleep brought Nighteyes' old nightmares of a filthy cage and a keeper who beat him.

The Skill is a magic which demands physical strength, a clear mental focus, and a strong will to perform. I had none of those. Waves of Skill-sendings from Dutiful struck me and washed through me, leaving no clear residue of thought. I knew only that he tried to reach me, and I wished heartily that he would stop. I wanted silence and stillness so I could hide from my pain. Sometimes I was aware of Nettle, too. I doubt that she sensed she had reached me.

In between those glimpses of waking life and nightmare plagued sleep, I lived another life. The rounded hillsides were smooth and white with snow under a grey sky. There were no trees, no bushes, and not even an upthrust of stone. Only the snow, the whispering wind and the ever-twilight. The only break in the smoothness of the snow were Nighteyes' tracks going on before me. I followed them doggedly. I would find him and I would join him. He could not be that far ahead. Once the wind turned to wolves howling in the distance, and I tried to hurry. That effort only woke me to the cold stink of the prison cell. I had moved and something hot and foul was trickling from my wound. I closed my eyes again and sought for the peace of the snowy hills.

It would be weeks before I pieced together the whole sequence of events. Lord Golden's missing purse of raw gemstones was found in Laudwine's cottage. Not that he was known as Laudwine in Buckkeep Town. Starling had been correct. To his neighbours, the one-armed man was known as Keppler. A witness attested that he had seen a man who might have been me pursue someone who might have been Padget into Keppler's cottage. Obviously, I had been robbed of my master's purse on my way to taking them to a gem-cutter for him. I had followed the thieves, they had fought me, and I'd killed them all, taking a grievous injury myself. Then I had valiantly killed the rabid horse before it could break free of the shed and injure people in the street. From being an accused triple-murderer, I was suddenly elevated to the status of loyal servant willing to risk his life for his master's property. As no one came forward to contradict this fabrication, or even to claim the bodies of 'Keppler' and Padget, it became the acknowledged truth in Buckkeep Town. The goatherd neighbours soon spoke of how it seemed to them that Keppler had many visitors who came and went at odd hours.

And so Lord Golden was allowed to claim what was left of me. He sent two serving-men to fetch me home. Stinking and semi-conscious, I was loaded onto a litter for a cold and jolting trip up to Buckkeep Castle. I did not know the men who came to fetch me, and they cared little for me. I felt each step they took, and would have wept if I had had the strength. The pain was such that it kept jolting me back to wakefulness. The stoutly-muscled men who trudged up the hill commented that they were grateful for the cold, still air, for it made the smell of my pus-running wound less. They delivered me to Lord Golden's door. He held a scented handkerchief over his mouth and nose as he commanded them to put me on my bed. Then he paid the men generously and thanked them for bringing me home to die. In the blackness of my closed room, I shut my eyes and tried to do just that.

Fragments of speech whirled like falling leaves in my memory. They flowed into my head and filled it up like other people's furniture moved into a once-familiar room. I could not disengage from them. Something held me there as firmly as the hand that gripped mine.

'. . . Can't move him again, even if you could get a litter up those stairs. You'll have to do it here.'

'I don't know how. I don't know how. I don't know how!' This from Dutiful. 'Eda and El, Chade, I'm not being stubborn. Don't you think I'd save him if I could? But I don't know how; I'm not even sure what you're asking me to do.'

Stinks worse than dogshit now. Thick was bored and wished he were anywhere else.

Chade, patiently explaining it yet again. 'It doesn't matter that you don't know how. He's going to die if we don't do anything. If you try and it kills him, well, at least it will be quicker than what he's enduring now. Now, I want you to look at these drawings carefully. They are my own work, from years ago. This shows you what those organs should look like, intact . . .'

I fell away from them. Blessed blackness for a time. Just as I found the snow-rounded hills, they tugged me back. Their hands were on me. My clothing was cut away. Someone retched, and Chade, tight-breathed, told them to get out of the room until called for. Then, harsh rags, water both cold and hot on my wound and close at hand a woman said sadly, 'It's hopelessly foul. Can't we just let him go peacefully?'

'No!' I thought the voice was King Shrewd's. Then I knew it could not be. It must be Chade, sounding so like his brother. 'Get the Prince back in here. It's time.'

Then I felt Dutiful's icy hands on my hot flesh, set to either side of the wound. 'Just Skill into his body,' Chade told him. 'Skill into him, look at what is wrong, and fix it.'

'I don't know how,' Dutiful repeated, but I felt him try. His mind battered against mine like a moth against a lamp's chimney. He was trying to reach my thoughts, not my body. I pushed feebly at him. That was a mistake.

For a moment, our minds touched and linked. *No.* I told him. *No. Leave me alone.*

His hands went away. 'He doesn't want us to do this,' Dutiful reported uncertainly.

'I don't care!' Chade's voice was furious. 'He isn't allowed to die. I won't permit it.' Suddenly, the words were louder, shouted right by my ear. 'Fitz, do you hear me? Do you hear me, boy? I'm not going to let you die, so you might as well cooperate. Stop feeling sorry for yourself and fight to live.'

'Fitz?' There was wonder and horror in Dutiful's voice.

A crack of silence opened. Then, harshly, Chade explained. 'He was born a bastard, just as I was. It's long been a joke between us, that the word only stings when it comes from someone who doesn't wear it also.'

Feeble, Chade. Feeble, I wanted to tell him, *and Dutiful knows you too well to be taken in by it.*

Someone stroked the hair back from my brow and took my hand. I thought it was the Fool. I tried to tighten my hand on his slender one, to somehow let him know that I would beg his pardon if I could. I suddenly thought of all the persons that I hadn't bid farewell. Hap. Kettricken. Burrich and Molly. I'd always meant to make everything right with everyone before I died. 'Patience, mother,' I said, but no one heard me. Perhaps I didn't even speak the words aloud.

'Show me the picture,' Lord Golden said. He let go of my hand and I swung abruptly into the blackness. I fell until I died. From the pillowed brow of a snow hilly, I glimpsed the summerland. A flash of grey moved in the tall grasses. Nighteyes! I called to him. He turned and looked back at me. He showed his teeth in a snarl, warning me back. I tried to move forward but again I was drawn back up to the surface. I thrashed helplessly, a fish on a line, but my body moved not at all.

'. . . done it before. At least, something like it. I was there when he used the Skill to heal his wolf. And years ago, I studied how a man's body is put together. And I don't have the Skill, myself, but I know Fi— Tom. If you can use the Skill through me, I'm willing to allow that.' The Fool was insistent.

'I have to use the privy.'

'Go, then, Thick, but come right back. Understand me? Come right back here when you have.' I can hear annoyance in Chade's voice. And uncertainty. 'Well, what can it hurt? Go ahead. Try.'

Then I felt the Fool's touch on my back. If Dutiful's hands had been cold to my fevered skin, then the Fool's fingers were as icicles. Their jabbing ice probed me. All eternity paused in anticipation of that dreaded, desired touch.

Long ago, the Fool had accompanied me into the Mountains on the quest to find Verity. In helping me tend our exhausted king, he had carelessly let his fingers come into contact with Verity's Skill-silvered hands. That physical manifestation of the Skill-magic had gleamed like quicksilver. The contact with the pure magic had jolted the Fool and forever marked him. The silvering magic had faded with time, yet enough of it remained on his fingertips that I had seen the Fool use it in his woodcarving. It allowed him to know, intimately, whatever those fingers touched, be it wood or plant or beast. Or me. Long ago, he had left his fingerprints on my wrist. Lord Golden's gloves always kept his Skill-fingers covered, protected from casual contact. Yet now the hands that touched the skin of my back were bared.

I knew the instant that his Skill-coated fingers made contact with my skin. Like little cold knives his touch plunged into me, cutting more sharply than the sword which had stirred my guts. It was neither pain nor pleasure; it was connection, pure and simple, as if we shared a skin. I lay still under that scrutiny, lacking even the strength to tremble, as I prayed he would go no further. I need not have feared. I felt the Fool's honour in that touch, an honour that was like armour between us. It was only my body he probed, not my heart or mind. I knew then with terrible guilt how my earlier accusations had wronged my friend. He would never seek anything from me that I did not first offer him. I heard him speak, and the words echoed through me even as they washed against my ears.

'I can see the damage, Chade. The muscles are like snapped cords that have pulled back on themselves. And where the blade cut him, there is rot and poison leaking from his own guts. His blood carries it through his body. It is not just this wound that is toxic. The wrongness gleams throughout his whole body, like dye spreading through water or decay that has reached up through a tree. It has overwhelmed him, Chade. The trouble is not just here, where the blade went in, but in other places where his own body tries to make it right and instead succumbs to the poison.'

'Can you repair it? Can you heal his body?' Chade's voice seemed choked and weak, but it could have been because the Fool's thoughts seemed so thunderously loud.

'No. I can see what is wrong but perceiving damage does not mend it. He is not a chunk of wood, so I cannot simply carve the rot away from what is sound.' The Fool fell silent, but I felt how he struggled within that silence. Then he spoke in a voice full of despair. 'We have failed him. He's dying.'

'No, oh no. Not my boy, not my Fitz. Please, no.' Light as leaves, the old man's hands settled on me. I knew how terribly he desired to make me right. Then his hands seemed to sink inside me and the heat of his touch burned like liquor running through my veins. Someone gasped, and then I felt, I felt the Fool join his mind to Chade's. They linked in me. It was a feeble thing, this Skilling effort. The old man's voice cracked as he cried out, 'Dutiful. Take my hand. Lend me strength.'

Dutiful joined them. It disrupted everything. Light exploded into blackness. 'Get Thick!' someone shouted. It didn't matter. I fell for a long time, getting smaller and smaller as I fell. I heard the howling of wolves. It grew louder.

Then I became aware of a light. The light was not hot, but it was terribly penetrating. I fell into it and became it. It seemed to come from inside my eyes themselves. There was no avoiding it. It was light that seared but did not illuminate. I could see nothing. It was unbearably bright, and then suddenly, the brilliance increased. I screamed, my whole body screamed with the force of the light surging through me. I was a broken limb jerked straight, a dammed river released, snarled hair roughly combed. Rightness tore through me. The cure was worse than the malady. My heart stopped. Voices cried out in dismay. Then my heart slammed into motion again. Air scorched into my lungs.

I passed through an instant of wild wakefulness in which I saw all, knew all, felt all. They surrounded me in a circle. The Fool's Skilled fingers were pressed to my back. Chade gripped his free hand, and in turn his hand held Dutiful's. Dutiful clenched Thick's chubby wrist in his hand and Thick stood, stock-still and stolid, immobile and yet roaring like a bonfire. Chade's eyes were wide, showing the whites all round and his clenched teeth were bared in a snarl of joy. Dutiful's face was white with fear, his eyes squeezed shut. And the Fool, the Fool was gold gleaming and joy and a flight of jewelled dragons across a pure blue sky. And the Fool screamed suddenly, shrill as a woman, 'Stop! Stop! Stop! It's too much, we've gone too far!'

They let me go. I raced on without them. I couldn't stop now. As a flash flood cuts down a ravine, clearing all debris along with the live trees that it tears up from the banks, so I raced. Healing? It was not a healing. Healing is gentleness and recovery and time. Healing, I suddenly knew, was not a thing that one man did to another. Healing was what a body did for itself, given the rest and time and sustenance to do it. If a man set fire to his feet to warm his hands, that would be like this healing was. My body sloughed rotted flesh and purged poisonous fluids from itself. Yet one cannot tear away from a structure without replacing it, and building bricks must come from somewhere. My body stole from itself and I felt it do it, but could not stop the process. And so I was made whole, but at a cost to the strength of that whole. Like a wall built without sufficient mortar, strength was sacrificed to the paucity of materials. When all was done and the world thundered to stillness around me, I lay looking up at them from the wash of filth and poison that my body had ejected, and I had not even the strength to blink.

They looked down at me, the four who had reconstructed my body. The old man, the golden lord, the prince and the idiot stared down at me, and in their gazes awe mingled with fear and satisfaction vied with regret. Thus was Dutiful's Coterie formed, and it was as poor a way for any five folk to be joined as I could imagine. Not since Crossfire's Coterie of cripples had there been such a sadly mismatched assortment of Skill-users. The Fool had no true Skill of his own, only the silver shadows on his fingertips and the thread of Skill-awareness we had shared for so long. Thick possessed it in ample quantity but had neither knowledge nor any ambition to gain knowledge to use it well. I had Skill, but as always it faded and then fountained unpredictably, untrained and unreliable. And Chade, gods help us all, had discovered his own talent in the waning of his years. He flourished it like a boy waving a wooden sword, with no concept of what a true edge could do. He had knowledge, and ambition like a floodtide, and yet he did not have the intrinsic understanding that Thick did. Only in our prince did Skill balance both intellect and ambition, and there it was Wit-tainted. I stared up at what I had wrought merely by virtue of nearly dying, and my courage left me. Catalyst indeed. A coterie should be able to lend its strength to the Farseer monarch in time of need. This one could not function without him. And it should have been built on the camaraderie of mutually-chosen companions. This was more like an accidental meeting of travellers in a tavern.

Some of the woe I felt must have shown in my eyes, for Chade knelt down by my bedside and took my hand. 'It's all right, boy,' he said reassuringly. 'You're going to live.'

I knew he meant it well. I closed my eyes to shut out the unholy glee shining in his face.

I slept for four days and four nights. I slept through them bathing my wasted body and clothing me anew. They told me later that I drank broth and wine and gruel in those days. Someone kept me clean. I don't recall it, and for that, I'm glad. I was later told that Starling checked on me several times, and that Wim came by and delivered a restorative potion from his grandmother's recipe. None of them were allowed to see me. I remember none of that, I am ashamed to say. Instead, I recalled memories I had not known I held. I ran with a pack of wolves, shadowing them over the hills. I watched their lives and longed to join them. But always, somewhere, a thread tugged at me, reminding me that eventually I would have to come back.

I do recall one interlude. Someone put her arm around my shoulders and hauled me up and held a mug of warm milk to my mouth. I have never cared for warmed milk, and I tried to turn aside from it when I smelled it, but she was determined. It was drink or drown, and most of it went down my throat. It was only when she lowered me back to my pillows that I recognized that strength of will as my queen's. I opened my eyes to slits. 'Sorry,' I croaked as Kettricken wiped the spilled milk from my scruff of beard and nightshirt.

She smiled at me and I saw relief in her eyes. 'That's the first time you've had the strength to be difficult. Should I take it that you are recovering and will soon be your old self?' She asked the question teasingly, but for all that relief quivered in her words. She set the cloth aside and gathered my hands in hers. I felt my bones rub together in her gentle grip; all flesh had fallen from my hands, leaving them like talons. I could not bear to look at them, or at the tenderness in her blue gaze. I glanced past her and frowned, not recognizing my surroundings. Her eyes followed my gaze. 'I changed it,' she said. 'I could not abide for you to lie in this cell as it was.'

There was a thick rug of Mountain weave on the floor. I lay on a low couch, while my exalted queen sat cross-legged on a plump cushion on the floor beside me. In the corner, a spiralling rack held tiers of scented candles that warmed and lit the room. A chest of drawers, the front ornamented with carving, supported a graceful ewer and wash bowl. I saw the lacy edge of some piece of weaving beneath the pitcher. A low table beside the bed held the empty mug and a bowl of torn bread softened in broth. The smell made me hungry. Kettricken must have seen my eyes go towards it, for she immediately took it up and lifted a spoonful.

'I think I can feed myself,' I said hastily. I tried to sit up and shamed myself by needing her assistance. When I did so, I became aware of the tapestry on the wall facing me. It had been freshly cleaned and mended, but as ever an elongated King Wisdom stared down at me as he made treaty with the Elderlings. My shock must have shown on my face, for Kettricken smiled and said, 'Chade said you would be astonished and pleased. It seemed a rather dismal tapestry to me but he said it was an old favourite of yours.'

It took up the entire wall. Just as it had when it hung on the wall of my childhood bedroom, it struck me as nightmarish. And the old man knew that full well. Despite how weak I was, his rough jest brought a smile to my face. Still I protested, 'But this chamber should be kept as the humble room of a serving man. Except for the size and lack of windows, you have fitted it out as if for a prince.'

Kettricken sighed. 'Chade, too, rebuked me for that, but I refused to listen. Bad enough that you must be ill in such a small and gloomy chamber. I will not leave it pauperish and cold as well.'

'But your chamber is simple and sparse, in the Mountain fashion. I don't—'

'When you are well enough to have visitors, then you may have it all taken away if you wish. But for now, I will have you comfortable. In the Six Duchies style.' She spoke with asperity, then sighed. 'As usual, a lie has explained it away. Lord Golden rewards his serving-man for loyalty. So. Tolerate it.'

And there was no arguing with her tone. She propped me up with pillows and I ate the sodden bread. I could have eaten more, but she took the empty bowl from me and told me to take my recovery slowly. And then I was suddenly tired. I lay back, overcome with weariness yet astounded there was no pain. And I suddenly realized that I was on my back. My face must have changed, for Kettricken anxiously asked me if I were all right.

I rolled to my side and reached a cautious hand to my back. 'There is no pain,' I told her.

There were no bandages.

I felt the smooth flesh, and then the knobs of my spine and my ribs that stuck out like a starved dog's. I started to tremble, and my teeth to chatter. Kettricken pulled blankets closer around me. 'The wound is completely gone,' I rattled out the words.

'Yes,' she agreed. 'The flesh is closed and sound. Of the sword-thrust, there is no sign. It is one reason we have kept visitors away from you. Surely they would wonder at that, and also wonder why you are thin and wasted as from a weeks-long illness.' She paused then, and I thought she would say more, but she did not. She smiled at me tenderly. 'Don't be concerned about anything right now. You need to rest, Fitz, not to worry. Rest, and eat, and soon you'll be up and about.' The Queen touched my whiskery cheek and then smoothed back my hair.

A thousand questions suddenly crowded my mind. 'Does Hap know I'm all right? Has he come to see me; is he worried?'

'Hush. You are not all right, not yet. He has come here, but we judged it best not to let him see you. Lord Golden has spoken with him, assuring him that you will recover and are receiving the best of care. He told him how grateful he was for how Tom Badgerlock had attempted to defend his treasure at such a cost to himself, and made Hap promise that if he had any need while you are recuperating, he would let Golden know of it. And a woman named Jinna has come to visit, but also been turned aside.'

I understood the wisdom of it. Both Hap and Jinna would have been astounded at my present appearance, but I hoped my boy had not been made too anxious. And then, as if a gate had been opened, all my other questions assaulted me. 'Were there other Piebalds, beside Laudwine and Padget? I got the impression that Civil's mother was very nearly living under siege. And there is a spy still, the one who took Thick to see Laudwine, Chade must—'

'You must rest,' she said firmly. 'Others are dealing with all of that.' She stood fluidly. It took only two steps to cross my tiny room. She blew out all the candles save one, and that one she removed from the holder. I became aware that my queen was in a nightrobe and wrapper. Her hair hung in a thick gold braid down her back.

'It's night,' I said stupidly.

'Yes. Very late at night. Go to sleep now, Fitz.'

'What are you doing here so late at night?'

'Watching you sleep.'

It didn't make sense. She had deliberately wakened me. 'But the milk and the bread?'

'I had my page fetch them for me, telling him I could not sleep. Because, in truth, I could not. And then I brought them here, for you.' She sounded almost defensive. 'There is a good amidst all this evil that has befallen you. It has made me recall vividly just how much I owe you, and how much I value you.' She looked down at me for a moment. 'If I lost you,' she said unwillingly, 'I would lose the only one who knows the whole of my story. The only one who looks at me and knows all I went through with my king.'

'But Starling was there. And Lord Golden.'

She shook her head. 'Not for all of it. And neither of them loved him as we did.' Then, candle in hand, she stooped and kissed my brow. 'Go to sleep, FitzChivalry.' And when she kissed my mouth, it was like a long drink of cool water, and I knew the kiss was not for me, but for the man we both had lost. 'Rest and grow strong again,' she admonished me, then rose and left by the secret doorway. She took the mug and the bowl with her, leaving behind no trace of herself save her lingering scent in the darkness. I sighed, and sank into a sleep that was deep, but almost normal.

TWENTY-ONE

———◆◦◆———

Convalescence

The Witness Stones have stood on the cliffs near Buckkeep Castle for as long as Buckkeep Castle has existed, and likely for longer. Tall and black, the four stones thrust up in a quadrangle from the rocky earth. Either time or the hands of men have obscured the markings that once graced each side of each standing Stone. The runes are unreadable now. The stone itself appears very similar to the black blocks of Buckkeep Castle, save for silvery threads that run like flaws through each pillar. No one knows whence came the tradition of calling the Stones to witness either a vow or the truth of what a man was saying. Sometimes combats are fought before the Stones, in the belief that invoking their presence will enable the fighter whose cause is just to prevail. Many superstitions are associated with the space at the centre of the four. Some say that a barren woman can conceive a child there; others, that there a woman can ask the Stones to take away that which grows in her womb.

Lady Clarine's *Customs of Buck Duchy*

I rose from my sickbed the next day. In the blackness of my closed chamber, I walked the three steps to my clothing chest. Then I fell and could not find the strength to get up. I lay still, resolving not to call out for help but to wait until I could muster the energy to return to my bed. But almost immediately, the door to my room opened, admitting light and air and Lord Golden. He stood limned in the doorway and looked down on me with aristocratic disapproval. 'Tom, Tom,' he said, shaking his head. 'Must you always be so annoyingly stubborn? Back to your bed until Lord Chade says you are free of it.'

As always, the strength in his slender body surprised me. He did not help me to my feet but lifted me bodily and set me back on my bed. I groped for my blanket. He caught up the corner of one and flipped it over me. 'I can't just lie here for days and days,' I complained.

Lord Golden looked amused. 'I'd like to see you try to do anything else, for obviously you can't. I'll leave the door open so you have some light. Do you wish a candle as well?'

I shook my head slowly, chilled by his impersonal yet tolerantly kindly manner. He left me, but the door remained open. I could see the fire burning in his tidily-swept hearth. He resumed his seat at a small writing desk and took up his quill again. It scratched energetically over the paper.

In a short time, there was a tap at the door, and at his invitation to enter, his serving-boy came in bearing a breakfast tray. Char set it down on the table and carefully unloaded it. When he was finished, there remained several bowls and a mug on the tray. He picked it up and started towards my door but Lord Golden, without looking away from his writing, said, 'Leave it on the table, Char.' The boy left, and still Lord Golden scribbled. A short time later, there was another knock on the door. This time, the boy carried in buckets of water. A man with him had an armload of firewood. Lord Golden ignored them both as they went about their tasks. When they had both left, he sighed, stood up from his desk and went to the door and latched it. Then he spoke to me again.

'Will you eat in your room or at the table, Tom?'

For answer, I sat up in my bed. There was a new blue woollen robe across the foot of my bed. I pulled it on over my head, and then stood up. The low bed made this more difficult than it should have been, and for a moment I stood still, my head reeling. Then I began my cautious walk to the table. I paused once in the doorway, clinging to the jamb as I caught my breath, then moved to the table. Lord Golden had already seated himself and was uncovering the dishes the boy had set out for him. After a moment, I lowered myself into the chair opposite him.

They had given me an invalid's meal of broth and runny porridge and bread in milk. On Lord Golden's side of the table, there were shirred eggs and sausages, bread and butter and preserves and everything else I desired. I knew a moment of irrational fury at him. Then I ate everything they had given me, and washed it down with a cup of lukewarm chamomile tea. Afterwards, I rose and went back to my bed. We had not exchanged a single word. After a time, boredom lulled me into sleep.

I awoke to low voices. 'Then he is well enough to rise and eat?' Chade asked.

'Barely,' Lord Golden replied. 'Better to go slowly. He has no reserves of strength to call upon. Yet if you set tasks before him now, he will still—'

'I'm awake!' I called out. It came out as a croak. I cleared my throat and tried again. 'Chade, I'm awake.'

He came quickly to the door of the room and smiled in at me. His white hair gleamed in shining curls and he seemed vital and energetic. He looked down with disdain at Kettricken's cushion beside my bed. 'Let me get a chair, boy, and I'll sit and we'll chat a bit. You're looking much better.'

'I can get up.'

'Can you? Ah. Well, take my hand and up you come. No, let me help you, don't be stubborn. Shall we sit by the fire?'

Thus he spoke to me, as if I were a trifle simple. I accepted it as his concern for me, and allowed him to support me as I walked. I lowered myself into one of the cushioned chairs before the hearth. He took the other with a sigh. I looked about for the Fool, but Lord Golden was busy at his desk again.

Chade smiled at me and stretched his feet out towards the fire. 'I'm so glad to see you doing so well, Fitz. You gave us quite a scare. It took everything we could muster to pull you back.'

'And that is something we need to talk about,' I told him gravely.

'Yes, but not just now. For now, you are to take things slowly and not tax yourself. Sleep and food are what you chiefly need.'

'Real food,' I stipulated firmly. 'Meat. I won't gain any strength on that pap they sent up this morning.'

His eyebrows rose. 'Feeling crotchety, are we? Well, that's to be expected. I'll see you get meat at noon. All you had to do was tell us you were ready for it. After all, up until a few moments ago I hadn't even heard you speak since we brought you home.'

It was unreasonable, but I felt my temper rise. Tears stung my eyes. I turned away from him, trying to master myself. What was wrong with me?

Chade spoke as if in answer to my thought. 'Fitz. Boy. Don't expect too much of yourself just yet. I've seen you through a number of hard times, and this was the worst yet. Give your mind time to recover, as well as your body.'

I took a breath to tell him I was fine. Instead I said, 'I expected to die down there. Alone.' And my discordant memories of my jail cell rushed back to fill me. I recalled both my terror and my despair, and felt anger that I had to bear those memories. They had left me there. Chade, the Fool, Kettricken, Dutiful – all of them.

'I feared the same,' Chade said quietly. 'It was a hard time for all of us, but for you, worst of all. Still, if you had heeded me—'

'Well, of course, it was all my own fault. It always is.'

Lord Golden spoke over his shoulder to Chade. 'There's no talking to him when he's like this. You will only upset him more. Best to let it go for now.'

'Be silent!' I roared at him, but my voice cracked to a squeak on the second word.

Chade looked at me in wordless reproach and concern. I pulled my knees up to my chest so I was sitting in a ball in the chair. My breath was coming in shuddering gasps. I took a breath and wiped my sleeve across my eyes. I would not weep. They expected me to fall apart, but I would not. I had been ill, and I'd had a bad scare. That was all. I dragged in a steadying breath. 'Just talk to me,' I begged Chade. I unfolded my shaking legs and planted my feet on the floor again. I hated that such weakness had come over me. 'Tell me what is happening, without making me ask all the stupid questions. Start with Civil.'

Chade heaved a sigh. 'I don't think this is wise.' I began to protest but he held up his hand. 'Nevertheless, I'll let you have your way in this. Very well. Civil. He got to his horse and came back to Buckkeep Castle as swiftly as he could without drawing attention to himself. When he got to Dutiful, he could scarcely croak out a word for how he had been strangled. But he got it across that Lord Golden's serving-man had rescued him from murderers in Buckkeep Town. That was as much as he told Dutiful, then. It was enough for the Prince to bring to me, and for me to set other feet running.' He cleared his throat, and then admitted, 'It took us longer than it should have to find you. I had not expected you to kill nor had I thought you would let the city guard take you alive. But when I knew you had been arrested and charged, I got a man into the cell with you as quickly as we could. Unfortunately, they had already had a healer see you, so I could not send in one of my own. The captain was very stubborn about releasing you. He was sure you'd killed those three men and some brawl you'd previously been involved in had marked you as a troublemaker in his eyes. Lord Golden had to complain of his missing jewels thrice before any of the guards thought to search Laudwine's cottage and find them there. I'd already provided a witness that you hadn't started the fight. That was as far along as I could nudge it. By the time the captain put together that you'd been defending your master's property from thieves and released you to us, it was damn near too late.'

'As far as you could nudge them,' I said flatly. Alone and cold and dying. He'd 'nudged' them.

'The Queen wanted to do more. She wanted simply to march her own guard down there and remove you from the cell. I couldn't allow it, Fitz. For, yes, there were other Piebalds. The day after you killed Laudwine, there were scrolls posted in several places saying that Laudwine and Padget were Witted, and that agents of the Queen had killed both them and their Wit-beasts. And it mocked her avowed intent to end unjust persecution of the Witted. It warned any Old Blood not to be stupid enough to trust her and come to her Old Blood convocation. And it ended by saying that she and her minions would kill anyone who tried to speak the truth: that her own son was Witted.' He paused a moment. 'So you see now. I had to leave you there. I didn't want to, Fitz. And I shouldn't have to tell you that.'

I put my face down in my hands. Yes. I should have heeded Chade. I had precipitated this. 'I suppose I should have let them kill Civil. And then run and reported the murder.'

'That would have been one way,' Chade agreed. 'But I think it would have damaged your relationship with Dutiful, even if you had concealed that you could have prevented his friend's death. And now, I think that is enough for today. Back to bed with you.'

'No. Finish this, at least. What did you do about the scrolls accusing Dutiful?'

'Do? Nothing, of course. We ignored them as ridiculous. And we took great care that there was no royal interest in Lord Golden's serving-man confined in a cell. The city guard had their murderer. Let justice take its course. The posted accusations were ridiculous, a wild attempt by someone to smear the Prince's good name. It was doubly ridiculous, in that the Prince still bore the deep scratches from his good friend's hunting cat. Surely a coursing beast would not attack a Witted one. All know the power Witted have over animals. And so on. In time, it was shown that the dead men were no better than common thieves. There was nothing of the Wit in what had happened, and certainly no royal interference. Thieves had been killed by a good servant protecting his master's property.'

'So. The Wit accusation was why you had to leave me there to rot.' I tried to put acceptance into my words. Part of me understood. Part of me hated him.

He winced at my choice of words, but nodded. 'I'm sorry, Fitz. We had no choice.'

'I know. And my own actions had brought it upon me.' I tried to keep bitterness out of my voice and nearly succeeded. I was suddenly horribly tired, but there was more I needed to know. 'And Civil?'

'Once I discovered who was dead, I knew I had to question him. I squeezed it all out of him. And what had triggered his action also. His mother killed herself, Fitz. She had sent the lad a message, begging his forgiveness, but saying she could not go on as things were. That she could not live with what he must be doing to buy her safety, even when it was a false sanctuary where men assaulted her at will.'

The ugliness of what he implied sickened me. 'Then Civil had meant to let them kill him.'

'His mother was dead. I think he meant to kill them, not caring if he died in the attempt, but he didn't even know how to begin. He was full of lofty ideals of duels and fair challenges. Laudwine never even gave him a chance to demand his right of combat.'

'What now for Civil?'

Chade took a breath. 'It's complicated. Dutiful insisted on being with him while I questioned him. Civil is Dutiful's man now, heart and soul. His prince defended him to me. If he must have a Witted one serving him, we have at least pulled that one's teeth. The Prince is fully convinced, and I almost am, that the Bresingas acted under duress. If the Piebalds ever held any of Civil's loyalty, his mother's suicide and their previous treatment of her have purged it from him. He hates them more than we ever could. Lady Bresinga was pressured into presenting the cat to the Prince, under threat that the Piebalds would betray her son and herself as Witted. But once she had done so, she was completely within their power. She was not only Witted; she had committed a treasonous act against the Prince. The Piebalds separated them, mother from son. Civil was sent to Buckkeep. They ordered him to maintain his friendship with Dutiful, to draw him deeper into the Wit, and to spy for them. If he did so, they promised his mother would be safe. His mother's home, Galekeep, became her prison. The Piebalds swiftly became greedy. First, it was her home, her wine cellar, her wealth. If she did not accommodate them, they threatened her son. Eventually, some of the men evidently availed themselves of the lady herself. She could not live with that. I think they misjudged her strength of will, and that of her son.'

It was an ugly, sobering story. But I did not let my mind dwell on it. I had more immediate concerns. 'What of Henja? Did the Prince tell you that I saw her?'

His face grew more grave. 'He did. But . . . is it possible you were mistaken? For my spies in town have heard not a whisper of her.'

I forced myself to consider the memory of that glimpse. 'I was hurt and it was dark. But . . . I do not think I was mistaken. And

I believe she was the woman who was there when Thick was. She offered gold to Padget and Laudwine for the Fool and me . . . I think. It was hard to decide what she was trying to buy from them. Laudwine didn't like her. She seems to be involved in all of this somehow.'

Chade lifted a hand, palm up. 'If she is, she has covered her tracks well. There is no sign of her in Buckkeep Town that I can discover.'

That was small comfort. His spies had not found Laudwine either. I kept that complaint to myself.

'We still have a Piebald spy here in Buckkeep. The man who led Thick to Laudwine.'

Chade's voice was neutral. 'Civil's groom met with a most unfortunate accident. He was found dead in a stud horse's stall, kicked to death. Why he would have gone into the stall at all is a mystery.'

I nodded. Another thread tied off. 'And Civil's mother and his holdings?'

Chade looked away from me. 'The tragic news reached us the day after you were taken prisoner. Lady Bresinga died of food poisoning. A number of her guests and servants died with her. It was horribly sad, but not the least bit shameful or scandalous. Her body was discovered first, but over the next few days, others sickened and swiftly died. Tainted fish is what I heard. Lady Bresinga's body was sent to her mother's home for burial. Civil is attending to that sad duty. Prince Dutiful sent his own honour guard with him as a token of the high esteem he holds him in. Civil understands that when the details have been settled, he will return to Buckkeep, to remain at the castle until he reaches his majority. Galekeep will be shuttered, though our Lady Queen has lent Civil staff and a steward to maintain the place in his absence.'

I nodded slowly. The Prince might call Civil friend, but he would be Chade's well-kept and pampered prisoner for the next few years. It was an apt solution. He could perceive it as protection or as a cage. All had been neatly managed. I wondered if Lady Rosemary had found a sudden reason to visit her friend at Galekeep, or if the spy that Chade had in place there had done the poisoning. It would have been difficult for Rosemary to travel, burned as she was. Then I suddenly turned to look at Chade. He met my scrutiny with a puzzled expression. I leaned forward suddenly and before he could draw back, touched his cheek. No paint came off on my fingers. Sound, pink flesh. No trace of healing burns.

'Oh, Chade,' I rebuked him, and my voice shook with shock. 'Have a care, man! You charge in blindly and none of us know the cost. None of us.'

He allowed himself a smile. 'I care little for the cost, when I know the benefit so well already. My burns are healed. For the first time in years, I walk with no pains in my knees and hips. I sleep free of pain at night. I even see more clearly.'

'You are not doing this alone.'

He looked at me, refusing to answer, and I knew the answer.

'You've been tapping Thick's strength,' I accused him in a low voice.

'He doesn't mind.'

'You don't know the dangers. He doesn't understand the risks.'

'And neither do you!' he replied sharply. 'Fitz, there are times to be cautious and times to be bold. The time has come for us to take these risks. We need to discover all the Skill can truly do. When the Prince goes on his quest to slay Icefyre, you will go with him. And you must know the Skill's powers by then, and must be capable of wielding them. This,' and he slapped his chest soundly, 'This is a miracle and a wonder. If we had had this at our disposal when Shrewd was ill, he never would have died. Think what that would have meant!'

'Yes, think,' I rejoined. 'Think of Shrewd, alive still and ruling here. Then ask yourself, why isn't that so? For he was not trained by Galen. Solicity was his Skillmistress. Can not we assume that he knew far more of the Skill than we do? Perhaps even how to prolong his life? So then, let us ask, why did he not do it? Why did not Solicity herself do it? Did they know that there was a price attached to that, a price too high to pay?'

'Or did he merely lack a coterie to assist him in his efforts?' Chade countered.

'He could have used Galen's Coterie, if that was the case.'

'Pah! You don't know that, and neither do I. Why must you be so pessimistic? Why must you always assume the worst?'

'Maybe I learned caution from a wise old man. One who is now behaving foolishly.'

Chade's cheeks flushed pink. Anger lit his eyes. 'You are not yourself. Or, perhaps it is even worse than that. You *are* yourself. Listen to me, you whelp. I watched my brother die. I watched King Shrewd dwindle, and I was beside him in the days when he did not know that his mind wandered, and I was beside him in the days when he was cognizant of the weakness of his body and his mind, and shamed to tears by it. I do not know which days were worse to witness. If he had had the Skill to change that, he would have done it, no matter the cost. This is Skill-knowledge that was lost to us. I intend to regain it. And to use it.'

I think he expected me to roar back at him. I half-expected myself to, and perhaps I would have if I had not felt such a combination of weakness, despair and fear. Chade had frightened me badly when his health and mind were failing and I feared we might lose his wealth of information and connections. Now, health-filled and bright-eyed, with ambition burning in him, he terrified me. I had known this side of Chade existed, known that he had always hungered to master the Skill. I had never known I'd have to confront that appetite. I took two deep breaths and spoke quietly. 'Is that decision yours to make?'

A frown furrowed his brows. 'What do you mean? Who else should make it?'

'The Skillmaster, perhaps, should say how the Skill is applied at Buckkeep. Especially among inexperienced students.' I met his gaze sternly. In truth, he was the one who had pushed me into accepting the responsibility of the position. I wondered if he winced now at how his own stubbornness in this had turned to bite him.

He was incredulous. 'You're saying you'd forbid me this? And expect me to obey you?' Hands on his knees, he leaned forward in his chair to confront me.

I did not want to meet him head-on in a clash of wills. I had not the strength just now. I turned the question. 'There was another Farseer who tried to use the Skill to his own ends. He himself was neither strong nor talented with the Skill, but he used the strength of his coterie to gain his ends. He used them ruthlessly, regardless of what it did to them, how it drained them or twisted their own wills. Will you become another Regal?'

'I am nothing like Regal!' Chade spat at me. 'For one thing, his interest was all for himself. You know that I have spent my entire life labouring tirelessly for the Farseer reign. And for another difference, I *will* develop my own Skill. I will not long be dependent on another's strength.'

'Chade.' My voice came out in a cracked whisper. I cleared my throat, but still spoke weakly. 'Perhaps you will develop your own Skill. But not if you go on as you have, experimenting alone, taking chances with yourself, and now risking Thick, who has no concept of the danger you may represent.' I wasn't sure he was listening to me. He was staring past me, his green eyes going far. I spoke on anyway, hearing my own voice failing and starting to rasp. 'You need to learn the dangers of the magic, Chade, before you wade into it and start using it for your own ends. The Skill is not a toy, nor is it something that any user should employ solely for his own benefit.'

'It wasn't fair!' Chade protested suddenly. 'They denied me the teaching, the teaching that I should have had. I was as much a Farseer as Shrewd. I should have been taught.'

I was tiring rapidly. I had to win this, or at least fight him to a draw before I collapsed back into my bed. 'No. It wasn't fair,' I agreed. 'But using Thick as your crutch and tool is not fair either. Nor will it replace the proper teaching you should have had. That you must get for yourself. Thick is strong with the Skill, and has no concept of what dangers that may present to him. Nor has he the will to resist you using his magic for your own purposes. He will not warn you when you are taking too much from him, and you will not know you have taken it until it is too late. It is wrong of you to tap his strength as if he were a bullock hitched to your cart. He may be simple, but in Skill at least he is our equal. He's a member of our coterie. As such you should be brothers, regardless of your varying abilities.'

'Coterie?' The slack-jawed look of astonishment on Chade's

face suddenly made me realize that he had not seen what was obvious to me.

'Coterie,' I repeated. 'You. Me. Dutiful. The Fool. And Thick.' I paused, waiting for him to say something. Instead, I heard the soft sound of the Fool's chair being pushed back from his desk. And the even quieter sounds of his feet as he crossed the room to stand near us. I wondered what expression he wore, but I didn't look away from Chade's gaze. When he continued to bet, I reminded him, 'Chade. I was there. I was not in full possession of myself, I know, but I would have had to be dead to have been unaware of what happened to me. What you all united to do to me. Didn't you understand that that was how a coterie functioned? The pooling of strength and abilities to achieve some goal. That was what you did. Thick's strength. Your knowledge of a man's internal structure. Dutiful's control and purpose. And the Fool's link to me. All were necessary to do what you did. And can do again, if needed. Dutiful has his coterie. Not much of one, in many ways, but a coterie, nonetheless. But only if we function as one. If you lead Thick astray, to use him as your personal reservoir of strength, you'll destroy us before we find our potential.'

I halted. My mouth was dry, and I'd run out of breath. At any other time, I would have been horrified to discover how weak I was. At the moment, I could not afford to spare it a thought. I felt I had come to a balancing point with the old man. For so many years, he had been my mentor and guide. As his apprentice, I had seldom questioned his wisdom or his ways; I had always been certain that he knew what was best. Yet, since summer, I had seen that his bright mind was failing and his memory not as tightly taloned as once it had been. But worse for both of us, I had begun to consider his decisions and even his thought processes from a man's perspective. I was no longer willing to concede to him that he knew best in everything. And when I applied the perspective of my thirty-odd years to the decisions he had made for me and for the Farseers in the past, I was not sure that I agreed with them any longer. Now that I could see his wisdom was not absolute, I felt more justified in demanding that he recognize there were areas in which I knew more than he did. It was a strange equality I sought to claim, one that did not assert I knew as much as he did, but rather that, although he was still wiser than I in many things, there were areas in which he must give way to me.

For so long he had been my mentor and above question. Now it was hard for both of us that I saw him as a man. I hated that I had become aware of his flaws. I never wanted to be the one to hold a mirror to him and point them out. I had to admit to myself, difficult as it was, that he had always been ambitious and eager for power. Limited by politics in his quest for his magic, scarred by an accident that doomed him to working unseen, he had still become a powerful force. It was his will that had sustained the Farseer throne in the days when King Shrewd was failing and his two remaining sons vied for his throne. It had been Chade's network of spies and servants who had assisted Queen Kettricken in retaining her power until her son could come of age. He was close now, so close, to putting another Farseer-orn heir on the throne.

Yet I could look at him and see that these successes would not be enough for him. He would not count any achievement a true victory until he had acquired for himself the things he had always hungered for. Power he had now, and the trappings that went with it. He could openly wield it, and folk accepted it as his right as the Queen's Councillor. Yet within the esteemed advisor there still lurked the deprived bastard, the disinherited child. No triumph would ever be enough for him until he mastered the Skill, yes, and let others know that he had mastered it.

I feared he would undermine all else he had engineered in attaining that one goal. His determination could blind him. And so I watched him as he weighed my words and thought his own thoughts about them. I studied him as I waited. He could not reverse the march of the years. Not even the Skill could make him young again. But perhaps, as Kettle had done, he could halt the progression of ageng, and repair the damage it had done to him. His hair was as white, the lines in his face graven as deep. But the knobbiness of his knuckles had subsided, and his cheeks were flushed with robust health. The whites of his eyes were clear.

As I watched him, I saw him come to a decision. And my heart sank as he rose hastily, for in his rush to leave I saw his desire to end the conversation. 'You are not well yet, Fitz,' he said as he stood. 'It will be days until you are strong enough to continue teaching Dutiful and Thick what you know of the Skill. And those days represent time I am not willing to waste. Therefore, while you are recuperating, I will continue my own explorations of the Skill. I will be circumspect, I promise you. I will risk no one except myself. But having begun this, having felt the first touch of what it can mean to me, I will not draw back. I will not.'

He started towards the door. I drew a ragged breath. I was very nearly at the end of my strength. 'Don't you understand, Chade? What you feel is the pull all students of the Skill are warned against! You venture into the Skill-current at your peril. If we lose you, the strength of the whole coterie is diminished. If you take Thick with you, the coterie is destroyed entirely.'

His hand was on the latch. He did not turn to look back at me. 'You need your rest, Fitz, not to work yourself up like this. When you are feeling better, then we will discuss this again. You know I am a cautious man. Trust me in this.' And then he was gone, closing the door behind him. He moved swiftly, like a child hurrying out of the room to escape a scolding. Or a man fleeing a truth he did not want to hear.

I sagged back into the chair. My throat and mouth were dry, my head pounding. I lifted my hands to shut out the light from my eyes. Into that small darkness, I asked, 'Have you ever suddenly realized that there was someone you loved, but presently did not like very much?'

'Strange you should ask *me* that,' the Fool observed dryly from close behind me. Then I heard him walk away.

I must have fallen asleep there. When I awoke, it was afternoon, and I ached from my cramped position in the chair. There was a tray of food on a table beside the chair. Even covered, it had gone cold. Fat was congealed in little floating lumps on top of the broth. There was meat, but it had gone cold. After two bites, the chewing of it wearied me. I forced myself to finish it, but felt that it sat like a lump in my stomach. They had given me watered wine, and bread in milk again as well. I didn't want it, yet could not have said what I did want. I forced myself to eat it.

The terrible weakness that was on me made me feel childishly weepy. I tottered back to my room. I wanted to wash my face to see if I could rouse myself from my lethargy. There was water in the pitcher, and a cloth to dry on, but my looking-glass was gone, probably tidied away when Kettricken changed my room. I washed, but felt no livelier for it. I went back to bed.

Two more days passed in the same haze of weakness and lassitude. I ate and I slept, but my strength seemed terribly slow to return. Chade did not visit me. I was not surprised at that, but Dutiful did not come either. Had Chade ordered him to stay away from me? Lord Golden had little to say to me, and turned my visitors away with the warning that I was still not well enough to see them. Twice I heard Hap's anxious tones, and once I heard Starling. I had no energy to move, but the inactivity made me ache. I lay alone in my bed, or sat on the chair near the fireside. I was both worried and bored. I thought about the Skill-scrolls up in Chade's old chamber, but the challenge of all the stairs daunted me. Nor could I bring myself to ask that favour of the Fool. It was not just that he never ventured forth from Lord Golden's façade. It was that we were both mired into coolly and correctly ignoring one another. It could only make our quarrel worse, and yet I could not bend enough to try any other way. It seemed to me I had already made enough efforts to mend things and been rebuffed by him. I wanted him to show some sign of wishing to make things right between us. But he did not. So two slow days of misery trickled past.

The next day I arose determined to put myself to rights. Perhaps if I stood and moved about as if I were healthy, I would begin to feel so. I began by washing myself, and then decided I would shave. The accumulation of whiskers was approaching a fair beard. I walked slowly to the door of my chamber and looked round. Lord Golden sat at the table, inspecting a dozen silk kerchiefs in different shades of yellow and orange and trying them against one another. I cleared my throat. He did not move. Very well, then.

'Lord Golden, pardon me if I disturb you. I seem to have misplaced my shaving mirror. Could I perhaps borrow one?'

He did not look round. 'Do you think that's wise?'

'Borrowing a mirror? Shaving without one strikes me as less wise.'

'I meant, do you think it's wise to shave?'

'I think I'm past due for it.'

'Very well, then. It's your choice.' His tone was neutral and chill, as if I did a risky thing and he wanted no part in it. He went to his room, and returned shortly with his own elaborate silver-framed hand-mirror.

I held it up, dreading what it would show me of my wasted face. The shock of my appearance numbed me; I dropped the mirror. Only good fortune decreed that it did not break when it fell to the rug. I have fainted from pain before, but never, I think, from pure surprise. As it was, I did not lose consciousness completely, but crumpled to sit in a heap on the floor.

'Tom?' Lord Golden asked in annoyance and surprise.

I had no attention for him. I slid the mirror across the rug to me and stared down into it. Then I touched my face. The scar I had borne for so long was gone. My nose was not precisely straight, but the long-ago break was far less evident. I thrust my hands inside my robe and felt my back. The sword-wound was gone, yes, but gone also was the ancient, pulling scar the festered arrowhead had left in my back. I inspected the place where my neck met my shoulder. Years ago, a Forged one had bitten a chunk from me there, leaving a puckered scar. The flesh was smooth.

I looked up to find Lord Golden regarding me with consternation.

'Why?' I asked him wildly. 'Why, in Eda's name, did you do this to me? All will mark this change in me. How will I explain it?'

He came a step closer. There was confusion in his eyes. Lord Golden spoke reluctantly. 'But Tom Badgerlock, we did nothing to you.' I do not know what my face looked like at his words but he recoiled from me. In a neutral voice, he continued, 'Truly, we did not do this to you. We worked to close the wound in your back and to clean your blood of poisons. When I saw your other scar start to pucker and then to expulse bits of flesh, I cried out to them we had to stop. But even after we dropped hands and stepped back from you . . .'

I tried to remember that moment, and could not. 'Perhaps what you set in motion, my body and Skill continued. I don't recall.'

He covered his mouth with a hand as he stood looking down on me. 'Chade—' He hesitated, then forced himself to go on. His voice was nearly the Fool's. 'I think Lord Chade felt . . . I should not surmise what he felt. Only I think he believes you knew how to do this, and that you kept it a secret from him.'

'Eda and El in a tangle,' I groaned. Chade was right. I never had been good at discerning what people felt unless they told me directly. I had sensed there was some knot between us, but this was the last thing I'd expected. Even if I'd known my body had been cleared of scars, I would not have suspected that Chade would feel slighted over some imagined secret. That was what was behind his huffy retreat; his resolution was that he would continue to discover whatever I'd concealed from him. I gathered my legs under me and stood without assistance. Not that Lord Golden had offered me any. I proffered the mirror to him and turned back to my room.

'So. Changed your mind about shaving, Badgerlock?' Lord Golden asked me.

'For now, yes. I'm going up to Chade's old chamber. If you could let him know that I'd like to see him there, I'd be appreciative.' I spoke to him as if he were the Fool. I didn't expect a reply and I didn't get one.

I simply had no strength. I stopped to rest so many times on the stairs that I thought my candle would burn out and leave me in darkness. When I did reach the chamber, I had lost all ambition. At the door, the ferret leaped out to challenge me. Gilly did a wild dance, inviting me to battle for the territory. 'You can have it,' I told him. 'You'd probably win anyway.' Ignoring his rushes at my feet, I went and sat on the edge of the bed, then lay down and almost immediately fell asleep. I think I slept for a long time.

When I awoke, the ferret was sleeping under my chin. The moment I stirred, Gilly fled. It was plain someone had come and gone. It disturbed me that I could sleep through that; when I had been bonded to my wolf, his mind had always kept watch through my senses. He would have wakened me as soon as he perceived I was hearing an intruder. I had grown too dependent on those wild senses, I decided as I swung my legs over the edge of the bed. I had grown too dependent on everything and everyone.

There were dishes and a bottle of wine on the cleared end of the table. A pot of soup had been left warming at the edge of the hearth, and the wood had been replenished for the fire. I got up and went directly to the food. I ate and drank and waited. And while I waited, I perused the scrolls that had been left out for me. There was a report from someone about Icefyre and Outislander dragons. Another spy report on doings in Bingtown and their war with Chalced. An old scroll that showed a sketch of the muscles in a man's back had been updated. The details and notes were in Chade's hand. Well, at least my journey through death's jaws had provided new knowledge. Beside that scroll were three more, bundled together. Tattered and faded they were, and all in the same hand. It was a set of Skill-exercises, designed specifically for the Solo. I scowled at that, wondering what they meant. A few minutes of reading enlightened me. These were exercises for the Skill-practitioner who had no coterie. It had never occurred to me before that there would be such, but when I thought about it, I saw it must be so. I had become one, hadn't I? There had always been people who had been socially inept, or simply preferred solitude. When coteries were formed, it would be likely there would be some excluded. These exercises were for ones such as those.

In reading it, I found it likely that they had most often been used as spies or healers. The exercises in the first scroll seemed to focus especially on subtle uses of the Skill either to listen in or implant suggestions in someone's thoughts. The second scroll dealt with repairing another's body. This fascinated me, not just because I had recently undergone it, but because it confirmed a thing I had suspected. What a man started with the Skill and his will, the body often took over. The body understood healing. Yet it also understood that sometimes hasty repairs were more important than perfect ones, that closing the wound might be more important than smooth skin afterwards. So the scroll put it. The body understood conserving one's strength and reserves against tomorrow's needs. The scroll cautioned Skill-users to be wary of ignoring the body's own tendencies, and to be circumspect with how ardently they pursued a repair. I wondered if Chade had read that part.

The third scroll dealt with maintaining one's own body. On this last scroll, the clear notes in Chade's hand contrasted strongly with the faded old inking. It chronicled his early failed efforts as well as his recent successes. This was what he had wanted me to see; these notes were why he had left it out. He wished me to know that ever since the Skill-scrolls had come into his possession, he had been trying and failing to repair his own body. He had been successful only since he had witnessed the healing of mine, and discovered that he could tap Thick's Skill-talent to supplement his faltering and groping efforts.

I read the diary of his frustration, and knew the fear that had accompanied it. I knew only too well what it was to live within a damaged body. And in witnessing Nighteyes' decline, I had tasted what it must be to grow old. Chade had resumed a normal life only in the last decade. He had spent his prime sequestered here, in this room, working from the shadows and in disguise. How bitter would it be to emerge into a world of people and music, dancing and conversation and, yes, power and the wealth to enjoy it, only to have one's declining body threaten to take it all away again? I could not blame him for what he had done, despite the risks he had taken. I understood it only too well. I dreaded the day when I would have to face such a decision, for I feared I would decide the same.

I read carefully, several times, the scroll that had to do with repairs to the body using the Skill. It told me much that was useful, but not all I needed to know. I knew with sad certainty why Chade had held these scrolls back from me. If I had seen them, I would have known that he was pursuing a lone quest to master the Skill. And he had obviously begun it years before I had been enticed to return to Buckkeep.

I leaned back in my chair and tried to put myself in the old man's place. What had he imagined, what had he dreamed? I pushed myself back through the years. The war with the Red Ships has finally ended. The raiders have been driven back by the Six Duchies dragons. Peace has returned to the land, the Queen is gravid with the Farseer heir, Regal has not only returned the missing library of Skill scrolls, but has conveniently died after renewing his loyalty to the crown. And Chade, after so many years spent in the shadows, can emerge as the Queen's trusted councillor. He can move freely about Buckkeep, enjoying food and drink and the companionship of the nobility. What is there left for him to desire? Only that which had been denied to him so many years ago.

The Skill was not taught to royal bastards, even if they had the aptitude for it. Some kings ruthlessly administered elfbark to illegitimate youngsters, to kill the Skill-ability in them. I did not doubt that other Farseer monarchs had saved time and simply killed the bastards. I had only been taught the Skill because both Lady Patience and Chade had pleaded on my behalf. Even then, if the need for a coterie had not been so desperate, I am sure King Shrewd would have refused me.

Chade had never been taught. And in the ways that boys do, I had always simply accepted that piece of knowledge about my master. I had never asked him, 'Were you ever tested for Skill-ability? Did you ask to be taught and were refused, or did you never even ask?' I had never asked for the details. Yet I knew that he had longed for that forbidden knowledge. I knew it in how ardently he had pursued it for me, and how badly he had hoped that I would succeed at it. My failure to master the magic had smarted as keenly for him as it had for me.

Yet I had never, until now, considered what these factors might mean when those scrolls came into his hands. Ever since he had come to my cottage, I had known that he had been reading the scrolls. Knowing Chade, I should have known that with or without a teacher, he would try to master what he read there. I should have offered to teach him what I knew. Every time he had brought up the question of Skill-candidates, had he secretly hoped I would look at him? And why hadn't I ever seriously considered the idea? Oh, yes, once I had thrown it out, as a man throws a bone to a hungry dog to appease it. But I had not truly considered him capable of learning it. Why not?

I had more questions about myself than I did about Chade. While I was pondering them, I heated water and found his looking-glass. In Chade's assassin's armoury were any number of knives sharp enough to shave with. I made a credible job of it, taking my time and watching my unscathed face emerge. I was sitting at the table, looking at myself in the mirror when Chade entered. I didn't wait for him to speak.

'I didn't realize that my old scars were gone. I think the coterie started the wheels turning, and after that my healing was like a runaway cart on a steep street. It just kept going on its own. I don't even really know how it was done.'

He spoke as humbly as I did. 'So Lord Golden managed to convey to me.' Then he came closer. When he stood over me, he studied my face, cocking his head to one side. When I looked up at him, he smiled reminiscently. 'Oh, my boy. You do look like your father. Far too much for our purposes now. You should not have shaved; the beard at least covered some of the changes in your face. Now you must wait until it grows back enough to disguise how much you've changed before you can go about the keep again.'

I shook my head. 'It wouldn't do, Chade. Not even a heavy beard would be enough.' I took a long final look at myself as I might have been. Then I laughed and pushed the mirror away. 'Come sit down. We both know what must be done. I've read your scrolls, but they don't seem to apply. In this effort tonight, we are going to have to feel our way.'

We did not work well together. I think by nature we were both Solos, and yet we would have to learn to function together as part of Dutiful's Coterie. And so we made a number of false starts, and irritably blamed Galen's fogging of me and my use of elfbark and those short-sighted folk who had not trained Chade when he was a boy. But at length, the Skill flowed hesitantly between us, and as I so often had before, I trusted myself to his long-fingered hands. I fed him strength and the Skill itself, for his ability was as yet only a sporadic trickling of the magic. Chade's knowledge of how a man's body was put together combined with my own body's awareness of itself to guide what we did. In some ways it was a more difficult task than my healing had been, for each piece had to be done separately, and in defiance of what my body felt was correct. But we prevailed.

And when we had finished, I took up the mirror again. My new scar was less noticeable than the old one, and my nose not quite as crooked. But it would suffice. The marks were there. As were the old bite scar on my neck, the star from the arrowhead near my spine, and a new web of scarring where the sword-wound should have been. These new scars were easier to tolerate than the old ones, for we involved only the skin and did not anchor them to the muscles underneath. Still, they pulled irritatingly. I knew I'd eventually get used to them. It was Chade who noticed that my 'badgerlock' was now growing in dark at the roots. He shook his head over that. 'I've no idea how to change that. Nothing in the scrolls mentions a change in the colour of hair. Dye the whole shock of white hair black is my advice. Let that change be obvious. Folk will think you've become vain. Vanity is easy to explain.'

I nodded and set the mirror down. 'But later. Right now, I'm exhausted,' I said, and spoke the simple truth.

He looked at me oddly. 'And your headache?'

I frowned and lifted a hand to my brow. 'Is no worse than an ordinary headache, despite all the Skilling we've done tonight. Perhaps you were right. Perhaps it only took getting used to.'

He shook his head slowly and came around the table to set his hands to my skull. 'Here,' he said, tracing the now non-existent scar that had birthed my badgerlock of white hair. 'And here.' He prodded an area near my eye-socket.

I winced from habit, then sat still. 'It doesn't hurt. My head always hurt, when I combed my hair, and my face always ached if I was long in the cold. I never thought about it before.'

'I'd date the injury by your eye to when Galen tried to kill you on the tower top. In the Queen's garden, when you were his student. Burrich said you nearly lost the vision in that eye. Have you forgotten the beating he gave you?'

I shook my head silently.

'Neither had your body. I've seen you from the inside out, Fitz. Seen the damage done to your skull in Regal's dungeons, and other long-healed fractures in your face and spine. The Skill-healing seems to have put right a lot of old damage. It interests me that you do not have a headache after Skilling. It will interest me even more if you cease having to fear seizures.'

He left my side and went to his scroll-rack. He returned with a copy of that most horrific of books, *Man's Flesh* by Verdad the Flayer. It was a beautifully-made thing, layers of paper bound between carved covers of hinkwood, and still smelled of its inks. Obviously this copy had been recently created. That corrupt and ruthless Jamaillian priest had flayed and dismembered bodies for years in a monastery in that distant land, but when his depravity was discovered, his notoriety spread even as far as the Six Duchies. I had heard of this treatise, but never before seen a copy.

'Where did this come from?' I asked in surprise.

'Some years ago, I sent for it. It took me two years to find one. And the text is obviously corrupted. Verdad never referred to himself as "the flayer" as this manuscript does. And I doubt that he rejoiced in the smell of rotting flesh, as this claims he did. No, I sought it out for the copies of his illustrations, not the words others have added.'

Chade opened it reverently and set it before me. As he had bidden me, I ignored the ornate Jamaillian lettering and focused instead on the detailed depictions of the interiors of bodies. As a boy, I had seen the sketches that Chade had made, and those he had from his master before him, but they had been crude things compared to these. Charts that show the most swiftly lethal places to thrust a dagger are not to be compared with a map of a man's exposed vitals. The colours were very true. It was strange to look at them and find myself reminded of the steaming entrails of a gutted deer. How can I explain how vulnerable I suddenly felt? All these soft structures, deep red and glistening grey, gleaming liver and intricately coiled intestines fit so precisely inside my body. Then Laudwine had thrust a sword blade through my back and into them. Without thinking, I set a hand to the false sword scar on my lower back. No ribs had shielded me there, only overlapping strands of muscle. Chade saw the gesture. 'Now you see why I feared so for you. From the start, I suspected that only the Skill could restore you to health.'

'Close it, please,' I said, and turned away from his treasured book, feeling ill. He ignored me, turning a page to yet another drawing. This was of a hand, skin and muscle pulled aside and pinned to show the bone and hinges.

'I studied this before I tried to repair my hands. I do not think his drawings are precisely correct, and yet I feel they were helpful to me. Who would have imagined there were so many individual bones in a man's hands and fingers?' Then he finally glanced up and, becoming aware of my discomfort, closed the tome. 'When you are better recovered, I recommend you study this, Fitz. I think perhaps every Skilled one should.'

'Even Thick?' I asked wryly.

He surprised me by lifting a shoulder. 'It would not hurt to show it to him. Sometimes he is capable of very fixed thought, Fitz. Who knows how much he retains in that misshapen skull?'

This brought a new thought to me. 'Misshapen. Do you think, then, that the Skill might be used on Thick? To repair what is wrong and make him normal?'

Chade shook his head slowly. '"Different" is not "wrong", Fitz. Thick's body recognizes itself as correct. His differences are no more to him than . . . well, here I am guessing, but I suspect that just as one man is tall and another is short, so it is with Thick. His body grew to some plan of its own. Thick is what he is. Perhaps we should just be grateful that we have him, even if he is different.'

'You have been investigating this most thoroughly, then.' I tried to keep condemnation from my voice.

'You cannot imagine what this is like for me, Fitz,' he affirmed quietly. 'It is as if a cell door has opened and I am allowed to walk free in the world. I am dazzled by all that I see. A blade of grass is as wonderful to such a freed prisoner as is the wide spread of a valley. I resent everything that calls me away from this exploration. I do not want to sleep or pause for meals. It is difficult for me to force my mind to the Queen's business. What do I care of Bingtown Traders and dragons and Narcheskas? The Skill has seized my imagination and my heart. Exploring it is all I truly want to do.'

My heart sank. I recognized Chade's obsession for what it was. Often and often had I seen him go through such fevers of fascination. Once his mind seized on an area of study, he would pursue it until he grasped it thoroughly. Or until another frenzy stole his attention away. 'So.' I attempted to speak lightly. 'Does this mean you will set aside your explosive experiments for a time?'

For an instant, he looked puzzled, as if he had completely forgotten. Then, 'Oh. That. I think I've discovered what I was attempting to discern about that. There are ways it may be useful, but it is too difficult to regulate to rely upon it.' He dismissed it with a wave of his hand. 'I have set it aside. This is far more important for me to grasp now.'

'Chade.' I spoke quietly. 'You must not venture alone into this. Even more, you must not draw Thick in after you. I hope you can see now that I speak for concern for you, not to hold you back from any selfish secret of mine.' I took a breath. 'You need a foundation. When I have my strength back, when Dutiful and Thick and I resume studying together, you must come to the tower with us.'

He was silent for a time, studying me. 'And Lord Golden?' He cocked his head at me. 'You did say before that he, too, was a member of this coterie.'

'Did I?' I feigned confusion for a moment. 'Oh. He was there, at my healing. And I thought I felt . . . do you think he truly contributed to my healing?'

Chade looked at me oddly. 'Don't you think you would be a better judge of that than I? You told me he did, but a day ago.'

I looked at my strange but strong reluctance to bring the Fool into our Skill lessons. He would not come anyway, I told myself, and then wondered if I were right. 'I could tell he was there, but I could not tell what he was doing,' I amended.

Chade's manner was grave. 'Guiding us, I thought. He said he had been part of something similar once, when Nighteyes was stricken.' He paused, then said without inflection, 'He knows you well. I think that was what he contributed most. He knows you well and he seemed to know . . . a way into you.' He sighed. 'Fitz, you have already admitted as much.'

'He was there when I used both the Wit and the Skill to heal the wolf. But he did not help with the healing. He helped me recover myself afterwards.' Then I stopped. After a time, I said, 'The reticence and secrecy. Does it become a habit? I swear, Chade, I don't know why . . . Damn this. Yes. The Fool and I have a Skill-bond. Thin but there, a remnant from when he first got the Skill on his fingers when he touched Verity and then me. And when he used it to pull me back to my body, it grew stronger. I suspect that if I considered it, I would find it stronger still since this healing. I rather doubt that he has any true Skill of his own. Only what is on his fingers, and perhaps his bond can only be with me.'

Chade smile almost guiltily. 'Well. A double relief. To hear you speak truth to me, and to let me know that . . . well. I've known the Fool a long time. I value him. But there is still about him a strangeness, even when he masquerades as Lord Golden that can make me uneasy at times. He knows too much, it sometimes seems, and at other times, I wonder if the things that matter to us concern him at all. Now that I have experienced the Skill a bit, and realized how open it makes us to one another . . . well. As you say, reticence and secrecy become a habit. A habit we both must preserve if we are to live. I am as reluctant to make the Fool privy to all my secrets as I am to share his.'

His honesty jolted me, and his opinion confounded me. And yet, he was right. It felt good to know there was honesty between us. 'I will speak to Lord Golden myself about what place he holds in our coterie,' I said. 'Much depends on what he is willing to do. No one can be forced to aid us.'

'Yes. And patch this foolish quarrel between you at the same time. Being in the same room with you two is as comfortable as standing between two snarling dogs. Who knows who will get bitten when they finally decide to rush one another?'

I ignored that. 'And you will join us in the Skill-tower for our lessons?'

'I will.'

I waited, then decided that this, too, was a thing that must be spoken openly. 'And your private Skill experiments?'

'They will go on,' he said quietly. 'As they must. Fitz, you know me. And you know the pattern of my years. Always I have learned alone and quietly, and always when I discovered a thread of learning that I felt I must possess, I pursued it ardently. Do not ask me to change that now. I cannot.'

And I truly believe he spoke the truth there, also. I sighed

515

heavily, but did not dare try to forbid it to him. 'Go carefully then, my friend. Go very carefully. The currents are strong and the footing treacherous. If you are ever swept away . . .'

'I'll be careful,' he said. And then he left me, and I crawled into the bed that was now more mine than his, and dropped into a deep, dreamless sleep.

TWENTY-TWO

Connections

Your estimation of the funds needed for this journey has fallen far short of the reality, nor would I have undertaken this inquiry if I had fully known about the foul weather, foul food and fouler people who inhabit these islands. I shall expect exceptional remuneration when I return.

I succeeded at last in visiting your demon-blasted island. Securing passage to visit that piece of ice and rock took the last of my insufficient funds, plus a day's labour of my stacking salt cod for a foul-tempered sea-bitch. The boat offered was leaky and unwieldy, of a kind I have never before seen and without proper oars. It was a miracle that I was able to navigate the icy waters to reach Aslevjal. Once there, I landed on a black and rocky shore. The glacier that once covered the entire island right down to the tideline seems to have retreated. An abandoned dock and pilings are visible, but all pieces that were easily scavenged are gone. The beach gives onto a wasteland of black stone. Tiny pockets of soil support little more than moss and scrubby grasses. There may have been crude buildings here at some time, but like the docks, anything usable was taken. Stone quarrying has evidently taken place here in the past but from the look of the place has been abandoned for at least a decade. Immense blocks of stone were cut and lined up end-to-end as for an immense wall, but it is a wall that begins and ends with a single run of blocks. Apparently efforts were made to chisel this run of stone into some sort of a horizontal statue, but the attempt was abandoned before it was even a quarter finished. It was impossible for me to discern what it was meant to be.

I walked as much of the beach as was bared and ventured briefly onto the glacial ice before nightfall caught me there. I saw no dragon, neither alive nor trapped in ice, nor anything even remotely resembling a live creature. I groped my way back to the beach and spent an icy night

517

sheltered behind the stone blocks. Not a scrap of driftwood could I find for a fire. I slept poorly, being troubled by horrendous dreams in which I was one of a mob of Six Duchies folk trapped in a dreadful stone prison. When dawn came, I was thankful to leave. Any others who venture here should take care to bring with them everything to supply their needs, for this island certainly offers nothing to a man.

Report to Chade Fallstar, unsigned

Restoring my scars had delayed the recovery of my strength. For the next three days, I withdrew into myself and focused solely on regaining my health. I slept and ate and slept again. I remained in the workroom. Chade himself brought meals to me. They followed no regular schedule, but he brought ample quantities of food when he did come, and I had the hearth for making tea or heating soup so it mattered little.

There were no windows in the workroom, and time lost all meaning for me. I returned to the wolfish habits I had shared for years. At dawn and at twilight I was most alert, and during those times I studied the scrolls. Then I ate, and dozed in front of the fire, or slept in the bed for the rest of the day's circle. Not all my waking hours were spent in reading. I amused myself and Gilly by hiding bits of meat when he was not in the room and then watching him ferret them out when he returned. I did simple projects such as suited my fancy. I made a board for playing the Stone game, burning the lines into it, and then carved the markers from a whale tusk that Chade had said I might use. I dyed them red and black, and left an equal quantity unmarked. I hoped for a game with Chade in vain, however. He spoke little to me of his Skill-studies, and when he came and went he seemed always in a hurry. Likely it was for the best. I slept more deeply when I was left alone.

He was very close-mouthed about the other news of the keep. What little I squeezed out of him worried me. The Queen was still in negotiations with the Bingtown Traders, but had graciously given the Dukes of Shoaks and Farrow permission to pressure Chalced along their borders as they wished. There would be no formal declaration of warfare, but the normal harrying and raiding that went on along that boundary would be increased, with her tacit blessings. There was little new in this: the slaves of Chalced had known for generations that they could claim freedom if they could manage to escape to the Six Duchies. Once free, they often turned against their old masters, raiding across the border the flocks and herds that once they had tended. For all that, trade between Chalced and duchies remained lively and prosperous. For the Six Duchies to side openly with Bingtown could put an end to that.

The Bingtown war with Chalced had horribly disrupted Chade's flow of spy information from that area. He had to rely on second- and third-hand accounts and, as with all such heavily-handled information, there were contradictions. We were both sceptical of the 'facts' we received. Yes, the Bingtown Traders had a dragon-breeding plantation far up the Rain Wild River. One, or perhaps two, full-grown dragons had been seen in flight. They were variously described as blue, silver or blue and silver. The Bingtown Traders fed the dragons, and in return, the dragons guarded Bingtown Harbour. But they would not fly out of sight of shore; which was why the Chalcedean ships still were able to menace and plunder Bingtown's trading fleet. The dragon-breeding farm was tended by a race of changelings, half-dragon and half-human. It was in the midst of a beautiful city, where wondrous gems glowed from the walls at night. The humans who also dwelt there preferred to live in lofty timber castles high in the tops of immense trees.

Such information more frustrated than enlightened us. 'Do you think they lied to us when they told us about the dragons?' I asked him.

'They likely told us their truth,' Chade replied tersely. 'That is the whole purpose of spies: to give us the other truths of the story, so that from all of them, we can cobble together our own truth. There is not enough meat here to make a meal from, only enough to torment us. What can we deduce for certain from these rumours? Only that a dragon has been seen, and that something peculiar is going on somewhere on the Rain Wild River.'

And that was as much as he would say on that subject. But I suspected he knew far more than he admitted, and that he had other irons in the fire than the ones he discussed with me. So my days passed in sleep, study and rest. Once, when rustling through Chade's scrolls for one I recalled on the history of Jamaillia, I found the feathers from the treasure-beach. I stood looking at them in the dimness, and then carried them over to Chade's worktable and examined them there in a better light. Just touching them was unsettling. They stirred to life memories of my days on that desolate beach, and awoke a hundred questions.

There were five feathers in all, about the size of the curving feathers in a cockerel's tail. They were carved in extreme detail, so that each separate rib of the feather lay against the next. They seemed to be made from wood, though they weighed oddly heavy in my hands. I tried several blades against them; the sharpest one made only a fine silvery scratch. If this was wood, it was near as hard as metal. Some trick of their carving seemed to catch the light strangely. The feathers were plain and grey and yet, seen from the tail of my eye, colour seemed to run over them. They had no discernible smell. Setting my tongue to one gave me a faint taste of brine followed by bitterness. That was all.

And having tested all of my senses against them, I surrendered to the mystery. I suspected they would fit the Fool's Rooster Crown. I wondered again whence that strange artefact had originated. He had unwrapped it from a length of fabric so wondrous that it could only have come from Bingtown. Yet the old wooden circlet seemed too humble to have come from a city of marvels and magic. When he had shown the ancient crown to me, I had recognized it immediately, having seen it once before, in a dream. In my vision, it had been colourfully painted and bright feathers had stood up above the circlet to nod in the breeze. A woman had worn it, pale even as the Fool had been pale then, and the folk of some ancient Elderling city had paused in their celebration to listen and laugh at her mocking words. I had interpreted her status as a jester. Now I wonder if I had missed a subtler meaning. I looked at them, spread like a fan, and a sudden shiver ran over me. They linked us, I knew with a sudden chill. They linked the Fool and me, not only to one another, but to another life. Hastily I wrapped them in a cloth and hid them under my pillow.

I could not decide what it meant that the feathers had come to me; but I did not want to discuss them with Chade. The Fool might have the answers, I suspected, and yet I felt a shamed reluctance to take them to him. There was not only the gulf of our present quarrel between us, but the fact that I had had them for so long and hadn't spoken of them to him. I knew that neither of those things would be improved by waiting longer, yet I truly felt too weak to present them to him. So I slept with them under my pillow each night.

In the deeps of my third night in the workroom, Nettle invaded my sleep. She came as a weeping woman. In my dream, a statue stood in a stream of the tears she had shed. Her tears were a silvery gown that she wore, and her mourning was a fog around her. I stood for a time, watching her cry. Each silver tear that ran down her cheeks splashed into a thread of gossamer that became part of her raiment before it turned into the stream that flowed past her. 'What is wrong?' I asked the apparition at last.

But she only continued to weep. I approached her, and finally put my hand on her shoulder, expecting to encounter cold stone. Instead she turned to me with eyes that were grey as fog. Her eyes were made of tears. 'Please,' I said. 'Please talk to me. Tell me why you weep?'

And suddenly she was Nettle. She leaned her brow on my shoulder and wept on. Always before, when I had encountered her in dreams, I had had the feeling she was seeking for me. This time I sensed that I had come to her, drawn by her sorrow into some other place that was usually private to her. I think my coming surprised her. Yet I was not unwelcome, only unlooked for.

What is it? Even in my sleep, I knew I Skilled to her.

'They quarrel. Even when they do not speak, their quarrel hangs like cobwebs in the room. Every word anyone says gets tangled in the quarrel. They act as if I cannot love them both, as if I must choose between them. And I cannot.'

Who quarrels?

'My father and my brother. They came home safely, as you said they would. But as soon as they got down from the horse, I felt the storm hanging between them. I don't know what it is about. My father refuses to speak of it, and he has forbidden my brother to tell me. It is something shameful and dark and horrid. Yet my brother wishes to do it. He desires it with all his heart. I cannot imagine why. Swift has always been such a good boy; quiet and meek and obedient. What can he have discovered that he longs to do and my father so abhors?'

I could almost feel her mind groping towards dark suspicions. She longed to know what had so disgraced her gentle brother in her father's eyes. Her imagination could not conjure anything sufficiently evil that a boy of his years could possibly do. That led her towards the idea that her father was being irrational. Yet that concept, too, was untenable for her. And so her speculation wobbled between two unacceptable ideas. And all the while the tension in the household grew heavier and heavier.

'He does not allow my brother to go outside by himself. All day long, he must accompany my father as he goes about his chores. Yet he is not allowed to help him exercise or groom the horses. Instead, he must simply stand and watch. It makes no sense to me, or to my brothers. But if we ask about it, my father becomes very strict and silent. It is making all of us miserable and I do not know how much longer my brother can stand it. I fear he will do something desperate.'

What do you fear he might do?

'I don't know. If I knew it, I could prevent it.'

I do not know of any way I can help you with this. I framed the thought very carefully, fencing it off from all I knew. What would she think of Swift if she knew he was Witted? How did Burrich and Molly speak of that magic in their home, if they spoke of it at all? She had not mentioned how her mother had reacted to the situation and I could not find the courage within me to ask.

'I did not think you could, Shadow Wolf. That was why I did not come to you. But I am grateful you came to me, even if you cannot help me.' A sigh. 'When you wall me out, I feel more isolated than I can explain, even to myself. For so long, you were always there, at the edges of my dreams, watching them through me. Then, you took yourself away. And I do not know why. Nor do I know who or what you truly are. Will not you explain yourself to me?'

I cannot. I heard the harshness of my own refusal and felt in a Skill-echo her hurt at my words. Against my will, I felt myself try. *I cannot explain. In some ways, I am a danger to you, and so I seek to stay away from you. You do not truly need me. Yet, in all ways that I can, I will watch over you and protect you. And come to you when I think you need me.*

'You contradict yourself. You are a danger that will protect me? I do not need you, yet you will come to me when I need you? You make no sense!'

No. I don't, I admitted humbly. *And hence I cannot explain myself to you, Nettle. All I can offer you is this. What is between your father and brother is between your father and brother. Do not let it stand between you and either of them, difficult as that might be. Do not lose faith in either of them. Or stop loving either of them.*

'As if I could,' she said bitterly. 'If I could stop loving them, I could stop grieving for what they do to each other.'

And there we left it as I faded from her dream. There was no comfort for me in such contact with my daughter and very little comfort for her, I am sure. Her worry became mine. Burrich had always been strict, yet fair within his own sense of fairness. He had often been rough with me, but never harsh. An irritated cuff, an impatient shove, he might have given, but he had seldom beaten me. The few thrashings I had suffered at his hands had been intended to teach a lesson, never to harm me. The times he had physically punished me I now saw as justified. Yet I feared that Swift would defy him openly as I had not, and I did not know what effect that would have on the man. He believed that one boy entrusted to his care had died horribly because he had failed to beat the Wit out of him. Would he see it as his duty to protect his own son from a similar fate, no matter how harsh he must be to do it? I feared for them both, and had no outlet for that worry.

At dawn of the fourth day, I awoke feeling stronger and restless. Today, I decided, I was well enough to get out and move around the keep a bit. It was time for me to resume my life. I took the feathers from beneath my pillow and went down to Tom Badgerlock's chamber to get some fresh clothing. I had scarcely closed the door to the hidden staircase behind me before there was a tap on the connecting door. I reached it in two steps and opened it. Lord Golden took a startled step backwards. 'Well, I suppose he is awake after all. And dressed, too, I see. So. Are you feeling more yourself, Tom Badgerlock?'

'A bit,' I replied, trying to look past him to discover for whom this mummery was played out. I barely had time to take in the shock on his face as he stared at my renewed scars before Hap almost shouldered him aside to get to me. My boy seized me by the shoulders and stared up at me in horror.

'You look terrible. Go back to bed, Tom.' Then, almost without drawing breath, he turned to Lord Golden. 'Sir, I beg your pardon. You were right, I had thought that you were deceiving me as to how ill he was. But you were right to keep all visitors from his door. I see that now. I most humbly beg your pardon for my ill words.'

Lord Golden gave a small harrumph. 'Well. I scarcely expect court manners from a country boy, and I understand that you have been so worried about your father. So, little as I have enjoyed your rousing me at such ungodly hours, or your churlish manners when I forbade you access, I shall forgive your behaviour. And I'm sure that you will both excuse me while you enjoy your visit.'

He turned away and left us alone in my small chamber. It did not take much urging from Hap to get me to sit down on the low bed. The long trek down Chade's winding stairs had tired me. Hap kept one hand on my shoulder as he sat down beside me. His gaze wandered over my face, and he squinted in pity at my gauntness. 'I'm so glad to see you,' he said tightly. For a moment longer he stared at me, face taut with some emotion. Then his eyes brimmed suddenly and he buried his face in both his hands and rocked back and forth on my bed. 'Tom, I thought you were going to die,' he managed to say through his fingers. And then he sat panting, fighting the sobs that threatened to overtake him. I put my arm around his shoulders and hugged him close. Dry sobs broke from him. He was suddenly my boy again, and very frightened he had been. He spoke in gasps. 'I've been here before dawn every day since they brought you here, and every day Lord Golden has told me that you were too weak for visitors. At first, I tried to be patient, but the last few days—' He gulped suddenly. 'I've been very rude to him, Tom. I was horrid. I hope he won't take it out on you. It was just—'

I spoke by his ear, calmly and reassuringly. 'I've been very ill, and my recovery is still slow. But I'm not going to die, son. Not this time. I'll be here for you for some time yet. And Lord Golden has already told you that he forgives you. So. Don't worry about any of that.'

He reached up to grip my hand tightly in both of his. After a moment, he straightened and turned to face me. Tears tracked his face. 'I thought you would die and I'd never get the chance to tell you I was s-s-sorry. For how I behaved. I knew you'd nearly given up on me, in that you hardly spoke to me nor came to see me any more. And then you were hurt, and I could not get to you in that jail. Nor afterwards, when they brought you up here. And all I could think was that you would die believing me both stupid and ungrateful for all you had done for me. You were right, you know. I should have listened to you. I wanted so badly to tell you that. You were right. And I've learned.'

'About what?' I asked, but my heart sank with the answer I already knew.

He sniffed, looking aside from me. 'About Svanja.' His voice grew deeper and thicker. 'She's cast me off, Tom. Just like that. And I've already heard that there is someone else for her – or maybe always was. A sailor on one of those big trading ships.' He looked down at the floor between his feet. He swallowed. 'I suppose they had been . . . close, before his ship last sailed, in the spring. Now he's back, with silver earrings for her, and fancy cloth and a spice perfume from far away. Gifts for her parents, too. They like him.' His voice grew softer and softer as he spoke, so that his last words were barely audible. 'If I'd known,' he said, and then his voice trailed away.

It was a very good time for me to be silent.

'I waited for her one night, and she just didn't come. And I got very worried, frightened for her. I was scared that something bad had happened to her on her way to meet me. And finally I got up the courage and went to her house. Just as I was going to knock on her door, I heard her laughing inside. I didn't dare to knock because her father hates me so much. Her mother didn't used to hate me, but then you got into that fight with her father and— Well. Anyway. I thought it was just that she hadn't been able to get out, well, sneak out to meet me. Because her father had started to be very watchful, you know.' He halted, face flushing. 'It's strange. Looking back at it now it seems shameful and childish. Us sneaking about, hiding from her father, her lying to her mother to get time to spend with me. It didn't seem like that at the time, not at all. It seemed romantic and, well, fated. That was what Svanja always said. That we were fated to be together, and should let nothing stand between us. That lies and deceit didn't matter, because together we were a truth that no one could deny.' He rubbed his brow with the heels of his hands. 'And I believed it. I believed it all.'

I sighed, yet admitted, 'If you had not believed it, Hap . . . well, then it would have been worse than foolish to do as you did.' And then I halted, wondering if I had just made it worse.

'I feel such a fool,' he admitted after a time. 'And the worst part is, I'd take her back in a breath if she came to me. Faithless as I know she is, first to him and now to me, I'd still take her back. Even if I had to wonder ever after if I could hold her.' After a time, he asked quietly, 'Is this how you felt when I told you Starling was married?'

A hard question, but mainly because I didn't want to tell him that I had never truly loved Starling. So I just said, 'I don't think any two pains are ever exactly the same, Hap. But the part about feeling a fool, oh, yes.'

'I thought I would die from it,' he declared passionately. 'The next day I was out on an errand for Master Gindast. He's come to trust me with making his purchases about town, because I am very exact with what he wants and what he will pay for it. So, I was hurrying, and then I saw a couple coming towards me. And I thought, "she looks so much like Svanja, she could be her sister." And then I saw it *was* Svanja, but wearing silver earrings and a shawl dyed such a violet as I had never seen. And the man beside her held her arm and she was looking up at him exactly as she looked up at me. I could not believe it. I stood gawking, and as they went by, she glanced at me. Tom, she blushed red, but pretended not to know me. I . . . I didn't know what to do. We have had to sneak about so much that I thought, well, perhaps this is her uncle or a man her father knows, and she must pretend not to know me. But even then, I knew it was not so. And when I went into the Stuck Pig two days later, in the hope of seeing her, the men in the tavern mocked me, asking how it felt to be small fry now that the big fish was biting again. I did not know what they meant, but they soon explained it to me. In detail. Tom, I have never been so humiliated. I all but fled, and I've been too ashamed to go back, lest I encounter them. A part of me wants to, a part of me yearns to tell her sailor how faithless she is, and to tell her that I've discovered how worthless she is. Yet another part of me longs to fight and best him, to see if that would bring her back to my side. I feel both a fool and a coward.'

'You are neither,' I told him, knowing he could not believe me. 'Walking away from it is the wisest thing to do. Fight him and win her back, and what do you have? A woman no better than a bitch in season that goes with the strongest dog. Confront her and have her disdain you, and you will only have added to your humiliation. Think of it this way, if it comforts you at all. She will always wonder at how easily you seemed to let her go.'

'A sour comfort. Tom, is there any such thing as a true woman?' He asked this so wearily that it twisted my heart to see him so soon disillusioned.

'Yes, there is,' I asserted. 'And you are young yet, with as good a chance as any of finding one.'

'Not really,' he declared. He stood up abruptly. A tired smile twisted his mouth. 'For I've no time to look for one. Tom, I'm so sorry to come and visit so briefly, but I must run now to be back at the woodshop on time. Old Gindast is a taskmaster. Since I discovered you were hurt, he's given me time each dawn to come and try to see you, but he insists I make up the work in the evening.'

'He's wise. Work is the best cure for worry. And for heartbreak. Throw yourself into your tasks, Hap, and don't berate yourself for foolishness. Every man makes his share of mistakes in that area.'

He stood looking at me for a time longer. Then he shook his head. 'Every time I think I've grown up a bit more, I look around and see myself acting like a child again. I came here to see you, sick with worry, and the instant that I saw you could stand, all I did was bend your ear with my woes. You've told me nothing of all you went through.'

I managed a smile. 'And that is how I'd like to leave it, son. Nothing there that I care to remember. Let's put it behind us.'

'For now, then. I'll come back and see you again tomorrow.'

'No, no, don't do that. If you've been coming every day, as I know you have, then I know you must be wearied of it. I'm mending nicely, as you can see. Soon enough I'll be down to visit with you, and then I'll ask Gindast to give you an afternoon off and we can sit and talk together.'

'I'd like that,' he said, and the sincerity in his voice gave me heart. He hugged me before he left and I feared his youthful strength would snap my weakened bones. Then he left me and I sat staring after him. For the first time in months, I felt I had my Hap back again, I thought as I laboriously took out clean clothing and clambered into them. My relief at regaining him was tinged with guilt. I couldn't keep him a boy. I shouldn't expect him to be 'my Hap' any more than Chade should hope me to be his 'boy'. To be relieved that his heartbreak and disappointment had brought him back to me and convinced him of my wisdom was a sort of betrayal on my part. Next time I saw him, I'd have to admit to him that I hadn't known that Svanja would be false to him, only that she distracted him from his apprenticeship. I didn't relish the idea.

Dressed, I left my room and went out into Lord Golden's chamber. I was no longer tottering about, but it was more comfortable to move slowly and carefully. His serving-boy hadn't brought breakfast up yet. The table was bare. He sat before the fire, looking weary. I nodded to him, and then set the cloth-wrapped feathers on the table. 'I think these were meant for you,' I said. I put no inflection in my voice. As I unrolled the cloth, he rose from his chair and came to see what I was doing. He watched, not saying a word as I nudged the feathers into a row.

'They are extraordinary. How came you by these, Badgerlock?' he asked at last, and I felt my silence had dragged the question from him. It burned me that he still spoke with Golden's Jamaillian accent.

'When Dutiful and I went through the Skill-pillar, it took us to a beach. I picked these up along the tideline there. They were lying amongst the driftwood and seaweed like flotsam. As I walked the beach I found them, one after the other.'

'Indeed. Never have I heard such a tale.'

There was an unspoken question in his neutral comment. Had

I concealed these from him deliberately or dismissed them as unimportant? I answered as best I could. 'The time spent on that beach still seems strange to me. Disconnected from all else. When I did get back, so much happened all at once: the fight to regain Dutiful, and Nighteyes' death and then our journey back here, with no privacy to speak to one another. Then, once we got to Buckkeep, there was the betrothal and all.' Even as I made my excuses, they seemed weak. Why hadn't I told him about the feathers? 'I put them away up in Chade's workroom. And the time never seemed right.'

He was just staring at them. I looked at them again. Set out in a row on the rough cloth, their flat greyness made them even more unremarkable. Yet at the same time they seemed profoundly strange, artefacts too perfect to have been shaped by men's hands and yet obviously manufactured. I felt oddly reluctant to touch them.

'I see,' Lord Golden said at last. 'Well. Thank you for showing them to me.' He turned and walked back towards the hearth.

I couldn't comprehend what had just happened. I tried again. 'Fool. I think they belong in the Rooster Crown.'

'Doubtless, you are correct,' he replied levelly, without interest. He sat down in front of the fire again and stretched his legs out toward it. After a moment, he crossed his arms on his chest and sank his chin down. He stared into the flames.

A flash of anger, cleansing as flame, washed through me. For an instant I wanted to seize him and shake him, to demand that he be the Fool again for me. Then the fury was gone and in its wake I stood trembling and sick. I felt then that I'd killed the Fool somehow, that I had destroyed him when I had demanded answers to the questions that had always floated unasked between us. I should have known that I could never understand him as I understood other people. Explanations had seldom worked between us. Trust had. But I had broken that, like a child who takes something apart to see how it works and ends up with a handful of pieces. Perhaps he could not be the Fool again, any more than I could go back to being Burrich's stableboy. Perhaps our relationship had changed too profoundly for us to relate as Fitz and the Fool. Perhaps Tom Badgerlock and Lord Golden were all that was left to us.

I felt suddenly weary and weak again. Without a word, I rolled the feathers up in the cloth again. Carrying them in my fist, I went back into my chamber and shut the door behind me. I opened the secret door, closed it behind me, and began the long climb back up to my workroom.

I was shaking with weariness by the time I reached my bed. Without undressing, I crawled back under the covers. After a time, I fell into a deep sleep. When I awoke hours later, I was hungry and the fire had almost burned out. Waking up, eating and feeding the fire: none of it seemed worth the effort. I shouldered deeper into the bed and fled back into unconsciousness.

The next time I awoke, it was because someone was bending over me. I came awake with a yell of alarm and had seized the Prince by the throat before I knew it was he. An instant later, I was sitting back on my bed, panting as my panic subsided. 'Sorry, sorry,' I managed.

The Prince stood well away from the bed, rubbing his throat and staring at me. 'What is the matter with you?' he croaked, caught between anger and alarm.

I gulped air in a dry throat, feeling sweaty and shaky. My eyes and mouth were sticky. 'Sorry,' I managed again. 'You woke me too suddenly. I was startled.' I struggled free of my blankets and staggered out of bed. I could not catch my breath. My alarm seemed a continuation of a nightmare I could not recall. I felt bleary and disoriented as I looked about my chamber. Thick was sitting in Chade's chair, his shoes stretched out towards the fire. His tunic and trousers were servant-blue, but they looked new and as if they had been cut to fit him. How long ago had I intended to get him shoes and better clothing? Chade must have done it. The fire burned merrily on the hearth and there was a tray of food on the table.

'Did you do this? Thank you.' I made my way to the table and poured wine into a glass.

The Prince shook his head in confusion. 'Do what?'

I lowered the glass I had drained. My mouth still felt dry. I poured another glass of wine and drank it down, then drew a breath. 'The food and the fire,' I explained. 'The wine.'

'No. That was there when we came in.'

My senses were gradually coming back to me and my heart was

resuming its normal rhythm. Chade must have come and gone while I was asleep. Then, as it dawned on me, 'How did you get here?' I demanded of the Prince.

'Thick brought me.'

At his name, the simpleton turned his head. He and the Prince exchanged conspiratorial grins. I sensed something pass between them, too swift and controlled for me to follow. Thick chuckled and turned back to the fire with a sigh.

'You are not supposed to be here,' I said heavily. I sat down at the table and poured more wine. I put my hand on the covered pot of soup on the tray. It was barely warm. Eating it seemed like too much trouble anyway. I drank the wine.

'Why shouldn't I be here? Why shouldn't I know the secrets of the castle where I shall some day be King? Am I considered too young, too stupid or too untrustworthy?'

That was a sorer point than I had expected to touch. I suddenly realized I had no good answer to his query. I said mildly, 'I thought Chade didn't want you up here.'

'He probably doesn't.' He came to sit down beside me at the table as I poured more wine. 'There are probably a lot more things that Chade would just as soon keep to himself. That man loves secrets. He has stuffed Buckkeep full of secrets like a magpie collecting shiny pebbles. And for the same reason, solely that he loves to have them.' He regarded me critically. 'The scars are back. Did the Skill-healing wear off, then?'

'No. Chade and I put them back. We judged it the most sensible thing to do. Fewer questions, you know.'

He nodded, but continued to stare at me. 'You look both better and worse than you did. You shouldn't be drinking all that wine before you've eaten.'

'The food's cold.'

'Well, it's simple enough to heat it.' He spoke with impatience for my stupidity. I thought he would put Thick to the task. Instead, he took up the pot himself, gave it a stir and covered it again. As if well practised at such things, he attached it to the hook and swung it over the fire again. He tore the small loaf of bread in half, and set it on a plate near the flames to warm. 'Do you want water for tea? It would do you more good than all that wine you're slogging down.'

I set my empty glass down on the table but did not fill it again. 'You amaze me sometimes. The things you know, for a prince, are surprising.'

'Well, you know how my mother is. Servant of the people. When I was younger, she wished me educated in the way her people educate their Sacrifice, that is, that I should know how to do the most common tasks as well as any peasant boy would. When she had a hard time teaching me all she wished to know at Buckkeep, she decided to foster me out, away from servants who leapt to my every desire. She wished to send me to the Mountains for a time, but Chade urged her to keep me in the Six Duchies. That left her only one choice, she decided. And so when I was eight, she sent me to Lady Patience, to page for her for a year and a half. Needless to say, I was not treated like a coddled princeling there. For the first two months, she kept forgetting my name. Yet Lady Patience taught me a wonderful array of things.'

'You didn't learn cooking skills from Lady Patience,' I observed before I could guard my tongue.

'Ah, but I did,' he replied with a grin. 'It was by necessity. She would want something heated, late at night in her room, and if left to herself, she burned it and filled the apartments with smoke. I learned a great deal from her, actually, but you are right. Cooking was not her strongest talent. Lacey taught me how to warm a meal at a hearth. And other things, as well. I can crochet better than half the ladies of the court.'

'Can you?' I asked in a voice of neutrally friendly interest. His back was to me as he stirred the pot. It suddenly smelled good. My small lapse had passed unnoticed.

'Yes, I can. I'll teach you some day, if you like.' He fished the soup back from the flames, stirred it again, and brought it back to the table with the bread. As he set it before me as if he were my page, he observed, 'Lacey said that you never learned as a boy. That you were too impatient to sit still that long.'

I had taken up my spoon. I set it down again. He went back to the hearth and checked the teakettle. 'Not quite hot enough yet,' he said, and then added, 'Lacey always told me that the steam should stand out a full handspan from the spout if the tea is to be brewed well. But I'm sure she said as much to you. Both Lady Patience and Lacey told many tales about you. I'd heard little about you here at Buckkeep. You were mentioned as often with a curse here as with regrets. But when I got there, it was as if they couldn't help themselves, even though it often made Patience break down and weep. That's the one thing I don't understand about all this. She thinks you are dead and she mourns you. Every single day. How can you let her do that? Your own mother.'

'Lady Patience is not my mother,' I said weakly.

'She says she is. Was,' he corrected himself sourly. 'She was always telling me what I *actually* wanted to eat or do or wear. And if I protested that my true preference was different, she would declare, "Don't be ridiculous. I know what you want. I know about boys! I had a son of my own, once." She meant you,' he added heavily in case the inference had escaped me.

I sat there, silent. I told myself that I was not a well man yet, that the cold, painful days in the prison and the Skill-healing and the remaking of my scars, and yes, even the Fool's rejection of my overtures of peace had weakened and drained me. Thus I trembled and my throat closed and I could not think what to do when a secret so well and truly kept was suddenly spoken aloud. A terrible darkness engulfed me, worse than anything elfbark had ever produced. Tears welled in my eyes. Perhaps, I thought, if I do not blink, they will not spill. Perhaps if I sat very still long enough, somehow my eyes would re-absorb the tears.

The kettle began to puff clouds of steam and Dutiful got up to tend to it. Hastily, I blotted my eyes on my sleeve. He brought the grumbling kettle to the table and poured hot water over the herbs in the teapot. As he carried it back to the fire, he spoke over his shoulder. Something in his subdued voice told me that my stillness had not deceived him. I think he sensed how close he had come to breaking me and it distressed him. 'My mother told me,' he said, almost defensively. 'She and Chade were both frantic over you being hurt and in prison. They were angry at one another and could not agree on anything. I was in the room when they had an argument. She told him that she was simply going to go down and take you out of there. He said she must not, that it would only put you and me into greater danger. So then she said she was going to tell me who was dying for me down there; he tried to forbid that. She said it was time I knew what it was to be Sacrifice for one's people. Then they sent me out of the room while they argued about it.' He set the kettle back by the hearth and came back to sit at the table with me. I didn't meet his eyes.

'Do you know what it means when she names you Sacrifice like that? Do you know how my mother thinks of you?' He pushed the bread toward me. 'You should eat. You look awful.' He took a breath. 'When she names you Sacrifice, it means that she thinks of you as the rightful king of the Six Duchies. She probably has since my father died. Or went into his dragon.'

That jerked my eyes to him. Truly, she had told him all, and it shocked me to my spine. I glanced over at Thick dozing before the fire. The Prince's eyes followed mine. He said nothing, but Thick suddenly opened his eyes and turned to face him. 'This is terrible food,' the Prince observed to him. 'Do you think you could get us better in the kitchens? Something sweet, perhaps?'

A wide grin spread over Thick's face. 'I can get that. I know what they got down there. Dried berry and apple pie.' He licked his lips. When he stood, I saw with surprise the Farseer Buck sigil on the breast of his tunic.

'Go the way we came, and come back the same way, please. It's important to remember that.'

Thick nodded ponderously. 'Important. I remember. I know that a long time now. Go through the pretty door, come back through the pretty door. And only when no one else can see.'

'Good man, Thick. I don't know how I ever got along without you.' There was satisfaction in the Prince's voice, and something else. Not condescension, but . . . ah. I grasped it. Pride in possession. He spoke to Thick as a man might speak to a prized wolfhound.

As the half-wit left, I asked him, 'You've made Thick your man? Openly?'

'If my grandfather could have a skinny albino boy as a jester and companion, why should I not have a half-wit as mine?'

I winced. 'You do not let folk mock him, do you?'

'Of course not. Did you know he could sing? His voice gives the music an odd tone, but the notes are true. I do not keep him by me always, but often enough that no one remarks him any longer. And it helps that he and I can speak privately, so that he knows when I wish him by me and when I wish him to go.' He nodded, well pleased with himself. 'I think he is happier now. He has discovered the pleasures of a hot bath and clean clothes. And I give him simple toys that please him. Only one thing worries me. The woman who helps him take care of himself told me that she has known two others like him in her life. She says they do not live as long as an ordinary man does, that Thick might already be close to the end of his days. Do you know if that is true?'

'I've no idea, my prince.'

I offered the honorific without thinking. It made him grin. 'And what shall I call you, if you call me that? Honoured cousin? Lord FitzChivalry?'

'Tom Badgerlock,' I reminded him flatly.

'Of course. And Lord Golden. I confess, it is much easier for me to accept you as Lord FitzChivalry than for me to imagine Lord Golden as a jester in motley.'

'He has travelled a far journey from those days,' I said, and tried to keep regret from my voice. 'When did the Queen decide to tell you all the family secrets?'

'The night after we healed you. She brought me back later through the secret corridors to your chamber, and we spent all night sitting by your bed. After a time, she just started talking. She told me that, with your scars erased, you looked very like my father. That sometimes, when she looked at you, she saw him in your eyes. And then she told me all of it. Not in one evening. I think it was three nights before the tale was told out. And all the while she sat by your bed on a cushion and held your hand. She made me sit on the floor. She allowed no one else in the room.'

'I did not even know you had been there. Nor she.'

He lifted one shoulder. 'Your body was healed, but the rest of you was as close to dead as make no difference. I could not reach you with the Skill, and to my Wit you were like the spark at the end of a candlewick. At any moment, you could have winked out. But while she held your hand and spoke, you seemed to burn brighter. I think she sensed that as well. It was as if she tried to anchor you to life.'

I lifted my hands and let them fall helplessly back to the table. 'I don't know how to deal with this,' I confessed abruptly. 'I don't know how to react to your knowing all these things.'

'I should think you'd feel relieved. Even if we must still maintain the charade of Tom Badgerlock about the keep for some time yet. At least here, in private, you can be who you are and not worry so much about guarding your tongue. Which you don't do very well in any case. Eat your soup. I don't want to have to warm it again.'

It seemed a good suggestion and bought me time to think without having to speak. Yet he sat watching me so intently that I felt like a mouse under a cat's eye. When I scowled at him, he laughed aloud and shook his head. 'You cannot imagine how it feels. I look at you, and wonder, will I be that tall when I am grown? Did my father scowl like that? I wish you had not put the scars back. It makes it harder for me to see myself in your face. You sitting there and me knowing who and what you are . . . it is as if my father has walked into my life for the first time.' The lad bounced and wiggled in his chair as he spoke, as if he were a puppy that longed to jump up on me. It was hard to meet his eyes. Something burned there which I was not prepared for. I did not deserve the Prince's adulation.

'Your father was a far better man than I am,' I told him.

He took a deep breath. 'Tell me something about him,' he begged. 'Something that only you and he would know.'

I sensed the importance of this request and could not refuse him. I cast about in my mind. Should I tell him that Verity had not loved Kettricken at first sight, but rather had grown to love her? It sounded too much like a comparison to his lack of feelings for Elliania. Verity had not been a man for secrets, but I didn't think Dutiful was asking for a secret. 'He loved good ink and paper,' I told him. 'And cutting his pens himself. He was very particular about his pens. And . . . he was kind to me when I was small. For no reason at all. He gave me toys. A little wooden cart, and some carved soldiers and horses.'

'He did? That surprises me. I thought that he had to keep his distance from you. I knew he watched over you, but in his letters to your father, he complains that he scarce sees the little Tom-cat save when he is trotting at Burrich's heels.'

I sat very still. It took a moment for me to recall how to breathe and then I asked, 'Verity wrote about me? In letters to Chivalry?'

'Not directly, of course. Patience had to explain to me what it meant. She showed the letters to me when I complained that I knew little of my father. They were very disappointing. Only four of them, and they were short and boring for the most part. He is fine, he hopes Chivalry and Lady Patience are well. Usually he is asking his brother to have a word with one duke or another, to smooth over some political difference. Once he asks him to send him an accounting of how the taxes were apportioned in a previous year. Then there would be a few lines about the harvest or how the hunting has been. But there was always a word or two about you at the end. "The Tom-cat that Burrich adopted seems to be making himself at home." "Near stepped on Burrich's Tom-cat as he ran through the courtyard yesterday. He seems to get bigger every day." That's how they named you in the letters, against spies and even, at first, against Patience reading them. In the last one, you are just "Tom". "Tom had crossed Burrich and been walloped for it. He seemed remarkably unrepentant. In truth, Burrich is the one I pitied." And at the end of each letter, a few lines about looking forward to the new moon or hoping that the full moon tides will be good for clamming. Patience explained that was how they set up a time to Skill to one another, when they could go apart from other people and be undisturbed. Our fathers were very close, you know. It was very difficult for them to be separated when Chivalry moved to Withywoods. They missed one another deeply.'

Tom. And Patience had, I thought, so carelessly hung that name on me. And I had kept it and little known its history. The Prince was right. Buckkeep Castle was stuffed full of secrets, and half of them were not secrets at all. They were only the things we dared not ask one another for fear the answers would be unbearably painful. I had never asked Patience to tell me about my father; never asked her or Verity what Chivalry had thought of me. Reluctance to ask metamorphosed into secrets. Silence had let me assume the worst of my father. He had never come to see me. Had he watched me through his brother's eyes? Should I blame them for not telling me what they, perhaps, had assumed I knew? Or should I blame myself for never demanding to know?

'The tea is brewed,' Dutiful announced, and lifted the teapot. For the first time, I became aware that the boy was serving me, much as I would have served Chade or Shrewd at his age. With respect and deference. 'Stop,' I said, and put out a hand to cover his. I forced the teapot back to the table. As I picked it up and poured my own tea, I warned him, 'Dutiful, my prince. Listen to me. I must be Tom Badgerlock to you, in every way. Today, for now, we will speak of this. But after this, I must revert to my role as Tom Badgerlock. You must see me as him, and you must see Lord Golden only as Lord Golden. You have been handed a blade with no handle. There is no safe way to grip nor wield this secret that you know now. You rejoice in knowing who I am, and in seeing me as a link to your father. I wish, with all my heart, that it was as simple and good as that. But this secret, breathed in the wrong company, brings us all down. We know that our queen would try to protect me. Think what it would do. I am not only a known user of the Wit, but also the supposed murderer of King Shrewd. Not to mention that I killed several of Galen's Coterie, before a room full of witnesses. Nor am I as dead as many think I should be. For me to be revealed as living would stir the hatred and fear of the Witted to new heights just as our Queen is trying to put an end to their persecution.'

'To our persecution,' the Prince corrected me mildly. He sat back in his chair and pondered it a bit, as if working out the consequences for himself. He looked uncomfortable as he said, 'You've already accidentally put a crimp in the Queen's plans. Despite all Chade's efforts to take no official interest in your fate, there were still rumours that the death of "Keppler", Padget and that other man went unpunished simply because they were suspected to be Witted.'

'I know. Chade told me. And that you were accused of having the Wit as well.'

The Prince bowed his head to that. 'Yes. Well, I do, don't I? And the Piebalds know that, and perhaps some of those who style themselves Old Blood know it as well. Right now, the Old Blood have an interest in keeping my secret. They want this convocation as much as the Queen does. But the deaths of those three men have made them far more cautious. They talk now of demanding more sureties before they will commit to endangering themselves by coming here.'

'They want hostages.' My mind made the leap. 'They want an exchange of people, some of ours to hold at risk while their folk are in our hands. How many?'

The Prince shook his head. 'Ask that of Chade. Or my mother. From the way they argue, I suspect that she communicates directly with the Old Bloods, and only tells the old man what she thinks he needs to know. It frustrates him. I think she has managed to calm their fears and reschedule the meeting. Chade swore that it would be impossible without granting them ridiculous demands. Yet she had done it. But she will not tell Chade how, and that agitates him. She has reminded him that she is Mountain-bred, and that granting a demand he would see as "ridiculous", or accepting a risk that he would declare "unacceptable" are for her a matter of principle. '

'I can't think of anything he would find more upsetting than to see a pie he couldn't get his fingers into.' I spoke mildly even as I wondered uneasily where Kettricken's Mountain ethics on being Sacrifice for her people might lead us.

Dutiful seemed to sense my reservations. 'I agree. And yet, in this, I will side with my mother. It is time she forced him to cede the upper hand to her. If she does not insist upon it now, it does not bode well for me to have any real power when I come to the throne.'

His words put a chill down my spine. He was right. The only reassuring part was that he could look at it so levelly and coolly. Then a wry thought twisted my perception. The Prince could see Chade's machinations because he was as much Chade's student as he was Kettricken's Mountain son. He spoke on as casually as if we were discussing the weather.

'But, that is not what we were talking about. You say your true identity cannot become known. I agree that cannot happen right now. There would definitely be a faction interested in ensuring your death. A great many people would hate and fear you. And the

Farseers would be accused of sheltering a regicide simply because you were one of the family. Even more interesting might be how it would affect both the Old Bloods and the Piebalds. The Witted Bastard has been a rallying point for them for years, and the rumour of your survival is like a revered legend amongst them. To hear Civil speak of you, you are almost a god.'

'You haven't discussed me with Civil?' Alarm flooded me.

'Of course not! Well, not you as you. The legend of FitzChivalry, the Witted Bastard, is what we have discussed. And only in passing, I assure you. Though I think your identity would be as safe with Civil as it is with me.'

I sighed, heartsick and weary. 'Dutiful. Your loyalty is admirable. But I doubt Civil's. The Bresingas have betrayed you twice. Will you allow them to do it a third time?'

He looked stubborn. 'They were coerced, Tom . . . It feels strange to call you that, now.'

I refused to be distracted. 'Become accustomed to it again. And if Civil is threatened again, and again spies for them, or worse?'

'He has no one left for them to threaten.' He halted suddenly and looked at me. 'You know, I have neither apologized nor thanked you. I sent you to Civil's aid without considering that it might be a risk to you. And you went, and you saved my friend's life, even though you yourself don't like him much. As a result, you nearly died.' He cocked his head at me. 'How do I thank you for that?'

'You don't need to. You are my prince.'

His face grew very still. Kettricken lurked in his eyes as he said, 'I don't much like that. It seems to make us more distant. I would that you and I were only cousins.'

I looked at him closely as I asked, 'And do you think that would make a difference? That I would have refused to help your friend because you were "only" my cousin?'

He smiled at me, and then gave a sigh of vast satisfaction. 'I still don't quite believe it's real,' he said quietly. A look somewhat like guilt crossed his face. 'And Thick and I are not supposed to be coming to visit you yet. Chade forbade it, or any attempts to Skill to you until you were stronger. I didn't mean to wake you when we came up here. I only wanted to look at you again. And when I saw the scars were back, I leaned too close.'

'I'm glad you did.'

I sat for a time in silence, uncomfortable and yet basking in his regard. How strange to be loved simply for who I was. It was almost a relief when Thick reappeared, pushing the secret door open with his shoulder. His hands were full and he was puffing with effort from his trot up the stairs. He had helped himself to a whole pie intended to serve a dozen men.

I watched him with satisfaction as he brought his loot to the table. He was grinning broadly, well pleased with himself. I realized I had never seen that expression on his face before. His small, separated teeth and protruding tongue in that round, wide face gave him the look of a cheerful goblin. If I had not known him, I probably would have found the result appalling, but his smirk was answered by a conspiratorial grin from the Prince, and I found myself smiling on both of them.

Thick set the pie down with a clack on the worktable, officiously pushing my dishes to one side to give himself room to work. He hummed as he set to work, and I recognized the refrain of his Skill-song. His surliness seemed to have vanished. I noticed that the knife he used to cut the staggeringly large portions of pie was the one I had bought for him in town on that horrid day. So somehow my purchases had made it up to Buckkeep and to him. The Prince found plates and Thick plopped the servings onto them. He took great care not to soil his new clothes while he did so, and later ate with a caution worthy of a great lady in a new gown. We divided that monstrous pie and left nothing in the pan, and for the first time since I had been injured food tasted good to me.

TWENTY-THREE

Revelations

The unWitted often tell fearsome tales of Witted ones who take on the forms of animals for nefarious reasons. Those of Old Blood will flatly state that no human, no matter how tightly bonded to his animal partner, can take on the shape of that animal. What Old Bloods speak about only reluctantly is that a human can inhabit the body of his beast partner. Usually this happens temporarily and only in extreme circumstances. The body of the human does not vanish; indeed, it remains very vulnerable at such times and may even appear dead. Extreme physical damage to a human's body or imminent death may make a human consciousness take refuge in his Wit-beast's body. Old Blood folk disparage this practice and strongly urge against it.

Among Old Blood, it is strictly forbidden that such an arrangement become permanent. An Old Blood human who flees his dying body and takes refuge in that of his Wit-partner becomes an outcast from the Old Blood community. The same is true for a human who takes in the fleeing soul of his animal partner. Such an act is regarded as extreme selfishness as well as being both immoral and unwise. All who grow up in the Old Blood communities are warned that no matter how tempting the circumstance, no happiness will result for either partner. Death is better.

In this significant way, Old Blood practitioners of the magic differ from the so-called Piebalds. Piebalds relegate their Wit-beasts to a lesser status than their human partners, and see nothing wrong with a human choosing to extend his life by sharing the body of his Wit-partner after his own human body has perished. In some cases, the human becomes the dominant spirit in the animal's body, all but driving it out of its own flesh. Given the long life span of some creatures such as tortoises, geese and certain tropical birds, an unscrupulous human could take such a

*partner late in life with the deliberate intention of providing himself with
a body after his own death. In such a way, a human could extend his
life for a century or more.*

Badgerlock's *Old Blood Tales*

I emerged from my convalescence like a new-hatched thing crawling out into the sunlight for the first time. The world dazzled and
overwhelmed me, and I felt amazement at my life. More, Dutiful's
new regard for me was something that I wore like a warm coat. I
felt that affirmation the next morning as I stood in the courtyard
of Buckkeep Castle and watched the folk of the keep come and go
around me at their daily tasks. The day seemed very bright, and to
my surprise, I could smell the end of winter in the air. The trodden
snow underfoot seemed heavier and denser and the blue of the sky
overhead deeper. I drew in a deep breath and then stretched and
heard my joints crackle from disuse. Today I'd cure that.

I still didn't trust my legs to carry me down to Buckkeep Town,
so I went to the stables. The stable-boy who regularly cared for
Myblack took one look at me and told me he'd ready my mare
for me. I leaned gratefully on her manger and watched him. He
treated her well and she was docile under his touch. When I took
the reins from him, I thanked him for caring for the horse I had
neglected. He gave me a puzzled look and confided, 'Well, I can't
say that she's seemed to miss you. Content with her own company,
that's this one.'

Halfway down the steep hill-path to town, I began regretting
my decision to ride. Myblack seemed bent on arguing with the
reins and showed me just how little strength had come back to my
hands and arms. Despite our little battle of wills, she did carry me
to Gindast's shop. There I was both disappointed and elated to find
that Hap had little time to visit. Although he came swiftly to me
when he saw me at the door, he explained apologetically that one
of the journeymen was allowing him to help with the roughing-in
of a carving on a headboard. If he went with me, the man would
likely choose one of the other apprentices for the task. I assured him
that another day would be soon enough and that I had no news for

him other than that I was feeling better. I watched him hurry off, chisel and scribe in hand, and felt only pride in my boy.

As I remounted Myblack, I glimpsed three of the younger apprentices. They were peering at me around the corner of a shed and whispering to one another. Well, I was known in Buckkeep Town now as a man who had killed three other men. Murder or justified slaying, it mattered not. I'd have to expect a certain amount of finger-pointing and gossip. I hoped it would not hurt Hap's standing among them. I pretended not to notice them and rode off.

I went next to Jinna's cottage. When she opened her door to me, she first gave a little breathless gasp at sight of me. She stared at me for a moment, then looked past me and up and down the street, as if expecting Hap. 'I'm alone today,' I said. 'May I come in?'

'Well. Tom. Of course. Come inside.' She stared at me as if my wasted appearance rattled her. Then she stepped back to allow me into her house. Fennel snaked into the cottage between my feet.

Inside, I sank down into the chair by her fireside gratefully. Fennel immediately settled in my lap. 'So sure of your welcome, aren't you, Cat? As if the world was made for you.' I stroked him and then looked up to find Jinna watching me apprehensively. Her concern touched me. I managed a smile. 'I'm going to be all right, Jinna. I had both feet in death's mouth but I managed to step back. I'll be myself again, with time. Right now, I'm a bit dismayed at how tired I am just from the ride down here.'

'Well.' Her hands tangled together as she spoke. Then she gave herself a little shake as if coming back to herself. She cleared her voice and spoke more strongly. 'It doesn't surprise me a bit. You're no more than bones, Tom Badgerlock. Look how your shirt hangs on you! Sit still a bit and I'll make you a strengthening tisane.' At the look on my face, she amended that to, 'Or perhaps just a cup of tea. And some bread and cheese.'

Fish? Fennel asked me.

Jinna says cheese.

Cheese isn't fish, but it's better than nothing.

'Tea and bread and cheese sounds good. I grew very weary of broth and tisanes and mush when I was recovering. In truth, I am most tired of all of being an invalid. I'm determined that I'll get up and move around a bit every day from now on.'

'Probably the best thing for you,' she agreed distractedly. She cocked her head and stared at me. 'But what's this? Your Badgerlock is gone!' and she pointed at my hair.

I managed a blush. 'I've dyed it. In an effort to look more youthful, I'm afraid. My sickness has taken a grave toll on my appearance.'

'It has, I must agree. But to dye your hair as a remedy . . . well. Men. Now.' She gave her head a small shake as if to clear it. I wondered what was troubling her, but an instant later she seemed to have set it aside. 'Have you heard what has happened between Hap and Svanja?'

'I have,' I assured her.

'Well. I saw it coming.' And then, as she put water on to heat, she went on to tell me, with many tongue cluckings, what I already knew: that Svanja had forsaken Hap for her returning sailor, and had shown her silver earrings to every other girl in town.

I let her explain it all to me as she sliced bread and cheese for us. When she had finished her say, I observed, 'Well, it's likely the best for both of them. Hap is more focused on his apprenticeship, and Svanja has a suitor her parents approve of. His heart is a bit bruised over it, but I think he'll recover.'

'Oh, aye, he'll recover, while Svanja's sailor boy is in port,' Jinna observed sourly as she brought a tray to the little table between the chairs. 'But you mark my words. The moment that lad has a deck under his feet again, Svanja will be after Hap once more.'

'Oh, I doubt that,' I observed mildly. 'And even did she come to him, I think Hap has learned his lesson. Once burnt, twice shy.'

'Hmph. Once bedded, ever eager, would be a better saying in this case. Tom, you need to warn him and warn him severely. Don't let him fall to her wiles again. Not that she's a wicked girl, only one that wants what she wants, when she wants it. She does as much damage to herself as she does to those young men.'

'Well. I hope my lad has more common sense than that,' I observed as she took the other chair.

'So do I,' she rejoined. 'But I doubt it.' Then, as she looked at me, her voice and face lapsed into stillness again. She looked at me as if she saw a stranger. I saw her start to speak twice and then each time still her words.

'What?' I asked finally. 'Is there more to this Svanja-sailor tale that I don't know? What's wrong?'

After a heavy silence, she asked quietly, 'Tom, I— We've been friends for a time, now. And we know more than just a bit about each other. I've heard . . . Never mind what I've heard. What really happened that afternoon on Falldown Street?'

'Falldown Street?'

She looked aside from me. 'You know the place. Three men dead, Tom Badgerlock. And some tale of a stolen purse of gemstones and a serving-man determined to get them back. Another might believe it. But then, half-dead yourself, you stop to kill a horse?' She got up to take the purring kettle off the fire and poured water into the teapot. In a very soft voice, she said, 'I'd been warned off you the week before, Tom. Someone told me you were a dangerous man to befriend. That something bad might befall you soon, and it would be better for me if it didn't happen in my house.'

I gently pushed the cat from my lap and took the kettle of hot water from her shaking hands. 'Sit down,' I suggested gently. She sat and folded her hands in her lap. As I put the kettle back on the hearth, I tried to think calmly. 'Will you tell me who warned you?' I asked as I turned back to her. I already knew the answer.

She looked down at her hands. Then she shook her head slowly. After a moment, she said, 'I was born here in Buckkeep Town. I've done my fair share of wandering about, but this is home when the snow comes down. The people here are my neighbours. They know me and I know them. I know . . . I know a great many people in this town, people of all kinds. Some of them I've known since I was just a girl. I've read the hands of many of them and I know many of their secrets. Now, I like you, Tom, but . . . you killed three men. Two of them Buckkeep Town men. Is that true?'

'I killed three men,' I admitted to her. 'If it makes a difference to you, they would have killed me first, if I'd let them.' A cold was creeping through me. Suddenly it seemed that perhaps her hesitations and apprehension today weren't concern for me at all.

She nodded to that. 'I don't doubt that. But it remains that you went to where they were. They didn't hunt you down. You went to them, and you killed them.'

I tried on the lie Chade had supplied for me. 'I pursued a thief, Jinna. Once I was there, they gave me no choice. It was kill or be killed. I didn't enjoy it. I didn't seek it.'

She just sat and looked at me. I sat back down in my chair. Fennel stood, waiting for me to invite him back into my lap, but I didn't. After a moment, I said, 'You'd rather that I didn't come here anymore.'

'I didn't say that.' There was an edge of anger in her voice, but I think it was anger that I'd stated it so flatly. 'I . . . it's difficult for me, Tom. Surely you can see that.' Again, that telling pause. 'When we first came together, well . . . I thought that the, that the differences between us would make no difference. I've always said that all that things that folk said of Witted ones were mostly lies. I've always said that!'

She snatched the teapot up and poured tea defiantly, for both of us, as if to prove she still welcomed me there. She sipped from her cup and then set it down. The she picked up a piece of bread, put a piece of cheese with it and set it down. She said, 'I'd known Padget since we were babes. I played with his girl-cousins when we were children. Padget was many things, and a number of them I didn't like. But he wasn't a thief.'

'Padget?'

'One of the men that you killed! Don't pretend you don't know his name! You had to know who he was to find him. And I know that he knew who you were. And his poor cousins were too frightened even to claim his body. For fear of being linked with him. Because it might make people think they were like him. But that is what I don't understand, Tom.' She paused, and in a quiet voice said, 'Because you are like he was. You're one, too. Why hunt and kill your own kind?'

I had just lifted up my teacup. I set it down carefully and took a breath, thinking I would speak. Then I let it out, waited, and began again. 'I'm not surprised there is gossip about this. What folk say to the guard and what they say to one another are two different things. And I know there were Piebald scrolls put about town, claiming all sorts of wild things. So. Let us speak bluntly. Padget was Witted. Like me. That isn't why I killed him, but it is true. It is also true that he was a Piebald. Which I am not.' At her look of confusion, I asked her, 'Do you know what a Piebald is, Jinna?'

'Witted are Piebalds,' she said. 'Some of your kind say "Old Blood" instead. It's all one.'

'Not quite. Piebalds are Witted who betray other Witted. They are the ones who post the little notices that say, "Jinna is Witted and her beast is a fat yellow cat".'

'I am not!' she exclaimed indignantly.

I perceived she thought that I had threatened her. 'No,' I agreed calmly. 'You are not. But if you were, I could destroy your livelihood and perhaps even take your life by making it public. That is what the Piebalds do to other Witted.'

'But that makes no sense. Why would they do that?'

'To make the other Witted do what they want.'

'What do they want them to do?'

'The Piebalds are seeking to gather power to themselves. To gain that, they need money and people willing to do what they tell them.'

'I still don't understand what they want.'

I sighed. 'They want the same things most Witted want. They want to exercise their magic openly, without fear of the noose or flame. They want to be accepted, not to have to live with their talents hidden. Suppose you could be killed simply for being a hedge-witch. Would not you want to change that?'

'But hedge-witches do no harm to anyone.'

I watched her face carefully as I said, 'Neither do Witted.'

'Some do,' she rejoined instantly. 'Oh, not all of them, no. But when I was but a child my mother kept two milk goats. They both up and died on the same day. And only the week before that she had refused to sell one to a Witted woman. So you see, Witted are like anyone else. Some of them are vengeful and cruel, and use their magic to that end.'

'The Wit doesn't work that way, Jinna. That is like me saying a hedge-witch could look in my hand, and put a line there that would make me die sooner. Or blaming you because you looked at my son's hand, said he had a short lifeline and then he died. Would that be your fault? For saying what you'd seen there?'

'Well, of course not. But that's not the same as killing some-one's goats.'

'That is what I'm trying to tell you. I can't use the Wit to kill anyone.'

She cocked her head at me. 'Oh, come, Tom. That great wolf of yours would have killed that man's pigs if you'd told him to, wouldn't he?'

I sat a long time silent. Then I had to say, 'Yes. I suppose he would have. If I were that sort of a man, I might have used the wolf and my Wit that way. But I'm not.'

Her silence lasted even longer than mine did. At last, very unwillingly, she said, 'Tom. You killed three men. And a horse. Wasn't that the wolf in you? Wasn't that your Wit?'

After a time, I stood up. 'Goodbye, Jinna,' I said. 'Thank you for your many kindnesses.' I walked towards the door.

'Don't go like this,' she begged me.

I halted, miserable. 'I don't know any other way to go. Why did you even let me inside your door today?' I asked bitterly. 'Why did you try to see me when I was hurt? It would have been a greater kindness simply to turn away from me than to show me what you truly thought of me.'

'I wanted to give you a chance,' she said dismally. 'I wanted . . . I hoped there was some other reason. Something besides your Wit.'

Hand on the latch, I paused. I detested my last lie, but it had to be told. 'There was. There was a purse that belonged to Lord Golden.' I did not look back to see if she believed me. She already had more truth than was safe for her to own.

I closed her door softly behind me. The day had clouded over abruptly and the shadows on the snowy ground were dark grey. All had changed in that sudden way that early spring days can. Somehow Fennel had managed to slip out with me. 'You should go back inside,' I told him. 'It's getting cold out here.'

Cold isn't so bad. Cold can only kill you if you stand still. Just keep moving.

Good advice, cat. Good advice. Goodbye, Fennel.

I mounted Myblack and turned her head towards Buckkeep Castle. 'Let's go home,' I told her.

She was willing enough to head for her stall and manger. I let her set her own pace while I sat in the saddle and pondered my life. Yesterday I had felt Dutiful's worship. Today, Jinna's fear and rejection. More, today Jinna had shown me how deep and wide the prejudice against the Witted might go. I had thought she had accepted me for who and what I was. But she hadn't. She had been willing to make an exception for me, but when I killed, I had proved her rule. The Witted were not to be trusted; they used their magic for evil. I felt myself sinking into despair as I realized the depth of it. For there was more than that. I had learned, yet again, that I could not serve the Farseers and still claim a life for myself.

Not this again, Changer. How could the moments of your life belong to anyone but you? You are the Farseers, blood and pack. See the whole of it. It is neither a binding nor a separation. The pack is the whole of you. The wolf's life is in the pack.

Nighteyes, I breathed. And yet I knew that he was not there. As Black Rolf had told me it would be, it was. There were moments when my dead companion came back to me as more than a memory, yet less than his living part of me. The part of me that I had given to the wolf lived on. I sat up straighter in the saddle and took charge of my horse. She snorted, but accepted it. And then, because I thought it might be good for both of us, I put heels to her and sent her surging up the snowy road to Buckkeep Castle and home.

I stabled Myblack and saw to her myself. It took me twice as long as it should have done. It shamed me to be out of the habit of caring for my own horse, and shamed me more that she should be so wilful that she made it difficult. Then I forced myself to go to the practice courts. I had to borrow a blade. I had gone into Buckkeep Town today unarmed save for the knife at my hip. Foolish, perhaps, but I'd had no alternative. I'd visited my room today, intending to get my ugly sword, only to discover it was missing. Most likely it was lost or adopted by an opportunistic city guardsman. The bright blade the Fool had given me was still hanging on the wall. I'd considered it but I could not bring myself to buckle it on. It was a symbol of an esteem he no longer extended to me. I'd decided I'd no longer wear it save in my role as his bodyguard. For practice, a dummy sword was best anyway. Dulled blade in hand, I went looking for a partner.

Wim was not about but Delleree was. In a very short time, she had killed me so many times I lost count, using either of her weapons at will. I felt it was all I could do to hold my sword up, let alone swing it. Finally, she stopped and said, 'I can't do this any more. I feel like I'm fighting a stickman. Each time I hit you, I feel my blade clack against your bones.'

'So do I,' I assured her. I managed to laugh and thank her, and then limped away to the steams. The looks of pity I received from the guardsmen there made me wish I had never disrobed. From the steams, I went directly to the kitchens. A cook's helper named Maisie told me she was glad to see me on my feet again. I am sure it was pity for me that made her cut an outside slice off a joint that was still roasting on the spit. She gave it to me on a slab of bread from the morning's baking, and then told me that Lord Golden's serving-boy had been looking for me earlier in the day. I thanked her but did not rush to my lord's summoning. Instead I stood outside, my back to the courtyard wall, and watched the folk of the keep while I wolfed down the food she had given me. It had been a very long time since I had just stood still and watched the folk of Buckkeep. I thought of all the other things I had not seen or done since I had returned to my childhood home. I had not visited the Queen's Garden at the top of the tower. Not once had I gone walking in the Women's Garden. I suddenly hungered to do simple things of that sort. Ride Myblack through the forested hills behind Buckkeep. Sit in the Great Hall of an evening and watch the fletchers work on their arrows and speculate on hunting prospects. To be a part of it all once more rather than a shadow.

My hair was still damp and there was not enough flesh on me to stay warm for long standing still on a wintry afternoon. I heaved a sigh and went inside and up the stairs, both dreading and anticipating an encounter with Lord Golden. It had been days since he had expressed any personal interest in me. His benevolent dismissal of me was worse than if he had maintained a sulky silence. It was as if he truly had ceased caring about the rift between us. As if who we were now, Lord Golden and Tom Badgerlock, was all we had ever been. A tiny flame of anger leapt up in me, and then as swiftly expired. I did not have the energy to maintain it, I realized. And then, with an equanimity I had not known I possessed, I suddenly accepted it. Things had changed. All my roles had shifted, not just with Prince Dutiful and Jinna and Lord Golden. Even Chade saw me differently. I could not force Lord Golden to revert to being the Fool. Perhaps he could not, even if he had wished to. Was it so different for me? I was as much Tom Badgerlock as FitzChivalry Farseer now. Time to let it go.

Lord Golden was not in his chambers. I went into my room and put on a shirt that wasn't sweated through. I took off the charm necklace Jinna had given me. When Dutiful's cat had attacked me, his teeth had left nicks in two beads. I hadn't noticed that before. For a short time I looked at it, and found that I was still grateful to Jinna for this gesture of goodwill. Yet that gratitude was not enough to allow me to continue wearing it. She had given it to me because she liked me, despite my Wit. That thought would always taint it now. I dropped it into the corner of my clothing chest.

As I was leaving my chambers, I encountered Lord Golden entering his. He halted at the sight of me. I had neither seen nor spoken to him since the feather incident. Now he looked me up and down as if he had never seen me before. After a moment, he said stiffly, 'It is good to see you up and about again, Tom Badgerlock. But from the look of you, I think it will still be some days before you are fit to resume your duties. Take some time to recover yourself.' There seemed something odd in his diction, as if he could not quite get his breath.

I offered him a servant's bow. 'Thank you, my lord and thank you for the additional time. I shall put it to good use. I've already been down to the practice courts today. As you observed, it may be some days before I am able to serve effectively as a bodyguard again.' I paused, then added, 'I was told in the kitchens that you had sent a boy to seek for me earlier today?'

'A boy? Oh. Yes. Yes, I did. Actually, I sent him at Lord Chade's behest. In truth, I near forgot. Lord Chade came here seeking you, and when you were not in your room, I set a boy running to see if you were in the kitchens. I think he wanted you to come to him.

I didn't . . . in truth, we had some talk that has . . .' Lord Golden's voice tottered to an uncertain halt. A silence fell. Then, in a voice that was almost the Fool's, he said, 'Chade came here to talk to me about something that he'd asked you to discuss with . . . There's something I want you to look at. Have you a moment to spare?'

'I am at your service, my lord,' I reminded him.

I expected some response to that little jab. Instead, looking distracted, he said, 'Of course you are. A moment, then.' His Jamaillian accent had faded from his words. He went into his bedchamber, shutting the door behind him.

I waited. I walked over to the fire, poked it up a bit, and added a log. Then I waited some more. I sat down in a chair, noticed that my fingernails had grown and pared them back with my belt-knife. I continued to wait. Finally, I rose and with a sigh of exasperation, went to tap on the door. Perhaps I had misunderstood. 'Lord Golden. Did you wish me to wait here?'

'Yes. No.' Then, in a very uncertain voice, 'Would you come in here, please? But first make sure the corridor door is well bolted.'

It was. I rattled it to be sure and then opened the door to his room. The room was dim, the windows shuttered. Several candles illuminated Lord Golden standing with his back to me. He wore a sheet from his bed like a cape. He glanced at me over his shoulder and someone I had never met looked out of those golden eyes. When I was three steps into the room, he said quietly, 'Stand there, please.'

With one hand, he lifted his hair up and out of the way to bare the nape of his neck. The sheet fell away from his naked back, but his free hand continued to clutch it to his chest. I gasped and took an inadvertent step closer. He flinched away but then stood his ground. In a small shaky voice, he asked, 'The Narcheska's tattoos. Were they like these?'

'May I come closer?' I managed to say. I didn't really need to. If his tattoos were not identical to hers, then they were at least extremely similar. He nodded jerkily, and I took another step into the room. He did not look at me but stared off into a dim corner. The room was not cold, but he was shivering. The exotic needling began at the nape of his neck and covered every part of his back before vanishing beneath the waistband of his leggings. The twining serpents and wingspread dragons sprawled in exquisite detail over his smooth golden back. The shining colours had a metallic gleam to them, as if gold and silver had been forced under his skin to illuminate them. Every claw and scale, every shining tooth and flashing eye was perfect. 'They are very alike,' I managed to say at last. 'Save that yours lie flat to your skin. One of hers, the largest serpent, stood swollen from her back as if inflamed. And it seemed to cause her great pain.'

He drew in a shuddering breath. His teeth were near to chattering as he observed bitterly, 'Well. Just when I thought there was no way she could increase her cruelty, she finds one. That poor, poor child.'

'Do yours hurt?' I asked cautiously.

He shook his head, still without looking at me. Some of his hair fell free of his grasp to brush across his shoulders. 'No. Not now. But the application of them was extremely painful. And of great duration. They held me very still, for hours at a time. They apologized and tried to comfort me as they did it. That only made it worse, that people who otherwise treated me with such love and regard could do that to me. They were meticulously careful to needle them in just as she instructed them. It is a horrible thing to do to a child. Hold him still and hurt him. Any child.' He rocked slightly, his shoulders hunched. His voice was distant.

'They?' I asked very softly.

His voice was tight, all melody gone from it. He shuddered out his words. 'I was at a place rather like a school. Teachers and learned folk. I told you about it before. I ran away from it. My parents sent me there, parting from me with both pride and sorrow, because I was a White. It was a long way from our home. They knew they would probably never see me again, but they knew it was the correct thing to do. I had a destiny to fulfil. But my teachers insisted there already was a White Prophet for this time. She had already studied with them, and already set forth to fulfil her destiny in the far north.' He turned his head suddenly and met my eyes. 'Do you guess of whom I speak?'

I nodded stiffly. I felt cold. 'The Pale Woman. Kebal Rawbread's adviser during the Red Ship War.'

He returned my nod as stiffly. Again he looked away from me, staring into a darkened corner of the room. 'So, a White I might be, but I could not be the White Prophet. Therefore, I must be an anomaly. A creature born out of my time and place. They were fascinated by me and listened to my every word and recorded every dream I spoke. They treasured me and treated me very well. They listened to me, but they never heeded what I said. And when she heard of me, she commanded that they keep me there. And they did. Later, she commanded that I be marked this way. And so they did.'

'Why?'

'I don't know. Save, perhaps, that we had both dreamed of these creatures, of sea serpents and dragons. But perhaps it is what you do with an extra White Prophet. Cover him over so he is no longer white.' His voice tightened until the words were hard as knots. 'It has shamed me so to be marked like this, at her will. It is worse now, to know that the Narcheska is also decorated with the Pale Woman's markings. As if she claimed us as her tool, her creatures . . .' His words faded away.

'But why did they obey her? How could anyone do a thing like that?'

He laughed bitterly. 'She is the White Prophet, come to set time in a better path. She has a vision. You do not question her will. Questioning her command can have severe repercussions. Ask Kebal Rawbread. You do as the Pale Woman tells you.' His shivering had become a wild shaking.

'You're cold.' I would have put a blanket around him, but to do so I would have had to step closer. I don't think he could have allowed me to do that.

'No.' He gave me a sickly smile. 'I'm afraid. I'm terrified. Please. Please go out while I get dressed again.'

I withdrew, shutting the door quietly behind myself. Then I waited. It seemed to take him a long time to put a shirt on.

When he emerged, he was meticulously attired, every strand of his hair restored to its rightful place. Still, he did not look at me. 'There's brandy by the fire for you,' I told him.

He crossed the room in short nervous steps and took up the glass but did not drink from it. Instead, arms crossed as if he were cold, he stood very close to the fire, hugging his cup to him. He stared fixedly at the floor.

I went into his room and took one of his thick woollen cloaks from the wardrobe there, then he came back and I put it around him. I pulled his chair closer to the hearth, then took him by the shoulders and sat him down in it. 'Drink the brandy,' I told him. My voice sounded harsh. 'I'll put on the kettle for tea.'

'Thank you.' He whispered the words. Horribly, tears began to track down his face. They cut runnels in his carefully-applied paint, and dripped paleness onto his shirt.

I spilled water and burned myself putting the kettle on the hook. When it was in place, I dragged my chair close to his. 'Why are you so scared?' I asked him. 'What does it mean?'

He sniffled, an incongruous sound from dignified Lord Golden. Worse, he took the corner of the cloak and wiped his eyes with it. It smeared his Jamaillian cosmetics, and I saw his bare skin. 'Convergence,' he said hoarsely. He drew a breath. 'It means convergence. All comes together. I'm on the right path. I feared I had strayed. But this confirms it. Convergence and confrontation. And time set aright.'

'I thought that was what you wanted. I thought that was what White Prophets do.'

'Oh, yes. That is what we do.' An unnatural calm came over him. He looked at me and met my eyes. I looked into a sorrow older and deeper than I wished to know. 'A White Prophet finds his Catalyst. The one on whom great events may turn. And he uses him, ruthlessly, to turn time out of his track. Once more my tracks will converge with hers. And we will set our wills against one another, to see who prevails.' His voice suddenly strangled. 'Again, death will try to take you.' His tears had stopped but moisture still glistened on his face. He caught up the hem of the cloak and smeared his face with it again. 'If I don't succeed, we'll both just die.' Hunched miserably in his chair, he looked up at me. 'Last time was too close.

Twice, I felt you die. But I held you and refused to let you go to peace. Because you are the Catalyst, and I win only if I keep you in this world. Alive no matter how. A friend would have let you go. I heard the wolves calling you. I knew you wanted to go to them. But I didn't let you. I dragged you back. Because I had to use you.'

I tried to speak calmly. 'That is the part that I have never understood.'

He looked at me sadly. 'You understand. You simply refuse to accept it.' He paused for a moment, then stated it simply. 'In the world that I seek to sculpt, you live. I am the White Prophet and you are my Catalyst. The Farseer line has an heir and he reigns. It is but one factor, but it is a key factor. In the world the Pale Woman seeks to advance, you do not exist. Failing that, you do not survive. There is no Farseer heir. The Farseer line fails completely. There is no renegade White.' He dropped his head into his hands and spoke through his fingers. 'She engineers your death, Fitz. Her machinations are subtle. She is older than I am, and far more sophisticated. She plays a horrible game. Henja is her creature. Make no mistake about that. I do not understand her ploy there, nor why she offers the Narcheska to Dutiful. But she is behind it all, I am certain. She sends death for you, and I try to snatch you out of the way. So far, we have always matched her, you and I. But it has been more your luck than my cleverness that has saved you. Your luck and your . . . dare I say it? Your magics. Both of them. Still, always, always the odds are against your survival. And the deeper we go in this game, the worse the odds become. This last time . . . This last time was too much. I don't want to be the White Prophet any more. I don't want you to be my Catalyst.' His voice had degraded to a cracked whisper. 'But there isn't any way to stop. The only thing that stops this is if you die.' He suddenly looked about frantically. I found the brandy bottle and set it within his reach. He didn't even bother to pour. He uncorked it and drank from the bottle. When he set it down, I reached over and took it.

'That won't help anything,' I told him severely.

He gave me a loose-lipped smile. 'I can't go through another one of your deaths. I can't.'

'*You* can't?'

He gave a giggle of despair. 'You see. We're trapped. I've trapped you, my friend. My beloved.'

I tried to fit my mind around what he was telling me. 'If we lose, I die,' I said.

He nodded. 'If you die, we lose. It's all the same.'

'What happens if I live?'

'Then we win. Not much chance of that, now. Not much chance and getting worse all the time, I'd say. Most likely we lose. You die and the world spirals down into darkness. And ugliness. Despair.'

'Stop being so cheerful.' This time I drank out of the bottle. Then I passed it to him. 'But what if I do live? What if we win? What then?'

He parted the bottle's mouth from his. 'What then? Ah.' He smiled beatifically. 'Then the world goes on, my friend. Children run down muddy streets. Dogs bark at passing carts. Friends sit and drink brandy together.'

'Doesn't sound much different from what we have,' I observed sourly. 'To go through all this and make no difference at all.'

'Yes.' He agreed beatifically. His eyes filled with tears. 'Not much different from the wondrous and amazing world that we have now. Boys falling in love with girls that aren't right for them. Wolves hunting on the snowy plains. And time. Endless time unwinding for all of us. And the dragons, of course. Dragons sliding across the sky like beautiful jewelled ships.'

'Dragons. That sounds different.'

'Does it?' His voice dropped to a whisper. 'Does it really? I think not. Remember with your heart. Go back, go back, and go back. The skies of this world were always meant to have dragons. When they are not there, humans miss them. Some never think of them, of course. But some children, from the time they are small, they look up at a blue summer sky and watch for something that never comes. Because they know. Something that was supposed to be there faded and vanished. Something that we must bring back, you and I.'

I put my face in my hand and rubbed my brow. 'I thought we had to save the world. What has that got to do with dragons?'

'It's all connected. When you save any part of the world,

you've saved the whole world. In fact, that's the only way it can be done.'

I hated his riddles. Hated them passionately. 'I don't know what you want from me.'

He was silent. When I lifted my face to regard him, he was watching me calmly. 'It's safe for me to tell you. You won't believe me.' He drew a steadying breath. He had the brandy bottle cradled in one arm as if it were his babe. 'We have to go on the Prince's quest with him. To Aslevjal. To find Icefyre. Then we must prevent the Prince from slaying him. Instead we must free the black dragon trapped beneath the ice so he can rise, to become Tintaglia's consort. So that they can mate and there can be real dragons in the world again.'

'But . . . I can't do that! Dutiful must cut off the dragon's head and bring it to the hearth of Elliania's motherhouse. Otherwise, she will not wed him. All these negotiations and hopes will have been for naught.'

He looked at me and I think he knew how torn I was. He spoke quietly. 'Fitz. Set it out of your mind. Don't think of it for now. The Convergence and the confrontation await us. We need not rush towards them. When the time comes, I promise, you alone will be the one to choose. Do you keep your vowed loyalty to the Farseers or do you save the world for me?' He paused. 'One other thing I shall tell you. I should not, but I will. So you do not think that it is your fault when the time comes. Because, I promise you, it will not be. I prophesied it long ago, not understanding what I spoke of until this business of the tattoos was made clear to me. I dreamed it long ago, a child's wild nightmare. Soon I will live it. So when it happens, you must promise me not to torment yourself with it.'

His shivering had returned as he spoke. His words came out between chattering teeth.

'What is it?' I asked with dread, already knowing.

'This time, on Aslevjal.' A terrified smile trembled at the corners of his mouth. 'It is my turn to die.'

TWENTY-FOUR

Connections

The legend of the White Prophet and his Catalyst might be better described as a religion from the far south, only echoes of which have reached Jamaillia. Like many philosophies from the south, it is riddled with superstitions and contradictions, so that no thinking man could subscribe to such foolishness. At the core of the White Prophet heresy is the concept that for 'every age' (and this space of time is never defined) there is born a White Prophet. The White Prophet comes to set the world on a better course. He or she (and in this duality of gender we may see some borrowing from the true faith of Sa) does this by means of his or her Catalyst. The Catalyst is a person chosen by the White Prophet because he stands at a juncture of choices. By changing what happens to the Catalyst in his lifetime, the White Prophet enables the world to follow a truer, better course of history. Any thinking man can see that, as there is no way to compare what has happened to what might have happened, White Prophets can always claim to have bettered the world. Nor can any of the adherents of this heresy explain the idea that the world and time roll in a circular track, endlessly repeating itself. A perusal of the history that we have recorded shows quite clearly that this is not so, yet adherents of this false belief will still cling to it.

Delnar, the wise old priest of Sa, has written in his Opinions that not only the followers of this heresy are to be pitied, but also the 'White Prophets' themselves. He proves conclusively that such self-deluded fanatics are actually suffering from a rare disorder that drains all pigment from their flesh, at the same time inducing hallucinations of prophetic dreams sent by gods.

Wiflen, priest of Sa, Jorepin Monastery
Cults and Heresies of the Southlands

CHADE! I need you, I need you now! Come to me in the workroom.
CHADE! Please hear me, please come!

I Skilled the summons wildly as I staggered up the stairs to my workroom. I do not even recall what urgent errand I had invented for my departure. I'd left him, the Fool and yet no longer the Fool, sitting by his fire with the brandy bottle. Now, heart hammering, I cursed my wasted body as I forced my legs to bend and push me along. I could not tell if Chade could hear me. Then I cursed myself and shifted my attention to Dutiful and Thick. *I need to see Lord Chade immediately. With the greatest urgency. Find him and send him to me in my workroom.*

Why? This from Dutiful.

Just do it!

Then, when I did stagger, sweating and puffing, into the workroom, I found Chade sitting impatiently by the hearth. He turned to glare at me. 'What has kept you? I heard you'd come back into the castle, and I know Lord Golden would pass on my message. I don't have all day to wait on you, boy. Important things are afoot, things that require your presence.'

'No,' I gasped. And then, 'I talk first.'

'Sit down,' he growled at me. 'Breathe. I'll get you some water.'

I made it to the chair by the fire before I collapsed. I'd tried to force my body too much today. The ride and the practice bout by itself were enough to exhaust me. Now I was shaking as badly as the Fool had been.

I drank the water Chade brought me. Before he could begin to speak, I told him everything that the Fool had told me. When I had finished, I was still panting. He sat thinking while my breathing gradually slowed.

'Tattoos,' he muttered in disgust. 'The Pale Woman.' He sighed. 'I don't believe him. And I don't dare disbelieve him.' He scowled as he pondered my tale. Then, 'You saw my spy's report? He found no trace of a dragon on Aslevjal.'

'I don't think he made a very thorough search.'

'Perhaps not. That is the trouble with hired men. When the money trickles away, their loyalty goes with it.'

'Chade. What are we going to do?'

He gave me an odd look. 'The obvious. Really, Fitz, you do need to recover your health. You are so easily rattled these days. Though I confess that the Fool's tattoos are as great a surprise to me as to you. As is the connection he makes of them. When I spoke to him earlier today, to ask if he knew anything of such tattoos as an Outisland custom, he said he did not and calmly changed the subject. I can scarcely believe he would so dissemble to me, but . . .' I watched Chade reorder to himself all that he knew of both the Fool and Lord Golden. Then he sighed heavily and admitted, 'We do know there was a Pale Woman advising Kebal Rawbread for much of the Red Ship Wars. But we assumed that she perished alongside him. What could she have to do with Elliania? And even if she had lived, why should she attempt to be a part of our matchmaking, let alone have an interest in you or Lord Golden? It is all too far-fetched.'

I swallowed. 'The maid, Henja. Elliania's servant. She spoke of a "she", as did Elliania and Blackwater. Those two spoke of her with dread. Perhaps this "she" is the Pale Woman, and perhaps she is the Fool's "other White Prophet". Then she could have plans of her own, plans that cross our own in ways we cannot foresee.'

I watched the old assassin mentally work through all the permutations of such a situation. Then he shrugged. 'Regardless,' Chade replied ruthlessly. 'Our solution remains the same.' He held up two fingers. 'One. The Fool promised you that it would be your decision, to keep your oath to the Farseers or try to save this frozen dragon for him. So. You'll keep your oath. I don't doubt your loyalty.'

It did not seem that simple to me at all. I kept silent.

He touched his second finger. 'Two. Lord Golden does not go to Aslevjal with us. Therefore, if we discover a dragon in the ice, which I very much doubt, he doesn't try to interfere with Dutiful killing the dragon. Or at least chopping the frozen head off some ancient carcass, which I consider far more likely. Then, even if this "Pale Woman" does still exist and is a threat to him, he never comes near her. Hence, Lord Golden doesn't die.'

'What if he comes to Aslevjal anyway, with or without us?'

Chade gave me a look. 'Fitz. Think, lad. Aslevjal is not an easy island to visit, even from the other Outislands. Not that he'll get that far. Don't you think I can issue an order that forbids Lord

Golden to take passage on any ship outbound from Buckkeep Town? I'll do it subtly, of course. But it will be done.'

'What if he changes his appearance?'

He raised a white eyebrow at me. 'Do you wish me to have him locked in a dungeon while we are gone? I suppose I could arrange that, if it would put your mind at rest. A comfortable dungeon, of course. All the amenities.' His tone plainly said that he thought I was worrying unnecessarily. Confronted with his calm scepticism, I found it difficult to support the frantic fear the Fool had raised in me.

'No. Of course I don't want that,' I muttered.

'Then trust me. Trust me as you used to. Have a little confidence in your old mentor. If I don't want Lord Golden to take ship from Buckkeep, then he won't.'

I CAN'T FIND HIM. WHAT SHOULD I DO? Dutiful sounded panicked.

Chade cocked his head. 'Did you hear something?'

'A moment.' I held up a finger to Chade. *Never mind, Dutiful. He's with me; it will be all right now.*

What's it all about?

Never mind, I tell you. Never mind. I shifted my attention from Dutiful to Chade. 'That which you "heard" was Dutiful shouting at me that he couldn't find you. A widespread Skilling, such as he still does when he's anxious.'

A slow smile dawned over Chade's features, even as he said, 'Oh, you must be mistaken. I was sure I heard a shout in the distance.'

'So the Skill can seem at first. Until your mind learns to interpret what it senses.'

'Oh, my,' Chade said quietly. He looked afar, smiling pensively. Then he came back to me with a jolt. 'I'd nearly forgotten why I'd summoned you. The Queen's convocation of the Witted. It is actually going to happen, much to my surprise. We've had word to expect them in six days. It's taken them time to gather themselves, and they ask that the Queen send her own guard to bring them in under a safe passage flag. They asked for an exchange of hostages too, of course, but I told her that was nonsense! Six days from now, they will send us a bird telling us where to meet them. They promise it will be within a day's ride of Buckkeep. When we get to the rendezvous, they will come to us. They will be cloaked and hooded to protect their identities. I'd like you to go with them when they ride out.'

'Wouldn't that seem very odd? Lord Golden's personal bodyguard riding out with the Queen's Guard on such a delicate mission?'

'It would, but for one thing. By then, you will have left Lord Golden's service, and taken a position with the Queen's Guard.'

'Won't that be a rather abrupt change? How do we explain that? And when did you decide that, you old fox?'

'Easily enough. Captain Fairgood will be anxious to secure your services, as he was so impressed with your ability to slay three men merely for attempting to steal your master's pouch. A man that good with a blade would always be a welcome addition to the Queen's Guard. If anyone asks, you can say that they offered you excellent wages, and that Lord Golden was only too willing to gain favour with the Queen by allowing her to hire his man away from him. Perhaps he is now comfortable enough at our court to see that he never needed a bodyguard at all.'

Chade stacked his logic nicely. I suspected he had a stronger motive than simply to have more access to me as a spy. I wondered if he wanted to separate me from Lord Golden lest he make any inroads on my loyalty to the Farseers. I edged around the question, asking him, 'Why is it so essential to you that I ride with the Queen's Guard now?'

'Well, for one thing, it will make it much easier to explain why you are chosen to accompany the Prince to the Outislands in spring. You'll be one of the lucky ones whose lot is chosen for the honour. But mostly because the Witted have asked that, as a token that we mean them no harm, Prince Dutiful ride out as part of their escort.'

I was instantly distracted. 'Do you think that's safe? It could be a trap to lure him into danger.'

He smiled grimly. 'Why do you think I want you riding at his heels? Of course, it's possible it's a trap. But the Witted must fear the same thing, must they not? So they ask for him, knowing that we would not risk the sole Farseer heir if there were any chance of a skirmish.'

'Old Blood,' I told him. 'You must learn to say "Old Blood" not "Witted". Then you'll send him out to escort them in?'

Chade scowled and admitted, 'He has little choice in that, as little as I do. The Queen has already promised it to them.'

'In spite of your disapproval.'

Chade gave a snort of disdain. 'My approval or disapproval means little to the Queen these days. She thinks, perhaps, that she has outgrown her need for me as a councillor. Well. We shall see.'

I could think of nothing to say to that. Truth to tell, and though it cost me a pang of disloyalty, I secretly rejoiced in my queen's assertion of her strength.

The days to come were so full that the tensions of them almost crowded from my mind my concerns for the Fool. Despite the fragility of my health, Chade, Thick, Dutiful and I began to meet every morning in the Seawatch Tower. The Fool was not included in our meetings. Chade made no comment on this; given what I had told him, perhaps he viewed it as more desirable that the Fool not be a part of our coterie. I never brought the topic up. Only we four gathered, and there we pursued the Skill with an avidity that frightened me and enthused the rest of them. We made progress, careful and controlled progress that satisfied no one except me. Thick learned to confine his music, though it seemed to distress him in a way he could not explain. Dutiful became better at directing his Skill-messages to individuals. Chade, as was to be expected, lagged behind the other two pupils. If we were physically touching, he could reach my mind faintly, and I his. Thick could direct an onslaught at him that would catch his attention but convey nothing. Dutiful could not seem to find him. Or Chade couldn't be aware of him. I could not tell which problem it was so we worked on both. The mornings were exhausting and nerve-wracking. I still got headaches, though they did not compare to the ones that had previously afflicted me.

Under Chade's strict directions, I ate a nourishing meal of bland and healthful food every noon. I might have taken control of his Skill-magic, but he still remained my mentor and believed he knew best where my physical health was concerned. It was at this time that he confronted me about the elfbark and carryme that he had found and removed from my room when I was recovering from my 'healing'. It was a sharp quarrel between us, and uncomfortable for us both. He maintained that I had a duty not to do anything that might injure or inhibit my Skill, especially now that I was Skillmaster to the Prince and his coterie. I maintained that I had a right to the privacy of my possessions. Neither of us either conceded or apologized. It simply became an area we avoided discussing.

Lord Golden had dismissed me from his service shortly after Chade had suggested he might. I was offered employment with the Queen's Guard and accepted it with alacrity. They accepted me into their midst with an equanimity that surprised me. Evidently I was not the first odd man that Chade had slipped into their ranks. I wondered how many of them were more than what they seemed. They asked me few questions, but measured me instead with their routine drills and practices. Early afternoons I spent with the Queen's Guard on the practice grounds. I was often found lacking, and wore the bruises to show for it

Ostensibly, I had a bunk in the barracks with the rest of the guards but as often I slept in my workroom. If anyone wondered at my oddly loose attachment to the Queen's Guard, no one commented on it to me. When I encountered Wim at the practice court, he congratulated me on 'being an honest fighter again'. In dress, I went back to the plain blue of a Buck guardsman, with a purple and white tunic for the times when I must show myself as belonging to the Queen. I derived an inordinate amount of pleasure from openly wearing her fox badge on my breast. It matched the fox pin I wore within my shirt and above my heart.

I seemed to weary more swiftly and heal much more slowly than I ever had before, but despite Chade's suggestions I did not attempt to use the Skill to speed that process. Late afternoons, while Chade was busy with diplomacy, Thick raided the kitchens for me. Together we gorged ourselves on sweets and rich pastries and fat meat. We discovered that Gilly loved raisins as much as Thick did. The ferret's pleading dance for them could reduce Thick to tears of laughter. We all began to put on flesh, Thick probably more than was good for him. He became as round and his hair as glossy as a noble lady's fat little lapdog. Blessed now with food, care and acceptance, a placid and sweet nature sometimes showed in the little man. I enjoyed those simple hours with him.

I even managed several evenings with Hap. We did not go to the Stuck Pig, but to a quiet alehouse, relatively new, called the Wrecked Red Ship. There we ate cheap and greasy tavern food and talked like the old friends we were becoming. It reminded me of my days with Burrich in the time just before Regal killed me. We recognized one another as men now. On our best evening, he regaled me with a long account of how Starling had swept into the woodshop, dazzled Master Gindast with her charm and fame, and carried him off for a day in Buckkeep Town. 'It was so strange, Tom,' he told me in a sort of wonder. 'She behaved as if there had never been any quarrel nor hard words between us. And so what could I do, save do the same? Do you think she has actually forgotten what she said to me?'

'I doubt she has forgotten,' I told him thoughtfully. 'A forgetful minstrel soon starves to death. No. With Starling, I think she believes that if she pretends hard enough that something is so, it becomes so. And, as you have seen, sometimes it works for her. Have you forgiven her, then?'

He looked nonplussed for a moment. Then, with a wry grin, he asked, 'Would she notice if I hadn't? She was so adept at persuading Gindast that she was all but a mother to me that I was half-convinced myself.'

I had to laugh and shrug to that. Starling had taken him to an inn frequented by travelling minstrels and there introduced to a number of musical young ladies. They had fed him mincemeat pastries and filled him up with ale and their songs, vying for his attention. I warned him facetiously about the soft and easy ways of minstrels and their stony hearts. It was a mistake. 'I've no heart left to give to any girl,' he informed me soberly. Nonetheless, from his descriptions of several of them, it seemed to me that even if he did not have the heart, he still had an eye for them. And so I silently blessed Starling and prayed for a swift healing for my lad.

Both the Fool and Lord Golden assiduously avoided me. On several evenings when I quietly descended from the workroom to enter

Lord Golden's apartments through my old bedroom, I found him not at home. Dutiful told me that he gamed more frequently now, in Buckkeep Town where such amusements were gaining popularity as well as at private parties in the keep. I missed him, but also dreaded confronting him eventually. I did not want him to read in my eyes that I had betrayed him to Chade. It was for his own good, I excused myself. Dragons be damned. If simply keeping him away from Aslevjal would keep him alive, then his displeasure would be a small cost. That was what I told myself at the times when I found myself believing his wild prophecies. At other times, I was sure there was no frozen dragon and no Pale Woman and hence no reason for him to go to Aslevjal at all. And thus I justified it that I plotted with Chade against him. As for why he avoided me, I suspected he harboured some odd sense of shame about the tattoos that I now knew he bore. I knew I could not demand his company, nor force mine upon him. I could only hope that as days passed, the healing rift between us would further close.

And so the days ticked by.

I would not have admitted it to anyone, but my newfound dread of the Prince's quest to Aslevjal Island was behind my renewed dedication to teaching him to Skill. No matter how I counted the days to our spring sailing, there were never enough of them. I now concurred with Chade that the Prince must have a coterie, one with at least a basic working knowledge of their magic. And so I applied myself to developing our Skill-talents, with varying degrees of success. Chade's Skill-level slowly increased at our morning lessons. He was very dissatisfied with his progress, and that made it more difficult for him to focus. I could not get him to relax, no matter how I tried to force him into a calm and empty state. Dutiful seemed to find my arguments with my elderly student amusing while Thick was elaborately bored by them. Neither attitude helped Chade to be less irascible with me. My kindly and patient teacher, I discovered, was a terrible student, headstrong and insubordinate. Finally I succeeded in opening him to the Skill after four days of unrelenting effort. At his first awareness of the Skill-current, he rushed headlong into it. I had no choice but to go after him. Sternly forbidding Dutiful and Thick to follow, I plunged into the Skill.

I do not like to recall that mishap. It was not just that Chade was unfurling in the Skill. It was that there was so much of him to unfurl. Every moment of all his years of life streamed away from him. After struggling for a time to gather him in, I realized that the Skill was not shredding him. Rather, the old man was sending seeking threads of himself. Like the roots of a thirsty plant, he spread himself in every direction, heedless of the way the Skill-current tore and scattered his filaments. Even as I gathered the bits of him, he was glorying in the wild rush of connection. At length I tore him from the cataract of the Skill, powered as much by my great anger as by any magic. When at last we came back to my bodies, I found mine under the great table, trembling and twitching at the edge of a convulsion.

'You stupid, stubborn old bastard!' I gasped at him. I had not the strength to shout. Chade himself was sprawled in his chair. As his eyelids fluttered and he came to awareness of himself, he muttered only, 'Magnificent. Magnificent.' And then he dropped his head down onto the table and sank into a deathly sound sleep from which there was no rousing him.

Dutiful and Thick hauled me out from under the table and back into my chair. Dutiful poured me a brimming glass of wine with shaking hands while Thick stood regarding me with his round little eyes very wide. When I had drunk half the wine, Dutiful said in an abashed voice, 'That was the most frightening thing I've ever witnessed. Was that what it was like when you came in after me?'

I was too shaken and angry with both Chade and myself to admit to the Prince that I didn't know. 'Let it be a lesson to the both of you as well,' I scolded. 'Any one of us who commits such a foolish act risks all of us. Well do I understand now why the Skillmasters of old might put a pain barrier between the Skill and a wilful student.'

The Prince looked shocked. 'You would not do such a thing to Lord Chade?' His tone was as if I had proposed clapping the Queen in irons for her own good.

'No,' I admitted grudgingly. I rose shakily and circled the table. I nudged the snoring old man, and then prodded him. His eyes opened to slits. He smiled at me, head still on the table. 'Ah. There you are, my boy.' His smile grew fatuously wider. 'Did you see me? Did you see me fly?' And then, I was not sure if his eyes rolled up or his lids closed, but he was gone again, as exhausted as a child after a day at a fair. I despaired that he seemed to have carried away no sensation at all of tragedy narrowly averted. It was an hour before he awoke, and then, for all his apologies, there was a gleam in his eye that filled me with trepidation. Even after he promised me to make no wild experiments on his own, I privately impressed on Thick that if he sensed Chade Skilling, he must contact me at once. Thick's earnest assent was a bare comfort to me; such promises did not usually stay long in his mind.

The next morning was to bring me no greater serenity. Exhorting Chade to do nothing this time, save witness as best he could, I attempted to guide Dutiful in borrowing Thick's strength to increase his own use of the Skill. Although they all had experienced in my healing what their joined strength could do, none of the three could really explain how they had tapped it or what had happened. It seemed to me that Dutiful at least needed to be able to reliably draw on Thick's power. So I set them a simple exercise, or so I thought.

Alone, Dutiful could reach Chade's mind only as the barest whisper. He could make Chade aware of his efforts, but not of the message he sought to convey. I was not sure if this indicated that Chade was still too closed to the Skill, or if Dutiful could not sufficiently target him. I wanted to see if by tapping Thick's strength, Dutiful could make Chade hear him. 'Prince Verity told me that a coterie member or solo used in such a fashion was referred to as a King's Man. So. Thick will be serving as King's Man to Dutiful. Shall we try this?' I asked them.

'He's the Prince. Not a king,' Thick interrupted anxiously.

'Yes. And?'

'Can't be a King's Man then. It won't work.'

I found my patience. 'It's all right, Thick. It will work. You will be serving as a Prince's Man.'

'Serving. Like a servant?' He was instantly affronted.

'No. Helping. Like a friend. Thick will be helping Dutiful as a Prince's Man. Shall we try this?'

Dutiful was grinning, but it did not mock his man. Thick turned to him, caught the grin from him and settled himself next to the Prince. 'It should be easy for both of you,' I suggested. I didn't know if I lied or not. 'Thick must simply be open to the Skill, but not making any effort. Dutiful should draw strength from him and use the Skill to try to reach Chade. Dutiful. Go slowly. And if I tell you to stop, you must break the contact immediately. Now. Begin.'

I thought I had planned for every possibility. I had sweet foods such as Thick loved and brandy if we needed a restorative. Both waited on the table. I wondered now if that had been a bad idea. Thick's eyes kept wandering to some current buns. Would they distract him too much from his Skilling? I had wanted to have elfbark and hot water ready as well, but Chade had sternly over-ruled me. 'Far better if the Prince's coterie is never exposed to such a destructive drug,' he opined righteously. I didn't remind him that he had taught me the use of it.

I hovered anxiously behind the Prince as he set his hand upon Thick's shoulder. If it appeared he were draining the little man, I was prepared to physically break the link between them. Well did I know that a Skill-user could deliberately kill that way. I wanted no tragic accidents.

We waited. After a time, I gave Chade a significant look. He raised his eyebrows.

'Begin,' I suggested to the two of them.

'I'm trying,' said Dutiful in exasperation. 'I can Skill to Thick. But I don't know how to draw his strength off and use it.'

'Hmm. Thick, can you help him?' I suggested.

Thick opened his eyes and looked at me. 'How?' he asked.

I didn't know. 'Just be open to him. Think of sending him your strength.'

Again, they settled. I watched Chade's face, hoping for some sign that Dutiful had touched minds with him. But after a short time, Dutiful lifted his eyes to mine. His mouth twisted in a small smile. 'He's Skilling "strength, strength, strength" to me,' he confided.

'You said to!' Thick protested angrily.

'Yes. So I did,' I assured him. 'Calm down, Thick. No one is mocking you.'

He glared at me, breathing through his nose. *Dogstink.*

Dutiful flinched. Chade's lips twitched but he managed not to smile. 'Dog stink. Is that the message you wished to convey to me?'

'I believe Thick intended that comment for me,' I said carefully.

'But it went through me to Chade, my target. I felt it,' Dutiful said excitedly.

'Well. At least we make progress,' I said.

'Can I have a bun now?'

'No, Thick. Not yet. We all need to work on this.' I pondered a moment. Dutiful had directed Thick's Skill. Did that mean he had actually taken strength from Thick to break through to Chade, or that he had simply diverted Thick's message intended for me to Chade?

I didn't know. I didn't think there was any way I could be absolutely certain of what had happened. 'Try it together,' I suggested. 'Both of you attempt to send the same message to Chade, and only Chade. Try to make a concerted effort.'

'Concerted?'

'Do it together,' Dutiful supplied to Thick. There was a moment of silent conference between the two. I suspected they chose a message. 'Now,' I suggested and watched Chade's face.

He furrowed his brow. 'Something about a bun.'

Dutiful gave a sigh of exasperation. 'Yes, but that wasn't what we were supposed to be conveying. Thick is having a bit of difficulty concentrating.'

'I'm hungry.'

'No, you aren't. You just want to eat,' Dutiful told him. Which put Thick into a sulk. No amount of prodding or persuasion would induce him to try again. We eventually allowed him the food and resolved to take a lesson from it on the morrow.

Yet the next morning we seemed doomed to have as little luck as before. Spring was in the air. I had thrown the window shutters open wide to the dawn. As yet, the sun was only a promise on the horizon, but the wind off the ocean had a lively and freshened air to it that spoke of life and change in the seasons. I stood breathing it in for a long time while I waited for the others to arrive.

I was no more at ease in conscience over what I had planned against Lord Golden. I had begun to wish I had not divulged that conversation to Chade, nor told him of the Fool's tattoos. Surely if he had wished Chade to know of them, he would have told him during the course of their conversation about the Narcheska's tattoos. I had a deep and profound sense of having made a wrong choice. There was no way to undo it, and confessing it to the Fool seemed unimaginable. The only thing more unimaginable was to allow him to go to Aslevjal if he believed he would die there. So, childish though it felt, I had decided that I would simply hold my tongue and leave the matter in Chade's hands. He would be the one who would not allow Lord Golden to accompany us. I drew another deep breath of spring air, hoping it would make me feel rejuvenated. Instead, I only felt more deeply anxious.

Civil Bresinga had returned to Buckkeep. The guard that had accompanied him on his journey was nominally to express Farseer sympathy at the loss of his mother. Yet he still knew, even if others did not, that he could look forward to years of being monitored at Buckkeep. He would remain at the castle until he reached his majority, with the crown benevolently managing his lands. Galekeep was closed save for a skeleton staff provided by the Queen. It seemed to me a mild rebuke compared to his treasonous conduct. His Wit had been kept confidential; I supposed that the revelation of it could be used as a threat to discourage him from further wrongdoing. He had not been connected at all to the deaths of three men in Buckkeep Town. I seethed that he had got off so lightly for exposing my Prince to so much danger. From what Chade had told me, Dutiful had insisted that Civil had passed on very little information about the Prince to the Piebalds, and most of it was knowledge that even the humblest serving-boy in the keep would have. It did not comfort me. Even more unsettling was that not only Laudwine but Padget had expressed an avid interest in whatever information Civil could discover about both me and Lord Golden. He knew little, so he had told them little. Still, Civil had confessed to the Prince that their interest made him very curious about us.

I'd spied on Civil in his rooms shortly after his return. He had looked like a forlorn and devastated young man. A single family servant remained with him at Buckkeep. He was a lad stripped of family and home, whittled down to his barest possessions, and his Wit-beast consigned to the stables. The simplicity of the chamber and furnishings offered to him was appropriate to a minor noble, but doubtless he had enjoyed far better at home. He had spent a good portion of his evening sitting and staring at the fire. I suspected he communed with his cat, but had not detected a flow of Wit between them. Instead, I had felt his misery as an almost tangible weight in his chamber.

I still didn't trust him.

I was still staring out the window when I heard the Prince's footfalls on the stairs. A moment later, he entered, shutting the door firmly behind him. Chade and Thick would be coming soon, by the secret passage, but for now I had a moment or two alone with him. I didn't look at him as I asked him, 'Does Civil's cat speak to you?'

'Pard? No. He's a cat, so he could, of course, if he wished. But it would be regarded as . . . rude, I suppose.' He made a considering noise. 'It's an odd thing to think of. Among the Old Blood who prefer cats, there are a number of shared customs. I would never attempt to initiate speech with someone else's cat partner. It would be like, well, like flirting with someone's intended. In all the time I've known Pard, he has never shown any interest in communicating with me. Of course, he did convey to me, that one time, that Civil was in danger. But that was more in the nature of a threat. Civil had brought him to me in a great canvas sack. I gathered from what Civil told me that he'd tricked the cat into getting into the sack in the course of some rough game they were playing. Only then Civil tied the sack shut and dragged him up the stairs to my chamber. And I do mean dragged. Pard's a big cat.'

He heaved a sudden sigh. 'I should have known, from that alone. If Civil had not been distraught, he never would have treated Pard so disrespectfully. But Civil seemed so distressed and in such a hurry that I agreed to keep the cat in my chamber until he returned for it and asked few questions. But then, after he'd gone, I couldn't stand to hear Pard snarling and doing that singsong whine. He was trying to gut his way out of the sack with the claws on his hind feet, but

Civil had chosen a very heavy canvas. After a while, he just lay there, panting, and I began to fear that he would suffocate. He sounded as if he were in distress. But the moment I opened the mouth of the bag, he came out clawing and knocked me down. He grabbed me here,' and Dutiful's hand measured the side of his throat, 'and dug his hind claws into my belly. He swore he'd kill me if I didn't let him out of the room. Then, before I could take any action, he yowled and raked his claws down me. That was when Civil was attacked. He said it was my fault and he'd kill me for it unless I saved him. So I Skilled to you.'

He had joined me at the window, looking out over the water's wrinkling face as the sunrise coaxed colour out of the black waves. He stared for a time in silence.

'Then what happened?' I nudged him.

'Oh. I suppose I was thinking of what must have been happening to you then. Why didn't you Skill to me? Don't you think I would have sent you aid?'

His question startled me. I took a moment to find the answer within myself. I laughed. 'I suppose you would have, if I'd thought of it. But, for so many years, it was just the wolf and me. And when I lost Nighteyes . . . I never thought that I could call out to you for help. Or even let you know where I was. It just never occurred to me.'

'I tried to reach you. When they were . . . strangling Civil, his cat went wild. Pard leapt off me and went racing around the room, killing everything within reach. I had no idea of the damage his claws could do. The bed curtains, clothing . . . There's still a tapestry rolled up under my bed that I haven't had the courage to tell anyone about. I think it's ruined. And I suspect it was priceless.'

'Don't worry. I've got one you can have.' He looked puzzled at my lop-sided smile.

'I tried to Skill to you. Even as Pard was shredding my room. But I couldn't get through to you.'

I recalled something that I hadn't in a long time. 'Your father had the same complaint about me. That, when I went into battle, I could not sustain a Skill-link to him. Nor could he establish one with me at such times.' I shrugged. 'I'd near forgotten that.'

Without thinking, I fingered the bite-scar at the angle of my neck. Then I realized Dutiful was staring at me with that look of boyish admiration and I snatched my hand down.

'And that is the only time that Pard has ever spoken to you?'

He shrugged. 'Almost. Abruptly he stopped tearing up my things. Then he thanked me. Very stiffly. I think it must be difficult for a cat to thank anyone. After that, he got up into the middle of my bed and ignored me. He stayed there until Civil came for him. My room reeks of cat still. I think Pard sprays when he fights.'

From the little I knew of cats, it seemed likely. I said as much. Then, delicately, because this was a topic that was tender between us, I asked him, 'Dutiful? Why do you trust Civil? I can't understand why you allow him in your life after what he's done.'

He gave me a puzzled glance. 'He trusts me. I don't think anyone could trust a man as he does me, and not be worthy of my trust in return. Besides. I need him if I am to understand the Old Blood people of my kingdom. My mother pointed that out to me. That I must know at least one, very well, if we are to treat with them at all.'

I hadn't thought of that, but I knew what he meant. The Old Blood lifestyle was a culture hidden within our own Six Duchies culture. I'd had a glimpse of it, but I could not explain it to Dutiful, as could someone born and raised in it. Still, 'There must be someone else who could serve you that way. I still do not see what Civil has ever done to deserve your regard of him.'

Dutiful gave a small sigh. 'FitzChivalry. He entrusted his cat to me. If you knew you were going forth to die, and you did not want Nighteyes to die alongside you, where would you leave him? Who would you entrust him to? A man you had willingly betrayed? Or a friend whom you trusted to see past all shams?'

'Oh,' I said, when his question had sunk in to my mind. 'I see. You are right.'

No man would entrust half his soul to a man he cared nothing for.

In a short time Chade and Thick emerged from the mantelpiece. The old man was scowling and shaking cobwebs from his elaborate sleeves. Thick was humming to himself, odd notes that filled in the gaps in a song that he Skilled to the morning. He seemed to be taking a great deal of pleasure in it. If I listened only with my ears, he seemed to be merely making annoying random sounds. What a difference access to another's mind could make in my understanding of him.

Thick's eyes went immediately to the table and I sensed his disappointment that no pastries awaited him. With a sigh, I hoped that his dashed expectations would not interfere with today's efforts. I seated my students as I had the day before, with Chade on one side of the table and Dutiful and Thick close beside each other on the other side. As before, I stood behind Dutiful and Thick, ready to fall on them and physically separate them if necessary. I knew Dutiful regarded this as somewhat dramatic, and even Chade seemed to think me overly anxious. But neither of them had ever been near drained of life by another Skill-user.

As before, Dutiful set his hand to Thick's shoulder. As before, they tried to reach Chade with a simple message and could not. Dutiful could reach my mind, as could Thick, but even in the familiar task of reaching me, they could not unite. I was beginning to think it was hopeless. One of the most basic tasks of a coterie was to be able to join their Skill and make it available to their king. We could not even do that. And the repeated failures were beginning to make us fractious with one another.

'Thick. Stop your music. How can I concentrate with your music running continually in the back of my mind?' Dutiful demanded after our latest effort had yielded naught.

Thick flinched to his prince's rebuke. As his eyes filled with tears, I realized suddenly how deep and powerful a bond he had formed with Dutiful. I think the Prince realized his error also, for an instant later he shook his head at himself and commented, 'It's the loveliness of the music that distracts me, Thick. I don't wonder that you always want to share it with the world. But for now, we must focus on our lessons. Do you see?'

Chade's eyes suddenly kindled to green sparks. 'No!' he exclaimed. 'Thick, do not stop your music. For I have never heard it, though I have often heard from Dutiful and Tom how lovely it is. Let me hear your music, Thick, just this once. Put your hand on Dutiful's shoulder and send your music to me. Please.'

Dutiful and I gawked at Chade, but Thick beamed. He did not hesitate for an instant. Almost before Dutiful had dropped his hand from Thick's shoulder, the little man had seized Dutiful's in a firm grip. Eyes fixed on Chade, mouth wide open with delight, he gave Dutiful no time to focus. Music filled us all like a flood. Vaguely, I saw Chade reel with the impact of it. His eyes widened, and even though triumph dawned on his features, I also saw a shadow of fear.

I had not underestimated Thick's strength. Never had I witnessed such an outpouring of Skill. Up to now, Thick's music had been always in the undercurrent of his thoughts, as unconscious as his breathing or the beating of his heart. Now he flung himself out wide to the world, rejoicing in his mother-song.

As a muddy river in flood time can colour the whole bay it drains into, so did Thick's song dye the great Skill-current. His song entered the flow and changed it. I had never imagined anything like it. Gripped by it as I was myself, I found myself powerless to take command of my body. The overwhelming fascination of Thick's music drew me into it and wrapped me in his rhythm and melody. Somewhere, I sensed that Dutiful and Chade were with me, but I could not discern them for the curtain of beckoning music. Nor was I the only one so drawn. I sensed others in the Skill-curtain. Some were single threads, a trailing tendril of magic from those barely Skilled at all. Perhaps somewhere a fisherman wondered at the odd tune running in the back of his mind, or a mother changed the lullaby she hummed. Others were more engaged. I sensed folk who halted in the midst of what they were doing and looked round blindly, trying to locate the source of the whispering music.

There were not many, but some were there, their awareness of the Skill a constant in their lives, a background hush of muted voices that they had schooled themselves to ignore. But this rush of music broke through all such habitual barriers, and I sensed them turn towards us. Some likely shouted aloud in shock; others may have fallen to the ground. Only one voice did I hear, clear and unencumbered by fear: *What is this?* Nettle demanded. *Whence comes this waking dream?*

From Buckkeep, Chade answered joyously. *From Buckkeep comes this call, oh ye Skilled ones! Awake and come to Buckkeep, so that your magic may be awakened and you may serve your prince!*

To Buckkeep? Nettle echoed.

And then, like a trumpet call from the distance, a far voice: I know you now. I see you now.

Perhaps nothing else could have broken me from those shackles of Skill-fascination. I parted Dutiful from Thick with a force that astonished all three of us. With a crash, the music halted. For a second I was blinded and deafened by the absence of the Skill. My heart went yearning after it. It was a far purer connection to the world than my feeble senses. But I soon came back to myself. I offered Dutiful my hand, for my shove had sent him sprawling to the floor. Dazedly he gripped my hand and came to his feet, asking as he did so, 'Did you hear that girl? Who was she?'

'Oh, just that girl that cries all the time,' Thick dismissed her and I felt gratitude that his answer filled the gap. Then, 'Did you hear my music? Did you like it?' he was demanding of Chade.

Chade didn't answer immediately. I turned to see him slumped in his chair. He wore a foolish smile yet his brow was furrowed. 'Oh, yes, Thick,' he managed. 'I heard it. And I liked it very much.' He put his elbows on the table and propped his head in them. 'We did it,' he breathed. He lifted his eyes to me. 'Does it always feel like that? The exuberance, the sense of completeness, of joining oneself to the world?'

'It's a thing to be wary of,' I warned him immediately. 'If you go into the Skill seeking that sense of connection, it may sweep you away entirely. A Skill-user must always keep his purpose in the forefront of his mind. Otherwise you can be swept away and lost—'

'Yes, yes,' Chade interrupted me impatiently. 'I haven't forgotten what happened to me last time. But I do think that this is an event that deserves a celebration.'

The others seemed to share his sentiments. I am sure they thought me curmudgeonly and grumpy for my silence. Still, I brought forth the covered basket I had concealed beneath the table, and within it even Thick found enough to be satisfied. We had brandy all round, though I think Chade was the only one who truly needed restoring. The old man's hands shook as he lifted the glass to his mouth, but nonetheless he smiled and offered a toast before he drank: 'To those who may come, to form a true coterie for Prince Dutiful!' He gave me no sly glances and I joined with the others in drinking, even as I hoped Burrich would firmly keep Nettle at home.

Then I asked warily, 'What do you think that other voice was? The one that said, "I know you now".'

Thick ignored me and went on nibbling raisins with his front teeth. Dutiful gave me a puzzled glance. 'Another voice?'

'Do you mean the girl who Skilled so clearly?' Chade asked, plainly shocked that I would call her to their attention. I think he had already deduced that she was Nettle.

'No,' I said. 'That other voice, so foreign and strange. So . . . different.' I could not find words to express the wariness it had roused in me. It was like a dark premonition.

A moment of silence followed my words. Then Dutiful said, 'I only heard the girl who said "To Buckkeep?"'

'And I the same,' Chade assured me. 'There was no coherent thought after hers. I thought she was why you broke our linking.'

'Why would he do that?' Dutiful demanded.

'No,' I insisted, ignoring the Prince's question. 'Something else spoke. I tell you, I heard . . . something. Some kind of a being. Not human.'

This was an extraordinary enough statement to distract Dutiful from prying for Nettle's identity. But as the other three all vowed they had sensed nothing, my claims were not taken seriously, and by the end of the session, I had begun to wonder if I had deceived myself.

TWENTY-FIVE

Convocation

. . . and nothing would do but that the Princess would have the dancing bear for her very own. Such a begging has not been heard for many a year, but at last she prevailed and her father gave the bear's keeper a whole handful of gold coins for the beast. And the Princess herself took hold of the chain that went to the bear's ring, and led the great, hulking creature up to her own bedchamber. But in the depth of the night, while all else in the keep slept, the boy rose up and threw off his bearskin. And when he showed himself to the Princess, she found him as comely a youth as she had ever seen. And it was not so much that he had his way with her, as that she had hers with him.

The Bear-boy and the Princess

One afternoon, the birches flushed pink and the packed snow of the courtyard turned to slush. Spring came that quickly to Buckkeep that year. By the time the sun went down, there were bare patches of earth showing on some of the best-trodden tracks. It was cold that night, and winter stilled everything with its touch, but the next morning the land awoke to the sound of trickling water and a warm sweeping wind.

I had slept in the barracks and slept well despite the snoring and night-shifting of two dozen other men. I rose with the others, ate a hearty breakfast in the guardroom and then returned to the barracks to don the purple and white of the Queen's Guard. We buckled on our swords, collected our horses, and gathered in the courtyard.

Then there was the inevitable wait for the Prince to emerge. When he did come out, Councillor Chade and Queen Kettricken accompanied him. The Prince looked both polished and uncomfortable. Perhaps a dozen lesser nobles were there to see him off. Amongst the well-wishers were the six representatives the Six Duchies had originally sent to the Queen for her discussion of the Witted problem. I could tell by their faces that they had never expected to be involved in a face-to-face confrontation with the Witted, and they did not look forward to it. Lord Civil Bresinga was among those who stood in the slushing snow to bid the Prince farewell. From the back rank of the Queen's Quard, I watched his still face and wondered how he felt about what was happening. By the Queen's express command, no one would leave Buckkeep save the guard and the Prince. She would take no chances of frightening away the already-cautious Old Blood delegation.

The Queen gave brief instructions to her commander. I could not hear her words to Marshcroft, our leader, but I saw his face change. He made a sincere bow but disapproval was in every line of his face. And I was shocked to the core when a woman on horseback suddenly joined us leading the Queen's mount. It took me a moment to recognize Laurel. She had cropped her hair short and dyed it black. Chade stepped forward, remonstrating, but the Queen looked adamant. She spoke briefly to him. I could not hear her words, but I saw the set line of the Kettricken's jaw and Chade's rising colour. With a final curt nod to her councillor she mounted, and signalled her readiness to Marshcroft. At his command, we all mounted, and then we followed our prince and Marshcroft as they led us out of the gates of Buckkeep. I glanced back to find Chade staring after us in horror. *Why is she going with us?* I Skilled frantically to Chade, but if he received my thought, he made no response.

I asked the same question of the Prince.

I do not know. She merely told Chade there had been a change in plans, and that she left it up to him to be certain that no one followed us. I do not like this.

Nor do I.

I watched as Dutiful said something to his mother. She merely shook her head at him. Her lips were firmly closed. Laurel rode looking straight ahead. My brief glimpse of her had shown me that there were new lines in her brow, and less flesh to her face. So, she had been the Queen's emissary to the Witted. Was that how she fought the Piebalds? Trying to win more political power for a more temperate group? It made sense, but it could not have been an easy task for her, or a safe one. I wondered when she had last slept soundly.

The melting slush gave way unevenly beneath our horses' hooves. We left by the west gate. Ostensibly, only the Prince and Marshcroft knew our destination. The bird with the message had arrived yesterday. In reality, I shared that knowledge. There had been mutterings and discontent about the Queen consenting to meet with emissaries of Old Blood. It had been judged wiser to keep our rendezvous location a secret lest any of the more intractable nobles sabotage our plans.

The wind promised either rain or wet snow to come. Sap had flushed the leafless trees to life. We did not take the fork of the road that led down to the river but instead took the branch that led into the forested hills behind Buckkeep Castle. A lone hawk patrolled the sky, perhaps in search of venturesome mice. Or perhaps not, I thought to myself. As the trees drew closer to the road, Marshcroft gave us the order to reform so that the Prince and the Queen rode now in our midst instead of before us. My dread grew. Not by any word or sign had Dutiful indicated that he was aware that I rode at his back, but I was glad of the tight Skill-awareness that hung between us.

We rode on through the morning, and at each fork in the road we took the less trafficked one. I was not pleased that the narrowing passage through the trees forced us into a long and straggling line. Myblack detested keeping a steady pace following the horse in front of her and I had a constant battle to keep her from moving up on him. Her wilfulness was an unwelcome distraction as I tried to expand my Wit-awareness of the forest around us. Given the men and horses around me, it was a near-impossible task to be aware of anything beyond them, much like trying to listen for the squeaking of a mouse while surrounded by barking dogs. Nonetheless, I cursed myself and sent a sharp Skill-warning to the Prince when I first became aware of the outriders flanking us. They had done a wonderful job. I was suddenly aware of two of them, and before

I could draw breath, noticed three more ghosting alongside us through the trees. They were on foot, their faces hooded against recognition. They carried bows.

This is not where we were told they'd await us, Dutiful Skilled anxiously as Marshcroft called an abrupt halt. We formed up as well as we could around the Prince. The Witted I could see had arrows nocked, but the bows were not drawn.

Then, 'Old Blood greets you!' a voice rang through the forest.

'Dutiful Farseer returns greeting,' Dutiful replied clearly when the Queen kept silent. He sounded very calm, but I could almost feel the hammering of his heart.

A short, dark woman came striding through her archers to stand before us. Unlike the others, she was unarmed and her face uncovered. She looked up at the Prince. Then she turned her gaze to the Queen. Her eyes widened and a tenuous smile came to her face. Then, 'FitzChivalry' she said clearly. I stiffened, but Dutiful relaxed.

He nodded to Marshcroft as he said, 'That was the agreed password. These are the folk we promised to meet and escort.' He turned back to the woman. 'But why are you here rather than at our arranged rendezvous?'

She laughed lightly, but bitterly. 'We have learned a measure of caution in the past, my lord, in dealing with Farseers. You will forgive us if we still employ it. It has saved many a life here.'

'You have not always been fairly dealt with, so I will excuse your suspicion. I am here, as you requested, to assure you that we offer the emissaries safe passage to Buckkeep Castle.'

The woman nodded. 'And have you brought for us a hostage, one nobly born, as we requested?'

For the first time, the Queen spoke. 'He is here. I give you my son.'

Dutiful went white. Marshcroft burst out, 'My Queen, I beg you, no!' He turned back to the Old Blood woman. 'Lady, if it please you, I was told nothing of a hostage. Do not take my prince from my protection. Take me instead!'

Did you know of this? I demanded of Dutiful.

No. But I understand her reasoning. His response was oddly calm.

He spoke his next words aloud, but they were for me as much as for the guard. 'Peace, Marshcroft. This is my mother's decision, and I will obey it. No one will fault you for following your queen's will. For in this, I am Sacrifice for my people.' He turned to look at his mother. His face was still pale, but his voice was firm. He was proud of this moment, I knew suddenly. Proud to serve in this way, proud that she had thought him mature enough to face this challenge. 'If it is my mother's will, then I put my life in your hands. And if any of your folk are harmed, then I am willing to forfeit.'

'And I, too, will remain as surety for my queen's word.' Laurel's soft voice rang clear in the shocked silence that followed. The Old Blood woman nodded gravely. Laurel was obviously well known to her.

My thoughts raced as I tried to put it all together. Of course the Old Blood folk would have asked for a hostage. Safe passage and hidden identities would not protect their chosen leaders once they were inside Buckkeep's walls. Despite Chade's dismissal of their request, I should have known that someone would have to serve. But why did it have to be the Prince? And why could not the Queen have chosen me to remain at his side instead of Laurel? I looked at Kettricken with new eyes. The subterfuge surprised me, as did her circumvention of Chade. Well I knew he would never have agreed to this. How had she arranged it all? Through Laurel? Marshcroft flung himself from his horse and knelt at her feet in the sogging snow, begging her not to do this, to let him be hostage instead, or at least to let him and five chosen men remain with the Prince. But she was adamant. Dutiful stepped down from his mount and drew Marshcroft to his feet. 'No one will ever fault you for this, even if it goes awry,' he sought to assure him. 'My lady mother is here to give me over; that was why she came. All will know it was her will, not yours, that this be done. I beg you, good man, remount and take our queen safely home.' He raised his voice, 'Yes, and all who ride back with you, hear me. Guard these folk as if my life depended on it, for I assure you that it does. That is how you can best serve me.'

The Old Blood woman spoke then to Marshcroft, saying, 'I promise both you and his mother that he will be treated well, so long as our own are treated similarly. On this you have my word.'

Marshcroft looked little comforted by it.

I was in a quandary as I sat and watched the exchange happen. *I will double back and follow*, I promised the Prince.

No. My mother has given her word that we will treat fairly with them, and so we shall. If I have need of you, I shall let you know. This I promise you. But for now, let me do this thing she has entrusted to me.

By then our emissaries were trickling in from the forest in twos and threes. Some brought their Wit-beasts. I heard the high cry of a hawk overhead, and knew that I had guessed correctly earlier that day. Another man rode with a spotted dog at his stirrup. One woman came towards us leading a milk-cow heavy with calf. But of the dozen folk, faces swathed and variously mounted, who came to join us, most were alone. I wondered if they had left their animals behind or were currently unpaired.

One man immediately caught my attention. He was probably about fifty, but he wore his years well as some active men do. He walked with a sailor's roll, leading a horse that he obviously mistrusted. Both the hair of his head and his short-trimmed beard were steely grey, and his eyes the same but with a hint of blue. Other than the woman who had first greeted us, he was the only Old Blood who went unmasked. Yet it was not his appearance that struck me so much as the deference the other Old Bloods accorded him. They stepped back for him as if he were either holy or mad. The Old Blood woman who had first greeted us indicated him with a flourish.

'You have entrusted us with Prince Dutiful. This we little expected you would do, despite the word that was sent to us. Yet I was determined that if you gave us a hostage that indicated you had true respect for us, we would do the same. We give you Web. He is of the oldest Old Blood, an unmingled bloodline and the last of that heritage. We have no nobility amongst ourselves, no kings nor queens. But from time to time we do have one such as Web. He does not rule us, but he does listen to us, and we listen to him. Mind that you treat all my people well, but Web treat as if he were your prince.'

It seemed a very strange introduction to me. I knew little more about the man than I had when she started speaking, and yet all the Old Blood behaved as if she had bestowed a gift upon us. I saved it up to expound on to Chade.

I thought of Skilling ahead to Thick to ask him to tell Chade what the Queen had done, but I decided against it. The little man often scrambled messages, and I did not want Chade spurred into rash action. I'd seen enough of that for one day. As our two groups parted, leaving the Prince and Laurel sitting their horses and surrounded by armed Witted, the rain suddenly came pelting down. The woman who had spoken called after us, 'Three days! Return my people unharmed in three days!'

The Queen turned back and nodded to her gravely. The reminder had scarcely been needed. It already seemed far too long a time to entrust the well-being of our prince to them.

Marshcroft did his best to form up his troops protectively about the Old Bloods, but they were more than we had expected and his guard was spread thin. I was towards the end of the procession, riding behind the woman who led her Wit-cow. I had thought the bearded man would insist on some sort of honoured place in the formation, perhaps riding alongside the Queen. Instead, Web rode towards the rear, right in front of me. I glanced back for a final glimpse of my prince sitting his horse in the freezing rain. When I looked forward again, I found the man watching me.

'Braver than I thought a boy of his years would be. Tougher than I thought a prince would be,' Web observed to me. The guardsman to my right scowled, but I nodded gravely. Web held my eyes for a time before he looked away. I felt uneasy that he had singled me out for his words.

Before we reached Buckkeep, I was soaked through. The rain turned to a sloppy snow, making the trail treacherous and slowing our progress. The guards at the gate admitted us without question or delay, but as we rode past, I saw one's eyes widen and read his lips as he whispered to his fellow, 'The Prince is gone!' So the rumour fled before us into Buckkeep.

In the courtyard, Marshcroft assisted the Queen's dismount. Chade was there to meet us. He lost control for an instant when he realized the Prince had not returned. His sharp green gaze sought me immediately. I avoided meeting it, as much because I had no information for him as because I did not want folks to connect us. It was not difficult. The courtyard had become a place of trampled snow and mud, full of milling folk and animals. The milk-cow's distressed intermittent mooing mingled with the general discord of voices. There were folk from our stables waiting to take our beasts and those of our guests, but they had not been prepared for the pregnant cow, nor for a soaking and masked woman who would not leave her animal but feared to enter our stables alone.

At length both Web and I volunteered to accompany her. I found an empty stall and made her weary cow as comfortable as she could be made in an unfamiliar place. The woman, Sally, said little to either of us, instead seeming completely concerned for the cow's welfare. But Web was affable and talkative, not just to me, but to the horses in their stalls and the stable boys that I sent running for water and fresh hay. I introduced myself as Tom Badgerlock of the Queen's Guard.

'Ah,' he said, and nodded as if confirming something he had already suspected. 'You would be Laurel's friend, then. She spoke well of you, and commended you to my attention.'

On that unnerving note, he turned back to his exploration of the stables. He seemed interested in all that was going on around him, asking questions not just about how many animals were stabled here, but what sort of a horse was that and had I been a guardsman long and did I look forward to a set of dry clothes and something hot to drink as much as he did?

I was taciturn in my response without being rude, but it was still a relief to escort them into the keep and up to the east wing where the Queen had decided to quarter all her Old Blood guests. Those quarters offered them privacy from the rest of the keep folk. There was a large room where they could dine together unmasked, once the food was set out and the serving folk were banished. They all seemed very concerned that their identities remain hidden. All save Web. I escorted him and the cow-woman up to the floor where the bedchambers were. There a maid greeted them and asked them to follow her. Sally left without a backwards glance, but Web clasped wrists with me heartily and told me that he expected we'd have a chance to talk again soon. He wasn't three steps away from me before he was asking the chambermaid if she enjoyed her work and had she lived at the castle long and wasn't it a shame the spring day had ended in such a downpour.

My duties discharged, this wet and weary guardsman went immediately to the guardroom. There, all was in an uproar as the Queen's decision was discreetly discussed at the top of our lungs. The hall was packed, not only with the guards who had just come in but with all who wanted to hear the tale at first hand. It was too late for that, however. Amongst guardsmen, tales multiply faster than rabbits. As I wolfed down stew and bread and cheese, I heard how we had been surrounded by a force of three score Witted ones with bows, swords and at least one wild boar, tusking and snorting and eyeing us all the while. I had to admire the last addition to the tale. At least the man shouting out his account most loudly told how brave and cool our prince had been.

Still dripping and cold, I left the guardroom and headed down a corridor that led past the kitchens and towards the pantries. In a quiet moment, I slipped inside Thick's small room, and from thence into the hidden corridors of the keep. I fled to my workroom as swiftly as I could and changed into dry clothes, spreading my wet ones to drip over the tables and chairs. The tiny note from Chade said merely, 'Queen's private council room'. From the splattered ink, I deduced he had been in high temper when he penned it.

And so I made another hurried dash through the twisting labyrinth. I cursed its construction, wondering if the men who had built it had been as short as the ceilings seemed to indicate, even as I knew that no one had ever planned this whole maze. Rather it utilized not only gaps between walls but abandoned servants' stairs as well as bits added deliberately in the course of repairing the old keep. I was out of breath when I reached the secret entrance to the Queen's private chambers. I halted to catch my breath before knocking, and became aware of the fierce argument on the other side of the concealed door.

'And I am the Queen!' Kettricken stated in fierce reply to whatever Chade had said. 'As well as his mother. In either capacity, do you think I would risk heir or son if I had not thought it of the highest importance?'

I didn't hear Chade's reply. But Kettricken's was clear and almost strident. 'No, it has nothing to do with my "damnable Mountain upbringing". It has to do with me forcing my nobles to treat with the Old Bloods as if they had something to lose. You witnessed how they trivialized my efforts before. Why? Because it cost them nothing to leave things as they were. The injustice did not bother them. None of their sons or wives were at stake. They had never lain awake at night, fearing that someone they cared about would be found out as Witted and murdered for it. But I have. I will tell you something, Chade. My son is in no more danger as hostage to the Witted than he was yesterday, here in the keep, where proof of his Wit could have turned his own dukes against him.'

In the silence that followed her words, I rapped overly-loud on the door. In a moment, I heard, 'Enter,' and did so, to find them both pink-cheeked but composed. I felt as if I were a child who had walked in on his parents' secret quarrel. But in an instant, Chade endeavoured to make it mine.

'How could you allow this to happen?' he demanded of me. 'Why didn't you keep me informed? Is the Prince well? Has he been harmed?'

'He is fine—' I began, but Kettricken cut in suddenly with, 'How could *he allow* this to happen? Councillor, you go too far. For many years you have advised me, and you have advised me well. But if you forget your place again, we will part company. You are to counsel, not to make decisions and certainly not to circumvent my will! Do you think I have not considered well every aspect of this? Follow my thoughts, then, you who taught me to plot this way. Fitz is here, and through him I shall know if my son suffers even an indignity. At my son's side is a woman familiar with Old Blood ways, a woman loyal to me, and capable of handling a weapon if she must. In my possession are a dozen folk, all at risk if anything befalls Dutiful, plus one man who seems of great significance to them. You dismissed their request for a hostage, saying that if we failed to offer one, they might protest but in the end would still vouchsafe their people to us. Laurel counselled me otherwise; she knows well the distrust they have for the Farseers, and the generations of abuse it is founded on. She said we must offer a hostage, one of good standing. Who, then, could I offer? Myself? That was my first thought. But then, who remains here to treat with them? My son, seen by many as an untried lad? No. I had to remain here. I pondered my other choices. A noble, fearful and disdainful of them, over the protests of my other dukes? You? Then I would be bereft of your counsel. FitzChivalry? To make him valuable enough, his identity would have to be revealed. And so I settled on my son. He is valuable to both sides, and most valuable alive. They have made no secret to me in these negotiations of the fact they know he is Witted. Hence, in some ways, he is one of their own as much as he is ours. He is sympathetic to their situation, for he shares it. I doubt not that while he is with them, he will learn more than he would if he had stayed here by my side during these formal negotiations. And what he learns will make him, ultimately, a better king for all his people.' She halted. A bit breathlessly, she added, 'Well, Councillor. Show me my error.'

Chade sat looking at her, mouth ajar. I did not bother to conceal my admiration. Then Kettricken grinned at me, and I saw green sparks ignite in Chade's eyes.

He shut his mouth with a snap. 'You might have told me first,' he said bitterly. 'I do not relish being made to look like a fool.'

'Then choose to look merely surprised, like the rest,' Kettricken advised him tartly. More gently, she added, 'Old friend, I know that I have made you concerned for my son's safety and hurt your feelings. But if I had taken you into my confidence on this, you would have prevented me from doing it. Wouldn't you?'

'Perhaps. But that still . . .'

'Peace,' she hushed him. 'It is done, Chade. Now accept it. And I beg you, do not let it hinder you from being just and resourceful as we enter into this negotiation.' As quickly as that, she silenced him. She turned to me. 'You I shall want behind the wall, FitzChivalry, witness to everything. And of course, it is also your function to monitor my son's well-being. He may be able to convey to you information that can put us at an advantage.' She pretended calmness as she asked, 'Are you aware of him right now?'

'Not in a direct way,' I admitted. 'Not riding with him as once Verity rode with me. That is an aspect of the Skill that he has not yet fully acquired. But . . . a moment.' I took a breath and reached for him. *Dutiful? I am with Chade and the Queen. All is well with you?*

We are fine. Is Chade very angry with her?

Don't be concerned with that. She deals well with him. They merely wanted to be sure we could reach one another.

That we can. I am in a conversation with Fleria, their leader. Let me pay attention to it now, or she will think I am more half-wit than Witted.

When I brought my attention back to Chade and Kettricken, the old man was scowling at me. 'And what makes you smile?' he demanded, as prickly as if I had mocked him.

'My prince made a jest with me. He is well. And as the Queen surmised, he is conversing with their leader. Fleria.'

The Queen turned to Chade triumphantly. 'There. Do you see? Already he has her name, a bit of information long denied us.'

'You mean, she has told him some name to call her by,' Chade rejoined irritably. Then, to me, 'Why cannot I hear him? What must I do, to perfect my talent to work as I need it to?'

'The fault may not be with you. Dutiful has finally mastered directing his thoughts only to me. Not even Thick would have been aware of his Skilling to me, I think. It could be that, as you and the Prince work together, you will establish a stronger link of your own. And you may become more receptive to the magic as you work with it more often. But, until then—'

'Until then, you must wait to discuss this later. Even the most laggardly of our guests should be warm and clad in dry garb by now. Come, Chade. We are to meet them in the east gathering hall. And you, Fitz, off to your post. If we hear anything that will affect my son's safety, I wish him to know of it immediately.'

Another woman might have waited for Chade, or have gone to a looking-glass briefly. Not Kettricken. She rose and swept from the room, completely confident that her councillor would be on her heels and that I would scuttle off to my spy-post. The look Chade shot me as he left mingled pride and chagrin.

'I may have taught her too well,' he observed to me in a whisper.

I re-entered the rat-warren of corridors. In the workroom, I provided myself with sufficient candles and a cushion for my comfort. As I made my roundabout way to my listening-post, Gilly joined me. He was disappointed to discover I had no raisins with me today, but contented himself with the adventure instead.

All the negotiations I have ever witnessed begin with at least a day of boredom. This was no exception. Despite the mystery of the masked Old Bloods, that first long afternoon was a morass of manoeuvring and suspicion cloaked behind extreme courtesy and reserve. The delegates did not wish to reveal where in the Six Duchies each came from, let alone their names. That was nearly all that was resolved by the end of that first session: that they must at least name the duchy each came from, and that complaints of treatment in that duchy must be documented with the name of the person who was wronged as well as dates and specific details.

Web remained the exception to every rule in this. He furnished the only moment that was interesting to me that entire first day. He introduced himself as coming from Buck, from a small coastal town on our border with Bearns. He was a fisherman by trade, and the last scion of what had once been a large Old Blood family. Most of his immediate family had perished during the Red Ship Wars, with his aged grandmother surrendering to her years only last spring. He was unmarried and childless, but did not count himself alone as he was bonded to a sea-bird, one that was even now riding the winds over Buckkeep Castle. Her name was Risk, and if the Queen was interested in meeting her, he would be happy to call her down to one of the tower tops.

He alone lacked the reserve and the suspicion that the rest of the Old Blood shared. His loquaciousness more than made up for the silence of many of the others. He seemed to take Queen Kettricken at her word that she wished to put an end to Old Blood persecution. He not only took some moments to publicly thank her for that, but also for making this gathering possible. He said she had brought together Old Blood people in a way that had not happened for generations, not since they had been forced to hide their magic and no longer live together in communities. From there, he launched into the importance of Old Blood children being able to acknowledge openly their magic so that they might learn it completely. He included Prince Dutiful amongst them, and said he shared her sorrow that her son's magic must remain both hidden and uneducated.

He paused then. I wondered what he expected. That the Queen would thank him for his sympathy and concern? I saw Chade's tension. Despite what the Old Blood claimed to 'know', Chade had counselled Kettricken not to admit to them that her son was Witted. The Queen skirted the issue nicely, telling her that she shared his concern for children that must grow up in an atmosphere of secrecy, their talents uneducated.

And so it went for that long evening. Web was the only one who seemed not only willing but insistent to share information about himself and his Wit. I began to recognize the distance that the Old Blood folks kept from him. It was as much confusion as awe. Like many a man labelled either god-touched or mad, folk were unsure what to make of him. He made them uneasy; they were not sure if they should emulate him or drive him from their midst. I swiftly deduced that alone of the folk there, he had come on his own. No community had selected him to represent them; he had simply heard of the Queen's summoning and answered it. The woman in the forest had seemed to set great store by him, but I was not at all sure that every Witted person in the room shared her high regard. And then he won my queen.

'A man with nothing to lose,' he said at one point, 'is often in the best position to sacrifice himself for the gain of others.'

That set Kettricken's eyes to shining at him, and I knew that both Chade and I wished that he had chosen any other word but 'sacrifice'.

The talk lasted until the evening meal. Chade and the Queen left them to eat in privacy, but I did not scruple to watch them remove their hoods and masks. I saw no one I recognized either from my contacts with Rolf's Old Bloods or from the Piebalds I had hunted. They ate well, commenting freely on how good the food was. One small Wit-beast that had passed by me unnoticed now emerged. A woman had a squirrel that came out and scampered about on the table, foraging amongst the serving dishes without remonstrance from anyone. This meal and the casual conversation were what the Queen and Chade truly wished me to witness. I was not surprised when Chade soon joined me at my post.

Silently we listened to our guests discuss the direction of the conversation and if they thought the Queen was truly listening to them. There were two Old Bloods, a man calling himself Boyo and a woman using the name Silvereye, who were particularly vocal. I sensed that they knew one another well, and perceived themselves as the leaders of this group. They attempted to rally the others into taking a firm stance with the Queen. Boyo recited a list of demands they should make, with Silvereye enthusiastically nodding to each one. Several were unrealistic and others raised difficult questions. Boyo claimed descent from a noble family which had been stripped of title and estates during the time of the Piebald Prince frenzy. He wanted all restored to him, with the promise that those who helped him insist on it would be made welcome as dwellers and workers on his family lands. Surely all could see that a noble of acknowledged Old Blood could improve conditions for all of them. I myself did not see that clear connection, but some of them nodded at his words.

Silvereye had more vengeance then restitution in mind. She proposed that those who had executed Witted ones should themselves receive the same treatment. Both were adamant that the Queen must offer reparations for old wrongs before any discussion of how Witted and unWitted could live peaceably alongside one another.

My heart sank at these words. In the dim light of our hooded candle, Chade looked weary. I knew the Queen had hoped to take the opposite approach and attempt to solve today's problems and eliminate tomorrow's rather than go back scores of years and try to render justice. Chade leaned over close to me to whisper in my ear, 'If they hold that line, then all of this will have been for naught. Three days will not suffice even to discuss such things. And even a presentation of such demands will drive the dukes to equally stringent demands of their own.'

I nodded. I set my hand upon his wrist. *Let us hope they are but*

*two, and that calmer heads will prevail. That Web, for instance. He did
not seem bent on revenge.*

Chade's brow had furrowed when I began my Skill-attempt. After
I had finished, he nodded his head slowly. I got the gist of his
returned thought *Where . . . Web?*

In the far corner. Just watching them all.

And indeed he was. It appeared almost as if he were dozing, but
I suspected that he was watching and listening as carefully as we
were. For a time longer, Chade and I crouched there together. Then
he suggested to me quietly, 'Go and eat. I'll keep watch while you're
gone. We shall want you to remain at this post as long as you can
this evening.'

And so I did. When I returned, I brought more cushions and
a blanket, a bottle of wine and a handful of raisins for the ferret
who accompanied me. Chade gave a sniff, plainly indicating that
he thought I indulged myself, and then vanished. The Old Bloods
re-masked themselves before they allowed the servants into the
room to clear away. Musicians and jugglers followed, and the Queen
and Chade joined them for this entertainment. Also included were
the dukes' representatives. These were all fairly young men and
they did not make a good showing. They clustered together, plainly
uneasy at the thought of spending the evening in the company of
Witted folk, and spoke mostly amongst themselves. They were
supposed to join the Queen and Chade in a discussion tomorrow
with the Old Bloods. I foresaw that little progress would be made
and felt some concern for my prince.

I reached for him, and in a moment felt his acknowledgment.
Where are you and what are you doing?

*I'm sitting and listening to an Old Blood minstrel sing songs from olden
days. We're at a sort of shelter at the head end of a valley. From the look of it,
I would say it was thrown together especially for this purpose. I guess they did
not want to take us to any of their real homes for fear of later reprisals.*

Are you comfortable?

*A bit cold, and the food is very basic. But it's no worse than an
overnight hunt would be. They are treating us well. Let my mother
know I am safe.*

I shall.

And how goes it at Buckkeep?

Slowly. I'm sitting behind a wall watching Old Bloods watch a juggler. Dutiful, I doubt that any real progress will be made in the next three days.

I suspect you are right. I think we should take the attitude of one old man here. He keeps telling everyone it will be a triumph if we have these talks at all without bloodshed. And that will be more than any Farseer has offered Old Blood in his lifetime.

Hmm. Perhaps he has something there.

The Old Bloods I watched made an early night of it. Doubtless they were weary both from the journey and from the tension. I was glad to seek my own bed but first decided on a trip down to the guardroom to see what gossip might be offered. The guardroom, I had long ago discovered, was the best place to hear rumour and innuendo, and to judge the temper of the folk at large.

On my way there, I was shocked to encounter Web wandering about in the quiet night halls of the castle. He greeted me warmly by name. 'Are you lost?' I asked him courteously.

'No. Only curious. And my head too full of thoughts to sleep. Where are you going?'

'To find a late meal,' I told him, and he suddenly decided that was the very thing he needed himself. I was reluctant to take one of our Old Blood emissaries into the guardroom, but he refused the suggestion that he find a quiet hearth in the Great Hall and wait there for me. As he walked beside me, dread rose in me that we might face some sort of encounter there, but he seemed immune to such fears, asking me endless questions about the tapestries, banners and portraits we passed.

When we entered the guardroom, all talk died for a moment. My heart sank at the hostile glances we received, and sank still more when I saw Blade Havershawk at the end of the table nearest the hearth. I averted my face as I observed, 'Our queen's guest would like a slice off the joint, fellows, and a mug of ale.' I made this heavy-handed reminder of the hospitality we owed in the hopes it would warm the room. It didn't.

'Rather we was sharing it with our prince,' someone said portentously.

'As would I,' Web agreed heartily. 'For I scarce got the chance to say two words to him before he rode off with my comrades. But as he dines with them tonight and listens to their tales, so I would break bread with you and hear the stories of Buckkeep Castle.'

'Don't know as we feed Witted at the table round here,' someone observed snidely.

I took breath, knowing I must make some reply and find some way to get Web out of the room uninjured, but Blade spoke before me. 'Once we did,' he said slowly. 'And he was one of our own and we loved him well, until we were stupid enough to let Regal take him from us.'

'Oh, not that old tale!' someone groaned, and another chimed in with, 'Even after he killed our king, Blade Havershawk? Did you love him well then?'

'FitzChivalry didn't kill King Shrewd, you young knot-head. I was there and I know what happened. I don't care what a drove of snake-tongued minstrels have sung since. Fitz didn't kill the King he loved. He did kill those Skill-users, and I warrant it was as he claimed. They killed Shrewd.'

'Aye. That's how I always heard the tale, too,' Web sounded enthused. As I watched in horror, he squeezed past men who pointedly did not step out of his way until he reached Blade's side. 'Is there room beside you on that bench, old warrior?' he asked amiably. 'For I would hear it told again, from the lips of a man who was there.'

There followed for me the longest evening I'd ever spent in the guardroom. Web was full of curiosity, and stopped Blade a hundred times in his telling of that fateful night to pose piercing questions that soon had the men around the table asking questions of their own. Had the torches truly burned blue and the Pocked Man been seen on that night when Regal claimed the throne was rightfully his? And the Queen had fled that night of blood, had she not? And when she returned to Buckkeep, had she shed no light on those events?

Full strange it was to hear that debate, and know that speculation still raged after all the years. The Queen had always asserted FitzChivalry had murdered in justified rage the true killers of the

King, but no proof had ever been offered that was so. Still, the men agreed, their queen was no fool, nor had she reason to lie on that topic. As if one Mountain bred as she was would ever lie! And from there they clambered on to the hoary tale of how I had clawed my way out of the grave, leaving an empty coffin behind. The empty coffin at least had been shown, though no man could say if my body had been spirited away or if I had truly transformed into a wolf and escaped it. The gathered guards were sceptical of Web's claim that no Witted one could transform in that way. From there, the talk went to his own beast, a gull of some sort. Again, he extended the invitation that any who wished might meet his bird on the morrow. A few shook their heads in superstitious fear, but others were plainly intrigued and said they would come.

'Fer what's a birdie agonna do t'you?' one drunkenly demanded of a less courageous fellow. 'Shittapon you, praps? You oughta be 'customed to that, Reddy. That woman of yers does it oft enou'.'

And that made for a brief and very cramped fistfight at that end of the table. When the combatants had been ejected by their fellows into the chilly night, Web declared that he'd had all the ale and stories he could hold for one evening, but he'd be pleased to join them again tomorrow, if he were welcome. To my dismay, Blade and several others heartily decided he was welcome, Witted or not, yes, and his bird, too.

'Well, my Risk's not one for coming within walls, nor for flight by dark. But I'll see you get a chance to meet her tomorrow, if you've a mind.'

As we parted from them and crossed the castle to the east apartments, it gradually came to me that Web had probably done more to further the cause of the Witted tonight than all the talk of the earlier day had. Perhaps he truly was a gift to us.

TWENTY-SIX

Negotiations

One man armed with the right word may do what an army of swordsmen cannot.

Mountain proverb

I reported on Web to Chade, of course, and in turn he reported to the Queen. And thus at the next day's meeting, in front of the Six Duchies representatives, she made certain that Web had the first opportunity to speak. I crouched behind the wall, my eye to the crack and listened to him. She introduced him to the delegates before he spoke, saying that he represented the oldest of the Old Blood lines, and that she desired that he be treated with all courtesy. Yet when she yielded her audience to him, he assured them all that he was only a humble fisherman who happened to be descended of parents far wiser than he would ever be. Then, with an abruptness that left me gasping, he introduced his proposals for ending the unjust persecution of the Witted. He spoke as much to the Witted as he did to our queen as he suggested that perhaps her best method to begin to bring the two groups together would be to admit some Witted into her own household.

As he spoke, he sounded more like a Jhaampe wise-man settling a dispute than a spokesman for the Old Blood. My queen's eyes shone as she listened to him. I caught not just Chade, but at least two of the Six Duchies men, nodding thoughtfully at what he proposed. Step by step, he revealed the reasoning behind his suggestion. He attributed much of the unjust persecution to fear, and much of the fear to ignorance. The ignorance he blamed on the Witted's need to remain hidden for their own safety. Where better to begin an end to ignorance than in the Queen's own household? Let an Old Blood woman with birding-skills assist in the mews, and a Witted dog-boy come to help her Huntswoman. Let her have a Witted page or maid, for no other reason than to let folk discover that they were no different from unWitted pages and maids. Let other nobles see that these folk did no harm to her household or to others, but rather prospered them. The Queen would, of course, commit to their protection from persecution until others had been won firmly to the cause. The Old Blood thus placed would take oath to initiate no strife.

Then, with a smoothness which left me gasping, he offered his own services to the Queen. This he did as courteously and correctly as any court-trained noble's son, so that I wondered uneasily if he had truly come of a fishing family. Down on one knee he sank before her, and begged to be allowed to remain at Buckkeep when the others departed. Let him live in the keep, and both learn and teach. Carefully keeping the secret of the Prince's Wit when speaking before her Six Duchies councillors, he nonetheless offered himself as 'a rough tutor, admittedly but one who would love to educate the Prince in how our folk live and in our customs, that he might know this group of his subjects more thoroughly'.

Chade objected. 'But if you do not return to your folk as we promised, will not some say we kept you hostage against your will?' I suspected my old mentor did not desire an Old Blood man counselling the Prince.

Web chuckled at his concern. 'All in the room have witnessed that I offer myself. If after they leave me here, you choose to chop and burn me, well, then let it be said that it was due to my own wooden-headedness, that I trusted wrong. But I do not think that will be so. Will it, my lady?'

'Of a certainty, not!' Queen Kettricken declared. 'And whatever else may come of these meetings, I will count it a benefit that I have added such a clear-minded fellow to my household men.'

His careful pondering of the situation and his suggestions had taken all the morning. When it was time for the noon meal, Web declared that he would eat with his new friends in the guardroom and then introduce them to his bird. Before Chade could suggest that would not be wise, the Queen announced that indeed she and Chade and her Six Duchies councillors would join him there, for she too wished see his Risk.

How I longed to be present for that, not just to witness it, but also to see the reaction of the guards when they found themselves honoured with the Queen at their table. It could not damage Web's standing with him that he had brought about such a thing. And I did not doubt that more would come to meet his bird if the Queen herself did not fear his Wit-beast.

But I was trapped in my watching-place, being Chade's eyes when he was not in the room. I saw the Old Bloods unmask after their food had been brought in. As before, Boyo and Silvereye spoke loudly of injustices done and the need for retribution, but theirs were not the only voices raised. Some spoke of Web's performance with amazement. I heard at least one woman say to another that, having met Kettricken, she would not mind entrusting a son to her to be her page, for she had heard that all children in the Keep were given a chance to learn both numbers and writing. And a young man, clearly a minstrel from his voice, wondered aloud what it would be like to sing the Old Blood songs at the Queen's own hearth, and if such a thing would not truly be the best way to teach the unWitted that his people were neither fearsome nor monstrous.

A crack had been opened. Tomorrow's possibilities were gaining strength, growing in the light of Web's optimism. I wondered if they could grow enough to cast their shadows over the weeds of yesterday's wrongs.

The afternoon, however, was a disappointment, long and tedious. When the Queen and her councillors returned with Web, Boyo rose to claim his turn to speak. Forewarned about him by Chade and myself, Kettricken listened calmly as he detailed first all the generalized wrongs the Farseers had ever done to the Old Bloods, and then the specifics of his case. There, at least, my queen was able to muffle him. Firmly but courteously, she told him that now was not the time for her to settle personal wrongs. If lands and wealth had been unjustly taken from his family, then that was a matter to be settled before her on a judging day rather than at this time. Chade would help him to make an appropriate appointment, and would also tell him what documentation he would need. Most of it would likely relate to the need for him to define a clear line of succession from his dispossessed ancestor to himself, including a minstrel that could attest to his being of the line of the eldest child of an eldest child for the intervening generations.

Very neatly she made it seem that he was putting his own interests ahead of the others at the meeting, as indeed he was. She did not refuse to find justice for him, but relegated his seeking of it to the path which any Six Duchies citizen would have to follow. She reminded them all that this convocation was intended to allow all to join their thoughts as to how unjust persecution of the Old Bloods might be ended.

Silvereye stirred a muck more difficult to settle. She spoke of those who had murdered her family. As she spoke, her voice rose in anger and hatred and pain, and I saw those emotions echoed in many faces around her. Web looked sick and sorrowful, and my Queen's face grew very still. Chade's features were graven in stone. But anger most often begets anger, and the faces of Queen Kettricken's Six Duchies representatives became set in surly expressions. The vengeance and punishment she demanded were far too steep for anyone to consider granting.

It was as if she set a jump that no negotiator could clear and then declared that she could be satisfied with nothing less. This, she declared, was the only way to end persecution of the Old Blood. Make it a crime so hideously punished that none would consider committing it again. Further, search out and eliminate all who had ever committed or tolerated such treatment of Old Bloods. Out of her personal sorrow Silvereye expanded her grievance to include all Witted executed in the last century. She demanded both punishment and restitution, with the punishment to mirror exactly what had befallen their victims. Kettricken had the wisdom to allow her to keep speaking until she had run out of words. Surely I could not have been the only one to hear the edge of madness in her demands. And yet if grief powered that madness, then who was I to criticize it?

By the time Silvereye had finished, there were many other Old

Bloods anxious to take up the tally of all that had been lost to the persecution. Names were called out of folk who deserved death, and the anger in the room swirled like a gathering storm. But my queen held up a hand and asked them quietly, 'Then where should it end?'

'When every last one has been punished!' Silvereye declared passionately. 'Let the gallows sway with their weight, and the smoke of their burning blacken the skies all summer. Let me hear their families wail aloud in a sorrow like the sorrows that we have been forced to conceal, lest others know us for Old Bloods. Let the punishment be apportioned exactly. For every father killed, let a father die. For every mother, a mother. For every child, a child.'

The Queen sighed. 'And when those who have suffered your vengeance come seeking from me a vengeance of their own? How then could I turn them aside? You propose that if a man has killed the children of an Old Blood family, then the children of his family should die alongside him. But what of the cousins of those children and the grandparents? Should not they then come before me and ask of me what you now demand? Would not they be just as right in saying that innocents had died in mad persecution? No. This cannot be. You ask what I cannot give you, and well you know it.'

I saw hatred and fury leap into Silvereye's gaze. 'So I knew it would be,' she declared bitterly. 'Empty promises are what you offer us.'

'I offer you the same justice that anyone in the Six Duchies may seek,' the Queen said wearily. 'Come before me on a judging day, with witnesses to the wrongs done to you. If murder has been done, then the murderer will be punished. But not his children. There is no justice in what you seek, only revenge.'

'You offer us nothing!' Silvereye declared. 'Well you know that we do not dare come before you seeking justice. Too many would stand between us and Buckkeep Castle, anxious to silence us with death.' She paused. Queen Kettricken remained still in the face of her wrath, and Silvereye made the mistake of pressing what she thought was her advantage. 'Or has that always been your intention, Farseer Queen?' Silvereye swept the gathering with a righteous glance. 'Does she lure us out into the open with empty promises so that she can do away with all of us?'

A brief silence followed her words. Then Kettricken spoke quietly. 'You throw words that you do not yourself believe. Your intention is to wound. Yet, if your accusations had any basis in fact, I would not be wounded by them, but would rather feel justified in hating Old Bloods.'

'Then you admit that you hate Old Bloods?' Silvereye demanded with satisfaction.

'That is not what I said!' Kettricken responded both in horror and anger.

Tempers were rising, and not just among the Old Bloods. Kettricken's Six Duchies councillors looked both insulted and uneasy at the brewing storm in the room. I do not know what would have become of the negotiation if fate had not intervened in the person of Sally, the cow-woman. She stood abruptly, saying, 'I must go to the stables. It is Wisenose's time, and she wishes me to be there.'

Someone in the back of the room laughed resignedly, and someone else cursed at her. 'You knew she was due to calve. Why did you bring her?'

'Would you have me leave her alone at home, then? Or that I stay away entirely, Briggan? Well do I know that you think me scatter-brained, but I've as good a right to be here as you.'

'Peace,' Web said suddenly. He croaked the word, then cleared his voice and tried again. 'Peace. It is as good a time as any to let tempers and hearts cool, and if Wisenose has need of her partner, then surely no one here will argue that she must go. And I will accompany her, if she wishes it. And perhaps by the time we return, all here will recall that we seek a solution to our present problems, not a way to change what is past, however grievous it may be.'

It struck me then that Web had a firmer control over this meeting than the Queen herself, but I doubt that any within the room noticed it. That is the advantage to watching from the outside, as Chade had often told me. Then it all becomes a show, and one scrutinizes the players equally. I observed them now as the Six Duchies delegation filed out behind the Queen and Chade, and then Web accompanied Sally down to the stables. I remained at my post, for I judged that what would follow might be most revealing of all.

And it was. Some, including the minstrel and the woman who had earlier spoken of her son paging for the Queen, asked Silvereye if she would destroy their future for the sake of a past that could not be remedied. Even Boyo seemed inclined to think Silvereye had taken their argument too far. 'If this Farseer queen holds to her word, then perhaps our grievances could be brought before her at a judging. I have heard it said she is fair in her decisions. Perhaps we should accept her offer.'

Silvereye all but hissed. 'Cowards, all of you. Cowards and boot-lickers! She offers you bribes, safety for one or two of your children, and in return you are ready to let the whole past be forgotten. Do you forget the screams of your cousins, do you forget coming to visit friends and finding only a scorched patch by a stream? How can you be so false to your own blood? How can you forget?'

'How can we forget? It isn't a matter of forgetting. It is a matter of remembering.' This from an Old Blood I had not particularly noted before. He was a man of middle years and slight build, a man with the look of a town about him. He was not a good speaker; he gulped his words and looked nervously about, but folk still listened to him. 'I will tell you what I remember. I remember that when my parents were taken from their cottage, it was because Piebalds betrayed them. Yes, and a Piebald rode with those who hanged and quartered them. Laudwine's cult dared to call my parents traitors to Old Blood and threatened to punish them because they would not offer haven to those who stir the hatred against us. Well, who was the true traitor that day? My parents who wished only to live in what peace they could find, or the Piebald betrayer who carried the torch that burned their bodies? We have worse enemies than this Farseer queen to fear. And what I intend to ask of her when she comes back is justice against those who terrorize and betray us. Justice against the Piebalds.'

A silence thick as congealing blood filled up the room. The minstrel came and set a hand on the slight man's sleeve. 'Bosk.

She cannot help us with that. That is for us to deal with. All you would do is put yourself at greater risk; yes, and your wife and daughters, too.' The minstrel glanced about the room, almost fearfully. And my heart sank at what I realized. The Old Bloods feared their own. There might be Piebald informers in that very room. The thought spread silently, chilling all of them. Soon some of them made excuses to visit their own chambers, and in a short time the room was nearly empty. Silvereye sat staring silently into the fire. The minstrel wandered aimlessly about the room. There was little talk among the few that remained.

I heard a scuffling noise down the passage behind me, and in a moment Chade crept up to join me. 'Anything important?' he whispered.

I set my hand to his wrist and conveyed all I had seen. His face grew thoughtful. After a moment he said softly, 'Well. That sets my thoughts in a new track. It would not be the first time I had turned an error to an advantage. Keep your watch here, Fitz.' Then, almost as an afterthought, 'Are you getting hungry?'

'A bit. But I'll be fine.'

'And our prince?'

'I've no reason to think he is otherwise.'

'Ah, but you do. If there may be Piebald informers in that room, then there may be Piebalds amongst those who hold him hostage. Warn him, lad. And keep watch.'

And then he was gone, shuffling along bent almost double in the passage. I watched him go and wondered what he had in mind. Then I reached for Dutiful.

All was well with him. He was cold, he was bored, but no one had offered him insult let alone injury. Most of the talk today had been about what might be happening at Buckkeep. Evidently a bird, perhaps Risk or the hawk, had been ferrying notes back and forth. So far, all tidings had been reassuring. But Dutiful said that the air was one of waiting and worry.

The cow had an easy labour and dropped a fine bull calf. Sally was just as glad that she'd had the benefit of a tight stable and a warm stall, for the calf was born unseasonably early. By the time she and Web returned to the east gathering hall, it was time for another meal. I watched the Old Bloods congregate again as their meal was brought in, and watched them as they unmasked after the servants had left. I studied every face more carefully, but if there were any who had been in Laudwine's band, I did not recognize them.

The meal was almost finished when there was a tap at the door. Several of the Old Bloods cried out to the supposed servants that they had not yet finished eating. Then a voice at the door said quietly, 'Let me in. Old Blood greets Old Blood.'

Web was the one who rose and went to the door. He unlatched it and opened it to admit both Civil Bresinga and his cat. The squirrel on the table chittered in panic and then ran up his partner to hide under her hair. Pard didn't bat an eye, but strolled into the room, glanced about, and then went over to the hearth where he made himself comfortable. No one could have watched the cat's entrance and doubted that he was Wit-partnered to the boy who closed the door quietly behind himself and then turned to face the assembly.

The gazes he met would have daunted anyone. But again Web rose to the challenge, setting a friendly hand to Civil's shoulder and loudly exclaiming, 'Old Blood welcomes Old Blood. Come in and join us, lad. And you might be?'

He took a breath and squared his shoulders. 'I am Civil Bresinga. Lord Civil Bresinga, now, of Galekeep. I am a loyal subject of Queen Kettricken, and friend and companion to Prince Dutiful Farseer. I am Old Blood. And both my queen and my prince know that I am.' He let them have a moment to consider that they looked at a Witted noble of the Farseer court. 'I have come, at Councillor Chade's behest, to tell you of how I am treated here. And to tell you, too, of my dealings with the Piebalds. And how I would have died at their hands, were it not for Farseer intervention.'

I watched in a sort of awe. The boy's story was obviously unrehearsed. He wandered through it, often having to go back and explain earlier events. When he spoke of what his mother had endured and how she had died, he choked and could not go on. Web sat him down then and gave him a glass of wine and patted his back soothingly as if he were no more than a child. And I blinked and saw myself at fifteen, plunged into intrigue far beyond my ability to manage. Civil *was* little more than a child, I saw suddenly. Witted and constantly at risk, manoeuvred into spying in a desperate bid to save his mother and his family fortune. He'd failed. Now he was deprived of parent and home; adrift: a very minor noble in a very political court. And the only reason he was alive, truly, was that possessed the friendship of a Farseer. One that he had betrayed not once, but twice, and yet each time, he had been forgiven.

'They have extended asylum to me,' he finished his tale. 'The Queen and the Prince and Councillor Chade are all full aware that I am Old Blood. And they know how I was used against them. And what it cost me.' He paused and shook his head. 'I am not skilled with words. I cannot draw all the parallels that I would like you to see. Only . . . they have not judged me by what I did in the past. They have not judged the Old Bloods by what the Piebalds attempted against the Prince. The Queen has not flinched from her Witted son. Cannot we do as much for them? Deal with the Farseers for who they are now, without looking too deeply into the past?'

Silvereye gave a contemptuous snort. But Boyo, perhaps seeing a kinship in this Witted noble and the title he hoped to reclaim, nodded thoughtfully. Civil suddenly looked at Web, and I sensed that something had just come into his mind, some idea of his own. As if in answer to my fervent wish, I heard the scuff of Chade's tread again. I motioned to him frantically to join me at the spy-post, even as I signalled silence to him. The boy was speaking to Web. His words barely carried to us.

'Councillor Chade told me what you suggested. That if Old Bloods could come to Buckkeep and live openly here alongside these ungifted folk, they might discover that we are not monsters to be feared. He also told me what you said. "A man with nothing to lose is often in the best position to sacrifice himself for the gain of others." I have not had much time to ponder that, but I do not think I need much time to see that I am truly a man with nothing to lose. The only threat that remains is to me alone. I have no family left to suffer consequences for what I do.' He glanced around the room. 'I know that many of you fear that if you venture out of hiding your neighbours kill you. For long and long, it has been a valid fear. And one I have shared, as did my mother.' His words died suddenly. Then he forced himself to go on, his voice cracking. 'And so we stayed in hiding. And by doing so, we made it possible for our "friends" to kill us instead. I see no point in hiding any more.' I could not decide if emotion choked him or if he paused to consider what he would say next. He glanced at Web again and then nodded as if to himself.

'All in the keep have heard now of Web the Witted, who walks amongst us unafraid and unthreatening. I feel almost shamed that he, a stranger here, has stepped out into the light while I, who know Prince Dutiful best, have crept along in the shadows at the edge of the room. Tomorrow, I will change that. I will proudly declare my Old Blood and vow that I will demonstrate that such a one as I can be completely devoted to my prince, as he well deserves of me.

'I have taught him of our ways, and willingly has Prince Dutiful learned. He has said that when he goes in the spring to the Outislands, to slay a dragon and claim a bride, that I may go with him. When I do, I shall go as his Witted companion. There is no Skillmaster at Buckkeep, and my prince will go alone, with no Skill-coterie such as Farseer kings of old had to aid them. Bereft of that magic, I will instead put ours at his service, and prove it every bit as able, I warrant. I will put my Old Blood magic before them all, proudly.'

Chade's tight grip on my wrist told me that all of this was new to him, not just that Civil planned to reveal himself but also that Dutiful had said his friend might accompany him on his quest. His Skilling was erratic, but it reached me. *Did I say I would turn an error to an advantage? I may have succeeded too well, and our advantage overshot into yet another error. I merely wanted the boy to say the Queen had treated him well and fairly, not make himself the ambassador for Old Blood at court.*

I joined my thoughts to his. *He does not perceive it is a risk for the Prince to admit to an Old Blood friend. He sees only the danger to himself, and that he would gladly risk it for Dutiful. Do you think you can talk him out of it?*

I'm not sure I'd be wise to, Chade conveyed to me. *His spirit has captured their imagination. Look.*

It was not an overwhelming outpouring of support. Web was the only one who was grinning wildly and proclaiming how proud he was of young Lord Bresinga. The others, with the notable exception of the scowling Silvereye, were more reserved in their approval, and it varied over a wide spectrum of levels. Both the minstrel and Boyo looked enthused. Sally, partly won over already by how her beast had been treated, was smiling gently. Others were discussing it more pragmatically. The Queen couldn't very well let him be put to death, not when he'd already claimed asylum and she had promised that no Witted ones would be killed solely because of their magic. Likely he was as safe as he could possibly be. And well it might be that a young man both noble and handsome might win some hearts over to the Old Blood side. His declaration could not hurt their cause.

Then the town man, Bosk, came to stand before Civil. He was twisting his fingers together as if he might unscrew them from his hands. Then, in an uncertain voice, he asked, 'Farseers killed Piebalds. Are you sure?'

'I'm very sure,' Civil said softly. His hand went up and touched his throat. 'Very sure indeed.'

'Their names,' the man whispered. 'Do you know their names?'

Civil stood still and silent for a moment. Then, 'Keppler. Padget. And Swoskin. Those were the names I knew them by. But Prince Dutiful called Keppler by another name, from his time amongst the Piebalds. He called him Laudwine.'

Bosk shook his head, plainly disappointed. But someone else in the room asked loudly, 'Laudwine?' She pushed to the front and I recognized Silvereye. 'That can't be so! He was the leader of the Piebalds. If he'd been killed, I'd have heard of it.'

'Oh, would you?' the minstrel asked curiously. The look on his face was not pleasant.

'I would,' she snapped. 'Make of that what you will. I know folk who know Laudwine, and yes, some of them are Piebalds. I am not one, myself, though my recent conversations here have made me see what drove them to such extreme acts.' She turned a shoulder to the minstrel, excluding him as she demanded of Civil, 'How long ago did this happen? And what proof do you have that what you say is true?'

The lad took a step back from her, but he answered. 'Well over a month ago. As for proof . . . what proof can you expect me to give? I saw what I saw, but I fled as soon as I could. It shames me to admit it, but it is so. Still, I doubt what is common talk in Buckkeep Town is false. A one-armed man and his horse were killed, as well as a small dog. And the other two men in the house.'

'His horse, too!' Silvereye exclaimed, and I saw her take it as a double loss.

'If this is so, it is a major blow to the Piebalds,' Bosk declared. 'It might well mean the end of them.'

'No. It will not!' Silvereye was adamant. 'The Piebalds are stronger than a single man. They will not give up this fight until we have had justice. Justice and revenge.'

Bosk stood up and walked towards her slowly, his fists knotted. His threat would have been pathetic if it had not been so sincere. 'Maybe I should take my revenge where I can get it,' he suggested breathlessly. His voice nearly broke on the next words. 'If I posted your name as Witted, and you were hanged and burned, would it scald your Piebald friends? Perhaps I should take your advice. Do to them exactly what was done to me.'

'You are so stupid! Can't you see they are fighting for all of us, and deserve our support? I had heard rumours that Laudwine had discovered something, something that could topple the Farseers from power. Perhaps that secret died with him, but perhaps it did not.'

'Now you are the one being stupid,' Civil broke in determinedly. 'Topple the Farseers? Now there is a plan! Bring down the only queen who has ever tried to halt the hanging and burning. And what will that gain us? Only widespread persecution, with no fear of reprisals or guardsmen coming to intervene. If Old Blood attempts to overthrow the monarchy, it will be seen as proof that we are as evil and untrustworthy as our enemies have claimed. Are you mad?'

'She is,' Web said quietly. 'And for that we should pity her, not condemn her.'

'I don't want your pity!' Silvereye spat out. 'I need no one's pity. Nor do I need your help. Grovel to this Farseer Queen. Forgive all that has been done to you, and let them use you as their servants. I do NOT forgive, and in my time I will have my revenge. I will.'

'We've done it,' Chade whispered by my ear. 'Or perhaps I should say that Silvereye has done it for us. She has driven into our fold any who do not dream of blood and burning. And that is most of them, I think. See if I am not right.'

And with that he left me, scuttling off like a grey spider through the tunnels. It wasn't until late that night that I finally left my post to go and find food and then to take some sleep. But it went as he had said it would. Civil remained with the Old Bloods, and when the Queen, Chade and the Six Duchies delegates returned, he stood before them and greeted them as a Witted noble. I saw the discomfort on the faces of the delegates as he assured them that in every duchy there were Witted nobility, forced for generations to keep their magic small and silent. Several of the young men he spoke to now knew him well. They had ridden with him, drunk with him and gamed at table with them. They exchanged glances with one another, and their plain message was, 'if he is Witted, who else might be also?' But Civil either did not see or ignored their reservations as he pushed on with his proclamation. He intended now to let his magic burn bright for the good of Prince Dutiful and the Farseer reign. He pledged himself to this, and I thought I saw grudging admiration on three of the delegates' faces. Perhaps this Old Blood youth could act as a proof against their prejudice.

The last day of Kettricken's Witted convocation showed solid progress. The minstrel appeared unmasked, and asked her permission to remain at court. The Queen presented to her Six Duchies delegates a proclamation that from this date henceforward, executions could only be carried out legally under the aegis of each of her ducal houses, with the head of each house liable for any injustices which occurred in his own duchy. Each duchy was to have only one gallows, and that was to be under the control of the ruling house. Not only was each duchy to prevent local officials from executing prisoners, but dukes and duchesses must review individually every such execution. Killings carried out otherwise would be seen as murders, and the Queen's judgement would be available against such killers. It did not solve the problem of how

Old Bloods could safely bring such charges without fear of reprisals, but at least it established consequences formally for them.

Of such tiny steps, Chade assured me, would our progress be made. When I rode forth with the Queen's guard to escort our Old Blood delegates back to their friends and receive our Prince and Laurel in return, I marked a solid change in the folk. There was talk and laughter amongst themselves as they rode, and some interchanges even with the guard. Sally, her cow and her calf trailing her, rode alongside Lord Civil Bresinga, and seemed to feel great honour at this fine young lord's conversation with her. On his other side rode Boyo. His evident efforts to claim equality with Lord Bresinga were rather undermined by that young man's egalitarian attitude towards Sally. Civil's cat rode on his saddle behind him.

All around us in the forest, the snow had melted down to thin, icy fingers clawing at the soil in the shadows. New green things were beginning to brave the sunlit world, and the breeze that flowed past us indeed seemed the wind of change. Amongst all this, Silvereye rode alone in our midst. Web rode alongside me and made conversation about everything, for both the Queen and Chade had insisted that he must make the journey so that all Old Bloods might witness that he returned to Buckkeep Castle of his own free will.

When we made our rendezvous, Civil and Pard seemed equally glad to see their Prince. Dutiful professed himself surprised and pleased to have them come to meet him. His warm welcome of his friend and his Wit-beast impressed the Old Bloods, both those who had been to Buckkeep Castle and those who awaited them. He had, of course, known of Civil's coming through my Skill.

When we returned to Buckkeep Castle, not only the Prince and Laurel returned with us, but also Web and the minstrel, whose name was Cockle. He sang as he rode with us, and I gritted my teeth at his rendition of 'Antler Island Tower'. That stirring and maudlin lay told the tale of the Antler Island defence against the Red Ship raiders, with much emphasis placed on the role that Chivalry's bastard son had played. It was true that I had been there, but I doubted half the exploits attributed to my axe. Web laughed aloud at my pained expression. 'Don't sneer so, Tom Badgerlock. Surely the Witted Bastard is a hero both our folk can share, being both a Buckkeep man and Old Blood.' And his bass joined the minstrel on the next refrain about 'Chivalry's son, with eyes of flame, who shared his blood if not his name'.

Didn't Starling write that ballad? Dutiful asked with false concern. *She considers it her property. She may not take kindly to Cockle singing it at Buckkeep.*

She wouldn't be alone in that. I may strangle him myself to save her the time.

Yet on the next refrain, not only Civil and Dutiful lifted their voices, but half the guardsmen as well. That, I told myself, is the effect a spring day can have on people. I hoped it would wear out soon.

TWENTY-SEVEN

Spring Sailing

In the beginning of the world, there were the Old Blood folk and the beasts of the fields, the fish in the water and the birds of the sky. All lived together in balance if not in harmony. Among the Old Blood folk, there were but two tribes. One was comprised of the blood-takers, who were the people who bonded to creatures who ate the flesh of other creatures. And the other folk were the blood-givers, and they bonded to those who ate only plants. The two tribes had nothing to do with each other, no more than a wolf has to do with a sheep; that is, they met only in death. Yet each respected the other as an element of the land, just as a man respects both a tree and a fish.

Now, the laws that separated them were stern laws and just. But there are always people who think they know better than the law, or think that in their special situation, an exception should be made for them. So it was when the daughter of a blood-taker, bonded to a fox, fell in love with the son of a blood-giver, bonded to an ox. What harm, they thought, could come of their love? They would do no injury to one another, neither woman to man nor fox to ox. And so they both went apart from their own peoples, lived in their love and in time brought forth children of their own. But of their children, the first son was a blood-taker and the first daughter was a blood-giver. And the third was a poor witless child, deaf to every animal of every kind and doomed always to walk only in his own skin. Great was the sorrow of the family when their eldest son bonded to a wolf and their eldest daughter to a deer. For his wolf killed her deer, and she took the life of her brother in recompense. Then they knew the wisdom of the oldest ways, for a predator cannot bond with prey. But worse was to come, for their witless child sired only witless children, and thus were born the folk who are deaf to all the beasts of the world.

Badgerlock's Old Blood Tales

Spring overwhelmed the land. Pale green hazed the trees on the hills behind the castle. Over the next two days, the leaves unfurled and grew, and the forest cloaked the hills again. The grasses rushed up from the earth, displacing the dry brown stalks of last year. The startling white of new lambs appeared amongst the grazing flocks. Folk began to talk of Springfest. It shocked me that only a year had passed since I had allowed Starling to take Hap off to Buckkeep from our quiet cottage. Too much had happened. Far too much had changed.

Within the keep, all was bustle and excitement. It was far more than the ordinary preparations for Springfest. During that auspicious time, the Prince would take ship to the Outislands, and all must be prepared for that. The captain and crew of the *Maiden's Chance* were pleased that their ship had been chosen as the transport vessel. There was much vying amongst the guardsmen to be among those chosen for the Prince's own guard. In the end, too many volunteered, myself amongst them, and the Prince was reduced to having the guardsmen draw lots to see who would be among the fortunate few. I was not surprised to be chosen; after all, Chade had given me the lot I would 'draw' the night before.

Civil Bresinga would indeed be going with us. Chade was also part of the company, as was Thick, much to the surprise of the Prince's court. Web, rapidly on his way to becoming a favourite with the Queen, had begged her permission to accompany her son and been granted it. He promised that his sea-bird would range far ahead of the vessel and keep a watch on the weather.

Civil was not the only noble hoping to accompany the Prince. Quite a number of his lords and ladies expressed the intent of going along. It quickly put me in mind of the immense expedition that had set out for the Mountains so many years ago when Kettricken was Verity's bride-to-be. Now, as then, every noble brought with them an entourage of servants and beasts. Secondary ships were rapidly hired. Nobles who could not afford the time or money to accompany the Prince would still make their presence felt. Gifts were also amassing at Buckkeep Castle, not just for the Narcheska but for her mother's house and her father's clan.

In Verity's tower, the Skill-lessons continued, but all my pupils were distracted and difficult. Thick sensed too well Dutiful's anxiety and anticipation and responded to it with excitability that made it well-nigh impossible to get him to concentrate on anything. Prince Dutiful arrived and left with a harried air. He seemed constantly to have a clothing fitting that he must go to, or a lesson in Outislander courtesy or language to attend.

I pitied him, but pitied myself more as I struggled to learn all I could from scrolls in the evening. Even Chade was distracted. He puppeteered far too many situations within Buckkeep to be able to leave the castle easily. Despite his keen interest in pursuing the Skill, much of his attention was given over to selecting folk to handle his responsibilities while he was gone. I was relieved that Rosemary would not be accompanying us, yet felt unhappy with the idea that she would be left in charge of much of Chade's spy network. I suspected that Chade was also burning some night oil with further experiments on his explosive powder, but the less I knew of that, the more contented I was.

Our imminent departure was more than enough to fill my mind, and yet life never allows a man to focus on one task at a time. Dutiful and Civil also had nightly lessons with Web in the history and customs of the Old Blood folk. These were held before a hearth in the Great Hall, and Web had made it plain that any who were interested were welcome to attend. The Queen herself had been present on several occasions. At first, his 'lessons' were sparsely attended, and many of the faces were set in disapproving lines. But Web was a masterful storyteller and many of his tales were new to the folk of Buckkeep. He rapidly gained an audience, especially amongst the children of the keep. And soon those who were ostensibly busy carding wool or fletching arrows or mending garments began to set up those tasks within earshot of Web's voice. I do not know that many became convinced the Old Blood were not to be feared, but at least they learned more of how such people lived and thought.

Web had one other student at those sessions, one I had never thought to see again at Buckkeep. Swift, Burrich's son, often sat silently on the outskirts of Web's circle.

Word that Queen Kettricken would welcome Witted folk had

gone out. Few had responded. The difficulty was plain. How could one offer his son or daughter as page without revealing that the Wit was in the family bloodline? Here at court, the Queen might be able to protect such a child, but what of his kin at home? Lord Brant, a lesser noble of Buck, had brought his ten-year-old son and sole heir. He had presented him to the Queen as Old Blood, but claimed that the magic came from his mother, dead these six years and with few surviving kin. The Queen had accepted him at his word. I also suspected one seamstress who had recently come to Buckkeep, but if she did not wish to openly declare her Wit, I would not ask.

The Queen's other new page was none other than Swift. He had come, alone and on foot, wearing new boots and a new jacket and bearing a letter from Burrich. I had witnessed him presenting it to the Queen from my usual vantage point. The letter ceded the boy to the Farseers, admitting that Burrich had done his best with the lad but failed to shake him from his course. If he would not leave that base magic, then let him embrace it, and his father was done with him. He could not afford to have the boy around his younger brothers. It also directed that the lad not be known as Burrich's son at the court. When Queen Kettricken gently asked of him how he wished to be known then, Swift had lifted his pale face and answered quietly but firmly, 'Witted. It is what I am and will not deny.'

'Swift Witted it shall be then,' she had replied with a smile. 'And I think it a name that will fit you well. I turn you over to my councillor, Chade, now. He will find appropriate duties for you, and lessons as well.'

The boy had given a small sigh, and then bowed deeply, obviously relieved that the ordeal of his royal audience was over. He had walked very stiff and straight as he left the audience chamber.

That Burrich would discard the boy shocked me to the depths of my soul, but I was also relieved. While Swift remained in Burrich's household and the Wit was a point of contention between them, it could lead only to strife and misery. I suspected the decision had been both difficult and bitter for Burrich, and I lay awake nearly all of one night wondering what Molly thought of it and if she had wept at her son's departure. I was sorely tempted to reach out to Nettle but had refrained from doing so since the day of Thick and Dutiful's wild Skilling. It was not only that I did not wish to connect what we shared with that Skill-summons. I still feared the echoing memory of that alien voice. I would not chance a strong sending that would draw its attention to myself or to my daughter.

Yet on that night, as if my heart betrayed my mind, Nettle's mind touched mine. It seemed almost a chance encounter, as if we had happened to dream of one another at the same moment. I wondered again at how effortlessly our minds could unite with the Skill, and wondered if Chade were correct. Perhaps this was something I had taught her from the time she was small. I dreamed of her sitting on the grass beneath a spreading tree. She held something in her cupped hands, something secret and small, and stared at it sorrowfully.

What troubles you? I asked her. Even as I spoke to her and she focused on me, I felt my dream self assume the shape she always gave me. I sat down and curled my tail around my forefeet. I grinned at her wolfishly. *I do not look like this, you know.*

How would I know what you look like? she asked me peevishly. *You tell me nothing about yourself.* Abruptly, there were daisies growing at her feet. A tiny blue bird alighted in a branch over her head and sat fanning its delicate wings.

I asked her curiously.

Her hands closed around the treasure she clasped. She pressed it to her chest, concealing it within her heart. Had she fallen in love, then?

Let me see if I can guess yours, I offered playfully. It pleased me unreasonably to think of my daughter in love and treasuring that first secret realization. I hoped the young man was worthy of her.

She looked alarmed. *No. Stay away from it. It isn't even mine. It was only entrusted to me.*

Has a young man, perhaps, spoken his heart to you? I hazarded merrily.

Her eyes widened in dismay. *Go away! Don't guess.* A wind stirred the tree branches above her head. We both looked up just as the blue bird changed into a bright blue lizard. Its silver eyes sparkled and whirled as it scuttled closer, coming down the trunk almost to her hair. 'Tell me,' it chirruped. 'I love secrets!'

She looked at me disdainfully. *Your ruse does not deceive me.* She flapped a hand at the lizard. *Go away, pest.*

Instead the creature leapt into her hair. It dug its claws in, tangling itself in her tresses. It grew suddenly larger, the size of a cat, and wings sprouted from its shoulders. Nettle shrieked and swatted at it, but it clung there. It lifted its head, suddenly at the end of a long neck and regarded me with spinning silver eyes. Small but perfect, a blue dragon sneered at me. Its voice changed terribly. Alien and freezing, it rasped against my soul. 'Tell me your secret, Dream Wolf!' it demanded. 'Tell me of a black dragon and an island! Tell me now or I tear her head from her shoulders.'

The voice tried to set hooks in me. It endeavoured to seize me and know me exactly as I was. I sprang to my feet and shook myself. I willed the wolf to fly free of me so that I could escape the dream, but it held me. I felt the creature's regard, the prying of another mind at mine, as it demanded silently that I give up my true name.

Suddenly, Nettle stood up. Reaching out, she seized the hissing creatures in both hands and glared at me. *It's only a dream. This is only a dream. You will not trick any secrets from me this way. This is only a dream and I break it and I awake. NOW!*

I do not know what she did. It was not so much that she shifted her shape out of the dream as that she trapped the dragon. It became blue glass in her hands, and then she flung it from her. It struck the soil at my feet and exploded in a storm of sharp fragments. The pain of the cuts it dealt me jabbed me back into wakefulness. I sat up with a gasp, throttling Chade's old blanket between my hands, then sprang from the bed and brushed my hands down my chest, expecting to sweep away shards of glass and feel the sting of bloody cuts. But there was only sweat. I shivered suddenly, and then shook as with an ague and spent the rest of the night sitting up before the fire wrapped in a blanket and staring into the flames. Try as I might, I could make no sense of what I had experienced. What parts were a dream, what parts a Skill-sharing with Nettle? I could not draw any lines, and I feared. I feared not only that something from the Skill-current had found us both, but also I feared the

Skill-talent I had sensed in Nettle as she had saved us both from its deadly regard.

I told no one of that dream. I knew what Chade's answer would be to my concerns. 'Bring the girl to Buckkeep where we can protect her. Teach her to Skill.' I would not. It had just been the bizarre ending to a dream in which my worst fears mingled. With all the strength I possessed, I believed that, as if my belief could make it the truth.

By daylight, it was easier to shelve those fears. I had many other concerns to occupy me, and much to arrange before my departure. I went down to Gindast and paid far ahead on Hap's education. My lad seemed to be prospering at his apprenticeship. Gindast himself told me that the boy surprised him almost daily. 'Now that he has put his mind to his learning,' he added heavily, and I heard there the master's rebuke of my slovenly parenting. But it was Hap who had applied the discipline to himself, and I gave him full credit for it. Every third or fourth day, I would make time in my schedule to visit him at least briefly. We did not speak of Svanja, only of how his work progressed and the approaching Springfest and the like. I had not yet told him that I would be leaving Buckkeep with the Prince. If I had, I was sure he would tell the other apprentices and perhaps pass it on to Jinna as well, for he was still occasionally a guest in her home. Habit made me wish to keep my travelling plans quiet until close to my departure date. Just as well not to connect me with the Prince, I told myself. I did not want to admit that part of that was my own dread at being parted from my foster son for that long, especially as I expected to be going into danger.

I had taken the Fool's warning to heart. In addition to raiding Chade's armoury for an impressive array of small and deadly items, I had undertaken modifying my clothing to accommodate them. It was a lengthy and frustrating process and I often missed the Fool's deft suggestions and defter hands. I saw little of him in those days. I might glimpse Lord Golden about the halls and courtyards of the keep, but other young and dashing nobles of the court always accompanied him. The halls of Buckkeep seemed to be swarming with such youngsters. The Prince's quest seemed to have a fascination for a certain type of young man, one eager both to prove himself and to spend his ancestral fortune on amusing himself at the same time. They were attracted to Lord Golden as moths are to a lamp. Then I heard a rumour that Lord Golden was completely enraged that Chalcedean vessels were disrupting trade and delaying the arrival of the Jamaillian cloaks that he had specially commissioned for the Outislander expedition wardrobe. They were, according to gossip, to have been patterned with dragons in black, blue and silver thread.

I asked Chade about it. He had come up to the tower that evening to help me work on speaking basic Outislander. The language shared many words with the common tongue of the Six Duchies, but the Outislanders twisted them and spoke gutturally. My throat was sore from my attempts. 'Did you know that Lord Golden still plans to accompany us?' I asked him.

'Well, I've given him no reason to think otherwise. Use your head, Fitz. He's a very resourceful man. As long as he thinks he will simply take ship with the Prince, he will make no alternate arrangements. And the less time we give that one to think of alternate arrangements, the less chance that he can circumvent our will.'

'I thought you said you could prevent him from taking ship from Buckkeep.'

'I did. I can. But he seems to have a goodly supply of coin at his command, Fitz, and that can make many things possible. Why give him any extra time to plan?' He glanced away from me. 'When the time comes to board, he will simply be told that there has been a miscalculation. There is no room for him. Perhaps he can follow on a later vessel. But I will be sure that there are no such vessels with available space.'

I was silent for a time. I tried to imagine that scene, and winced. Then I said softly, 'It seems a hard way to treat a friend.'

'We treat him thus precisely because he is your friend. You were the one who wished him stopped. He told you he had foreseen his death on Aslevjal, and that you must somehow prevent the Prince from slaying the black dragon. As I told you then, I put little weight on either event happening. If Lord Golden does not accompany us, he cannot die there. Nor can he provoke you into interfering with

Dutiful's mission. I doubt it will be much of an adventure, anyway. He will have missed only some cold and difficult work. I think that the Prince's "slaying" may be no more than chopping free the head of something that was buried in the ice ages ago. How are you two getting along lately?'

He added the final question so adroitly that I answered it without thinking. 'Not well and not poorly. Mostly I don't see much of him.' I looked down at my fingers and scraped at a hanging nail. 'It's as if he has become someone else, someone I don't know very well. And would have no reason to know, in this life we live now.'

'And I the same. I've the feeling that he has been very busy of late, and yet I am not sure with what. The common gossip tells me only that he has begun to gamble heavily on games of chance. He spends his money lavishly, on dinners and gifts of wine and fine garment for his friends, but even more on gambling with them. No fortune will withstand that for long.'

I scowled. 'That does not sound like the man I know. He so seldom does anything without a purpose, yet I see no reason for that.'

Chade laughed without humour. 'Well, so many say when they see a friend fall to a weakness. He would not be the first intelligent man I've known to succumb to an unreasoning appetite for games of chance. And in a way, you may blame yourself. Since Dutiful introduced the Stone game, it has roared into popularity. The young men call it, "the Prince's Stones". As with all such caprices, what started out as simple has become terribly expensive. Not only do opponents wager against each other, but now men back favourite players, and the wagers on a single game may mount to a small fortune. Even the game-cloths and stones have increased in value. Instead of a cloth, Lord Valsop has created a board of polished walnut set with lines of ivory, and his playing pieces are of jade, ivory and amber. One of the better taverns in town has refitted its upper room exclusively for Stones players. It is expensive even to enter it. Only the finest wine and foods are served there, by only the comeliest servants.'

I was appalled. 'All this from a simple game supposed to help Dutiful focus his mind on the Skill.'

Chade laughed. 'One never knows where such things will lead.'

It recalled another question to my mind. 'Speaking of something that led to something else: of those we felt stir when Dutiful and Thick Skilled out, have any come to Buckkeep?'

'Not yet,' Chade replied, and tried to keep disappointment from his voice. 'I had hoped they would hasten here, but I suppose that summons was both too strange and too abrupt. We should make a time when we can all sit down and intentionally reach forth in that way again. Last time, it only occurred to me in that instant that we could summon those we had wakened. My thoughts to them were rushed and unclear. And now we have so little time before we sail that there is no point in calling them here now. Nonetheless, it should be one of the first things we attend to when we return. How I wish that our prince were setting out with a traditional coterie of six trained Skill-users at his beck and call. Instead we are five, and one is the Prince himself.'

'Four, for we leave Lord Golden behind,' I pointed out.

'Four,' Chade agreed sourly. He looked at me and Nettle's name hung, unuttered, between us. Then, as if to himself, he said, 'And there is no time now to train any others. In truth, there is scarcely time enough to train those we have.'

I cut him off before he could voice his frustration with himself. 'It will come with time, Chade. I am convinced you cannot force it, any more than a swordsman can use will alone to make himself better. It must be coupled with endless practice and with drills that seemingly have nothing to do with his goals. Patience, Chade. Patience with yourself, and with us.'

He still could not hear any individual of the coterie Skill to him, unless there was physical contact as well. He was aware of Thick's Skilling but it was like the humming of a gnat by his ear; it conveyed nothing. I did not know why we could not break through to him, and I did not know why he could not reach out to us. He had the Skill. Both my healing and my scarring had proven that he possessed great talent with it in that specialized area. But Chade was a man consumed by his ambition, and he would not rest until he had mastered the full spectrum of his magic.

But my efforts to reassure Chade had only turned his thoughts into a different channel. 'Would you rather have an axe?' he asked me abruptly.

I goggled at him for a moment, and then grasped his thought. 'I haven't fought with an axe in years,' I told him. 'I suppose I could try to get some practice in before we sailed. But I thought you just told me that this would probably be more drudgery than battle. After all, what enemy do we expect to fight?'

'Even so. Still, an axe might prove more useful against the ice around the dragon than a sword. Request one from the Weaponsmaster tomorrow. And begin some drill with it to refresh your skills.' He cocked his head at me and smiled. I knew that smile. I was already braced when he added, 'You'll be teaching weapons to Swift, along with reading and numbers. He is not doing well in the hearth classes with the other children. Burrich has taught him ahead of his years, so he is bored when put with the lads his own age and uncomfortable with the older boys. Kettricken has decided he would do best with an individual tutor. The Queen chose you.'

'Why me?' I demanded. What I had seen of the boy at Web's lessons did not make me anxious to take him on as a student of anything. He was a dark and moody child, who sat solemn through stories that had other children rolling with laughter. He spoke little and looked much with Burrich's black eyes. He carried himself as stiffly as a guardsman who had just taken a lashing, and had as much cheerfulness, also. 'I am not suited to be a tutor. Besides, I think the less I have to do with the boy, the better for both of us. What if Burrich came to visit him and the boy wished him to meet his teacher? It would cause great difficulties.'

Chade shook his head sorrowfully. 'Would that there was a chance of that happening. In the ten days the boy has been here, there has not been one word from his father to say he regretted sending him. I think Burrich has well and truly disowned him. That is one reason why Kettricken thinks it so important that one man take him over. He needs such a man in his life. Give him a sense of belonging, Fitz.'

'Why me?' I asked again sourly.

Chade smiled even wider. 'I think the symmetry of it pleases Kettricken. And I confess to seeing a certain rough justice there, as well.' Then he took a breath and spoke more seriously. 'Where else would you have us put him? With someone who despises the Wit? With someone who finds him a burden but has no sense of obligation to him? No. He's yours, now, Fitz. Make something of him. And teach him the axe. The lad should have Burrich's build when he is grown. Right now, he's just skin over bone. Take him to the practice courts each day and put some muscle on his frame.'

'In my spare time,' I promised him sourly. I wondered if Burrich had regarded me with as much dread as I did his son. I considered it probable. Yet no matter how much I dreaded it, Chade's words had made it inevitable. The moment he had asked me 'where else should I put the boy?' I had known dread of what might befall Swift in someone else's hands. It was not that I wanted an extra responsibility, least of all now. It was that I could not bear the thought of someone else taking him and being cruel or ignoring him. Such is the conceit all men have once they have been parents. One becomes convinced that no one else is better suited to the task.

I thought with dread of taking up the axe again. That was going to hurt. Yet Chade was right. It had always been my best weapon. Fine blades were wasted on me. I thought with regret of the beautiful sword that the Fool had given me. It had remained with him, along with my extravagant wardrobe, when I had left his service. I had not been comfortable masquerading as his servant, but now I found that I missed it. At least it had given me an opportunity to spend time with him. Our last conversation had healed some of the rift between us, but in another way it had created a distance of its own. I had come face to face with the fact that the Fool was but one aspect of the man I had thought I'd known. It was, I reflected sourly, like being friends with a puppeteer's puppet and trying to ignore the man that gave it speech and made it dance.

Yet, late that same night, I went to his chamber door and tapped lightly. Dim light seeped from beneath it, but I stood long in the hall before a voice within asked irritably, 'Who is there?'

'Tom Badgerlock, Lord Golden. Might I come in?'

After a pause, I heard the latch lifted. I entered a room that I scarcely recognized. Reserved elegance had become sprawling opulence. Rich carpets overlapped one another on the floor. The candlesticks on the table were gold, and the perfume that the burning tapers gave off breathed as expensively as if he burned coins. The man who stood before me was robed in lavish silk and adorned with jewels. Even the hangings of the walls had been changed. The simple hunting scenes common to so many Buckkeep tapestries had been replaced with ornate depictions of Jamaillian gardens and temples.

'Will you come in and close the door, or did you merely wish to stand there and gawp?' he demanded peevishly. 'It is late at night, Tom Badgerlock. Scarcely the hour for casual visitors.'

I shut the door behind me. 'I know. I apologize for that, but when I've come round at more reasonable times, you haven't been here.'

'Did you forget something when you left my service and moved out of your chambers? That hideous tapestry, perhaps?'

'No.' I sighed and decided that I would not let him force me back into that role. 'I missed you. And I've regretted, over and over, that stupid argument I began with you when Jek was here. It is as you warned me. I've been doomed to remember it every day, and every day wished I could unsay those words.' I walked over to his hearth and dropped into one of the chairs by the dwindling fire. There was a decanter of brandy on a small table beside it and a glass with a drop or two left in the bottom.

'I've no idea what you are talking about. And I was just about to seek my bed. So. Your business here, Badgerlock?'

'Be angry with me if you wish. I suppose I deserve it. Be whatever you have to be with me. But stop this charade and be yourself. That's all I ask.'

He stood silent for a moment, looking at me with haughty disapproval. And then he came to take the other chair. He poured himself more brandy without offering me any. I could smell that it was the apricot one that we had shared in my cabin less than a year ago. He sipped it and then observed, 'Be myself. And who would that be?' He set down the glass, leaned back in his chair and crossed his arms on his chest.

'I don't know. I wish you were the Fool,' I said quietly. 'But I think we have come too far to go back to that pretence. Yet, if we could, I would. Willingly.' I looked away from him. I kicked at the end of a hearth log, pushing it further into the fire and waking new flames in a gust of sparks. 'When I think of you now, I do not even know how to name you to myself. You are not Lord Golden to me. You never truly were. Yet you are not the Fool any more either.' I steeled myself as the words came to me, unplanned but obvious. How could the truth be so difficult to say?

For a teetering instant, I feared he would misunderstand my words. Then I knew that he would know exactly what I meant by them. For years, he had shown that he understood my feelings, in the silences he kept. Before we parted company, I had to repair, somehow, the rift between us. The words were the only tool I had. They echoed of the old magic, of the power one gained when one knew someone's true name. I was determined. And yet, the utterance still came awkward to my tongue.

'You said once that I might call you Beloved, if I no longer wished to call you Fool.' I took a breath. 'Beloved, I have missed your company.'

He lifted a hand and covered his mouth. Then he disguised the gesture by rubbing his chin as if he thought something through carefully. I do not know what expression he hid behind his palm. When he dropped his hand from his face, he was smiling wryly. 'Don't you think that might cause some talk about the keep?'

I let his comment pass for I had no answer to it. He had spoken to me in the Fool's mocking voice. Even as it soothed my heart, I had to wonder if it was a sham for my benefit. Did he show me what I wished to see, or what he was?

'Well,' he sighed, 'I suppose that if you were going to have an appropriate name for me, it would still be Fool. So let us leave it at that, Fitzy. To you, I am the Fool.' He looked into the fire and laughed softly. 'It balances, I suppose. Whatever is to come for us, I will always have these words to recall now.' He looked at me and nodded gravely, as if thanking me for returning something precious to him.

There were so many things I wanted to discuss with him. I wanted to review the Prince's mission and talk about Web and ask him why he now gambled so much and what his wild extravagances meant. But I suddenly wanted to add no more words to what we had said tonight. As he had said, it balanced now. It was a hovering scale between us; I would chance no word that might tip it awry again. I nodded to him and rose slowly. When I reached the door, I said quietly, 'Then, good night, Fool.' I opened the door and went out into the corridor.

'Good night, beloved,' he said from his fireside chair. I shut the door softly behind myself.

EPILOGUE

The hand that once wielded both sword and axe now aches after an evening of the quill. When I wipe the tip of one clean, I often wonder how many buckets of ink I have used in a lifetime? How many words have I set down on paper or vellum, thinking to trap the truth thereby? And of those words, how many have I myself consigned to the flames as worthless and wrong? I do as I have done so many times. I write, I sand the wet ink, I consider my own words. Then I burn them. Perhaps when I do so, the truth goes up the chimney as smoke. Is it destroyed, or set free in the world? I do not know.

I used to doubt the Fool when he told me that all of time was a great circuit, and that we are ever doomed to repeat what has been done before. But the older I get, the more I see it is so. I thought then that he meant one great circle entrapped all of us. Instead, I think we are born into our circuits. Like a colt on the end of a training line, we trot in the circular path ordained for us. We go faster, we slow down, we halt on command and we begin again. And each time we think the circle is something new.

My father's raising was given over, all those many years ago, to my grandfather's half-brother, Chade. In his turn, my father gave me over to his right-hand man to rear. And when I became a father, I entrusted that the same hand could best raise my daughter in safety. Instead, I took in another man's son and made Hap mine. Prince Dutiful, my son and yet not mine, also came to be my student. And in time, Burrich's own son came to me, to learn from me that which his own father would not teach him.

Each circle spins off a circle of its own. Each one seems a new thing but in truth it is not. It is just our most recent attempts to correct old errors, to undo old wrongs done to us and to make up for things we have

631

neglected. In each cycle, we may correct old errors, but I think we make as many new ones. Yet what is our alternative? To commit the same old errors again? Perhaps having the courage to find a better path is having the courage to risk making new mistakes.